THE JOHN DIC[illegible]

OMNIBUS

The John Dickson Carr Omnibus

a&b

This Omnibus edition first published in 2000
by Allison & Busby Limited
114 New Cavendish Street
London W1M 7FD
http://www.allisonandbusby.ltd.uk

A catalogue record for this book is available
from the British Library

ISBN 0 7490 0428 2

Printed and bound by Biddles Limited,
Guildford, Surrey.

Contents

DR. GIDEON FELL, DETECTIVE

> He comes striding towards us now, beaming like Old King Cole. You can probably hear him chuckle. If he wheezes a little, that's due to his weighing more than three hundred pounds . . . You notice the three chins, and the bandit's mustache, and the eyeglasses on the black ribbon. He removes his hat with old-school courtesy. Don't try to bow, doctor! He is Gideon Fell, Doctor of philosophy and expert on crime.

In these words, the narrator of one of John Dickson Carr's radio-plays introduced Dr. Gideon Fell. As Anthony Boucher remarked, "the detective story in the grand manner demands a Great Detective," and Dr. Fell is a memorable sleuth. He is larger-than-life both in his appearance and in his actions. Although he is not fiction's most gargantuan crime-solver – that prize belongs to the four hundred pounds of Paul McGuire's Superintendent Fillinger – he puts most detectives literally in the shade. But, to be fair, Carr may have exaggerated Fell's weight for radio audiences; normally he is described as being a relatively svelte twenty stone. It is, however, more than his size which allows Fell to dominate his cases: "A huge joy of life, a piratical swagger merely to be hearing and seeing and thinking, glowed from him like steam from a furnace. It was like meeting Father Christmas." Everything about Fell is in large proportions. He smokes a meerschaum which he fills from an obese pouch. He consumes countless tankards of beer and is fond of whiskey ("It would be very interesting to find any whiskey that could take the top of my head off"), and he has a tremendous fund of miscellaneous knowledge about obscure subjects.

At the time of HAG'S NOOK, Dr. Fell has been working for six years on his magnum opus, *The Drinking Customs of England from the Earliest Days.* It was eventually published in 1946, Carr said, by a publishing house with the evocative name of Crippen & Wainwright. Fell is also the author of *Romances of the Seventeenth Century* and a book on the supernatural in English fiction. He spends his spare time, he explains on several occasions, improving his mind with sensational fiction.

Dr. Fell's name came from the seventeenth-century bishop and dean of Christ Church, Oxford, who was immortalized in Thomas Brown's famous doggerel:

I do not like thee, Doctor Fell.
The reason why I cannot tell,
But this I know, and know full well,
I do not like thee, Doctor Fell.

Fell himself sometimes quotes this verse, and so do the murderers he tracks down, but otherwise he does not take after his rather stern namesake. His appearance and personality were based on Carr's literary idol, G. K. Chesterton, the essayist and author of the Father Brown detective stories. The formality of Fell's speech was borrowed from Dr. Samuel Johnson, a fact which probably explains why Fell is described in HAG'S NOOK as a lexicographer. Fell is, as students of his cases know, a historian, Fellow of the Royal Historical Society with degrees from Harvard, Oxford, and Edinburgh. He has occasionally lectured at American universities on such topics as "The Effects of King's Mistresses on Constitutional Government."

In the Mystery Writers of America Anthology *Four-and-Twenty Bloodhounds* (1950), Carr contributed a "Detective's Who's Who" entry about Dr. Fell. We learn that he was born in Lincolnshire in 1884 the second son of Sir Digby and Lady Fell; his aristocratic connections help us to understand why he never seems to be earning a living during his cases and why he was able to afford several different residences. Besides Yew Cottage in Lincolnshire, where Fell is living during the events of HAG'S NOOK, he resides at Number 1 Adelphi Terrace in London and, later, at 12 Round Pond Place, Hampstead. In one short story, he has a house in Chelsea. Carr added a few more details: Fell is the recipient of the French Grand Cross Legion of Honor and he is a member of the Garrick, Savage, and Detection Clubs – organizations, incidentally, to which Carr also belonged. (The Detection Club is a society of detective-story writers; Carr was the only American member.)

But what is most noteworthy about the "Detective's Who's Who" is how much Carr left unsaid. We hear nothing about his wife, who plays a subsidiary role in HAG'S NOOK and is mentioned in passing in three or four other cases. Nothing is revealed about Sir Digby Fell's first son or, indeed, of Dr. Fell's other relatives. Like Sir Arthur Conan Doyle (but unlike many modern Holmesians), Carr realized that much of a detective's life should be left vague. A larger-than-life character can be part of this world, but he should not be limited by it. It is insignificant that Hercule Poirot must have been as old as Methuselah in his final cases. Poirot, like Holmes and Fell, has gained an immortality that is unaffected by mere chronological considerations. Glimpses of a detective's background are more effective than elaborate biographical details. Thus Doyle referred to Holmes's unrecorded cases, and Carr mentioned that Fell was involved in such matters as the "Weatherby Grange affair," the "six blue coins which hanged Paulton of Regent Street," and "the still more curious problem of the inverted room at Waterfall Manor." Tolkien understood in LORD OF THE RINGS the importance of referring to other events which are not detailed in the narrative. Such hints contribute a feeling of depth and timelessness, what Tolkien called "a large history in the background, an attraction like that of viewing far off an unvisited island."

Carr was only twenty-six years old when he wrote HAG'S NOOK, the first Gideon Fell story. He was born in Uniontown, Pennsylvania, on November 30, 1906. Beginning in preparatory school and continuing through his studies at Haverford College, he wrote detective stories and historical romances along with occasional poems and comic tales. After living in Paris in the late 1920s, he returned to the United States and published his first novel, *It Walks by Night,* featuring the French detective Henri Bencolin. But Carr believed that England – the land of Holmes and Watson, of Fu Manchu and Nayland Smith, of Dr. Thorndyke and Reggie Fortune and the transplanted Belgian Hercule Poirot – was the natural home for a detective-story writer. In 1932, he married an Englishwoman, Clarice Cleaves, moved to England, and began a regimen of writing four or five detective novels a year featuring English sleuths. Under the pseudonym "Carter Dickson" he wrote a series of books about Sir Henry Merrivale, and under his own name he wrote about Gideon Fell, who eventually appeared in twenty-three novels, four short stories, and four radio-plays.

HAG'S NOOK is told from the viewpoint of Tad Rampole, a young American visiting England who clearly represents Carr's own feelings, and it is filled with Anglophilic warmth. I know of no writing that conveys so sensitively the love of England and of the past than the second paragraph of HAG'S NOOK. Rampole will appear in two other Fell cases, *The Mad Hatter Mystery,* and *The Three Coffins,* in which his name is unaccountably altered to "Ted." It is the feeling for the past and how it influences the present that dominate HAG'S NOOK. Carr believed that "to write good history is the noblest work of man," and like Fell he loved the romance of the past. In 1936, he wrote the finest true-crime book, *The Murder of Sir Edmund Godfrey,* about an unsolved murder of 1678, and later in his career he became the master of the historical detective novel. According to Dr. Fell "the talent for deduction developed by judicious historical research can just as well be applied to detective work."

HAG'S NOOK also reflects Carr's affection for the works of G. K. Chesterton. Dorothy Sayers wrote of Carr's novels: "Chestertonian . . . are the touches of extravagance in character and plot, and the sensitiveness to symbolism, to historical association, to the shapes and colours of material things, to the crazy terror of the incongruous." Not only Dr. Fell's appearance but his love of paradoxes come directly from Chesterton.

John Dickson Carr was famed for the "miracle crime" – the impossible disappearance and the locked-room murder; indeed he found so many ways to explain tricks and impossibilities that as Anthony Boucher remarked, "his own career seems a miraculous event demanding some rational explanation." The seeming impossibilities in HAG'S NOOK are handled subtly, more hinted at than proclaimed. Few tales so perfectly combine atmosphere, mystery, ingenuity, and an extraordinarily well-concealed murderer.

Douglas G. Greene
Norfolk, Virginia
April, 1985

Acknowledgements: I am grateful to Dr. James E. Keirans and to the late Larry L. French for material on Dr. Fell which appears in this introduction.

Series Consultant Douglas G. Greene is Director of the Institute of Humanities at Old Dominion University. Dr. Greene is working on a multi-volume history of the detective story. He has edited two anthologies of John Dickson Carr's work, and is widely recognized as *the* authority on that writer.

Hag's Nook

1

The old lexicographer's study ran the length of his small house. It was a raftered room, sunk a few feet below the level of the door; the latticed windows at the rear were shaded by a yew tree, through which the late afternoon sun was striking now.

There is something spectral about the deep and drowsy beauty of the English countryside; in the lush dark grass, the evergreens, the grey church-spire and the meandering white road. To an American, who remembers his own brisk concrete highways clogged with red filling-stations and the fumes of traffic, it is particularly pleasant. It suggests a place where people really can walk without seeming incongruous, even in the middle of the road. Tad Rampole watched the sun through the latticed windows, and the dull red berries glistening in the yew tree, with a feeling which can haunt the traveller only in the British Isles. A feeling that the earth is old and enchanted; a sense of reality in all the flashing images which are conjured up by that one word "merrie." For France changes, like a fashion, and seems no older than last season's hat. In Germany even the legends have a bustling clockwork freshness, like a walking toy from Nuremberg. But this English earth seems (incredibly) even older than its ivy-bearded towers. The bells at twilight seem to be bells across the centuries; there is a great stillness, through which ghosts step, and Robin Hood has not strayed from it even yet.

Tad Rampole glanced across at his host. Filling a deep leather chair with his bulk, Dr. Gideon Fell was tapping tobacco into a pipe and seemed to be musing genially over something the pipe had just told him. Dr. Fell was not too old, but he was indubitably a part of this room. A room – his guest thought – like an illustration out of Dickens. Under the oak rafters, with smoke-blackened plaster between, it was large and dusky; there were diamond-paned windows above great oak mausoleums of book-shelves, and in this room, you felt, all the books were friendly. There was a smell of dusty leather and old paper, as though all those stately old-time books had hung up their tall hats and prepared to stay.

Dr. Fell wheezed a little, even with the exertion of filling his pipe. He was very stout, and walked, as a rule, with two canes. Against the light from the front windows his big mop of dark hair, streaked with a white plume, waved like a war-banner. Immense and aggressive, it went blowing before him through life. His face was large and round and ruddy, and had a twitching smile somewhere above several chins. But what you noticed there was the twinkle in his eye. He wore eyeglasses on a broad black ribbon, and the small eyes twinkled over them as he bent his big head forward; he could be fiercely combative or slyly chuckling, and somehow he contrived to be both at the same time.

"You've got to pay Fell a visit," Professor Melson had told Rampole. "First, because he's my oldest friend, and, second, because he's one of the great institutions of England. The man has more obscure, useless, and fascinating information than any person I ever met. He'll ply you with food and whiskey until your head reels; he'll talk interminably, on any subject whatever, but particularly on the glories and sports of old-time England. He likes band music, melodrama, beer, and slapstick comedies; he's a great old boy, and you'll like him."

There was no denying this. There was a heartiness, a *näiveté*, an absolute absence of affectation about his host which made Rampole at home five minutes after he had met him. Even before, the American had to admit. Professor Melson had already written to Gideon Fell before Rampole sailed – and received an almost indecipherable reply decorated with little drawings of a hilarious nature and concluding with some verses about prohibition. Then there had been the chance meeting on the train, before Rampole arrived at Chatterham. Chatterham, in Lincolnshire, is some hundred and twenty-odd miles from London, and only a short distance away from Lincoln itself. When Rampole boarded the train at dusk, he had been more than a little depressed. This great dun-coloured London, with its smoke and its heavy-footed traffic, was lonely enough. There was loneliness in wandering through the grimy station, full of grit and the iron coughing of engines, and blurred by streams of hurrying commuters. The waiting-rooms looked dingy, and the commuters, snatching a drink at the wet-smelling bar before train time, looked dingier still. Frayed and patched, they seemed, under dull lights as uninteresting as themselves.

Tap Rampole was just out of college, and he was, therefore, desperately afraid of being provincial. He had done a great deal of travelling in Europe, but only under careful parental supervision on the value-received plan, and told when to look. It had consisted in a sort of living peep-show at the things you see on post cards, with lectures. Alone he found himself bewildered, depressed, and rather resentful. To his horror, he found himself comparing this station unfavourably with Grand Central – such comparisons, according to the Better American Novelists, being a sin.

Oh, well, damn it! . . .

He grinned, buying a thriller at the bookstall and wandering towards his train. There was always the difficulty in juggling that money; it seemed to consist of a bewildering variety of coins, all of inordinate dimensions. Computing the right sum was like putting together a picture puzzle; it couldn't be done in a hurry. And, since any delay seemed to him to savour of the awkward or loutish, he usually handed over a bank note for the smallest purchase, and let the other person do the thinking. As a result, he was so laden with change that he jingled audibly at every step.

That was when he ran into the girl in grey.

He literally ran into her. It was due to his discomfort at sounding so much like an itinerant cash-register. He had tried jamming his hands into his pockets, holding them up from underneath, walking with a sort of crab-like motion, and becoming generally so preoccupied that he failed to notice where he was going. He bumped into somebody with a startling thud; he heard somebody gasp, and an "Oh!" beneath his shoulder.

His pockets overflowed. Dimly he heard a shower of coins tinkle on the wooden platform. Fiery with embarrassment, he found himself holding to two small arms and looking down into a face. If he had been able to say anything, it would have been, "Gug!" Then he recovered himself to notice the face. Light from the first-class carriage beside which they stood shone down upon it – a small face, with eyebrows raised quizzically. It was as though she were looking at him from a distance, mockingly, but with a sympathetic pout of her lips. A hat was pulled down anyhow, in a sort of rakish good-humour, on her very black, very glossy hair; and her eyes were of so dark a blue that they seemed almost black, too. The collar of her rough grey coat was drawn up, but it did not hide the expression of her lips.

She hesitated a moment. Then she spoke, with a laugh running under it: "I say! You *are* wealthy . . . Would you mind letting go my arms?"

Acutely conscious of the spilled coins, he stepped back hastily.

"Good Lord! I'm sorry! I'm a clumsy ox; I – Did you drop anything?"

"My purse, I think, and a book."

He stooped down to pick them up. Even afterwards, when the train was rushing through the scented darkness of a night just cool enough, he could not remember how they had begun talking. A dim train-shed, misted with soot and echoing to the rumble of baggage trucks, should not have been the place for it; yet it seemed, somehow, to be absolutely right. Nothing brilliant was said. Rather the opposite. They just stood there and spoke words, and Rampole's head began to sing. He made the discovery that both the book he had just bought and the book he had knocked out of her hands had been written by the same author. As the author was Mr. Edgar Wallace, this coincidence was hardly stupefying enough to have impressed an outsider, but Rampole made much of it. He was conscious of trying desperately to hold to this subject. Each moment, he felt, she might break away. He had heard how aloof and unapproachable Englishwomen were supposed to be; he wondered whether she were just being polite. But there was something – possibly in the dark-blue eyes, which were wrinkled up at him – of a different nature. She was leaning against the side of the carriage, as carelessly as a man, her hands shoved into the pockets of the fuzzy grey coat: a swaggering little figure, with a crinkly smile. And he suddenly got the impression that she was as lonely as himself.

Mentioning his destination as Chatterham, he inquired after her luggage. She straightened. There was a shadow somewhere. The light throaty voice, with its clipped and slurred accent, grew hesitant; she spoke low:

"My brother has the bags." Another hesitation. "He – he'll miss the train, I expect. There goes the horn now. You'd better get aboard."

That horn, tooting thinly through the shed, sounded inane. It was as though something were being torn away. A toy engine began to puff and stammer; the bumping shed winked with lights.

"Look here," he said, loudly, "if you're taking another train –"

"You'd better *hurry*!"

Then Rampole grew as inane as the horn. He cried in a rush: "To hell with the train! I can take another. I'm not going anywhere, as it is. I –"

She had to raise her voice. He got the impression of a smile, bright and swashbuckling and pleased. "Silly! – I'm going to Chatterham, too. I shall probably see you there. Off you go!"

"Are you sure?"

"Of course."

"Well, that's all right, then. You see –"

She gestured at the train, and he swung aboard just as it got under way. He was craning out of one corridor window, trying to get a glimpse of her, when he heard the throaty voice call something after him, very distinctly. The voice said an extraordinary thing. It called:

"If you see any ghosts, save them for me."

What the devil! Rampole stared at the dark lines of idle carriages sweeping past, the murky station lights which seemed to shake to the vibration of the train, and tried to understand that last sentence. The words were not exactly disturbing, but they were a little – well, cockeyed. That was the only way to express it. Had the whole business been a joke? Was this the English version of the needles, the raspberry, or any similar picturesque and delicate term? For a moment his neckband grew warm. No, damn it! You could always tell. A train guard, passing through the corridor at this moment, perceived an obviously American Young Gen'lman thrusting his face blindly out of the window into a hurricane of cinders, and breathing them with deep joyous breaths, like mountain air.

The depressed feeling had vanished. This little, swaying train, almost empty of passengers, made him feel like a man in a speedboat. London was not big and powerful now, nor the countryside a lonely place. He had drunk strong liqueur in a strange land, and he felt suddenly close to somebody.

Luggage? He froze for a moment before remembering that a porter had already stowed it into a compartment somewhere along here. *That* was all right. Under his feet he could feel the floor vibrating; the train jerked and whirled with a clackety roar, and a long blast of the whistle was torn backwards as it gathered speed. This was the way to begin adventure. "If you see any ghosts, save them for me." A husky voice – which somehow suggested a person standing on tiptoe – drifting down the platform . . .

If she had been an American, now, he could have asked her name. If she had been an American . . . but, he suddenly realized, he didn't want her to be an American. The wide-set blue eyes, the face which was just a trifle too square for complete beauty, the red and crinky-smiling mouth; all were at once exotic and yet as honestly Anglo-Saxon as the brick staunchness of Whitehall. He liked the way she pronounced her words, as though with a half mockery. She seemed cool and clean, like a person swinging through the countryside. Turning from the window, Rampole had a strong desire to chin himself on the top of one of the compartment doors. He would have done so but for the presence of a very glum and very rigid man with a large pipe, who was staring glassily out of a near-by window, with the top of his travelling-cap pulled over one ear like a beret. This person looked so exactly like a comic-strip Englishman that Rampole would have expected him to exclaim, "What, what, what, what?" and go puffing and stumping down the corridor, had he seen any such athletic activity indulged in here.

The American was to remember this person presently. For the moment, he knew only that he felt hilarious, hungry, and in need of a drink. There was, he remembered, a restaurant-car ahead. Locating his luggage in a smoking-compartment, he groped his way along narrow corridors in search of food. The train was clattering through suburbs now, creaking and plunging and swaying under the shrillness of its whistle, and lighted walls streamed past on either side. To Rampole's surprise, the restaurant-car was almost full; it was somewhat cramped, and smelt heavily of beer and salad oil. Sliding into a chair opposite another diner, he thought that there were rather more crumbs and blotches than were necessary; whereupon he again damned himself for provincialism. The table shook to the swaying of the train, lights jolted on nickel and woodwork, and he watched the man opposite skilfully introduce a large glass of Guinness under a corresponding moustache. After a healthy pull, the other set down the glass and spoke.

"Good evening," he said, affably. "You're young Rampole, aren't you?"

If the stranger had added, "You come from Afghanistan, I perceive," Rampole could not have been more startled. A capacious chuckle enlivened the other man's several chins. He had a way of genially chuckling, "Heh-heh-heh," precisely like a burlesque villain on the stage. Small eyes beamed on the American over eyeglasses on a broad black ribbon. His big face grew more ruddy; his great mop of hair danced to the chuckles, or the motion of the train, or both; and he thrust out his hand.

"I'm Gideon Fell, d'ye see? Bob Melson wrote me about you, and I knew you must be the person as soon as you walked in the car. We must have a bottle of wine on this. We must have two bottles of wine. One for you, and one for me, d'ye see? Heh-heh-heh. *Waiter*!"

He rolled in his chair like a feudal baron, beckoning imperiously.

"My wife," continued Dr. Fell, after he had given a Gargantuan order – "my wife would never have forgiven me if I'd missed you. She's in a stew as it is, what with plaster falling off in the best bedroom, and the new revolving sprinkler for the lawn, which wouldn't work until the rector came to call, and then it doused him like a shower-bath. Heh-heh. Have a drink. I don't know what kind of wine it is, and I never ask; it's wine, and that's enough for me."

"Your health, sir."

"Thank'e, my boy. Permit me," said Dr. Fell, apparently with some vague recollections of his stay in America, "to jump the gutter. *Nunc bibendum est.* Heh. – So you're Bob Melson's senior wrangler, eh? English history, I think he said. You're thinking of a Ph.D., and then teaching?"

Rampole suddenly felt very young and very foolish, despite the doctor's amiable eye. He mumbled something noncommittal.

"That's fine," said the other. "Bob praised you, but he said, 'Too imaginative by half'; that's what he said. Bah! give 'em the glory, *I* say; give 'em the glory. Now, when I lectured at your Haverford, they may not have learned much about English history, but they cheered, my boy, they cheered when I described battles. I remember," continued the doctor, his vast face glowing as with a joyous sunset, and puffing beneath it – "I remember teaching 'em the Drinking Song of Godfrey of Bouillon's men on the First Crusade in 1187, leading the chorus myself. Then they all got to singing and stamping on the floor, as it were; and a maniacal professor of mathematics came stamping up with his hands entangled in his hair – as it were – and said (admirably restrained chap) would we kindly stop shaking the blackboards off the wall in the room below? 'It is unseemly,' says he; 'burpf, burpf, ahem, very unseemly.' 'Not at all,' says I. 'It is the "Laus Vini Exercitus Crucis."' 'It is, like hell,' says he. 'Do you think I don't know "We Won't Be Home until Morning" when I hear it?' And then I had to explain the classic derivation . . . Hallo, Payne!" the doctor boomed, breaking off to flourish his napkin at the aisle.

Turning, Rampole saw the exceedingly glum and rigid man with the pipe, whom he had noticed before in the corridor of the train. The cap was off now, to show a close-shaven skull of wiry white hair, a long brown face, and a general air of doddering down the aisle, looking for a place to fall. He grumbled something, not very civilly, and paused by the table.

"Mr. Payne, Mr. Rampole," said Dr. Fell. Payne's eyes turned on the American with a startling flash of their whites; they seemed suspicious. "Mr. Payne is Chatterham's legal adviser," the doctor explained. "I say, Payne, where are your charges? I wanted young Starberth to have a glass of wine with us."

A thin hand fluttered to Payne's brown chin, and stroked it. His voice was dry, with a premonitory rasp and difficulty, as though he were winding himself up.

"Didn't arrive," replied the lawyer, shortly.

"Humf. Heh. Didn't arrive?"

The rattle of the train, Rampole thought, must shake Payne's bones apart. He blinked, and continued to massage his chin.

"No. I expect," said the lawyer, suddenly pointing to the wine-bottle, "he's had too much of that already. Perhaps Mr. – ah – Rampole can tell us more about it. I knew he didn't fancy his little hour in the Hag's Nook, but I hardly thought any prison superstitions would keep him away. There's still time, of course."

This, Rampole thought, was undoubtedly the most bewildering gibberish he had ever heard. "His little hour in the Hag's Nook." "Prison superstitions." And here was this loose-jointed brown man, with the deep wrinkles round his nose, turning the whites of his eyes round and fixing Rampole with the same pale-blue, glassy stare he had fixed on the corridor window a while ago. The American was already beginning to feel flushed with wine. What the devil was all this, anyhow?

He said, "I – I beg your pardon?" and pushed his glass away.

Another rasp and whir in Payne's throat. "I may have been mistaken, sir. But I believe I saw you in conversation with Mr. Starberth's sister just before the train started. I thought perhaps – ?"

"With Mr. Starberth's sister, yes," said the American, beginning to feel a pounding in his throat. He tried to seem composed. "I am not acquainted with Mr. Starberth himself."

"Ah," said Payne, clicking in his throat. "Just so. Well –"

Rampole was conscious of Dr. Fell's small, clever eyes watching through the joviality of his glasses; watching Payne closely.

"I say, Payne," the doctor observed, "he isn't afraid of meeting some one going out to be hanged, is he?"

"No," said the lawyer. "Excuse me, gentlemen. I must go and dine."

2

The rest of that ride often came back to Rampole as a sinking into the deep countryside; a flight into cool and mysterious places as the lights of towns went out with the hours, and the engine's whistle called more thinly against an emptier sky. Dr. Fell had not referred to Payne again, except to dismiss him with a snort.

"Don't mind him," he said, wheezing contemptuously. "He's a stickler for things. Worst of all, the man's a mathematician. *Pah!* A mathematician," repeated Dr. Fell, glaring at his salad as though he expected to find a binomial theorem lurking in the lettuce. "*He* oughtn't to talk."

The old lexicographer did not even manifest any surprise at Rampole's acquaintance with the unknown Starberth's sister, for which the American felt grateful. Rampole, in his turn, refrained from asking questions about the odd statements he had heard that evening. He sat back, pleasantly padded by the wine, and listened to his host talk.

Although he was no critic in the matter of mixing drinks, he was nevertheless a trifle appalled at the way Dr. Fell poured down wine on top of stout, and followed both with beer towards the close of the meal; but he kept up valiantly with every glass. "As for this beverage, sir," said the doctor, his great voice rumbling down the car, "as for this drink, witness what the Alvismal says: 'Called ale among men; but by the gods called beer.' Hah!"

His face fiery, spilling cigar-ashes down the front of his necktie, rolling and chuckling in his seat, he talked. It was only when the waiters began to hover and cough discreetly round the table that he could be persuaded to leave. Growling on his two canes, he lumbered out ahead of Rampole. Presently they were established facing each other in corner seats of an empty compartment. Ghostly in the dim lights, this small place seemed darker than the landscape outside. Dr. Fell, piled into his dusky corner, was a great goblin figure against the faded red upholstery and the indistinguishable pictures above the seats. He had fallen silent; he felt this unreal quality, too. A cool wind had freshened from the north and there was a moon. Beyond the flying click of the wheels, the hills were tired and thick-grown and old, and the trees were mourning bouquets. Then Rampole spoke at last. He could not keep it back. They had chugged in to a stop at the platform of a village. Now there was absolute silence but for a long expiring sigh from the engine . . .

"Would you mind telling me, sir," said the American, "what Mr. Payne meant by all that talk about 'an hour at the Hag's Nook,' and – and all the rest of it?"

Dr. Fell, roused out of a reverie, seemed startled. He bent forward, the moon on his eyeglasses. In the stillness they could hear the engine panting in hoarse breaths, and a wiry hum of insects. Something clanked and shivered through the train. A lantern swung and winked.

"Eh? – Why, Good Lord, boy! I thought you knew Dorothy Starberth. I didn't like to ask . . ."

The sister, apparently. Handle with care. Rampole said:

"I just met her today. I scarcely know her at all."

"Then you've never heard of Chatterham prison?"

"Never."

The doctor clucked his tongue. "You've got something out of Payne, then. He took you for an old friend . . . Chatterham isn't a prison now, you know. It hasn't been in use since 1837, and it's falling to ruin."

A baggage truck rumbled. There was a brief glare in the darkness, and Rampole saw a curious expression on the doctor's big face, momentarily.

"Do you know why they abandoned it?" he asked. "It was the cholera, of course; cholera – and something else. But they said the other thing was worse."

Rampole got out a cigarette and lighted it. He could not analyse his feeling then, though it was sharp and constricting; he thought afterwards that it was as though something had gone wrong with his lungs. In the dark he drew a deep breath of the cool, moist air.

"Prison," continued the doctor, "particularly prisons of that day, were hellish places. And they built this one round the Hag's Nook."

"The Hag's Nook?"

"That was where they used to hang witches. All the common malefactors were hanged there, of course. H'mf." Dr. Fell cleared his throat, a long rumble. "I say witches because that fact made the most impression on the popular mind . . .

"Lincolnshire's the fen country, you know. The old British called Lincoln *Llyn-dune*, the fen town; the Romans made it *Lindum-Colonia.* Chatterham is some distance from Lincoln, but then Lincoln's modern nowadays. We're not. We have the rich soil, the bogs and marshes, the waterfowl, and the soft thick air – where people see things, after sunset. Eh?"

The train was rumbling out again. Rampole managed a little laugh. In the restaurant-car this swilling, chuckling fat man had seemed as hearty as an animated side of beef; now he seemed subdued and a trifle sinister.

"See things, sir?" the other repeated.

"They built the prison," Fell went on, "round a gallows . . .

Two generations of the Starberth family were governors there. In your country you'd call 'em wardens. It's traditional that the Starberths die of broken necks. Which isn't a very pleasant thing to look forward to."

Fell struck a match for his cigar, and Rampole saw that he was smiling.

"I'm not trying to scare you with ghost stories," he added, after he had sucked wheezingly on the cigar for a time. "I'm only trying to prepare you. We haven't your American briskness. It's in the air; the whole countryside is full of belief. So don't laugh if you hear about Peggy-with-the-Lantern, or the imp on Lincoln cathedral, or, more particularly, anything concerned with the prison."

There was a silence. Then Rampole said: "I'm not apt to laugh. All my life I've been wanting to see a haunted house. I don't believe, of course, but that doesn't detract from my interest . . . What *is* the story concerned with the prison?"

"'Too imaginative by half,'" the doctor muttered, staring at the ash on his cigar. "That was what Bob Melson said. – You shall have the full story tomorrow. I've kept copies of the papers. But young Martin has got to spend his hour in the Governor's Room, and open the safe and look at what's in there. You see, for about two hundred years the Starberths have owned the land on which Chatterham prison was built. They still own it; the borough never took it over, and it's held in what the lawyer chaps call 'entail' by the eldest son – can't be sold. On the evening of his twenty-fifth birthday, the eldest Starberth has got to go to the prison, open the safe in the Governor's Room, and take his chances . . ."

"On what, sir?"

"I don't know. Nobody knows what's inside. It's not to be mentioned by the heir himself, until the keys are handed over to *his* son."

Rampole shifted. His brain pictured a grey ruin, an iron door, and a man with a lamp in his hand turning a rusty key. He said: "Good Lord! it sounds like –" but he could not find words, and he found himself wryly smiling.

"It's England. What's the matter?"

"I was only thinking that if this were America, there would be reporters, news-reel cameras, and a crowd ten deep round the prison to see what happened."

He knew that he had said something wrong. He was always finding it out. Being with these English was like shaking hands with a friend whom you thought you knew, and suddenly finding the hand turned to a wisp of fog. There was a place where thoughts never met, and no similarity of language could cover the gap. He saw Dr. Fell looking at him with eyes screwed up behind his glasses; then, to his relief, the lexicographer laughed.

"I told you it was England," he replied. "Nobody will bother him. It's too much concerned with the belief that the Starberths die of broken necks."

"Well, sir?"

"That's the odd part of it," said Dr. Fell, inclining his big head. "They generally do."

No more was said on the subject. The wine at dinner seemed to have dulled the doctor's rolling spirits, or else he was occupied with some meditations which were to be seen only in the slow, steady pulsing and dimming of his cigar from the corner. Over his shoulders he pulled a frayed plaid shawl; the great mop of hair nodded forward. Rampole might have thought him asleep but for the gleam under his eyelids, the bright shrewd steadiness behind those eyeglasses on the black ribbon . . .

The American's sense of unreality had closed in fully by the time they reached Chatterham. Now the red lights of the train were sinking away down the tracks; a whistle fluttered and sank with it, and the air of the station platform was chill. A dog barked distantly at the passage of the train, followed by a chorus which sullenly died. Their footsteps crunched with startling loudness on gravel as Rampole followed his host up from the platform.

A white road, winding between trees and flat meadows. Marshy ground, with a mist rising from it, and a gleam of black water under the moon. Then hedgerows, odorous with hawthorn; the pale green of corn stretching across rolling fields; crickets pulsing; the fragrance of dew on grass. Here was Dr. Fell, in a rakish slouch-hat, and the plaid shawl over his shoulders, stumping along on two canes. He had been up to London just for the day, he explained, and he had no luggage. Swinging a heavy valise, Rampole strode beside him. He had been startled, momentarily, to see a figure ahead of them – a figure in a nondescript coat and a travelling-cap, beating along the road, with sparks from a pipe flying out behind. Then he realized it was Payne. Despite his doddering walk, the lawyer covered ground with speed. Unsociable dog! Rampole could almost hear him growling to himself as he walked along. Yet there was small time to think of Payne; here *he* was, singing with adventure under a great alien sky, where not even the stars were familiar. He was very small and lost in this ancient England.

"There's the prison," said Dr. Fell.

They had topped a slight rise, and both of them stopped. The country sloped down and out, in flat fields intersected by hedgerows. Some distance ahead, muffled in trees, Rampole could see the church spire of the village; and farmhouses slept, with silver windows, in the rich night-fragrance of the soil. Near them and to the left stood a tall house of red brick, with white window-frames, austere in its clipped park beyond an avenue of oaks. ("The Hall," Dr. Fell said over his shoulder.) But the American was staring at the promontory to the right. Incongruous in this place, crude and powerful as Stonehenge, the stone walls of Chatterham prison humped against the sky.

They were large enough, though they seemed much bigger in the distortion of moonlight. And "humped," Rampole thought, was the word; there was one place where they seemed to surge and buckle over the crest of a hill. Through rents in the masonry vines were crooking fingers against the moon. A teeth of spikes ran along the top, and you could see tumbled chimneys. The place *looked* damp and slime-painted, from occupation by lizards; it was as though the marshes had crept inside and turned stagnant.

Rampole said suddenly: "I can almost feel insects beating against my face. Does it get you that way?"

His voice seemed very loud. Frogs were croaking somewhere, like querulous invalids. Dr. Fell pointed with one cane.

"Do you see that" – queer how he used the same word – "that hump up there, on the side where there's the fringe of Scotch firs? It's built out over a gully, and that's the Hag's Nook. In the old days, when the gallows used to stand on the edge of the hill, they'd give the spectators a show by attaching a very long rope to the condemned man's neck and chucking him over the brink with a sporting chance to tear his head off. There was no such thing as a drop-trap, you know, in those days."

Rampole shivered, his brain full of images. A hot day, with the lush countryside burning dark green, the white roads smoking, and the poppies at the roadside. A mumbling concourse of people in pigtails and knee-breeches, the dark-clad group in the cart creaking up the hill, and then somebody swinging like an unholy pendulum above the Hag's Nook. For the first time the countryside really seemed to be full of those mumbling voices. He turned, to find the doctor's eyes fixed on him.

"What did they do when they built the prison?"

"Kept it. But it was too easy to escape that way, they thought; walls built low, and several doors. So they made a kind of well below the gallows. The ground was marshy anyhow, and it filled easily. If somebody got loose and tried a jump he'd land in the well, and – they didn't pull him out. It wouldn't have been pleasant, dying with the things down there."

The doctor was scuffling his feet on the ground, and Rampole picked up the valise to go on. It was not pleasant, talking here. Voices boomed too loudly; and, besides, you had an uncomfortable sensation that you were being overheard . . .

"That," added Dr. Fell, after a few wheezing steps, "was what did for the prison."

"How so?"

"When they cut down a person after they'd hanged him, they just let him drop into the well. Once the cholera got started . . ."

Rampole felt a qualm in his stomach, almost a physical nausea. He knew that he was warm despite the cool air. A whispering ran among the trees, lightly.

"I live not far from here," the other continued, as though he had mentioned nothing out of the way. He even spoke comfortably, like one pointing out the beauties of a city. "We'rc on the outskirts of the village. You can see the gallows side of the prison very well from there – and the window of the Governor's Room too."

Half a mile on, they turned off the road and struck up through a lane. Here was a crooked, sleepy old house, with plaster and oak beams above, and ivy-grown stone below. The moon was pale on its diamond-paned windows; evergreens grew close about its door, and the unkempt lawn showed white with daisies. Some sort of night bird complained in its sleep, twittering in the ivy.

"We won't wake my wife," said Dr. Fell. "She'll have left a cold supper in the kitchen, with plenty of beer. I – *What's the matter?*"

He started. He wheezed, and gave an almost convulsive jump, because Rampole could hear the slither of one cane in the wet grass. The American was staring out across the meadows to where – less than a quarter of a mile away – the side of Chatterham prison rose above the Scotch firs round Hag's Nook.

Rampole felt a damp heat prickling out on his body.

"Nothing," he said, loudly. And then he began to talk with great vigour. "Look here, sir, I don't want to inconvenience you. I'd have taken a different train, except there isn't any that gets here at a reasonable hour. I could easily go to Chatterham and find a hotel or an inn or –"

The old lexicographer chuckled. It was a reassuring sound in that place. He boomed, "Nonsense!" and thumped Rampole on the shoulder. Then Rampole thought, "He'll think I've got a scare," and hastily agreed. While Dr. Fell searched after a latch-key, he glanced again at the prison.

These old woman's tales might have influenced his outlook. But, just for a moment, he could have sworn that he had seen something looking over the wall of Chatterham prison. And he had a horrible impression that the something was *wet* . . .

3

Sitting now in Dr. Fell's study, on the afternoon of his first day at Yew Cottage, he was inclined to question everything in the nature of the fanciful. This solid little house, with its oil-lamps and its primitive plumbing, made him feel as though he were on a vacation in some hunting-lodge in the Adirondacks, say; that presently they would all go back to New York, and that a car door would slam, to be opened only by the doorman of his own apartment house.

But here it was – the bees astir in a sunlit garden, the sun-dial and bird-houses, the smell of old wood and fresh curtains; not like anything except England. Bacon and eggs had a savour here that he had never fully appreciated before. So had pipe tobacco. The countryside here didn't look artificial, as country has a habit of looking when you live in it only during the summer; nor did it at all resemble the shrubs on the roof of a penthouse.

And here was Dr. Fell, pottering about his domain in a broad-brimmed white hat, looking sleepily amiable and doing nothing with an engrossed thoroughness. Here was Mrs. Fell, a very small and bustling and cheerful woman who was always knocking things over. Twenty times in a morning you would hear a small crash, whereupon she would cry, "Bother!" and go whisking on with her cleaning until the ensuing mishap. She had, moreover, a habit of sticking her head out of windows all over the house, one after the other, to address some question to her husband.

You would just place her at the front of the house when out she would pop at a rear window, like a cuckoo out of a clock, to wave cheerfully at Rampole and ask her husband where something was. He always looked mildly surprised, and never knew. So back she would go, previous to her reappearance at a side window with a pillow or a dust-cloth in her hand. To Rampole, lounging in a deck-chair under a lime tree and smoking his pipe, it suggested one of those Swiss barometers where the revolving figures are for ever going in and coming out of a chalet to indicate the weather.

The mornings and a part of the afternoons Dr. Fell usually devoted to the composition of his great work, *The Drinking Customs of England from the Earliest Days*, a monumental labour into which he had put six years of scholarly research. He loved to trace out the origin of such quaint terms as drinking *supernaugulum*; carouse the hunter's hoop; quaff *upse freez crosse*; and with *health*, *gloves*, *mumpes*, *frolickes*, and other curious terms of the tankard. Even in speaking of it to Rampole, he took violent issue with the treatises of such authors as Tom Nash (*Pierce Pennilesse,* 1595) and George Gascoigne (*A delicate Diet for daintie mouthed Dronkardes, wherein the fowle Abuse of common carowsing and quaffling with hartie Draughtes is honestlie admonished,* 1576).

The morning passed, with the blackbirds piping from the meadow and drowsy sunlight drawing all suggestion of evil from Chatterham prison. But the mellowness of afternoon brought him to the doctor's study, where his host was tapping tobacco into a pipe. Dr. Fell wore an old shooting-jacket, and his white hat was hung on a corner of the stone mantelpiece. On the table before him were papers, at which he kept stealing furtive glances.

"There will be guests to tea," said the doctor. "The rector is coming, and young Martin Starberth and his sister – they live at the Hall, you know; the postman tells me they got in this morning. Perhaps Starberth's cousin, too, though *he's* a sullen sort of dog for your money. I suppose you'll want to know more about the prison?"

"Well, if it's not –"

"Violating any confidence? Oh no. Everybody knows about it. I'm rather curious to see young Martin, myself. He's been in America for two years, and his sister has run the Hall since their father died. A great girl, that. Old Timothy died in rather a curious way."

"A broken neck?" Rampole inquired, as the other hesitated.

Dr. Fell grunted. "If he didn't break his neck, he broke most of the rest of him. The man was fearfully smashed up. He was out riding just after sunset, and his horse threw him – apparently while he was coming down Chatterham prison hill near the Hag's Nook. They found him late that night, lying in the underbrush. The horse was near by, whinnying in a kind of terror. Old Jenkins – that's one of his tenants – found him, and Jenkins said the noises his horse was making were one of the worst things he'd ever heard. He died the next day. He was fully conscious, too, up to the end."

Several times during his stay Rampole had the suspicion that his host might have been making game of him as an American. But he knew differently now. Dr. Fell was plodding through these gruesome anecdotes because something worried him. He talked to relieve himself. Behind the shiftings of his eyes, and his uneasy rollings in the chair, there was a doubt – a suspicion – even a dread. His asthmatic breaths were loud in the quiet room, turning dusky against the afternoon sun.

Rampole said, "I suppose it revived the old superstition."

"It did. But then we've always had superstitions hereabouts. No, this business suggested something worse than that."

"You mean –"

"Murder," said Dr. Fell.

He was bending forward. His eyes had grown large behind the glasses, and his ruddy face looked hard. He began to speak rapidly:

"Mind! I say nothing. It may be fancy, and it's no concern of mine. H'mf. But Dr. Markley, the coroner, said he'd got a blow across the base of the skull which might have been caused by the fall, and then again might not. He looked, it seemed to me, less as though he'd had a fall than that somebody had trampled on him. I don't mean by a horse, either. Another thing: it was a damp evening in October, and he was lying in marshy ground, but that didn't seem to account wholly for the fact that the body was *wet.*"

Rampole looked steadily at his host. He found that his fingers had closed on the arms of his chair.

"But you say he was conscious, sir. Didn't he speak?"

"I wasn't there, of course. I got the story from the rector, and from Payne, too; you remember Payne? Yes, he spoke. He not only spoke, but he seemed to be in a sort of ghoulish high spirits. Just at daybreak they knew he was dying. He had been writing, Dr. Markley said, on a board propped across him; they tried to prevent it, but he just showed his teeth. 'Instructions for my son,' he said – Martin was in America, as I told you – 'there's the ordeal to be gone through, isn't there?'"

Dr. Fell stopped to light his pipe. He pulled the flame down fiercely into the bowl, as though it might give him clearer sight.

"They hesitated in calling Mr. Saunders, the rector, because Timothy was an old sinner and a furious hater of the Church. But he always said Saunders was an honest man, even if he didn't agree with him, so they brought him out at dawn to see whether the old man would agree to prayers for the dying. He went in to see old Timothy alone, and after a while he came out wiping the sweat off his forehead. 'My God!' says the rector, as though he were praying, 'the man's not in his right mind. Somebody go in there with me.' 'Will he hear the commitment?' says Timothy's nephew, who was looking queer. 'Yes, yes,' says the rector, 'but it isn't that. It's the way he's talking.' 'What did he say?' asks the nephew. 'I'm not allowed to tell you that,' says the rector, 'but I wish I could.'

"In the bedroom they could hear Timothy croaking gleefully, though he couldn't move for the splints. He called out to see Dorothy next, alone, and after that Payne, his lawyer. It was Payne who called out that he was going fast. So just as daylight was growing outside the windows, they all went into the big oak room with the canopied bedstead. Timothy was nearly speechless now, but he said one clear word, which was, 'Handkerchief,' and he seemed to be grinning. The rest of them knelt down while the rector said the prayers, and just as Saunders was making the sign of the cross, some froth came out of Timothy's mouth, and he jerked once and died."

During a long silence, Rampole could hear the blackbirds piping outside. The sun was growing long and wan in the branches of the yew.

"It's odd enough," the American assented at length. "But if he said nothing, you've hardly any grounds to suspect murder."

"Haven't I?" said Dr. Fell, musingly. "Well, maybe not . . . The same night – of the day he died, I mean – the same night there was a light in the window of the Governor's Room."

"Did anybody investigate?"

"No. You couldn't get any of the villagers near there after dark for a hundred pounds."

"Oh, well! A superstitious imagination –"

"It wasn't a superstitious imagination," the doctor affirmed, shaking his head. "At least, I don't think so. I saw the light myself."

Rampole said, slowly, "And tonight your Martin Starberth spends an hour in the Governor's Room."

"Yes. If he doesn't funk it. He's always been a nervous chap, one of the dreamy kind, and he was always a little ticklish about the prison. The last time he was in Chatterham was about a year ago, when he came home for the reading of Timothy's will. One of the specifications of the inheritance, of course, was that he should pass the customary 'ordeal.' Then he left his sister and his cousin Herbert in charge of the Hall, and returned to America. He's in England only for the – the merry festivities."

Rampole shook his head.

"You've told me a lot about it," he said; "all but the origin. What I don't see is the reason behind these traditions."

Dr. Fell took off his eyeglasses and put on a pair of owlish reading-spectacles. For a moment he bent over the sheets of paper on his desk, his hands at his temples.

"I have here copies of the official journals, made from day to day like a ship's log, of Anthony Starberth, Esquire, Governor of Chatterham Prison 1797–1820, and of Martin Starberth, Esquire, Governor 1821–1837. The originals are kept at the Hall; old Timothy gave me permission to copy them. They ought to be published in book form, one day, as a sidelight on the penal methods of that day." He remained for a time with his head down, drawing slowly on his pipe and staring with brooding eyes at the inkwell. "Previous to the latter part of the eighteenth century, you see, there were very few *detention* prisons in Europe. Criminals were either hanged outright, or branded and mutilated and turned loose, or deported to the colonies. There were exceptions, like the debtors, but in general no distinction was made between those who had been tried and those who were awaiting trial; they were flung in willy-nilly, under a vicious system.

"A man named John Howard started an agitation for detention prisons. Chatterham prison was begun even before Milbank, which is generally supposed to be the oldest. It was built by the convicts who were to occupy it, of stone quarried from the Starberth lands, under the muskets of a redcoat troop commissioned by George III for that purpose. The cat was freely used, and sluggards were hung up by their thumbs or otherwise tortured. Every stone, you see, has meant blood."

As he paused, old words came unbidden to Rampole's mind, and he repeated them: "'There was a great crying in the land . . .'"

"Yes. A great and bitter one. The governorship, of course, was given to Anthony Starberth. His family had been active in such interests for a long time; Anthony's father, I believe, had been deputy sheriff of Lincoln Borough. It has been recorded," said Dr. Fell, a long sniff rumbling up in his nose, "that every day during the building, light or dark, sun or sleet, Anthony would come riding out on a dappled mare to oversee the work. The convicts grew to know him, and to hate him. They would always see him sitting on his horse, up against the sky and the black line of the marshes, in his three-cornered hat and his blue camlet cloak.

"Anthony had one eye put out in a duel. He was a bit of a dandy, though very miserly except where his person was concerned; he was stingy and cruel; he wrote bad verses by the hour, and hated his family for ridiculing them. I believe he used to say they would pay for making fun of his verses.

"They finished the prison in 1797, and Anthony moved in. He was the one who instituted the rule that the eldest son must look at what he'd left in the safe of the Governor's Room. His governorship, I needn't tell you, was a trifle worse than hellish; I'm deliberately toning down the whole recital. His one eye and his grin . . . "it was a good job," Dr. Fell said, putting his palm down flat on the papers as though he were trying to blot out the writing – "it was a good job, my boy, that he made his arrangements for death when he did."

"What happened to him?"

"Gideon!" cried a reproachful voice, followed by a fusillade of knocks on the study door which made Rampole jump. "Gideon! *Tea!*"

"Eh?" said Dr. Fell, looking up blankly.

Mrs. Fell stated a grievance. "Tea, Gideon! And I wish you'd let that horrible beer alone, though goodness knows the butter-cakes are bad enough, and it's so stuffy in there, and I see the rector and Miss Starberth coming up the road as it is." There was the sound of a deep breath being drawn, whereupon Mrs. Fell summed it up saying, "Tea!"

The doctor rose with a sigh, and they heard her fluttering down the passage, repeating, "Bother, bother, bother!" like the exhaust of an automobile.

"We'll save it," said Dr. Fell.

Dorothy Starberth was coming up the lane, moving with her free stride beside a large and bald-headed man who was fanning himself with his hat. Rampole felt a momentary qualm. Easy! – Don't act like a kid, now! He could hear her light, mocking voice. She was wearing a yellow jumper with a high neck, and some sort of brown skirt and coat into whose pockets her hands were thrust. The sun glimmered on her rich black hair, caught carelessly round her head; and as she turned her head from side to side you could see a clear profile, somehow as poised as a bird's wing. Then they were coming across the lawn, and the dark-blue eyes were fixed on him under long lashes . . .

"I think you know Miss Starberth," Dr. Fell was saying. "Mr. Saunders, this is Mr. Rampole, from America. He's staying with us."

Rampole found his hand grasped with the vigour of muscular Christianity by the large and bald-headed man.

Mr. Thomas Saunders was smiling professionally, his shaven jowls gleaming; he was one of those clergymen whom people praise by saying that they are not at all like clergymen. His forehead was steaming, but his bland blue eyes were as alert as a scoutmaster's. Mr. Saunders was forty years old, and looked much younger. He served his creed, you felt, as clearly and unthinkingly as he had served Eton (or Harrow, or Winchester, or whatever it was) on the playing-fields. Round his pink skull a fringe of fair hair fluffed like a tonsure, and he wore an enormous watch-chain.

"I am delighted to make your acquaintance, sir," the rector boomed, heartily. "I – ah – was pleased to know many of your countrymen during the war. Cousins over the sea, you know; cousins over the sea!"

He laughed, lightly and professionally. This air of professional smoothness and ease irritated the American; he murmured something and turned towards Dorothy Starberth . . .

"How do you do?" she said, extending a cool hand. "It's jolly seeing you again! – How did you leave our mutual friends, the Harrises?"

Rampole was about to demand, *"Who?"* when he caught the expectant innocence of her glance and the half-smile which animated it.

"Ah, the Harrises," he said. "Splendid, thank you, splendid." With a startling burst of inspiration he added. "Muriel is cutting a tooth."

As nobody seemed impressed by this intelligence, and he was a trifle nervous about the ring of authenticity he had put into it, he was about to add further intimate details of the Harris household when Mrs. Fell suddenly shot out of the front door in another of her cuckoo-like appearances, to take charge of them all. She made a variety of unintelligible remarks which seemed to be chiefly concerned with beer, butter-cakes, and the dear thoughtfulness of the rector; and had he quite recovered from being drenched by that horrible water-sprinkler; and was he *sure* he hadn't got pneumonia? Mr. Saunders coughed experimentally, and said he hadn't.

"Dear me . . . bother!" said Mrs. Fell, walking into some plants. "So near-sighted, blind as a bat, dear Mr. Saunders . . . And my dear," whirling on the girl, "where is your brother? You said he'd be here."

Momentarily the shade was back on Dorothy Starberth's face, as Rampole had seen it last night. She hesitated, putting a hand to her wrist as though she would like to look at her watch; but taking it away instantly.

"Oh, he'll be here," she said. "He's in the village – buying some things. He'll be along directly."

The tea table was set out in the garden behind the house; it was shaded by a large lime tree, and a singing stream ran a few yards away. Rampole and the girl lagged behind the other three on the way.

"Baby Eadwig," said Rampole, "is down with mumps –"

"Smallpox. Ugh, you beast! I thought you were going to give me away. And in a community like this – I say, how did they know we'd met?"

"Some old fool of a lawyer saw us talking on the platform. But I thought you were going to give *me* away."

At this extraordinary coincidence they both turned to look at each other, and he saw her eyes shining again. He felt exhilarated, but prickly. He said, "Ha!" rather like Dr. Fell, and noticed the dappling of shadows that trembled on the grass, and they both laughed. She went on in a low voice:

"I can't tell you – I was feeling desperately low last night, what with one thing and another. And London is so big, and everything was wrong. I wanted to talk to somebody. And then you bumped into me and you looked nice, so I did."

Rampole felt a desire to give somebody a joyous poke in the jaw. In imagination he lashed out triumphantly. He had a sensation as though somebody were pumping air into his chest.

He said, not wittily, but – be honest with yourself, sneering peruser! – very naturally:

"I'm glad you did."

"So am I."

"Glad?"

"Glad."

"HAH!" said Rampole, exhaling the air in triumph.

From ahead of them rose Mrs. Fell's thin voice. "– Azaleas, petunias, geraniums, hollyhocks, honeysuckle, and eglantine!" she shrilled, as though she were calling trains. "I can't see 'em, on account of being so nearsighted, but I know they're there." With a beaming if somewhat vague smile she grasped the newcomers and urged them into chairs. "Oh, Gideon, my love, you're not going after that horrible beer, are you?"

Dr. Fell was already bending over the stream. Puffing laboriously, he extracted several beaded bottles and hauled himself up on one cane.

"Notice, Mr. Rampole," said the rector, with an air of comfortable tolerance. "I often think," he continued, as though he were launching a terrible accusation but slyly smiling to mitigate it – "I often think that the good doctor can't be English at all. This barbarous habit of drinking beer at tea-time – my dear sir! It isn't – well, it isn't English, you know!"

Dr. Fell raised a fiery face.

"Sir," he said, "it's tea that isn't English, let me inform you. I want you to look at the appendix of my book, Note 86, Chapter 9, devoted to such things as tea, cocoa, and that unmentionably awful beverage known as the ice-cream soda. Tea, you will find, came into England from

Holland in 1666. From Holland, her bitter enemy; and in Holland they contemptuously called it hay-water. Even the French couldn't stand it. Patin calls tea *'l'impertinente nouveauté du siècle,'* and Dr. Duncan, in his *Treatise on Hot Liquors* –"

"And in front of the rector, too!" said Mrs. Fell, wailing.

"Eh?" said the doctor, breaking off with some vague idea that she thought he was swearing. "What, my dear?"

"Beer," said Mrs. Fell.

"Oh, hell!" said the doctor, violently. "Excuse me, excuse me." He turned to Rampole. "Will *you* have some beer with me, my boy?"

"Why, yes," the other answered, with gratitude. "Thanks, I will."

"– and coming out of that cold water, it'll probably give you both pneumonia," Mrs. Fell said, darkly. She seemed to have an *idée fixe* on the subject of pneumonia. "What it's coming to I don't know – more tea, Mr. Saunders, and there are the cakes beside you – with everybody catching pneumonia the way they are, and that poor young man having to sit up in that draughty governor's place tonight; *he'll* probably have pneu –"

There was an abrupt silence. Then Saunders began talking very smoothly and easily about the flowers, pointing to a bed of geraniums; he seemed to be trying to alter their minds by altering the direction of their gaze. Dr. Fell joined in the discussion, glowering at his wife. She was quite unconscious of having opened that forbidden subject. But constraint had come upon the party under the lime tree, and would not go away.

A soft pink afterglow had crept across the garden, though it would be yet light for several hours. In silver flakes through the tree branches the west glowed clear and warm. All of them, even Mrs. Fell, were silent, staring at the tea-service. A wicker chair creaked. Distantly they could hear the clank and jangle of bells; and Rampole pictured the cows, somehow lonely in a vast meadow, being driven home through mysterious dusk. A deeper hum pulsed in the air.

Dorothy Starberth rose suddenly.

"Stupid of me!" she said. "I'd almost forgot. I must go in to the village and get some cigarettes before the tobacconist closes." She smiled at them, with an affected ease which deceived nobody; the smile was like a mask. She glanced with elaborate carelessness at her watch. "It's been divine being here, Mrs. Fell. You must come over to the Hall soon. I say," with an air of inspiration, to Rampole, "wouldn't you like to walk along with me? You haven't seen our village yet, have you? We've rather a good early Gothic church, as Mr. Saunders would tell you."

"Yes, indeed." The rector seemed to hesitate, looked at them in a heavily paternal way, and waved his hand. "Go along, do. I'll have another cup of tea, if Mrs. Fell doesn't mind. It's so comfortable here," he beamed on his hostess; "makes one ashamed of being lazy."

He sat back with a smug air, as of one who murmurs, "Ah, I was young once!" but Rampole had the impression that he didn't like it at all. It suddenly struck the American that this patronizing old bald-head (*sic,* in Rampole's inflamed thoughts) had a more than clerical interest in Dorothy Starberth. Why, damn the man – ! Come to think of it, the way he had hung over her shoulder, smoothly, as they walked down the lane . . .

"I had to get out of there," the girl said, half breathlessly. Their quick footsteps rustled in the grass. "I wanted to walk, fast."

"I know."

"When you're walking," she explained, in that same breathless voice, "you feel free; you don't feel you have to keep things in the air, like a juggler, and strain yourself not to drop one . . . Oh!"

They were going down the shadowed lane, where the grass muffled their footsteps. Its junction with the road was hidden by the hedgerows, but they became aware of feet scuffling in the dust out there, and a murmur of conversation. Abruptly one voice rose. It came twitching through the soft air, alive and ugly.

"You know the word for it right enough," the voice said. "The word is *Gallows*. Yes, and you know it as well as I do."

The voice laughed. Dorothy Starberth stopped, and her face – sharp against the dark-green hedge – was a face of fear.

4

"I shall have to hurry to catch that tobacconist," the girl declared, instantly. Her small voice was raised, insistent to be heard. "Good Lord! it's past six o'clock! – But then he always reserves a box of my special brand, every day, and if I'm not there . . . I say! Hullo, Martin!"

She stepped out into the road, motioning Rampole to follow. The murmur of voices had frozen. Standing in the middle of the road, still with his hand half lifted, a slightly built young man had twisted round to face her. He had the spoiled, selfconscious face of one who generally gets his way with women, with dark hair and a contemptuous mouth; and he was a little drunk. He swayed a little now. Behind him Rampole could see a crooked track in the white dust to show his progress.

"Hello, Dot!" he said, abruptly. "You can certainly sneak up on a fellow. What's the idea?"

He spoke with a strong attempt at an American accent. Laying a hand on the arm of the person with him, he assumed dignity. This latter was obviously a relation; his features were blunt where the other's were delicate, his clothes rode high on him, and his hat did not have the same careless curve as Martin Starberth's, but there was an undeniable resemblance. He looked embarrassed, and his hands seemed too big.

"Been – been in to tea, Dorothy?" he asked, fumbling. "Sorry we're late. We – we were detained."

"Of course," the girl said, impassively. "May I present: Mr. Rampole, Mr. Martin Starberth, Mr. Herbert Starberth. Mr. Rampole's a countryman of yours, Martin."

"You an American?" demanded Martin, in a brisk manner. "That's good. Whereya from? New York? That's good. I just left there. I'm in the publishing business. Whereya staying? – Fell's? *That* old codger. Look here, come on up to the house and I'll give you a little drink."

"We're going to tea, Martin," Herbert said, with a sort of stolid patience.

"Ah, t'ell with that tea stuff. Listen, you come up to the house –"

"You'd best not go to tea, Martin," said his sister; "and, please, no more to drink. I wouldn't care, but you know why."

Martin looked at her. "I'm going to tea," he said, sticking out his neck, "and, what's more, I'm going to have another little drink. Come on, Bert."

He had forgotten Rampole, for which the American was grateful. He adjusted his hat. He brushed his arms and shoulders, though there was no dust on him, and straightened up, clearing his throat. As the stolid Herbert guided him on, Dorothy whispered: "Don't let him go there, and see that he's all right by dinner-time. Do you hear?"

Martin heard it, too. He turned, put his head on one side, and folded his arms.

"You think I'm drunk, don't you?" he demanded, studying her.

"Please, Martin!"

"Well, I'll show you whether I'm drunk or not! Come on, Bert."

Rampole quickened his step beside the girl as they moved off the other way. As they turned a bend in the road he could hear the cousins arguing, Herbert in a low voice, and Martin vociferously, his hat pulled down on his eyebrows.

For a time they walked in silence. That momentary encounter had jarred against the fragrance of the hedgerows, but it was swept away by the wind over the grass in the meadows that surrounded them. The sky was watery yellow, luminous as glass, along the west; firs stood up black against it, and even the low bog water had lights of gold. Here were the lowlands, sloping up into wolds; and from a distance the flocks of white-faced sheep looked like toys out of a child's Noah's ark.

"You mustn't think," the girl said, looking straight ahead of her and speaking very low – "you mustn't think he's always like that. He isn't. But just now there's so much on his mind, and he tries to conceal it by drinking, and it comes out in bravado."

"I knew there was a lot on his mind. You can't blame him."

"Dr. Fell told you?"

"A little. He said it was no secret."

She clenched her hands. "Oh no. That's the worst of it. It's no secret. Everybody knows, and they all turn their heads away. You're *alone* with it, do you see? They can't talk about it in public; it isn't done. They can't talk about it to me. And *I* can't mention it either . . ."

A pause. Then she turned to him almost fiercely.

"You say you understand, and it's nice of you; but you don't! Growing up with the thing . . . I remember, when Martin and I were tiny children, mother holding us each up to the window so that we could see the prison. She's dead now, you know. And father."

He said, gently, "Don't you think you're making too much of a legend?"

"I told you – you wouldn't understand."

Her voice was dry and monotonous, and he felt a stab. He was conscious of searching desperately for words, feeling his inadequacy every time he found one; yet groping after a common point with her, as he might have groped after a lamp in a haunted room.

"I'm not intelligent about practical things," he said, blankly. "When I get away from books or football, and up against the world, I'm just mixed up. But I think that, whatever you told me, I would understand it, provided it concerned you."

Across the lowlands drifted a clangor of bells. A slow, sad, ancient clangor, which swung in the air and was a part of it. Far ahead, the church-spire among the oaks caught the last light. Birds twittered into flight from its belfry as the bell notes clashed with iron weariness, and a rook was cawing . . . They had stopped by a stone bridge over a broad stream. Dorothy Starberth turned and looked at him.

"If you can say that," she said, "it's all I could ask."

Her lips moved slowly, with a faint smile, and the breeze was smoothing her dark hair.

"I hate practicality," she went on, with sudden vehemence. "I've had to be practical ever since father died. Herbert's a good old dependable horse, with about as much imagination as that hayrick over there. And there's Mrs. Colonel Granby, and Leutitia Markley, and Mrs. Payne who uses the ouija board, and Miss Porterson who almost gets round to reading the new books. There's Wilfrid Denim, who comes to pay me attentions every Thursday night at nine P.M. precisely, runs out of new conversational matter at nine five, and continues to talk about a play he saw in London three years ago, or else illustrates tennis strokes till you think he's jolly well got St. Vitus' dance. Oh yes – and Mr. Saunders. St. George for merrie England, and if Harrow beats Eton this year the country's in the hands of the Socialists. *Woof!*"

She wound up breathlessly, again shaking her head with vehemence until she had to smooth back the cloudy hair.

Then she smiled, rather shame-facedly. "I don't know what you'll think of me for talking like this –"

"I think you're absolutely right!" Rampole returned, enthusiastically. He had particularly relished that crack about Mr. Saunders. "Down with ouija boards. *À bas le* tennis. I hope Harrow knocks Eton for a row of brick – ahem! What I mean to say is, you're absolutely right and long live Socialism."

"I didn't say anything about Socialism."

"Well, say something about it, then," he offered, magnanimously. "Go on, say something about it. Hurrah for Norman Thomas! God bless –"

"But *why*, silly? Why?"

"Because Mr. Saunders wouldn't like it," explained Rampole. The thesis seemed to him a good one, if vague. But another idea struck him, and he inquired, suspiciously: "Who is this Wilfrid person who comes round to see you every Thursday night? 'Wilfrid' is a lousy name, anyway. It sounds like somebody with marcelled hair."

She slid off the coping of the bridge, and she seemed somehow set free in the strength of her small body. Her laughter – real and swashbuckling, as he had heard it the night before – had got out of its prison, too.

"I say! We'll *never* get those cigarettes if we don't hurry . . . I feel the way you talk. D'you want to run for it? But take it easy; it's a quarter of a mile."

Rampole said, "What ho!" and they clipped out past the hayricks with the wind in their faces, and Dorothy Starberth was still laughing.

"I hope I meet Mrs. Colonel Granby," she said, breathlessly. She seemed to think this a wicked idea, and turned a flushed face over her shoulder, eyes dancing. "It's nice, it's nice. – Ugh! I'm glad I have on low-heeled shoes."

"Want to speed it up?"

"Beast! I'm warm already. I say, are you a track man?"

"Hmf. A little."

A little. Through his brain ran white letters on black boards, in a dusky room off the campus, where there were silver cups in glass cases and embalmed footballs with dates painted on them. Then, with the road flying past, he remembered another scene of just such an exhilaration as he felt now. November, with a surf of sound beating, the rasp of breathing, and the quarterback declaiming signals like a ham actor. Thick headache. Little wires in his legs drawn tight, and cold fingers without feeling in them. Then the wheeze and buckle of the line, and thuds. Suddenly the cold air streaming in his face, a sensation of flying over white lines on legs wired like a puppet's, and a muddy object he plucked out of the air just under the goal-posts . . . He heard again that stupefying roar, and felt his stomach opening and shutting as the roar lifted the dusky air like a lid off a kettle. That had been only last autumn, and it seemed a thousand years ago. Here he was on a weirder adventure in the twilight, with a girl whose very presence was like the tingle of those lost, roaring thousand years.

"A little," he repeated, suddenly, drawing a deep breath.

They were into the outskirts of the village, where thick-waisted trees shaded white shop-fronts, and the bricks of the sidewalks ran in crooked patterns like a child's writing-exercise. A woman stopped to look at them. A man on a bicycle goggled so much that he ran into the ditch and swore.

Leaning up against a tree, flushed and panting, Dorothy laughed.

"I've had enough of your silly game," she said, her eyes very bright. "But, O Lord! I feel better!"

From the furious excitement which had possessed them, neither knowing why, they passed to deep contentment and became carefully decorous. They got the cigarettes, the tobacconist explaining as 'ow he had stopped there after hours, and Rampole gratified a long-cherished wish to buy a church-warden pipe. He was intrigued by the chemist's shop; with its large glass vats of red and green and its impressive array of drugs, it was like something out of a mediaeval tale. There was an inn, called The Friar Tuck, and a public-house called The Goat and Bunch of Grapes. Rampole was steered away from the latter only by the girl's (to him) inexplicable refusal to accompany him into the bar. All in all, he was much impressed.

"You can get a shave and a hair-cut in the cigar store," he continued to muse. "It isn't so different from America, after all."

He felt so fine that even the trials were nothing. They ran into Mrs. Theodosia Payne, the lawyer's wife, who was stalking grimly along the High Street with her ouija board under her arm. Mrs. Payne had a formidable hat. She moved her jaws like a ventriloquist's dummy, but spoke like a sergeant-major. Nevertheless, Rampole listened with Chesterfieldian politeness while she explained the vagaries of Lucius, her "control" – apparently an erratic and dissipated member of the spirit world, who skidded all over the board and spelled with a strong cockney accent. Dorothy saw her companion's face looking dangerously apoplectic, and got him away from Mrs. Payne before they both exploded into mirth.

It was nearly eight o'clock before they started back. Everything pleased these two, from the street lamps (which resembled glass coffins, and burnt a very consumptive sort of gas) to a tiny shop with a bell over the door, where you could get gilt-covered gingerbread animals and the sheets of long-forgotten comic songs. Rampole had always had a passion for buying useless junk, on the two sound principles that he didn't need it and that he had money to spend; so, finding a kindred spirit who didn't think it was childish, he indulged. They went back through a luminous dusk, the song-sheets held between them like a hymnal, earnestly singing a lament called, "Where Was You, 'Arry, on the Last Bank 'Oliday?" – and Dorothy was sternly ordered to repress her hilarity in the pathetic parts.

"It's been glorious," the girl said when they had almost reached the lane leading to Dr. Fell's. "It never occurred to me that there was anything interesting in Chatterham. I'm sorry to go home."

"It never occurred to me, either," he said, blankly. "It just seemed that way this afternoon."

They meditated this a moment, looking at each other.

"We've got time for one more," he suggested, as though that were the most important thing in the world. "Do you want to try 'The Rose of Bloomsbury Square'?"

"Oh *no*! Dr. Fell's an old dear, but I've got to preserve *some* dignity. I saw Mrs. Colonel Granby peeping through the curtains all the time we were in the village. Besides, it's getting late . . ."

"Well –"

"And so –"

They both hesitated. Rampole felt a little unreal, and his heart was pounding with enormous rhythm. All about them the yellow sky had changed to a darkling light edged with purple. The fragrance of the hedgerows had become almost overpowering. Her eyes were very strong, very living, and yet veiled as though with pain; they went over his face with desperate seeking. Though he was looking only there, he somehow felt that her hands were extending . . .

He caught her hands. "Let me walk home with you," he said, heavily; "let me –"

"*Ahoy there!*" boomed a voice from up the lane. "Hold on! Wait a minute."

Rampole felt something at his heart that was like a physical jerk. He was trembling, and he felt through her warm hands that she was trembling, too. The voice broke such an emotional tensity that they both felt bewildered; and then the girl began to laugh.

Dr. Fell loomed up, puffing, out of the lane. Behind him Rampole saw a figure that looked familiar; yes, it was Payne, with the curved pipe in his mouth. He seemed to be chewing it.

Dread, coming back again after a few brief hours . . .

The doctor looked very grave. He stopped to get his breath, leaning one cane up against his leg.

"I don't want to alarm you, Dorothy," he began, "and I know the subject is taboo; all the same, this is a time for speaking straight out –"

"Er!" said Payne, warningly, making a rasp in his throat. "The – er – guest?"

"He knows all about it. Now, girl, it's none of my business, I know –"

"Please tell me!" She clenched her hands.

"Your brother was here. We were a bit worried about the state he's in. I don't mean the drinking. That'll pass off; anyway, he was sick, and he was almost cold sober when he left. But it's the fright he's in; you could see it in the wild and defiant way he acted. We don't want him to get wrought up and do himself an injury over this silly business. Do you see?"

"Well? Go on!"

"The rector and your cousin took him home. Saunders is very much upset about this thing. Look here, I'll be absolutely frank. You know, of course, that before your father died he told Saunders something under a sort of seal of confession; and Saunders just thought he was out of his head at the time? But he's beginning to wonder. *Now there may not be anything in this*, but – just in case – we're going to keep guard. The window of the Governor's Room is plainly visible from here, and this house isn't much over three hundred yards from the prison itself. Do you see?"

"Yes!"

"Saunders and I, and Mr. Rampole, if he will, are going to be on the watch all the time. There'll be a moon, and we can see Martin when he goes in. All you have to do is walk to the front of the lawn, and you have a good view of the front gates. Any noise, any disturbance, anything at all suspicious – Saunders and the young 'un here will be across that meadow before a ghost could vanish." He smiled, putting his hand on her shoulder. "This is all moonshine, I know, and I'm just a crazy old man. But I've known your people a long time – you see? Now, then, what time does the vigil commence?"

"At eleven o'clock."

"Ah, I thought so. Now, then, just after he's left the Hall *telephone us.* We'll be watching. Naturally, you're not to mention this to him; it isn't supposed to be done, and if he knew it he might be in just such a state of nervous bravado to go the other way and block our plans. But you might suggest to him that he sit somewhere near the window with his light."

Dorothy drew a deep breath. "I knew there was something in it," she said, dully. "I knew you were all keeping something from me . . . O my God! why does he have to go, anyway? Why can't we break a silly custom, and –"

"Not unless you want to lose the estate," Payne said, gruffly. "Sorry. But that's the way it's arranged. And I have to administer it. I have to deliver several keys – there's more than one door to be got through – to the heir. When he returns them to me, he must show me a certain thing from inside that vault, never mind what, to show me he's really opened it."

Again the lawyer's teeth gripped his pipe hard. The whites of his eyes looked luminous in the dusk.

"Miss Starberth knew all that, gentlemen, whether the rest of you did or not," he snapped. "We grow frank. Very well. Permit me to shout *my* affairs from the church spire. My father held this trust from the Starberths before me. So did my grandfather, and his grandfather. I state these details, gentlemen, so as not to seem a fool for technicalities. Even if I wanted to break the law, I tell you frankly I wouldn't break the trust."

"Well, let him forfeit the estate, then! Do you think any of us would care a snap of our fingers –"

Payne cut her short, testily: "Well, *he* isn't such a fool, however you and Bert feel about it. Good Lord! girl, do you want to be a pauper as well as a laughingstock? This procedure may be foolish. Very well. But it's the law and it's a trust." He brought the palms of his hands together with a sort of hollow *thock*. "I'll tell you what is more foolish. Your fears. No Starberth has suffered harm like that since 1837. Just because your father happened to be near the Hag's Nook when his horse threw him –"

"Don't!" the girl said, wretchedly.

Her hand quivered, and Rampole took a step forward. He did not speak; his throat felt hot and sanded with fury. But he thought, If I hear that man's voice a minute longer, by God! I'll break his jaw.

"You've said enough, Payne, don't you think?" grunted Dr. Fell.

"Ah," said Payne. "Just so."

Anger was in the air. They heard a small noise of Payne sucking his leathery jaws in against his teeth. He repeated, "Just so!" in his low, dry voice, but you knew that he felt the licking flames.

"If you will excuse me, gentlemen," he continued, very impassive, "I shall accompany Miss Starberth . . . No, sir," as Rampole made a movement, "on this occasion, no. There are confidential matters I must express. Without interference, I hope. I have already discharged a part of my duty in handing over the keys to Mr. Martin Starberth. The rest remains. As – ah – possibly an older friend than the rest of you," his thin voice went high and rasping, and he almost snarled, "I may possibly be permitted to keep *some* matters confidential."

Rampole was so mad that he came close to an absurd gulp. "Did you say 'manners'?" he asked.

"Steady," said Dr. Fell.

"Come along, Miss Starberth," said the lawyer.

They saw him shoot in his cuffs and hobble forward, and the white flash of his eyes as he glanced back over his shoulder. Rampole pressed the girl's hand; then both of them were gone . . .

"Tut, tut!" complained the doctor, after a pause. "Don't swear. He's only jealous of his position as family adviser. I'm much too worried to swear. I had a theory, but . . . I don't know. It's going all wrong. All wrong . . . Come along to dinner."

Mumbling to himself, he led the way up the lane. Something cried aloud in Rampole's heart, and the dusk was full of phantoms. For a moment the released, laughing creature with the wind in her hair as she raced; the wistfulness of the square sombre face, wry-smiling on a bridge; the practicality, the mockery, the little Puckish humours; then suddenly the pallor by the hedge, and the small gasp when these terrors crept back. Don't let anything happen to her. Keep good watch, that no harm may touch her. Keep good watch, for this is her brother . . .

Their footfalls rustled in the grass, and the insect-hum pulsed in shrill droning. Distantly, in the thick air to the west, there was a mutter of thunder.

5

Heat. Heat thick and sickly, with breezes that came as puffs out of an oven, made a gust in the trees, and then died. If this cottage had really been a Swiss barometer, the little figures would have been wildly swinging in their châlet now.

They dined by candlelight, in the little oak room with the pewter dishes round the walls. The room was as warm as the dinner, and the wine warmer than both; Dr. Fell's face grew redder as he kept filling and refilling his glass. But his blowings and easy oratory were gone now. Even Mrs. Fell was quiet, though jumpy. She kept passing the wrong things, and nobody noticed it.

Nor did they linger over coffee, cigars, and port, as was the doctor's custom. Afterwards Rampole went up to his room. He lighted the oil-lamp and began to change his clothes. Old soiled tennis-flannels, a comfortable shirt, and tennis shoes. His room was a small one with a sloping roof, under the eaves, its one window looking out towards the side of Chatterham prison and the Hag's Nook. Some sort of flying beetle banged against the window-screen with a thump that made him start, and a moth was already fluttering round the lamp.

It was a relief to be doing something. He finished dressing and took a few restless strides about. Up here the heat was thick with a smell of dry timber, like an attic; even the paste behind the flowered wall-paper seemed to give out a stifling odour; and the lamp was worst of all. Putting his head against the screen, he peered out. The moon was rising, unhealthy and yellow-ringed; it was past ten o'clock. Damn the uncertainty! – A travelling-clock ticked with irritating nonchalance on the table at the head of his four-poster bed. The calendar in the lower part of the clock-case showed a staring figure where he had been last July 12th, and couldn't remember. Another gust of wind swished in the trees. Heat, prickling out damply on him and flowing over the brain in dizzy waves; *heat* . . . He blew out the lamp.

Stuffing pipe and oilskin pouch into his pocket, he went downstairs. A rocking-chair squeaked tirelessly in the parlour, where Mrs. Fell was reading a paper with large pictures. Rampole groped out across the lawn. The doctor had drawn two wicker chairs round to the side of the house looking towards the prison, where it was very dark and considerably cooler. Glowing red, the bowl of the doctor's pipe moved there; Rampole found a cold glass put into his hand as he sat down.

"Nothing now," said Dr. Fell, "but to wait."

That very distant thunder moved in the west, with a noise which was really like a bowling-ball curving down the alley, never to hit any pins. Rampole took a deep drink of the cold beer. That was better! – The moon was far from strong, but already the cup of the meadow lay washed in a light like skimmed-milk, which was creeping up the walls.

"Which is the window of the Governor's Room?" he asked, in a low voice.

The red bowl gestured. "That large one – the only large one. It's in an almost direct line from here. Do you see it? Just beside it there's an iron door opening on a small stone balcony. That's where the governor stepped out to oversee the hangings."

Rampole nodded. The whole side was covered with ivy, bulging in places where the weight of the masonry had made it sink into the crest of the hill. In the skimmed-milk light he could see tendrils hanging from the heavy bars in the window. Immediately beneath the balcony, but very far down, was another iron door. In front of this door, the limestone hill tumbled down sheer into the pointed fir trees of the Hag's Nook.

"And the door below," he said, "is where they took the condemned out, I suppose?"

"Yes. You can still see the three blocks of stone, with the holes in them, that held the framework of the gallows . . . The stone coping of the well is hidden in those trees. They weren't there, of course, when the well was in use."

"All the dead were dumped into it?"

"Oh yes. You wonder the whole countryside isn't polluted, even after a hundred years. As it is, the well is a rare place for bugs and vermin. Dr. Markley had been agitating about it for the last fifteen years; but he can't get the borough or council to do anything about it, because it's Starberth land. Hmf."

"And they won't let it be filled in?"

"No. That's a part of the old mumbo-jumbo, too; a relic of the eighteenth-century Anthony. I've been going over Anthony's journal again. And when I think of the way he died, and certain puzzling references in the journal, I sometimes think . . ."

"You haven't yet told me how he died," Rampole said, quietly.

As he said it he wondered whether he wanted to know. Last night he thought, he was certain, that something wet had been looking down from the prison wall. In daytime he had not noticed it, but now he was aware of a distinct marshy smell, which seemed to be blowing across the meadow from the Hag's Nook.

"I forgot," muttered the old lexicographer. "I was going to read it to you this afternoon when Mrs. F. interrupted us. Here." There was a rustle of paper, and a thick bundle of sheets was put into his hand. "Take it upstairs later; I want you to read it and form your own opinions."

Were those frogs croaking? He could hear it plainly above the twitching and pulsing of insects. By God! that marshy odour *was* stronger; it was no illusion. There must be some natural explanation of it – the heat of the day released from the ground, or something. He wished he knew more about nature. The trees had begun to whisper uneasily again. Inside the house, a clock bonged out a single note.

"Half-past ten," grunted his host. "And I think that's the rector's car coming up the lane."

Unsteady headlights were gleaming there. Bumping and rattling, a high old Model T Ford – the kind they used to tell the jokes about – swung round to a stop, the rector looking huge on his perch. He hurried over in the moonlight, catching up a chair from the front of the lawn. His bluff and easy airs were not so much in evidence now; Rampole had a sudden feeling that they were assumed, for social purposes, to cover an intense self-consciousness. They could not see his face well in the gloom, but they knew he was perspiring. He panted as he sat down.

"I snatched a quick meal," he said, "and came straightway. Did you arrange everything?"

"Everything. She'll telephone when he leaves. Here, have a cigar and a glass of beer. How was he when you saw him last?"

A bottle jittered and clicked against the side of a glass. "Sober enough to be frightened," the rector answered. "He went for the sideboard as soon as we reached the Hall. I was of two minds as to whether to stop his drinking. Herbert's got him in hand, though. When I left the Hall he was sitting up in his room lighting one cigarette from the end of the last; he must have smoked a whole box just while I was there. I – er – I pointed out the deleterious effect of so much tobacco –

No, thanks; I won't smoke – on his system, and he flew at me."

They all fell silent. Rampole found himself listening for the clock. Martin Starberth would be watching it, too, in another house.

Inside the house, the telephone rang stridently.

"There it is. Will you get the message, my boy?" asked Dr. Fell, breathing a little faster. "You're more spry than I am."

Rampole almost fell over the front steps in his hurry. The telephone was of the ancient type you crank up, and Mrs. Fell was already holding out the receiver to him.

"He's on his way," the voice of Dorothy Starberth told him. It was admirably calm now. "Watch the road for him. He's carrying a big bicycle lamp."

"How is he?"

"A little thick-spoken, but sober enough." She added, rather wildly, "*You're* all right, aren't you?"

"Yes. Now don't worry, please! We'll take care of it. He's in no danger, dear."

It was not until he was on his way out of the house that he remembered the last word he had quite unconsciously used over the phone. Even in the turmoil it startled him. He had no recollection whatever of using it at the time.

"Well, Mr. Rampole?" the rector boomed out of the dark.

"He's started. How far is the Hall from the prison?"

"A quarter of a mile beyond, in the direction of the railway station. You must have passed it last night." Saunders spoke absently, but he seemed more at his ease now that the thing was begun. He and the doctor had both come round to the front of the house. He turned, big and bold-shining in the moonlight. "I've been imagining – dreadful things – all day. When this business was far off, I laughed at it. Now that it's here . . . Well, old Mr. Timothy Starberth . . ."

Something was worrying the good rector's Eton

conscience. He mopped his forehead with a handkerchief. He added:

"I say, Mr. Rampole, was Herbert there?"

"Why Herbert?' the doctor asked, sharply.

"It's – ah – it's only that I wish he were here. That young man is dependable. Solid and dependable. No nerves. Admirable; very English, and admirable."

Again the rumble of thunder, prowling stealthily and low down along the sky. A fresh breeze went swishing through the garden, and white blossoms danced. There was a flicker of lightning, so very brief that it was like an electrician flashing on footlights momentarily to test them before the beginning of a play.

'We'd better watch to see that he gets in safely," the doctor suggested, gruffly. "If he's drunk, he may get a bad fall. Did she say he was drunk?"

"Not very."

They tramped up along the lane. The prison lay in its own shadow on that side, but Dr. Fell pointed out the approximate position of the gateway. "No door on it, of course," he explained. But the rocky hill leading up to it was fairly well lighted by the moon; a cow-path meandered almost into the shadow of the prison. For what seemed nearly ten minutes nobody spoke. Rampole kept trying to time the pulse of a cricket, counting between rasps, and got lost in a maze of numbers. The breeze belled out his shirt with grateful coolness.

"There it is," Saunders said, abruptly.

A beam of white light struck up over the hill. Then a figure, moving slowly but steadily, appeared on the crest with such weird effect that it seemed to be rising from the ground. It tried to move with a jaunty swing, but the light kept flickering and darting – as though at every slight noise Martin Starberth were flashing it in that direction. Watching it, Rampole felt the terror which must be running in the slight, contemptuous, tipsy figure. Very tiny at that distance, it hesitated at the gates. The light stood motionless, playing on a gaping archway. Then it was swallowed inside.

The watchers went back and sank heavily into their chairs.

Inside the house, the clock began to strike eleven.

"– if she only told him," the rector had been running on for some time, but Rampole only heard him now, "to sit near that window!" He threw out his hands. "But, after all, we must be sensi – we must – What *can* happen to him? You know as well as I do, gentlemen . . ."

– *Bong*, hammered the clock slowly. *Bong*, three, four, five –

"Have some more beer," said Dr. Fell. The rector's smooth, unctuous voice, now raised shrilly, seemed to irritate him.

Again they waited. An echo of footfalls in the prison, a scurry of rats and lizards as the light probed; in Rampole's taut fancy he could almost hear them. Some lines in Dickens came back to him, a sketch of prowling past Newgate on a drizzly night and seeing through a barred window the turn-keys sitting over their fire, and their shadows on the whitewashed wall.

A gleam sprang up now in the Governor's Room. It did not waver. The bicycle lamp was very powerful, cutting a straight horizontal band against which the bars of the window leapt out. Evidently it had been put down on a table, where it remained, sending its beam into one corner of the room without further movement. That was all – the tiny shaft of brightness behind ivy-fouled bars, lonely against the great ivy-fouled hulk of the prison. The shadow of a man hovered there, and then vanished.

It seemed to have an incredibly long neck, that shadow. To his surprise, Rampole discovered that his heart was bumping. You had to do something; you had to concentrate . . .

"If you don't mind, sir," he said to his host, "I'd like to go up to my room and look at these journals of the two governors. I can keep my eye on the window from there. And I want to *know*."

It suddenly seemed vitally important to know how these men had come to death. He fingered the sheets, which were damp from his hand. They had been there, he remembered, even when he held the receiver of the telephone in the same hand. Dr. Fell grunted, without seeming to hear him.

The thunder went rattling, with a suggestion of heavy carts shaking the window panes, when he ascended the stairs. His room was now swept by a thick breeze, but still exhaling heat. Lighting the lamp, he drew the table before the window and put down the manuscript sheets. He glanced round once before he sat down. There were the copies of those comic songs, lying scattered on the bed, which he had bought this afternoon; and there was the church-warden pipe.

He had a queer, vague idea that if he were to smoke that pipe, the relic of lightheartedness, it might bring him closer to Dorothy Starberth. But he felt foolish, and cursed himself, the moment he picked it up. When he was about to replace it there was some noise; the brittle clay slipped through his fingers and smashed on the floor.

It shocked him, like breaking a living thing. He stared at it for a moment, and then hurried over to sit down facing the windows. Bugs were beginning to tick and swarm against the screen. Far across the meadow was that tiny, steady lamp in the window of the prison, and he could hear the voices of the rector and Dr. Fell mumbling in conversation just below.

A. Starberth, Esquire, His Journal.

PRIVATE.

(Eighth September, 1797. This being the First Year in the Good Works of Chatterham Gaol, in the Shire of

Lincoln; like-wise the Thirty-Seventh in the Reign of His Sovereign Majesty, George III).

Quae Infra Nos Nihil Ad Nos.

These typewriter sheets carried a more vivid suggestion, Rampole felt, than would have the yellowed originals. You imagined the handwriting to have been small, sharp, and precise, like the tight-lipped writer. There followed some fancy composition, in the best literary style of the day, on the majesty of justice and the nobility of punishing evil-doers. Suddenly it became business-like:

TO BE HANGED, Thursday, the tenth inst., the following, viz.:

John Hepditch. For Highway Robbery.
Lewis Martens. For Uttering Forged Notes, the amt. £2.

Cost of timber for erecting gallows, 2s 4d. Parson's fee 10d, which I would readily do away with but that it is subscribed by law, these being men of low birth and with small need of ghostly consolation.

This day I have overseen the digging of the well to a commodious depth, viz., 25 feet, and 18 feet across at the wide lip – it being rather a moat than a well proper, and being designed to hold the bones of evil-doers, thus saving any unnecessary cost of burial, as well as a most praiseworthy safeguard for that side. Its edge has been buttressed by a row of sharpened iron spikes, by order of me.

I am much vexed, in that my new suit of scarlet, together with the laced hat, which I ordered these six weeks ago, did not arrive by the mail-coach. I had resolved to present a good appearance – scarlet, like a judge, would (I am convinced) make an imposing figure – at the hangings, and have prepared words to speak from my balcony. This John Hepditch (I have heard) has a pretty talent for the making of speeches, though of low birth, and I must take care he doth not outshine me.

I am informed by the chief turnkey that there is some discontent, and a striking upon cell-doors, in the underground corridors, due to a species of large grey field-rat which eats the bread of those confined, and is not easily frightened away; these men further complain that, due to natural darkness, they are unable to see such rats until the rats are upon their arms and snatch at food. Master Nick. Threnlow asked me, What he should do? To which I replied, That it was through the instigation of their own wicked habits that they had come to such a pass, and must endure it; and I further counselled that any unwarranted noises should be met by such Floggings as would induce the malefactors to preserve their proper chastened demeanour.

This evening I began writing a new ballade, in the French manner. I think it very good.

Rampole moved in his chair, and looked up uneasily, to be met by the staring light across the meadow. Below him on the lawn he heard Dr. Fell expounding some point in connection with the drinking customs of England, and the protesting rumble of the rector. Then he continued reading, skimming the pages. They were far from complete. A number of entire years were omitted altogether, and in others there were merely some jottings. But the parade of horror, cruelty, high-sounding preachments, and miserly chucklings over twopence saved, while old Anthony scribbled away at his verses . . . these were only a prelude.

A change was coming over the writer. He began to scream to his journal.

> They call me a "limping Herrick," do they? [he writes in 1812]. A "Dryden in falsetto." But I begin to think of a plan. I do heartily abhor and curse each of those to which I have the misfortune to be bound by ties of blood. There are things one can buy and things one can do to defeat them. *By which I am reminded that the rats are growing thicker lately.* They come into my room, and I can see them beyond the circle of my lamp as I write.

He has grown a new literary style with the passing years, but his rage grows like a mania. Under the year 1814 there is only one entry:

> I must go slowly with the buying. Each year, each year. The rats seem to know me now.

Out of all the rest of them, one passage brought Rampole up with a shock.

> June 23. I am wasting, and I find it difficult to sleep. Several times I have believed to hear a knocking on the outside of the iron door which leads to my balcony. But there is no person there when I open it. My lamp smokes worse, and I believe to feel things in my bed. *But I have the beauties safe.* It is good that I am strong in the arms.

Now the wind rushed fully in at the window, almost blowing the sheets from Rampole's hands. He had a sudden horrible feeling as though they had been jerked away from him; and the ticking and scrambling of the bugs outside did not add to his easiness. The lamp flame jumped slightly, but resumed its steady yellow glow. Lightning illuminated the prison, followed in an instant by a full crash of thunder.

Not yet through with Anthony's journal, and the diary of another Starberth still to come. But he was too fascinated to read faster; he had watched the one-eyed old governor shrivel up with the years, wearing now his tall hat and tight-waisted coat, and carrying the gold-headed cane he mentioned frequently. All of a sudden, the dogged quiet of the diary was broken!

July 9. Oh Lord Jesus, sweet dispenser of mercy to the helpless, look upon me and aid me! I do not know why, but my sleep is gone, and I can thrust a finger between the bones of these ribs. Will they eat my pets?

Yesterday we hanged a man for murder, as already noticed. He wore a blue-and-white striped waistcoat to the gallows. The crowd booed me.

I sleep now with two rush-lights burning. There is a soldier on guard at my door. But last night, the while I was making out my report upon this execution, I heard patterings in my room, to the which I tried to pay no heed. I had trimmed my bedside candle, put on my nightcap, and prepared to read in bed, when I noted a movement among the bedclothes. Whereupon I took my loaded pistol from the table and called to the soldier to throw back the clothes. And when he had done it, doubtless thinking me mad, I saw in the bed a large grey rat looking up at me with his eyes. He was wet, and there was a large pool of black water there; and the rat was gorged fat, and seemed to be trying to shake loose from his sharp teeth a flimsy of blue-and-white striped cloth.

This rat the soldier killed with the butt of his musket, the rat being not well able to run across the floor. Nor would I sleep in the bed that night. I had them kindle a great fire, and dozed before it in a chair with warm rum. I thought that I was just falling asleep when I heard a murmur as of many voices on the balcony outside my iron door – though this is impossible, so many feet from the ground – and a low voice whispered at the keyhole, *"Sir, will you come out and speak with us?"* And, as I looked, methought there was water running under the door.

Rampole sat back with a constriction at his throat and the palms of his hands damp. He was not even startled when the storm broke, the rain sheeting down into the dark lawn and hissing among the trees. He heard Dr. Fell cry: "Get those chairs in! We can watch from the dining-room!" – and the rector replying with something unintelligible. His eyes were fixed on the pencilled note at the end of the journal; Dr. Fell's handwriting, for it bore the initials G.F.

He was found dead on the morning of Sept. 10, 1820. The night before had been stormy, with a high wind, and it is improbable that the turnkeys or soldiers would have heard any cry had he made one. He was found lying with his neck broken across the stone coping around the well. Two of the spikes on this coping had been driven entirely through his body and impaled him with his head pointing down into the well.

There was some suggestion of foul play. No signs of any struggle were visible, however; and it was pointed out that, had he been attacked, even several assailants would have had their hands full. Despite his age, he was widely celebrated for the almost incredible strength of his arms and shoulders. This is a curious fact, since he seemed to develop it after he had taken over the governorship of the prison, and it steadily increased with the years. Latterly he remained always at the prison, rarely visiting his family at the Hall. The eccentric behavior of his later life influenced the findings of the coroner's jury, which were: "Death by misadventure while of unsound mind."

– G.F., Yew Cottage, 1923.

Putting his tobacco-pouch on the loose sheets to keep them from blowing, Rampole sat back again. He was staring out at the drive of the rain, visualizing that scene. Automatically he lifted his eyes to the window of the Governor's Room. Then he sat for an instant motionless . . .

The light in the Governor's Room was out.

Only a sheet of rain flickering in darkness before him. He got up spasmodically, feeling so weak that he could not push the chair away, and glanced over his shoulder at the travelling-clock.

It was not yet ten minutes to twelve. A horrible sensation of unreality, and a feeling as though the chair were entangled in his legs. Then he heard Dr. Fell's shout from downstairs somewhere. They had seen it, too. It couldn't have been out more than a second. The face of the clock swam; he couldn't take his eyes from those placid small hands, or hear anything but the casual ticking in a great silence . . .

Then he was wrenching at the knob of the door, throwing it open, and stumbling downstairs, in a physical nausea which made him dizzy. Dimly he could see Dr. Fell and the rector standing bareheaded in the rain, staring towards the prison, and the doctor still was carrying a chair under his arm. The doctor caught his arm.

"Wait a minute! What's the matter, boy?" he demanded. "You're as white as a ghost. What –"

"We've got to get over there! The light's out! The –"

They were all panting a little, heedless of the rain splashing into their faces. It got into Rampole's eyes, and for a moment he could not see.

"I shouldn't go so fast," Saunders said. "It's that beastly business you've been reading; don't believe in it. He may have miscalculated the time . . . Wait! You don't know the way!"

Rampole had torn from the doctor's grasp and was running through the soggy grass towards the meadow. They heard Rampole say, "I promised her!" – and then the rector was pounding after him. Despite his bulk, Saunders was a runner. Together they slithered down a muddy bank; Rampole felt water gushing into his tennis shoes as he bumped against a rail fence. He vaulted it, plunged down a slope and up again through the long grass of the meadow. He could see little through the blinding cataract of rain, but he realized that unconsciously he was bearing to the left, toward the Hag's Nook. That wasn't right; that wasn't the way in; but the memory of Anthony's journal burned too vividly in his brain. Saunders cried out something behind him, which was lost under the crackle and boom of thunder. In the ensuing flash of lightning he saw a gesticulating Saunders running away from him to the right, towards the gate of the prison, but he still kept on his way.

How he reached the heart of the Hag's Nook he could never afterwards remember. A steep slippery meadow, grass that twisted the feet like wires, then brambles and underbrush tearing through his shin; he could see nothing except that he was bumping into fir trees with a gutted precipice looming up ahead. Breath hurt his lungs, and he stumbled against sodden bark to clear the water from his eyes. But he knew he was *there*. All around in the dark was a sort of unholy stirring and buzzing, muffled splashes, a sense of things that crawled or crept, but, worst of all, an odour.

Things were flicking against his face, too. Throwing out his hand, he encountered a low wall of rough stone, and felt the rust of a spike. There must be something in the feel of this place that made your head pound, and your blood turn thin, and your legs feel weak. Then the lightning came with broken illumination through the trees . . . He was staring across the wide well, on a level with his chest, and hearing water splash below.

Nothing there.

Nothing hanging head down across the edge of the well, impaled on a spike. In the dark he began groping his way round the side of the well, holding to the spikes, in a frenzy to know. It was not until he was just beneath the edge of the cliff, and beginning to gasp with relief, that his foot kicked something soft.

He started groping in the dark, so numb that he groped with hideous care. He felt a chilly face, open eyes, and wet hair, but the neck seemed as loose as rubber, because it was broken. It did not need the lightning-flare immediately afterwards to tell him it was Martin Starberth.

His legs gave, and he stumbled back against the cliff – fifty feet below the governor's balcony, which had stood out black against the lightning a moment before. He shuddered, feeling drenched and lost, with only one sick thought – that he had failed Dorothy Starberth. Everywhere the rain ran down him, the mud thickened under his hands, and the roar of the shower deepened. When he lifted stupid eyes, he suddenly saw far across the meadow, at Dr. Fell's cottage, the yellow lamp in the window of his room. There it was, plain through a gap in the fir trees; and the only images that stuck in his mind, wildly enough, were the scattered music sheets across the bed – and the fragments of a brittle clay pipe, lying broken on the floor.

6

Mr. Budge, the butler, was making his customary rounds at the Hall to see that all the windows were fastened before he retired to his respectable bachelor bed. Mr. Budge was aware that all the windows were fastened, had been fastened every night during the fifteen years of his officiation, and would continue so until the great red-brick house should fall or Get Took By Americans – which latter fate Mrs. Bundle, the housekeeper, always uttered in a direful voice, as though she were telling a terrible ghost story. None the less, Mr. Budge was darkly suspicious of housemaids. He felt that, when his back was turned, every housemaid had an overpowering desire to sneak about, opening windows, so that tramps could get in. His imagination never got so far as burglars, which was just as well.

Traversing the long upstairs gallery with a lamp in his hand, he was especially careful. There would be rain before long, and much weighed on his mind. He was not worried about the young master's vigil in the Governor's Room. That was a tradition, a foregone conclusion, like serving your country in time of war, which you accepted stoically; like war, it had its dangers, but there it was. Mr. Budge was a reasonable man. He knew that there were such things as evil spirits, just as he knew there were toads, bats, and other unpleasant things. But he suspected that even spooks were growing mild and weak-voiced in these degenerate days when housemaids had so much time off. It wasn't like the old times of his father's service. His chief concern now was to see to it that there was a good fire in the library, against the young master's return; a plate of sandwiches, and a decanter of whiskey.

No, there were more serious concerns on his mind. When he reached the middle of the oaken gallery, where the portraits hung, he paused as usual to hold up his lamp briefly before the picture of old Anthony. An eighteenth-century artist had depicted Anthony all in black, and the decorations on his chest, sitting at a table with a skull under his hand. Budge had kept his hair and was a fine figure of a man. He liked to imagine a resemblance to himself in the pale, reserved, clerical countenance of the first governor, despite Anthony's history; and Budge always walked with even a more dignified gait when he left off looking at the portrait. Nobody would have suspected his guilty secret – that he wept during the sad parts at the motion pictures, to which he was addicted; and that he had once tossed sleepless for many nights in the horrible fear that Mrs. Tarpon, the chemist's wife, had seen him in this condition during a performance of an American film called "Way Down East" at Lincoln.

Which reminded him. Having finished with the upstairs, he went in his dignified Guardsman's walk down the great staircase. Gas burning properly in the front hall – bit of a sputter in that third mantle to the left, though; they'd be having in electricity one of these days, he shouldn't wonder! Another American thing. Here was Mr. Martin already corrupted by the Yankees; always a wild one, but a real gentleman until he began talking in this loud gibberish you couldn't understand, nothing but bars and drinks named after pirates – made with gin, too, which was fit for nobody but old women and drunkards; yes, and carrying a revolver, for all *he* knew! "Tom Collins"; that was the pirate one, wasn't it, or was the pirate called John Silver? And something called a "sidecar." . . .

Sidecar. That suggested Mr. Herbert's motorbike. Budge felt uneasy.

"Budge!" a voice said from the library.

Habit cleared Budge's mind as it cleared his face. Setting down his lamp carefully on the table in the hall, he went into the library with just the proper expression of being uncertain he had heard.

"You called, Miss Dorothy?" said the public face of Mr. Budge.

Even though his mind was a sponged slate, he could not help noticing a startling (almost shocking) fact. The wall safe was open. He knew its position, behind the portrait of Mr. Timothy, his late master; but in fifteen years he had never seen it indecently naked and open. This he observed even before his automatic glance at the fireplace, to see that the wood was drawing well. Miss Dorothy sat in one of the big hard chairs, with a paper in her hands.

"Budge," she said, "will you ask Mr. Herbert to step downstairs?"

A hesitation. "Mr. Herbert is not in his room, Miss Dorothy."

"Will you find him, then, please?"

"I believe Mr. Herbert is not in the house," said Budge, as though he had given some problem deep consideration and were arriving at a decision.

She dropped the paper into her lap. "Budge, what on earth do you mean?"

"He – er – mentioned no prospective departure, Miss Dorothy? Thank you."

"Good Heavens, no! Where would he be going?"

"I mentioned the matter, Miss Dorothy, because I had occasion to go to his room shortly after dinner on an errand. He appeared to be packing a small bag."

Again Budge hesitated. He felt uneasy, because her face had assumed an odd expression. She got up.

"When did he leave the house?"

Budge glanced at the clock on the mantel-shelf. Its hands pointed to eleven-forty-five. "I am not certain, Miss Dorothy," he replied. "Quite soon after dinner, I think. He went away on his motor-bicycle. Mr. Martin had asked me to get him an electric bicycle-lamp as being – ah – more convenient for his sojourn across the way. That is how I happened to notice Mr. Herbert's departure. I went out to the stable to detach a lamp from one of the machines, and – ah – he drove past me . . ."

(Odd how Miss Dorothy was taking this! Of course, she had a right to be upset, what with Mr. Herbert's unheard-of departure without a word to anybody, and the safe standing open for the first time in fifteen years; but he did not like to see her show it. He felt as he had once felt when he peeked through a keyhole and saw – Budge hastily averted his thoughts, embarrassed at remembering his younger days.)

"It's strange I didn't see him," she was saying, looking at Budge steadily. "I sat on the lawn for at least an hour after dinner."

Budge coughed. "I was about to say, Miss Dorothy, that he didn't go by the drive. He went out over the pasture, towards Shooter's Lane. I noticed it because I was some time in finding a proper lamp to take to Mr. Martin, and I saw him turning down the lane then."

"Did you tell Mr. Martin of this?"

Budge permitted himself to look slightly shocked. "No, Miss Dorothy," he answered, in a tone of reproof. "I gave him the lamp, as you know, but I did not think it within my province to explain –"

"Thank you, Budge. You needn't wait up for Mr. Martin."

He inclined his head, noting from a corner of his eye that the sandwiches and whiskey were in the proper place, and withdrew. He could loosen his grammar now, like a tight belt; he was Mr. Budge again. A queer one, the young mistress was. He had almost thought, "pert little piece," but that it would be disrespectful. All stiffness and high varnish, with her straight back and her coolish eyes. No sentiment. No 'eart. He had watched her growing up – let's see; she was twenty-one last April – since she was six. A child not condescending or sure of getting her way, like Mr. Martin, or quietly thankful for attention, like Mr. Herbert, but odd . . .

It was thundering more frequently now, he noted, and little streaks of lightning penetrated dark places of the house. Ah, a good job he'd lit that fire! The grandfather clock in the hall wanted winding. Performing that office, he kept thinking of what a hodd child Miss Dorothy had been. A scene came back: the dinner table, with himself in the background, when the master and the mistress were alive. Master Martin and Master Herbert had been playing war in Oldham orchard, with some other boys; in talking of it at dinner, Master Martin had twitted his cousin about not climbing into the branches of the highest maple as a look-out. Master Martin was always the leader, and Master Herbert trotted after him humbly; but this time he refused to obey orders. "I wouldn't!" he repeated at the table. "Those branches are rotten." "That's right, Bert," said the mistress, in her gentle way. "Remember, even in war one must be cautious." And then little Miss Dorothy had astonished them all by suddenly saying, very violent-like, though she hadn't spoken all evening: "When I grow up, *I'm* going to marry a man without any caution at all." And looked very fierce. The mistress had reproved her, and the master had just chuckled in his dry, ugly way; queer to remember that now . . .

It was raining now. As he finished winding the clock, it began to strike. Budge, staring at it vacantly, found himself surprised, and wondered why. Midnight, the clock was striking. Well, that was all right, surely . . .

No. Something was wrong. Something jarred at the back of his small, automatic brain. Troubled, he frowned at the landscape painted on the clock-face. Ah, he had it now! Just a few minutes ago he had been talking to Miss Dorothy, and the library clock had said eleven forty-five. The library clock must be wrong.

He drew out his gold watch, which had not erred in many years, and opened it. Ten minutes to twelve. No, the library clock had been right; this old grandfather, by which the housemaids set the other time-pieces in the house, was precisely ten and a half minutes fast. Budge permitted a groan to go backwards down his windpipe, and thus remain unheard. Now, before he could retire with an undisturbed conscience, he must go about and inspect the other clocks.

The clock struck twelve.

And then, presently, the telephone rang. Budge saw Dorothy Starberth's white face in the library door as he went to answer it . . .

7

Sir Benjamin Arnold, the chief constable, sat behind the writing-table in Dr. Fell's study, his bony hands folded on it like a schoolmaster. He looked a little like a schoolmaster also, but for the burnt color and horsiness of his face. His thick greyish hair was combed pompadour; his eyes looked sharp behind a pince-nez.

"– I thought it best," he was saying, "to take personal charge. It was suggested that an inspector be sent down from Lincoln. However, I have known the Starberths, and Dr. Fell in particular, for such a long time that I thought it best to drive over and superintend the Chatterham police myself. In that way we may save any scandal, or as much beyond what the inquest is bound to bring out."

He hesitated, clearing his throat.

"You, Doctor – and you, Mr. Saunders – are aware that I have never had occasion to handle a murder case. I am almost certain to being out of my depth. If everything fails, we shall have to call in Scotland Yard. But among us we may be able to straighten this unfortunate business out."

The sun was high in a clear, warm morning, but the study still held little light. During a long silence they could hear a police constable walking up and down the hall outside. Saunders nodded ponderously. Dr. Fell remained frowning and glum. Rampole was too tired and muddled to pay much attention.

"You – ah – said 'murder case,' Sir Benjamin?" the rector inquired.

"I know the Starberth legend, of course," answered the chief constable, nodding. "And I confess I have a theory about it. Perhaps I should not have said 'murder case' in the properest sense. Accident we may put out of the question. But I will come to that presently . . . Now, Doctor."

He squared himself, drawing in his lips and tightening fingers round his bony knuckles; shifting a little, like a lecturer about to commence on an important subject.

"Now, Doctor. You have told everything up to the time the light went out in the Governor's Room. What happened when you went up to investigate?"

Moodily Dr. Fell poked at the edge of the writing-table with his cane. He rumbled and bit at his moustache.

"I didn't go. Thanks for the compliment, but I couldn't move like these other two. H'mf, no. Better let them tell you."

"Quite . . . I believe, Mr. Rampole, that you discovered the body?"

The clipped, official lines of this procedure made Rampole feel uneasy. He couldn't talk naturally, and felt that anything he said might be used against him. Justice! – it was a big, unnerving thing. He felt guilty of something without knowing what.

"I did."

"Tell me, then: why did it occur to you to go directly to the well, instead of through the gate and up to the Governor's Room? Had you reason to suspect what had happened?"

"I – I don't know. I've been trying to figure it out all day. It was just automatic. I'd been reading those journals – the history of the legend, and all that – so . . ." He gestured, helplessly.

"I see. What did you do afterwards?"

"Well, I was so stunned that I sort of fell back against the hill and sat there. Then I remembered where I was and called for Mr. Saunders."

"And you, Mr. Saunders?"

"For for myself, Sir Benjamin," the rector said, giving the title its full value, "I was almost to the gate of the prison when I – ah – heard Mr. Rampole's summons. I thought it somewhat odd that he should go directly towards the Hag's Nook, and tried to beckon him. But there was scarcely time to – think much." He frowned judicially.

"Quite. When you stumbled on the body, Mr. Rampole, it was lying at the edge of the well, directly beneath the balcony?"

"Yes."

"How lying? – I mean, on its back or face?"

Rampole reflected, closing his eyes. All he could think of was the wetness of the face. "On his side, I think. Yes, I'm certain."

"Left or right?"

"I don't know . . . Wait a minute! Yes, I do. It was the right."

Doctor Fell bent forward unexpectedly, poking the table sharply with his cane. "You're sure of that?" he demanded. "You're sure of it, now, boy? Remember, it's easy to be confused."

The other nodded. Yes – feeling that dead man's neck, bending over and finding it all squashed into his right shoulder; he nodded fiercely, to drive away the image. "It was the right," he answered. "I'll swear to it."

"That is quite correct, Sir Benjamin," the rector affirmed, putting his finger tips together.

"Very well. What did you do next, Mr. Rampole?"

"Why, Mr. Saunders got there, and we weren't certain what to do. All we could think of was getting him out of the wet. So first we thought we'd carry him down to the cottage here, and then we didn't want to frighten Mrs. Fell; so we took him up and put him in a room just inside the prison. Oh, yes – and we found the bicycle lamp he'd been using for a light. I tried to work it so as to give us some light, but it had been smashed by the fall."

"Where was this lamp? In his hand?"

"No. It was some distance away from him. It looked as though it had been pitched over the balcony; I mean, it was too far away for *him* to have been carrying it."

The chief constable tapped his fingers on the table. A spiral of wrinkles ascended his leathery neck as he kept his head sideways, staring at Rampole.

"That point," he said, "may be of the utmost importance in the coroner's verdict between accident, suicide, or murder . . . According to Dr. Markley, young Starberth's skull was fractured, either by the fall or by a heavy blow with what we generally term a blunt instrument; his neck was broken, and there were other contusions of a heavy fall. But we can go into that later . . . What next, Mr. Rampole?"

"I stayed with him while Mr. Saunders went down to tell Dr. Fell and drive to Chatterham after Dr. Markley. I just waited, striking matches and – I mean, I just waited."

He shuddered.

"Thank you. Mr. Saunders?"

"There is little more to add, Sir Benjamin," Saunders returned, his mind on details. "I drove to Chatterham, after instructing Dr. Fell to telephone to the Hall, speak to Budge, the butler, and inform him what had happened . . ."

"That fool –" Dr. Fell began explosively. As the rector glanced at him in shocked surprise he added: "Budge, I mean. Budge isn't worth a two-ounce bottle in a crisis. He repeated what I said over the phone, and I heard somebody scream; and, instead of keeping it from Miss Starberth until somebody could tell her gently, she knew it that minute."

"As I was saying, Sir Benjamin – of course you're right, Doctor; it was most inopportune – as I was saying," the rector went on, with the air of a man trying to please several people at once, "I drove to get Dr. Markley, stopping only at the rectory to procure myself a raincoat; then we returned, taking Dr. Fell to the prison with us. After a brief examination, Dr. Markley said there was nothing to do but notify the police. We took the – the body to the Hall in my car."

He seemed about to say more, but he shut his lips suddenly. There was an enormous pressure of silence, as though everyone had checked himself in the act of speaking, too. The chief constable had opened a large claspknife and begun to sharpen a pencil; the small quick rasps of the knife against lead were so loud that Sir Benjamin glanced up sharply.

"You questioned the people at the Hall?" he asked.

"We did," said Dr. Fell. "*She* was bearing up admirably. We got a clear, concise account of everything that had happened that evening, both from her and from Budge. The other servants we did not disturb."

"Never mind. I had better get it first hand from them. – Did you speak to young Herbert?"

"We did not," the doctor responded, after a pause. "Just after dinner last night, according to Budge, he packed a bag and left the Hall on his motor-cycle. He has not returned."

Sir Benjamin laid down knife and pencil on the table. He sat rigid, staring at the other. Then he took off his pince-nez, polished it on an old handkerchief; his eyes, from being sharp, suddenly looked weak and sunken.

"Your implication," he said at length, "is absurd."

"Quite," echoed the rector, looking straight ahead of him.

"It's not any implication. Good God!" Dr. Fell rumbled, and slapped the ferrule of his cane against the floor. "You said you wanted facts. But you don't want facts at all. You want me to say something like, 'Of course there is the little point that Herbert Starberth went to Lincoln to the cinema, taking some clothes to leave at the laundry, and that he left the theatre so late he undoubtedly decided to spend the night with a friend.' Those implications would be what you call the facts. But I give you the plain facts, and you call them implications."

"By Jove!" the rector said, thoughtfully, "he might have done just that, you know."

"Good," said Dr. Fell. "Now we can tell everybody just what he did. But don't call it a fact. That's the important thing."

The chief constable made an irritable gesture.

"He didn't tell anybody he was going?"

"Not unless he mentioned it to somebody other than Miss Starberth or Budge."

"Ah. Well, I'll talk to them. I don't want to hear anything more . . . I say, there were no bad feelings between him and Martin, were there?"

"If there were, he concealed 'em admirably."

Saunders, stroking a plump pink chin, offered: "He may have come back by this time, you know. We haven't been at the Hall since last night."

Dr. Fell grunted. Rising with obvious reluctance, Sir Benjamin stood and worked with the point of his knife at the table blotter. Then he made a schoolmaster's gesture, compressing his lips again.

"If you gentlemen don't mind, we'll go and have a look at the Governor's Room. I take it none of you went up there last night? . . . Good. Then we shall begin with unprejudiced minds."

"I wonder," said Dr. Fell.

Something said, "Oooo-o!" and gave a fluttering jump as they left the study, and Mrs. Fell went scuttling down the hall. They could see by the police constable's distracted expression that she had been talking to him; and the constable was holding, with obvious embarrassment, a large doughnut.

"Put that thing down, Withers," the chief constable rasped, "and come with us. You've posted a man at the prison? . . . Good. Come along."

They went out into the highroad, Sir Benjamin in the lead with his old Norfolk jacket flying and a battered hat stuck on the side of his head. Nobody spoke until they had climbed the hill to the great gate of the prison. The iron grating which had once barred it sagged open in rusty drunkenness; Rampole remembered how it had jarred and squeaked when they had carried Martin Starberth's body inside. A dark passage, cold and alive with gnats, ran straight back. Coming in here out of the sunlight was like entering a spring-house.

"I've been in here once or twice," the chief constable said, peering round curiously, "but I don't remember the arrangement of the rooms. Doctor, will you lead the way? . . . I say! The Governor's Room part of the place is kept locked, isn't it? Suppose young Starberth locked the outer door of the room when he went in; how do we manage it? I should have got the keys from his clothes."

"If somebody chucked him over that balcony," Dr. Fell grunted, "you can rest assured the murderer had to get out of the Governor's Room afterwards. He didn't try to make a fifty-foot jump from the window, either. Oh, we shall find the door open, right enough."

"It's confoundedly dark in here," said Sir Benjamin. Craning his long neck, he pointed to a door at the right. "Is that where you carried young Starberth last night?"

Rampole nodded, and the chief constable pushed a rotting oak door a little way open to peer inside.

"Not much in there," he announced. "Ugh! Damn the cobwebs. Stone floor, grated window, fireplace, what I can see of it. Not much light." He slapped at some invisible bugs before his face.

"That was the turnkeys' waiting-room, and the prison office beyond it," Dr. Fell amplified. "There was where the governor interviewed his guests and recorded 'em before they were assigned their quarters."

"It's full of rats, anyway," Rampole said, so suddenly that they all glanced at him.

The earthy, cellary smell of the place still seemed to be about him as it had been last night. "It's full of rats," he repeated.

"Oh, ah – undoubtedly," said the rector. "Well, gentlemen?"

They pushed forward along the passage. These walls were uneven with ragged stones, and dark green moss patched the cracks; a rare place, Rampole thought, for typhoid fever. Now scarcely anything could be seen, and they blundered forward by holding to one another's shoulders.

"We should have brought a flashlight," growled Sir Benjamin. "There's an obstruction –"

Something struck the weedy stone floor with a dull crash, and they jumped involuntarily.

"Manacles," said Dr. Fell from the gloom ahead. "Leg irons and such. They're still hanging from the wall along here. That means we're entering the wards. Look sharp for the door."

It was impossible, Rampole thought, to straighten out the tangle of passages; though some small light filtered in once they had passed the first of the inner doors. At one point a heavily grated window, sunk in the five-foot thickness of the wall, looked out upon a dank, shaded yard. It had once been paved, but it was now choked in weeds and nettles. Along one side a line of broken cell-doors hung like decayed teeth. Weirdly, just in the centre of this desolate yard grew a large apple tree in white bloom.

"The condemned ward," said Dr. Fell.

Nobody spoke after that. They did not explore, nor did they ask their conductor to explain the meaning of certain things they saw. But, in one airless room just before they came to the staircase for the second floor, they saw the Iron Maiden by the light of matches; and they saw the furnaces for certain charcoal fires. The Iron Maiden's face wore a drowsy, glutted smile, and spiders swung in webs from her mouth. There were bats flopping around in that room also, so that they did not linger.

Rampole kept his hands clenched tightly; he did not mind anything but the things that flicked against his face, briefly, or the feeling that something was crawling up the back of his neck. And you could hear the rats. When they stopped at last before a great door, bound in iron, along a gallery on the second floor, he felt that he was out of it; he felt as though he had just plunged into clear cool water after sitting on an anthill.

"Is it – is it open?" asked the rector, his voice startlingly loud.

The door rasped and squealed as Dr. Fell pushed it back, the chief constable lending him a hand; it was warped, and difficult to jar backwards along the stone floor. A sifting of dust shook round them.

Then they stood on the threshold of the Governor's Room, looking round.

"I dare say we shouldn't be going in here," Sir Benjamin muttered, after a silence. "All the same! – Any of you ever seen the room before? . . . No? I didn't expect so. H'm. They can't have changed the furniture much, can they?"

"Most of the furniture was old Anthony's," said Dr. Fell. "The rest of it belonged to his son Martin, who was governor here until he – well, died – in 1837. They both gave instructions that the room wasn't to be altered."

It was a comparatively large room, though with rather a low ceiling. Directly opposite the door in which they stood was the window. That side of the prison was in shadow, and the ivy twined round the window's heavy grating did not admit much light; puddles of rain water still lay under it on the uneven stone floor. Some six feet to the left of the window was the door giving on the balcony. It was open, standing out almost at right-angles to the wall; and trailing strands of vine, ripped apart when the door had been opened, drooped across the entrance; so that it allowed but little more light than the window.

There had evidently been an effort, once upon a time, to lend a semblance of comfort to this gloomy place. Black-walnut panelling, now rotting away, had been superimposed on the stone walls. In the wall towards the left of the watchers, just between a tall wardrobe and a bookcase full of big discoloured volumes in calfskin, was a stone chimneypiece with a couple of empty candlesticks on its ledge. A mildewed wing-chair had been drawn up before the fireplace. There (Rampole remembered) would be where old Anthony sat in his nightcap before the blaze, when he heard a knocking at the balcony door and a whispered invitation to come out and join dead men . . .

In the centre of the room was an old flat desk, thick with dust and debris, and a straight wooden chair drawn up beside it. Rampole stared. Yes, in the dust he could see a narrow rectangular space where the bicycle-lamp had stood last night; there, in that wooden chair facing the right-hand wall, was where Martin Starberth had sat with the ray of his lamp directed towards . . .

So. In the middle of the right-hand wall, set flush with it, was the door to the vault or the safe or whatever it was called. A plain iron door, six feet high and half as wide, now dull with rust. Just under its iron handle was a curious arrangement like a flattened box, with a large keyhole in one end, and in the other what resembled a metal flap above a small knob.

"The reports were correct, then," Dr. Fell said, abruptly. "I thought so. Otherwise it would have been too easy."

"What?" asked the chief constable, rather irritably.

The doctor pointed with his cane. "Suppose a burglar wanted to key into that thing. Why, with only a keyhole in plain sight, he might get an impression of the lock and have a skeleton key made; though it would be an infernally big key . . . But with *this* arrangement, he couldn't have got in short of blowing the whole wall out with dynamite."

"With what arrangement?"

"A letter combination. I'd heard there was one. It isn't a new idea, you know. Metternich had one; and Talleyrand speaks of, *'Ma porte qu'on peut ouvrir avec un mot, comme les quarante voleurs de Scheherazade.'* You see that knob, with the sliding metal thing above it? The metal piece covers a dial, like a modern safe, except that there are the twenty-six letters of the alphabet instead of numbers. You must turn that knob and spell a word – the word arranged on – before the door can be opened; without that word, a mere key is useless."

"Provided anybody wanted to open the dashed thing," said Sir Benjamin.

They were silent again, all uncomfortable. The rector was mopping his forehead with a handkerchief, a sure sign, and regarding a large canopied bed against the right-hand wall. It was still laid with moth-eaten, decaying clothes and bolster; and fragments of the curtains hung on black brass rings about the tester. There was a night table beside it, with a candlestick. Rampole found himself thinking of lines out of Anthony's manuscript: "I had trimmed my bedside candle, put on my nightcap, and prepared to read in bed, when I saw a movement among the bedclothes . . ."

The American removed his eyes quickly. Well, one more person had lived and died in this room since Anthony. Over beyond the safe there was a desk-secretary with glass doors; on top of it he could see a bust of Minerva and a huge Bible. None of them, with the exception of Dr. Fell, could quite shake off a sense that they were in a dangerous place where they must walk lightly and not touch. The chief constable shook himself.

"Well," Sir Benjamin began, grimly, "we're here. I'm hanged if I see what we do now. There's where the poor chap sat. There's where he put his lamp. No sign of a struggle – nothing broken –"

"By the way," interposed Dr. Fell, thoughtfully, "I wonder if the safe is still open."

Rampole felt a constriction in his throat.

"My dear Doctor," said Saunders, "do you think the Starberths would quite approve . . . Oh, I say!"

Dr. Fell was already lumbering past him, the ferrules of his canes ringing on the floor. Turning sharply to Saunders, Sir Benjamin drew himself up.

"This is murder, you know. We've got to see. But wait! – Wait a minute, Doctor!" He strode over, earnest and horsy, with his long head poked forward. In a lower voice he added, "Do you think it's wise?"

"I'm also curious," the doctor was ruminating, without seeming to hear him, "as to what letter they have the combination on now. Will you stand aside a moment, old man? Here . . . By Jove! the thing's *oiled*!"

He was working the metal flap up and down as they crowded about him.

"It's set on the letter 'S.' Maybe that's the last letter of the word, and maybe it isn't. Anyhow, here goes."

He turned, with a sleepy grin among his chins, peering at them mockingly over his glasses, as he seized the handle of the safe.

"Everybody ready? Look sharp, now!"

He twisted the handle, and slowly the door creaked on its hinges. One of his canes fell down with a sharp clatter.

Nothing came out . . .

8

Rampole did not know what to expect. He held his ground at the doctor's elbow, though the others had instinctively backed away. During an instant of silence they heard rats stirring behind the wainscot.

"Well?" demanded the rector, his voice high.

"I don't see anything," said Dr. Fell. "Here, young fellow – strike a match, will you?"

Rampole cursed himself when he broke off the head of the first match. He struck another, but the dead air of the vault extinguished it the moment he put it inside. Stepping inside, he tried another. Mould and damp, and a strand of cobweb brushing his neck. Now a tiny blue flame burnt in the cup of his hand . . .

A stone enclosure, six feet high and three or four feet deep. Shelves at the back, and what looked like rotting books. That was all. A sort of dizziness went from him, and he steadied his hand.

"Nothing," he said.

"Unless," said Dr. Fell, chuckling, "*unless it got out.*"

"Cheerful blighter, aren't you?" demanded Sir Benjamin. "Look here – we've been wandering about in a nightmare, you know. I'm a business man, a practical man, a sensible man. But I give you my word, gentlemen, that damned place put the wind up me for a moment. It did for a fact."

Saunders ran his handkerchief round under his chin. He had suddenly become pink and beaming, drawing a gusty lungful of air and making a broad unctuous gesture.

"My dear Sir Benjamin," he protested, boomingly, "nothing of the kind! As you say – practical men. As a servant of the Church, you know, I must be the most practical person of all in regard to – ah – matters of this kind. Nonsense! Nonsense!"

He was altogether so pleased that he seemed about to shake Sir Benjamin's hand. The latter was frowning over Rampole's shoulder.

"Anything else?" he asked.

The American nodded. He was holding the flame of the match down against the door, and moving it about. Clearly something had been there, by the outline in the heavy dust: a rectangular outline about eighteen by ten inches. Whatever it was, it had been removed. But he hardly heard the chief constable's request to close the vault again. The last letter of the combination was "S." Something was coming back to him, significant and ugly. Words spoken over a hedge at twilight, words flung at Herbert Starberth by a drunken, contemptuous Martin when the two were coming home from Chatterham yesterday afternoon. "You know the word for it right enough," Martin had said. "The word is *Gallows*." . . .

Rising and slapping dust from his knees, he pushed the door shut. Something had been in that vault – a box, in all likelihood – and the person who killed Martin Starberth had stolen it.

"Somebody took –" he said, involuntarily.

"Yes," said Sir Benjamin. "That seems fairly clear. They wouldn't hand down such a piece of elaborate mummery all these years without any secret at all. But there may be something else. Has it occurred to you, Doctor?"

Dr. Fell was already lumbering round the centre table, as though he were smelling it. He poked at the chair with his cane; he bent down, his big mop of hair flying, to peer under it; and then he looked up vacantly.

"Eh?" he muttered. "I beg your pardon. I was thinking of something else. What did you say?"

The chief constable assumed his schoolmaster's air again, drawing in his chin and compressing his lips to indicate that a deep subject was coming. "Look here," he said, "look here. Don't you think it's more than a coincidence that so many of the Starberth family have died in this particular way?"

Dr. Fell looked up with the expression of a man who has just been hit on the head with a club in a movie comedy.

"Brilliant!" he said. "Brilliant, my boy! – Well, yes. Dense as I am, the coincidence gradually begins to obtrude itself. What then?"

Sir Benjamin was not amused. He folded his arms.

"I think, gentlemen," he announced, seeming to address everybody, "that we shall get forrader in this investigation if we acknowledge that I am, after all, the chief constable, and that I have been at considerable trouble to take over –"

"Tut! I know it. I didn't mean anything." Dr. Fell chewed his moustache to keep back a grin. "It was your infernally solemn way of saying the obvious, that's all. You'll be a statesman yet, son. Pray go on."

"With your permission," conceded the chief constable. He tried to retain his schoolmaster's air; but a smile crept up his speckled face. He rubbed his nose amiably, and then went on with earnestness: "No, see here now. You were all sitting on the lawn watching this window, weren't you? You'd have seen anything untoward that happened up here, certainly – a struggle, or the light knock over, or something. Eh? You'd certainly have heard a cry."

"Very probably."

"And there wasn't any struggle. Look where young Starberth was sitting. He could see the only door in the room; it's exceedingly likely he had it locked, too, if he was as nervous as you say. Even if a murderer could have got into the room first, there was no place for him to hide – unless – Hold on! That wardrobe . . ."

He strode across and opened the doors, disturbing thick dust.

"That's no good, either. Nothing but dust, mouldy clothes . . . I say, here's one of your frogged greatcoats with the beaver collars; George IV style – spiders!" Closing the doors with a slam, he turned back. "Nobody hid there, I'll swear. And there was no place else. In other words, young Starberth couldn't have been taken by surprise, without fight or at least outcry . . . Now, then, how do you know the murderer didn't come in here *after* young Starberth had fallen from the balcony?"

"What the devil are you taking about?"

Sir Benjamin's mouth assumed a tight mysterious smile.

"Put it this way," he urged. "Did you actually see this murderer throw him over? Did you see him fall?"

"No, as a matter of fact, we didn't, Sir Benjamin," put in the rector, who evidently felt he had been neglected long enough. He looked thoughtful. "But then we wouldn't have, you know. It was very dark and raining hard, and the light was out. I am of the opinion that he could have been thrown over even while the light was on. You see . . . here's where the light was, on the table. The broad end of the lamp is here, meaning that the beam was directed on the safe. Six feet to the other side, where the balcony door is, and a person would have been in complete darkness."

The chief constable drew up his shoulders and stabbed one long finger into the palm of his head.

"What I am trying to establish, gentlemen, is this: There may have been a murderer. But that murderer did not necessarily creep in here, smash him over the head, and pitch him down to his death; I mean, there may not have been *two* people on the balcony at all . . . What about a death-trap?"

"Ah!" muttered Dr. Fell, hunching his shoulders. "Well –"

"You see, gentlemen," Sir Benjamin went on, turning to the others in an agony of verbal precision, "I mean . . . At least two Starberths have met their deaths off that balcony before this one. Now suppose there were something about that balcony – a mechanism – eh?"

Rampole turned his eyes towards the balcony door. Beyond the torn ivy he could see a low stone wall, balustraded, suggestive. The very room seemed to grow darker and more sinister.

"I know," he nodded. "Like the stories. I remember one I read when I was a kid, and it made a powerful impression on me. Something about a chair bolted to the floor in an old house, and a weight that swung down out of the ceiling and killed whoever sat under it But, look here! That sort of thing doesn't happen. Besides, you'd have to have somebody to work a thing like that . . ."

"Not necessarily. There may have been a murderer; but the 'murderer' may have been dead two hundred years." Sir Benjamin's eyes opened wide, and then narrowed. "By George! I'm getting rather good at this sort of thing! – It just occurred to me: Suppose young Martin opens the safe, finds a box there, and in it directions to do something *on the balcony*? Well, something happens; the box flies out of his hand, down into the well – the lamp goes in another direction, where you find it later – eh?"

Any enthusiastic theory could generally carry Rampole with it. Again he found himself thinking of lines out of Anthony's manuscript: "But I begin to think of a plan. I do heartily abhor and curse each of those to whom I have the misfortune to be bound by ties of blood . . . By which I am reminded that the rats are growing thicker lately."

And yet – no. Even in his excitement, doubts rattled round inside this smooth hypothesis.

"But look here, sir," he protested, "you can't seriously mean that Anthony wanted to plan a death-trap for all his descendants! Even if he did, it wouldn't be very practical. He would just have got one person with it. The victim takes the box out, reads the paper or whatever it is, gets pitched off the balcony. All right. But the next day they discover the secret, don't they?"

"On the contrary. That's exactly what they haven't discovered. Suppose the instructions were like this: Read this paper, put it back in the box, close the safe again, and then do as directed therein . . . But this time," said Sir Benjamin, growing so excited that he began to poke Rampole in the chest with a long forefinger – "this time the victim, from whatever cause, takes box and paper along – and down they go into the well."

"Well, then, what about the other Starberths who haven't died in that way? There have been several between Martin in 1837 and Martin in 1930. Timothy got his neck broken in the Hag's Nook, but there's no means of knowing . . ."

The chief constable settled his pince-nez more firmly, even benignantly. He was the professor aiding a favourite pupil.

"My dear Mr. Rampole," he said, with a class-room clearing of his throat, "surely you expect too much of the man's mechanical devices to think it will catch *all* his descendants? No, no. It wouldn't always work, of course, from one cause or another. Anthony may have died in testing it out . . . Of course, you can take the first theory I outlined, if you prefer it. I confess I'd forgotten that, momentarily. I mean a murderer who wants to steal something from that safe. He has prepared this death-trap on the balcony, using old Anthony's for his own modern use. He waits until young Martin had opened the safe. Then – by some means – he sees to it that Martin is lured out in the balcony, where the mechanism tips him over. The light is thrown and broken. The murderer (who has never actually touched his victim) takes his booty and departs. There, I submit, are two theories, both revolving round a death-mechanism created in the past by Anthony Starberth."

"HEY!" boomed a thunderous voice.

By this time the two parties to the argument had become so engrossed with tapping each other on the shoulder or squaring away to emphasize a point that they had entirely forgotten the others. The violent exclamation from Dr. Fell brought them up with a start. It was followed by heavy rappings of a cane on the floor. Rampole turned to see Dr. Fell's great bulk spread out on the chair beside the table; he was glowering at them and shaking the other cane in the air.

"You two," said the doctor, "have the most brilliantly logical minds I ever listened to. You're not trying to solve anything. You're simply arguing about what would make the best story."

He made a tremendous challenging sound in his nose, like a battle-cry. Then he went on more mildly:

"Now, I'm very fond of such stories, myself. I have been improving my mind with fiction of the Bloody Hand variety for the last forty years. So I know all the conventional death-traps: the staircase that sends you down a chute in the dark, the bed with the descending canopy, the piece of furniture with the poisoned needle in it, the clock that fires a bullet or sticks you with a knife, the gun inside the safe, the weight in the ceiling, the bed that exhales the deadly gas when the heat of your body warms it, and all the rest of 'em . . . probable or improbable. And I confess," said Dr. Fell, with relish, "that the more improbable they are, the better I like 'em. I have a simple melodramatic mind, gentlemen, and I would dearly love to believe you. Have you ever seen 'Sweeney Todd, the Demon Barber of Fleet Street'? You should. It was one of the original thriller plays, well known in the early eighteen-hundreds; all about a devilish barber's chair which dropped you into the cellar so that the barber could cut your throat at his leisure. *But* –"

"Hold on!" said Sir Benjamin irritably. "All this just means, then, that you think the notion is too far-fetched?"

"The Gothic romance in particular," pursued Dr. Fell, "is full of such – eh?" he broke off, lifting his eyes. "Far-fetched? God bless my soul, no! Some of the most far-fetched of the death-traps have been real ones, like Nero's collapsing ship, or the poisoned gloves that killed Charles VII. No, no. I don't mind your being improbable. The point is that you haven't any grounds to be improbable *on.* That's where you're far behind the detective stories. They may reach an improbable conclusion, but they get there on the strength of good, sound, improbable evidence that's in plain sight. – How do you know there was any 'box' inside that safe?"

"Well, we don't, of course; but –"

"Exactly. And you no sooner have the box, than you get an inspiration of a 'paper' inside it. Then you get the paper, and you put 'instructions' on it. Then young Starberth goes over the balcony; the box becomes inconvenient, so you drop it after him. Splendid! Now you've not only created the box and the paper, but you've made them disappear again, and the case is complete. As our American friends say, Horse-blinders! It won't do."

"Very well, then," the chief constable said, stiffly. "You can examine that balcony, if you like. I'm jolly certain *I* won't."

Dr. Fell hoisted himself to his feet. "Oh, I'm going to examine it. Mind, I don't say there wasn't any death-trap; you may be right," he added. He stared straight ahead of him, his big red face very intent. "But I want to remind you that there's only one thing we're absolutely sure of – that Starberth was lying under that balcony with his neck broken. That's *all.*"

Sir Benjamin smiled in that tight way of his which seemed to pull the corners of his mouth down rather than up. He said, ironically:

"I'm glad you see at least a little virtue in the notion. I have advanced two perfectly good theories of the death, based on a trap –"

"They're rubbish," said Dr. Fell. He was already staring across at the door to the balcony, and he seemed preoccupied.

"Thank you."

"Oh, all right," the doctor murmured, wearily. "I'll show you, if you like. Both of your ideas, then, are based on young Starberth's being lured out on that balcony, either (A) by instructions he found in the safe, or (B) by the stratagem of some person who wanted to rob the safe, and so got him out there to let the balcony do its villainous job. EH?"

"Quite right."

"Now, then, put yourself in young Starberth's place. You're sitting at this table, where he sat, with your bicycle-lamp beside you; as nervous as he was, or as cool as you might be – either way. Got it? Got the scene?"

"Perfectly, thank you."

"For whatever purpose, you get up to go over to that door, which hasn't been opened in God knows how many years; you're not only trying to open a sealed door, but you're going out on a balcony that's blacker than pitch . . . What do you do?"

"Why, I pick up the lamp and I –"

"Precisely. That's it. That's the whole story. You hold your lamp while you're opening the door, and flash it out on the balcony to see where you're going, before you've even set foot out there . . . Well, that's precisely what our victim didn't do. If so much as a crack of light had shown through this door anywhere, we should have seen it from my garden. But we didn't."

There was a silence. Sir Benjamin pushed his hat over to one side of his head and scowled.

"By Jove!" he muttered, "that sounds reasonable, you know. Still – Oh, look here! There's something wrong. I don't see any earthly way a murderer could have come in this room without an outcry on Starberth's part."

"Neither do I," said Dr. Fell. "If that encourages you any. I . . ." He broke off, a startled expression coming into his eyes as he stared at the iron door to the balcony. "O Lord! O Bacchus. O my ancient hat. This won't do."

He went stumping over to the door. First he knelt down and examined the dusty, gritty floor, where bits of dirt and stone had fallen when the door was opened. He ran his hand along them. Rising, he examined the outer face of the door; then he pushed it partly shut and looked at the keyhole.

"Opened with a key, right enough," he mumbled. "Here's a fresh scratch in the rust where it slipped . . ."

"Then," snapped the chief constable, "Martin Starberth did open that door, after all?"

"No. No, I don't think so. That was the murderer." Dr. Fell said something else, but it was inaudible because he had stepped through the sheathing ivy out upon the balcony.

The rest of them looked at one another uneasily. Rampole found himself more afraid of that balcony than he had even been of the safe. But he found himself moving forward, with Sir Benjamin at his elbow. The rector, he discovered as he glanced over his shoulder, was intently examining the titles of the calf-bound books in the shelves to the right of the fireplace; he seemed reluctant to drag himself away, though his feet appeared to be moving in the direction of the balcony.

Pushing aside the vines, Rampole stepped out. The balcony was not large; hardly more than a stone shelf about the base of the door, with stone balustrades built waist-high. There was little more room than would comfortably accommodate the three of them as he and Sir Benjamin stepped to either side of the doctor.

Nobody spoke. Over the top of the prison the morning sun had not yet struck; these walls, the hill, and the Hag's Nook below were still in shadow. Some twenty feet down, Rampole could see the edge of the cliff jutting out in mud and weeds, and the triangle of stone blocks which had once supported the gallows. Through the little door down there they had brought out the condemned from the pressroom, where the smith had struck off their irons before the last jump. From up here Anthony had watched it, in his "new suit of scarlet and laced hat." Bending over, Rampole could see the well gaping among the firs; he thought he could discern the green scum upon its water many feet farther down, but it was in heavy shadow.

Only that gaping pit, ringed in spikes, fifty feet below the balcony. Beyond it the northern meadows were sunlit, and starred with white flowers. You could see across the lowlands, cut with hedgerows like a rolling checkerboard; the white road, the stream glimmering, the white houses among trees, and the church spire. Peace. The meadows were not now black with faces to watch a hanging. Rampole could see a hay-wagon dawdling along the road.

"– it seems solid enough," Rampole heard Sir Benjamin saying, "and we've quite a lot of weight on it. I don't like messing about with it, though. Steady! What are you doing?"

Dr. Fell was grubbing among the ivy over the black balustrades.

"I've always wanted to examine this," he said, "but I never thought I should have the opportunity. H'm. It wouldn't wear, or would it?" he added to himself. There followed a sound of ripping ivy.

"I should be careful, if I were you. Even if –"

"Ha!" cried the doctor, loosing his breath in a gust. "What ho! *'Drinc heil!'* – as the Saxon toast was. Mud in your eye! I never thought I should find it, but here it is. Heh. Heh-heh-heh." He turned a beaming face. "Look here, on the outer edge of the balustrade. There's a worn place I can put my thumb in. And another, not so worn, on the side towards us."

"Well, what about it?" demanded Sir Benjamin. "Look here, I shouldn't mess about with that. You never know."

"Antiquarian research. We must celebrate this. Come along, gentlemen. I don't think there's anything more out here."

Sir Benjamin looked at him suspiciously as they re-entered the Governor's Room. He demanded:

"If you saw anything, I'm hanged if I did. What has it got to do with the murder, anyhow?"

"Nothing whatever, man! That is," said Dr. Fell, "only indirectly. Of course, if it weren't for those two worn places in the stone . . . Still, I don't know." He rubbed his hands together. "I say, do you remember what old Anthony's motto was? He had it stamped on his books, and his rings, and Lord knows what all. Did you ever see it?"

"So," the chief constable said, narrowing his eyes, "we come back to Anthony again, do we? No. I never saw his motto. – But unless you have anything more to suggest, we'd better get out of here and pay a visit to the Hall. Come, now! What's this all about?"

Dr. Fell took a last glance about the gloomy room.

"The motto," he said, "was *'Omnia mea mecum porto'* – 'All that belongs to me I carry with me.' Eh? Think it over. Look here, what about a bottle of beer?"

9

A gravel walk, winding. Grey pigeons that waddled suspiciously under elms. Shaven lawns, and the shadows of birds under the sun. The tall, bluff house of mellowed red brick, with white facings and a white cupola surmounted by a gilt weather-vane, growing old gracefully since the days when Anne was queen. Bees somewhere, droning, and a sweet smell of hay in the air.

Rampole had not seen it thus the night before. It had been raining when the rector's Ford drew up here then, and he and Saunders had carried the light, stiffening body up those steps. Before him had opened the mellow hallway, as though he had been suddenly thrust on a lighted stage with that dripping burden, before a thousand people. As he walked up the drive with his companions now, he shrank from meeting Her again. That was how it had been: thrust upon a stage, without lines, dazed and futile; unclothed, the way you feel in dreams sometimes. She hadn't been in the hall then. There had been only that butler – what was his name? – stooping slightly forward, his hands clasped together. He had prepared a couch in the drawing-room.

She had come out of the library, presently. Her red eyes showed that she had been crying desperately, in one of those horrible paroxysms; but she was steady and blank-faced then, squeezing a handkerchief. He hadn't said anything. What the devil was there to say? A word, a motion, anything would have seemed crude and clumsy; he didn't know why; it just would have seemed so. He had merely stood wretchedly by the door, in his soaked flannels and tennis shoes, and left as soon as he could. He remembered leaving: it had just stopped raining a moment before, and the grandfather clock was striking one. Through his wretchedness he remembered fastening foolishly on a small point: the rain stopped at one o'clock. The rain stopped at one o'clock. Got to remember that. Why? well, anyway –

It wasn't as though he could feel any sorrow at the death of Martin Starberth. He hadn't even liked Martin Starberth. It was something he stood for; something lost and damned in the girl's face when she walked in to look at her dead; a squeeze of a flimsy handkerchief, a brief contortion of a face, as at pain too great to be borne. The immaculate Martin looked queer in death: he wore an ancient pair of grey flannels and a torn tweed coat . . . And how would Dorothy feel now? He saw the closed shutters and the crape on the door, and winced.

Budge opened the door to them now, looking relieved when he saw the chief constable.

"Yes, sir," he said. "Shall I call Miss Dorothy?"

Sir Benjamin pulled at his lower lip. He was uneasy.

"No. Not for the moment, anyhow. Where is she?"

"Upstairs, sir."

"And Mr. Starberth?"

"Upstairs also, sir. The undertaking people are here."

"Anybody else here?"

"I believe Mr. Payne is on his way, sir. Dr. Markley was to call; he told me that he wished to see you, sir, as soon as he had finished his morning round."

"Ah yes. I see. By the way, Budge . . . those undertakers: I shall want to see the clothes Mr. Starberth wore last night, and the contents of his pockets, you know."

Budge inclined his flattish head towards Dr. Fell. "Yes, sir. Dr. Fell mentioned that possibility last night. I took the liberty of preserving them without removing anything from the pockets."

"Good man. Get them and bring them to the library now . . . And I say, Budge – !"

"Yes, sir?"

"If you should happen to see Miss Starberth," said Sir Benjamin, fidgeting, "just – er – convey my deepest . . . you know? Yes." He hesitated, this honest police official, growing slightly red in the face at what he apparently considered deception on friends. "And I should like to see Mr. Herbert Starberth as soon as is convenient."

Budge was impassive. "Mr. Herbert has not yet returned, sir."

"Oh, ah! I see. Well, get me those clothes."

They went into a darkened library. It is women who are most efficient in a house of death, where emotionalism runs high; men, like these four, are tongue-tied and helpless. Saunders was the only one who showed any degree of calmness; he was getting back his smooth manners, and seemed as unctuous as though he were opening a Prayer-book to read.

"If you'll excuse me, gentlemen," he said, "I think I had better see whether Miss Starberth will receive me. It's a trying time, you know; a trying time; and if I can be of any assistance . . ."

"Quite," said the chief constable, gruffly. When the rector had gone, he began to pace up and down. "Of course it's a trying time. But why the devil talk about it? I don't like this."

Rampole thoroughly agreed with him. They all fidgeted in the big old room, and Sir Benjamin opened some shutters. Silver chimes rang with fluid grace from the great clock in the hall, sounding as though they were striking through the vault of a cathedral. In this library everything looked old and solid and conventional; there was a globe-map which nobody ever spun, rows of accepted authors which nobody ever read, and above the mantelpiece a large mounted swordfish which (you were convinced) nobody had ever caught. A glass ball was hung up in one window, as a charm against witches.

Budge returned presently, carrying a laundry-bag.

"Everything is here, sir," he announced, "with the exception of the underclothing. Nothing has been removed from the pockets."

"Thank you. Stay here, Budge; I shall want to ask you some questions."

Dr. Fell and Rampole came over to watch as Sir Benjamin put the bag on the centre table and began taking things out. A grey jacket, stiff with mud, the lining frayed and torn, and several buttons missing.

"Here we are," the chief constable muttered, feeling in the pockets. "Cigarette-case – handsome one, too. Full of . . . these look like American cigarettes. Yes. Lucky Strike. Box of matches. Pocket flask, brandy, a third gone. That's the lot."

He rummaged again.

"Old shirt, nothing in the pocket. Socks. Here are the trousers, also in disrepair. He knew it would be a dusty job, poking about that prison. Here's his wallet, in the hip pocket." Sir Benjamin paused. "I suppose I'd better look inside. H'm. Ten-shilling note, two pound notes, and a fiver. Letters, all sent to him in America, American postmark. 'Martin Starberth, Esq., 470 West 24th St., N.Y.' Look here, you don't suppose some enemy might have followed him from America . . . ?"

"I doubt it," said Dr. Fell. "But you might put them aside."

"Notebook of some sort, full of figures. 'A. & S.,' 25, 'Good Roysterers,' 10, 'Roaring Caravans,' 3, 'Oedipus Rises'; 'Bloomingdales,' 25 'Good – ' What's all this?"

"Probably salesman's orders," said Rampole. "He told me he was in the publishing business. Anything else?"

"A number of cards. 'The Freedom Club, 65 West 51st St.' All clubs of some sort; dozens of them. 'Valhalla Cordial Shop, We Deliver, 342 Bleecker – '"

"That's all right," said Rampole. "I understand."

"That finishes the wallet, and the clothes, too. Wait! By Jove! here's his watch in his watch-pocket. And still running. His body broke the force of the fall, and the watch –"

"Let me look at that," Dr. Fell interposed, suddenly. He turned over the thin gold watch, whose ticking was loud in the quiet room. "In the stories," he added, "the dead man's watch is always very conveniently smashed, thus enabling the detectives to fix the wrong time of death because the murderer has set the hands at a different hour. Behold an exception from life."

"So I see," replied the chief constable. "But why are you so interested? In this case, the time of death isn't at all important."

"Oh, yes it is!" said Dr. Fell. "More important than you think. Er – at present this watch says five-and-twenty minutes past ten." He peered up at the clock on the mantelpiece. "That clock also says five-and-twenty minutes past ten, to the second . . . Budge, do you happen to know whether that clock is right?"

Budge inclined his head. "Yes, sir. It is right. I can answer positively about that score, sir."

The doctor hesitated, peering sharply at the butler, and then put the watch down.

"You look confoundedly earnest, man," he said. "Why are you so positive?"

"Because an unusual thing happened last night, sir. The grandfather clock in the hall was ten minutes fast. I – er – happened to notice it by comparing it with the clock in here. Then I went round to look at all the other clocks in the house. We generally set our watches by the grandfather clock, sir, and I fancied –"

"You did?" demanded Dr. Fell. "You looked at the others, did you?"

"Why – yes, sir," said Budge, slightly shocked.

"Well? Were they all right?"

"That, if I may say so, sir, is the curious part of it. They were. All of them except the grandfather. I can't imagine how it came to be wrong, sir. Somebody must have set it that way. In the hurry and rush, I have not had an opportunity to enquire . . ."

"What's this all about?" asked the chief constable. "According to what you've told me, young Starberth arrived at the Governor's Room on the tick of eleven – his watch is right – everything is right . . ."

"Yes," said Dr. Fell. "Yes. That's what makes it wrong, you see. Just one more question, Budge. Is there a clock in Mr. Martin's room?"

"Yes, sir. A large one on the wall."

Dr. Fell nodded his head several times, in communication with himself. Then he went to a chair and lowered himself into it with a sigh.

"Carry on, old man. I may seem to ask a number of foolish questions at odd times, and I shall probably be doing it all day, to every one of your witnesses. Bear with me, will you? – But, Budge! when Sir Benjamin has finished talking to you, I wish you'd try to dig up the person who changed that clock in the hall. It's rather important."

The chief constable was tapping his fingers impatiently on the table. "You're sure you're quite through?" he asked. "If not –"

"Well, I might point out," said the doctor, raising one cane to point, "that the murderer has certainly pinched something out of those clothes. What? – Why, his keys, man! All the keys he had to have! You didn't find 'em, did you?"

Sir Benjamin remained silent, nodding to himself; then he made a gesture and turned resolutely to Budge. Again they were to go over the same bare ground as last night. Rampole did not want to hear it. He already knew Budge's bare story, as the doctor had elicited it; and he wanted to see Dorothy Starberth. The rector would be up there with her now, shovelling out platitudes like a pious stoker, with the idea that in quantity there was consolation. He could imagine Saunders saying the conventional things in just the smooth, unthinking fashion which makes women murmur, "Such a help, you know!" – and remarking how beautifully he behaved.

Why weren't people silent in the presence of death? Why, from everybody, this invariable ghoulish murmuring of, "So-natural-looking, isn't-he?" and all the comments which only started the women to weeping afresh? No matter. What he disliked was the idea of Saunders being so kind and big-brotherly (Saunders would enjoy that role, too) up there with Her. Budge's professionally serene visage was an annoyance, too; and Budge's carefully fashioned sentences where the h's were automatically clipped on, like caps upon bottles, as the words issued from the machine. Bad form or not, he couldn't sit here. Whatever the rest of them thought, he was somehow going to get closer to her. He slipped from the room.

But where would he go? Obviously not upstairs; that would be a little too much. But he couldn't prowl about the hall, as though he were looking for the gas-meter or something. Did they have gas-meters in England? Oh, well! Wandering towards the back of the dusky hall, he saw a door partly open near the stairs. A figure blocked the light and Dorothy Starberth was beckoning to him . . .

He met her in the shadow of the stairs, clasping her hands hard, and he could feel her trembling. At first he was afraid to look at her face, because he was afraid, in the thickness of his throat, that he might blurt out, "I've failed you, and I shouldn't have failed you," and to say that – no! Or he might say, "I love you," here in the shadow, beneath the mellow ticking of the great clock; and the thought of what he might have said struck deep, with a barbed and shaking hurt.

But there were no words, and only the clock murmured in this quiet cathedral, and something sang within him, crying: Great God, why must there be all this nonsense about the glory of strength and self-reliance in such as she? I would not wish her so. This small body, which I might hold in my arms now for a moment, I would shield and guard; and the whisper she might give me would be as a war-cry in the night; and against this shield, as I held her forever, even the gates of hell should not prevail. But he knew that this ache in the blood must be stifled now. He was only thinking crazy things; laugh-provoking things, so they said; and through the muddle of dreams he could be only his clumsy self, and say:

"I know . . ."

A foolish whisper, as he patted her hand. Then somehow they were inside the door, in a small office with drawn blinds.

"I heard you come in," she said, in a low voice, "and I heard Mr. Saunders coming upstairs, and I couldn't talk to him; so I let Mrs. Bundle stop him – she'll talk his ears off – and came down the back stairs."

She sat down on an old horsehair sofa, her chin propped in the palm of her hand, her eyes heavy and dull. A silence. The closed, darkened room was thick with heat. When she started to speak again, with a little spasmodic movement of her hand, he touched her shoulder.

"If you'd rather not talk . . ."

"I've got to talk. It seems days since I've slept. And I must go in there, in a moment, and go over the whole thing again with Them."

His fingers tightened. She raised her head.

"You needn't look like that," she said, softly. "Would you – would you believe that I was never tremendously fond of Martin? It isn't that so much – his dying, I mean. He was never very close to any of us, you know. I ought to feel worse about it than I do."

"Well, then . . ."

"Either one of the two is just as bad!" she cried, her voice rising. "It's either – We can't help ourselves; we're haunted; we're damned, all of us, in the blood; retribution; I never believed it, I won't believe it; or else –"

"Steady! You've got to snap out of this."

"Or else – maybe it's both. How do we know what's in a person's blood? Yours or mine or anybody's? There may be a murderer's blood just as well as a ghost; more so. Is that door shut?"

"Yes."

"Any of us. Why" – her voice grew vague, and she put her hands together as though she were uncertain of their position, "I might – kill *you.* I might take the gun out of that desk drawer, just because I couldn't help myself, and all of a sudden . . ." She shuddered. "Why, if all those old people weren't damned to suicide, or being thrown off the balcony by destiny – ghosts – I don't know – then somebody was damned to kill them – in the family . . ."

"You've got to stop this! Look here! Listen – !"

She nodded gently, touched her eyelids with her finger tips, and looked up. "Do you think Herbert killed Martin?"

"No! No, of course not. And it wasn't any foolery about ghosts, either. And – you know your cousin couldn't have killed Martin. He admired him; he was solid and dependable –"

"He talked to himself," the girl said, blankly. "I remember now; he talked to himself. It's the quiet people I'm afraid of. They're the ones who go mad, if it's tainted blood to begin with . . . He had big red hands. His hair wouldn't stay down, no matter how much he slicked it. He was built delicately, like Martin, but his hands were too big. He tried to look like Martin. I wonder if he hated Martin?"

A pause, while she plucked at the edges of the sofa.

"And he was always trying to invent something that never worked. A new churn. He thought he was an inventor. Martin used to laugh at him . . ."

The dim room was full of personalities. Rampole saw two figures standing in the middle of a white road at dusk, so like in appearance and yet so vitally unlike. Martin, drunk, a cigarette hanging from his lips. Herbert gawky and blunt-featured, with a badly fitting hat set exactly high and straight on his head. You felt that if Herbert smoked a cigarette, too, it would protrude from the exact centre of his mouth, and waggle awkwardly.

"Somebody opened the wall safe in the library last night," said Dorothy Starberth. "That was something I didn't tell Dr. Fell last night. I didn't tell him so much that was important. I didn't tell him that at dinner Herbert was more flustered than Martin . . . it was Herbert who opened that library safe."

"But –"

"Martin didn't know the combination. He's been away two years, and he never had occasion to. The only ones who knew it were myself and Mr. Payne – and Herbert. I saw it standing open last night."

"Something was taken?"

"I don't think so. There was never anything valuable left in there. When father built this office here, he stopped using it. I'm sure he hadn't opened it for years, and none of the rest of us ever did. It was just full of some old papers for years back . . . It wasn't that anything had been taken; at least, anything I know of. It was something I found."

He wondered whether she were becoming hysterical. She rose from the sofa, opened a secretary-desk with a key hung round her neck, and took out a yellowed piece of paper. As she handed it to him, he fought down a desire to take her in his arms.

"Read it!" she said, breathlessly. "I trust you. I won't tell the others. I must tell somebody . . . Read it."

He glanced down, puzzled. It was headed, "Feb. 3, 1895. My copy of the verses – Timothy Starberth," in faded ink. It read:

How called the dwellers of Lyn-dun?
Great Homer's tale of Troy,
Or country of the midnight sun –
What doth all men Destroy?

Against it man hath dashed his foot;
This angel bears a spear!
In garden-glade where Lord Christ prayed
What spawns dark stars and fear?

This place the white Diana rose,
Of this, Dido bereft;
Where on four leaves good fortune grows
East, west, south – what is left?

The Corsican was vanquished there,
Oh, mother of all sin!
Find green the same as shiretown's name,
Find Newgate Gaol, and win!

"Well," said Rampole, muttering over the lines, "it's very bad doggerel, and it doesn't make the slightest sense so far as I can see; but that's true of a lot of verse I've read . . . What is it?"

She looked at him steadily. "Do you see the date? February 3 was father's birthday. He was born in 1870, so in 1895 he would have been –"

"Twenty-five years old," interposed Rampole, suddenly.

They were both silent, Rampole staring at the enigmatic words with a slow comprehension. All the wild surmises which he and Sir Benjamin had been making, and which Dr. Fell had so violently ridiculed, seemed to grow substantial before him.

"Now let me lead *you* on," he suggested. "If that's true, then the original of this paper – it says 'my copy' – was in the vault in the Governor's Room. So?"

"It must be what the eldest sons were intended to see." She took the paper out of his hands as though she felt a rage against it, and would have crumpled it in her hand but that he shook his head. "I've thought about it, and thought about it, and that's the only explanation I can see. I hope it's true. I had fancied so many ghastly things that *might* be there. And yet this is just as bad. People still die."

He sat down on the sofa.

"If there was an original," he said, "it isn't there now."

Slowly, omitting nothing, he told her of their visit to the Governor's Room. "And that thing," he added, "is a cryptogram of some sort. It's got to be. Could anybody have killed Martin just to get at this?"

There was a discreet knock at the door, and they both started like conspirators. Putting her finger on her lips, Dorothy hastily locked the paper in the desk.

"Come in," she said.

Budge's smooth countenance floated in at the opening of the door. If he were surprised to find Rampole here, there was no sign of it.

"Excuse me, Miss Dorothy," he said. "Mr. Payne has just arrived. Sir Benjamin would like to see you in the library, if you please."

10

There had been high words in the library a moment before; so much was plain from the constraint and tensity there, and the slight flush on Sir Benjamin's face. He stood with his back to the empty fireplace, his hands clasped behind him. In the middle of the room, Rampole saw, stood his own pet dislike – Payne, the lawyer.

"I'll tell you what you'll do, sir," said Sir Benjamin. "You'll sit down there like a sensible man, and you'll give your testimony when it's asked for. Not before."

Payne whirred in his throat. Rampole saw the short white hair bristle on the back of his head.

"Are you familiar with the law, sir?" he rasped.

"Yes, sir, I am," said Sir Benjamin. "I happen to be a magistrate myself, you know. Now will you obey my instructions, or shall I –"

Dr. Fell coughed. He inclined his head sleepily towards the door, hoisting himself up from his chair as Dorothy Starberth entered. Payne turned jerkily.

"Ah, come in, my dear," he said, pushing out a chair. "Sit down. Rest yourself. Sir Benjamin and I" – the whites of his eyes flashed over towards the chief constable, "will talk presently."

He folded his arms, but he did not move from the side of her chair, where he had taken up his stand like a guardian. Sir Benjamin was ill at ease.

"You know, of course, Miss Starberth," he began, "how we all feel about this tragic business. As long as I've known you and your family, I don't think I need say more." His sincere old face looked muddled and kindly. "I dislike intruding on you at this time. But if you feel up to answering a few questions . . ."

"You don't have to answer them," said Payne. "Remember that, my dear."

"You don't have to answer them," agreed Sir Benjamin, controlling his temper. "I only thought to save you trouble for the inquest."

"Of course," said the girl. She sat quietly, her hands in her lap, while she told the story she had told last night. They had finished dinner a little before nine o'clock. She had tried to entertain Martin and keep his mind off the forthcoming business; but he was moody and distraught, and had gone up to his room immediately. Where was Herbert? She did not know. She had gone out on the lawn, where it was cooler, and sat there for the better part of an hour. Then she had gone in to the office to look over the day's household accounts. In the hall she had met Budge, who informed her that he had taken a bicycle-lamp up to Martin's room, as Martin had asked. Several times, during the half-hour or three-quarters ensuing, she had been on the point of going up to Martin's room. But he had expressed a desire to be left alone; he was sullen, and had been bad-tempered at dinner; so she had refrained from doing so. He would feel better if nobody saw his state of nerves.

At about twenty minutes to eleven she had heard him leave his room, come downstairs, and go out the side door. She had run after him, reaching the side door as he was going down the drive, and called to him – afraid that he might have taken too much to drink. He had called back to her, snapping some words she did not catch; his speech was rather thick, but his step seemed fairly steady. Then she had gone to the telephone and communicated with Dr. Fell's house, telling them that he was on the way.

That was all. Her slow, throaty voice never faltered as she told it, and her eyes remained fixed on Sir Benjamin; the full pink lips, devoid of make-up, hardly seemed to move at all. At the conclusion, she sat back and looked at the sunlight in one unshuttered window.

"Miss Starberth," said Dr. Fell, after a pause, "I wonder if you'd mind my asking a question? . . . Thank you. Budge has told us that the clock in the hall out there was wrong last night, though none of the others were. When you say that he left the house at twenty minutes to eleven, do you mean the time by that clock, or the right time?"

"Why –" she looked at him blankly; then down at her wristwatch and up at the clock on the mantelpiece. "Why, the right time! I'm positive of it. I never even glanced at the clock in the hall. Yes, the right time."

Dr. Fell relapsed, while the girl regarded him with a slight frown. Evidently nettled at this irrelevancy being brought in again. Sir Benjamin began to pace up and down the hearth rug. You felt that he had been nerving himself up to ask certain questions, and the doctor's interruption had scattered his resolves. Finally he turned.

"Budge has already told us, Miss Starberth, about Herbert's entirely unexplained absence . . ."

She inclined her head.

"Think, if you please! You are positive that he never mentioned the possibility of leaving suddenly – well, that is, you can think of no reason for his doing so?"

"None," she said, and added, in a lower voice: "You needn't be so formal, Sir Benjamin. I understand the implications as well as you do."

"Well, to be frank, then: the coroner's jury is likely to put an ugly interpretation on it, unless he returns immediately. Even so – you see? Has there been any ill-feeling between Herbert and Martin in the past?"

"Never."

"Or more recently?"

"We hadn't seen Martin," she answered, interlacing her fingers, "since about a month after father died, up until the time we met his boat at Southampton the day before yesterday. There has never been the slightest ill-feeling between them."

Sir Benjamin was plainly at a loss. He looked round at Dr. Fell, as though for prompting, but the doctor said nothing.

"At the moment," he went on, clearing his throat, "I can think of nothing else. It's – ah – very puzzling. Very puzzling indeed. Naturally, we don't want to subject you to any more of an ordeal than is necessary, my dear; and if you care to go back to your room . . ."

"Thanks. But if you don't mind," said the girl, "I should prefer to remain here. It's more – more . . . Well, I should prefer to remain."

Payne patted her on the shoulder. "*I'll* attend to the rest of it," he told her, nodding towards the chief constable with dry, vicious satisfaction.

There was an interruption. They heard a nervous, whispering jabber in the hall outside and a voice which suddenly croaked, "Nonsense!" with a shrillness so exactly like a talking crow that everybody started. Budge came sailing in.

"If you please, sir," he said to the chief constable, "Mrs. Bundle is bringing one of the housemaids who knows something about that clock."

"– now you march!" squawked the crow's voice. "You march right in there, young lady, and you speaks to 'em. It's a *nice* state of affairs, it's a *nice* state of affairs, I say, if we can't 'ave truth-telling people in the 'ouse, I say . . . *Pop!*" concluded Mrs. Bundle, making a noise with her lips like a cork pulled out of a bottle.

Escorting a frightened housemaid, she came rolling through the door. Mrs. Bundle was a little lean woman with a sailor's walk, a lace cap coming down into her bright eyes, and a face of such extraordinary malevolence that Rampole stared. She glared upon everybody out of a dusty face, but she seemed less to be damning everybody than to be meditating some deep wrong. Then she assumed a wooden stare, which gave her a curious cross-eyed look.

"'Ere she is," said Mrs. Bundle. "And what I say is this: things being what they are, I say, we might as well all be murdered in our beds or Get Took By Americans. It's all the same. Many's the time I've said to Mr. Budge, I've said, 'Mr. Budge, you mark my words, there's no good a-going ter come of mucking about with them ghosters. 'Tain't in natur,' I've said, 'for this 'ere tenement of clay (which we all is) to be alwis a-trying to beard them ghosters by their beards,' I says. *Pop.* You'd think we was Americans. *Pop!* And them ghosters, now –"

"Of course, Mrs. Bundle, of course," the chief constable said, soothingly. He turned to the little housemaid, who trembled in Mrs. Bundle's grip like a virgin ensnared by a witch. "You know something about the clock – er – ?"

"Martha, sir. Yes, sir. Truly."

"Tell us about it, Martha."

"They chews gum. Drat 'em!" cried Mrs. Bundle, with such ferocious malignancy that she gave a little hop.

"Eh?" said the chief constable. "Who?"

"They takes pies and hits people," said Mrs. Bundle. "Eee! Squee! Pop! Drat 'em! . . ."

The housekeeper showed a tendency to hold forth on this theme. She was not talking about the ghosters, it seemed, but about the Americans, whom she proceeded to describe as "nasty cowboy people with straw hats on." The ensuing monologue she delivered, shaking a bunch of keys in one hand and Martha in the other, was a trifle clouded in meaning, due to the listeners' inability to tell when she was referring to the Americans and when she was referring to the ghosters. She had concluded a lecture which seemed to deal with the ghosters' impolite habit of squirting one another in the face with soda-water from syphons, before Sir Benjamin summoned enough courage to interfere.

"Now, Martha, please go on. It was you who changed the clock?"

"Yes, sir. But he told me to do it, sir, and –"

"Who told you?"

"Mr. Herbert, sir. Truly. I was crossing the hall, and he comes out of the library a-looking at his watch. And he says to me, 'Martha, that clock's ten minutes slow; set it right,' he says. Sharp-like. You know. I was that astonished you could have knocked me over with a feather. Him speaking sharp-like, and all. Which he never does. And he says, 'See to the rest of the clocks, Martha; set 'em right if they're wrong. Mind!'"

Sir Benjamin looked over at Dr. Fell.

"It's your enquiry," said the chief constable. "Carry on."

"Hmf," said Dr. Fell. His rumbling from the corner startled Martha, whose pink face turned a trifle pinker. "When was this, did you say?"

"I didn't, sir, truly I didn't say, but I will, because I looked at the clock. Naturally. Changing it like he told me, and all. It was just before dinner, sir, and the rector had just went after bringing Mr. Martin home, and Mr. Martin was in the library, he was; and so I changed the clock, and it said five-and-twenty minutes past eight. Only it wasn't. Being ten minutes fast after I changed it. I mean –"

"Yes, of course. And why didn't you change the others?"

"I was a-going to, sir. But then I went into the library, and Mr. Martin was there. And he says, 'What are you doing?' and when I told him he says, 'You let them clocks alone,' he says. And of course I did. Him being the master, and all. And that's all I know, sir."

"Thank you, Martha . . . Mrs. Bundle, did you or any of the housemaids see Mr. Herbert leaving the house last night?"

Mrs. Bundle thrust out her jaw. "When we went to the fair at Holdern," she replied, malignantly, "Annie Murphy's purse was stole by thiefpockets. And they put me on a thing what goes round and round, it did; round and round; and then I walks upon boards which shakes, and stairs which collapses, and in the dark, and me 'airpins comes loose, which is that the way to treat a lady? Eeee! Drat 'em!" squawked the housekeeper, shaking her keys ferociously. "It was a in-vention, that's what it was, a dratted in-vention! All them inventions is like that, which I told Mr. Herbert about it many's the time, and when I see him going out to the stable last night –"

"You saw Mr. Herbert leave?" demanded the chief constable.

"– to the stable where he keeps them inventions which to be sure *I* don't look at stairs which shakes out me very 'airpins. Do I?"

"What inventions?" said the chief constable, rather helplessly.

"It's all right, Sir Benjamin," said Dorothy. "Herbert is always tinkering with something, without any success. He had a workshop out there."

Further than this no information could be elicited from Mrs. Bundle. All inventions, she was convinced, had to do with certain contraptions which threw one about in the dark at the Holdern fair. Apparently somebody with a primitive sense of humour had led the good lady into the Crazy House, where she had screamed until a crowd assembled, got caught in the machinery, hit somebody with an umbrella, and was finally escorted out by the police. Just as, after a tempestuous review of the matter without enlightenment for her hearers, she was led out by Budge.

"Waste of time," growled Sir Benjamin, when she had gone. "There's your question about the clock answered, Doctor. Now I think we can proceed."

"I think we can," Payne interposed, suddenly.

He had not moved from his position beside the girl's chair; small, his arms folded, ugly as a Chinese image.

"I think we can," he repeated. "Since you seem to get nowhere with this aimless questioning, I fancy that some explanations are due *me.* I hold a trust in this family. For a hundred years nobody except members of the Starberth family have been allowed in the Governor's Room on any pretext whatsoever. This morning, I am given to understand, you gentlemen – one of you a perfect stranger – violated that law. That in itself calls for an explanation."

Sir Benjamin shut his jaws firmly. "Excuse me, my friend," he said. "I don't think it does."

The lawyer was beginning, in a furious voice: "What you think, sir, is of minor –" when Dr. Fell cut him short. He spoke in a tired and indolent voice.

"Payne," said Dr. Fell, "you're an ass. You've made trouble at every turn, and I wish you wouldn't be such an old woman . . . By the way, how did you know we were up there?"

The tone in which he spoke, one of mild expostulation, was worse than any contempt. Payne glared.

"I have eyes," he snarled. "I saw you leaving. I went up after you to be sure your meddling ways had interfered with nothing."

"Oh!" said Dr. Fell. "Then you violated the law too?"

"That is not the question, sir. I am privileged. I know what is in that vault . . ." He was so angry that he grew indiscreet, and added, "It is not the first time I have been privileged to see it."

Dr. Fell had been staring blankly at the floor. Now he rolled up his big lionlike head, still with that vacant expression, to regard the other.

"That's interesting," he murmured. "I rather thought you had. too. H'mf. Yes."

"I must remind you again," said Payne, "that I hold a trust –"

"Not any longer," said Dr. Fell.

There was a pause, which somehow seemed to make the room cold. The lawyer opened his eyes wide, jerking his head towards Dr. Fell.

"I said, 'not any longer,'" the doctor repeated. raising his voice slightly. "Martin was the last of the direct line. It's all over. The trust, or the curse, or whatever you care to call it, is done with for ever; and for that part of it I can say, thank God . . . Anyhow, it needn't be a mystery any longer. If you were up there this morning, you know that something has been taken from the safe . . ."

"How do *you* know that?" demanded Payne, sticking out his neck.

"I'm not trying to be cute," the doctor responded, wearily. "And I wish you wouldn't try to be, either. In any case, if you want to help justice, you'd better tell us the whole story of your trust. We shall never know the truth about Martin's murder unless we know that. Go on, Sir Benjamin. I hate to keep butting in like this."

"That's the position exactly," said Sir Benjamin. "You'll withhold no evidence, sir. That is, unless you want to be held as a material witness."

Payne looked from one to the other of them. He had had an easy time of it, you felt, up to now. Few people had crossed him or sat upon him. He was wildly trying to keep his cool dignity, like a man striving to manage a sail-boat in a high wind.

"I will tell you as much as I think fit," he said with an effort, "and no more. What do you want to know?"

"Thank you," said the chief constable, drily. "First, you kept the keys to the Governor's Room, did you not?"

"I did."

"How many keys were there?"

"Four."

"Damn it, man," snapped Sir Benjamin, "you're not on the witness-stand! Please be more explicit."

"A key to the outer door of the room. A key to the iron door giving on the balcony. A key to the vault. And, since you have already looked inside that vault," said Payne, biting his words, "I can tell you the rest. A small key to a steel box which was inside the safe."

"A box –" Sir Benjamin repeated. He glanced over his shoulder at Dr. Fell; his eyes had verified a prediction, and there was a small, knowing, rather malicious smile in them. "A box. Which, we know, is gone . . . What was inside the box?"

Payne debated something in his mind. He had not unfolded his arms, and the fingers of one hand began to tap on his biceps.

"All that it was my duty to know," he answered after a pause, "is that there are a number of cards inside, each with the eighteenth-century Anthony Starberth's signature on it. The heir was instructed to take out one of those cards and present it to the executor next day, as proof that he had actually opened the box . . . Whatever else there may have been inside –" He shrugged.

"You mean you don't know?" asked Sir Benjamin.

"I mean that I prefer not to say."

"We will return to that in a moment," the chief constable said, slowly. "Four keys. Now, as to the word which opens the letter-lock . . . neither are we quite blind, Mr. Payne . . . as to the word: you are intrusted with that also?"

A hesitation. "In a manner of speaking, I am," the lawyer returned, after considering carefully. "The word is engraved on the handle of the key which opens the vault. Thus some burglar might get a duplicate key made for the lock; but without the original key he was powerless."

"Do you know this word?"

A longer hesitation. "Naturally," said Payne.

"Did anybody else know it?"

"I consider that question an impertinence, sir," the other told him. Small brown teeth showed under his upper lip. His face had become all wrinkles and ugliness, the grey cropped hair drawn down. He hesitated again, and then added, more mildly: "Unless the late Mr. Timothy Starberth communicated it to his son by word of mouth. He never took the tradition very seriously, I am bound to say."

For a moment Sir Benjamin went prowling up and down before the fireplace, flapping his hands behind his back. Then he turned.

"When did you deliver the keys to young Starberth?"

"At my office in Chatterham, late yesterday afternoon."

"Was anybody with him?"

"His cousin Herbert."

"Herbert was not present during the interview, I take it?"

"Naturally not . . . I delivered the keys, and gave the only instructions left me: that he open the safe and the box, examine what was inside, and bring me one of the cards inscribed with Anthony Starberth's name. That was all."

Rampole, sitting far back in the shadow, remembered those figures in the white road. Martin and Herbert had been coming from the lawyer's office when he saw them, and Martin had uttered that inexplicable taunt, "The word is *Gallows*." And he thought of that paper, written over with the queer meaningless verses, which Dorothy had shown him; it was fairly clear, now, what had been inside the box, despite Dr. Fell's ridicule of a "paper." Dorothy Starberth sat motionless, her hands folded; but she seemed to be breathing more rapidly . . . Why?

"You refuse to tell us, Mr. Payne," the chief constable pursued, "what was inside that box in the vault?"

Payne's hand fluttered up to stroke his chin; that gesture, Rampole remembered, he always used when he was nervous.

"It was a document," he responded at length. "I cannot say more, because, gentlemen, I do not know."

Dr. Fell got to his feet, a bulky walrus coming to the surface.

"Ah," he said, blowing out his breath and hitting one stick sharply on the floor, "that's what I thought. That's what I wanted to know. The document was never allowed to leave that iron box, was it, Payne? . . . Good! Very good! Then I can go on."

"I thought you didn't believe in any document," said the chief constable, turning with a still more satiric expression.

"Oh, I never said that," the other protested, mildly. "I only protested at your guessing, without any logical reasons, that there was a box and a document. I never said you were wrong. On the contrary, I had already arrived at your own conclusions, with good and logical evidence to support them. That's the difference, you see."

He lifted his head to look at Payne. He did not raise his voice.

"I'll not trouble you about the document that Anthony Starberth left for his heirs in the early nineteenth century," he said. "But, Payne, what about the *other* document?"

"Other – ?"

"I mean the one that Timothy Starberth, Martin's father, left in the steel box, in that same vault, less than two years ago."

Payne made a small motion of his lips, as though he were blowing out tobacco smoke slowly. He shifted his position, so that the floor creaked, and you could hear it plainly in the great stillness of the room.

"What's this? What's this?" gabbled Sir Benjamin.

"Go on," said Payne, softly.

"I've heard the story a dozen times," Dr. Fell went on, nodding his head in a detached, meditative fashion. "About old Timothy's lying there writing, just before he died. Sheets upon sheets he was writing – though his body was so smashed he could scarcely hold a pen. Propped up with a writing-board, cackling and howling with glee, determined to go on . . ."

"Well?" demanded Sir Benjamin.

"Well, what was he writing? 'Instructions for my son,' he said, but that was a lie. That was to throw some of you off the track. His son, by the nature of the so-called 'ordeal,' didn't need any instructions – he only needed to get the keys from Payne. In any event, he didn't need page after page of closely written script. Old Timothy wasn't copying anything, because he didn't need to do that, either . . . this 'document' of Anthony's, Payne says, never left the safe. So what was he writing?"

Nobody spoke. Rampole found himself moving out towards the edge of the chair. From where he sat he could see Dorothy Starberth's eyes, unwinking, fixed on the doctor. Sir Benjamin spoke, loudly:

"Very well. then. What *was* he writing?"

"The story of his own murder," said Dr. Fell.

11

"It isn't every day, you know," the doctor explained, apologetically, "that a man gets the opportunity to write the story of his own murder."

He looked round the circle, leaning heavily on one cane, his big left shoulder hunched high. The broad ribbon on his eyeglasses hung almost perpendicular to the floor. A wheezing pause . . .

"I don't need to tell you that Timothy Starberth was a strange man. But I wonder if any of you appreciate just how strange? You knew his bitterness, his rather satanic humours, his exquisite appreciation of this sort of jest; in many respects – you'll agree – he was a throwback to old Anthony himself. But you possibly didn't think he would conceive of a thing like this."

"Like what?" asked the chief constable, in a curious voice.

Dr. Fell raised his cane to point.

"Somebody murdered him," he answered. "Somebody killed him and left him in the Hag's Nook. In the Hag's Nook – remember that! The murderer thought he was dead. But he lived a good many hours after that. And there you have the point of the joke.

"He could have denounced the man who killed him, of course. But that would have been too easy, don't you see? Timothy didn't want him to get off so lightly. So he wrote out the whole story of his own murder. He arranged that it should be sealed up and put – where? In the safest place of all. Behind key-locks, and letter-locks, and (best of all) in a place where nobody would suspect it – in the vault of the Governor's Room.

"For two whole years, you see – until Martin's opening of that vault on his birthday – everybody should still think he died by accident. *Everybody, that is, but the murderer.* He would take pains to get the knowledge conveyed to the murderer that this document was there! There was the joke. For two years the murderer would be safe, and suffering the tortures of the damned. Every year, every month, every day would narrow down the time when, inexorably, that story should come to light. Nothing could prevent it. It was like a death-sentence – slowly coming on. The murderer couldn't get at it. The only way he could have reached that damning paper would have been to blow the vault down with a charge of nitro-glycerin which would have taken the roof off the whole prison – not a very practical way out. It may sound feasible for a skilful cracksman, and in the city of Chicago; but it isn't very practical for an ordinary human being in an English village. Even in the doubtful event that you know something about cracking safes, you can't go playing about with burglar's tools and importing high explosives into Chatterham without exciting considerable comment. In simple terms, the murderer was powerless. So can you conceive of the exquisite agony he has undergone, as Anthony meant him to?"

Sir Benjamin, jarred thoroughly, shook his fist in the air.

"Man," he said, "you – you're – this is the insanest – ! You've no evidence he was murdered! You –"

"Oh, yes I have," said Dr. Fell.

Sir Benjamin stared at him. Dorothy Starberth had risen, her hand making a gesture . . .

"But, look here," the chief constable said, doggedly, "if this crazy surmise is true – I say *if* it's true – why, then, two years . . . The murderer would just have run away, wouldn't he, and be beyond pursuit?"

"Thereby," said Dr. Fell, "admitting his guilt beyond all doubt, once the paper was found . . . Confession! That's what it would be. And wherever he went in the world, wherever he hid himself, he would always have that hellish thing hanging over him; and sooner or later they'd find him out. No, no. His only safe way, the only thing he could possibly do, was to stay here and try to lay hands on that accusation. If the very worst came, he could always deny it and try to fight it. In the meantime, there was always the dogged hope that he could destroy it before they knew." The doctor paused, and added in a lower voice:

"We know now that he has succeeded."

There were heavy footfalls on the polished floor. The noise fell so eerily into the dusky room they all looked up . . .

"Dr. Fell is quite right, Sir Benjamin," said the voice of the rector. "The late Mr. Starberth spoke to me before he died. He told me about the person who murdered him."

Saunders paused by the table. His large pink face was a blank. He spread out his hands and added, very slowly and simply:

"God help me, gentlemen. I thought he was mad."

The silver chimes of the clock ran fluidly in the hall . . .

"Ah," said Dr. Fell, nodding. "I rather thought he'd told you. You were supposed to pass the information on to the murderer. Did you?"

"He asked me to speak to his family, but to nobody else. I did that much, as I'd promised," said Saunders, pressing a hand over his eyes.

From the shadow of the great chair, in which she had sat down again, Dorothy said:

"That was the other thing I was afraid of. Yes, he told us."

"And you never mentioned it?" cried the chief constable, with abrupt shrillness. "You knew a man was murdered, and none of you – ?"

There was no heartiness or smooth bumptiousness about

Saunders now. He seemed to be trying to apply the rules of English sports, suddenly, to a dark and terrible thing; and he could not find their application. His hand groped.

"They tell you things," he said, with an effort, "and you don't know – you can't judge. You – Well, I tell you, I simply thought he was out of his head. It was incredible, more than incredible. It was something nobody would ever *do,* don't you see?" His baffled blue eyes moved round the group, and he tried to catch at something in the air. "It just isn't so!" he went on desperately. "Up until last night I couldn't believe it. And then suddenly I thought – what if it were true, after all? And maybe there was a murderer. And so I arranged to watch, with Dr. Fell and Mr. Rampole here, and now I know . . . I know. But I don't know what to do about it."

"Well, the rest of us do," snapped the chief constable. "You mean he told you the name of the person who killed him?"

"No. He only said – it was a member of his family."

Rampole's heart was beating heavily. He found himself wiping the palms of his hands on the knees of his trousers, as though he were trying to dislodge something from them. He knew now what had been on the rector's mind last night; and he remembered that puzzling, quick question, "Where is Herbert?" which Saunders had asked when Dorothy Starberth had phoned to say Martin had left the house. Saunders had explained it, rather lamely, by saying Herbert was a good man to have around in a pinch. But he explained it much better now . . .

And there was Dorothy, with her burnt-out eyes, and her small, wry, vacant smile, as one who says, "Oh, well!" And Dr. Fell poking at the floor with his stick. And Saunders looking into the sun as though he were trying to do a penance by staring it out of the sky. And Payne humped, drawn into his little grey shell. And Sir Benjamin looking wry-necked at them all, like a horse round the corner of its stall.

"Well," said the chief constable, in a matter-of-fact voice,

"I suppose we shall have to send out the drag-net for Herbert, after all . . ."

Dr. Fell glanced up mildly.

"Isn't there something you've forgotten?" he enquired.

"Forgotten?"

"For instance," the doctor said, thoughtfully, "you were questioning Payne a moment ago. Why not ask him what he knows about it? Somebody had to take Timothy's statement over to the vault in the Governor's Room, you know. Does he know what was in it?"

"Ah," said Sir Benjamin, jerked out of his thoughts. "Ah yes. Of course." He adjusted his pince-nez. "Well, Mr. Payne?"

Payne's fingers flicked to his chin. He coughed.

"It may be so. Personally – I think you're talking nonsense. If Starberth had done any such thing, I think he ought to have told *me* about it. I was the logical one to tell. Not you, Mr. Saunders. Not you. – It is perfectly true, however, that he gave me a sealed envelope, inscribed with his son's name, to take to the vault."

"That's what you meant, is it, when you said you had been there before?" asked Dr. Fell.

"It is. The whole proceeding was most irregular. But" – the lawyer made gestures of discomfort, as though his cuffs were sliding down over his hands and impeding them – "but he was a dying man, and he said this envelope was vitally concerned with the ceremony the heir had to go through. Not knowing what was in the *other* document, I naturally could not judge. His death was sudden; there might have been things which he had left undone, and which must be done under the terms of my trust. So I accepted. I was the only one who could undertake the mission, of course; I had the keys."

"But he said no word about murder to you?"

"No. He only asked me to scribble a note testifying that he was in his right mind. He seemed so to me. The note he put into the envelope along with his manuscript, which I did not look at."

Dr. Fell brushed up the corners of his moustache, keeping on nodding in that monotonous toy-figure way.

"So this is the first time you have ever heard the suspicion mentioned?"

"It is."

"And when did you put the document in the steel box?"

"That night; the night of his death."

"Yes, yes," put in the chief constable, impatiently, "I can see all that. But we're off the subject. Hang it, look here! We've got a motive, right enough, as to why Herbert should have killed Martin. But why should Herbert have killed his uncle, at the start of the whole business? It's getting worse confused . . . And if he killed Martin, why did he run away? When he'd had to keep his nerve for two years, and kept it successfully, why did he cut along just when he was safe? And what's more – look here! – where was he going on his bicycle, down a back lane and with a bag packed. several hours *before* the murder? It doesn't look right, somehow . . ."

He drew a deep breath, scowling.

"In any case, I shall have to get busy. Dr. Markley wants to hold the inquest tomorrow, and we'll let them decide . . . In the meantime, I had better have the number and description of that bicycle for a general alarm, Miss Starberth. I'm sorry. But it's necessary."

Sir Benjamin was clearly so bewildered that he wanted to break up the conference as soon as possible. You could see a whiskey-and-soda in his eye even more clearly than any suspicions. They made their farewells rather awkwardly, with a tendency to bow to the wrong people. Rampole lagged behind at the door as Dorothy Starberth touched his sleeve.

If the questioning had strained her nerves, she did not show it. She was only thoughtful, like a sombre child. She said in a low voice:

"That paper I showed you – the verses – we know now, don't we?"

"Yes. Directions of some kind. The heir was supposed to figure them out . . ."

"But what for?" she asked, rather fiercely. "What for?"

One statement, made rather carelessly by the lawyer, had been at the back of Rampole's mind for some time. Something he had been groping for; it showed itself now, and asked a question.

"There were four keys –" he began, and glanced at her.

"Yes."

"To the door of the Governor's Room. That's reasonable. To the vault, and to the box inside it; those three are natural enough. But – why a key to the iron door going out on the balcony? What would anybody need that one for? Unless those directions, rightly interpreted, would lead the person out on the balcony . . ."

Back again crept the formless surmises in which Sir Benjamin had been indulging. Every indication pointed to that balcony. He was thinking of the ivy, and the stone balustrade, and the two depressions in the stone which Dr. Fell had discovered. A deathtrap . . .

Startled, he discovered that he had spoken aloud. He was aware of it by the quick look she turned on him, and he cursed himself for letting the words slip out. What he had said was:

"Herbert, they all say, was an inventor."

"You believe that he – ?"

"No! I don't know what I meant!"

She turned a pale face in the dimness of the hall. "Whoever did this killed Father, too. You all think so. And, listen! There was a reason. I *know* there was a reason now. And it's ghastly – and awful – and all that, but, O my God! I hope it's true! . . . Don't stare at me like that. I'm not mad. Really."

Her low voice was growing a trifle thick, and she spoke as

one who begins to see shapes in a mist. The dark blue eyes were eerie now.

"Listen. That paper – it gives directions for something. What? If father was killed, murdered by somebody – no curse, but deliberately murdered – what then?"

"I don't know."

"But I think I do. If Father was murdered, he wasn't murdered for following out directions in those verses. But maybe *somebody else* had fathomed the verses. Maybe there's something hidden – something those verses have a clue to – and the murderer killed Father because Father had surprised him at work . . . !"

Rampole stared at her tense face, and her hand groping before her as though she touched a secret, lightly. He said:

"You're – you're not talking about anything so wild as buried treasure?"

She nodded. "I don't care about that . . . What I mean is, if that *is* true, don't you see, there isn't any curse – there isn't any madness – I'm not tainted, nor any of us. That's what I care about." In an even lower voice: "You've only got to wonder whether there's any horrible seed in your blood, and brood about it, to go through the worst hell –"

He touched her hand. There was a pent-up silence, a sense of fears pattering in a dark room, and windows that needed to be opened to daylight.

"– that's why I say I hope to God it's true. My father is dead, and so is my brother, and that can't be helped now. But at least it was something clean; it was something you could understand, like an auto wreck. Do you see?"

"Yes. And we've got to find the secret of that cryptogram, if there is a secret. Will you let me have a copy?"

"Come back and copy it now before the rest of them get away. I mustn't see you for a while . . ."

"But you can't – I mean, you've got to! We've got to see each other, if only for a few minutes – !"

She looked up slowly. "We can't. People would talk." Then, as he nodded blankly, she put out the palms of her hands as though she would put them against his breast, and went on in a strained voice: "Oh, do you think I don't want to as much as you? I do. More! But we can't. They'd talk. They'd say all sorts of horrible things, and that I was an unnatural sister, and – maybe I am." She shivered.

"They always said I was a strange one, and I'm beginning to think it's true. I shouldn't be talking like this, with my brother just dead, but I'm human – I – Never mind! Please go and copy out that paper. I'll get it for you."

They said no more as they went down to the little office, where Rampole scribbled down the verses on the back of an envelope. When they returned to the hall everybody had disappeared except a shocked and open-eyed Budge, who passed them with an air of not having seen them at all.

"You see?" she enquired, lifting her eyebrows.

"I know. I'll go, and I won't try to see you until you give the word. But – do you mind if I show this thing to Dr. Fell? He'll keep it a secret. And you know from today how good he is at this sort of thing."

"Yes, show it to Dr. Fell. Do! I hadn't thought of that. But not to anybody else – please. And now you must hurry along . . ."

When she opened the great door for him, it seemed surprising to find the placid sunlight on the lawns as though this were only an English Sunday and no dead man lay upstairs. We are not touched so deeply by tragedy as we think. As he went down the drive to join his companions, he glanced back once over his shoulder. She was standing in the doorway, motionless, the breeze stirring her hair. He could hear doves in the tall elms, and sparrows bickering among the vines. Up on its white cupola, the gilt weather-vane had turned fiery against the noonday.

12

"We find," said the inquest, "that the deceased met his death as the result of –" The formal words had a habit of singing through Rampole's mind with thoughtless and irritating refrain. What they meant was that Herbert Starberth had killed his cousin Martin by throwing him from the balcony of the Governor's Room. Since the autopsy revealed blood in the nostrils and mouth, and a contusion at the base of the brain not explicable by the position in which he had fallen, it was pointed out by Dr. Markley that the deceased had in all likelihood been rendered insensible by a heavy blow before the actual murder took place. Martin's neck and right hip had been broken, and there were other pleasant details which had hung with cold ugliness in the stolid air of the inquest-room.

It was over now. In the London press Chatterham's wonder had not even lasted nine days; it blossomed into pictures, speculations, and hectic news stories, and then sank back among the advertisements. There remained only a man-hunt, baying after Herbert, and Herbert had not been found. That enigmatic figure on the green bicycle slid through England as through a mist. He was seen, of course, in a dozen places, but it never turned out to be Herbert Starberth. Assuming that he had ridden in the direction of Lincoln to take a train, it had been so far found impossible to trace his movements, nor was there any trace of the green motor-bike. Scotland Yard moved so quietly that it was as invisible as the fugitive, but there was no word of capture from the grim building above Westminster Pier.

A week after the inquest, and Chatterham slept again. All day the rain fell, sheeting these lowlands, droning on the eaves, and sputtering in chimneys where fires had been lighted against the damp. The ancient rain of England, which brought out old odours like ghosts, so that black-letter books, and engravings on the wall, seemed more alive than real people. Rampole sat before a coal fire in the grate of Dr. Fell's study. But for its creakings, Yew Cottage was quiet. Dr. and Mrs. Fell had gone to Chatterham for the afternoon; their guest, alone in an easy chair by firelight, wanted no lamps. He could see the rain thickening beyond grey windows, and he could see things in the fire.

The arch of the grate, black-shining; the flames, and Dorothy Starberth's face at the inquest – never turned towards him. There were too many rumours. Chairs rasping on the sanded floor; the voices that struck across the inquest-room sharply, like voices inside a stone jug. She had gone home, afterwards, in an old car driven by Payne, with its side curtains down. He had watched the dust that followed its jolting passage, and he had seen faces peering out slyly from the windows of houses along the way. Gossip had been a sly postman tapping at every door. The damned fools, he thought, and suddenly felt very miserable.

But the rustle of the shower deepened, a few drops hissing in the fire. He stared at the paper across his knee – those inane verses he had copied from the paper she had shown him. He had mentioned them to Dr. Fell, but the old lexicographer had not seen them yet. Decently, in view of the turmoil and later the funeral, they had been able to drop the puzzle for the time being. Yet now Martin Starberth was tucked away, out there under the rain . . . Rampole shivered. Platitudes went through his brain; he knew them now to be terrifyingly true. And other words.

"Though worms destroy this body . . ." the strong, calm words uttered under an empty sky. Again in his memory the earth fell upon the coffin, thrown as with the motion of a sower of grain. He saw the sodden willows tossing against a grey horizon, and the sing-song intonation of the service was as weirdly moving as when once – long ago, as a child – he had heard at twilight distant voices singing "Auld Lang Syne."

What was that? He had been almost hearing again things lost far back in childhood, when he knew that there had been a real noise. Somebody was knocking at the outer door of Yew Cottage.

He got up, kindled the lamp on the table beside him, and carried it to light his way out into the hall. Raindrops blew into his face as he opened the door, and he held the lamp high.

"I came to see Mrs. Fell," said the girl's voice. "I wondered if she would offer me tea."

She looked up seriously from under her sodden hat-brim. The lamplight brought her close out of the rain. She spoke with an innocent, apologetic glance past him into the hall.

"They're out," he said. "But please don't let that stop you from coming in. I – I don't know whether I can manage making tea the right way . . ."

"I can," she told him.

All the stiffness vanished. She smiled. So presently the wet hat and coat were hanging in the hall, and she was hurrying about the kitchen in a highly practical manner while he tried to give a decent appearance of being busy. There is never, he reflected, such a guilty feeling as standing in the middle of a kitchen during the preparation of food; it is like watching somebody change a tire. Whenever you try to move about, as though you were actually doing something, you run into the other person with a bump; and then you feel as though you had shoved the tire-changer over on his face for sheer devilment. They did not talk much, but Dorothy addressed the tea-things vigorously.

She laid the cloth on a small table before the fire in the doctor's study. The curtains were drawn, the blaze piled again with coal. Intent, her brows puckered, she was buttering toast; he could see the shadows under her eyes in the yellow lamplight. Hot muffins, marmalade, and strong tea; the rasp of the knife on toast, steadily, and the warm sweet odour of cinnamon spread on it . . .

She looked up suddenly.

"I say, aren't you going to drink your tea?"

"No," he said flatly. "Tell me what's been happening."

The knife tinkled on the plate as she put it down, very quietly. She answered, looking away: "There isn't anything. Only, I had to get out of that house."

"*You* eat something. I'm not hungry."

"Oh, don't you see I'm not either?" she demanded. "It's so nice here; the rain, and the fire –" She flexed her muscles, like a cat, and stared at the edge of the mantelpiece. The teacups smoked between them. She was sitting on an old sagging sofa, whose cloth was of a dull red. Thrown down on the hearth, face upwards, lay the paper on which he had copied the verses. She nodded towards it.

"Have you told Dr. Fell about that?"

"I've mentioned it. But I haven't told him your idea that there is something hidden . . ."

He realized that he had no idea what he was talking about. On an impulse that was as sudden as a blow in the chest, he rose to his feet. His legs felt light and shaky, and he could hear the teakettle singing loudly. He was conscious of her eyes, bright and steady in the firelight, as he went round to the sofa. For a moment she stared at the fire, and then turned towards him.

He found himself looking at the fire, its heat fierce on his eyes, listening vaguely to the singing kettle and the dim tumult of the rain. For a long time, when he had ceased to kiss her, she remained motionless against his shoulder, her eyes closed and waxen-lidded. Fear that he would be repulsed had lifted, and slowed the enormous pounding of his heart into a peace that was like a blanket drawn about them. He felt madly jubilant and, at the same time, stupid. Turning, he was startled to see her looking at the ceiling with a blank, wide-open stare.

His voice sounded loud in his own ears. "I –" he said, "I shouldn't have –"

The blank eyes moved over to his. They seemed to be looking up from some great depth. Slowly her arm moved up round his neck, and drew his face down again. A close, heart-pounding interval while the kettle ceased to sing and somebody seemed to be murmuring incoherently into his ear, through a warm mist. Then suddenly she broke away from him and got to her feet with a spasmodic motion. Walking back and forth in the lamplight, her cheeks flushed, she stopped before him.

"I know it," she said, breathlessly, in a hard voice. "I'm a callous little beast. I'm a rotter, that's all. To be doing that – with Martin . . ."

He got up sharply and took her by the shoulders.

"Don't think about that! Try to stop thinking about it," he said. "It's over and done with, don't you see? Dorothy, I love you."

"And do you think I don't love you?" she demanded. "I never will, I never could, love anybody as much as I do you. It scares me. It's the first thing I think of when I wake up in the morning, and I even dream about it at night. That's how bad it is. But it's horrible of me to be thinking about that now . . ."

Her voice shook. He found that he had tightened his grip on her shoulders, as though he were trying to hold her from a jump.

"We're both a little crazy," she went on. "I won't tell you I care for you. I *won't* admit it. We're both upset by this ghastly business . . ."

"But it won't be for long, will it? My God! can't you stop brooding? You know what all these fears amount to. Nothing. You heard Dr. Fell say so."

"I can't explain it. I know what I'll do – go away. I'll go away now – tonight – tomorrow – and I'll forget you –"

"Could you forget? Because, if you could –"

He saw that her eyes were full of tears, and cursed himself. He tried to make his voice calm. "There isn't any need to forget. There's only one thing we've got to do. We've got to explain all this tommyrot, murders and curses and foolishness and everything, and then you'll be free. We'll both go away then, and –"

"Would you want me?"

"You little fool!"

"– Well," she said, plaintively, after a pause, "I only asked . . . Oh, damn it, when I think of myself reading books a month ago, and wondering whether I might be in love with Wilfrid Denim and not know it, and wondering how they could make such a fuss about it; and then I think of myself now – I've played the silly fool, I'd have done anything – !" She shook her head fiercely and then smiled. The impish look came back; she spoke banteringly, yet it was as though she were pricking a knife-point against her flesh, half fearful that she might draw blood. "I hope you mean it, old boy. I rather think I should die if you didn't."

Rampole started in, oratorically, to tell how worthless he was; young men always feel impelled to do this, and Rampole even went so far as to mean it. The effect was somewhat marred by his putting his hand into the butter-dish at the height of the peroration, but she said she didn't care if he rolled in the butter, and laughed at his humiliation. So they decided they ought to eat something. She kept saying everything was "'ridiculous,'' and Rampole seized recklessly on the idea.

"Have some of this damn silly tea," he suggested. "Take a little of this maundering, bughouse lemon and a *soupçon* of senile sugar. Go on, take it. It's a curious thing, but I feel like throwing the loony toast at you precisely because I love you so much. Marmalade? It has a very low I.Q. I recommend it. Besides –"

"Please! Dr. Fell will be in any moment. Do stop dancing about! – And would you mind opening a window? You beastly Americans like everything so stuffy. Please!"

He strode across to a window beside the fireplace and threw back the curtains, giving a very fair imitation of her accent as he continued his monologue. The rain had slackened. Throwing open the leaves of the window, he poked his head out, and instinctively looked towards Chatterham prison. What he saw caused him not a shock of surprise or fear, but a calm, cold jubilation. He spoke with pleasure and deliberateness.

"This time," he said. "I'm going to get the son – I'm going to get him."

He nodded as he spoke, and turned a queer face to the girl as he pointed out into the rain. Again there was a light in the Governor's Room of Chatterham prison.

It looked like a candle, small and flickering through the dusk. She took only one glance at it before she seized his shoulder.

"What are you going to do?"

"I've told you. Heaven willing," said Rampole, briskly, "I'm going to kick hell out of him."

"You're not going up there?"

"No? Watch me! That's all I ask, just watch me."

"I won't let you! No, I'm serious. I mean it! You can't –"

Rampole emitted a laugh modelled on the pattern of a stage villain. He took the lamp from the table and hurried out towards the hall, so that she was forced to follow. She seemed to be fluttering around him.

"I asked you not to!"

"So you did," replied the other, putting on his raincoat. "Just help me with the sleeve of this thing, will you? . . . Good girl! Now what I want," he added, inspecting the hatstand, "is a cane. A good heavy one . . . Here we are. 'Are you armed, Lestrade?' 'I am armed.' Plenty."

"Then, I warn you, I'll go along!" she cried, accusingly.

"Well, get your coat on, then. I don't know how long that little joker will wait. Come to think of it, I'd better have a flashlight; the doctor left one here last night, as I remember . . . Now."

"Darling!" said Dorothy Starberth. "I was hoping you'd let me go . . ."

Soaked, splattering through mud, they cut down across the lawn and into the meadow. She had some difficulty manoeuvring the fence in her long raincoat; as he lifted her over it, he felt a kiss on his wet cheek, and the exultation of confronting that person in the Governor's Room began to leave him. This wasn't a joke. It was ugly, dangerous work. He turned in the dimness.

"Look here," he said, "seriously, you'd better go back. This isn't any lark, and I won't have you taking chances."

There was a silence while he heard the rain beating on his hat. Only that lonely light shone over the rain-sheets flickering white across the meadows. When she answered, her voice was small and cool and firm.

"I know it as well as you do. But I've got to know. And you've got to take me, because you don't know how to get to the Governor's Room unless I show you the way. – Checkmate, dear."

She began to splash ahead of him up the slope of the meadow. He followed, slashing at the soggy grass with his cane.

They were both silent, and the girl was panting, when they reached the gates of the prison. Away from firelight, you needed to deny to yourself several times that there could be nothing supernatural about this old house of whips and hangings. Rampole pressed the button of his flashlight. The white beam ran along that green-fouled tunnel; probed it, hesitated, and moved forward.

"Do you suppose," the girl whispered, "it's *really* – the man who – ?"

"Better go back, I tell you!"

"It's worn off," she said in a small voice. "I'm afraid. But I'd be more afraid to go back. Let me get a grip on your arm and I'll show you the way. Careful. – What do you suppose he's doing up there? He must be crazy to risk it."

"Do you suppose he can hear us coming?"

"Oh no. Not yet; it's miles and miles."

Their footfalls made sounds like the squish of oozing water. Rampole's light darted. Small eyes regarded them, scuttling away as the beam pried open dark corners. There were gnats flicking round their faces, and somewhere close there must have been water, for the croaking of frogs beat harshly in guttural chorus. Again that interminable journey wound Rampole through corridors, past rusty gates, down stone stairs and twisting up again. As the flashlight's beam found the face of the Iron Maiden, something whirred in the darkness . . .

Bats. The girl ducked, and Rampole struck viciously with his stick. He had miscalculated, and the cane clanged against iron, sending a din of echoes along the roof. From a flapping cloud, the squeaks of the bats shrilled in reply. Rampole felt her hand shaking on his arm.

"We've warned him," she whispered. "I'm afraid. We've warned him . . . No, no, don't leave me here! I've got to stay with you. If that light goes out . . . Those ghastly things; I can almost feel them in my hair . . ."

Though he reassured her, he felt the thick knocking of his own heart. If there were dead men walking in the stone house where they had died, he thought, they must have faces just like that big, empty, spider-hung countenance of the Iron Maiden. The sweat of the old torture-room seemed to linger. He tightened his jaws as though he were biting on a bullet, as soldiers did to stifle the pain of an amputation in Anthony's day.

Anthony . . .

There was a light ahead. They could see it dimly, just at the top of a flight of stairs leading to the passage which ran outside the Governor's Room. Somebody was carrying a candle.

Rampole snapped off his light. He could feel Dorothy shaking in the dark as he put her behind him and began to edge up the stairs along the left-hand wall, the stick free in his right hand. He knew with cold clarity that he was not afraid of a murderer. He would even have liked to swing the heavy cane against a murderer's skull. But what made the small wires jerk and jump in his legs, what made his stomach feel cold as a squeezed rag, was the fear that this might be somebody else.

For a moment he was afraid the girl behind him was going to cry out. And he knew that he, too, would have cried out if there had been a shadow across that candle-light, and the shadow had worn a three-cornered hat . . . Up there he heard footsteps. Evidently the other person had heard them coming, and then believed he must have been mistaken, for the sounds were going back in the direction of the Governor's Room.

Somewhere there was the tapping of a cane . . .

Silence.

Slowly, during interminable minutes, Rampole moved up the staircase. A dim glow shone from the open door of the Governor's Room. Putting the electric torch in his pocket, he took Dorothy's cold and wet hand. His shoes squeaked a trifle, but the rats were squeaking, too. He moved down the corridor and peered round the edge of the door.

A candle in a holder was burning on the centre table. At the table, Dr. Fell sat motionless, his chin in his hand, his stick propped against his leg. On the wall behind him the candlelight reared a shadow which was curiously like that of the Rodin statue. And, sitting up on its haunches beneath the canopy of old Anthony's bed, a great grey rat was looking at Dr. Fell with shiny, sardonic eyes.

"Come in, children," Dr. Fell said, scarcely glancing at the door. "I confess I was reassured when I knew it was you."

13

Rampole let the stick slide through his hand until its ferrule clanged on the floor; then he leaned on it. He said, "Dr. –" and found that his voice had gone into a crazy key.

The girl was laughing, pressing her hand to her mouth.

"We thought –" Rampole said, swallowing.

"Yes," nodded the doctor, "you thought I was the murderer, or a ghost. I was afraid you might see my candle from Yew Cottage and come over to investigate, but there was no way to block the window. Look here, my dear girl, you'd better sit down. I admire your nerve in coming up here. As for me –"

From his pocket he took an old-style derringer revolver and weighed the heavy weapon in his palm reflectively. He wheezed, nodding again.

"Because, children, I rather think we're up against a very dangerous man. Here, sit down."

"But what are *you* doing here, sir?" Rampole asked.

Dr. Fell laid the pistol on the table beside the candle. He pointed to what looked like a stack of manuscript ledgers, rotten and mildewed, and to a bundle of brown dry letters; with a large handkerchief he tried to mop the dust from his hands.

"Since you're here," he rumbled, "we might as well go into it. I was ransacking . . . No, my lad, don't sit on the edge of that bed; it's full of unpleasant things. Here, on the edge of the table. You, my dear," to Dorothy, "may have the straight chair; the others are full of spiders.

"Anthony kept accounts, of course," he continued. "I fancied I should find 'em if I poked about . . . The question is, what was Anthony hiding from his family. I must tell you, I think we're in for another old, old story about buried treasure."

Dorothy, sitting very quiet in her wet raincoat, turned slowly to look at Rampole. She only observed:

"I knew it. I said so. And after I found those verses –"

"Ah, the verses!" grunted Dr. Fell. "Yes. I shall want to look at those. My young friend mentioned 'em. But all you have to do is read Anthony's diary to get a hint about what he did. He hated his family; he said they'd suffer for ridiculing his verse. So he turned his verse into a means to taunt them. I'm no very good accountant, but I can see from these," he tapped the ledgers, "that he left 'em precious little cash out of a large fortune. He couldn't beggar them, of course, because the lands – the biggest source of revenue – were entailed. But I rather think he put a gigantic sum beyond their reach. Bullion? Plate? Jewels? I don't know. You'll remember, he keeps referring in the diary to *'the things one can buy to defeat them,'* meaning his relatives; and again he says, 'I have the beauties safe.' Have you forgotten his signet, 'All that I have I carry with me?' – 'Omnia mea mecum porto.'"

"And left the clue in the verses?" asked Rampole. "Telling where the hiding-place is?"

Dr. Fell threw back his ancient box-pleated cape and drew out pipe and tobacco-pouch. Reeling out the black ribbon, he adjusted his glasses more firmly.

"There are other clues," he said, meditatively.

"In the diary?"

"Partly. 'M. For instance, why was Anthony so strong in the arms? He was rather puny when he became governor;

nothing about him developed except his arms and shoulders. We know that . . . Eh?"

"Yes, of course."

The doctor nodded his big head. "Then again, you saw that deeply worn groove in the stone railing of the balcony over there. Eh? It was about of a size to contain a man's thumb," added the doctor, examining his own thumb reflectively.

"You mean a secret mechanism?" asked Rampole.

"Again," said the doctor, "again – and this is important – why did he leave behind him a key to the balcony door? Why the *balcony* door? If he left those instructions in the vault, all that his heirs would need to get at them would be three keys: one to the corridor door of this room, one to the vault, and one to the iron box inside the vault. Why, then, include that fourth key?"

"Well, clearly because his instructions entailed going out on the balcony," said Rampole. "That was what Sir Benjamin said when he was talking about a death-trap out there . . . Look here, sir! By that groove the size of a man's thumb, do you mean a spring, a mechanism, to be pressed so that –"

"Oh, nonsense!" said the doctor. "I didn't say a man's thumb went there. A man's thumb, even in the course of thirty years, wouldn't have worn that groove. But I'll tell you what would have done it. A rope."

Rampole slid off the edge of the table. He glanced over at the balcony door, closed and sinister in the faint light of the candle.

"Why," he repeated aloud – "Why was Anthony so strong in the arms?"

"Or, if you want more questions," boomed the doctor, sitting up straight, "why is the destiny of everybody so intimately concerned with that well? Everything leads straight to the well. – There's Anthony's son, of course, the second

Starberth who was a governor of this prison. He's the one who threw us all off the track. *He* died of a broken neck, like his father, and started the tradition. If he'd died in bed, there wouldn't have been any tradition, and we could examine the death of Anthony, his father, without any hocus-pocus. We could see it as the isolated problem it is. But it didn't happen that way. Anthony's son had to be governor of this prison when the cholera wiped out most of its inmates, and those poor devils went mad down in their airless cells. Well, the governor of the prison went mad from the same fever. He had it, too, and his delusions were too strong for him. You know what an effect that diary of his father's had on all of us? Then what sort of effect do you imagine it had on a nervous, bogey-ridden man who had been stricken with cholera in the bogey-ridden nineteenth century? What do you suppose is the effect on the brain of living just above the exhalations of a swamp where hanged men have been thrown to rot? – Anthony could hardly have hated his own son enough to want him to get up from his bed in delirium and throw himself from that balcony. But that's what the second governor did."

Rumbling, Dr. Fell exhaled his breath so hard that it almost blew out the candle, and Rampole jumped. For a moment the big room was quiet: dead men's books, dead men's chairs, and now the ancient sickness of their brains had become as terrible here as the face of the Iron Maiden. A rat scurried across the floor. Dorothy Starberth had put her hand on Rampole's sleeve; you would have said that she saw ghosts.

"And Anthony – ?" Rampole put in, with an effort.

For a time Dr. Fell sat with his big shock of hair bowed.

"It must have taken him a long time," he remarked, vacantly, "to have worn so deep a groove in the stone. He had to do it all alone, and in the dead of night-time, when nobody could see him. Of course, there were no guards on that side of the prison, so he could escape unnoticed . . . Still, I'm inclined to think he had a confederate for the first few years, until he could develop his own strength. His own terrific strength would come with patience, but until then he had to have a confederate up raise and lower him . . . Probably, afterwards, he did away with the man . . ."

"Wait, please!" said Rampole, hitting the table. "You say that the groove was worn by a rope because Anthony spent years . . ."

"Hauling himself up and down it."

"Into the well," the other observed, slowly. He had a sudden vision of a weird spiderish figure in black, swinging on a rope under the night sky. A lamp or two would be burning in the prison. The stars would be out. And Anthony would dangle by night where dead men dangled in daytime, working his way down to the well . . .

Yes. Somewhere down in that broad well, God knew where, he had spent years in hollowing out a cache. Or possibly every night he had swung down to examine his treasures there. The reek from the well would dissolve his own sanity as it later dissolved his son's; but more subtly, for he was a harder man. He would see dead men climbing up from the well to knock at his balcony door. He would hear them whispering together at night, because he had decked their flesh with his wealth, and planted gold among their bones. Many nights he must have seen the rats eating in the well. It was only when he saw the rats in his own bed that he believed the dead men were coming to carry him down with them, soon.

Rampole's damp coat felt repulsive against him. The room was full of Anthony's presence.

Dorothy spoke in a clear voice. She did not look afraid now.

"And that," she said, "went on until – ?"

"Until he grew careless," answered Dr. Fell.

The rain, which had almost died away, crept up on the prison once more; it rustled in the ivy at the window, splattering the floor; it danced through the prison, as though it were washing things away.

"Or perhaps," resumed the doctor, looking suddenly at the balcony door, "perhaps he didn't grow careless. Perhaps somebody knew of his visits, without knowing what they were about, and cut that rope. Anyway, the knot of his rope slipped, or was cut. It was a wild night, full of wind and rain. The rope, freed, went down with him. Since its edge was on the inside lip of the well, it slid over into the well; nobody would have cared to examine anything down there, so they didn't suspect a rope. But Anthony didn't fall into the well."

And Rampole thought: Yes, a rope that was cut. Much more probable than a noose that slipped. Perhaps there was a lamp burning in the Governor's Room, and the man with the knife was looking over the balcony rail, and saw Anthony's face momentarily as he went whirling down towards the spikes on the edge of the well. In Rampole's mind it was as horribly vivid as a Cruikshank print – the white, staring eyeballs, the outflung arms, the shadowy murderer.

A cry against the wind and rain; then the noise, however it had sounded; and a lamp blown out. It was all as dead as one of those books in the shelves. Ainsworth might have imagined it, just as it took place, in the eighteen-twenties . . .

Distantly he heard Dr. Fell say: "There, Miss Starberth. There's your damned curse. There's what's been worrying you all this time. Not very impressive, is it?"

She rose without speaking, and began to walk about the room, her hands thrust into her pockets, just as Rampole remembered her that first night at the train. Pausing in front of Dr. Fell, she took a folded paper from her pocket and held it out. The verses.

"Then," she asked, "this? What about this?"

"A cryptogram, undoubtedly. It will tell us the exact place . . . But don't you see that a clever thief wouldn't have needed that paper, he wouldn't even need to have known of its existence, to know that there was something hidden in the well? He could have used just the evidence *I* used. It's all available."

The candle was getting low, and a broad sheet of flame curled about it, throwing momentary brightness. Dorothy went to where the rain was making splattered pools below the window, and stared blankly at the vines.

"I think I see," she said, "about my father. He was – wet, wet all over, when they found him."

"You mean," said Rampole, "that he caught the thief at work?"

"Well, is there any other explanation?" Dr. Fell growled. He had been making ineffectual efforts to light his pipe, and now he laid it down on the table. "He was out riding, you know. He saw the rope going down into the well. We can assume that the murderer didn't see him, because Timothy went down into the well. So – ?" He glared ferociously.

"There's some sort of room, or hollowed-out place," Rampole nodded. "And the murderer didn't know he was there until he came down."

"Humph. Well. There's another deduction, but let it go. Excuse me, Miss Starberth: your father didn't fall. He was beaten, coldly and viciously, and then thrown into the bushes for dead."

The girl turned. *"Herbert?"* she demanded.

With his forefinger Dr. Fell was making a pattern in the dust of the table, like a child drawing, with the utmost absorption. He muttered:

"It can't be an amateur. The thing's too perfect. It can't be. But it's got to be, unless they tell me differently. And if he isn't, it must be a high stake."

Rampole somewhat irritably asked what he was talking about.

"I was talking," the doctor replied, "about a visit to London."

With an effort he hoisted himself to his feet on the two canes; he stood fiery and lowering, blinking about the room behind his glasses. Then he shook one stick at the walls like a schoolmaster.

"Your secret's out," he rumbled. "You can't scare anybody now."

"There's still a murderer," Rampole said.

"Yes. And, Miss Starberth, it's your father who has kept him here. Your father left that note in the vault, as I explained to you the other day. The murderer thinks he's safe. He has waited nearly three years to get that condemning paper back. Well, he isn't safe."

"You know who it is?"

"Come along," said the doctor, brusquely. "We've got to get home. I need a cup of tea or a bottle of beer, preferably the latter. And my wife will be returning from Mrs. Payne's before long . . ."

"Look here, sir," Rampole persisted; "do you know who the murderer is?"

Dr. Fell pondered.

"It's still raining hard," he responded, at length, with the air of one meditating a move at chess. "Do you see how much water has accumulated under that window?"

"Yes, of course, but –"

"And do you see," he indicated the closed door to the balcony, "that none has got in through there?"

"Naturally."

"But if that door were open there would be much more water there than under the window, wouldn't there?"

If the doctor were doing all this merely for the purpose of mystification, Rampole could not tell it. The lexicographer was looking through his glasses in a rather cross-eyed fashion, and pinching at his moustache. Rampole grimly resolved to hang on to the coat-tails of the comet.

"Undoubtedly, sir," he agreed.

"Then," said the other, triumphantly, "why didn't we see his light?"

"O God!" said Rampole, with a faint groan.

"It's like a conjuring trick. Do you know," enquired Dr. Fell, pointing with one cane, "what Tennyson said of Browning's 'Sordello'?"

"No, sir."

"He said that the only things you could understand in the poem were the first line and the last – and that both of 'em were lies. Well, that's the key to this business. Come along, children, and have some tea."

There might still have been terror in the house of whips and hangings. But Rampole did not feel it when he led the way down again with his light.

Back in the lamplit warmth of Dr. Fell's house, they found Sir Benjamin Arnold waiting for them in the study.

14

Sir Benjamin was moody. He had been cursing the rain, and, afterwards, the presence of strong language was still as palpable as a whiskey breath. They found him looking hungrily at the cold tea-things before the study fire.

"Halloa!" said Dr. Fell. "My wife not back yet? How did you get in?"

"I walked in," the chief constable responded, with dignity. "The door was open. Somebody's been neglecting a jolly good tea . . . I say, what about a drink?"

"*We* – ah – had tea," said Rampole.

The chief constable was aggrieved. "I want a brandy-and-soda. Everybody is pursuing me. First the rector. His uncle – New Zealander – old friend of mine; I got the rector the parish here – is making his first trip to England in ten years, and the rector wants me to meet him. How the devil can I go away? The rector's a New Zealander. Let *him* go to Southampton. Then Payne . . ."

"What's wrong with Payne?" asked Dr. Fell.

"He wants the door of the Governor's Room sealed up with bricks for good. Says its purpose is over now. Well, I only hope it is. But we can't do it yet. Payne always has a kind of mental toothache about something. Finally, since the last Starberth male heir is dead, Dr. Markley wants the well filled up."

Dr. Fell puffed out his cheeks. "We certainly can't do *that*," he agreed. "Sit down. There's something we've got to tell you."

While the doctor was pouring out stiff drinks at the sideboard, he told Sir Benjamin everything that had happened that afternoon. During the recital, Rampole was watching the girl's face. She had not spoken much since Dr. Fell had begun to explain what lay behind the Starberths; but she seemed to see peace.

Sir Benjamin was flapping his hands behind his back. His damp clothes exhaled a strong odour of tweed and tobacco.

"I don't doubt it, I don't doubt it," he grumbled. "But why did you have to be so confoundedly long about telling this? We've lost a lot of time. – Still, it doesn't alter what we've got to face – that Herbert's the only one who could be guilty. Inquest said so."

"Does that reassure you?"

"No. Damn it. I don't think the boy's guilty. But what else can we do?"

"No trace of him yet?"

"Oh, he's been reported everywhere; but they haven't found him. In the meantime, I repeat, what else can we do?"

"We can investigate the hiding-place Anthony made, for one thing."

"Yes. If this infernal cipher, or whatever it is . . . Let's have a look. I suppose we have your permission, Miss Starberth?"

She smiled faintly. "Of course – now. But I am inclined to think Dr. Fell has been overconfident. Here's my own copy."

Dr. Fell was seated spread out in his favourite arm-chair, his pipe glowing and a bottle of beer beside him. With white hair and whiskers, he could have made a passable double for Father Christmas. He watched benignly as Sir Benjamin studied the verses. Rampole's own pipe was drawing well, and he sat back comfortably on the red sofa where, in an unobtrusive way, he could touch Dorothy's hand. With his other hand he held a drink. Thus, he reflected, there were all the requisites of life.

The chief constable's horsy eyes squinted up. He read aloud:

"How called the dwellers of Lyn-dun;
Great Homer's tale of Troy?
Or Country of the midnight sun –
What doth all men destroy?"

Slowly he read the lines again, in a lower voice. Then he said with heat:

"Look here, this is nonsense!"

"Ah!" said Dr. Fell, like one who savours a rare bouquet of wine.

"It's just a lot of crackbrain poetry –"

"Verse," corrected Dr. Fell.

"Well, it certainly isn't any cryptogram, whatever it is. Have you seen it?"

"No. But it's a cryptogram, all right."

The chief constable tossed the paper across to him. "Righto, then. Tell us what it means. 'How called the dwellers of Lyn-dun; Great Homer's tale of Troy?' It's a lot of rubbish . . . Hold on, though!" muttered Sir Benjamin, rubbing his cheek. "I've seen those puzzles in the magazines. And I remember in the stories – you take every other word, or every second word, or something – don't you?"

"That won't work," said Rampole, gloomily. "I've tried all the combinations of first, second and third words. I've tried it as an acrostic, down the whole four verses. The first letters give you 'Hgowatiwiowetgff.' With the last letters you produce 'Nynyfrdrefstenen.' The last one sounds like an Assyrian queen."

"Ah," said Dr. Fell, nodding again.

"In the magazines –" began Sir Benjamin.

Dr. Fell settled himself more deeply into his chair, blowing an enormous cloud of smoke.

"By the way," he observed. "I have a quarrel to pick with those puzzles in the magazines and illustrated papers. Now, I'm very fond of cryptograms myself. (Incidentally, you will find behind you one of the first books on cipher-writing: John Baptist Porta's *De Furtivis Literarum Notis,* published in 1563.) Now, the only point of a good cryptogram is that it should conceal something which somebody wanted to keep a secret in the first place. That is, it is really a piece of secret writing. Its message should be something like, 'The missing jewels are hidden in the archdeacon's pants,' or, 'Von Dinklespook will attack the Worcestershire Guards at midnight.' – But when these people in the illustrated papers try to invent a cryptogram which will baffle the reader, they don't try to baffle you by inventing a difficult cryptogram at all. They only try to baffle you by putting down a message which nobody would ever send in the first place. You puzzle and swear through a gigantic mass of symbols, only to produce the message: 'Pusillanimous pachyderms primarily procrastinate procreative prerogatives.' *Bah!*" stormed the doctor. "Can you imagine an operative of the German secret service risking his life to get a message like that through the British lines? I should think that General Von Googledoffer would be a trifle nettled when he got his dispatch decoded and found that cowardly elephants are in the habit of putting off any attempt to reproduce their species."

"That isn't true, is it?" inquired Sir Benjamin, with interest.

"I'm not concerned with the natural history of the statement," returned the doctor, testily; "I was talking about cryptograms." He took a long pull at his beer-glass, and went on in a more equable tone:

"It's a very old practice. of course. Plutarch and Gellius mention secret methods of correspondence used by the

Spartans. But cryptography, in the stricter sense of substituting words, letters, or symbols, is of Semitic origin. At least, Jeremiah uses it. A variant of this same simple form is used in Caesar's *'quarta elementorus littera,'* where –"

"But look at the blasted thing!" exploded Sir Benjamin, picking up Rampole's copy from the hearth and slapping it. "Look here, in the last verse. It doesn't make sense. *'The Corsican was vanquished here, Great mother of all sin.'* If that means what I think it does, it's a bit rough on Napoleon."

Dr. Fell took the pipe out of his mouth. "I wish you'd shut up," he said, plaintively. "I feel like lecturing, I do. I was going on from Trithemius to Francis Bacon, and then –"

"I don't want to hear any lecture," interposed the chief constable. "I wish you'd have a look at the thing. I don't ask you to solve it. But stop lecturing and just *look* at it."

Sighing, Dr. Fell came to the centre table, where he lighted another lamp and spread the paper out before him. The pipe smoke slowed down to thin, steady puffs between clenched teeth.

"H'm," he said. There was another silence.

"Wait a bit," urged Sir Benjamin, holding up his hand as the doctor seemed about to speak. "Don't begin talking like a damned dictionary, now. But do you see any lead there?"

"I was about to ask you," replied the other, mildly, "to pour me out another bottle of beer. However, since you mention it . . . the old-timers were children to our modern cryptographers; the war proved that. And this one, which was written in the late eighteenth or early nineteenth century, shouldn't be so difficult. The rebus was a favorite form then; it isn't that, I know. But it's a bit more difficult than the ordinary substitution cipher Poe was so fond of. It's something like a rebus, only . . ."

They had gathered round his chair and were bending over the paper. Again they all read the words:

How called the dwellers of Lyn-dun;
Great Homer's tale of Troy?
Or country of the midnight sun –
What doth all men destroy?

Against it man hath dashed his foot;
This angel bears a spear!
In garden glade where Lord Christ prayed
What spawns dark stars and fear?

In this the white Diana rose;
Here was Dido bereft –
Where on four leaves good fortune grows;
East, south, west, what is left?

The Corsican was vanquished here,
Great mother of all sin;
Find green the same as shiretown's name,
Find Newgate Gaol, and win!

Dr. Fell's pencil worked rapidly, making unintelligible symbols. He grunted, shook his head, and returned to the verses again. Reaching to a revolving bookshelf beside him, he took down a black-bound volume labelled, "L. Fleissner, *Handbuch der Kryptographik*," and glanced at the index, scowling again.

"Drafghk!" he snapped, like one who says "damn." "That works out to 'drafghk,' which is nonsense. I'll swear the thing isn't a substitution cipher at all. I'll try Latin as well as English on the tests. I'll get it. The classical background always triumphs. Never, young man," he said, fiercely, "forget that . . . What's the matter, Miss Starberth?"

The girl was leaning both hands on the table, her dark hair gleaming under the light. She let out a small laugh as she glanced up.

"I was only thinking," she returned, in a puzzled way, "that, if you disregarded punctuation . . ."

"What?"

"Well . . . look at the first verse. 'Homer's tale of Troy.' That's the Iliad, isn't it? 'Country of the midnight sun.' That's Norway. If you took each of the lines separately, and put down the definition for each – I hope I'm not being silly," she hesitated, "and put down the definition for each as a separate word . . ."

"My God!" said Rampole, "it's a cross-word puzzle!"

"Nonsense!" shouted Dr. Fell, growing more red in the face.

"But look at it, sir," insisted Rampole, and bent over the paper suddenly. "Old Anthony didn't know he was doing a cross-word puzzle; but, in effect, that's what it is. You said it was a form of the rebus –"

"Come to think of it," rumbled Dr. Fell, clearing his throat, "the process was not unknown –"

"Well, work it!" said Sir Benjamin. "Try it that way. 'What called the dwellers of Lyn-dun?' I supposed that means, 'What were the dwellers of Lyn-dun called?' Does anybody know?"

Dr. Fell, who had been puffing out his moustache and acting like a sulky child, took up the pencil again. He answered, shortly:

"'Fenmen,' of course. Very well, we'll try it. As Miss Starberth has suggested, our next two words are 'Iliad' and 'Norway.' 'What doth all men destroy?' I can't think of anything except Death. So there we are – FENMEN ILIAD NORWAY DEATH."

There was a silence.

"That doesn't seem to make much sense," muttered Sir Benjamin, dubiously.

"It makes the most sense of anything yet, at least," Rampole said. "Let's go on. 'Against it man hath dashed his foot . . .' That sounds familiar. 'Lest he dash his foot against a – ' Got it! Try 'stone.' Now, what angel bears a spear?"

"That's Ithuriel," Dr. Fell pointed out, recovering his good humour. "The next line is obviously 'Gethsemane.' Let's see what we have now – FENMEN ILIAD NORWAY DEATH STONE ITHURIEL GETHSEMANE."

Then a broad grin creased up the folds of his many chins. He twisted his moustache like a pirate.

"It's all up now," he announced. "I've got it. Take the first letter of each word separately . . ."

"F I N D –" Dorothy read, and then looked round, her eyes very bright. "That's it. S I G – What comes next?"

"We need an N. Yes. 'What spawns dark stars and fear?'" the doctor read. "The next word is 'Night.' Next, the place where the white Diana rose – Ephesus. The next line is bad, but Dido's city was Tyre. So we have FIND SIGNET. I told you it would be simple."

Sir Benjamin was repeating, "By Jove!" and slapping his fist into his palm. He had a burst of inspiration, and added:

"Good fortune growing on four leaves: that must mean a shamrock, or clover, or whatever they call the dashed things. Anyway, the answer is Ireland."

"And," Rampole put in, "after you've taken away east, west, and south, the only thing left is north. North. That adds an N. FIND SIGNET IN –"

Dr. Fell's pencil added four words and then four letters.

"Complete," he said. "In the last verse, the first word has to be 'Waterloo.' The second is 'Eve.' That line about a green the same as the shiretown's name – why, Lincoln, of course. Lincoln green. Finally, we find Newgate Gaol in London. The whole word is WELL." He threw down his pencil. "Crafty old devil! He kept his secret for over a hundred years."

Sir Benjamin, still muttering imprecations, sat down blankly. "And we solved it in half an hour . . ."

"Let me remind you, sir," rumbled Dr. Fell, thoroughly roused, "that there is absolutely nothing in this cipher I couldn't have told you already. The explanation was all made. This is only proof of the explanation. If this cryptogram had been solved without that previous knowledge, it would have meant nothing. Now we know what it means, thanks to – ah – that previous knowledge." He finished his beer with a swashbuckling gesture, and glared.

"Of course, of course. But what does he mean by signet?"

"It could be nothing but that motto of his, 'All that I have I carry with me.' It's been helpful so far. And it'll help us again. Somewhere down in that well it's carved on the wall . . ."

Again the chief constable was rubbing his cheek and scowling.

"Yes. But we don't know where. And it's an unhealthy place to go foraging, you know."

"Nonsense!" the doctor said, sharply. "Of course we know where it is."

As the chief constable only looked sour, Dr. Fell settled back again to a comfortable lighting of his pipe. He went on in a thoughtful voice:

"If, for example, a heavy rope were to be run round the balcony railing in the groove of old Anthony's rope, and its end dropped into the well as Anthony's rope was . . . Well, we shouldn't be very far from the place, should we? The well may be large, but a line dropped from that groove would narrow our search down to a matter of feet. And if a stout young fellow – such as our young friend here – were to take hold of it at the mouth of the well and swarm down . . ."

"That's sound enough," the chief constable acknowledged. "But what good would it do? According to you, the murderer has long ago cleaned out whatever might have been in there. He killed old Timothy because Timothy surprised him, and he killed Martin because Martin would have learned his secret if he'd read the paper in the vault . . . What do you expect to find down there now?"

Dr. Fell hesitated. "I'm not sure. But we should have to do it, anyhow."

"I dare say." Sir Benjamin drew a long breath. "Well. Tomorrow morning I'll get a couple of constables –"

"We should have all Chatterham round us if we did it that way," said the doctor. "Don't you think this had better be kept among ourselves and done at night?"

The chief constable hesitated. "It's damned risky," he muttered. "A man could easily break his neck. What do you say, Mr. Rampole?"

It was an alluring prospect, and Rampole said so.

"I still don't like it," grunted the chief constable; "but it's the only way to avoid unpleasantness. We can do it tonight if the rain clears off. I'm not due back at Ashley Court until tomorrow, and I dare say I can put up at the Friar Tuck . . . Look here. Won't lights in the prison, when we go up to attach that rope – well, won't they attract attention?"

"Possibly. But I'm pretty sure nobody will bother us. Anybody from the village would be too frightened."

Dorothy had been looking from one to the other, the lids tightening down over her eyes. There were small lines of anger round her nostrils.

"You're asking him to do this," she said, nodding at Rampole, "and I know him well enough to be sure he will. *You* can be cool. And you say none of the villagers will be there. Well, you may have forgotten somebody who *is* very apt to be there. The murderer."

Rampole had moved round to her side, and unconsciously he had taken her hand. She did not notice it; her fingers closed over his. But Sir Benjamin noticed it, with a startled expression which he tried to conceal by saying,

"Hem!" and teetering on his heels. Dr. Fell looked up benevolently from his chair.

"The murderer," he repeated. "I know it, my dear. I know it."

There was a pause. Nobody seemed to know what to say. The expression of Sir Benjamin's eyes seemed to indicate that it wasn't British to back out now. In fact, he looked downright uncomfortable.

"Then I'll be on my way," he said at length. "I shall have to take the magistrate at Chatterham into my confidence, by the way; we need ropes, spikes, hammers – things like that. If the rain holds off, I can return here about ten o'clock tonight."

He hesitated.

"But there's one thing I want to know. We've heard a great deal of talk about that well. We've heard of drowned men, and ghosts, and bullion and jewels and plate and God knows what. Well, doctor; what are *you* looking for down in that well?"

"A handkerchief," said Dr. Fell, taking another drink of beer.

15

Mr. Budge had been spending an edifying evening. Three nights a month he had to himself. Two of these he generally contrived to spend at the motion pictures in Lincoln, watching people being placed on the spot with gratifying regularity, and refreshing his memory anew with such terms as "scram," "screwey," and other expressions which might be useful to him in his capacity as butler at the Hall. His third evening out he invariably spent with his good friends, Mr. and Mrs. Rankin, butler and house-keeper at the home of the Paynes in Chatterham.

In their snug rooms downstairs, the Rankins greeted him with a hospitality whose nature rarely varied. Mr. Budge had the best chair, a squeaky rush rocker whose top towered far above the head of any sitter. Mr. Budge was offered a drop of something – port from upstairs, from the Paynes' own table, or a hot toddy in wet weather. The gaslights would sing comfortably, and there would be the usual indulgent baby-talk to the cat. Three rocking-chairs would swing in their separate tempos – Mrs. Rankin's quick and sprightly, her husband's more judicially, and that of Mr. Budge with a grave rolling motion, like an emperor being carried in his litter.

The evening would be spent in a discussion of Chatterham and the people of Chatterham. Particularly, when the pretence of formality was dropped about nine o'clock, the people of the big houses. At shortly after ten they would break up. Mr. Rankin would recommend to Mr. Budge's attention some worth-while book which his master had mentioned in the course of the week; Mr. Budge would gravely make note of it, put on his hat with the exactitude of a war helmet, button up his coat, and go home.

This evening, he reflected as he started up the High Street towards the Hall, had been unusually refreshing. The sky had cleared, pale and polished and gleaming, and there was a bright moon. Over the lowlands hung a faint smokiness, and the moist air smelt of hay. On such a night the soul of Mr. Budge became the soul of D'Artagnan Robin Hood Fairbanks Budge, the warrior, the adventurer, the moustache-twister – even, in mad moments, Budge the great lover. His soul was a balloon, a captive balloon, but still a balloon. He liked these long walks, where the stars were not merry at the antics of the other Budge; where a man could take a savage pass at a hayrick with an imaginary sword, and no housemaid the wiser.

But, while his footfalls were ringing on the hard white road he was delaying these pleasant dreams as a luxury for the last mile of his walk. He reflected on the evening. He reflected particularly on the enormous news at the end of it . . .

There had been at first the usual talk. He himself had discussed Mrs. Bundle's lumbago with affection. On the other hand, there had been the news that Mr. Payne was going on another of his trips to London for a legal conference. Mr. Rankin had dwelt upon this fact in the most impressive terms, and mentioned mysterious brief-cases which were as awesome as the wigs of judges. What impressed them all most about the legal profession was that you had to read so many books in order to become a member of it. Mrs. Payne was in a rare bad temper, but what could you expect, she being her?

Then, again, it had been bruited about the village that the rector's uncle from Auckland was coming to visit him. One of Sir Benjamin Arnold's oldest friends, he was; got the rector his appointment, he did; and he (the uncle) and Sir Benjamin had been with Cecil Rhodes in the Kimberley diamond-fields years ago. There was speculation about that. There was also a little speculation about the murder, but a very little, because the Rankins respected Mr. Budge's feelings. Budge felt grateful for that. He was morally certain Mr. Herbert had committed the murder, but he refused to think about it. Each time the ugly subject popped up in his mind, he closed it like the lid of a jack-in-the-box repressed, but it could be held down . . .

No, what he was thinking about most concerned the rumour of an Affair. The capital letter was logical; it had a much more sinister sound, even in the imagination, and sounded almost French. An affair between Miss Dorothy and the young American who was stopping at Dr. Fell's.

At first Budge had been shocked. Not about the affair, but about the American. Odd – very odd, Budge reflected with a sudden start. Walking here, under the swishing tireless trees in the moonlight, things seemed different from their normal appearance at the Hall. Possibly it was Budge the swash-buckler, who could wink at an indiscretion as easily as ("*canaille!*") he spitted a varlet on a rapier-point. The Hall was as stuffy and orderly as a game of whist. Here you wanted to kick over the table and sweep off the cards. It was only . . . Well, these confounded Americans, and Miss Dorothy!

Good Lord! Miss Dorothy!

His earlier words came back to him, as they had formed in his mind that night Mr. Martin was murdered. Miss Dorothy: he had almost said a cold little piece. Dominating everything, what would Mrs. Bundle say? The idea would have turned him cold at the Hall. But here the beams of the silver screen made the soul of Mr. Budge gleam like armour.

He chuckled.

Now he was passing some hayricks, monstrous black shadows against the moon, and he wondered that he had come so far. His boots must be covered with dust, and his blood was heating from the rapid walk. After all, the young American had seemed a gentleman. There had been moments, certainly, when Budge had suspected him of the murder. He came from America; Mr. Martin had spent several years in America; there was an ominous inference. Even, for a delightful moment, there had been the suspicion that he might have been what Mrs. Bundle described as a gunster.

But the hayricks had turned to castles for the Duc de Guise's cannon, and the night as soft as the velvet a swordsman wore; and Mr. Budge grew sentimental. He remembered Tennyson. He could not at the moment think of anything Tennyson said, but he was sure Tennyson would have approved a love-affair between Miss Dorothy and the Yankee. Besides, Lord! what a secret satisfaction to see somebody bring her to life! – Ah! She had been absent from the Hall that afternoon, saying she wanted no tea. She had been absent from tea-time almost until the hour Budge had left for Chatterham. Ha! Budge was her protector by this time. (*Had she been absent,* demanded the police magistrate, deadly notebook at attention. And the dauntless Budge smiled at disaster, and replied, *No.*)

He stopped. He stopped exactly in the middle of the road, and a trembling quivered down one knee, and he was looking across the meadows to his left.

Ahead of him towards the left, clear against the moon-lit sky, rose Chatterham prison. The light was so pale-sharp that he could even distinguish the trees of the Hag's Nook. A yellow gleam was moving among those trees.

For a long time Budge stood motionless in the middle of the white road. He had some vague idea that if there were dangers ahead, and you stood absolutely still, they could not hurt you – as, they said, a fierce dog would not attack a motionless man. Then, very meticulously, he moved his bowler hat and wiped his forehead with a clean pocket handkerchief. One queer little idea was twisting through his brain, almost pathetic in its intensity. Over there, where the goblin-light fluttered, was a test for the adventurer Budge. He had come home in the high night with the swagger within him. So, later on, the butler Budge must look at his white bed with a small shame, and realize that he was only the butler Budge, after all . . .

Whereupon Mr. Budge did what, for his butler-self majestically moving in the Hall, would have seemed an insane thing. He climbed the stile, bending low, and began to move up across the slope of the meadow towards the Hag's Nook. And it is to be recorded that his heart suddenly sang.

It was still squashy from the recent rain. He had to climb the slope in full moonlight, and too late he remembered that he could have approached the Hag's Nook by a more circuitous route. Still, it was done now. He found himself puffing, with little saw-like cuts being drawn up and down in his throat; and he was hot and damp. Then, with an obedience which an eighteenth-century Budge would have accepted without thanks and even without comment, the moon slid behind a cloud.

He found himself on the edge of the Hag's Nook. There was a beech tree ahead, against which he leaned with a feeling as though his bowler were tightening against his brain, and a throat sore from running. He panted now.

This was mad.

Never mind the adventurer Budge. This was mad.

Ahead, the gleam showed again. He could see it near the well, some twenty or thirty feet ahead, through the twisted boles of trees. It flashed as though for a signal. Evidently in reply, another gleam winked out high above and away. Budge, craning his neck upwards, could have no doubt: it was from the balcony of the Governor's Room. Somebody had set down a light there. He saw the shadow of a very stout man bending over the railing, and this shadow seemed to be doing something to the rail.

A rope shot downwards, curling and darting with such suddenness that Budge jumped back. Hitting the side of the well with a dull *plop,* it straggled and then slid over the edge. Fascinated, Budge poked his head forward again. Now the light beside the well had turned into a steady beam; it seemed to be held by a small figure – almost, he thought, like a woman. A face moved into the beam; a face craning upwards, and a hand was waved towards the balcony far above.

The Yankee.

Even at that distance, there could be no doubt about it. The Yankee, with his strange, grinning, reckless face. His name was – Mr. Rampole. Yes. Mr. Rampole seemed to be testing the rope. He swung round on it, drawing up his legs. Climbing a few feet up the rope, he hung there with one hand and pulled at it with the other. Then he dropped to the ground and waved his hand again. Another light, like a bull's-eye lantern, flashed on. He hitched it to his belt, and into that belt he seemed to be thrusting other things – a hatchet and an instrument like a diminutive pick.

Sliding his body between two of the wide spikes on the edge of the well, he sat on the inner edge for a moment, holding the rope. He was grinning again, at the small figure which held the other light. Then he swung off the edge and down into the well; his lamp was swallowed. But not before the small figure had darted to the edge, and, as the beam of Rampole's lamp struck upwards for an instant, Budge saw that the face bending over the well was the face of Miss Dorothy . . .

The watcher at the edge of the Hag's Nook was not now the adventurer Budge or even the butler Budge. He was simply a stooping, incredulous figure who tried to understand these amazing things. Frogs complained loudly, and there were bugs brushing about his face. Edging forward between the trees, he crept closer. Miss Dorothy's light went out. The thought went through his head that he would have a rare wild story to tell to the Rankins a month hence, over the port.

From the well a few broken reflections glimmered, as of a lamp sizzling out in water, but never quite extinguished. Momentarily the pointed leaves of a beech tree were outlined, and once (Budge thought) Miss Dorothy's face. But the cool moon had come out again, ghostly against the wall of the prison. Afraid of making a noise, tight-chested and sweating, Budge moved still closer. The chorus of frogs, crickets, God knew what! – this chorus was so loud that Budge wondered how any noise could be heard. It was cold here, too.

Now, it is to be urged that Budge was not, and never has been, an imaginative man. Circumstances do not permit it. But when he glanced away from the flickers of light dancing deep in the well, and saw a figure standing motionless in the moonlight, he knew it was an alien presence. Deep within him Budge knew that the presence of Miss Dorothy and the American was *right,* as right as gravy over roast beef, and that the other presence was wrong.

It was – Budge tells it to this day – a small man. Standing some distance behind Miss Dorothy, a crooked shadow among the shadows of the trees against the moon, he seemed to grow into weird proportions, and he had something in his hand.

A muffled noise bubbled up from the well. There had been other noises, but this was definitely a cry or a groan or a strangling of breath . . .

For a time Budge remembered nothing very clearly. Afterwards he tried to determine how long a time had elapsed between that booming echo and the time that a head appeared over the edge of the well once more, but he could never be sure. All he could be sure of was that Miss Dorothy, at some period or other, had snapped on her light. She did not point it down into the well. She kept it steady, across the mouth of the rusty spikes . . . And up from the well, now, another lamp was strengthening as somebody climbed . . .

A head appeared, framed between the spikes. At first Budge did not see it very clearly, because he was trying to peer into the darkness to find that alien figure on the outer edge; that motionless figure which somehow gave an impression of wire and hair and steel, like a monster. Failing to see it, Budge looked at the head framed between the spikes, coming higher and higher above the well.

It was not Mr. Rampole's face. It was the face of Mr. Herbert Starberth, rising up over the spikes of the well; and the jaw was fallen, and by this time Budge was so close he could see the bullet-hole between the eyes.

Not ten feet away from him he saw this head rising, horribly, as though Mr. Herbert were climbing out of the well. His sodden hair was plastered down over his forehead; the eyelids were down and the eyeballs showed white beneath; and the colour of the bullet-hole was blue. Budge staggered, literally staggered, for he felt one knee jerk sideways beneath him, and he thought he was going to be sick.

The head moved. It turned away from him, and a hand appeared over the edge of the well. Mr. Herbert was dead. But he seemed to be climbing out of the well.

Miss Dorothy screamed. Just before her lamp went out, Budge saw another thing which loosened his horror like a tight belt, and saved him from being sick. He saw the young American's head propped under Mr. Herbert's shoulder; and he saw that it was the Yankee's hand which had seized the wall, carrying a stiff corpse up out of the depths.

Silver-blue like the glow for a pantomime, the moonlight etched a Japanese tracery of trees. All of it had been done in pantomime. Budge never knew about the other figure, the *alien* figure he had seen standing beyond the well and peering towards the spikes. He never knew whether this man had seen the young American's head beneath Mr. Herbert's body at all . . . But he did hear a flopping and stumbling among the brush, a wild rush as of a bat banging against walls to get out of a room. Somebody was running, with inarticulate cries, through the Hag's Nook.

The gauzy dimness of the pantomime was ripped apart. Far above, from the balcony of the Governor's Room, glared a bright light. It cut down through the trees, and the boom of a voice roared out from the balcony.

"There he goes! Grab him!"

Wheeling, the light made a green and black whirlpool among the trees. Saplings crackled, and feet sloshed on marshy ground. Budge's thoughts, in this moment, were as elementary as the thoughts of an animal. The only distinct impression in his mind was that here, crackling through these bushes, ran Guilt. He had a confused idea that there were several flash-lamps darting beams around the runner.

A head and shoulders were suddenly blocked out against the moon. Then Budge saw the runner sliding down a slippery bank, and the runner was coming straight for him.

Budge, fat and past fifty, felt the flesh shaking on his big body. He was neither Budge the swashbuckler nor Budge the butler; he was only an unnerved man leaning against a tree. Now, when the moonlight fell as with a shining of raindrops, he saw the other man's hand; it was encased in a big gardener's glove, and the forefinger was jammed through the trigger-guard of a long-barrelled pistol. Through Budge's mind went a vision of youth, of standing on a broad football field, wildly, and seeming to see figures coming at him from every direction. It was as though he were naked. The other man plunged.

Budge, fat and past fifty, felt a great pain in his lungs. He did not drop behind the tree. He knew what he had to do; he was solid, with a quiet brain and a very clear eye.

"All right," he said aloud. "All right!" and dived for the other man.

He heard the explosion. There was a yellowish spurt, like a bad gas-range when you apply a match to it. Something hit him in the chest, swirling him off balance as his fingers ripped down the other man's coat. He felt his finger nails tear in cloth, falling, and his hip was suddenly twisted into weakness. There was a sensation as though he were flying through the air. Then his face squashed into dead leaves, and he dimly heard a thud as of his own body hitting the ground.

That was how Budge the Englishman went down.

16

"I don't think he's dead," said Rampole, going down on his knees beside the flattened figure of the butler. "Buck up, please! Hold your light down here while I roll him over. Where the devil is what's-his-name – Sir Benjamin?"

Budge was lying on his side, one hand still stretched out. His hat was crushed along one side with an almost rakish effect, and his respectable black coat had burst a button. Tugging at the dead weight, Rampole wrenched him over. The face was like dough and the eyes were closed, but he was breathing. Since the wound was high along the left breast, blood had begun to soak through.

"Haloa!" Rampole shouted. "Halloa, there! Where are you?"

He lifted his head to glance at the girl. He could not see her distinctly; she was looking away, but the light did not waver much.

There was a crackling in the bushes. Sir Benjamin, his cap crushed down like a gangster in a motion picture, pushed through. His long arms dangled out of his sleeves, and you could see the freckles against the muddy pallor of his face.

"He – he got away," the chief constable said rather hoarsely. "I don't know who he was. I don't even know what happened. Who's this?"

"Look at him," said Rampole. "He must have tried to stop . . . the other one. Didn't you hear the shot? For God's sake let's get him to your car and down to the village. Take his feet, will you? – I'll get his head. Try not to jolt him."

It was a heavy weight. It had a habit of sagging between them, as when two people try to move a large mattress. Rampole found his chest tight and his muscles aching. They staggered through the scratching arms of bushes and out across the long slope to where Sir Benjamin's Daimler was parked in the road.

"You'd better stay here on guard," the chief constable said, when they had steadied Budge in the tonneau. "Miss Starberth, will you ride in to Dr. Markley's with me and hold him on the rear seat? Thank you. Steady, now, while I turn round."

The last sight Rampole had was of her holding Budge's head in her lap as the motor churned into life, and the big headlamps swung. When he turned to go back towards the prison, he found he was so weak that he had to lean against the fence. His brain, tired and stupid, moved round like a creaky wheel. So there he was, clinging to the fence in the clear moonlight, and still holding Budge's crushed hat in one hand.

He glanced at it, dully, and let it fall. Herbert Starberth –

A light was coming closer. Dr. Fell's bulk waddled above the grey meadow.

"Halloa there!" the doctor called, poking his chins forward. He came up and put his hand on Rampole's shoulder. "Good man," he said after a pause. "Well? What happened? Who was hurt?"

The doctor tried to speak levelly, but his voice grew high. He went on:

"I saw most of it from the balcony. I saw him run, and called out, and then I thought he fired at somebody . . ."

Rampole put a hand to his head. "That butler fellow – what's his name – Budge. He must have been watching us from the wood. God knows why. I'd just hoisted him – you know, the dead one – over the edge of the well, and I heard you call, and somebody start to run. Budge got in his way, and took it in the chest."

"He isn't – ?"

"I don't know," the American answered, despairingly. "He wasn't dead when we put him in the car. They've taken him in to Chatterham."

Both of them stood silent for a while, listening to the crickets. The doctor took a flask from his pocket and held it out. Cherry brandy went down Rampole's throat with a choking bite, and then crawled along his veins in a way that made him shudder.

"You've no idea who the man was?" Dr. Fell asked.

Rampole said, wearily: "Oh, to hell with who it was. I didn't even get a glimpse of him; I just heard him running. I was thinking about what I'd seen down there . . . Look here, we'd better get back to the dead one."

"I say, you're shaking. Steady on –"

"Give me a shoulder for a second. Well, it was this way –"

Rampole swallowed again. He felt that his nostrils would never be free of the odour from that well, or from crawling things. Again he saw the rope curling down from the balcony, and felt the stone against his corduroy trousers as he swung himself over the edge . . .

"It was this way," he went on, eagerly. "I didn't have to use the rope very far. About five or six feet down there are stone niches hacked into the side, almost like steps. I'd figured it wouldn't be very far down, because heavy rains might flood out any hiding place Anthony had made. You had to watch yourself, because the niches were slimy; but there was one big stone scraped almost clean. I could see an 'om' and a 'me' cut into a round inscription. The rest was almost obliterated. At first I thought I couldn't move the stone block, but when I braced myself, and tied the rope round my waist, and put the edge of the trench-mattock into the side, I found it was only a thin slab. You could push it in fairly easily, and if you kept it upright there was a hole at one side where you could get in several fingers to pull it back again . . . The place was full of waterspiders and rats . . ."

He shuddered.

"I didn't find a room, or anything elaborate. It was just an opening hollowed out of the flat stones they'd used for the well, and a part of the earth around; and it was half full of water, anyway. Herbert's body had been squeezed into it along the back. The first thing I touched was his hand, and I saw the hole in his head. By the time I had hauled him out I was as wet as he was. He's pretty small, you know, and by keeping the rope tied round my waist to brace me I could hoist him on my shoulder. His clothes were full of some kind of overblown flies, and they crawled on me. As for the rest of it . . ."

He slapped at himself, and the doctor gripped his arm.

"There wasn't anything else, except – oh yes, I found the handkerchief. It's pretty well rotted, but it belonged to old Timothy; T. S. on the edge, bloody and rolled in one corner. At least, I think it's blood. There were some candle-ends, too, and what looked like burnt matches. But no treasure; not a box, not a scrap. And that's all. It's cold; let me go back and get my coat. There's something inside my collar . . ."

The doctor gave him another drink of brandy, and they moved on heavy legs towards the Hag's Nook. Herbert Starberth's body lay where Rampole had deposited it beside the well. As they looked down at it under the doctor's light, Rampole kept wiping his hands fiercely up and down the sides of his trousers. Small and doubled, the body had its head twisted on one side, and seemed to be gaping at something it saw along the grass. The cold and damp of the underground niche had acted like an ice-house; though it must have been a week since the bullet had entered his brain, there was no sign of decomposition.

Rampole, feeling as though his brain were full of dull bells, pointed.

"Murder?" he asked.

"Undoubtedly. No weapon, and – you know."

The American spoke words which sounded idiotic even to him in the way he felt. "This has got to stop!" he said, desperately, and clenched his hands. But there was nothing else to say. It expressed everything. He repeated: "This has got to stop, I tell you! Yes, that poor devil of a butler . . . or do you suppose he was in on it? I never thought of that."

Dr. Fell shook his head.

"No. No, there is only one man concerned in this. I know who he is."

Leaning against the coping of the well, Rampole groped in his pocket after cigarettes. He lit one with a muddy hand on the match, and even the cigarette smelt of the depths down there. He said:

"Then we're near the end – ?"

"We're near the end," said Dr. Fell. "It will come tomorrow, because of a certain telegram." He was silent, meditating, with his light directed away from the body. "It took me a long time to realize it," he added, abruptly. "There is one man, and only one man, who could have committed these murders. He has killed three men already, and tonight he may have killed a fourth . . . Tomorrow there is an afternoon train arriving from London. We will meet that train. And there will be an end to the murderer."

"Then – the murderer doesn't live here?"

Dr. Fell raised his head. "Don't think about it now, young fellow. Go down to Yew Cottage and get a bath and a change of clothes; you need it. I can watch."

An owl had begun to cry over the Hag's Nook. Rampole moved through the brush, back along the trampled trail where they had carried Budge. He glanced back only once. Dr. Fell had switched off his flashlamp. Against the blue and silver of the moonlight, Dr. Fell was standing motionless, a massive black silhouette with a leonine head, staring down into the well.

Budge was conscious only of dreams and pain. He knew that he was lying on a bed somewhere, with deep pillows under his head. Once he thought he saw a white-lace curtain blowing at a window; he thought that a lamp was reflected in the window-glass, and that somebody was sitting near him, watching.

But he could not be sure. He kept dozing off to sleep, without seeming to be able to move. There were noises like the shiver of beaten gongs. Somebody was arranging a prickly blanket about his neck, though he felt too hot already. At the touch of the hands he felt terrified, and again he tried to lift his arms without success; the gong-noises and the swing of phantom rooms dissolved in a jerk of pain which ran through him as though it were flowing along his veins. He smelt medicine. He was a boy on a football field, under a dinning of shouts; he was winding clocks and measuring port from a decanter; and then the portrait of old Anthony, from its frame in the gallery at the Hall, leapt out at him. Old Anthony wore a white gardener's glove . . .

Even as he retreated, he knew that it was not old Anthony. Who was it? Somebody he had seen on the motion-picture screen, associated with fighting and gunplay; and a whole genie-bottle of shadowy faces floated past. Nor yet was it any of these, but some person he had known a long time. A familiar face –

It was bending over him now, in his bed.

His scream became a croak.

Impossible that it should be there. He was unhurt, and this was a fancy coloured with the smell of iodoform. The linen of the pillow felt cool and faintly rough to his cheek. A clock struck. Something was shaken and flashing, thin glass in lamplight, and there were tiptoeing footfalls. Distinctly he heard a voice say:

"He'll live."

Budge slept. It was as though some subconscious nerve had been waiting for those words, so that afterwards sleep descended, and wound him rigid as in a soft dark bail of yarn.

When at length he awoke, he did not know at first how weak he was, nor had the morphine quite worn off. But he did know that a low sun was streaming in at the window. Bewildered and a little frightened, he tried to make a move; he knew with ghastly certainty that he had slept into the afternoon, a thing unheard-of at the Hall . . . Then he saw that Sir Benjamin Arnold, a smile on his long face, was bending over the bed. Behind him was a person whom he did not at first recognize, a young man . . .

"Feeling better?" asked Sir Benjamin.

Budge tried to speak, and only croaked. He felt humiliated. A bit of remembrance swirled down into his consciousness, like a rope . . .

Yes. He remembered now. It swept in such vivid colours that he closed his eyes. The young Yankee, the white gloves, the pistol. What had he done? – it rushed over him that he had been a coward, as he had always felt, and the taste of that thought was like nauseous medicine.

"Don't try to say anything," Sir Benjamin said. "You're at Dr. Markley's; he said you couldn't be moved. So lie still. You got a nasty bullet wound, but you'll pull through. We'll clear out now." Sir Benjamin seemed embarrassed. He fingered the iron post at the foot of the bed. "As to what you did, Budge," he added, "well, I don't mind telling you – well, it was damned sporting, you know."

Moistening his lips, Budge at last achieved speech.

"Yes, sir," he said. "Thank you, sir."

His half-closed eyes opened in wonder and some anger when he saw that the young American had almost laughed . . .

"No offense, Budge," Rampole hastily put in. "It was just that you rushed his gun like an Irish cop, and now you act as if somebody had just offered you a glass of beer . . . I don't suppose you recognized him, did you?"

(Some struggle in the brain; a half-face, cut into whorls like water over sand. Budge felt dizzy, and there was something hurting inside his chest. The water washed out the face.)

"Yes, sir," he said, with an effort. "I shall remember it – soon. Just now I can't think . . ."

"Of course," Rampole interposed, hurriedly. He saw somebody in white beckoning them from the doorway. "Well, good luck, Budge. You've got plenty of nerve."

At the smiles of the others, Budge felt a responsive smile drawing at his own lips like a nervous twitch. He felt drowsy again, and his head sang, but he was floating pleasantly away now. He was not sure what had happened; but warm satisfaction lulled him for the first time in his life. What a story! If only those housemaids wouldn't leave windows open . . .

His eyes closed.

"Thank you, sir," said Budge. "Please tell Miss Dorothy that I shall be back at the Hall tomorrow."

Rampole closed the door of the bedroom behind them, and turned to face Sir Benjamin in the dim upper hallway of Dr. Markley's house. He could see the white skin of a nurse descending the stairs ahead.

"He saw whoever it was," the chief constable said, grimly. "Yes, and he'll remember. What the devil, though, was he doing up there, to begin with?"

"Just curiosity, I suppose. And now what?"

Sir Benjamin opened the case of a big gold watch, glanced at it rather nervously, and shut it up again.

"It's Fell's show. I'm dashed if *I* know." His voice grew querulous. "He's gone over my head completely – mine! I mean to say, he has quite a stand-in with Sir William Rossiter, the High Commissioner at the Yard; he seems to be on intimate terms with everybody in England. And he's been pulling wires . . . All I know is that we're to meet the five-four train from London, and nab somebody who gets off it. Well, I hope everybody's waiting. Come along."

Dr. Markley was still on his afternoon round, and they did not linger. As they went down into the High Street, Rampole was rather more nervous than the chief constable. Neither last night nor today could he elicit anything more from Dr. Fell.

"What's more," the chief constable grumbled, in the same tone, "I will not go to Southampton to meet the rector's uncle. I don't care if he is an old friend; the rector is going instead. I have business in Manchester – that's Thursday – and I've got to be away a week at the least. Dash it! Something always comes up. I can't find Payne, either; he has some papers I must take to Manchester along with me. Dash it! Here I've wasted all this time with the blasted case, when I could easily turn it over to the proper people, and Fell takes the whole thing out of my hands . . ."

He was talking rather desperately, Rampole sensed, talking away at anything that came into his head, so that he would not be forced to think. And the American agreed with him.

Sir Benjamin's grey Daimler was waiting in the elm-shadowed street. It was tea-time, and few people were abroad. Rampole wondered whether the news of Herbert's death had yet filtered into Chatterham; the body had been conveyed to the Hall late last night, and the servants warned with awesome threats to say nothing until they were given permission, but that was no guarantee at all. Last night, to keep away the horrors, Dorothy had stayed with Mrs. Fell. Until almost daybreak Rampole had heard them talking in the room next to his. Exhausted and yet unable to sleep, he had sat at the window, smoking innumerable cigarettes, and staring with smarting eyelids at the whitening dawn . . .

Now the grey Daimler swept through Chatterham, and the wind stroked his face with cool fragrance. In the sky the fiery streaks had paled; there were white, and violet, and a smokiness of shadow creeping up from the lowlands. There were a few dark clouds, like slow sheep. He remembered the first evening he had walked into Chatterham with Dorothy Starberth, through this mysterious hour of the gold-darkened sky and the faint jangling bells; when a wind ran across the green corn, and the smell of hawthorn grew stronger with dusk. Remembering it, he did not believe that it had been only ten days ago.

"Tomorrow there is an afternoon train from London," he could hear Dr. Fell speaking in the Hag's Nook. *"We will meet that train."*

The words had finality . . .

Sir Benjamin said nothing. The Daimler roared against the whipping breeze. Dorothy in New York. Dorothy as his wife. Lord! but it had a funny sound! – every time he thought of that, he thought of himself sitting in a class last year and thinking that if he flunked economics (which, like all intelligent people, he detested), it would be the end of the world. Possessing a wife, he would become suddenly a citizen, with a telephone number and a cocktail-shaker and everything; and his mother would have hysterics; and his father, up twenty-five floors in a law-office at Number One West Forty-Second Street, would drowsily lift an eyebrow and say, "Well, how much do you need?"

The Daimler stopped with a slur of tires in the road. They would have to wait for this respectable citizenship; they would have to wait for a murderer.

In the darkening lane which led to Yew Cottage several figures were awaiting them. Dr. Fell's voice boomed out:

"How is he? Getting better? – I thought so. Well, we're ready." He made a gesture with one cane. "Everybody who was on the scene the night Martin was murdered, everybody who can give evidence, is going to be in at the death now. Miss Starberth didn't want to come, and neither did the rector. But they're both here. I think there will be others waiting for us at the railway station." He added, testily, "Well, climb in, climb in!"

The rector's huge figure loomed out of the lane. He almost stumbled as he assisted Dorothy into the car.

"I'm quite willing, of course," he said. "But I don't understand what you said about *needing* me –"

They had come out of the lane's shadow now. Dr. Fell struck his stick in the dust. He said:

"That's the point. That's the whole point. I want you to identify somebody. There's something you can tell us, and I doubt whether you know it yourself. And, unless you all do exactly as I tell you, we shall never know. Do you hear?"

He glared at all of them. Sir Benjamin was racing his motor, keeping his stiff face turned away. He suggested in a cold voice that they be on their way. In the tonneau the rector was trying to arrange his large plump face along pleasant lines. Dorothy sat with her hands folded in her lap, looking straight ahead . . .

Rampole had not been to the railway station since he had arrived in that other age ten days ago. The Daimler fled along the curves of the road, its siren crying ahead. Chatterham prison fell away behind; they seemed more in touch with reality now. Up over the waves of corn rose the small brick station, and the rails were shimmering against a low, dull, yellow-gleaming sunset. The lamps along the platform had not yet been lighted, but there was a green-shaded light in the ticket window of the station. Dogs were barking, just as on that first night.

As Sir Benjamin stopped the car they heard, far down the tracks, the thin whistle of the train.

Rampole started. Stumbling on his canes, Dr. Fell had lurched out of the car. He wore his old black slouch-hat and box-pleated cape, which made him seem like a fat bandit; and a breeze waved the black ribbon on his eyeglasses.

"Now, listen," he said. "Stay with me. The only instructions I have are for you." He looked fiercely at Sir Benjamin. "I warn you that you may have a temptation. But, whatever you see or hear, *for God's sake don't speak!* Do you understand?" He was glaring now.

"As chief constable of this county –" Sir Benjamin was beginning, snapping the words out, when the doctor cut him short.

"Here comes the train. Walk up to the platform with me."

They could hear the thin, faint, clicking roar. It was rushing through Rampole's nerves now. He felt as though he were one of a herd of chickens being shooed into a pen by Dr. Fell. The headlight of the locomotive winked around a curve among the trees; the rails were shimmering, and they had begun to hum . . .

A stationmaster pulled open the door of the baggage-room with a long screech, emitting light on the boards of the platform. Rampole glanced in that direction. Against the eeriness of the dim yellow sky he saw a motionless figure standing near the station. Then, with a shock, he saw that there were several of these motionless figures in corners about the platform. All of them had their hands in the side pockets of their coats.

He turned sharply. Dorothy Starberth was at his side, staring up the tracks. The rector, his blue eyes pinched up, was swabbing at his forehead with a handkerchief, and seemed about to speak. Sir Benjamin looked sourly at the ticket window.

Swaying in a gush of cinders, the small train ground in to a stop, its headlight enormous now. There was a heavy sigh from the engine, and it panted in puffs of steam. A white lamp winked on over the entrance to the station. Past the yellow, grimed windows of the train there were flickers as of people moving out. The only noise was a subdued clanking, above the rumble of the baggage truck.

"There . . ." said Dr. Fell.

One passenger was alighting now. Rampole could not see his face because of the conflicting lights and the heavy backwash of steam. Then the passenger moved under the white station light, and the American stared.

He had never seen this man before. At the same time, he was conscious that one of the motionless men about the platform, his hand still in his pocket, had moved closer. But he was looking at this curious person from the train: a tall man, with an old-fashioned square derby and a grey moustache clipped sharp about a strong brown chin. The stranger hesitated, swinging a large valise from his right hand to his left . . .

"There," repeated Dr. Fell. He seized the rector's arm. "You see him? Who is he?"

The rector turned a puzzled face. He said: "You must be mad! I never saw him before. What on earth – ?"

"Ah," said Dr. Fell. His voice suddenly grew louder. It seemed to boom and echo along the platform. "You don't recognize him. But you should, Mr. Saunders; you should. *He's your uncle.*"

During an enormous silence one of the motionless men came up behind and put his hand on the rector's shoulder.

He said: "Thomas Saunders, I arrest you for the murder of Martin Starberth. I have to warn you that anything you say may be taken down and used in evidence against you."

He had taken his other hand out of his pocket, and it held a revolver. Rampole, even while his wits were whirling, saw that the motionless men were closing in, silently, from all corners of the platform.

17

The rector did not move, nor did his expression change. He continued to swab at his forehead with the handkerchief, that old trick of his; large and black-clad and comfortable, with his gold watch-chain swinging. But his blue eyes seemed to have shrunk. Not narrowed, but shrunk, as though they had really grown smaller. He was mustering up unction, ease, fluency, Rampole felt, as a man takes a deep inhalation before a swim underwater.

He said:

"This is absurd. I hope you realise that. But," a polite gesture, with the handkerchief, "we seem to be – ah – attracting some attention. I suppose you gentlemen are all detectives; even if you are so mad as to arrest me, you hardly needed so large a force . . . There's a crowd gathering!" he added, in a lower and angrier tone. "If you must keep your hand on my shoulder, let's go back to Sir Benjamin's car."

The man who had arrested him, a taciturn-looking person with heavy lines in his face, looked at Dr. Fell.

"This is the man, sir?" he asked.

"It's all right, Inspector," answered the doctor. "That's the man. You may as well do as he suggests. – Sir Benjamin, you see that man on the platform. You recognize him?"

"Good Lord, yes!" exclaimed the chief constable. "It's Bob Saunders, right enough. He's older than when I knew him, but I should recognize him anywhere . . . But I say, Fell!" He was sputtering like a boiling kettle. "You can't possibly mean – the rector – Saunders – !"

"His name isn't Saunders," said the doctor, composedly. "And I'm fairly sure he isn't a clergyman. Anyhow, you recognize the uncle. I was afraid you would blurt out something before I could enquire. There was always a chance that the bogus Saunders would resemble the real rector . . . Inspector Jennings, I suggest you take your prisoner over to that grey automobile on the other side of the road. Sir Benjamin, you might meet your old friend before the rest of us do. Tell him as much or as little as you like, and then join us."

Saunders took off his hat and fanned himself with it.

"Then you are behind this, Doctor?" he enquired, almost genially. "I – er – it surprises me. It even shocks me. I do not like you, Doctor Fell. Gentlemen, come along. You needn't keep hold of my arm, Inspector. I assure you I have no intention of running away."

In the darkening light, the little party moved across to the Daimler. Inspector Jennings turned his neck as though on a slow pivot.

"I thought I should bring a few of the men along with me, sir," he said to Dr. Fell. "You said he was a killer."

The ugly word, unemotionally spoken, caused a hush which was broken only by the plodding of large feet. Rampole, walking behind the rest of them with Dorothy, stared at the large back of the rector moving in confident strides. The bald spot on Saunders' head shone out of the fluff of yellowish hair. He heard Saunders laugh . . .

They put the prisoner in the tonneau of the car. Spreading himself comfortably, the rector drew a deep breath. The word "killer" was still sounding faintly in their ears. Saunders seemed to know it. His eyes moved slowly over them, and he was meticulously folding and unfolding his handkerchief. It was as though he were putting on pieces of armour.

"Now, then, gentlemen," he remarked, "pray let's make this appear to be a pleasant little chat in the rear of a motor-car . . . What, precisely, is the charge against me?"

"By God!" said Dr. Fell, striking the side of the car admiringly, "it's damned good, Saunders! – You heard the Inspector. Officially you are charged only with the murder of Martin Starberth. Eh?"

"Quite," agreed the rector, nodding slowly. "I am glad I have such a group of witnesses about me . . . Before I say anything, Inspector, this is your last chance. Are you sure you want to proceed with this arrest?"

"Those are my instructions, sir."

Again the other nodded pleasantly. "I rather think you'll regret it, then. Because three witnesses – excuse, four witnesses – will testify that it would have been absolutely impossible for me to have killed my young friend Martin. Or, indeed, anybody else."

He stalled.

"May *I* ask a question now? Dr. Fell, you seem to have caused this somewhat – pardon me – amazing procedure. On the night my young friend – ah – died, I was at your house, by your side, was I not? At what time did I arrive?" Dr. Fell, still resembling a fat bandit, was leaning against the side of the car. He seemed to be enjoying himself.

"First move," he said. "You're opening with a pawn instead of a knight. Stand by, Inspector; I like this. – You arrived in the vicinity of ten-thirty. More or less. I'll give you ten-thirty."

"Let me remind you" – the rector's voice had grown a trifle harsher; but he changed it in an instant, smoothly. "Ah, no matter. Miss Starberth, will you tell these gentlemen again what time your brother left the Hall?"

"There was a mix-up about clocks, you know," Dr. Fell put in. "The clock in the hall was ten minutes fast . . ."

"Quite so," said Saunders. "Well, at whatever time he left the Hall, I must have been at Dr. Fell's house? You know this to be a fact?"

Dorothy, who had been staring at him queerly, nodded. "Why . . . yes. Yes, naturally."

"And you, Mr. Rampole. You know that I was at the doctor's, and that I never left. You saw Martin coming up to the prison with his light while I was there; you saw his lamp in the Governor's Room while I was there? In short, I could not conceivably have killed him?"

Rampole had to say, "Yes." There was no denying it. During all that time, Saunders had been directly under his eyes; under Dr. Fell's eyes also. He did not like Saunders' look. There was too much of a sort of desperate hypnosis behind the smile of the big, pink, steaming face. All the same . . .

"You, too, must grant all this, Doctor?" the rector asked.

"I do admit it."

"And I employed no mechanical device, such as has several times been suggested in this investigation? There was no death-trap by which I could have killed Martin Starberth while I was not there?"

"There was not," the doctor replied. His blinking eyes had become steady. "You were with us the whole time you say you were. In the brief moments when you were separated from Mr. Rampole while you two ran up towards the prison, you did nothing whatever – Martin Starberth was already dead. Your conduct was clear. And yet you killed Martin Starberth with your own hand, and flung his body into the Hag's Nook."

Unfolding his handkerchief again, the rector wiped his forehead. His eyes seemed to watch for a trap. Anger was growing now . . .

"You'd better turn me loose, Inspector," he said, suddenly. "Don't you think we've had enough foolery? This man is either trying to play a joke, or . . ."

"Here comes Sir Benjamin with the man you say is your uncle," remarked Dr. Fell. "I think we had all better go back to my house. And then I'll show you how he did it. In the meantime – Inspector!"

"Yes, sir?"

"You have the search warrant?"

"Yes, sir."

"Send the rest of your men down to search the rectory, and come with us."

Saunders moved slightly. His eyes were reddish round the lids, and had an expression like marbles. He still wore his steady smile.

"Move over," Dr. Fell ordered, composedly. "I'll sit beside you. Oh, and by the way! – I shouldn't keep fiddling with that handkerchief, if I were you. Your constant use of a handkerchief is too well known. We found one of 'em in the hiding-place in the well, and I rather imagined the initials stood for Thomas Saunders instead of Timothy Starberth. The last word old Timothy said before he died was 'handkerchief.' He saw to it that a clue was left behind, even beside that manuscript."

Saunders, moving over to make room, calmly spread the handkerchief out on his knee so that it was in full view. Dr. Fell chuckled.

"You don't still insist your name is Thomas Saunders, do you?" he enquired. A motion of his cane indicated Sir Benjamin coming towards them with the tall brown man carrying the large valise. Piercing across the open space, a high and querulous voice was complaining:

"– about what the devil this means. I had some friends to visit, and I wrote Tom not to meet me until Thursday; then he cabled me to the boat to come down here directly, on a matter of life or death, and specified trains, and –"

"I sent the cable," said Dr. Fell. "It's a good thing I did. Our friend would have disappeared by Thursday. He had already persuaded Sir Benjamin to urge him to disappear."

The tall man stopped short, pushing back his hat.

"Listen," he said, with a sort of wild patience. "Is everybody stark, raving mad? First Ben won't talk sense, and now – who are *you*?"

"No, no. That's not the question," Dr. Fell corrected. "The question is, who is this?" He touched Saunders' arm. "Is it your nephew?"

"Oh, hell!" said Mr. Robert Saunders.

"Get into the car, then. Better sit up beside the driver, and he'll tell you."

In went the inspector on the other side of Saunders. Rampole and Dorothy sat on the small seats, and Robert Saunders up with Sir Benjamin. The rector only remarked:

"A mistake can be proved, of course. But such a mistake is very different from a murder charge. You can prove no murder charge, you know."

He had got rather white. Sitting with his knee almost touching the rector's, Rampole felt a little quiver of repulsion and almost of fear. The bulbous blue eyes were still wide open, the mouth hung somewhat loose. You could hear his breathing. A deadly quiet hung in the tonneau. Dusk had come on rapidly, and the wheels sang with the word "killer."

Then Rampole saw that the inspector had unobtrusively folded his pistol under one arm, and that its barrel was against the rector's side.

Down the lane to Yew Cottage, wild bumping, and Sir Benjamin was still talking in the front seat . . . They had just stopped before the house when Robert Saunders sprang out. His long arm reached into the tonneau.

He said: "You dirty swine, where is he? *What did you do to Tom?*"

The inspector seized his wrist. "Steady, sir. Steady. No violence."

"*He* claims to be Tom Saunders? He's a damned liar. He – I'll kill him. I –"

Without haste, Inspector Jennings pushed him away from the car door as it was opened. They were all around the rector now. With his tonsure and fluff of yellow hair, he looked like a decaying saint; he kept trying to smile. They escorted him into the house, where Dr. Fell was lighting lamps in the study. Sir Benjamin pushed the rector down into a chair.

"Now, then –" he began.

"Inspector," said Dr. Fell, gesturing with the lamp, "you'd better search him. I think he's wearing a money-belt."

"Keep away – !" Saunders said. His voice was growing high. "You can't prove anything. You'd better keep away . . . !"

His eyes were opened wide. Dr. Fell put the lamp down beside him, so that it shone on his sweating face.

"Never mind, then," the doctor said, indifferently. "No good searching him, Inspector . . . Saunders, do you want to make a statement?"

"No. You can't prove anything."

As though he were reaching after a piece of paper to take down a statement, Dr. Fell drew open the drawer of his study table. Rampole followed the movement of his hand. The others did not see it, because they were looking at Saunders; but the rector was hungrily following every gesture the doctor made.

There was paper in the drawer. There was also the doctor's old-fashioned derringer pistol. It had been broken open, so that the chambers lay exposed; and as the lamp light gleamed on it, Rampole saw that there was just one cartridge in the breech. Then the drawer closed.

Death had come into the room now.

"Sit down, gentlemen," urged Dr. Fell. Saunders' blank eyes were still on the closed drawer. The doctor glanced over at Robert Saunders, who was standing with a stupid expression on his brown face and his fists clenched. "Sit down, gentlemen. I must tell you how he did these murders, if he refuses to tell, himself. It isn't a pretty story. If you, Miss Starberth, would care to withdraw . . . ?"

"Please go," said Rampole, in a low voice. "I'll go along."

"No!" she cried, and he knew that she was fighting down hysteria. "I've stood it so far. I won't go. You can't make me. If he did it, I want to know . . ."

The rector had recovered himself, though his voice was husky.

"By all means stay, Miss Starberth," he boomed. "You are the one with a right to hear this madman's story. He can't tell you – he, or anybody else, can't tell you how I could be sitting with him in this very house – and still throw your brother off the balcony of the Governor's Room."

Dr. Fell spoke loudly and sharply. He said:

"I didn't say you threw him from the balcony. He was never thrown from the balcony at all."

There was a silence. Dr. Fell leaned against the mantelpiece, one arm stretched along it and his eyes half shut. He went on, thoughtfully:

"There are several reasons why he wasn't. When you found him, he was lying on his right side. And his right hip was broken. But his watch, in the watch-pocket of his trousers, was not only unbroken, but still kept ticking without a flaw. A drop of fifty feet – it can't be done, you know. We will come back to that watch in a moment.

"Now, on the night of the murder it rained heavily. It rained, to be exact, from just before eleven o'clock until precisely one. The next morning, when we went up to the Governor's Room, we found the iron door to the balcony standing *open*. You remember? Martin Starberth was, presumably, murdered about ten minutes to twelve. The door, presumably also, was open then, and remained open. An hour's heavy rain, we must assume, drove in at that door. Certainly it drove against the window – a much smaller space, and choked with ivy. The next morning there were large rain-water pools under the window. *But not a drop of rain had come in at the door;* the floor around it was dry, gritty, and even dusty.

"In other words, gentlemen," the doctor said, calmly, "the door had not been opened until after one o'clock, after the rain had stopped. It didn't blow open; it is so heavy that you can barely wrench it out. Somebody opened it afterwards, in the middle of the night, to set his stage."

Another pause. The rector sat stiffly upright. The lamplight showed a twitching nerve beside his cheekbone.

"Martin Starberth was a very heavy smoker," continued Dr. Fell. "He was frightened, and nervous, and he had been smoking steadily all that day. In a vigil of the sort he had to undergo it is not too far fetched to believe that he would have smoked even more heavily during his wait . . . A full cigarette-case and matches were found on his body. There was not one single cigarette-stub on the floor of the Governor's Room."

The doctor spoke leisurely. As though his recital had given him an idea, he produced his own pipe.

"Undoubtedly, however, there had been *somebody* in the Governor's Room. And just there is where the murderer's plan miscarried. Had they gone according to schedule, there would have been no necessity for a wild dash across the meadow when the light went out. We should have waited, and found Martin's body after a decently long interval, when he did not reappear. But – remark this, as Mr. Rampole has – the light went out *just ten minutes too soon*.

"Now it was fortunate that the murderer, in smashing Martin's hip to simulate a fall from the balcony, did not smash Martin's watch. It was running, and it had the right time. Let us suppose (for the sake of a hypothesis) that it had really been Martin waiting in the Governor's Room. When his vigil was ended, he would have switched off his lamp and gone home. *He* would have known, at ten minutes to twelve, that his time was not yet up. But, if there were somebody else keeping vigil in his place, and this somebody's watch happened to be ten minutes fast . . . ?"

Sir Benjamin Arnold got up from his chair like a man groping blindly.

"Herbert –" he said.

"We knew that Herbert's watch was just ten minutes fast," the doctor said. "He ordered the housemaid to set the grandfather clock; but she discovered that it was wrong, and left the other clocks as they were. And while Herbert was keeping the vigil for the cousin who was too frightened to do it, his cousin was already lying with his neck broken in the Hag's Nook."

"But still I don't see how –" Sir Benjamin paused bewilderedly.

The telephone in the hall rang with a suddenness that made them all jump.

"You'd better answer it, Inspector," suggested the doctor; "it's probably your men phoning here from the rectory."

Saunders had risen now. His fleshy jowls had the look of a sick dog's. He started to say. "Most preposterous! Most – in a way that sounded horribly as though he were burlesquing his usual voice. Then he stumbled against the edge of the chair and sat down again . . .

They could hear Inspector Jennings talking in the hall. Presently he came back into the study, with an even more wooden face.

"It's all up, sir," he said to Dr. Fell. "They've been down in the cellar. The motor-bicycle is broken in bits and buried there. They've found a Browning pistol, a pair of gardener's gloves, some valises full of –"

Sir Benjamin said, incredulous, "You swine . . ."

"Wait!" cried the rector. He had gotten to his feet again, his hand moving like some one scratching at a door. "You don't know the story. You don't know anything – just guesses – part of it –"

"I don't know *this* story," snarled Robert Saunders, "and I've kept quiet long enough. I want to know about Tom. Where is he? Did you kill him, too? How long have you been posing here?"

"He died!" the other said, desperately. "I had nothing to do with it. He died. I swear to God I never did anything to him. I just wanted quiet, and peace, and respect, and I took his place . . ."

Aimless fingers were fumbling in the air. "Listen. All I want is a little time to think. I only want to sit here and close my eyes. You caught me so suddenly . . . Listen. I'll write you out everything, the whole story, and you'd never know it if I didn't. Not even you, Doctor. If I sit down here, now, and write it, will you promise to stop?"

He was almost like a huge and blubbering child. Looking at him narrowly, Dr. Fell said:

"I think you'd better let him, Inspector. He can't get away. And you can walk about the lawn, if you like."

Inspector Jennings was impassive. "Our instructions from Sir William, sir, at the Yard, were to take orders from you. Very well."

The rector drew himself up. Again that weird burlesque of his old mannerisms. "There is – ah – only one other thing. I must insist that Dr. Fell explain certain things to me, as I can explain certain things to you. In view of our past – friendship, will you be so good as to sit down here with me a few moments when the others have gone?"

A protest was almost out of Rampole's mouth. He was going to say, "There's a gun in that drawer! –" when he saw that Dr. Fell was looking at him. The lexicographer was casually lighting his pipe beside the fireplace, and his squinted eyes were asking for silence over the flame of the match . . .

It was almost dark now. A furious and wildly threatening Robert Saunders had to be led out by the inspector and Sir Benjamin. Rampole and the girl went out into the dim hallway. The last thing they saw was the doctor still lighting his pipe, and Thomas Saunders, his chin up and his expression indifferent, reaching towards the writing-table . . .

The door closed.

18

STATEMENT

6:15 P.M.

For Inspector Jennings, or whom it may concern: I have heard the whole story now, from Dr. Fell, and he has heard mine. I am quite composed. It vaguely occurs to me that on legal documents one is supposed to put down "of sound mind," or some such terms, but I trust I shall be forgiven if I do not adhere strictly to the prescribed form. I do not know it.

Let me try to be frank. This is easy, inasmuch as I shall shoot myself when I have finished writing. For a moment I had entertained the idea of shooting Dr. Fell during our talk a few minutes ago. However, there was only one bullet in the pistol. When I confronted him with it, he made a gesture of a rope being put about his neck; and upon reflection I could easily perceive that such a clean exit is better than hanging, so I put away the weapon. I hate Dr. Fell, I confess I genuinely hate him, for having exposed me, but I must think of my own welfare above all others, and I have no wish to be hanged. They say it is very painful, and I could never bear pain with fortitude.

To begin with, let me say in all justice to myself, as a last word, that I think the world has shabbily used me. I am not a criminal. I am a man of education and parts; an ornament, I believe, to any society in which I move. This has been partly my consolation. My real name I will not give, nor too much of my background, lest it should be traced: but I was actually, at one time, a student of theology. My dismissal from a certain seminary was due to unfortunate circumstances – such circumstance as may involve any young man of robust and healthy nature who is not enervated by worship from the appeal of a pretty girl. That I had stolen money I do to this day deny, or that I had attempted to place the blame on another of my fellow students.

My parents, not understanding, refused to sympathize. I could not help thinking even then that the world has a shabby treatment for its most favored sons. Let me be brief: I could not obtain employment. My gifts were such that I could have advanced rapidly had I had the *opportunity*, but I got no opportunities, save menial ones. I borrowed money from an aunt (she is dead now; *in pace requiescat!*); I went about the world, I knew poverty – yes, and for one day I was hungry – and I grew weary. I wished to settle down, to be comfortable, to be respected, to use my powers, and to taste the sweets of ease.

On a liner from New Zealand, something more than three years ago, I met young Thomas Audley Saunders. He told me that the influence of a certain Sir Benjamin Arnold, an old friend of his uncle's who had never seen the nephew, had obtained him this new and splendid position. Knowing theology well, I became his friend on the long voyage. I need not dwell on it. The poor fellow died shortly after he reached England. It was only then that the thought occurred to me that I should disappear and a new Thomas Saunders should appear at Chatterham. I did not fear discovery. I knew enough of his history to take his place, and his uncle never left Auckland. I should have to keep up a correspondence, of course, but by typing my infrequent letters and practising the signature on Saunders' passport until I had an excellent imitation, I was safe from discovery. He had been educated at Eton, but his collegiate and theological courses were taken at St. Boniface's in New Zealand, and it was unlikely that I should come upon an old friend.

The life, while pleasant and pastoral, was hardly stimulating. I was a gentleman, but – like all others – I wished to be a rich and roving gentleman. It was necessary. however, to keep a curb upon my appetites so that my sermons might be really instructive and sincere; I say with pride that I kept the parish accounts straight, and only once – on pain of severe necessity, when a serving-girl of the county threatened scandal for being attacked – did I tamper with these. But I wish to live a more pleasant life; say, in continental hotels, with many servants and a fling at amorousness now and then.

In my talk with Dr. Fell, I have learned that he knows almost everything. I had made the same deductions from old Anthony Starberth's diary – which Mr. Timothy Starberth kindly showed me – as Dr. Fell made over three years later. I determined that there must be money hidden in the well at the Hag's Nook. If it were negotiable – jewels or bullion, say – I could presently resign and disappear.

I need not dwell on this part. Chance, *vile* chance, entered again. Why does God permit such things? I had found the cache, and to my delight it proved to be precious stones. Through my earlier experiences I was aware of a trustworthy man in London who could engineer sales at Antwerp in a most satisfactory fashion . . . I dislike that word "engineer." It destroys what some have been so kind as to call the Addisonian purity of my prose style; but let it stand . . . Let me say again, I found the stones. I estimated that their value might be conservatively placed at about five thousand pounds.

It was (I remember it distinctly) the afternoon of the eighteenth of October when I made this discovery. As I was on my knees in the hiding-place, prying open the iron box which contained these stones, and shielding my candle from outside observation, I thought that I heard a noise in the well outside. I was just in time to see the rope quivering, and a thin leg disappear from the mouth of the opening, and I heard Mr. Timothy Starberth's unmistakable laugh. Undoubtedly he had noticed something amiss in the well. He had climbed down, seen me at work, and was now going up to laugh. I may here say that he had always a most inexplicable dislike, nay, hatred, for the church and all holy things, and his attitude had at times amounted almost to blasphemy. He, of all people, could work me the most harm. Even if he had not seen my find (and I did not doubt he had) his mirth at finding me thus employed would wreck all my hopes.

Here I must point out a curious feature of my own character. There are times when I seem absolutely to lose control over my reflex actions, and when I seem almost to enjoy inflicting physical pain. Even as a child I had buried rabbits alive and torn the wings from flies. In maturity this often amounts to a certain bewildered activity – which I find difficult to remember, and strive to conceal, and which has often frightened me . . . But let me go on. I found him standing at the top of the well, waiting for me when I came up, his riding-clothes soaking wet. He was doubled up in laughter and slapping his knee with his crop. The precious box was buttoned up in my coat; in my hand I had the small crowbar.

When his elaborate laughter had turned him almost with his back to me, I struck. I took delight in striking him many times, even after he had fallen. I cannot boast that at this time the plan I conceived was at full maturity; but it took shape presently, and I resolved to turn the Starberth legend of broken necks to profitable use.

I broke his neck with the iron bar, and left him in a thicket at twilight, whistling his horse near me.

My fright may be readily imagined when, later on and in a calmer moment, I learned that he was not dead and wished to see me. Dr. Fell has just recently told me that it was this fact which first made him suspicious of me – *i.e.*, that Timothy Starberth should ask for me to be summoned to his bedside, and that I should see him alone. My natural agitation after that interview, which I could scarcely conceal, did not go unnoticed by Dr. Fell. Mr. Starberth told me – in brief – what Dr. Fell already outlined to us all the other day, namely the plan for putting a statement of my guilt into the vault of the Governor's Room, so that a conviction for murder should hang over my head throughout three years. When I heard him tell me this, I did not know what course to pursue. I thought of flying at his throat, but that would only mean a cry and instant apprehension. Given three years, I thought, and I could surely find a means of circumventing his purpose. When I returned to the others, I was careful to implant in their minds the belief that the old man was mad – lest, in an unguarded moment, he should betray me before he died.

Nor need I discuss here the many plans I evolved for stealing that paper. They came to nothing. Instead of being able to resign and leave Chatterham, I was now powerless. In three years, certainly, I might put a deal of ground between myself and Lincolnshire, but there was this overwhelming reason against flight:

If I disappeared, an inquiry would be instituted for Thomas Saunders. It must inevitably be revealed that the real Thomas Saunders was dead – unless, of course, I could step forward whenever they searched for me, and stop investigations. If I were free, without this murder charge in the Governor's Room vault hanging over me, I could always step forward; I could be merely Thomas Saunders resigned from his pastorate. But if I were Thomas Saunders the fugitive – as I must be always – then they would discover what had happened to the real clergyman from Auckland and I should be thought guilty of foul play against *him*. In either case, I should be faced with a murder charge if I disappeared then. The only course was in some fashion to purloin that paper from the safe.

I therefore set about making a confidant of young Mr. Martin Starberth before his departure for America. Without being accused of lack of modesty, I think I may say that my powers of personality are sufficient to make a staunch friend of whomever I choose. I did this with Martin, whom I found a trifle conceited and headstrong, but otherwise a very amiable young man. He told me about the keys to the vault, the conditions, everything concerning his duties on the evening of his twenty-fifth birthday. Even at that date, some two years ago, he was uneasy. As time went on, I saw by his letters from America that the fear had become almost pathological (if I may use the word), and that I might turn to good account both this fact and the well-known devotion of his cousin Herbert to the more brilliant Martin. My purpose was, of course, to gain possession of the paper; it was unfortunate that I should be compelled to kill Martin in so doing – indeed, I liked the young man – and, as a corollary, to encompass the death of his cousin Herbert; but it will be seen that my position was precarious.

I have already indicated that my plan rested upon Martin's fear and Herbert's hero-worship, but there was a third element. These two young men were, in general build and appearance, surprisingly alike. At a distance, one might easily be mistaken for the other.

Taking them into my confidence, I disclosed the arrangement. It would not be necessary for Martin to subject himself to the terrors of such a vigil. On the designated night, immediately after dinner, they should go to their respective rooms; and – lest either of them be intruded upon to disclose the trick – Martin should make it clear that he wanted no interruptions. Herbert should dress himself in Martin's clothes, and Martin in Herbert's. To avoid a waste of time in resuming identities when the vigil was over (I suggested), Herbert should pack a suit of his and one of Martin's own clothes in a bag, and give it to Martin. This Martin should strap on the rear of Herbert's motor-bicycle, and immediately set out on the bicycle, by a back lane, for the rectory. At the appropriate time Herbert should set out for the Governor's Room, taking Martin's keys and going through the instructions as set down by the Starberth tradition.

This, it is to be understood, is what I told *them* to do. My own plans were different; but let me proceed. At just twelve o'clock Herbert was to leave the Governor's Room; and Martin, having changed into his own clothes at the rectory and driven back at this time, should be waiting for him, with the motor-bicycle, in the road before the prison. Whereupon Herbert would deliver to his cousin the keys, the lamp, and the written proof of the vigil, and Martin should return afoot to the Hall. Herbert should take the motor-bicycle, drive to the rectory, change his clothes, and also return – apparently after having taken only a drive through the countryside to relieve his feelings on the night of his cousin's ordeal.

My own design, I need not say, was: first, to provide an absolute and undeniable alibi for myself; and, second, to make the murder of Martin seem the work of Herbert. To this end I played strongly on family pride, which is in its own way a very admirable sentiment. I suggested that, even though the strict letter of the ordeal were broken, its spirit could be preserved. Herbert could open the iron box inside the vault, *but he must not examine any of its contents.* He must, instead, put them all into his pocket, and deliver them to Martin when they met at midnight outside the prison. Returning to the Hall, Martin could examine them at his leisure. If, on the morrow, Mr. Payne protested that he had removed from the iron box in the vault anything which should not be removed, Martin could credibly plead a blunder. A harmless blunder, since his conduct had in any event proved the purpose of the ordeal, *viz.*, that he had spent the hour in the Governor's Room.

My own course of action was clear. When Martin arrived at the rectory not later than nine-thirty, he could be disposed of there. I regretted that I could not make his death entirely painless; but a blow from an iron bar would render him unconscious while the neck was broken and the other injuries prepared. He could then be conveyed without suspicion in my car to the Hag's Nook, and arranged under the wall. The almanac had prophesied dark and wet weather, which proved to be a true prediction. After doing this, I should repair to Dr. Fell's. Having already suggested a party to watch the window of the Governor's Room, I felt that I could have no better alibi. When – at midnight – the light was extinguished in the Governor's Room, exactly on time, the uneasiness of the watchers would be set at rest. They would decide that Martin had come safely through his vigil. Shortly thereafter I should take my leave. Herbert, I knew, would wait patiently before the prison for as long as I liked, since he expected his cousin; and he would not let himself be seen. The longer I delayed, the better. When I left Dr. Fell's I should leave my car and join Herbert. I should inform him that, unfortunately, in my absence from the rectory his cousin had drunk himself into a bad state – a statement which his conduct would admirably bear out – and that it was necessary for Herbert to accompany me there and assist in getting Martin on his feet before Miss Starberth grew alarmed.

With the keys, the lamp, and the contents of the iron box, he would return with me to the rectory. There was no need for subterfuge in his case; a bullet would suffice. Later on in the night I could safely return to the prison and make sure that Herbert had overlooked nothing. I had tried to find an excuse for causing him to open the balcony door, but I feared lest he grow suspicious, and determined to accomplish this result myself.

What actually happened I need scarcely recapitulate. Although in one instance (which I shall indicate) my calculations went awry, I think I may say that presence of mind rescued me from a dangerous situation. It was only *chance* which defeated me. Herbert was seen by the butler while he was packing the change of clothes in the bag; this indicated flight. Martin – whom they thought to be Herbert – was seen driving away, down a back lane, on the motor-bicycle; another indication of flight. Miss Starberth happened to come out into the hall (unforeseen chance) when Herbert, posing as Martin, was leaving the house. But he was seen only from the rear, at a distance and in dim light; when addressed, he merely mumbled something to simulate drunkenness, and thus escaped undetected. Not once were either of these two directly addressed or confronted when assuming the identities of each other. When Budge took up the bicycle-lamp to Martin's room, where Herbert waited, he did not give it to anyone, as he has remarked; he merely left it outside the door. When Budge, in going to obtain the bicycle-lamp, saw Martin on the bicycle, it was in the obscurity of night – riding away.

I applied lethal measures to Martin. I confess that it was with a hesitation that I did so, for he was almost tearfully wringing my hand and thanking me for rescuing him from what he dreaded most. But a sudden blow, when he was bending over the spirits-decanter, and I felt stimulated to my work. He was a very light weight. I am counted a powerful man, and I had not the slightest difficulty later. A rear lane, behind Yew Cottage, took me to the vicinity of the prison; I arranged the body under the balcony and beside the well, and returned to Dr. Fell's. Though I had toyed with the idea of driving the spikes of the well through the body, as a more realistic detail and to confirm the ancient tale of Anthony's death, I abandoned it as being a trifle *too* apt, a trifle *too* studied a vindication of the Starberth curse.

My only fear was now that Herbert should get out of the house safely. Without wishing to speak ill of the dead, I think I may say that he was a dull, cloddish fellow, not overquick in an emergency. He had even been backward in taking up my plan, having several strong and almost bitter arguments with Martin about it . . . In any event, Dr. Fell tells me that, while waiting in his garden for the stroke of eleven, I overreached myself. My agitation, and my somewhat inessential question, "Where is Herbert?" at the critical period of the wait, caused him some speculation; but I dare assert that I had been through a period of strong emotional tension, and such manifestations were only to have been expected.

I now can discuss another effort of vile and devilish *chance* to overthrow me. I refer, of course, to the ten-minute difference in the clocks. For some time I have puzzled as to why, since Herbert shut off his lamp ten minutes too soon and thus almost precipitated catastrophe – I have puzzled, I say, as to why he had arrived in the Governor's Room almost on the stroke of the *real* eleven o'clock. But I saw my answer anticipated, I regret to say, by Dr. Fell's questioning of the servants at the Hall. Herbert carried a watch which was fast. But while he was waiting in Martin's room he not unnaturally kept his eyes on the clock there. He had ordered the housemaid to set all the clocks right, according to his own time, and he assumed she had done so. There was, as Dr. Fell discovered, a large clock with the right time in Martin's room. Thus Herbert left the Hall by the right time. In the Governor's Room he had only his watch, and he left by the wrong time.

At this point, through no fault of my own reasoning, but due sheerly to *chance*, the young American (for whom I have the highest respect) had been roused to a dangerous pitch of emotional tension. He determined on a dash across the meadow. I tried to dissuade him; it would have been fatal had he run into Herbert leaving the prison, and it would have proved my own undoing. Seeing, therefore, that it was useless to stop him, I followed. The spectacle of a hatless clergyman pounding through a thunderstorm like a boy at a country frolic did not go unobserved by Dr. Fell, but my mind was on other matters. And I saw what I had hoped for, and what was only natural – he was running towards the Hag's Nook, and not towards the gate of the prison.

Thereupon ensued the inspiration upon which I cannot pride myself, since it is a part of my character and no development of my own. I perceived how this danger could be turned into an advantage. I ran – as was natural for a man with nothing on his conscience – towards the prison gate. I had carefully cautioned Herbert that, while he must show his light in going *into* the prison, he must under no circumstances show it in going out; some stranger might observe him meeting Martin in the lane, and wonder.

It was timed with an accuracy I can only regard as the fruit of my own labours. What with the night and the rain, the American was lost; and I had ample time to meet Herbert. I made sure he had the documents. I told him briefly, standing there in the wild night, that he had miscalculated – happy invention! – that he was ten minutes too early, and Martin had not yet left the rectory. I told him further that the suspicions of the watchers were aroused and that they were all about us. He must hurry back to the rectory on foot, and by devious ways. I was genuinely afraid that he might show his light, so I jerked it from his hand, intending to get rid of it in the wood.

But another ray of imaginative insight showed me a better plan. Save by flashes of lightning, the American could see nothing. I therefore smashed the lamp with my foot, and in hurrying to join him I simply dropped it near the wall. It is in such crises as these that one's brain amazes one with the quickness and finely wrought artistry of its conceptions.

I had now nothing more to fear. Herbert would go afoot. It was impossible that the American should avoid finding Martin's body, but, if he did not, *I* was prepared to stumble upon it. Whereupon I, possessing the only automobile within reach, would be dispatched to Chatterham for either the doctor or the police. I should have ample time to anticipate Herbert at the rectory.

Need I say that so it worked out? I had a more than human task to do that night, but I had set myself to it coolly; and, once I had killed Martin, that deed might have impelled me by its inexplicable stimulus to a dozen others. Before getting Dr. Markley – as I later told the chief constable – I stopped at the rectory, quite naturally, for my raincoat.

I had been a trifle delayed, and I was scarcely a second before Herbert. It would have been more prudent to have come close to him and fired against his body, as conducive to less noise; but the rectory is isolated, without much danger of a revolver-shot being overheard; and it seemed, at that moment, more sporting to stand at a distance and shoot him between the eyes.

I then put on my raincoat and drove back to the prison with Dr. Markley.

All our labours were over by one o'clock. I had, then, several hours before dawn to complete my arrangements. Never have I felt so impelled to tidy up everything, as one takes pleasure in meticulously tidying up a room. I could have concealed Herbert's body – at least for the time being

– in the cellar where I had hidden the bicycle, the valise, and certain implements I had used on Martin. But I must go to bed with my house (so to speak) swept and garnished. Besides, I had wished to fix the murder of Martin Starberth on his cousin, and I must overlook no *chance.*

All that I did, I did that night. It was not heavy work, since the body was so light. Knowing my way so thoroughly, I did not even need a lamp. So many times I had taken solitary walks through the prison – standing on its walls (often, I fear, seen) – standing on its walls, I say, moving through its historic corridors with some apt quotation on my lips – that I knew my way in the dark. With the Starberth keys in my possession, I now had access to the Governor's Room. For a long time I had been uncertain as to whether or not the door to the balcony had ever been locked; in any case (as I have indicated) it could *be* unlocked. I did this, and my plan was complete.

One thing more. The iron box containing the documents in the vault I later dropped into the well. I did this because I still suspected (nay, I dare say feared) the diabolical cleverness of Timothy, whom I had killed. I feared another document, perhaps, a secret compartment; I wished to be sure.

It amuses me to think that last night I was almost caught. I became suspicious of those conferences at Dr. Fell's, and I watched, suitably armed. Some one tried to intercept me and I fired; I was relieved to learn today that it was only Budge, the butler. Earlier in this narrative I stated that I would be frank; I withdraw that statement now. There is one point upon which I cannot be frank, even knowing that in the next few minutes I must put a revolver to my temple and pull the trigger. Sometimes, at night, I have seen faces. Last night I thought I saw one, too, and momentarily it unnerved me. I will not discuss it. Such matters disrupt the nice logic of my plans. This is all I can bear to say.

And now, gentlemen who will read this, I have nearly done. My dealings with my friend the diamond salesman have been satisfactorily completed – not too often, lest I rouse suspicion – over a period of years. I was prepared. When, as a climax to the buffetings of evil chance, I received a letter from my "uncle" that he was visiting England for the first time in ten years, I could accept it with quiet resignation. In brief – I was weary. I had fought too long. I only wanted to leave Chatterham. So the news of my uncle's coming, with details, I told freely over all the country; as a subterfuge, I urged Sir Benjamin Arnold to meet him, knowing that he would refuse and insist that I go in his stead. I should have disappeared. For three years I had brooded so long over chance, and the malevolent turns it had dealt me, that a smoothly rounded life, without dangers, seemed no longer essential.

Dr. Fell has left me the pistol as a kindness. I do not want to use it yet. The man has too much power at Scotland Yard . . .

I wish, now, that I had shot him. When death is so close I think I could stand the idea of hanging, if it were only a few weeks away. The lamp gives not too much life, and I should have preferred to kill myself in a gentlemanly way, with a suitable flourish and at least more prepossessing clothes.

The fluency which has animated me in writing my sermons seems to desert my pen. Have I done blasphemy? A man of my parts, I tell myself, could not possibly do so, since my precepts – even though I am not ordained or likely to be ordained – were of the most approved order. Where was the flaw in my plans? I asked Dr. Fell. That was why I wanted to see him. His suspicion of me became a certainty when I, in a too rash moment, to cover up any doubts in their minds, said that Timothy Starberth on his death-bed had accused one of his own family of killing him. I was rash, but I was consistent. If I had been given the opportunity in this life, some chance for my brilliance – I *am* a great man. I can with difficulty bring myself to take the pen from the paper, because then I must pick up the other thing.

I hate everybody. I would wipe out the world if I could. Now I must shoot myself. I have blasphemed. I who have secretly not believed in God, I pray, I pray . . . God help me. I can write no more; I am sick.

THOMAS SAUNDERS.

He did not shoot himself. When they opened the door to the study, he was trembling in a fit – the pistol halfway to his temple, without courage enough to pull the trigger.

The Mad Hatter Mystery

Contents

Plan of the South Side of the Tower of London, Giving on the Thames Wharf, where the Action of this Story takes Place.

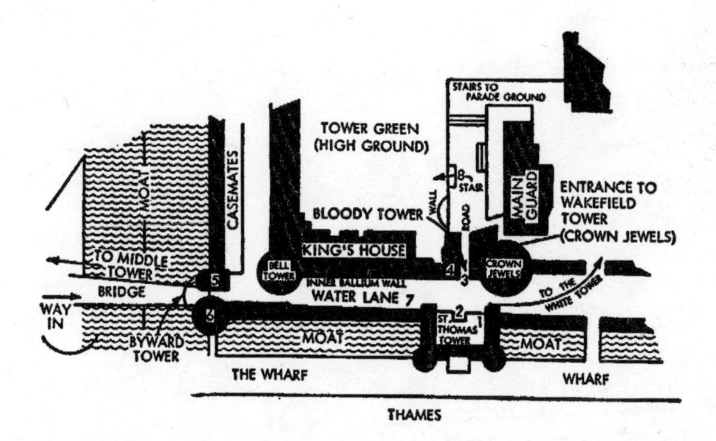

THE reader will please observe that the Bloody Tower, to which frequent reference is made, is built above the gate marked 3 in the plan; that the gate of this tower does not lead into the tower itself, but to a roadway going past the Wakefield Tower. The door of the Bloody Tower faces Tower Green, and is reached by a stairway from the roadway mentioned. (8)

1. Traitors' Gate.
2. Steps where body was found.
3. Gateway of Bloody Tower.
4. Window from which Parker saw Driscoll and the unknown.
5. Small Warders' Room, northern side of Byward Tower, where questioning took place.
6. Warders' Hall, southern side of Bloody Tower, where visitors were detained.
7. Where Mrs. Larkin stood.

1
A CAB HORSE IN A BARRISTER'S WIG

It began, like most of Dr. Fell's adventures, in a bar. It dealt with the reason why a man was found dead on the steps of Traitors' Gate, at the Tower of London, and with the odd headgear of this man in the golf suit. That was the worst part of it. The whole case threatened for a time to become a nightmare of hats.

Abstractly considered, there is nothing very terrifying about a hat. We may pass a shop-window full of them without the slightest qualm. We may even see a policeman's helmet decorating the top of a lamp-post, or a pearl-grey top-hat perched on the head of one of the lions in Trafalgar Square, with no more than an impression that some practical joker is exercising a primitive sense of humour. Young Rampole, when he saw the newspaper, was inclined to grin at the matter as just that.

Chief Inspector Hadley was not so sure.

They were waiting for Dr. Fell at Scott's, which is in the heart of Piccadilly Circus. You descend a flight of stairs from Great Windmill Street to a lounge like a club, brown panels and easy-chairs in red leather, with the brass-bound kegs behind the bar and the model of a ship on the ledge of the stone mantelpiece. Sitting in an alcove with a glass of beer, Rampole studied the chief inspector. He was wondering. He had only arrived from America that morning, and the press of events seemed rather sudden.

He said: "I've often wondered, sir, about Dr. Fell. I mean . . . his position. He seems to be all sorts of things."

The other nodded, smiling faintly. You could not, Rampole felt, help liking the chief inspector of the C.I.D. He was the sort of man who might be described as compact; not tall or heavy, yet giving the impression of being so; very neatly dressed, with a military moustache and smooth hair the colour of dull steel. If there was a quality about him you noticed at once, it was a quality of repose, of quiet watchfulness. His movements were deliberate. Even his eyes, which seemed to go from grey to black, had that deliberate faculty, and he rarely raised his voice.

"Have you known him long?" Hadley asked, examining his glass.

"As a matter of fact, only since last July." The American found himself rather startled to remember that. "Good Lord! it seems years! He . . . well, in a manner of speaking, he introduced me to my wife."

Hadley nodded. "I know. That would be the Starberth case. He wired me from Lincolnshire, and I sent the men he wanted."

A little more than eight months ago . . . Rampole looked back on those terrifying scenes in the Hag's Nook, and the twilight by the railway station where Dr. Fell had put his hand on the shoulder of Martin Starberth's murderer. Now there were only happiness and Dorothy. Now there was London in the cool, misty days of March, revisited for the first time since then.

Again the chief inspector smiled faintly. "And you, I believe," he continued in his deliberate voice, "carried off the young lady. I hear glowing reports of you from Fell . . . He did rather a brilliant piece of work in that affair," Hadley added abruptly. "I wonder . . ."

"Whether he can do it again?"

The other's expression grew quizzical. He turned his head. "Not so fast, please. You seem to be scenting crime again."

"Well, sir, he wrote me a note to meet you here . . ."

"And," said Hadley, "you may be right. I have a feeling," he touched a folded newspaper in his pocket, hesitated and frowned. "Still, I thought that this thing might be rather more in his line than mine. Bitton appealed to me personally, as a friend, and it's hardly a job for the Yard. I don't want to turn him down."

Rampole wondered whether he was supposed to know what his companion was talking about. The chief inspector seemed to be musing, in a hesitant fashion, and his hand kept straying to the newspaper in his pocket. He added:

"I suppose you've heard of Sir William Bitton?"

"The collector?"

"Ah," said Hadley; "I fancied you would. Fell said it would be in your line, too. The book-collector, yes. Though I knew him better before he retired from politics." He glanced at his watch. "He should be here by two o'clock, and so should Fell. There's a train from Lincoln which gets into King's Cross at one-thirty . . ."

A thunderous voice boomed, "AHA!" They were conscious of somebody flourishing a cane at them from across the room, and of a great bulk filling the stairway to the street. The bar had been very quiet; this entrance caused one white-jacketed bartender to start violently. The only other occupants of the room were two business men conversing in low tones in one corner, and they jerked round to stare at the beaming appearance of Gideon Fell.

All the old genial days, all the beer-drinking and fiery moods and table-pounding conversations, beamed back at Rampole in the person of Dr. Fell. The American felt like calling for another drink and striking up a song for sheer joyousness. There was the doctor, bigger and stouter than ever. He wheezed. His red face shone, and his small eyes twinkled over eyeglasses on a broad black ribbon. There was a grin under his bandit's moustache, and chuckling upheavals animated his several chins. On his head was the inevitable black shovel-hat; his paunch projected from a voluminous black cloak. Filling the stairs in grandeur he leaned on an ash cane with one hand and flourished another cane with the other. It was like meeting Father Christmas or Old King Cole. Indeed, Dr. Fell had frequently impersonated Old King Cole at garden pageants, and enjoyed the rôle immensely.

"Heh," he said. "Heh-heh-heh." He came rolling over to the alcove and wrung Rampole's hand. "My boy, I'm delighted. Delighted! Heh. I say, you're looking fine. And Dorothy? . . . Excellent; I'm glad to hear it. My wife sends her warmest regards. We're going to take you back to Chatterham as soon as Hadley tells me what he wants with me . . . Eh, Hadley? Here, let's all have a drink."

There are people before whom you instantly unbend. Dr. Fell was one of them. No constraint could exist before him; he blew it away with a superb puff; and, if you had any affectations, you forgot them immediately. Hadley looked indulgent, and beckoned a waiter.

"This might interest you," the chief inspector suggested, handing Dr. Fell a wine-card. He assumed a placid, innocent air. "The cocktails are recommended. There is one called an 'Angel's Kiss' . . ."

"*Hah*?" said Dr. Fell, starting in his seat.

". . . or a 'Love's Delight' –"

"Gurk!" said Dr. Fell. He stared at the card. "Young man, do you serve these?"

"Yes, sir," said the waiter, jumping involuntarily.

"You serve an 'Angel's Kiss,' a 'Love's Delight,' and – ah – if my eyes do not deceive me, a 'Happy Virgin'? . . .

"Young man," continued the doctor, rumbling and polishing his glasses, "have you never reflected on what American influence has done to stalwart England? Where are your finer instincts? This is enough to make decent tipplers shudder. Instead of saying, 'A bitter,' or 'A Scotch and splash, please,' like scholars and gentlemen, we are now expected to coo for . . . Hah!" He broke off and scowled ferociously. "Can you imagine Buffalo Bill striding into a Western saloon and roaring for an 'Angel's Kiss'? Can you fancy what Tony Weller would have said if he called for hot rum punch and received a 'Love's Delight'?"

"No, sir," said the waiter.

"I think you'd better order something," suggested Hadley.

"A large glass of beer," said the doctor. "Lager."

Snorting, he produced his cigar-case and offered it round as the waiter took away the glasses. But with the first healing puffs of smoke he settled himself back benignly against the alcove.

"I hadn't meant to draw a crowd, gentlemen," he rumbled, making an immense gesture with the cigar. Heads, which had been poked through the doorway to the restaurant adjoining, were discreetly withdrawn. One of the business men, who had almost swallowed the stick skewering the cherry in his drink, had settled down again to conversation. "But my young friend here will tell you, Hadley, that I have been working for seven years on the materials of my book, *The Drinking Customs of England from the Earliest Days*, and I blush to have to include such manifestations as these, even in the appendix. They sound almost bad enough to be soft drinks. I . . ."

He paused, small eyes blinking over his glasses. A quiet, impeccably-dressed man, who seemed like a manager of some sort, was hesitating near their alcove. He appeared to be ill-at-ease, and feeling slightly ridiculous. But he was contemplating Dr. Fell's very picturesque shovel-hat, which lay across the cloak on a chair. As the waiter brought three rounds of beer, this man entered the alcove.

"Excuse me, sir," he said, "but may I make a suggestion? If I were you, I should be very careful of this hat."

The doctor stared at him for a moment, his glass halfway to his lips. Then a bright and pleased expression animated his red face.

"Permit me, sir," he requested earnestly, "to shake your hand. You are, I perceive, a person of sound taste and judgment. I wish you could talk to my wife on this matter. It is, I agree, an excellent hat. But why should I exercise more than my usual care in guarding it?"

The man's face was growing pink. He said, stiffly: "I had no wish to intrude, sir. I thought you knew . . . That is to say, there have been several such outrages in this vicinity, and I did not wish to have our patrons incommoded. That hat – well, hang it!" the manager exploded, volplaning down into honest speech, "that thing would be too much. He couldn't miss. The Hatter would be bound to steal it."

"*Who*?"

"The Hatter sir. The Mad Hatter."

Hadley's mouth was twitching back, and he seemed about to burst out laughing or leave the table in haste. But Dr. Fell did not notice. He took out a large handkerchief and wiped his forehead.

"My dear sir," he said, "this is most refreshing. Let me see if I follow you. Am I to understand that there is in this neighbourhood a hatter of such notoriously unbalanced mind, that as I walk innocently past his shop, he would be apt to dash into the street and steal my hat? That is carrying the aesthetic sense too far. I must courteously but firmly refuse," continued Dr. Fell, raising his voice warmly, "to run up Piccadilly pursued by impassioned hatters. I am too old, my dear sir; and I am too fat; and, if you want still a third reason, I am convinced that among your friends you are known by the playful nickname of The March Hare."

In contrast to the manager's low, nervous tones, he had been trumpeting across the room. The business man with the cocktail gave a slight moan, put on his coat, and moved hastily towards the door. The other business man stayed grimly at his table.

Even the chief inspector, in his own quiet way, was flustered. He said, sharply: "Thank you very much. This gentleman has just arrived in London; he knows nothing about it. I can explain."

As the red-faced manager hurried towards the restaurant, Dr. Fell sighed.

"Now you've driven him away," he protested, querulously, "and I was just beginning to enjoy it. I perceive among London hatters a bustling, up-to-the-minute, go-get-'em spirit. Still, I hope you don't have mad tailors who rush out of their shops and remove the trousers of casual passers-by. That would be a trifle alarming." He took a deep drink of beer, and shook his great head of hair like a mane. Then he beamed on his companions.

"Blast you . . ." said the chief inspector. He struggled with dignity, and lost. "Oh well. Confound it, I hate scenes, and you seem to revel in them. All the same, he was talking perfect sense."

"Eh?"

"He was talking perfect sense," Hadley repeated, with some irritation. He fingered his close grey moustache. "It's a kid's prank, of course. But it keeps on and on. If he'd stopped at stealing one or two hats, and this infernal newspaper ragging hadn't begun, no harm would have been done. But it's making us look foolish. And it's got to stop."

The doctor adjusted his glasses.

"Do you mean to say," he demanded, "that a real hatter is going about London stealing . . ."

"'Mad Hatter' is what the newspapers call him. It was started by this young cub Driscoll, the free-lance. Driscoll is Bitton's nephew; it would be difficult to muzzle him and if we did try to muzzle him we should look foolish. *He's* doing the damage . . . Laugh, by all means!" Hadley invited, frigidly.

Dr. Fell lowered his chins into his collar. The twinkle in his eye had become more pronounced.

"And Scotland Yard," he asked, with suspicious politeness, "is unable to apprehend this villainous . . ."

Hadley retained his repose with an effort. Hadley said, in a quiet voice: "I don't give a damn, personally, if he steals the Archbishop of Canterbury's mitre. But the effect of a police force's being laughed at is not at all humorous. Besides, suppose we catch him? To the newspapers the trial would be much funnier than the offence. Can you imagine two solemn wigged counsels battling as to whether the defendant did, or did not, on the evening of March 5th, 1932, abstract the helmet of Police Constable Thomas Sparkle from the head of the said constable, in or about the premises of Euston Road, and did thereafter elevate the said helmet to the top of a lamp-standard before the premises of New Scotland Yard, S.W. – or whatever it is they say?"

"Did he do that?" Dr. Fell queried, with interest.

"Read it," said Hadley, and drew the newspaper from his pocket. "That's young Driscoll's column. It's the worst, but the others are almost as facetious."

Dr. Fell grunted. "I say, Hadley, this isn't the case you wanted to talk to *me* about is it? Because if it is, I'm damned if I help you. Why, man, it's glorious! It's like Robin Hood. It's like . . ."

Hadley was not amused. "That," he answered, coldly, "is not the case. But out of what I have on hand, I hope to put a brake on Driscoll. Unless . . ." He hesitated, turning something over in his mind. "Read it. It will probably delight you."

Rampole glanced over the doctor's shoulder as the latter read:

HAT-FIEND STRIKES AGAIN!

IS THERE A POLITICAL SIGNIFICANCE IN THE MOVEMENTS OF THE SINISTER MASTER MIND?

By PHILIP C. DRISCOLL, our special correspondent in charge of the latest Mad Hatter atrocities.

London, March 12. Not since the days of Jack the Ripper has this city been so terrorized by a mysterious fiend who strikes and vanishes without a clue, as in the exploits of the diabolical criminal genius known as the Mad Hatter. On Sunday morning fresh exploits of the Mad Hatter challenged the best brains of Scotland Yard.

Passing the cab-rank on the east side of Leicester Square about 5 A.M., P. C. James McGuire was struck by a somewhat unusual circumstance. A hansom-cab was drawn up at the kerb from which certain not untuneful noises indicated that the driver was asleep inside. The horse (whose name has subsequently been ascertained to be Jennifer) was chewing a large stick of peppermint and looking benevolently upon P. C. McGuire. What especially struck the quick-witted policeman, however, was the fact that on her head Jennifer wore a large white wig with flowing sides: in fact, a barrister's wig.

Though some caution was manifested in taking steps when Mr. McGuire reported to Vine Street Police Station the presence of a horse in a barrister's wig eating peppermint in Leicester Square, ultimate investigation proved it true. It became obvious that the Hat-Fiend was again at large.

Readers of the *Daily Herald* are already aware how, on the preceding day, a beautiful pearl-grey top-hat was discovered on the head of one of the lions on the Nelson Monument in Trafalgar Square, looking towards Whitehall. By its inscription it was found to belong to Sir Isaac Simonides Levy, of Curzon Street, the well-known member of the Stock Exchange.

Under cover of a light mist, that cloak of evil-doers, it had been twitched from Sir Isaac's head as he was leaving his home the preceding evening to address a meeting of the Better Orphans' League. It will be obvious that Sir Isaac, in a pearl-grey top-hat for evening wear, was (to say the least) conspicuous.

The origin of the wig on Jennifer's head was, therefore, clear to the authorities. At the present moment its owner has not been ascertained, nor has he come forward. This modesty has led to all sorts of speculations, but clues are few. Mr. Aylmer Valence, the driver of the hansom-cab, could shed no light on the matter. Detectives believe that the Mad Hatter must have been near the cab-rank only a few moments before the arrival of P. C. McGuire, inasmuch as the stick of peppermint was scarcely a third gone when the policeman first saw her. It is further inferred that the criminal was well acquainted with Leicester Square, and probably with the horse Jennifer, since he took advantage of her liking for peppermints to place the wig upon her head. Beyond this, the police have little to work on.

This is the seventh reported outrage in the last week. It would not be too far-fetched to wonder whether any sinister political scheme underlies this.

"There's more of it," Hadley said, when he saw Dr. Fell fold over the paper at this point, "but it doesn't matter. I hate this damned ragging, that's all."

"Undoubtedly," said Dr. Fell, sadly, "you police are a persecuted lot. And no clue, I suppose. I'm sorry I can't take the case. Perhaps, though, if you sent your best men to all the sweet-shops near Leicester Square, and inquire who bought . . ."

"I didn't bring you down from Chatterham," Hadley retorted, with asperity, "to talk about an undergraduate prank. But I may stop this young pup Driscoll from writing such tosh, and that will stop the rest of them. I wired you that it had something to do with Bitton; Bitton is this boy's uncle, and holds the pursestrings . . . One of the most valuable manuscripts in Bitton's collection, he tells me, has been stolen."

"Ah," said Dr. Fell. He put aside the paper, and sat back with his arms folded.

"The devil about these thefts of manuscripts or rare books," Hadley continued, "is that you can't trace them like an ordinary theft. In the case of precious stones, or plate, or even pictures, it's fairly simple. We know our pawnshops and our receivers of stolen goods too well. But you can't do it with books or manuscripts. When a thief takes something like that, he has a definite person in mind to whom he intends to dispose of it; or else he's acting under the buyer's orders, to begin with. In any case, you can be sure the buyer won't tell."

The chief inspector paused.

"And the Yard's intervention in the matter is further complicated by the fact that the manuscript stolen from Bitton was one to which he had – well, a rather dubious right himself."

"I see," murmured the doctor. "And what was it?"

Hadley picked up his glass slowly, and set it down hastily. Nobody, least of all the business man who remained drinking in one corner, was prepared for another stormy entrance to the bar that afternoon. Feet clattered on the brass stair-rods. A tall man in a flapping greatcoat strode down into the room; the bartender drew a deep breath, resignedly, and tried not to notice the wild look in the stranger's eye. The bartender murmured, "Good afternoon, Sir William," and returned to polishing glasses.

"It's not a good afternoon," Sir William Bitton announced, violently. He passed the end of his white scarf across his face, moist from the thickening mist outside, and glared. His white pompadour stood up like the foam on a beer-glass. "It's a hell of an afternoon, that's what it is . . . Ah, Hallo, Hadley! Now, look here, something's got to be done. I tell you I won't . . ." He strode into the alcove, and his eye fell on the paper Dr. Fell had discarded. "So you're reading about him, are you? You're reading about that swine who steals hats?"

"Quite, quite," said Hadley, looking about nervously. "Sit down, man! What's he done to you?"

"What's he done?" inquired Sir William, with deadly politeness. He raised the forelock of his white hair. "You can see for yourself what he's done. It was an hour and a half ago, and I'm still boiling. I boil every time I think of it. Right in front of my house – car standing there – chauffeur down buying cigarettes. *I* went out to it. Misty in the square. Saw what I thought was a sneak-thief putting his hand into the side pocket of the car door through the window in the tonneau. I said, 'Hi!' and jumped on the runningboard. *Then* the swine shot out his hand and . . ."

Sir William gulped.

"I had three appointments this afternoon before I came here; two of 'em in the City. Even going to make monthly calls. Call on Lord Tarlotts. Call on my nephew. Call – Never mind. But I couldn't and wouldn't go *anywhere,* because I hadn't got one. And I was damned if I'd pay three guineas for a third one that swine might . . . What's he done?" bellowed Sir William, breaking off again. "He's stolen my hat, that's what he's done! And it's the second hat he's stolen from me in three days!"

The business man in the corner uttered a faint noise, shook his head despondently, and hurried out of the bar.

2
MANUSCRIPTS AND MURDER

Hadley rapped on the table. "A double whiskey here," he said to the waiter. "Now sit down and calm yourself. People think this is a madhouse already . . . And let me introduce you to some friends of mine . . ."

"D'ye do?" said the other, grudgingly, and bobbed his head at the introductions. He resumed in his high, argumentative voice as he sat down. "It's infuriating. It's maddening. All those visits; make 'em regular as clockwork, every month. The only reason I came here was because I'd *got* to see you if I'd had to come without my boots. Ha. No other hat in the house. Think of that! My daughter'd made me give the others to my valet; wouldn't wear them in a pigsty; just bought two new hats last week – top-hat and Homburg. And Saturday night this maniac pinched the top-hat, and this afternoon he got the Homburg. By God! I won't have it! I tell you –" He glared round as the waiter appeared. "Eh? – Oh, whiskey. Just a splash, thanks. That'll do. My daughter said, 'Why not chase him?' *Me?* Chase my hat? Ha. Sheila has no brains. Never had."

Spluttering, he sat back to take a drink, and Rampole studied him. Everybody knew, by hearsay, of this man's fiery humours. Jingo newspapers frequently dwelt on his career: how he had begun in a draper's shop at the age of eighteen, become a whip in Parliament at forty-two, managed the armament policy of one Government, and had gone down still battling for a bigger navy in the peace reaction after the war. He had been the prince of jingoes; his speeches were full of reference to Drake, the long-bow, and hurrah for old England; and he still wrote letters vilifying the present Prime Minister. But his best-known activities were before the war, and he had retired completely from public life at little more than forty-five. Now Rampole saw a man hardly past his prime at seventy; wiry, vigorous, with a long neck thrust out of his wing collar, and uncannily shrewd blue eyes. His fingers were restless and tapping. The face was bony, with a high, frail forehead, the eyebrows like white moustaches, and the mouth at once thin and mobile – an orator's mouth.

Suddenly he put down his glass and stared at Dr. Fell with narrowed eyes. "Excuse me," he said, in his jerky but wonderfully clear fashion, "I didn't catch your name at first. Dr. Fell? Dr. Gideon Fell? – Ah, I thought so. I have been wanting to meet you. I have your work on the history of the supernatural in English fiction. But this damned business about hats . . ."

Hadley said, brusquely: "I think we've heard quite enough about hats, for the moment. You understand that according to the story you told me we can't take official cognizance of it at the Yard. That's why I've summoned Dr. Fell. There's no time to go into it now, but he has – helped us before. I am not one of those fools who distrust amateurs. And it is particularly in his line. All the same . . ."

The chief inspector was troubled. Suddenly he drew a long breath. His slow grey eyes were almost black now. Evenly he continued:

"Gentlemen, neither am I one of those fools who call themselves thoroughly practical men. A moment ago I said we had heard quite enough about hats; and before I saw Sir William I thought so. But this second theft of his hat . . . has it occurred to you that in some fashion (I do not pretend to understand it) this may relate to the theft of the manuscript?"

Sir William seemed about to utter a snort of protest, but the lines tightened round his eyes, and he kept silent.

"It had occurred to me, of course," Dr. Fell rumbled, beckoning the waiter and pointing to his empty glass, "that the theft of the hats was more than an undergraduate prank. It's quite possible that some scatterbrained chap might want to *collect* stolen hats; a policeman's helmet, a barrister's wig, any sort of picturesque headgear he could proudly display to his friends. I noticed the same habit when I was teaching in America, among the students. There it ran to signs and signboards of all kinds to decorate the walls of their rooms . . . Is that right, my boy?"

Rampole nodded. "Yes. And it went to fantastic lengths sometimes. I knew one chap who made a bet that he would steal the street-sign from the corner of Broadway and Forty-second Street in broad daylight. And he did it. He put on overalls, slung a bucket of paint over his arm, and carried a short ladder. Then he propped the ladder against the post, climbed up, unscrewed the sign, and walked away. There were thousands of people passing at the time, and nobody even glanced at him."

"For a collection, yes," said the doctor. "But this is a different thing, you see. This chap isn't a lunatic collector. He steals the hat and props it up somewhere else, like a symbol, for everybody to see. There's one other explanation . . ."

Sir William's thin lips wore a wintry smile as he glanced from Rampole to the absorbed face of the doctor; but shrewd calculation moved in his eyes.

"You're a quaint parcel of detectives," he said. "Are you seriously suggesting that a thief begins pinching hats all over London so that he can pinch a manuscript from me? Do you think I'm in the habit of carrying valuable manuscripts around in my hat? Besides, if I must become slightly crazy myself, I might point out that it was stolen several days before either one of my hats."

Dr. Fell ruffled his big dark mane with a thoughtful hand. "The repetition of that word 'hat,'" he observed, "has rather a confusing effect. I'm afraid I shall say 'hat' when I mean almost anything else . . . Suppose you tell us about the manuscript first – what was it, and how did you get it, and when was it stolen? It wasn't the one of Coleridge's *Kubla Khan*, was it?"

The other shook his head. He finished his whiskey and leaned back. For a moment he studied Dr. Fell sharply, with heavy-lidded eyes. Then a sort of dry, eager pride edged his look.

"I'll tell you what it was," he answered, in a low voice, "because Hadley vouches for you. Only one collector in the world – no, say two – know that I found it. One of them had to know; I had to show it to him to make sure it was genuine. The other I'll speak of presently. But I found it."

His dry bones seemed to stiffen. Rampole, who could never understand this ghoulish eagerness to finger and possess original manuscripts or first editions, regarded him curiously.

"I found it," Sir William repeated. "It is the manuscript of a completely unknown story by Edgar Allan Poe. Myself and one other person excepted, nobody except Poe has ever seen it or heard of it . . . Find that hard to believe, do you?" There was a frosty pleasure in his look, and he chuckled without opening his mouth. "Listen. It's happened before with Poe's work, you know. You've heard how the very rare first edition of *The Murders in the rue Morgue* was found in a trash-basket, haven't you? Well, this is better. Much better. I found it – by chance, yes. But it's real. Robertson said so. Ha. *Listen*."

He sat back, his hand moving along the polished table as though he were smoothing down sheets of paper. He resembled less the traditional figure of a collector than a pawnbroker explaining a particularly shrewd stroke of business.

"I've never collected Poe manuscripts. The American societies have a corner on those. But I have a first edition of the *Al Araaf* collection, published by subscription while he was at West Point, and a few copies of the *Southern Literary Messenger* he edited in Baltimore. Well! – I was poking about for odds and ends in the States last September, and I happened to be visiting Dr. Masters, the Philadelphia collector. He suggested that I have a look at the house where Poe lived there, at the corner of Seventh and Spring Garden Streets. I did. I went alone. And a jolly good thing I did.

"It was a mean neighbourhood, dull brick fronts and washing hung in gritty backyards. The house was at the corner of an alley, and I could hear a man in a garage swearing at a back-firing motor. Very little about the house had been changed, except that a door had been knocked through the one next to it and turned the two houses into one. It was unoccupied, too – they were altering it just *then.*

"From the alley I went through a gate in a high board fence, and into a paved yard with a crooked tree growing through the bricks. In the little brick kitchen a glum-looking workman was making some notations on an envelope; there was a noise of hammering from the front room. I excused myself; I said that the house used to be occupied by a writer I had heard of, and I was looking round. He growled to go ahead, and went on ciphering. So I went to the other room. You know the type; small and low-ceilinged; cupboards set flush with the wall, and papered over, on either side of a low black mantelpiece with an arched grate. But – Poe had scribbled there by candlelight, and Virginia plucked at her harp, and Mrs. Clemm placidly peeled potatoes."

Sir William Bitton obviously saw that he had caught his audience, and it was clear from his mannerisms and pauses that he enjoyed telling a story. The scholar, the business man, the mountebank – all these peered out of his bony face and showed in a rather theatrical gesture.

"They were altering the cupboards. The *cupboards,* mind you." He bent forward suddenly. "And again – a jolly good thing they took out the inner framework instead of just putting up plaster-board and papering them out. There was a cloud of dust and mortar in the place. Two workmen were just bumping down the framework, and I saw . . .

"Gentlemen, I went cold and shaky all over. It had been shoved down between the edges of the framework; thin sheets of paper, spotted with damp, and folded twice lengthwise. It was like a revelation, for when I had pushed open the gate, and first saw those workmen altering the house, I thought: *Suppose I were to find* . . . Well, I confess I almost lunged past those men. One of them said, 'What the hell!' and almost dropped the frame. One glance at the handwriting, what I could make out of it, was enough; you know that distinctive curly line beneath the title in Poe's MSS., and the fashioning of the E. A. Poe?

"But I had to be careful. I didn't know the owner of the house; and *he* might know the value of this. If I offered the workmen money to let me have it, I must be careful not to offer too much, or they would grow suspicious and insist on more . . ."

Sir William smiled tightly. "I explained it was something of sentimental interest to a man who bad lived here before. And I said, 'Look here, I'll give you ten dollars for this.' Even at that, they were suspicious; I think they had some idea of buried treasure, or directions for finding it, or something. The ghost of Poe would have enjoyed that." Again that chuckle behind closed teeth. Sir William swept out his arm.

"But they looked over it, and saw that it was only – 'a kind of a story, or some silly damn thing, with long words at the beginning.' I was in agony for fear they would tear the sheets; folded in that fashion, they were very apt to tear without their age and flimsiness. Finally they compromised at twenty dollars, and I took the manuscript away.

"As you may know, the leading authorities on Poe are Professor Hervey Allen of New York and Dr. Robertson of Baltimore. I knew Robertson, and took my find to him. First I made him promise that, no matter what I showed him, he would never mention it to anybody . . ."

Rampole was watching the chief inspector. During the recital Hadley had become – not precisely bored, but restive and impatient, with a frown between his brows.

"But why keep it a secret?" he demanded. "If there were any trouble about your right, you were at least first claimant; you could have bought it. And you'd made what you say is a great discovery. Why not announce it and get the credit?"

Sir William stared at him, and then shook his head. "You don't understand," he replied at length. "And I can't explain. I wanted *no* trouble. I wanted this great thing, a secret between Poe and myself, for *myself.* For nobody else to see unless I chose. *Mine,* can you understand? It would be almost like knowing Poe."

A sort of pale fierceness was in his face; the orator was at loss for words to explain something powerful and intangible, and his hand moved vaguely in the air.

"At any rate – Robertson is a man of honour. He promised, and he will keep his promise, even though he urged me to do as you say, Hadley. But, naturally, I refused . . . Gentlemen, the manuscript was what I thought; it was even better."

"And what was it?" Dr. Fell asked, rather sharply.

Sir William opened his lips, and then hesitated. When he spoke again, it was in a thin, wiry voice from deep down in his throat.

"One moment, gentlemen. It is not that I do not – ah – trust you. Of course not. Ha! But so much I have told openly, to strangers. Excuse me. I prefer to keep my secret a bit longer. Well enough to tell you what it was when you have heard my story of the theft, and decide whether you can help me. Besides, we have taken a great deal of time already."

"*You* have taken it," the chief inspector corrected, placidly. "Well, Doctor?"

There was a curious expression on Dr. Fell's face; not contemptuous, not humorous, not bored, but a mixture of the three. He rolled in his seat, adjusted his eyeglasses, and peered thoughtfully at the knight.

"Suppose you tell us," he suggested, "the facts of the theft, and whom you suspect. You do suspect somebody, don't you?"

Sir William had started to say, "Yes," and closed his mouth. He responded:

"It was taken from my house in Berkeley Square – let me see. This is Monday afternoon. It was taken at some time between Saturday afternoon and Sunday morning. Let me explain.

"Adjoining my bedroom upstairs I have a dressing-room which I use a good deal as a study. The greater part of my collection is, of course, downstairs in the library and my study there. I had been examining the manuscript in my upstairs study on Saturday afternoon . . ."

"Was it locked up?" Hadley inquired. He was interested now.

"No. Nobody – at least, so I thought – knew of it, and I saw no reason for unusual precautions. It was merely in a drawer of my desk, wrapped in tissue paper to preserve it."

"What about the members of your household? Did they know of it?"

Sir William jerked his head down in a sort of bow. "I'm glad you asked that, Hadley. Don't think I shall take umbrage at the suggestion; but I couldn't make it myself. At least – not immediately. Naturally I don't suspect them; ha!"

"Naturally," said the inspector, placidly. "Well?"

"At the present, my household consists of my daughter Sheila . . ."

A faint frown was on Hadley's face. He stared at the table. "As a matter of fact," he said, "I was referring to servants. But proceed."

He looked up, and the calm eyes met the knight's shrewd ones.

". . . of my daughter Sheila," the latter continued, "my brother Lester, and his wife. My nephew by marriage, Philip, has a flat of his own, but he generally eats Sunday dinner with us. That is all – with the exception of one guest. Mr. Julius Arbor, the American collector."

Sir William examined his finger nails. There was a pause.

"As to who knew about it," he resumed, waving a careless hand; "my family knew that I had brought back a valuable manuscript with me, of course. But none of them is in the least interested in such matters, and the mere words, 'another manuscript,' was sufficient explanation. I dare say I may have occasionally let fall hints, as one does in enthusiasm when he is sure nobody will understand. But . . ."

"And Mr. Arbor?"

Sir William said, evenly: "I had intended to show it to him. He has a very fine collection of Poe first editions. But I had not even mentioned it."

"Go on," said Hadley, stolidly.

"As I have said, I was examining the manuscript on Saturday afternoon; fairly early. Later I went to the Tower of London . . ."

"To the Tower of London?"

"A very old friend of mine, General Mason, is deputy governor there. He and his secretary have done some very fine research into the Tower records. They wanted me to see a recently discovered record dealing with Robert Devereux, Earl of Essex, who . . ."

"Quite," said Hadley. "And then?"

"I returned home, dined alone, and afterwards went to the theatre. I did not go into my study then, and after the theatre it was rather late; so I turned in immediately. I discovered the theft on Sunday morning. There was no attempt at burglarious entry at any time; all the windows were locked, and nothing else in the house had been touched. The manuscript was simply missing from the desk drawer."

Hadley pinched at the lobe of his ear. He glanced at Dr. Fell, but the latter was sitting with his chin on his chest, and did not speak.

"Was the drawer locked?" Hadley went on.

"No."

"Your rooms?"

"No."

"I see. What did you do then?"

"I summoned my valet." Sir William's bony fingers rapped flatly on the table; he twisted his long neck, and several times started to speak before he resumed. "And I must confess, Hadley, that I was at first suspicious of him. He was a new man; he had been in my employ only a few months. He had the closest access to my rooms and could prowl as he liked without suspicion. But – well, he seemed too earnest, too dog-like, too thoroughly stupid at anything beyond his immediate duties; and I flatter myself on my ability to judge men."

"Everybody does," Hadley agreed, wearily. "That's why *we* have so much trouble. Well?"

"As it happens, my judgment was correct," snapped Sir William. "My daughter Sheila engaged him. He had been fifteen years in the service of the late Marquess of Sandival; I spoke to Lady Sandival myself, yesterday, and she scoffed at the idea of Marks being a thief . . . As I told you, I was suspicious of him at first. He was obviously upset and tongue-tied, but that was a product of his natural stupidity."

"And his story?"

"He had no story," Sir William said, irritably. "He had noticed nothing suspicious, seen nothing whatever. I had difficulty getting it through his head how important the thing was; even what I was looking for. It was the same thing with the rest of the servants. They had noticed nothing. But I was not unduly suspicious, because they are all old retainers; I know the history of every one."

"What about the members of the – household?"

"My daughter Sheila had been out all Saturday afternoon. When she returned, she was in the house only a short time, and then she went out to dinner with the chap she's engaged to . . . General Mason's secretary, by the way. But," he added, with suspicious haste, "– ah – very well connected, I am told, young Dalrye is.

"What was I saying? Ah, yes. My brother Lester and his wife were visiting friends in the west of England; they only returned on Sunday evening. Philip – Philip Driscoll, my nephew – comes to see us only on Sundays. Consequently, nobody noticed anything suspicious at the time the manuscript could have been stolen."

"And this – Mr. Arbor?"

The other reflected, rubbing his dry hands together meditatively.

"A very fine – ah – specimen of the best Hebrew type," he answered, as though he were examining something for a catalogue. "Reserved, scholarly, a trifle sardonic at times. Quite a young man, I should say; scarcely more than forty – Ah, what were you asking? Mr. Arbor, yes. Unfortunately, *he* was not in a position to observe. An American friend of his had invited him to the country for the week-end. He left on Saturday, and did not return until this morning . . .

That's true, by the way," he added, dropping into normal speech and almost leering across the table; "I phoned up about it."

Rampole thought, "Damn you!" And then he thought: After all, the man has been robbed of his most valued possession; he has a right to suspect outsiders, even grave-faced book-collectors like himself. The thought of these solemn gentlemen scrabbling about like children after a manuscript brought a grin to his face. He suppressed it instantly as he caught Sir William's cold eye.

"– and I definitely don't want scandal," the knight concluded. "That's why I came to you, Hadley. So there it is. Plain, simple, and not a single damned clue."

Hadley nodded. He seemed to be debating something.

"I've brought you in a consulting expert," he said, slowly, nodding towards the doctor. "Dr. Fell has come some little distance as a favour to me. Hence I shall wash my hands of the business, unless you should find the thief and want to prosecute. As I – ah – hardly think you will. But I should like to ask a favour in return."

"A favour?" Sir William repeated, opening his eyes. "Good God! yes, of course! Anything in reason, I mean."

"You spoke of your nephew, Mr. Driscoll . . ."

"Philip? Yes. What about him?"

"– who writes for the newspapers . . ."

"Oh, ah. Yes. At least, he tries to. I've exerted considerable influence to get him a real position on a newspaper. Bah! Between ourselves, the editors tell me he can turn out a good story, but he hasn't any news sense. Harbottle says he would walk through rice an inch deep in front of St. Margaret's and never guess there'd been a wedding. So he's free-lancing. He won't believe what I say. Now if I *were* writing –"

Hadley turned an expressionless face and picked up the newspaper on the table. He was just about to speak when a waiter hurried to his side, glanced at him nervously, and whispered.

"Eh?" said the chief inspector. "Speak louder, man! Yes, that's my name . . . Right. Thanks." He drained his glass and looked sharply at his companions. "That's damned funny. I told them not to get in touch with me unless . . . Excuse me a moment, gentlemen."

"What the matter?" inquired Dr. Fell, rousing himself from some obscure meditation and blinking over his spectacles.

"Phone. Back in a moment."

They were silent as Hadley followed the waiter. In Hadley's look there had been a startled uneasiness which gave Rampole a shock. The American looked at Sir William, who was also staring curiously . . .

He returned in less than two minutes, and Rampole felt something tighten in his throat. The chief inspector did not hurry; he was as quiet and deliberate as ever; but his footfalls sounded louder on the tiled floor, and under the bright lights his face was pale.

Stopping a moment at the bar, he spoke a few words and then returned to the table.

"I've ordered you all a drink," he said, slowly. "A whiskey. It's just three minutes until closing-time, and then we shall have to go. I should appreciate it if you would accompany me."

"Go?" repeated Sir William. "Go where?"

Hadley did not speak until the waiter had brought the drinks and left the table. Then he said, "Good luck!" hastily drank a little whiskey, and set the glass down with care. Again Rampole was conscious of that tightening sense of terror . . .

"Sir William," Hadley went on, looking at the other levelly, "I hope you will prepare yourself for a shock."

"Yes?" said the knight. But he did not pick up his glass.

"We were speaking a moment ago of your nephew, Philip . . ."

"Yes? Well, good God! get on with it! What about him?"

"I am afraid I must tell you that he is dead. He has just been found at the Tower of London. There is reason to believe that he was murdered."

The foot of Sir William's glass rattled on the polished table-top. He did not move; his eyes were fixed steadily and rather glassily on Hadley, and he seemed to have stopped breathing. In the long silence they could hear motor horns hooting in the street outside . . .

A nerve in Sir William's arm kept twitching. He had to take his hand from the glass to keep it from rattling on the table. He said, with an effort:

"I – I have my car here . . ."

"There is also reason to believe," Hadley went on, "that what we thought a practical joke has turned into murder . . . Sir William, your nephew is wearing a golf suit. And on the head of his dead body somebody has put your stolen top-hat."

3
THE BODY AT TRAITORS' GATE

The Tower of London . . .

Over the White Tower flew the banner of the three Norman lions, when William the Conqueror reigned, and above the Thames its ramparts gleamed white with stone quarried at Caen. And on this spot, a thousand years before the Domesday Book, Roman sentinels cried the hours of the night from Divine Julius's Tower.

Richard of the Lion's Heart widened the moat about a squat grey fortress, fourteen acres ringed with the strength of inner and outer ballium walls. Here rode the kings, stiff-kneed in iron and scarlet; amiable Henry, and Edward, Hammer of the Scots; and the cross went before them to Westminster, and the third Edward bent to pick up a lady's garter, and Becket's lonely ghost prowled through St. Thomas's Tower. There were tournaments on Tower Green. There were torches for the feasts in William's hall. Up Water Lane moves now that shadowy company of eight hundred years, in the echo of whose names you can hear arrows sing, and the thud of weighted horses.

A palace, a fortress, a prison. Until Charles Stuart came back from exile it was the home of the kings, and it remains a royal palace today. Bugles sound before Waterloo Barracks, where once the tournaments were held, and you will hear the wheel and stamp of the Guards. In the green places under the trees, a raven comes to sit on a drinking-fountain, and looks across at the spot where men and women with bandaged eyes mounted a few steps to put their heads upon a block.

On certain dull and chilly days there creeps from the Thames a smoky vapour which is not light enough to be called mist nor thick enough to be called fog. The rumble of traffic is muffled on Tower Hill. In the uncertain light, battlements stand up ghostly above the brutish curve of the round-towers; boat whistles hoot and echo mournfully from the river; and the rails of the iron fence round the dry moat become the teeth of a prison. Low-lying under the shoulder of Tower Hill, the few white stones almost startling against dingy grey, these walls show thin slits for windows, and you think upon the unholy things which have gone on inside them. Of the two children smothered by lantern-light, and pale Raleigh walking the ramparts in ruff and feathered hat, and Sir Thomas Overbury racked with poison in the lower room of the Bloody Tower . . .

Rampole had visited the Tower before. He had seen it in the grace of summer, when grass and trees mellow the aisles between the walls. But he could visualize what it would be like now. The imaginings grew on him during that interminable ride in Sir William's car between Piccadilly Circus and the Tower.

When he thought about it afterwards, he knew that those last words Hadley spoke were the most horrible he had ever heard. It was not so much that a man had been found dead at the Tower of London. He had eaten horrors with a wide spoon during those days of the Starberth case in Lincolnshire. But a corpse in a golfing suit, on which some satanic hand had placed the top-hat stolen from Sir William, was a final touch in the hideous. After placing his stolen hats on cab horses, lamp-posts, and stone lions, this madman seemed to have created a corpse so that he could have at last a fitting place to hang his hat. The evil grotesquerie of the situation was enhanced because Rampole had already smiled at the antics of the thief as an undergraduate jest. With his memories of the Tower of London, it seemed an admirable choice of a place wherein to decorate a dead man thus.

The ride was endless. In the West End there had been a fairly light mist, but it thickened as they neared the river, and in Cannon Street it was almost dark. Sir William's chauffeur had to proceed with the utmost care. Hatless, his scarf wound crazily about his throat, strained forward with his hands gripping his knees, Sir William was jammed into the tonneau between Hadley and Dr. Fell. Rampole sat on one of the small seats, watching the dull light fall on the knight's face through the blurred panes of the limousine.

Sir William was breathing heavily . . .

"We'd better talk," Dr. Fell said in a gruff voice. "My dear sir, you will feel better . . . It's murder now, Hadley. Do you still want me?"

"More than ever," said the chief inspector.

Dr. Fell puffed out his cheeks meditatively. He was sitting forward, his hands clasping one cane so that his chin was almost upon them, and the shovel-hat shadowed his face.

"Then if you don't mind, I should like to ask . . . ?"

"Eh?" said Sir William, blankly. "Oh. No, no. Not at all. Carry on." He kept peering ahead into the mist.

The car bumped. Sir William turned and said: "I was very fond of the boy, you see," and then continued to crane his neck ahead.

There was a silence, while the horn honked savagely, and the three figures in the rear seat wove about before Rampole's eyes.

"Quite," said Dr. Fell, gruffly. "What did they tell you over the phone, Hadley?"

"Just that. That the boy was dead; stabbed in some way. And that he wore a golf suit and Sir William's top-hat. It was a relay call from the Yard. Ordinarily, I shouldn't have got the call at all. The matter would have been handled by the local police station, unless they asked the Yard for help or we intervened of our own accord. But in this case . . ."

"Well?"

"I had a feeling. I had a feeling that this damned hat business wasn't sheer sport. I left orders – and got smiled at behind my back for it – that if any further hat antics were discovered, they should be reported to the Yard by the local station, and sent through Sergeant Anders directly to me. There. *That's* what a fool I thought I was." Hadley jerked his head, and stared across at Dr. Fell with vindictive eyes. "But, by God! I told you I wasn't one of those fools who boasted about being a thoroughly practical man . . . And I'll take charge of this case myself."

"That's sensible. But I say, how did the people at the Tower know it was Sir William's hat?"

"I can tell you that," snapped Sir William, rousing himself. "I'm tired of picking up the wrong hat when I go out in the evenings. All top-hats look alike in a row, and initials only confuse you. I have *Bitton* stamped in gold inside the crown of the formal ones, opera hats and silk ones; yes, and bowlers too, for that matter." He was speaking rapidly and confusedly, and his mind was on other things. He seemed to utter what thoughts went through his head without thinking about them at all. "Yes, and come to think of it, *that* was a new hat, too. I bought it when I bought the Homburg, because my other opera hat got its spring broken . . . I'd only worn it once before . . . it was . . ."

He paused, and brushed a hand over blank eyes.

"Ha," he went on, dully. "Odd. That's odd. You said my 'stolen' hat, Hadley. Yes, the top-hat was stolen. That's quite right; how did you know it was the stolen hat they found on Philip?"

Hadley was irritable. "I don't know. They told me over the phone. But they said General Mason discovered the body, and so . . ."

"Ah," muttered Sir William nodding and pinching the bridge of his nose. He seemed dazed by trifles. "Yes. Mason was at the house on Sunday, and I dare say I told him. I . . ."

Dr. Fell leaned forward. In a subdued way he seemed excited.

"So," he said, "it was a new hat, Sir William? A new hat?"

"Yes. I told you."

"An opera hat," Dr. Fell mused, "which you were wearing for the first time . . . When was it stolen?"

"Eh? Oh. Saturday night. When I was coming home from the theatre. We'd turned off Piccadilly into Berkeley Street. It was a muggy night, rather warm, and all the windows of the car were down. Besides, it's rather dark along there . . . What was I saying? Oh, yes. Well, just opposite Lansdowne Passage Simpson slowed down to let some sort of blind man with a tray of pencils, or something, get across the street. Then somebody jumped out of the shadows near the entrance to the passage, thrust his arm into the rear of the car, twitched off my hat, and ran."

"What did you do?"

"Nothing. I was too startled. Just . . . just spluttered, I suppose. What the devil *can* one do when a person . . ."

"Did you chase the man?"

"And look a fool? Good God! no. Rather let him get away."

"So naturally," said Dr. Fell, "you didn't report it. Did you catch a glimpse of the man?"

"No. It was too sudden, I tell you. *Flick*, and it was gone. Ha. Damn him. And now . . . You see," Sir William muttered, hesitantly, turning his head from side to side – "you see . . . Never mind the hat; I'm thinking about Philip. I never treated him as I should. I was as fond of him as a son. But I always acted the Dutch uncle. Kept him on a starvation allowance, always threatened to cut him off, and always told him how worthless he was. I don't know why I did it, but every time I saw that boy I wanted to preach. He had no idea of the value of money. He . . ."

Sir William struck his knee with his fist. He added, in a dull voice:

"Never mind now. He's dead."

The limousine slid among gigantic red houses and street lamps made pale gleams through its windows in a canopy of mist. Emerging from Mark Lane, it swerved round the Monument and descended Tower Hill.

Rampole could see nothing more than a few feet ahead. Lamps winked in smoky twilight, and the immensity which should have been the river was full of short, sharp whistle blasts answered by deeper hootings from a distance. Cart wheels rattled somewhere. When the limousine passed through the gate in the rails surrounding the whole enclosure, Rampole tried to rub the blur from the window to peer out. Vaguely he saw a dry moat paved in white concrete, with a forlorn hockey-net near the middle. The drive swung to the left, past a frame building he remembered as the ticket-office and refreshment-room, and under an arch flanked by low, squat round towers. Just under this arch they were brought up short. A sentry, in the high black shako and grey uniform of the Spur Guard, moved out smartly and crossed his rifle on his breast. The limousine slithered to a halt and Hadley sprang out.

In the dim, ghostly half-light another figure emerged at the sentry's side. It was one of the Yeoman Warders, buttoned up in a short blue cloak and wearing the red-and-blue Beefeater hat. He said:

"Chief Inspector Hadley? . . . Thank you. If you'll follow me, sir . . . ?"

There was a quick, military precision about the whole proceeding which made Rampole shiver. But that, he reflected, was literally what it was. The Yeomen Warders were selected from sergeants of the Army of long and distinguished service, and rank as sergeant-majors with warrant rank. There would be no waste motion.

Hadley asked, shortly: "Who is in charge?"

"The chief warder, sir, under the orders of the deputy governor. These gentlemen . . . ?"

"My associates. This is Sir William Bitton. What has been done?"

The warder looked impassively at Sir William, and back to Hadley.

"The chief warder will explain, sir. The young gentleman's body was discovered by General Mason . . ."

"Where?"

"I believe it was on the steps leading down to Traitors' Gate, sir. You know, of course, that the warders are sworn in as special constables. General Mason suggested that, as – you were a friend of the young gentleman's uncle, we communicate directly with you instead of with the district police station, and deal with the matter ourselves until you arrived."

"Precautions?"

"An order has been issued that no one is to enter or leave the Tower until permission has been given, sir."

"Good! Good! You had better leave instructions to admit the police surgeon and his associates when they arrive."

"Yes, sir." He spoke briefly to the sentry, and led them under the arch of the tower.

A stone bridge led across the moat from this (called the Middle Tower) to another and larger tower, with circular bastions, whose arch formed the entrance to the outer-walls. Grey-black, picked out with whitish stones, these heavy defences ran left and right; but the damp mist was so thick that the entrance was entirely invisible. As he crossed the bridge with Dr. Fell, Hadley and Sir William striding ahead behind the warder, Rampole felt himself shivering once more. It was all at once ancient and modern, with the swift deadliness of both times.

Just under the arch of this next tower, another figure appeared with the same eerie suddenness as the others: a thick, rather short man with a straight back, his hands thrust into the pockets of a dripping water-proof. A soft hat was drawn down on his brows. He came forward, peering, as he heard their muffled footfalls on the road. He peered again in the mist and started slightly.

He said; "Good God, Bitton! How did *you* get here?" Then he hurried up to grasp Sir William's hand.

"Never mind," Sir William answered, stolidly. "Thanks, Mason. Where have you got him?"

The other man looked into his face. He wore a gingery moustache and imperial, drooping with the damp; there were furrows in his dull-coloured face and lines round his hard, bright unwinking eyes. For some moments he regarded Sir William with those unwinking eyes, his head slightly on one side. There were no echoes in this vast place. Only a querulous tug whistled on the Thames.

"Good man!" said the other, releasing his hand. "This is . . . ?"

"Chief Inspector Hadley. Dr. Fell. Mr. Rampole . . . General Mason," explained Sir William, jerking his head. "Where is he, Mason? I want to see him."

General Mason took his arm. "You understand, of course, that we couldn't disturb the body until the police arrived. He's where we found him. That's correct, isn't it, Mr. Hadley?"

"Quite correct, General . . . If you will show us the place . . . ? Thank you. I'm afraid we shall have to leave him there, though, until the police surgeon examines him."

"For God's sake, Mason," Sir William said, in a low voice, "*who* . . . I mean, how did it happen? *Who did it*? It's the insanest . . ."

"I don't know. I only know what we saw. Steady, now! Would you like a drink first?"

"No. No, thanks. I'm all right. How was he killed?"

General Mason drew a hand down hard over his moustache and imperial. It was his only sign of nervousness. He said:

"It appears to be a crossbow bolt, from what I can judge. There's about four inches projecting from his chest, and the point barely came out the other . . . Excuse me. A crossbow bolt. We have some in the armoury. Straight through the heart. Instantaneous death, Bitton. No pain whatever."

"You mean," said the chief inspector, "he was shot . . ."

"Or stabbed with it like a dagger. More likely the latter. Come and look at him, Mr. Hadley; and then take charge of my court" – he nodded towards the tower behind him – "in there. I'm using the Warders' Hall as a . . . what d'ye call it . . . third-degree room."

"What about visitors? They tell me you've given orders nobody is to leave."

"Yes. Fortunately, it's a bad day and there aren't many visitors. Also, fortunately, the fog is very thick down in the well around the steps of Traitors' Gate; I don't think a passer-by would notice him there. So far as I'm aware, nobody knows about it yet. When the visitors try to leave, they are stopped at the gate and told that an accident has happened; we're trying to make them comfortable until you can talk to them . . ." He turned to the warder. "Tell the chief warder to carry on until I return. Find out if Mr. Dalrye has got the names and addresses of all the visitors . . . This way, gentlemen."

Ahead of them the hard road ran arrow-straight. Towards the left, a little distance beyond the long arch beneath which they stood, Rampole could see the murky outlines of another round tower. Joining it, a high wall ran parallel with the road. And Rampole remembered now. This left-hand wall was the defence of the inner fortress roughly, a square within a square. On their right ran the outer wall, giving on the wharf. Thus was formed a lane some twenty-five or thirty feet broad, which stretched the whole length of the enclosure on the riverside. At intervals along the road, pale gas-lamps were strangled in the mist, and Rampole could dimly see the spiky silhouettes of tree branches.

Their footfalls rang in the hollow beneath the walls. On the right gleamed the lighted windows of a little room where post cards were sold; the head and hat of a Yeoman Warder were darkly outlined as he peered out. For perhaps a hundred yards along this road General Mason led them; then he stopped and pointed towards the right.

"St. Thomas's Tower," he said. "And that's the Traitors' Gate under it."

It was full of evil suggestion. The tower itself went almost unnoticed because of the great gateway over which it was built. Traitors' Gate was a long, flattened arch of stone, like the hood of an unholy fireplace in the thick wall. From the level of the road, sixteen broad stone steps led down to the floor of a large paved area which had once been the bed of the Thames. For originally this had been the gateway to the Tower by water; the river had flowed in at a level with the topmost steps, and barges had moved under the arch to their mooring. There were the ancient barriers closed as of old: two heavy gates of oaken timbers and vertical iron bars, with an oaken lattice stretching above them to fill in the arch. Thames-wharf had been built up beyond, and the vast area below was now dry.

It had made a powerful impression on Rampole when he saw it before. And he needed to reconstruct such details from his imagination, for the great arch was blurred with mist. Faintly he could see thc ugly teeth of the spikes on top of the gates, and flickers of white through the lattice. But, beyond the iron fence which guarded the descent, the area below was a smoky well.

General Mason took an electric torch from his pocket, snapped it on, and directed the beam towards the ground. A warder had been standing motionless near the fence; and the General gestured with his light.

"Stand at the gate of the Bloody Tower," he said, "and don't let anybody come near . . . Now, gentlemen. I don't think we need to climb this fence. I've been down once before."

Just before the beam of his flashlight moved down the steps, Rampole felt almost a physical nausea. He was holding tightly to the wet iron railing, and he wanted to shut his eyes or turn away. His chest felt tight and empty, and a small hammer pounded there. Then he saw it . . .

The thing lay with its head near the foot of the stairs, on its right side, and sprawled as though it had rolled down the entire flight of steps. Philip Driscoll wore a suit of heavy tweed, with plus fours, golf stockings, and thick shoes. Originally the suit must have been of a conspicuous light-brown colour, patterned broadly; now it was almost black with wetness. But the watchers scarcely saw these things. As General Mason's light moved along the body, they saw the dull gleam of several inches of steel projecting from the left breast. Apparently the wound had not bled much.

The face was flung up towards them, just as the chest was slightly arched to show the bolt in the heart. White and waxy, the face was, with eyelids nearly closed; it had a stupid, sponged expression which would not have been terrifying at all but for the hat.

The opera hat had not been crushed in the fall. It was much too large for Philip Driscoll; whether it had been jammed on or merely dropped on his head, it came down nearly to his eyes, and flattened out his ears grotesquely. To see the white face turned up, cheek against the stone step, and hat set at a sort of hideous rakish angle over one eye, drew from Sir William a sound which was less a sob than a snarl of fury.

General Mason switched off his light.

"You see?" he said out of the dimness. "If that hat hadn't looked so weird, I shouldn't have taken it off at all, and seen your name inside it . . . Mr. Hadley, do you want to make an examination now, or shall you wait for the police surgeon?"

"Give me your torch, please," the chief inspector requested, brusquely. He snapped on the light again and swung it round. "How did you happen to find him, General?"

"There's more of a story connected with that," the deputy governor replied, "than I can tell you. The prelude to it you can hear from the people who saw him here when he arrived, earlier in the afternoon."

"When was that?"

"The time he arrived? Somewhere about twenty minutes past one, I believe; I wasn't here . . . Dalrye, my secretary, drove me from the middle of town in my car, and we got here at precisely two-thirty. I remember, because I heard the clock at the barracks strike when we were driving under the Byward Tower." He pointed back along the road. "That's the Byward Tower, incidentally; the one where I met you.

"We drove along Water Lane . . . this road . . . and Dalrye let me out at the gate of the Bloody Tower, directly opposite us."

They peered into the gloom. The gate of the Bloody Tower was in the inner ballium wall, facing them across the road. They could see the teeth of the raised portcullis over it, and, beyond, a gravelled road which led up to higher ground.

"My own quarters are in the King's House, inside that wall. I was just inside the gate, and Dalrye was driving off down Water Lane to put the car away, when I remembered that I had to speak to Sir Leonard Haldyne . . ."

"Sir Leonard Haldyne?"

"The Keeper of the Jewel House. He lives on the other side of St. Thomas's Tower. Turn on your light, please; now move it over to the right, just at the side of Traitors' Gate arch . . . There." The misty beam showed a heavy iron-bound door sunk in the thick wall. "That leads to a staircase going up to the oratory, and Sir Leonard's quarters are on the other side.

"By this time, in addition to the fog, it was raining, and I could barely see. I came across Water Lane, and took hold of the railing here in front of the steps to guide me over to the door. What made me look down I don't know. This talk about a sixth sense is damned nonsense, of course, but when you've seen as much death as I have . . . Anyhow, I did glance down. I couldn't see anything clearly, but by what I did see I knew something was wrong. I climbed over the railing, went down cautiously, and struck a match. I found him."

The general's voice was precise, gruff, and dry. He lifted his heavy shoulders.

"What did you do then?"

"It was obviously murder," the general continued, without seeming to notice the question. "A man who stabs himself can't drive a steel bolt through his own chest so far that the point comes out under his shoulder-blade; certainly not such a small and weak person as young Driscoll. And he had clearly been dead for some time . . . the body was growing cold.

"As to his odd behaviour . . . No; you'll hear that from others. I'll tell you simply what *I* did. Young Dalrye was coming back from the garage then, and I hailed him. I didn't tell him who the dead man was. He's engaged to Sheila Bitton, and . . . well, you shall hear. But I told him to send one of the warders for Dr. Benedict . . ."

"Who is that?"

"The chief of staff in charge of the army hospital here. I told Dalrye to go to the White Tower and find Mr. Radburn, the chief warder. He generally finishes his afternoon round at the White Tower at two-thirty. I also told him to leave instructions that nobody was to leave the Tower by any gate. I knew it was a useless precaution, because Driscoll had been dead some time and the murderer had every opportunity for a getaway; but it was the only thing to do."

"Just a moment, General Mason," interposed Hadley. "How many gates are there through the outer walls?"

"Three, not counting the Queen's Gate; nobody could get through *there.* There's the main gate, under the Middle Tower, through which you came. And two more giving on the wharf. They are both in this lane, by the way, some distance farther down."

"Sentries?"

"Naturally. A Spur Guard at every gate, and a warder also. But if you're looking for a description of somebody who went out, I'm afraid it's useless. Thousands of visitors use those gates every day. Some of the warders have a habit of amusing themselves by watching and cataloguing the people who go in and out, but it's been foggy all day and raining part of the time. Unless the murderer is some sort of freak, he had a thousand-to-one chance of having escaped unnoticed."

"Damn!" said Hadley, under his breath. "Go on, General."

"That's about all. Dr. Benedict – he's on his rounds now – confirmed my own diagnosis. He said that Driscoll had been dead at least three-quarters of an hour when I found him, and probably longer. The rest you know."

General Mason hesitated.

"There's a strange, an incredible story concerned with Driscoll's activities here this afternoon. Either the boy went mad, or . . ." another sharp gesture. "I suggest that you look at him, Mr. Hadley; then we can talk more comfortably in the Warders' Hall."

Hadley nodded. He turned to Dr. Fell. "Can you manage the fence?"

Dr. Fell's big bulk had been towering silently in the background, hunched into his cloak like a bandit. Several times General Mason had looked at him sharply. He was obviously wondering about this stout man with the shovel-hat and the wheezy walk; wondering who he was and why he was there; wondering about the small shrewd eyes fixed on him behind eyeglasses on a black ribbon.

"No," said the doctor. "I'm not so spry as all that. But I don't think it's necessary. Carry on; I'll watch from here."

The chief inspector drew on his gloves and climbed the barrier. A luminous circle from his flashlight preceded him down the steps. Again Rampole gripped the rail and watched. Unruffled, sedate in blue overcoat and bowler, Hadley was running his light along the huddled figure.

First he carefully noted the position of the body, and made some sketches and markings in a notebook, with the torch propped under one arm. He flexed the muscles, rolled the body slightly over, and felt at the base of the skull; Philip Driscoll was rolled about like a tailor's dummy. Most meticulously he examined the pavement of the area; then he returned to the few inches of steel projecting from the chest. It had been polished steel, rounded and thin, and it was not notched at the end as in the case of an arrow. Now a film of damp overlay the polish.

Finally Hadley removed the hat. The wet face of the small, dandyish youth was turned full up at them, pitiful and witless. Tight reddish curls were plastered moistly against his forehead. Hadley did not even look at it. But he examined the hat carefully, and brought it up with him as he slowly mounted the stairs.

"Well?" demanded Sir William, in a harsh, thin voice.

Over the fence again, Hadley was silent for a long time. He stood motionless, his light off, slapping the torch with slow beats against his palm. Rampole could not see him well, but he knew that his eyes were roving about the lane.

A fog-horn blew one long blast on the river, and there was a rumbling of chains. Rampole shivered.

Hadley said: "There's one thing your surgeon overlooked, General. There's a contusion at the base of the skull. It could have come either from a blow over the head, or – which is more likely – he got it by being tumbled down those stairs after the murderer stabbed him."

The chief inspector peered about him slowly.

"Suppose he were standing at this rail, or near it, when the murderer struck. The rail is more than waist high and Driscoll is quite small. It's unlikely that even such a terrific blow with that weapon would have knocked him over the rail. Undoubtedly the murderer pitched him over to put him out of sight."

The chief inspector spoke deliberately, and the torch still slapped in measured beats against his palm.

"Still, we mustn't overlook the possibility that the bolt might have been fired instead of being used as a dagger. That's improbable; it's almost insane, on the face of it. If a crossbow is what I think it is, then it's highly unlikely that the murderer went wandering about the Tower of London carrying any such complicated apparatus. Why should he?"

"Well," said Dr. Fell, musingly, "why should he steal hats, for that matter?"

Rampole saw another jerk of General Mason's shoulders, as though he were trying to shake off a cloud of insane contradictions. But he did not speak, and Hadley went on in his imperturbable voice:

"A knife, or the blow of a blackjack in the fog, would have done just as well. And because of the fog – as you say,

General – it's impossible that a marksman could have seen his target very far: certainly not to put a bolt so cleanly through the heart. Finally, there's the hat." He took it from under his arm. "For whatever purpose, the murderer wanted to set his hat on the dead man's head. I think I may take it for granted that Mr. Driscoll wasn't wearing it when he came to the Tower?"

"Naturally not. The Spur Guard and the warder at the Middle Tower, who saw him come in, said he was wearing a cloth cap."

"Which isn't here now," the chief inspector said, thoughtfully. "But tell me, General. You said that so many people are always passing through here . . . how did they happen to notice Driscoll?"

"Because they knew him. At least, that warder had a nodding acquaintance with him; the guard, of course, is always changing. He's quite a frequent visitor. Dalrye has got him out of so many scrapes in the past that Driscoll came to count on him; that was why he was here today. Besides . . . the warder will tell you about it. *I* didn't see him."

"I see. Now, before we go into this matter of the weapon, there's something I want to know . . . To begin with, we must admit this: whether he was shot or stabbed, he was killed very close to these steps. The murderer couldn't walk about here, with all the warders present, carrying a dead body; these steps were made to order for concealment, and they were used. So let's assume the most improbable course. Let's assume (a) that he was shot with a crossbow; (b) that the force of the shot – and it was a very powerful one – knocked him over this rail, or that the murderer later pushed him over; and (c) that subsequently the killer decorated him with Sir William's hat. You see? *Then from where about here could that bolt have been fired*?"

General Mason massaged his imperial. They were peering at the wall across the way, at the gate of the Bloody

Tower just opposite, and the bulk of a higher round tower just beside it. Farther on, straight along the length of Water Lane, Rampole could discern another archway over the continuation of the lane.

"Well . . ." said the general. "Damn it all, man, it could have been fired from anywhere. From this lane, east or west, on either side of Traitors' Gate. From under the gate of the Bloody Tower; that's the most likely direction – a straight line. But it's tommyrot. It's out of the question. You can't go marching about here with a crossbow, as though it were a rifle. What's more, just on the other side of that gate is the entrance to the Wakefield Tower. We admit visitors, and there's always a warder on duty there. Good God! let's be sensible. It couldn't be done."

Hadley nodded placidly.

"I know it couldn't. But, as you say, that's the most likely direction. So what about windows or the top of a wall?"

"Eh?"

"I said, what about windows or roofs? Where could you stand and shoot a bolt from some such place? I shouldn't have asked, but I can't see anything beyond outlines in this fog."

The general stared at him. Then he nodded curtly. There was a hard, jealous, angry parade-ground ring in his voice when he spoke; it made Rampole jump.

"I see. If you're suggesting, Mr. Hadley, that any member of this garrison . . . !"

"I didn't say that, my dear sir," Hadley answered, mildly. "I asked you a perfectly ordinary question."

The general jammed his hands deeper in the pockets of his water-proof. After a moment he turned sharply and pointed to the opposite wall.

"Up there on your left," he said, "in that block of buildings jutting up above the wall proper, you may be able to make out some windows. They are the windows of the

King's House. It is occupied by some of the Yeomen Warders and their families; and by myself, I might add . . . Then the ramparts of the wall overlooking us run straight along to the Bloody Tower. That space is called Raleigh's Walk, and only a rather tall man can see over the rampart at all . . . Raleigh's Walk joins the Bloody Tower, in which there *are* some windows looking down at us. Next to the Bloody Tower on the right, and joined to it, you see that large round tower? That's the Wakefield Tower, where the Crown Jewels are kept. You will find some windows there. You will also – not unnaturally – find two warders on guard. Does that answer your question, sir?"

"Thanks," said the chief inspector; "I'll look into it when the mist clears a bit. If you're ready, gentlemen, I think we can return to the Warders' Hall."

4
INQUISITION

Gently General Mason touched Sir William's arm as they turned away. The latter had not spoken for a long time; he had remained holding to the rail and staring into the dimness of the area; and he did not speak now. He walked quietly at the general's side as they returned.

Still holding the hat under his arm, and propping flashlight against notebook, Hadley made several notations. His heavy, quiet face, with the expressionless dark eyes, was bent close over it in the torch-gleam.

He nodded, and shut up the book.

"To continue, General. About that crossbow bolt. Does it belong here?"

"I have been wondering how long you would take to get to that," the other answered, sharply. "I don't know. I am inquiring. There is a collection of crossbows and a few bolts here; it is in a glass case in the armoury on the second floor of the White Tower. But I am perfectly certain nothing has been stolen from there . . . However, we have a workshop in the Brick Tower, on the other side of the parade-ground, which we use for cleaning and repairing the armour and weapons on display. I've sent for the warder in charge; he should be here now. And he will be able to tell you."

"But *could* one of your display crossbows have been used?"

"Oh yes. They are kept in as careful repair as though we meant to use them as weapons ourselves."

Hadley fell to whistling between his teeth. Then he turned to Dr. Fell.

"For a person who enjoys talking as much as you do, Doctor," he said, "you have been incredibly silent. Have you any ideas?"

A long sniff rumbled in the doctor's nose. "Yes," he returned, "yes, I have. But they don't concern windows or crossbows. They concern hats. Let me have that topper, will you? I shall want to look at it when we get a good light."

Hadley handed it over without a word.

"This," General Mason explained, as they turned to the left at the Byward Tower, "is the smaller Warders' Hall; we have our enforced guests in the other." He pushed open a door under the arch, and motioned to them to pass.

It was not until Rampole entered the warmth of the room that he realised how chilled and stiff he was. A large coal fire crackled under a hooded fireplace. The room was circular and comfortable, with a groined roof from which hung a cluster of electric lights, and cross-slits of windows high up in the wall. There were chairs of hard leather, and bookshelves. Behind a large flat desk, his hands folded upon it, sat a straight-backed elderly man, regarding them from under tufted white eyebrows. He wore the costume of the Yeomen Warders, but his was much more elaborate than those Rampole had seen. Beside him a tall, thin young man with a stoop was making notes on a slip of paper.

"Sit down, gentlemen," said General Mason. "This is Mr. Radburn, the chief warder; and Mr. Dalrye, my secretary."

He waved his guests to chairs after he had performed the introductions, and produced a cigar-case. "What have you got now?"

The chief warder shook his head. He pushed out the chair in which he had been sitting for General Mason.

"Not much, I'm afraid, sir. I've just questioned the guards from the White Tower, and the head workman from the repair shop. Mr. Dalrye has the notes in short-hand."

The young man shuffled some papers and blinked at General Mason. He was still rather pale. And instinctively Rampole liked this Robert Dalrye. He had a long, rather doleful face, but a humorous mouth. His sandy hair bristled at all angles, apparently from a tendency to run his hand through it. His good-humoured, rather near-sighted grey eyes were bitter; he fumbled with a pair of pince-nez on a chain, and then stared down at his papers.

"Good afternoon, sir," he said to Sir William. "They told me you were here. I . . . I can't say anything, can I? You know how I feel."

Then still staring at his papers, he changed the subject with a rush. "I have the notes here, sir," he told General Mason. "Nothing has been stolen from the armoury, of course. And the head workman at the shop, as well as both warders from the second floor of the White Tower, are willing to swear that crossbow bolt is not in the collection and never has been in any collection here."

"Why? You can't positively identify a thing like that, can you?"

"John Brownlow got rather technical about it. And he's by way of being an authority, sir. It's here. He says" – Dalrye adjusted his pince-nez and blinked – "he says it's a much earlier type of bolt than any we have here. That is, judging from what he can see of it . . . in the body. Late fourteenth-century pattern. Ah, here we are. 'The later ones are much shorter and thicker and with a broader barb at the head. That one's so thin it wouldn't fit smoothly in the groove of any crossbow in the lot.'"

General Mason turned to Hadley, who was carefully removing his overcoat. "You're in charge now. So ask any questions you like. Give that chair to the chief inspector . . .

But I think that proves it wasn't fired, unless you believe the murderer brought his own bow. Then it couldn't have been shot from one of the crossbows here, Dalrye?"

"Brownlow says it could have been, but that there would be a hundred-to-one chance of the bolt going wild."

Mason nodded, and regarded the chief inspector with tight-lipped satisfaction. Rampole saw him for the first time in full light. He had removed his soggy hat and water-proof, and flung them on a bench; evidently there was about him none of that fussiness which is associated with the brass-hat. Now he stood warming his hands at the fire, and peering round his shoulder at Hadley: a straight, thick-set figure, rather bald, with ginger moustache and imperial, and a pair of hard, unwinking eyes.

"Well?" he demanded. "What's the first step now?"

Dalrye put down his papers on the table.

"I think you'd better know," he said, speaking between Mason and Sir William. "There are two people here among the visitors who are certain to have an interest in this. They're over with the others in the Warders' Hall. I wish you'd give me instructions, sir. Mrs. Bitton has been raising the devil ever since . . ."

"*Who*?" demanded Sir William. He had been staring at the fire, and he lifted his head suddenly.

"Mrs. Lester Bitton. As I say, she's been . . ."

Sir William rumpled his white pompadour and looked blankly at Mason. "My sister-in-law . . . What on earth would *she* be doing here?"

Hadley had sat down at the desk, and was arranging notebook, pencil, and flashlight in a line with the utmost precision. He glanced up in mild interest.

"Ah," he said, "I'm glad to hear it. It centres our efforts, so to speak. But don't trouble her for the moment, Mr. Dalrye; we can see her presently." He folded his hands and contemplated Sir William, a wrinkle between his brows.

"Why does it surprise you that Mrs. Lester Bitton should be here?"

"Why, *you* know . . ." Sir William began in some perplexity, and broke off. "No. As a matter of fact, you don't know her, do you? Well, she's of the sporting type; you'll see. I say, did you tell her about . . . about Philip, Bob?" He spoke hesitantly.

"I had to," Dalrye answered, grimly.

"What did she say?"

"She said I was mad. Among other things."

Hadley had picked up his pencil, and seemed intent on boring a hole in the desk top with its point. He asked:

"And the second person among the visitors, Mr. Dalrye?"

The other frowned. "It's a Mr. Arbor, Inspector. Julius Arbor. He's rather famous as a book-collector, and I believe he's stopping at Sir William's house."

Sir William raised his head. His eyes grew sharp again, for the first time since he had heard the news of the murder; it was curiously as though the colour had come back into them, like colour into a pale face. His narrow shoulders were a trifle raised, and now they squared.

He said: "Interesting. Damned interesting." And he walked over with a springy step to sit down in a chair near the desk.

"That's better," approved the chief inspector, laying down his pencil. "But for the moment we shan't trouble Mr. Arbor either. I should like to get the complete story of Mr. Driscoll's movements today. You said something, General, about a rather wild tale connected with it."

General Mason turned from the fire.

"Mr. Radburn," he said to the chief warder, "will you send to the King's House for Parker? Parker," he explained, as the other left the room, "is my orderly and general handy-man. He's been with me since the Boer War, and I know he's absolutely reliable . . . Meantime, Dalrye, you might tell the chief inspector about the wild-goose chase?"

Dalrye nodded. He looked suddenly older. Putting a hand over his eyes for a moment, he turned uncertainly to Hadley.

"You see, Inspector," he said, "I didn't know what it meant then, and I don't know now. Except that it was a frame-up of some sort against Phil. Do you mind if I sit down and smoke? . . . Thanks."

His long legs were shaking a trifle as he lowered himself into a chair. He got out a cigarette, and Hadley struck a match for him.

"Take your time, Mr. Dalrye," said the chief inspector. "Sir William – excuse me – has told us you are his daughter's *fiancé*. So I presume you knew young Driscoll well?"

"Very well. I thought a hell of a lot of Phil," Dalrye answered, quietly. He blinked as the smoke got into one eye. "And naturally this business isn't pleasant. Well – you see, he had the idea that I was one of these intensely practical people who can find a way out of any difficulty. He was always getting into scrapes, and always coming to me to help him out of them. Now, I'm not that sort at all. But he was the brooding sort, and any small difficulty seemed like the end of the world; he'd stamp and rave, and swear it was insufferable. You have to understand all this to understand what I'm going to tell you."

"Difficulties?" repeated the chief inspector. He was sitting back in his chair, his eyes half closed, but he was looking at Sir William. "What sort of difficulties?"

Dalrye hesitated. "Financial, as a rule. Nothing important. He'd run up bills, and things like that . . ."

"Women?" asked Hadley, suddenly.

"O, Lord! don't we all?" demanded the other, uncomfortably. "I mean to say . . ." He flushed. "Sorry. But nothing important there, either; I know that. He was always ringing me up in the middle of the night to say he'd met some girl at a dance who was the absolute One and Only. He would rave. It lasted about a month, generally."

"But nothing serious? Excuse me, Mr. Dalrye," said the chief inspector, as the other waved his hand, "but I am looking for a motive for murder, you know. I have to ask such questions. So there was nothing serious?"

"No."

"Please go on. You said that you helped him . . ."

"I was flattered, I suppose. And I liked to feel I was . . . well, helping somebody close to Sheila. We all do, hang it. We like playing the all-wise director of destinies; the Olympian angle. Bah! Anyway, as I say, you've got to understand his nature to understand today."

For a moment Dalrye drew deeply on his cigarette.

"He telephoned here early this morning, and Parker answered the telephone in the general's study. I wasn't up yet, as a matter of fact. He began talking rather incoherently, Parker says, and said they were to tell me he would be down here at the Tower at one o'clock sharp; that he was in bad trouble and needed help. In the middle of it I heard my name mentioned, and came out and talked to him myself.

"I thought it was probably nothing at all, but to humour him I said I should be here. Though, I told him, I had to go out early in the afternoon.

"You see, if it hadn't been for that . . . As it happened, General Mason had asked me to take the touring-car up to a garage in Holborn and have the horn repaired. It's an electric horn, and it got so that if you pressed it you couldn't stop the thing's blowing."

Hadley frowned. "A garage in Holborn? That's rather unnecessarily out of the way, isn't it?"

Again a dull anger was at the back of Mason's eyes. He was standing with his back to the fireplace, legs wide apart; he spoke curtly.

"Quite right, sir. You see it in a moment. But it happens to be run by an old army man; a sergeant, by the way, who did me rather a good turn once . . . I have all my motor repair work done there."

"Ah," said Hadley. "Well, Mr. Dalrye?"

Rampole, leaning against a row of bookshelves with an unlighted cigarette in his fingers, tried again to imagine that all this was real; that he was really being drawn again into the dodges and terrors of a murder case. Undoubtedly it was true. But there was a difference between this affair and the murder of Martin Starberth. He was not, now, vitally concerned in its outcome. Through chance and courtesy he was allowed to be present merely as a witness, detached and unprejudiced, of the lighted playbox where lay a corpse in an opera hat.

It was as bright as a play in the ancient room. There behind the desk sat the patient, watchful chief inspector, with his steel-wire hair and his clipped moustache, indolently folding his hands. On one side of him sat Sir William, his shrewdness glittering again behind impassive eyes; and on the other was the thin, wry-faced Robert Dalrye, staring at his cigarette. Still bristling, General Mason stood with his back to the fire. And in the largest chair over against the fireplace, Dr. Fell had spread himself out – and he was contemplating with an owlish and naïve gaze the opera hat in his hands. He hardly lifted his eyes from the hat; he turned it over and over, wheezing. This taciturnity irritated Rampole. He was used to hearing the doctor roar with a sort of genial wrath, and trample down everybody's opinions before him. No, it was unnatural; it worried the American.

He became aware that Dalrye was speaking, and jerked his thoughts back.

". . . so I didn't think much more about it. That was all, until somewhere about one o'clock, the time Phil said he would be here. The phone rang again, and Parker answered it. It was Phil, asking for me. At least," said Dalrye, squashing out his cigarette suddenly, "it sounded like Phil. I was in the record-room at the time, working on the notes for the general's book, and Parker transferred the call. Phil was more chaotic than he had been in the morning. He said that, for a reason he couldn't explain over the phone he couldn't come to the Tower, but that I had got to come to his flat and see him. He used his old phrase – I'd heard it dozens of times before – that it was a matter of life or death.

"I was annoyed. I said I had work to do, and I damned well wouldn't do it, and that if he wanted to see me he could come down here. Then he swore it really was a matter of life or death. And he said I had to come to Town, anyway; his flat was in Bloomsbury, and I had to take the car to a garage which wasn't very far away; it wouldn't be out of my way if I dropped in. That was perfectly true. I couldn't very well see a way out of it. So I agreed. I even promised to start at once."

Dalrye shifted in his chair. "I'll admit – well, it *did* sound more convincing than the other times. I thought he might really have got himself into a genuine mess this time. So I went."

"Had you any definite reason to believe this?"

"N-no. Yes. Well, make of it what you like." Dalrye's gaze strayed across to the corner, where Dr. Fell was still examining the top-hat with absorbed interest. Dalrye shifted uneasily. "You see, Phil had been in rather high spirits recently. That was why I was so surprised at this change of front. He had been making a play with his stories on this hat-thief thing . . . you know?"

"We have good reason to know," the inspector said. His look had suddenly become one of veiled interest. "Go on, please."

"It was the sort of story he could do admirably. He'd been free-lancing, and he hoped the editor might give him a permanent column. So, as I say, I was astonished when I heard him say what he did. And I remember, I said, 'What's the row, anyway? I thought you were following the hat-thief.' And he said, 'That's just it,' in a sort of queer, horrible voice. 'I've followed it too far. I've stirred up something, and it's got me.'"

Rampole felt a stab of something like fear. From Dalrye's description it was easy to picture the dapper, volatile Driscoll, white-faced, talking wildly into the telephone. The chief inspector leaned forward.

"Yes?" he prompted. "You gathered that Driscoll thought he was in danger from this hat-thief; is that it?"

"Something like that. Naturally, I joked about it. I remember asking, 'What's the matter; are you afraid he'll steal *your* hat?' And he said –"

"Well?"

"'It's not my hat I'm worried about. It's my head.'"

There was a long silence. Then Hadley spoke almost casually:

"So you left the Tower to go to his place. What then?"

"Now comes the odd part of it. I drove up to the garage; it's in Dane Street, High Holborn. The mechanic was busy on a job at the moment. He said he could fix the horn in a few minutes, but I should have to wait until he finished with the car he was working on. So I decided to walk to the flat, and pick up the car later. There was no hurry."

Hadley reached for his notebook. "The address of the flat?"

"Tavistock Chambers, 34, Tavistock Square, W.C. It's number two, on the ground floor . . . Well, when I got there I rang at his door for a long time, and nobody answered. So I went in."

"The door was open?"

"No. But I have a key. You see, the gates of the Tower of London are closed at ten o'clock sharp every night, and the

King himself would have a time getting in after that. So, when I went to a theatre or a dance or something of the sort, I had to have a place to stay the night, and I usually stopped on the couch in Phil's sitting-room . . . Where was I? Oh yes. Well, I sat down to wait for him. I supposed he was at a pub or something. But the fact is . . ."

Dalrye drew a long breath. He put the palm of his hand suddenly down on the table.

"About fifteen minutes or so after I had left the Tower, Phil Driscoll appeared at the general's quarters here and asked for me. Parker naturally said I had gone out in response to his phone message. Then, Parker says, Phil got as pale as death; he began to rave and call Parker mad. He had phoned that morning asking to see me at one o'clock . . . But he swore he had not changed the appointment. He swore he had never telephoned a second time at all."

5
THE SHADOW BY THE RAIL

Hadley stiffened. He laid down the pencil quietly, but there were tight muscles down the line of his jaw. It was silent in the stone room save for the crackle of the fire.

"Just so," he said, quietly, after a pause. "What then?"

"I waited. It was getting foggier, and it had started to rain, and I got impatient. I was cursing Phil and everybody else. Then the phone in the flat rang, and I answered it.

"It was Parker, telling me what I've just told you. He had called once before to get me, but I was at the garage and hadn't arrived. Phil was waiting for me at the Tower, in a hell of a stew. Parker said he wasn't drunk, and I thought somebody had gone mad. But there was nothing to do but return; I had to do that, anyway. I hurried over to get the car, and when I was leaving the garage I met the general . . ."

"You also," inquired Hadley, glancing up, "were in town, General?"

Mason was gloomily regarding his shoes. He looked up with a somewhat satiric expression.

"It would seem so. I had a luncheon engagement, and afterwards I went to the British Museum to pick up some books they had for me. As Dalrye says, it began to rain, so of course there weren't any taxis. And I hate travelling by tube or bus. No privacy. A man's packed in with the herd. Bah! Then I remembered the car would probably be at Stapleman's garage; or, if it weren't, Stapleman would lend me a car to go back in. It's not far away from the Museum, so I started out. And I saw Dalrye in the car, and hailed him . . . I've told you the rest of it. We got here at two-thirty, and found – him."

There was another long silence. Hadley was sitting forward with his elbows on the desk, rubbing his temples with heavy fingers. Then, from the corner, a curious, rumbling, thoughtful voice spoke.

"Was it a very important luncheon engagement, General Mason?" asked Dr. Fell.

The query was startling in its very naïveté, and they all turned to look at him. His round and ruddy face was sunk into his collar, the great white plumed mop of hair straggling over one ear, and Dr. Fell was staring through his glasses at the top-hat in a weirdly cross-eyed fashion. He looked quite vacant.

The general stared. "I don't think I understand, sir."

"Was it by any chance," pursued the doctor, still blankly, "a society of some sort, a board of directors' meeting, a gathering of . . ."

"As a matter of fact," said Mason, "it was." He seemed puzzled, and his hard eyes grew brighter. "The Antiquarians' Society. We meet for lunch on the first Monday of every month. I don't like the crowd. Gaa-a! Sedentary fossils of the worst type. Hit 'em with a feather pillow, and they'd collapse. I only stay in the organization because you get the benefit of their knowledge on a doubtful question. I have to attend the lunch to stay in, but I leave as soon as I can. Sir Leonard Haldyne – the Keeper of the Jewels here – drove me up in his car at noon. He's a soldier, and good company, and he feels as I do about it . . . But wait a bit. Why do you ask?"

"H'mf. Yes." The doctor nodded ponderously. "I suppose your membership in the society is well known?"

"All my friends know of it, if that's what you mean. It seems to amuse them at the Rag."

Hadley nodded slowly, contemplating Dr. Fell. "I begin to see what you're driving at . . . Tell me, General. You and Mr. Dalrye were the only people at the Tower whom young Driscoll knew at all well?"

"Ye-es, I suppose so. I think he'd met Sir Leonard, and he had a nodding acquaintance with a number of the warders, but . . ."

"But you were the only ones he'd be apt to call on, weren't you?"

"Probably."

Dalrye's mouth opened a trifle, and he sat up. Then he sank back into his chair. His fist hammered slowly on the arm.

"I see, sir. You mean, then – you mean the murderer had made certain both General Mason and I were out?"

The doctor spoke in a testy voice, ringing the ferrule of his cane as he hammered it on the floor:

"Of course he did. If you had been here, he'd certainly have been with you. If the general had been here in your absence, he might have been with the general. And the murderer wouldn't have any chance to lure him to a suitable spot in the fog and put an end to him."

Dalrye looked troubled. "All the same," he said, "I'm willing to swear it was really Phil's voice on the phone that second time. My God! man – excuse me, sir!" He swallowed, and as Dr. Fell only beamed blandly he went on with more assurance, "What I mean is, I knew that voice as well as I knew anybody's. And if what you say is true, it couldn't have been Phil's voice at all . . . Besides, how did this person, whoever it was, know that Phil had arranged to meet me down here at one o'clock? And why all the rigmarole about being 'afraid of his head'?"

"Those facts," said Dr. Fell composedly, "may provide us with very admirable clues. Think them over. – By the way, what sort of voice did young Driscoll have?"

"What sort of –? Well . . ." Dalrye hesitated. "The only way to describe it is incoherent. He thought so fast that he ran miles ahead of what he was trying to say. And when he was excited his voice tended to grow high."

Dr. Fell, his head on one side and his eyes half closed, was nodding slowly. He peered up as a knock sounded at the door, and the chief warder entered. He had moved through these events as unruffled as he might have moved on this afternoon round of inspection; a precise, mediaeval figure in blue-and-red uniform, with a long moustache carefully brushed.

"The police surgeon is here, sir," he said, "and several other men from Scotland Yard. Are there any instructions?"

Hadley started to rise, and reconsidered. "No. Just tell them the usual routine, if you please; they'll understand. I want about a dozen pictures of the body, from all angles. Is there any place the body can conveniently be taken for examination?"

"The Bloody Tower, Mr. Radburn," said General Mason. "Use the Princes' Room; that's very suitable. Have you got Parker here?"

"Outside, sir. Have you any instructions about those visitors? They're getting impatient, and . . ."

"In a moment," said Hadley. "Would you mind sending Parker in?" As the chief warder withdrew, he turned to Dalrye. "You have those visitors' names?"

"Yes. And I rather overstepped my rights," said Dalrye. He drew from his wallet a number of sheets of paper torn from a notebook. "I was very solemn about it. I instructed them to write down names, addresses, occupations, and references. If they were foreigners, their length of stay in the United Kingdom, the boat they landed on, and where they intended to go . . . Most of them were obvious tourists, and they got alarmed at the red tape; I don't think there's any harm in them, and they didn't show any fight. Except Mrs. Bitton, that is. And one other woman."

He handed the bundle of sheets to Hadley. The chief inspector glanced up sharply. "One other woman? Who was she?"

"I didn't notice what she wrote, but I remembered her name from the way she acted. Hard-faced party. You see, I had it all very official, to scare 'em into writing the truth. And this woman was wary. She said, 'You're not a notary, are you, young man?' and I was so surprised that I looked at her. Then she said, 'You've got no right to do this, young man. We're not under oath. My name is Larkin, and I'm a respectable widow, and that's all *you* need to know.' I said she could do as she liked, but if she found herself in jug it was no affair of mine. She said, 'Bah!' and glared a bit. But she wrote down something."

Hadley shuffled through the papers.

"Larkin," he repeated. "H'm. We must look into this. When the net goes out, we often get small fish we're not after at all . . . Larkin, Larkin – here it is. 'Mrs. Amanda Georgette Larkin.' The 'Mrs.' in brackets; she wants that clearly understood. Stiff handwriting. Address – Hallo!"

He put down the sheets and frowned. "Well, well! The address is 'Tavistock Chambers, 34, Tavistock Square.' So she lives in the same building as young Driscoll, eh? This is getting to be quite a convention. We'll see her presently. For the moment . . ."

Sir William had been rubbing his jaw uneasily. He said:

"Look here, Hadley, it isn't quite the thing . . . I mean, don't you think you'd better bring Mrs. Bitton away from the crowd? She's my sister-in-law, you know, and after all . . ."

"Most unfortunate," said Hadley, composedly. "Where's that man Parker?"

Parker was a most patient man. He had been standing hatless and coatless in the fog just outside the crack of the door, waiting to be summoned. At Hadley's remark he knocked, came inside, and stood at attention.

He was a square, brownish, grizzled man with a military cut. Like most corporals of his particular day, he ran largely to moustache; nor did he in the least resemble a valet. The high white collar pinioned his head, as though he were having a daguerreotype taken, and gave him a curious expression of seeming to talk over his inquisitor's head.

"Yussir," he said, gruffly and quickly.

"You are General Mason's –" Hadley was going to say "valet," as fitting to a retired commander, but he substituted "orderly." "You are General Mason's orderly?"

Parker looked pleased. "Yussir."

"Mr. Dalrye has already told us of the two phone calls from Mr. Driscoll . . . You answered the phone both times, I believe?"

Parker was ready. His voice was hoarse, but his aspirates under perfect control, and he tended, if anything, to be a trifle flowery. This was an important occasion.

"Yussir. On both occasions I had reason to go to the telephone, sir."

"So you had some conversation with Mr. Driscoll?"

"I did, sir. Our talks was not lengthy, but full of meat."

"Er – quite so," said the chief inspector. "Now could you swear it was Mr. Driscoll's voice both times?"

Parker frowned. "Well, sir, when you say, 'Could you swear it?' – that's a long word," he answered, judicially. "To the best of my knowledge and discernment from previous occasions, sir, it were."

"Very well. Now, Mr. Dalrye left here in the car shortly before one o'clock. Do you remember at what time Mr. Driscoll arrived?"

"One-fifteen, sir."

"How are you so positive?"

"Excuse me, sir," Parker said, stolidly. "I can inform you of everything that happens at the time which it happens, exact, sir, by the movements at the barracks. Or by the bugles. One-fifteen it was."

Hadley leaned back and tapped his fingers slowly on the desk.

"Now, take your time, Parker. I want you to remember everything that happened after Mr. Driscoll arrived. Try to remember conversations, if you can . . . First, what was his manner? Nervous? Upset?"

"Very nervous *and* upset, sir."

"And how was he dressed?"

"Cloth cap, light-brown golf suit, worsted stockings, club tie, sir. No overcoat . . ." He paused for prompting, but Hadley was silent and he went on: "He asked for Mr. Dalrye. I said Mr. Dalrye had gone to his rooms in response to his own message. He then demonstrated incredulity. He used strong language, at which I was forced to say, 'Mr. Driscoll, sir,' I said, 'I talked to you myself.' I said, 'When I answered the telephone you thought I was Mr. Dalrye; and you said all in a rush, "Look here, you've got to help me out – I can't come down now, and –" That's what you said.'" Parker cleared his throat. "I explained that to him, sir."

"What did he say?"

"He said, 'How long has Mr. Dalrye been gone?' I told him about fifteen minutes. And he said, 'Was he in the car?' and I said 'Yes,' and he said – excuse me, sir – 'Oh, my God! that's not long enough to drive up there on a foggy day.' But, anyway, he went to the telephone and rang up his own flat. There was no answer. He said to get him a drink, which I did. And while I was getting it I noticed that he kept looking out of the window . . ."

Hadley opened his half-closed eyes. "Window? What window?"

"The window of the little room where Mr. Dalrye works, sir, in the east wing of the King's House."

"What can you see from there?"

Parker, who had become so interested in his story that he forgot to be flowery, blinked and tried to right his thoughts "*See*, sir?"

"Yes! The view. Can you see the Traitors' Gate, for instance?"

"Oh. Yussir! I thought you was referring to . . . well, sir, to something *I* saw, which I didn't think was important, but now I get to thinking . . ." He shifted from one foot to the other.

"*You* saw something?"

"Yussir. That is, it was after Mr. Driscoll had left me, sir."

Hadley seemed to fight down a desire to probe hard. He had half-risen, but he sat back and said, evenly: "Very well. Now go on with the story, Parker, from the time you saw Mr. Driscoll looking out of the window."

"Very good, sir. He finished his drink, and had another neat. I asked him why he didn't go back to his flat, if he wanted to see Mr. Dalrye; I said he could take the tube at Mark Lane and it wouldn't be a very long ride. And he said, 'Don't be a fool; I don't want to take the chance of missing him again.' Which was sound sense, sir. He said, 'We'll keep ringing my place every five minutes until I know where he is.'"

Parker recounted the conversations in a gruff, sing-song voice, and in such a monotone that Rampole could tell only with difficulty where he was quoting Driscoll and where he spoke himself. The words were thrown steadily over Hadley's head.

"But he could not sit still, sir. He roamed about. Finally he said: 'My-God-I-can't-stand-this; I'm going for a walk in the grounds.' He instructed me to keep ringing his flat after Mr. Dalrye, and that he would keep close within call. So he went out."

"How long was he with you?"

"A matter of ten minutes, say, sir. No; it was less than that . . . Well, sir, I paid no more attention. I should not have seen anything, except . . ." Parker hesitated. He saw the veiled gleam in Hadley's eyes; he saw Sir William bent forward, and Dalrye pausing with a match almost to his cigarette. And he seemed to realize he was a person of importance. He gave the hush its full value.

". . . except, sir," he suddenly continued in a louder voice, "for the match-in-ashuns of fate. I may remark, sir, that earlier in the day there had been a light mist. But nothing of what might be termed important. It was possible to see some distance, and objects was distinct. But it was a-growing very misty. That was how I come to look out of the window. And that was when I saw Mr. Driscoll."

Hadley's fingers stopped tapping while he scrutinized the other. Then they began to tap again, more rapidly.

"How did you know it was Mr. Driscoll? You said the mist was thickening

"So it were. Yussir!" agreed Parker, nodding so vigorously that the points of his collar jabbed his neck. "I didn't say I saw his face. Nobody could have recognized him that way: he were just an outline. *But,* sir, wait! There was his size. There was his plus-fours, which he alwis wore lower-down than other gentlemen. And when he went out he was a-wearing his cap with the top all pulled over to one side. Then I saw him walking back and forth in Water Lane in front of the Traitors' Gate, back and forth, and I knew his walk . . ."

"But you can't swear it was actually he?"

"Yussir. I can. Becos, sir, he went to the rail in front of Traitors' Gate and leaned on it. And whereupon he struck a match to light a cigarette. And – mind you, sir, if you'll excuse me – not another man here has the eyesight *I* have, and just for a second I saw part of the face. It was one of them big sputtering matches, sir, if you know what I mean. Yussir, I'm positive. I know. I saw 'im just before the other person touched 'im on the arm.

"*What*?" demanded Hadley, with such suddenness that Parker took it for a slur on his veracity.

"Sir, so help me God. The other person that was standing over by the side of Traitors' Gate. And that come out and touched Mr. Driscoll on the arm. Mind, sir, I'm not sure of that, becos the match was out. But it looked as though –"

"I see," Hadley agreed, mildly. "Did you see this other person, Parker?"

"No sir. It was too dark there; shadowed, sir. I shouldn't even have seen Mr. Driscoll if I hadn't been watching him and saw 'im strike the match. It were what I should call a Shape."

"Could you tell whether this person was a man or a woman?"

"Er – no, sir. No. Besides," explained Parker, drawing in his neck again, "it were not in any manner of speaking as though I was *watching*, sir. I turned away then. I was not endowed with the opportunity to see no further occurrences."

"Quite. Do you know at what time this was?"

Parker screwed his face up into a grimace which was evidently regret. "Ah!" he said profoundly, "ah, I confess you've got me, sir. You see, it transpired between the quarter-hours of the clock. It were shortly past one-thirty. More I couldn't tell you, not if I wanted to, sir. Except I know it were not so late as a quarter to two. Becos that was when I phoned Mr. Driscoll's flat again and Mr. Dalrye had arrived there, and I told him Mr. Driscoll was here a-waiting."

Hadley brooded, his head in his hands. After a time he looked across at General Mason.

"And the doctor here said, General, that when you discovered the body at two-thirty Driscoll had been dead at least half an hour – probably three-quarters? Yes. Well, that's that. He was murdered within ten minutes or fifteen minutes after this so-called Shape touched his arm at the rail. The police surgeon will be able to tell us exactly. He's rather a wizard at that sort of thing."

He paused, and looked sharply at Parker.

"You didn't notice anything more, did you? That is, you didn't go to look for Mr. Driscoll, to tell him you'd found Mr. Dalrye?"

"No, sir. I knew he would come back and ask me, if he was that impatient, and, anyway, Mr. Dalrye was a-coming down here. Though he swore some. I thought it was funny Mr. Driscoll not coming up to ask, sir. Of course," Parker said, deprecatingly, "I can comprehend at the present juncture why he didn't."

"I think we all can," said the chief inspector, grimly. "Very well, Parker. That's all, and thank you. You've been most helpful."

Parker clicked his heels and went out glowing.

The chief inspector drew a long breath. "Well, gentlemen, there you are. That fixes us. The murderer had considerably over half an hour's time to clear out. And, as the general says, what between rain and fog the sentries at the gates wouldn't have been able to see anything of a person who slipped out. Now we get down to work. Our first hope . . ."

He picked up the sheets containing the names of the visitors.

"Since we have something to go on," he continued, "we can use our guests. We know the approximate time of the murder. Hallo!" he called towards the door, and a warder opened it. "Will you go down to the Bloody Tower and send up the sergeant in charge of the police officers who have just arrived? . . . Thanks."

"I hope it's Hamper," he added to his companions. "It probably is, too. First, we'll put aside the slips made out by the three people we want to interview ourselves – Mrs. Bitton, Mr. Arbor, and, just as a precaution, the careful Mrs. Larkin. Let's see, Larkin –"

"Mrs. Bitton didn't make out any, sir," Dalrye told him. "She laughed at the idea."

"Right, then. Here's the Arbor one. Let's see. I say, that's a beautiful handwriting; like the lettering on a calling-card. Fastidious, this chap." He examined the paper curiously. " 'Julius Arbor. 440 Park Avenue, New York City. No occupation . . .'"

"Doesn't need one," Sir William growled. "He's got pots."

"'Arrived Southampton, March 4th, S.S. *Bremen*. Duration of stay indefinite. Destination, Villa Seule, Nice, France.' He adds, very curtly, 'If further information is necessary, suggest communicating with my London solicitors, Messrs. Hillton and Dane, Lincoln's Inn Fields.' H'm."

He smiled to himself, put the sheet aside, and glanced hastily at the others.

"If you've ever heard any of these other names, gentlemen, sing out; otherwise I'll let the sergeant handle them.

"Mr. and Mrs. George G. Bebber, 291 Aylesborough Avenue, Pittsburgh, Pa., U.S.A. – Jno. Simms, High Street, Glytton, Hants. He adds, 'Of the well-known plumbers, as above.' – Mr. and Mrs. John Smith, Surbiton. Well, well! That's descriptive enough. – Lucien Lefèvre, 60 Avenue Foch, Paris. Mlle Clémentine Lefèvre, as above. – Miss Dorothea Delevan Mercenay, 23 Elm Avenue, Meadville, Ohio, U.S.A. Miss Mercenay adds *M.A.* to her name, underscored heavily. That's the lot. They sound harmless enough."

"Sergeant Betts, sir," said a voice at the door. A very serious-faced young man saluted nervously. He had obviously expected an inspector, and the presence of the chief was disturbing.

"Betts," said Hadley. "Betts . . . oh yes. Did you get a picture of the dead man's face?"

"Yes, sir. They've set up the outfit in that Tower place, and the pictures are drying now. Ready in two seconds, sir."

"Right. Take a copy of that picture and show it to all the people listed here; the warder will show you where they are. Ask them if they saw him today; when and where. Be particular about *anybody* they may have seen in the vicinity of the Traitors' Gate at any time, or anybody acting suspiciously. Mr. Dalrye, I should be obliged if you would go along and make shorthand notes of anything important. Thanks. And . . ."

Dalrye rose, reaching for pencil and notebook.

"I want particularly to know, Betts, where they were between one-thirty and one-forty-five o'clock. That's vital. Mr. Dalrye, will you kindly ask Mrs. Lester Bitton to step in here?"

6
THE SOUVENIR CROSSBOW BOLT

"Now, then," Hadley pursued. Again with meticulous attention he straightened the pencil, the notebook, and the flashlight before him. "The police surgeon will bring in the contents of Driscoll's pockets, and we can have a good look at the weapon. I'll leave it up to the chief warder to take charge of questioning the warders about whether they saw anything. How many warders are there altogether, General?"

"Forty."

"H'm. It's unlikely that Driscoll would have strayed far from the vicinity of the King's House; he was waiting for that phone call. Still, we shall have to go through with it."

General Mason bit off the end of a cigar. "If you're going to question the whole personnel of the Tower," he observed, "that's the least of your worries. There is a battalion of the Guards stationed here, you know, to say nothing of workmen and attendants and servants."

"If necessary," Hadley answered, placidly, "we'll do it. Now, gentlemen. Before we see Mrs. Bitton, suppose we try to clarify our ideas. Let's go around the circle here, and see what we all have to say. Sir William, what strikes *you* about the case?"

He addressed the knight, but out of the corner of his eye he was looking at Dr. Fell. The doctor, Rampole noted, again with vague irritation, was otherwise occupied. A large, damp, shaggy Airedale, with affectionate eyes and a manner as naïve as the doctor's, had wandered into the room and bounded instantly for Dr. Fell. The Airedale was sitting up, ears cocked expectantly, while the doctor bent over to ruffle his head.

Rampole tried to collect muddled thoughts. He was here purely by chance, and he had somehow to justify his presence. When Hadley again mentioned the weapon a moment ago, it stirred some question which had been at the back of his brain since Dalrye had read out the warder's description of the type of crossbow bolt with which Driscoll was slain. He saw once more the thin, polished steel protruding from the dead man's chest, and the question in his mind grew sharper. He was not sure he could explain it . . .

Sir William was speaking now. His face was still dull, but the deadness of shock was beginning to pass from it. Before long he would be again his sharp, jerky, impetuous self.

"That's easy," he said, twisting the ends of his white scarf. "You can't miss it. It's the absolute lack of motive. Nobody in the world had the slightest reason for killing Philip. If there was anything you *could* safely say about him, it was that everybody liked him."

"Yes. But you're forgetting one thing," Hadley pointed out. "We're dealing in some fashion with a madman. It's useless to deny that this hat-thief is mixed up in it. Whether he killed Philip Driscoll or not, he seems to have put that hat on his head. Now, from what Dalrye said, it's clear that Driscoll was on the hat-man's track pretty closely . . ."

"But, good God, man! You can't seriously suggest that this fellow killed Philip because Philip found out who he was! That's absurd."

"Quite. But worth looking into. Therefore, what's our obvious move?"

Sir William's hooded eyelids dropped. "I see. Philip was turning in regular copy to his newspaper. One of his articles appeared today, in the morning edition. That means he turned it in last night. And if he went to the office, he may have told his editor something . . . ?"

"Precisely. That's our first line of inquiry. If by any wild chance his agitation today was caused by some sort of threat, it would probably have been sent *to* the office; or at least he might have mentioned it there. It's worth trying."

There was a deep, delighted chuckle. Hadley looked up in some annoyance, to see Dr. Fell stroking the dog's head and beaming at him with one eye closed.

"Rubbish," said Dr. Fell.

"Indeed?" said the chief inspector, with heavy politeness. "Would you mind telling us why?"

The doctor made a capacious gesture. "Hadley, you know your own game, Heaven knows. But you don't know the newspaper business. I, for my sins, do. Did you ever hear the story of the cub reporter whose first assignment was to cover a big Pacifist meeting in the West End? Well, he came back with a doleful face. 'Where's your story?' says the city editor. 'I couldn't get one,' says the cub; 'there wasn't any meeting.' 'No meeting?' says the city editor. 'Why not?' 'Well,' says the cub, 'the first speaker had no sooner got started than somebody threw a brick at him. And then Lord Dinwiddie fell through the bass drum, and a fight started all around the platform, and they began hitting each other over the head with the chairs, and when I saw the Black Maria at the door I knew there wouldn't be any more meeting, so I left.'"

Dr. Fell shook his head sadly. "That's the sort of picture you're drawing, Hadley. Man, don't you see that if Driscoll had found out anything, or particularly been threatened, it would have been NEWS? News in capitals. 'HAT-FIEND THREATENS *DAILY SOMETHING* MAN.' Certainly he'd have mentioned it at the office; he was trying desperately to get on the staff, wasn't he? And the stupidest cub in Fleet Street wouldn't have passed up such an opportunity. Rest assured you'd have seen it today on the first page."

"He mightn't," Hadley said, irritably, "if he had been as nervous as he seems to have been. He'd have kept it to himself."

"Wait a bit. You're wrong there," put in Sir William. "Give the boy his due. Whatever he was, he wasn't a coward. His upsets never came because he feared any sort of violence; he was only upset over – well, messes, as you've heard."

"But he said . . ."

"That isn't the point, you see," Dr. Fell said, patiently. "To publish anything of the sort couldn't have done any harm. They might say they'd found a vital clue, or that there had been a threat. The first would only warn their victim. The second would have been more publicity, which the hat-fellow wanted in the first place; look at the way he acts. It would have done no harm, and assuredly it would have helped young Driscoll's job."

"Suppose he'd actually found out who the man was, though?"

"Why, the newspaper would have communicated with the police, and Driscoll would have got the credit and more assignments. Do you seriously think anybody would have been afraid, at the time, of a person who seemed to be a mere genial practical joker? – No, no. You're letting the hat on the corpse run away with your own sense of humour. It's unbalanced you. There's another explanation, I think. I'm willing to agree with Sir William's statement that the boy wasn't a coward; but what was it he *did* fear? There's a tip. Think it over."

Grunting, he returned his attention to the dog.

"I have something to say to you in a moment," the chief inspector told him. "But, for the moment, let's continue. Have *you* any suggestions, General?"

General Mason had been smoking glumly. He took the cigar out of his mouth and shook his head.

"None whatever. Except that it's fairly obvious now he was stabbed and not shot with that bolt. That's what I'd thought all along."

"Mr. Rampole?" Hadley saw that the American was ill at ease, and he raised his eyebrows encouragingly. "You've said nothing at all so far, which is wise. Any ideas?"

Three pairs of eyes were fixed on him, and he tried to be casual under the scrutiny. This might be the test as to whether he heard anything more of the case after today. He couldn't keep shoving his ideas at them like a cocksure schoolboy; and when he was asked for them, he had to talk sense.

"There was something," he said, feeling his voice a trifle unsteady. "Though it's probably not important. It's this. The crossbow bolt didn't come from the collection here and one of the warders said its pattern was late fourteenth century. Now, it isn't probable, is it, that Driscoll was really killed with a steel bolt made in thirteen hundred and something?" He hesitated. "I used to dabble a bit with arms and armour; one of the finest collections in the world is at the Metropolitan Museum in New York. In a bolt so old as that one, the steel would be far gone in corrosion. Would it be possible to get that bright polish and temper of the one used to kill Driscoll? It looks *new,* and not thinned at all. If I remember correctly, you have no arms exhibits here previous to the fifteenth century. And even your early-fifteenth-century helmets are worn to a sort of rusty shell."

There was a silence. "I begin to see," nodded the chief inspector. "You mean that the bolt is of recent manufacture. And if it is . . . ?"

"Well, sir, if it is, who made it? Certainly there aren't many smiths turning out crossbow bolts of fourteenth-century pattern. It may be a curio of some kind or there may be somebody who does it for amusement or for decorative purposes. I don't suppose it was made here?"

"By Gad!" General Mason said, softly, "I believe he's got something . . . No. No, young man, I'm pretty sure it wasn't made here, or they'd have mentioned it."

Hadley made a note in his black book. "It's a long shot," he remarked, shaking his head, "but undoubtedly there's something in it. Good work! Now we come to my usually garrulous colleague, Dr. Fell. For Lord's sake," he snapped, in exasperation, "let that damned dog alone, will you, and try to pay some attention? What are your erudite comments on the testimony we've heard?"

Dr. Fell cocked his head on one side. He seemed to meditate.

"The testimony," he repeated, as though he were coming upon a new angle of the case. "Ah yes. The testimony. Why, I'm afraid I wasn't paying a great deal of attention to it. However, I do want to ask one question."

"That's gratifying. What is it?"

"This hat." He picked up the topper and flourished it. "I suppose you noticed. When it was put on the boy's head, it slid down over his ears like the bowler on a Hebrew comedian in a comedy. Of course, he's very small, Sir William, and you're tall. But you have rather a long and narrow head. Wasn't it too large even for you?"

"Too . . ." The other looked bewildered. "Why, no! No, it wasn't too large. Hold on, though. I remember now. When I was trying on hats at the shop, I remember *one* I tried on, among others, was too large. But the one they sent me was quite all right: a good fit."

"Well, would you mind putting this one on?"

Sir William sat back. For a moment he seemed about to stretch out his hand, as General Mason took the hat from Dr. Fell and passed it across. Then he sat rigid.

"You'll have to excuse me," he said through his teeth. "I – sorry, but I can't do it."

"Well, well, it's of no consequence," Dr. Fell said, genially. He took back the hat, pressed it down so that it collapsed, and fanned his ruddy face with it. "Not for the moment, anyhow. Who are your hatters?"

"Steele's, in Regent Street. Why?"

"Mrs. Lester Bitton," said a voice at the door. The warder on guard pushed it open.

Mrs. Bitton was not backward. She came into the room with an assurance which betokened a free stride, and she radiated energy. Mrs. Bitton was a slim woman in the late twenties, with a sturdy, well-shaped figure like a swimmer's. If on close observation she was not exactly pretty, health and vigour made her seem so. Even in winter she seemed to have a suspicion of tan; she had level, rather shining brown eyes, a straight nose, and a humorous but determined mouth. Her light-brown hair was caught under the tilt of a tight blue hat; beneath a broad fur collar the tight-fitting coat showed off her full breasts and rather voluptuous hips . . . As she caught sight of Sir William she became less assured. The level eyes grew sombre.

"Hallo!" she said. The voice was quick and self-determined. "Bob didn't tell me you were here. I'm sorry you got here so soon." She studied him, and added, with complete seriousness: "You're not built for this sort of thing nowadays. It's bad for you. You ought to take it easy."

Sir William performed the introductions, and sat down again with the air of one who says, "You see? These modern women . . . !" Rampole set out a chair for her beside Hadley's desk. She sat down, subjected them all to an inspection, took a cigarette out of her purse, and lit it before anybody could offer her a match.

"So you're Mr. Hadley," she observed, studying him with her head slightly back. Then she looked at Sir William.

"I've heard Will speak of you." Once more she made a cool inspection of everybody in the room, finally craning round the better to see Dr. Fell. "And these are your inspectors or something. I'm afraid I kicked up rather a row across the way. It was stuffy in there, and some impossible woman kept talking to me. But then I didn't know. Even when Bob told me . . . told me it was Phil, I didn't believe him."

Despite her assurance Rampole got a definite impression that she was nervous and that she had made this strong initial rush to carry her over some sort of barrier. She knocked some ashes on the floor, and kept tapping her cigarette over it afterwards.

Hadley was impassive. "You know the circumstances, Mrs. Bitton?"

"What Bob was able to tell me. Poor Phil! I'd like to . . ." She paused, seeming to meditate punishments for a murderer, and jerked her hand to dislodge non-existent ashes from the cigarette. "Of course it was absurd asking me to fill out that silly paper. As though *I* had to explain."

"It was merely a matter of form. However, you understand that all the people who were here near the time of the tragedy must be questioned. We brought you here first," Hadley smiled, "because we wanted to get the routine business over with as soon as possible."

"Of course I understand that. I've read detective stories." She looked at him sharply. "When was Phil killed?"

"We'll come to that in a moment, Mrs. Bitton." Hadley smiled and made an urbane gesture. "Let's get things in order, if you don't mind . . . To begin with, I dare say this isn't the first time you've visited the Tower? Naturally, you're interested in the – er – historic treasures of the place?"

A rather humorous look crept into her face. "*That's* a gentleman's way of asking me my business," she approved. The eyes wandered to Sir William. "I imagine Will has already told you about me. He thinks I haven't any interest in musty ruins and things like that."

General Mason was stung. The word "ruins" had shocked him. He took the cigar out of his mouth.

"Madam," he interposed, warmly, "if you will excuse my reminding you . . ."

"Certainly," she agreed, with a bright smile, and looked back at Hadley. "However, that's not true. I *do* like them. I like to think about those people in armour, and the tournaments and things, and fights; provided nobody tries to give me a lot of dates or tell me what happened in them. I can't tell one king from another, and why should I? That's all out of date, as Lester says. But I was going to tell you why I was here. It wasn't the Tower, exactly. It was the walk."

"The walk?"

"I'm afraid, Mr. Hadley," she observed, critically, and took a cool survey of him, "that you don't walk enough. Good for you. Keeps you fit. Lester is getting a paunch; that's why I take him on walking tours as often as he'll let me. We just came back yesterday from a walking trip in the West Country. So today I decided to walk from Berkeley Square to the Tower of London."

Now she had succeeded in stinging Hadley, and she seemed unconscious of it. But the chief inspector only nodded.

"Of course I couldn't persuade Lester to come along. Lester is a Conservative. He is always upset over the state of the country. Every morning he looks at the newspaper, says, 'O my God,' and broods all day until he has his liver-trouble. I had him on a walking tour in the south of France last summer, and he was grousing about it every minute . . . So I came down here alone. And then I thought, 'So long as I'm here, I might as well look at the place.'"

She explained this carefully, almost querulously, and straightened her supple body in the chair.

"I see. Do you remember what time you arrived?"

"'M. I'm not sure. Is it important?"

"I should appreciate an answer, Mrs. Bitton."

She stiffened. "One o'clock or some time afterwards, I fancy. I had a sandwich in the refreshment-room up by the gate. That was where I bought the tickets for the towers; three of 'em. A white one, a pink one, and a green one."

Hadley glanced at General Mason. The latter said:

"For the White Tower, the Bloody Tower, and the Crown Jewels. There's an admission fee for those."

"'M, yes. Did you use these tickets, Mrs. Bitton?"

She held the cigarette motionless before her lips. For a moment, the movement of her full breast was quicker. Then her lip curled slightly. Hadley had remained impassive, but he had picked up his pencil.

"I had a look at the Crown Jewels," she replied, with an expression of candour. "I didn't think they were so" – she searched her memory – "so hot. They looked like glass to me. And I'll bet they're not real, either."

General Mason's face had assumed a brickish hue, and a strangled noise issued from him. Then he controlled himself and went on smoking in vicious puffs.

"May I ask why you didn't use the other tickets, Mrs. Bitton?"

"O Lord, how should I know? I didn't feel like it, I suppose; I changed my mind." She slid her body about in the chair, seeming to have lost interest. But her eyes looked strained. "I did wander about a bit in that inner courtyard up there . . . where the big stone buildings are, and the ravens. I liked the look of the soldiers. And I talked to one nice old Beefeater . . ."

This time General Mason did speak. He said, with cold courtesy:

"Madam, may I request you not to use that word? The guards at the Tower are called Yeomen Warders, not Beefeaters. The term is applied . . ."

Mrs. Bitton seemed to catch rather eagerly at the correction.

"I'm sorry. Of course I didn't know. You hear people talk, that's all. I pointed to that place where the stone slab is, where it says they used to chop people's heads off, you know and I asked the Bee . . . the man, 'Is that where Queen Elizabeth was executed?' And he nearly fainted. He cleared his throat a couple of times, and said, 'Madam . . . er . . . Queen Elizabeth had not the honour to be . . . ah . . . I mean, Queen Elizabeth died in her bed.' And then he reeled off a list of people who got their heads chopped off there; and I said, 'What did she die of?' and he said, 'Who, ma'am?' and I said, 'Queen Elizabeth,' and he made a sort of funny noise."

"They'll get their reward in heaven," General Mason said gloomily.

Hadley was not impressed. "Please keep to the subject, Mrs. Bitton. When did you leave?"

"My dear man, I don't carry a watch. But I know that I came down from the parade-ground under the arch of that big place called the Bloody Tower. And I saw a group of people standing over by the rail around these steps, and there was a Beefeater who asked me if I would mind going on. So I suppose it was after you found . . . Phil. Anyway, when I got to the front gate they wouldn't let me out. And that's all *I* know."

"Did you run into Mr. Driscoll at any time?"

"No. Naturally, I didn't know he was there."

Hadley absently tapped his fingers on the desk for some time. He resumed suddenly: "Now, Mrs. Bitton, according to your own statement you arrived here in the vicinity of one o'clock . . ."

"Sorry. I told you I didn't know *what* time it was."

"But it was shortly after one?"

"Perhaps. I may have been mistaken."

"The body was discovered at two-thirty, and of course you started to leave after that time, or you wouldn't be here. So you spent all that time looking at the Crown Jewels and wandering about the parade-ground in the fog? Is that correct?"

She laughed. Her cigarette had burnt down to her fingers, and she jumped a little as she felt the fire. Dropping it on the floor, she regarded Hadley with some defiance. But she was not so cool as before.

"I hope you don't think I'm afraid of a bit of mist or rain? That belongs in the days of Mr. Gladstone, you know. It's comical. Yes, I suppose that's what I must have done . . . Good Lord! you surely don't think *I* had anything to do with killing Phil, do you?"

"It is my duty to ask these questions, Mrs. Bitton. Since you carried no watch, I suppose you do not know whether you were anywhere near the Traitors' Gate between half-past one and a quarter to two?"

She crossed one silk-clad leg over the other and frowned. "The Traitors' Gate," she repeated. "Let's see. Which one is that?"

Hadley nodded towards her handbag. "May I ask what you have there, under the strap on the other side of your bag? Folded over, I mean; a greenish pamphlet of some sort?"

"It's . . . I say, I'd forgotten all about it! It's a guide to the Tower of London. I bought it for twopence at the ticket-window."

"Were you anywhere near the Traitors' Gate between half-past one and a quarter to two, Mrs. Bitton?"

She took out another cigarette, lighted it with a sweep of the match against the table, and regarded him with cold anger.

"Thanks for repeating the question," she returned. "It's most considerate. If by the Traitors' Gate you mean the one where Phil was found, as I assume you do, the answer is No. I was not near it at any time except when I passed it going in and coming out."

Hadley grinned. It was a placid, slow, homely grin, and it made his face almost genial. The woman's face had hardened, and there was a strained look about her eyes; but she caught the grin, and suddenly laughed.

"All right. *Touché.* But I'm hanged if I let you pull my leg again, Mr. Hadley. I thought you meant it."

"You're . . . ah . . . impulsive, Laura," Sir William put in, stroking his long chin. Aggressive as he was, he seemed bewildered by this sister-in-law of his. "Excuse me, Inspector. Go on."

"We now come to the inevitable. Mrs. Bitton, do you know anybody who would desire to take Mr. Driscoll's life?"

"I'll never forgive you," she replied in a low, fierce voice, "if you don't find out who killed him. Nobody would want to kill him. It's absurd. It's insane. Phil was wonderful. He was a precious lamb."

General Mason shuddered and even Hadley winced a trifle.

"Ah," he said. "He may have been . . . ah . . . as you say, a . . . never mind. Though I question whether he, or anybody else, would have relished the description. When did you last see him?"

"H'm. Well, it's been some time. It was before Lester and I went to Cornwall. He only comes to the house on Sundays. And he wasn't there yesterday, now that I come to think of it." She frowned. "Yes. Will was so cut up over losing that manuscript, and turning the house upside down . . . or did you know about that?"

"We know," Hadley answered, grimly.

"Wait a bit. Wait. I'm wrong," she corrected, putting her hand down on the desk. "He did come in for a short time rather late Sunday night, to pay his respects to us. He was on his way to the newspaper office to turn in his story, I remember: about the barrister's wig on the cab-horse. Don't you remember, Will?"

Sir William rubbed his forehead. "I don't know. I didn't see him, but then I was . . . occupied."

"Sheila told us about this new newspaper line of his chasing hats." For the first time Laura Bitton shuddered. "And I told him what Sheila told me, about Will's hat being stolen the night before."

"What did he say?"

"Say? . . . Well, he asked a lot of questions about where it had been stolen and when, and all about it and then I remember he started to pace up and down the drawing-room, and he said he'd got a 'lead,' and went hurrying away before we could ask what he meant."

At last Hadley was pleased. He glanced over at Dr. Fell, who had taken the dog in his lap now, but Hadley did not speak. A knock at the door preceded the appearance of an oldish, tired man carrying a bundle made out of a handkerchief. He saluted.

"Sergeant Hamper, sir. I have the dead man's belongings here. And the police surgeon would like to speak to you."

A mild-mannered, peering little man with a goatee doddered in at the door and regarded Hadley with a vague stare.

"Howdy!" he said, pushing his derby hat slightly back on his head with the hand containing his black satchel. In the other he held a straight length of steel. "Here's your weapon, Hadley. Hur-umph . . . No, no fingerprints. I washed it. It was messy. Hur-rumph."

He doddered over to the table, examined it as though he were looking for a suitable place, and put down the crossbow bolt. It was rounded, thin, and about eighteen inches long, with a barbed steel head.

"Funny-lookin' things they're usin' nowadays," commented the doctor, rubbing his nose. "Now I can see a use for the things my wife picked up at Margate. Harrumph."

"It's a crossbolt from the late fourteenth century."

"My eye," said the doctor, "and Betty Martin."

"What?"

"I said, 'My eye and Betty Martin.' Look what's engraved down it. *'Souvenir de Carcassonne, 1932.'* The pirate French sell 'em at little sourvenir booths. That's the curse of travellin', that is. Harrumph."

"But, Doctor . . ." said Sir William.

The other blinked at him. "My name," he observed, with a sudden querulous suspicion – "my name, sir, is Watson. Doctor Watson. And if any alleged humorist . . ." squeaked the doctor, flourishing his satchel – "if any alleged humorist makes the obvious remark, I'll brain him. For thirty years on this force I've been hearin' nothing else. And I'm tired of it. People hiss at me round corners. They ask me for needles and four-wheelers and Shag tobacco, and have I my revolver handy? Every fool of a plain-clothes constable waits patiently for my report so he can say, 'Elementary, my dear . . .'"

Laura Bitton had paid no attention to this tirade. She had grown a trifle pale, and she was standing motionless, staring down at the crossbow bolt. Even Dr. Watson broke off to look at her.

She said, in a voice she tried to keep matter-of-fact:

'I know where this belongs, Mr. Hadley."

"You've seen it before?"

"It comes," said Mrs. Bitton, in a careful voice, "from our house. Lester and I bought it when we were on that walking-trip in southern France."

7
MRS. LARKIN'S CUFF

"Sit down, everybody!" Hadley said, sharply. "This place is turning into a madhouse . . . You're certain of that, Mrs. Bitton?"

She seemed to recover herself from an almost hypnotized stare at the bright steel. She sat down again, drawing jerkily at the cigarette.

"I . . . I mean . . . of course I can't say. Things like that are on sale at Carcassonne, and hundreds of people must buy them."

"Quite," Hadley agreed, dryly. "However, you bought one just like it. Where did you keep it at your home?"

"I honestly don't know. I haven't seen it for months. I remember when we returned from the trip I ran across it in the baggage and thought, 'Now, why on earth did I buy *that* stupid thing?' My impression is that I chucked it away somewhere."

Hadley turned the bolt over in his hands, weighing it. Then he felt the point and sides of the head.

"Mrs. Bitton, the point and barb are as sharp as a knife. Was it like that when you bought it?"

"Good Lord, no! It was very blunt. You couldn't possibly have cut yourself with it."

"As a matter of fact," said the chief inspector, holding the head close, "I think it's been filed and whetted. And there's something else. Has anybody got a lens? . . . Ah, thanks, Hamper." He took the small magnifying glass which the sergeant passed over, and tilted up the bolt to scrutinize the engraving along the side. "Somebody has been trying to efface this *Souvenir de Carcassonne* thing with a file. H'm. And it isn't as though the person had given it up as a bad job. The s-o-u part is blurred and filed almost out, systematically. It's as though the person had been interrupted and hadn't finished his job."

He put down the bolt glumly. Dr. Watson, having evidently satisfied himself that nobody was in a joking mood, had grown more amiable. Removing a stick of chewing-gum from his pocket, he peeled off its wrapper and popped it into his mouth.

"Well, I'm goin'," he volunteered. "Anything you want to know? No use tellin' you that did for him. I'm not givin' you the technical gubble-gubble . . . I hate pedants," he explained to the company. "Clean puncture; plenty of strength behind it. Might have lived half a minute. Harrumph. Oh yes. Concussion. Might have got it failing down the steps, or maybe somebody batted him. That's your job."

"What about the time of death, Watson? The doctor here says he died between one-thirty and one-forty-five."

"Oh, he does, does he?" said the police surgeon. He took out an enormous gun-metal watch, peered at it, shook it beside his ear, and put it back with satisfaction. "Harrumph. Later. Yes. Wasn't a bad guess, though. He died about ten minutes to two. Maybe a few minutes this side, that side. I'll take him along in the ambulance for a good look, and let you know. Well – er – goo'-bye. Harrumph."

He doddered out, swinging his black bag.

"But look here!" protested Sir William, when the door had closed. "He can't possibly know it so exactly, can he? I thought doctors gave a good deal of leeway on a thing like that."

"*He* doesn't," said Hadley. "That's why he's so invaluable. And in twenty years I've never known him more than ten minutes wrong about the time of death. He says he conducts a physical examination after death . . . Still he was showing off. If we say one-forty-five or slightly less we shall be close to the mark."

He turned to Laura Bitton.

"To proceed, Mrs. Bitton. Let's assume that this bolt came from your house. Who knew it was there?"

"Why, everybody, I imagine. I don't remember, but I suppose I must have shown the junk we accumulated on that trip."

"Had you seen it before, Sir William?"

"I'm not sure," the other answered, slowly. His eyes were hazy. "I may have. But I can't recall ever having seen it. Ah yes. *Ha*! Now I know, Laura. You and Lester made the trip while I was abroad in the States, and I came back after you. That accounts for it."

Hadley drew a long breath. "There's no use speculating," he said. "We shall have to make inquiries at the house . . . and now, Mrs. Bitton, I don't think we need detain you any longer. One of the warders will escort you to a cab. Or perhaps Sir William will do it . . . And look here, old man" – he put his hand on the knight's arm – "you've a perfect right to stay, if you like; at least, *I* shan't try to drive you away. But you've had a trying day. Don't you think it would be better if you went home with Mrs. Bitton?"

"No. I'm waiting for something," Sir William answered, woodenly. "I'm waiting to hear what you have to say to Arbor."

"Which is exactly what you mustn't do, don't you see? It would spoil everything. I don't want to have to give you an order . . ."

"Tell you what, Bitton," the general suggested, gruffly, "go up to my rooms. Parker will give you a cigar and a brandy, and if there's any news we'll let you know. That Devereux record is in the portfolio in my desk; have a look at it."

Sir William rose to his great and stooping height. As he turned towards the woman, Rampole turned also; and Rampole was startled to see on Laura's face . . . for a space as brief as a snapping of your fingers . . . an expression of stark terror. It was not caused by anything she saw; it was the expression of one who remembers something momentarily forgotten; who stops breathless, eyes opening wide. It was gone immediately, and Rampole wondered whether Hadley had noticed it.

"I don't suppose I might be allowed to remain?" she asked, in her cool, clear voice. But two kinks were working at the corners of her nostrils, and she seemed almost to have stopped breathing. "I might be helpful, you know." As Hadley smiled and shook his head, she seemed to weigh something in her mind. Then she shrugged. "Ah, well. Excuse the morbid curiosity. And I *will* go home in a cab. I'm not in the state of mind to enjoy a good walk. Good afternoon, gentlemen."

She nodded curtly. Followed by her brother-in-law she swung out of the room.

"Hum!" said General Mason, after a long pause. The fire was getting low, and he kicked at it. Then he noticed Sergeant Hamper, who had been standing, patient and forgotten, since Dr. Watson's entrance; and the general did not continue.

"Oh, ah yes," the chief inspector coughed, as though he had just noticed it, too. "Sorry, Hamper, for keeping you waiting. Those are the contents of the pockets you have there, eh? Very well. Put them down here, and see if you can pick up any news from the chief warder."

"Yes, sir."

"But before you do, go across the way and find Mrs. Amanda Larkin. Wait about five minutes, and send her in here."

The sergeant saluted and withdrew. Hadley contemplated the small bundle on the desk before him, but he did not immediately open it. He glanced at Dr. Fell, who was regarding him benevolently, a pipe in his mouth and the front of his cloak full of hair from the demonstrative Airedale. The chief inspector's expression was sour.

"I say, Mr. Hadley," said the general, after scuffling his feet hesitantly. "What did you make of that woman?"

"Mrs. Bitton? I wonder . . . She's an old hand at evasion, and a very good one. She sees the traps as soon as you set them. And she has rather an ingenious counterattack. She either tries to make somebody angry and jar the proceedings out of line, or else she babbles. But she's not the babbling kind. H'm. What do you know about her?"

"I'd never met her. She seemed to take me for a police officer. But I know her husband slightly, through Bitton."

"What's this Lester Bitton like?"

"I don't like to say," the general answered, doubtfully. "Don't know the man well enough. He's older than she is; considerably, I should think. Can't imagine him enjoying these athletic activities of hers. I believe he made a lot of money in some financial scheme . . . And he doesn't smoke or drink. *Bah*!" said General Mason, blowing through his whiskers.

Hadley seemed about to reply, but he thought better of it. Instead he turned his attention to the handkerchief, knotted up like a bundle, which contained the dead man's effects.

"Here we are. Wrist-watch; crystal broken, but still running. Bunch of keys. Fountain-pen and stylo pencil. Banknotes, silver and coppers: a whole handful of coppers. Only one letter . . . O Lord! here it is. Pure trash . . . pale mauve envelope, and scented; woman's handwriting."

He drew out a single sheet of paper, and Rampole and the general bent over it as he spread it out on the table.

There was no date or heading. The message was written in the centre of the sheet: "Be careful. Tower of London, one-thirty. Suspect. Vital. – *Mary*."

Hadley read it aloud, scowling. "Mary?" he repeated. "Now we've got to find a Mary. Let's see. Postmarked London, W., ten-thirty last night. This thing is beginning to get on my nerves." Pushing the letter out on the desk, he turned to the contents of the handkerchief again. "I must say the sergeant is thorough. He even included the dead man's ring and tie-pin. But here's our hope. Loose-leaf notebook, black leather."

Opening the notebook, he let his eye run along the few scrawled lines on the first sheet. Then Hadley struck the desk despairingly.

"Listen to *this*! Notes of some sort, with dashes between. Apparently it's in Driscoll's handwriting:

"'*Best Place? . . . Tower? . . . Track down hat . . . Unfortunate Trafalgar . . . can't transfix . . . 10 . . . Wood . . . Hedges or shield . . . Find out.*'"

There was a silence.

"But that's gibberish!" General Mason protested, somewhat superfluously. "It doesn't mean anything. At least, it may have meant something, but . . ."

"But he's left out the connecting words," Hadley supplied. "I've often put things down that way. Still, even with the connectives, it would take a genuine puzzle artist to put that together. It seems to refer to some clue for following our hat-man. What clue, I don't know."

"Read that again!" Dr. Fell suddenly boomed from his corner. He had hauled himself up straight, and he was shaking his pipe at them. On his big face was a blank expression which slowly turned to something like amusement as the chief inspector repeated the words . . .

"Mrs. Larkin is here, sir," said the voice of Sergeant Hamper from the door.

A series of chuckles were running down the bulges of Dr. Fell's waistcoat. His small eyes twinkled, and ashes from his pipe were blown about him. He looked like the Spirit of the Volcano. Then his red and shining face sank down again, and he became decorous as the sergeant ushered in their next visitor. Hadley hastily closed the notebook, and General Mason retired again to the fireside.

Mrs. Amanda Georgette Larkin looked about carefully before she entered, rather as though she expected to find a bucket of water balanced on the top of the door. Then she marched in, saw the empty chair beside Hadley's desk, and sat sown without further ado. She was a tall, rather heavy woman, well dressed in dark clothes of the sort called "sensible"; which word, as in its usual context, means an absence of charm. Mrs. Larkin had a square face and suspicious dark eyes. She adjusted her arms on the chair in the manner of one expecting somebody to adjust straps over them, and waited.

Hadley hitched his own chair round. "Mrs. Larkin, I am Chief Inspector Hadley. Naturally, you understand, I dislike having to inconvenience any of you . . ."

"Oh yeah?" said Mrs. Larkin.

"Yes. But you may be able to give us some very important information."

"Maybe," grunted Mrs. Larkin hitching her shoulders. "I don't know *that.* But first, before you ask me any questions, either give me the usual warning or else give me your word anything I say will be treated as a confidence."

She had a way of flicking her head from side to side, and half closing her eyes, as she tossed out the words. Hadley considered gravely.

"Are you familiar with the 'usual warning,' Mrs. Larkin?"

"Maybe and maybe not. But I know the law, and what I say stands."

"Then I can only repeat what you already know. I can make no promises. If anything you say has a direct bearing on this investigation, I can't treat it as a confidence. Is that clear? . . . Besides Mrs. Larkin, I'm almost positive I've seen you somewhere before."

She shrugged. "Maybe you have, and maybe you haven't. That's as it may be. But there's no slop in the business who's got anything on *me.* I'm a respectable widow. I've got a life annuity from my old man all straight and in order, and I can give you a dozen character witnesses. I don't know anything about your investigation, and I haven't anything to tell you. So that's final."

All this time Mrs. Larkin seemed to be having some difficulty with her cuff. Under her dark coat she seemed to have on some sort of tailored suit, with turned-up white cuffs; whether the left-hand one was sliding down, or her capable fingers had a habit of playing with it, Rampole could not tell. If Hadley noticed it, he gave no sign.

"Do you know what has happened here, Mrs. Larkin?"

"Certainly I know. There was enough talk from the crowd over the way."

"Very well. Then you may know that the dead man is Mr. Philip Driscoll, of Tavistock Chambers, Tavistock Square. On the paper you filled out you say that you lived in this building also."

"I do. What about it?"

"What is the number of your flat?"

A brief hesitation. "Number 1."

"Number 1. Ground floor, I suppose? . . . Quite so. You must be an old resident, Mrs. Larkin?"

She blazed. "What the hell difference is it to you? It's none of your business whether I'm an old resident or not. I pay my rent. If you've got any complaint to make, make it to the manager of the flats."

Again Hadley gravely considered, his hands folded. "Who would also tell me how long you had been a resident, Mrs. Larkin. After all, it can't harm you to give us a bit of assistance, can it? You never know. Some time" – he raised his eyes – "some time it might help you a good deal."

Another hesitation. "I didn't mean to speak so sharp," she told him, moving sullenly in the chair. "Well, if it does you any good, I've been there a few weeks; something like that."

"That's better. How many flats on each floor?"

"Two. Two in each entry of the buildings; it's a big place."

"So," Hadley said, musingly, "you must have lived directly across the way from Mr. Driscoll. Did you know him?"

"No. I've seen him, that's all."

"Inevitable, of course. And passing in and out, you may have noticed whether he had visitors?"

"What's the use my telling you I didn't? Sure I did. I couldn't help it. He had lots of people coming to see him."

"I was thinking particularly of women, Mrs. Larkin."

For a moment she scrutinized him with an ugly eye. "Yes. There was women. But what about it? *I'm* no moralist. Live and let live, that's what *I* say. It was none of my business. They didn't disturb me, and I didn't disturb them. But if you're going to ask me who the women were, you can save your breath. I don't know."

"For instance," said Hadley. He glanced over at the sheet of mauve notepaper lying spread out under the bright lights. "You never heard the name 'Mary' used did you?"

She stiffened. Her eyes remained fixed on the notepaper, and she stopped fiddling with her cuff. Then she began talking rather volubly in her straight, harsh fashion:

"No. I told you I didn't know him. The only woman's name I ever heard in connection with him was on the up-and-up. It was a little blonde. Pretty little thing. She used to come with a big thin bird with eyeglasses on. One day she stopped me as I was coming in and asked me how she could find the porter to get into his flat. There's no hall-porter; it's an automatic lift. She said her name was Sheila and she was his cousin. And that's *all* I ever heard."

Hadley remained silent for a time, regarding the articles on his desk.

"Now, about this afternoon, Mrs. Larkin . . . How did you happen to come to the Tower of London?"

"I've got a *right* to come here if I want to. I don't need to explain why I go to a public building, do I? I just did." The reply was fired back so quickly that Rampole suspected it had been framed in advance, ready for the proper occasion.

"When did you arrive?"

"Past two o'clock. Mind, I don't swear to that! I'm not under oath. That's what time I think it was."

"Did you make the tour . . . go all around?"

"I went to two of them – Crown Jewels and Bloody Tower. Not the other one. Then I got tired and started out. They stopped me."

Hadley went through the routine of questions, and elicited nothing. She had been deaf, dumb, and blind. There were other people about her . . . she remembered an American cursing the fog . . . but she had paid no attention to the others. At length he dismissed her, with the warning that he would probably have future questions. Mrs. Larkin sniffed. She adjusted the collar of her coat, gave a last defiant glance about, and stalked out.

The moment she had disappeared Hadley hurried to the door. He said to the warder there:

"Find Sergeant Hamper and tell him to put a tail on the woman who's just left here. Hurry! If the fog's any thicker he'll miss her . . . Then tell Hamper to come back here."

He turned back to the desk, thoughtfully beating his hands together.

"Hang it all, man," General Mason burst out, impatiently, "why the kid-glove tactics? A little third degree wouldn't have hurt her. She knows something, right enough. And she probably is, or has been, a criminal."

"Undoubtedly, General. But I had nothing to hold over her; and, above all, she's much more valuable on the string. We'll play her out a bit. And I think we should discover something interesting . . . I think we'll find there is nothing against her at present at the Yard. And I'm almost sure we'll find she's a private detective."

"Ha!" muttered the general. He twisted his moustache. "A private detective. But why?"

Hadley sat down again and regarded the articles on his desk.

"Oh, I needn't be mysterious like my friend Dr. Fell. There are any number of indications . . . Clearly she has nothing to fear from the police; she challenged that with every word. She lives in Tavistock Square. The neighbourhood isn't 'flash' enough for her if she had that much money of her own to spend, and it isn't cheap enough if she had less. I know the type. She has lived there only a few weeks . . . just opposite Driscoll. She obviously had paid a great deal of attention to his visitors. She told us only one incident, the visit of his cousin Sheila, because that wouldn't help us; but you notice she had all the details.

"Then . . . did you see her fumbling at her cuff? She hasn't been in the business long; she was afraid it would show out of the arm of her coat, and she was afraid to take it off over in the Warders' Hall, for fear of looking suspicious."

"Her cuff?"

Hadley nodded. "These private snoopers who get material for divorces. They have to make notes of times and places quickly, and often in the dark. Oh yes. That's what she's up to. She was following somebody this afternoon."

The general said, "Hum!" He scuffled his feet a moment before asking, "Something to do with Driscoll?"

Hadley put his head down in his hands.

"Yes. You saw the start she couldn't help giving when she saw that note on my desk. She was close enough to have read it, but the colour of the paper was enough to identify it . . . if she'd ever seen any similar notes in connection with Driscoll. H'm, yes. But that's not the point. I strongly suspect that the person she was actually shadowing this afternoon was . . . whom do *you* say, Doctor?"

Dr. Fell relighted his pipe. "Mrs. Bitton, of course. I'm afraid *she* rather gave herself away, if you listened to what she said."

"But, good God!" muttered the general. He paused and stared round quickly. "Eh. That's better. I thought for a moment Bitton was here. You mean to say there's something between Driscoll and . . . H'm. Yes. It fits, I suppose. But where's your proof?"

"I haven't any proof. As I say, it's only a suspicion." Hadley rubbed his chin. "Still, let's take it as a hypothesis for the moment, and work back. Let's assume Larkin was shadowing Mrs. Bitton . . . Now, this White Tower, General. That's the biggest and most important one, isn't it? And it's some distance away from the Bloody Tower, isn't it?"

"Well, yes . . . it stands alone; it's in the middle of the inner ballium walls just beside the parade-ground."

"And I think you said that the tower where the Crown Jewels are kept is directly beside the Bloody Tower?"

"The Wakefield Tower. Yes . . . Wait a minute!" said Mason, excitedly. "I've got it. Mrs. Bitton went to see the Crown Jewels. So did Larkin. Mrs. Bitton said she wandered up through the arch of the Bloody Tower, inside the inner wall, and up to the parade-ground . . . Larkin went to the Bloody Tower. She couldn't keep too close to Mrs. Bitton. And if she went up the stairs of the Bloody Tower to Raleigh's Walk, she could have seen from a height where Mrs. Bitton was going."

"That's what I wanted to ask you," said Hadley, knocking his fists against his temples. "She couldn't have been very far in the mist, of course. It's more probable she did that – *if* she did – to keep up the illusion of being a tourist. Or she might have thought Mrs. Bitton had gone into the Bloody Tower. It's all supposition. But neither of them went to the White Tower, you see . . . Those may be coincidences, but when you couple them with the presence of those two women here, and the statements of Mrs. Bitton and Larkin, they sound pretty plausible indications."

"You're assuming," said the general, pointing to the table, "that Mrs. Bitton wrote that note?"

"And all the time," Hadley mused, "suspecting she was being watched. See what the note says: "Be careful. Suspect. Vital." She used an obviously crude and ordinary notepaper; but, you remember, Larkin gave a start on seeing it. The letter was posted at ten-thirty last night, in Mrs. Bitton's district, after Driscoll had paid a short visit that evening. Mrs. Bitton had just that day come back from a walking tour in Cornwall . . . and *why,* in God's name, a walking trip in Cornwall in the worst part of March, unless somebody wanted to get her away from a dangerous infatuation?"

He got up and began to pace about the room. As he passed General Mason, the latter silently handed him his cigar-case. Hadley took a cigar and put it into his mouth, but he did not light it.

"I'm running on, I suppose. Still if we assume all this, we must assume it *was* a dangerous infatuation. For here's a private detective who has been planted in a flat opposite Driscoll for some weeks, even during the time she and her husband were away! . . . Does that mean anything? And who planted her there? Offhand, of course, the husband."

"But the name, 'Mary'?" suggested General Mason.

"I've heard many more hilariously funny nicknames . . . whatd'yecallem . . . pet names . . . in my time," Hadley said, grimly. "And the handwriting's undoubtedly disguised. Even if it were stolen it couldn't be used as evidence against her. She's a clever woman, right enough. But look here . . ."

He struggled with a match to light his cigar.

"Do you see the deep waters we're in *now*? Come along, Mr. Rampole," he prompted, turning so suddenly that the American jumped; "do you see how it mixes everything up?"

Rampole hesitated. "I can see plenty of difficulties," he returned. "That letter would have been delivered fairly early this morning. Now we've been assuming ail along that the reason why Driscoll telephoned Mr. Dalrye had something to do with the hat-thief and his pursuit of the hat-thief. But Driscoll never actually *said* it did. Dalrye asked him jokingly, if I remember it right, whether he was afraid of his hat being stolen. But all Driscoll actually answered was, "It's not my hat I'm afraid of; it's my head." Dalrye thought it referred to the hat-affair; but did it?"

He looked bewilderedly at the chief inspector.

"I don't know," snapped Hadley. "But he makes that appointment with Dalrye for one o'clock. The appointment in the letter is for one-thirty. He has received the letter that morning; it's scared him, and he wants Dalrye's help . . . Then, what? Some *other* person carefully sends Dalrye on a wild-goose chase to Driscoll's fiat. Then Driscoll arrives here, in a bad state. He is seen by Parker *looking out of the window*, and later somebody touches him on the arm by Traitors' Gate.

"So what?" Hadley had got his cigar lighted now, after wasting several matches, and he regarded his companions more calmly. "What went on in the merry-go-round composed of Driscoll, Mrs. Bitton, Larkin, and a possible fourth party? Was it some sort of *crime passionel*? And if it was, can anybody on this side of sanity inform me why Driscoll's body should be found wearing Sir William's stolen top hat? It's the hat-thief angle that's mad and impossible; but the hat-thief is in on this somehow, and I hope you can explain him. I can't."

There was a pause. Dr. Fell took the pipe out of his mouth and spoke rather plaintively.

"I say, Hadley," he remonstrated. "You're working yourself up into a lather. Be calm. Endeavour to cultivate that philosophical outlook of which Marcus Aurelius speaks. So far you've reasoned closely and well; but – to put it pointedly – don't smash your bat over the wicket-keeper's head when you've already made over a century. It'll come out all right. Just keep on in your normal course."

The chief inspector regarded him bitterly.

"Unless our questioning of the other visitors turns up something," he said, "we have only one other person to interview. And thank God. I need a brandy. Several brandies. – But for the next few minutes, Doctor, I am going to exercise that philosophical spirit. *You* are going to be the chief inspector. With the next witness it becomes your case. In other words, you are going to examine Julius Arbor."

"With pleasure," said the doctor, "if you'll give me your chair." He hauled himself to his feet as Hadley summoned the warder on guard and gave instructions. "It's what I should have asked to do, in any case, Hadley. Because why? Because a good part of the case depends on it. And that side of the case – shall I tell you what that side of the case hinges on, Hadley?"

"You will, anyhow. Well?"

"It hinges on a stolen manuscript," said Dr. Fell.

8
MR. ARBOR'S AURA

Dr. Fell hung his cloak over the back of the chair. Then he squeezed himself into the chair and arranged his various ridges of stomach. Folding his hands over this, he twinkled amiably.

"I don't know whether I ought to let you do this" said Hadley. "I don't want the general to think we're both mad. And for the love of God try to control your deplorable sense of humour. This is serious business." He massaged his chin uncomfortably. "You see, General, in his own way Doctor Fell is invaluable. But he gets his ideas of police procedure from the cinema, and he is under the impression that he can act any sort of part. Whenever I let him question anybody in my presence he tries to give an imitation of me. The result sounds like a schoolmaster with homicidal mania trying to find out what fourth-former spread the axle grease on the stairs when the headmaster was coming down to dinner."

Dr. Fell grunted. "Ha," he said. "Your analogy, while classical, supports me rather than you. It seems to me, Hadley, that you are the one who is going about grimly determined to discover who put the barrister's wig on the cab-horse. I'm exactly the detective you want. – Besides, schoolboys are much more ingenious than that. Now, an outhouse of medium weight carefully substituted for the statue of the headmaster on the night before the public unveiling of the latter . . ."

General Mason shook his head. "Personally," he observed frowning at his cigar, "I remember my own schoolboy holidays in France. And I have always maintained that there is nothing more edifying than the experiment of placing a red lamp over the door of the mayor's house in a district full of sailors. Ahem!"

"Go ahead," Hadley said, bitterly. "Have a good time. I suppose if this case hadn't wound up in a murder you'd be stealing hats yourselves, and thinking up new places to hang them."

Dr. Fell rapped one of his canes sharply across the table. "Man," he said, "I tell you in all seriousness that it's less than a joke. If you were able to think along those lines, along the hat-man's lines, you'd see the explanation of at least one thing you regard as gibberish. You might know the whole explanation."

"Do *you* know it?"

"I rather think I do," Dr. Fell replied, modestly.

The general was frowning with an uncertain air. "Excuse me, sir," he said to Dr. Fell, "if I intrude on something that's none of my business. But, since this seems to be a sort of council of war, may I ask who you are? I don't think you're a police official. And yet you seem familiar, somehow; I've been puzzling about it all afternoon. It seems to me that I've met you somewhere, or seen you . . ."

Dr. Fell contemplated his pipe. For a time he wheezed heavily.

"I'm not sure what I am," he said. "Some people would say a Fossil. But in a manner of speaking you *have* come in contact with me, General. That would be some years ago. Do you remember Allerton, the naturalist?"

The general's hand stopped with the cigar halfway to his lips.

"He was a good man, Allerton was," Dr. Fell said, reflectively. "He'd been sending some beautiful and intricate drawings of butterflies to a friend of his in Switzerland. The patterns of the wings were perfect, in their way. They were plans of the British minefields in the Solent. But he got his Latin a trifle mixed in the notations . . . His real name was Sturmm, and I believe he was shot here in the Tower. I – er – accounted for him."

A rumbling sound apparently indicated a sigh.

"Then there was good old Professor Rogers, of the University of Chicago. If he'd known just a bit more about American history I don't think I should have been certain. I've forgotten his name, but he played a good game of chess and had a sound liking for drinking-bouts; I was sorry to see him go. He used to carry his information written infinitesimally small on the lenses of his spectacles . . . Or perhaps you recall little Ruth Wilisdale? I was her dear father-confessor. She would have a snapshot of herself taken at Portsmouth, with the newest thing in gun designs just in the background; but I hoped she wouldn't try to use it. If she hadn't shot that poor clerk, for no reason except that he was in love with her, I should have let her go."

Dr. Fell blinked at the steel crossbow bolt.

"But that was in the line of duty. I'm older now. Hadley insisted on that business of Cripps, the Notting Hill poisoner; and that chap Loganray, with the mirror inside his watch; and the Starberth affair was rather forced on me. But I don't like it. Heh. Hmf. No."

There was a knock at the door. Rampole, to whom all this was a revelation, jerked his thoughts back.

"Pardon me," said a calm, slightly edged voice. "I've knocked several times, and there seemed to be no answer. You sent for me, I think. If you don't mind, I'll come in."

Rampole had been wondering what to expect from the enigmatic Mr. Julius Arbor. He remembered Sir William's description earlier that afternoon: "Reserved, scholarly, a trifle sardonic." The American had been vaguely expecting some one tall and thin and swarthy, with a hooked nose. The man who entered now, slowly drawing off his gloves and looking about with cool curiosity, was somewhat swarthy. And in every movement he was austere. But that was all.

Mr. Arbor was not above middle height, and he was inclined towards pudginess. He was perfectly dressed, too well dressed: there was a white piqué edging to the front of his waistcoat, and a small pearl pin in his tie . . . His face was flattish, with heavy black eyebrows; and the rimless eyeglasses were such delicate shells that they seemed to blend with his eyes. At the moment he had an air of tolerance and false pleasantry. His expression, as he regarded Dr. Fell, conveyed surprise without a muscle moving in his face; conveyed it by a sort of aura.

"Am I addressing Chief Inspector Hadley?" he inquired.

"Good day," said Dr. Fell, waving his hand affably. "I'm in charge of the investigation, if that's what you mean. Sit down. I presume you're Mr. Arbor."

Dr. Fell hardly presented an imposing picture of a dreaded police official. The front of his waistcoat was littered with tobacco ash and dog's hair, and the Airedale itself now wandered over and lay down beside him. Arbor's eyes narrowed slightly. But he shifted his umbrella from the crook of one arm to hang it over the other; he moved across to the chair, inspected it for dust, and sat down. Carefully he removed his soft pearl-grey hat, placed it in his lap, and waited.

"That's better," said the doctor. "Now we can begin." From his pocket he took his battered cigar-case and extended it. "Smoke?"

"Thank you, no," the other answered. His manner appeared to be the utmost in courtesy. He waited until Dr. Fell had replaced the disreputable case. Then he produced an elaborately chased silver cigarette-case of his own, containing long and slender cigarettes with a cork tip. Snapping on a silver lighter, he applied it to a cigarette with nicety; then with all deliberation replaced lighter and case. He waited again.

So did Dr. Fell. The doctor studied him sleepily, hands folded over his stomach. He appeared to have endless patience. Arbor seemed to grow a trifle restless. He cleared his throat.

"I do not wish to hurry you, Inspector," he said at length, "but I should like to point out that I have been put to considerable inconvenience this afternoon. So far I have complied without hesitation to all requests. If you will tell me what you wish to know, I shall be happy to assist you in any way I can."

His voice was not precisely condescending. But he tried to convey an effect by concealing it. Dr. Fell nodded.

"Got any Poe manuscripts?" he inquired, rather like a customs officer asking for contraband.

The question was so sudden that Arbor stiffened. Hadley gave a faint groan.

"I beg your pardon?" said Arbor, after a slight hesitation.

"Got any Poe manuscripts?"

"Really, Inspector . . ." said the other. A faint frown ruffled his swarthy forehead. "I don't think I quite understand you. At my home in New York I certainly have a number of first editions of Edgar Allan Poe, and a few of the manuscript originals. But I scarcely think they would be of interest to *you*. I understand you wished to question me concerning a murder."

"Oh, the murder!" grunted Dr. Fell, with a careless wave of his hand. "Never mind that. I don't want to talk about the murder."

"Indeed?" said Arbor. "I had supposed that the police might have some curiosity concerning it. However, that is none of my affair. I must remark, with Pliny, '*Quot homines, tot sententiae*'."

"No, it wasn't," said Dr. Fell, sharply.

"I beg your pardon?"

"It wasn't Pliny," explained the doctor, testily. "That's an inexcusable blunder. And if you must use that deplorable platitude, try to pronounce it correctly. The 'O' in *homines* is short, and there's no long nasal sound to the 'en' in *sententiae* . . . But never mind that. What do you know about Poe?"

Hadley was making weird noises in the corner. Mr. Arbor's flattish face had stiffened; he said nothing, but the aura about him conveyed anger. He glanced round at the others, touching lightly his shells of eyeglasses. He seemed not quite certain what to say. Under his scrutiny Rampole tried to make a face like a grim inquisitor; Rampole was enjoying this. If Mr. Arbor could not be called a type, he was at least among a certain class of Americans who had always irritated Rampole, and who can only be described as Overcultured. They try to see everything and know everything in as correct a fashion as possible. They go to the right places at exactly the right time. Their pale, assured knowledge of the arts is like their well-groomed houses and their well-groomed selves. When a new Atlantic liner is launched, they discover the proper place to sit in the dining-salon, and sit there. They avoid errors, and never drink too much. – In short, Dr. Fell and General Mason and Rampole were not allies of theirs.

"I am not sure," Arbor said, quietly, "that I know what you are driving at or whether this is an elaborate joke. If so, kindly tell me. You are certainly the most extraordinary sort of policeman I have ever seen."

"I'll put it this way, then. Are you interested in Poe? If you were offered the authentic manuscript of one of his stories, would you buy it?"

This sudden swoop to the practical, Rampole felt, put Arbor right again. There was a trace of a smile on his face. But you knew he had been outraged; he had tried to impress a policeman with a casual retort, and instead he had been flicked across his poise. He would try to get his own back.

"Now I see, Mr. Hadley," he said to Dr. Fell. "This tribunal, then, was called because of Sir William Bitton's stolen manuscript. I was a bit puzzled at first." He smiled again, a mere wrinkle in his pudgy face. Then he considered. "Yes, I should certainly buy a Poe item if it were offered to me."

"H'm, yes. You know there has been a theft at Bitton's house, then?"

"Oh yes. And you, Inspector, know that I am stopping at Bitton's home. I should say," Arbor corrected himself, impassively, "I *was* stopping there. Tomorrow I shall remove myself to the 'Savoy.'"

"Why?"

Arbor glanced round for an ash-tray, saw none; then he held his cigarette out levelly so that, when the ashes fell, they should not fall on his trousers. "Let's be frank, Mr. Inspector," he suggested. "I am aware of what Bitton thinks. I am not insulted. We must accept these little things. *Amara temperet lento risu,* if I may again risk Scotland Yard's correction of my pronunciation. But I dislike awkwardness. You see; or don't you?"

"Do you know the nature of the manuscript that was stolen?"

"Perfectly. In point of fact, I had some intention of intending to buy it."

"He told you about it, then, did he?"

The flattish face was a polite mask of deprecation. Arbor put up a hand to touch his dark hair, which was brushed straight and flat across the big skull. "You know he didn't, Mr. Inspector. But Bitton is like a child, if I may say so. I have heard him let fall enough dark and mysterious hints at the dinner table for even his family to guess the nature of his find . . . However, I knew all about the manuscript before I left the States."

He chuckled. It was the first human sound Rampole had heard out of him.

"I dislike commenting on the infantile nature of some of these gentlemen, but I fear Doctor Robertson, who had been Bitton's confidant, was indiscreet."

Dr. Fell thoughtfully took the handle of his stick, which was lying across the desk, and poked at the crossbow bolt. Then he glanced up amiably.

"Mr. Arbor, would you have stolen that manuscript, if you were given the opportunity?"

Across the room Rampole saw the despairing expression on Hadley's face. But Arbor was not in the least perturbed. He appeared to consider the question from all angles, gravely.

"No, Inspector, I don't think I would," he replied. "It would entail so much awkwardness, you see. And I dislike violating hospitality in that fashion. Don't misunderstand me. I have no moral scruples," Mr. Arbor explained, gently, like one who says, "I am not a hard-hearted man," "and it might seriously be questioned as to whether Bitton has any right to it at all. Under the law, his possession of it could be questioned. But, as I say, I dislike unpleasantness."

"But suppose somebody offered to sell you that manuscript, Mr. Arbor?"

Arbor took off his delicate eyeglasses and polished them with a white silk handkerchief. To do so he was compelled to drop his cigarette on the floor, which he did with repugnance. He was easy, smug and half smiling now. The black eyebrows were wrinkled with amusement.

"Let me tell you a story, Inspector. The police should know it, to support my claim in case it is – ah – successful. Before I came to England I went to Philadelphia and looked up Mr. Joseph McCartney, of Mount Airy Avenue, who owns the property on which the manuscript was found. For the fact that it was found there I had the testimony of three honest labouringmen. I laid my case with a tolerable degree of frankness before Mr. McCartney. *He* was the owner. I informed him that if he would give me a three months' written option on that manuscript, wherever it might be, I would hand him one thousand dollars in cash. There was also another agreement. It specified that, if the manuscript proved to be what I wanted (the decision to rest with me), I should pay him four thousand dollars for a complete sale . . . In these matters, Inspector, it is never wise to be miserly."

Dr. Fell nodded ponderously, leaning forward with his chins in his fist.

"Actually, Mr. Arbor, what is the manuscript worth?"

"To me? Well, gentlemen, witness my frankness. I should be willing to go as high as, say, ten thousand pounds."

General Mason, who had been scowling and pulling at his imperial, interrupted. "But, my God! man, that's fantastic! No Poe manuscript . . ."

"I venture to predict," Arbor said, placidly, "that this one would. Has Bitton described it to you? Ah, I thought not. It would be rather revolutionary." His cool eyes travelled slowly about the group. "Since I seem in the presence of an unusually well-informed group of policemen, I may tell you that it is. It is the first analytic detective story in the history of the world. It antedates Poe's own *Murders in the rue Morgue.* Dr. Robertson informs me that even from an artistic point of view it surpasses Poe's other three Dupin crime tales . . . I say that I would give ten thousand pounds. I could name you off-hand three fellow collectors who would go as high as twelve or fifteen. And I enjoy thinking what it would fetch at auction – where, I need not tell you, I intend to place it."

Hadley had come up hurriedly to the side of the desk. He seemed almost on the point of tapping Dr. Fell on the arm and getting him out of the chair, to take over the interrogation. But he remained staring at Arbor.

Dr. Fell cleared his throat with a rumbling noise.

"This may be a lot of nonsense," he said, glowering. "Or it may not. How do you know this? Have you seen the manuscript?"

"I have the word of Dr. Robertson, the greatest living authority on Poe. I fear that the good doctor has a short eye to business, or he would have adopted my own course. He only told me all this because – well, Inspector, my wine-cellar is considered excellent. And even Imperial Tokay is cheap at the price. Of course, he regretted his indiscretion next day; he had promised Bitton, and he begged me to take no action. I was sorry."

Again Arbor drew out the silk handkerchief and lightly mopped his head.

"Then," said Dr Fell, "it wasn't a mere matter of a find you were interested in? You were after this manuscript to sell it?"

"I was, my dear Inspector. The manuscript – wherever it is – happens to belong to me. I may remind you . . . Shall I go on?"

"By all means."

"My business with Mr. McCartney was easily settled," Arbor continued comfortably. "He seemed staggered. It was incredible to him that any written document, save perhaps a blackmailing letter or one of 'them treaty things' to which he referred, could be worth five thousand dollars. I found in Mr. McCartney a great reader of sensational fiction . . . My next move – you follow it, Inspector?"

"You got yourself invited to Bitton's house," grunted Dr. Fell.

"Not exactly. I had a standing invitation there. At one time, I may remark, my friend Bitton thought highly of me. As a rule, of course, I do not stay with friends when I am in

London. I own a cottage in the suburbs, at which I often stay in summer; and in winter I go to a hotel. But, you see, I had to be tactful. He was a friend."

Again Arbor drew out his silver cigarette-case. But he seemed to remember that there was no ash-tray, and he put it back again.

"I could not, of course," he pursued, "say to him, 'Bitton, I think you have a manuscript of mine. Hand it over.' That would have been distasteful, and, I thought, unnecessary. I expected him to show me his find voluntarily. Then I would lead up to my subject by gradual degrees, explain the unfortunate circumstances, and make him a fair offer. Understand me! I was prepared to pay him his price, within reason, even for my own property. I wished no sort of undignified squabble.

"Now, Inspector – and gentlemen – that was difficult. You know Bitton? Ah. I knew him as a headstrong, stubborn and secretive fellow; rather a monomaniac on cherishing his discoveries. But I had not expected him to be quite so difficult. He did not speak of his find as I had expected. For some days I hinted. I thought he was merely obtuse, and I fear my hints grew so outrageously broad that they puzzled even his family. But I am aware now that he must have known, and suspected me. He merely kept his mouth more tightly closed. It was distasteful to me – but I was coming to the point where I should have had to claim my rights. Under the law," said Arbor, his leisurely voice growing suddenly harsh, "I was not required to pay him a penny for my property."

"The sale had not been concluded between you and McCartney, had it?" inquired Dr. Fell.

Arbor shrugged. "Virtually. I had my option. Of course, I was not willing to hand over five thousand dollars on a manuscript I had never seen, even on the word of Dr. Robertson; and a manuscript, besides, which might conceivably have been lost or destroyed by the time I came to claim it. However, to all intents and purposes it was mine."

"Did you tell Bitton you were the owner, then?"

Arbor's nostrils tightened with anger. "Obviously not. Or would he have been so mad as to do what he did – seek the aid of the police when it was stolen?

"But before that. Consider the difficulty of my position. I began to see that, if I asked him outright, this – ah – this lunatic might make all sorts of trouble. He would probably refuse, and question my rights. My rights could be proved; but it would mean delay and all sorts of unpleasantness. He might maintain he had lost the manuscript, and that would be worse. I imagine he would have been quite capable of summoning a policeman and having me thrown out of his house."

Mr. Arbor's aura conveyed an acute spasm of anguish at this thought. General Mason coughed, and Dr. Fell contrived to twist his moustache with a hand that hid his mouth.

"And at *this* juncture," continued the other, tapping the end of his umbrella on the floor, "everything blew up. The manuscript was stolen. And I, you notice, *I* was the loser.

"Now, gentlemen." He sat back and gazed about, fixing the eye of each in turn. "Now you will understand why I have gone into such thorough explanations, and why I wish to establish the ownership of that manuscript. Bitton undoubtedly thinks I stole it. I am not particularly concerned with what he thinks; I have not even bothered to undeceive him. But I cannot have the police thinking so.

"I was away over the week-end during which the manuscript was stolen, and I arrived back only this morning. I was visiting Mr. and Mrs. Spengler, some friends of mine who live close to that cottage of my own I mentioned, at Golder's Green. 'Ah,' says the cunning Bitton; 'an alibi.'

And he has the colossal impudence to telephone them in order to confirm it. 'Ah,' he says then; 'it was done by somebody in his employ.'

"Now, all this might be at least remotely possible in Bitton's wild imagination. But you know better. Why, in the name of Heaven, should I go to all the trouble of stealing a manuscript which was already mine?"

Arbor folded his hands with the air of an orator sitting down again.

There was a silence. Hadley, who had perched himself on the edge of the desk nodded.

"I suppose, Mr. Arbor," he said, "you are prepared to prove this claim of yours?"

"Naturally. An agreement between Mr. McCartney and myself was drawn up by my lawyer in New York and duly attested. A copy of this agreement is now filed with my solicitors in London. Should you care to verify what I say, I shall be happy to give you a card to them."

Hadley lifted his shoulders. "In that case, Mr. Arbor, there is nothing more to be said. Sir William simply took a chance that his discovery would go unnoted." Hadley spoke coldly and levelly. "Even if you had – hum – abstracted the manuscript, to avoid trouble at Sir William's hands, the law could do nothing. I should not call it very ethical. I tell you frankly, sir, I should call it pretty damned sneaking. But it is perfectly legal."

Mr. Arbor's aura radiated a sort of sputter, like a muffled wireless-key. He tried to draw himself up, but the eye of the chief inspector was a trifle too cold. Then Mr. Arbor became placid again.

"We'll let that pass," he observed, with an effort. "The absurdity of your suggestion is as evident as – ah – your somewhat noticeable manners. That a man of my well-known standing . . ." The aura sputtered again. Then Mr. Arbor recovered himself. "It would amuse some of my associates in New York," he said. "Ha, ha. Ha. Very amusing. But, as I think we agreed to begin with, perfectly legal."

"Not if it concerned a murder," said Dr. Fell.

There was an abrupt and rather terrible silence.

The doctor had spoken in a casual tone, and he was leaning over to stroke the head of the dog curled up beside his chair. In the stillness they could all hear the last rattle of coals falling in the grate, and, very faintly, the thin sudden note of a bugle from the parade-ground. General Mason automatically reached for his watch as he heard the bugle; but he stopped and stared.

Arbor had been gathering his coat about him to rise, and his hand jerked on the lapel. "I – I beg your pardon?" he said.

"I said, 'Not if it concerned a murder,'" Dr. Fell repeated in a louder voice. "Don't get up, Mr. Arbor. We're going to talk about the murder now. That doesn't surprise you, does it? You offered to talk about it a while ago, you know."

His half-closed eyes opened wide.

"Don't you know *who* was murdered, Mr. Arbor?" he pursued.

"I – I heard them talking over there," the other answered, regarding his interrogator fixedly. "I think I heard somebody say his name was Drakell or Driscoll or something of the sort. But I didn't mix with them. What has a man being killed at the Tower of London to do with *me*?"

"The name was Driscoll. Philip Driscoll. He was Sir William Bitton's nephew."

Whatever sort of effect Dr. Fell had hoped to produce, there was no question about an effect. Arbor's swarthy face turned white; literally white, for mottled blotches stood out against his pallor. The thin eyeglasses jerked on his nose, and he covered them with a shaking hand. Undoubtedly Arbor had a weak heart. The effect was as much physical as nervous. Hadley started forward in concern; but Arbor waved him back.

"You must – you must excuse me, gentlemen," he muttered. His voice grew stronger. "I – it was the shock of hearing the name of – somebody – I did know. This – this Driscoll, was he a small young man, with – let me see – with reddish hair?"

"Yes," said Dr. Fell stolidly. "You did know him, then?"

"I – Yes. That is, I met him – ah – Sunday before last, at dinner in Bitton's house. It was the day I arrived. I hadn't caught his last name. They all called him Phil; that's how I remembered. And a nephew of Bitton, by that name . . ."

General Mason pulled a flask out of his hip pocket and held it out. "Try this," he said, gruffly. "Brandy. Buck you up."

"Thank you, no," the other answered, with some dignity. "I'm quite all right. But I assure you I don't know anything about this ghastly business. How did he die?"

"He was stabbed with this crossbow bolt," said Dr. Fell, picking it up. "It comes from Bitton's house."

The other said, "Most – interesting –" in a way that sounded like a horrible burlesque. But he was better now. "I don't want you to think, gentlemen," he went on, with a sort of heavy facetiousness, "that *I* know anything of the poor boy's murder because I seemed – ah – upset when you mentioned it. After all, murderers don't do that, do they? It would be too easy if they did. A person with courage enough to use one of those vicious-looking things isn't apt to faint when it's produced afterwards. It was – ah – bringing the thing home, so to speak. The doctor warned me against shocks, gentlemen; I'm not as healthy as I look. Bitton . . . poor devil. Does he know?"

"He knows, Mr. Arbor. But about young Driscoll: you can't think of any reason for his murder?"

"My dear sir, no! No, of course not. I only met him once, at that dinner. I haven't seen him since."

"He was killed at the Traitors' Gate out there," pursued Dr. Fell, nodding, "and his body thrown on the steps. I don't suppose you noticed anything suspicious while you were here? People near the gate; anything of the sort?"

"No. What I – er – wanted to tell you when I first came in was that it was only by chance I was detained here at all. You see, I wanted to examine that copy of Sir Walter Raleigh's *History of the World* which is on display at the Bloody Tower, in the room where he wrote it. I arrived here shortly after one o'clock, and went directly to the Bloody Tower. I – er – I confess I was shocked at the way they allow such a valuable book to lie exposed and open all day in such a damp place. I presented my card to the warder on duty, and asked whether I might make a detailed examination. He said he was sorry, but that it was a part of the Tower exhibits and that I couldn't handle it without a written order from the resident governor or deputy governor . . ." Arbor seemed a trifle surprised at the interest depicted in the faces of the others. Nobody spoke; he went on talking volubly.

"Even then, he said, it was doubtful whether I could get the order. But I asked to be directed to where I might find either one. He sent me across the way . . ."

"*Inside* the inner ballium wall?" Hadley interrupted.

"Why – er – yes. Yes. To a row of buildings facing up towards the Green and the parade-ground. But it was foggy, and there were several doors, and I was uncertain. While I hesitated, a man came out one of the doors . . ."

He paused, puzzled and growing nervous under their eyes.

"A man in knickerbockers and cap?" Dr. Fell inquired.

"I don't know. Er – yes, I believe he did wear knickerbockers; I recall it because they seemed a bit absurd on such a day. But it was foggy, and I could not swear to it. I spoke to him to find out which door I should use, but he brushed past me without listening. Then another warder hailed me and told me that visitors were not permitted on the side of the grounds where I was walking. I explained.

He then said he was positive neither of the persons I wanted to see were in their quarters at the time."

"Quite correct," said General Mason dryly.

"But surely, gentlemen – !" Arbor protested, wetting his lips, "surely you can't be interested . . . You are? Well, let me see. I returned to the Bloody Tower and tried the judicious use of a bank-note. It was not accepted. So I determined to leave. On my way out to Water Lane I collided with a young lady who had just come under the arch of the gate from Water Lane and was walking very rapidly up the incline that goes towards the parade-ground . . . You said something?"

"No," said Dr. Fell. "Could you describe this young lady?"

Arbor was again entirely at his ease. By his expression, he seemed to regret his late weakness and to make up for it by clear, judicial telling of his own story. It was obvious that the import of the story puzzled him. But, at Dr. Fell's question, he reflected carefully.

"No. No, I'm afraid not. I scarcely glanced at her. All I remember is that she was in a great hurry, and that she wore some sort of fur collar, and that she seemed – ah – uncommonly solid. It gave me a jar when we bumped. My wrist-watch was a bit loose, and I thought it had slipped off. Well, I walked through the arch of the Bloody Tower, into Water Lane . . ."

"Now, Mr. Arbor, for the Lord's sake think! Think! Was there anybody near the railing around Traitors' Gate then? Did you see anybody standing there, or did it seem to be deserted?"

Arbor sat back. "I begin to see the drift," he answered, nervously. "I didn't go close to the rail, or look over . . . But there was nobody standing near it, Inspector. Nobody!"

"And could you remember the time then?"

"I can tell you the time precisely," said the other. "It was just twenty-five minutes to two."

9
THE THREE HINTS

It was the placid Hadley who was momentarily jarred out of his calm then. "But look here!" he protested, "the police surgeon said he died at a quarter to . . ."

"Hold on!" bellowed Dr. Fell. He struck the top of the desk such a sharp blow with his cane that the sheet of mauve notepaper fluttered off. "By God and Bacchus! That's what I wanted! That's what I was hoping and waiting for. And to think I never took this man's testimony of the murder before! I nearly passed it up. My friend, I am grateful. I am profoundly grateful . . . Now, you're absolutely positive of that time, are you?"

Arbor was growing mollified at being a person of such importance.

"Positive. As I told you, my encounter with the young lady had jarred my watch. I stepped back into the door of the Wakefield Tower to see whether it was in danger of slipping off, and I noted the time just before I walked down to Water Lane."

"Get out your watches, gentlemen," rumbled Dr. Fell, "and let's compare notes. *Eheu*! So! – it's a quarter past six. That's what I have, anyhow. What about the rest of you?"

"Quarter past six," said General Mason, "and I'm right. I know."

"Thirteen and a half minutes past," said Rampole.

"And I?" concluded Arbor. "Fifteen and one half minutes past, to the second. I never am wrong. This watch was made by . . ."

"Never mind," interposed Dr. Fell. "We shan't row about half a minute. That settles it. There is, however, one thing I should like to ask. You said you were on your way out at this time, Mr. Arbor. But the murder wasn't discovered until half-past two. How is it you were caught here when the detention order was issued?"

"That was what I wished to explain a moment ago," Arbor answered, "when I said it was chance. I left one of my gloves behind, on the railing round the Raleigh first-edition in the Bloody Tower. They're – ah – rather special gloves," he explained, carelessly. "Carter of Fifth Avenue does them for me, and I have no other pair of exactly this sort."

General Mason looked pained, and Arbor lifted the shiny grey hat from his lap and indicated the gloves.

"I was all the way to the Strand in my cab before I remembered, and I returned. It was about twenty minutes to three when I arrived, and then I couldn't get out."

"I hope that cabby isn't still waiting," the general mused. "It would be unfortunate, Mr. Arbor, if such an unfortunate witness got his head bashed in. Ah," he said, somewhat dreamily, "most unfortunate . . . Hold on! Wait! I remember now. There's something *I* wanted to ask you."

"With pleasure." Arbor frowned. "You are . . . ?"

"I'm the man you wanted to see," the general replied, with some asperity. "I'm the deputy governor of the Tower. And what's more, sir, I'm damned if I let you paw over that Raleigh book. General Sir Ian Hamilton presented that to us. What was I saying? Oh yes. About the Raleigh. You said you'd never seen it. Is this your first visit to the Tower?"

"It is."

"The reason I asked is that you have all the names down pat. You speak familiarly of 'Water Lane,' and the Green, and all the rest of it, when you didn't go any farther than the Bloody Tower."

"Perfectly simple," said Arbor, with the air of a detective speaking to his dull-witted assistant. "I dislike asking directions, my dear sir. It savours of *gaucherie.*" From his pocket he produced one of the green pamphlets. "This little guide, with a map, which I studied before entering the Tower at all, gave me a thorough working knowledge."

Dr. Fell pulled at his moustache.

"I've got just one more question, my friend, and then you are free to go. Are you acquainted with Mrs. Lester Bitton, your host's sister-in-law?"

"Unfortunately, no. You see, as I told you, I have never before stopped at Bitton's house. Mr. and Mrs. Bitton were away when I first arrived. They returned last night, I am told, but I only came back from my weekend this morning, and both were out of the house . . . I know Lester Bitton slightly. And I have heard Bitton himself speak of her and seen her portrait. But I've never met her."

"You wouldn't recognize her, then, if you saw her?"

"I'm afraid not."

"Before you go, though," Hadley suggested, "isn't there something you want to tell us?"

Arbor had risen with almost a shake of relief. He was buttoning his coat slowly, so as not to seem in a hurry; but he stopped. "Tell you? I don't understand."

"Any – hints, or instructions, Mr. Arbor? A valuable manuscript virtually belonging to you has been stolen, you know. Aren't you interested in recovering it? It would seem that you are very easily diverted from the loss of a ten-thousand-pound possession, considering the trouble you took to acquire it. Today you were down here, deeply interested in something else. Aren't you making any inquiries at all?"

Arbor, Rampole sensed, had been dreading that question. But he did not immediately speak. He adjusted his hat to a nicety, drew on his gloves, and hooked his umbrella over his arm. This sartorial adjustment seemed to lend him his old cool confidence and bearing.

Just so," he agreed. "But you are forgetting something. I want no unpleasantness in this matter, gentlemen; I have already outlined my reasons. I prefer not to use the assistance of the police. But I assure you I have not been idle. I have contacts and leads which are – excuse me – not open to *you.* As you say, it is not likely that I shall neglect to investigate." A thin smile on the swarthy face, a cool raising of the black brows, a slight bow. "If you wish to speak to me further, you will reach me at the Savoy. I thank you for – ah – a most instructive afternoon. Good day, gentlemen."

After he had gone there was a long silence. It had grown cold in the room, for the fire was almost out. An expression of malignancy was on General Mason's face. He moved his hands in the air after the fashion of a burlesque hypnotist.

"Hocus-pocus," he muttered. "Allagazam. I hope you haven't got any more witnesses, Hadley. That's enough. First hats, and then love-affairs, and now manuscripts. It hasn't helped any. It's only mixed us up worse . . . What did you make of our aesthete?"

"As a witness," said Hadley, "he was either too difficult or too easy at various times. He started off smoothly enough. Then he went into a complete funk at the mention of the murder. Finally, I'd swear he was telling the truth when he described what he knew of the happenings here."

"Meaning?" prompted the general.

Again Hadley began to stride about the room. He spoke irritably.

"Oh, I can see one obvious explanation. But *that* only complicates matters. See here. He obviously didn't know it was Driscoll who had been murdered here. At least, he didn't know it was the young chap he'd met at Sir William's. And it nearly knocked him over when he heard. Why?

"Put it this way. Arbor's clever, and he's tricky. He genuinely dislikes unpleasantness, because it upsets his own self-conscious dignity; but he has no more courage than a rabbit. You could see that in everything he said. Worst of all, he has an unholy horror of publicity. Agreed?"

"Without a struggle," said the general.

"All right. Now, he tried to make a joke out of the suggestion that he himself might have stolen that manuscript. But when you know Arbor's character, and Sir William's, it isn't quite so fantastic as it sounds. He knew the old man would raise thirty-eight different kinds of hell if he demanded his manuscript. There would be all the red-tape, delay, wrangling, and probably publicity, to say nothing of what Sir William's temper might do to Arbor's skin . . . But if the thing were stolen, Sir William could whistle for it. He had no case. Arbor could point all this out to him (by telephone, if necessary) after he'd safely got the manuscript and left the house. And Sir William wouldn't dare act. Aside from having no case, he'd show himself up in a ridiculous light. Respected ex-Cabinet Ministers can't stand that."

"I doubt whether Arbor would actually pinch the manuscript himself," said the general, shaking his head. "He wouldn't dare."

"Wait a minute. Now, he wasn't worried about that theft. He wasn't exerting himself, you see. Well, who might have stolen it for him?"

The general whistled. "You mean . . ."

"It can't be!" snapped the chief inspector, striking his fist into his palm. "It would be too much. But the possibility stares us right in the face, and we've got to think about it . . .

"Why, I mean this. Arbor said he talked Poe in that house until even the family began to wonder; broader and broader hints. He also said that with the dark and mysterious hints Sir William constantly let fall, everybody must have known about the manuscript. Certainly a clever young fellow like Driscoll couldn't have failed to know it. And Driscoll was there to dinner when Arbor did much of his talking . . ."

"Oh, look here!" General Mason protested in a distressed voice. "I mean to say – Well, it isn't done! An infernal counter-jumper like Arbor might have done it, of course. But if you're suggesting that young Driscoll . . . Purf! Burr! Bah! Out of the question. Absolutely."

"I didn't say it was true," Hadley said, patiently. "But consider. Driscoll was discontented. Driscoll was always short of money. Driscoll was invariably in a row with his uncle. Driscoll was a madcap, lunatic kid who might regard that manuscript as simply a foolish piece of paper. I confess I did myself, until I heard how much it's worth. So suppose Driscoll takes Arbor aside and says, 'Look here, if you happened to find that manuscript under your pillow one morning, what would it be worth to you?'" Hadley raised his eyebrows. "Perhaps Arbor then explained, as he might, that he was really the owner. Perhaps that didn't matter to Driscoll. But, since Arbor would have had to pay some sort of price to the old man if he bought it outright – well? It was a good chance for a stroke of business. The old man knew the full value of the manuscript. Driscoll didn't. And Arbor's an excellent man of business."

"NO!" boomed a thunderous voice.

Hadley jumped. There had been in that voice not only protest, but a sort of agonized appeal. They all turned to see Dr. Fell lumbering to his feet, his big hands spread out on the table.

"I beg of you," he said, almost imploring – "I beg and plead with you, whatever else you think of anything in this case, not to get that absurd idea. If you do, Hadley, I warn you, you'll never see the truth. Say whatever else you like. Say that the thief was Arbor, if you like. Say that it was General Mason or Father Christmas or Mussolini. But don't I entreat you, ever for a moment believe it was Driscoll."

The chief inspector was peevish. "Well, why not? I didn't say I definitely thought it was Driscoll, you understand. But, since you seem to have such a violent horror of the idea – why not?"

The doctor sat down again.

"Let me explain. By all means let me get that point straight, or you'll never understand the rest of it. Cast your minds back a couple of hours. Damn it where's my pipe? Ah. Well, we were speaking of Driscoll. And Sir William said he wasn't a coward. And I tried to give you a hint, if you recall. I said, What *was* he afraid of?

"Let me repeat that. I agree that Driscoll was far from a coward. I agree with your definition, Hadley, that he was a madcap, lunatic kid. But one thing he most definitely did fear."

"And that?"

"He feared his uncle," said Dr. Fell. After a pause, while he spilled a considerable amount of tobacco in filling his pipe, he went on wheezily: "Look here. Driscoll was an improvident sort, with expensive tastes. He lived entirely off his uncle's bounty. You heard Bitton speak of his 'allowance.' He got precious little from what small free-lance newspaper work he did, and Bitton helped him get along even with that.

"But – Bitton wasn't an indulgent uncle. Quite to the contrary. He was always quarrelling with his nephew on some point or other. And why? Because he was so fond of him. He had no son of his own. *He* had risen from small beginnings, and he wanted to see the boy exhibit some of his own violent energy. –And do you think Driscoll didn't know that? *Ha*!" said the doctor, snorting. "Of course he did. The old man might squeeze the purse-strings tighter than a slip-knot. But Driscoll knew he was the old man's favourite. And when it came to the last . . . I rather suspect Driscoll figured conspicuously in the old man's will. Didn't he, General Mason?"

"I happen to know," the general said, rather guardedly, "that he wasn't forgotten."

"So. Hadley, are you really mad enough to think the boy would have endangered all that? Why, that manuscript was literally Bitton's most cherished possession. You saw how he gloated. If Driscoll had stolen it, and he ever had the faintest suspicion Driscoll had stolen it, out the boy would have gone for ever. You know Bitton's temper and, above all, his stubbornness. He wouldn't have forgiven. There wouldn't have been a penny more from him, alive or dead . . . And what had Driscoll to gain? At most a few pounds from Arbor. Why should Arbor, a good man of business, give money to a thief for his own property? He would simply smile in that mincing way of his. 'A thousand guilders? Come, take fifty! Or I might tell your uncle where you got this manuscript.' – No, Hadley. The last thing in the world Driscoll would have done would have been to dare steal it. The person he feared most, I tell you, was his uncle."

Hadley nodded thoughtfully.

"Yes. Yes," he said, "that's true. And I have no doubt it's a very interesting lecture you're giving. But why are you so aggressive on the point? Why is it so important?"

Dr. Fell sighed. He was very much relieved.

"Because, if you understand that, you're halfway along the right track. I . . ." Wearily he raised his eyes to the door at another of the inevitable knocks. He went on, vigorously; "But I was going to say that I absolutely refuse to listen to another witness this afternoon. It's past six and the pubs are open. Come in!"

A very tired-looking Sergeant Betts entered.

"I've just been talking to the other visitors, sir," he said to Hadley. "And I'm afraid it's been a long job. They all wanted to talk, and I had to listen for fear of missing something. But not one of them knew anything whatever. All of them spent nine-tenths of their time in the white Tower. It takes quite a while to explore it thoroughly; and they weren't anywhere near the Traitors' Gate between one-thirty and two o'clock. They seemed straight, so I let them go. Was that correct, sir?"

"Yes. But keep those names and addresses in case you need them." Wearily Hadley passed a hand over his eyes. He hesitated, and then looked at his watch. "H'm. Well, it's getting late, sergeant, and we'll run along. I'll take charge of these articles on the table. In the meantime, I want you to cooperate with Hamper and find out what you can from the warders or anybody else who occurs to you. Use your own judgment. If you find out anything, communicate with the Yard. They'll know where I am."

He took down his overcoat and donned it slowly.

"Well, gentlemen," said General Mason, "that seems to be all for the moment. And I think we could all deal with a large brandy and soda. I can recommend my own, and I have some very passable cigars. If you'll do me the honour to come up to my rooms . . . ?"

Hadley hesitated; but he looked at his watch again, and shook his head.

"Thanks, General. It's good of you, but I'm afraid I can't. I have to get back to the Yard; I've the devil's own lot of routine business, you know, and I've taken far too much time as it is. I shouldn't be handling the affair at all." He frowned. "Besides, I think it's best that none of us go up. Sir William will be waiting for you, General. You know him best and you had better tell him everything. About Arbor, you see?"

"Hum! I'm bound to admit I don't like the job," the other said, uncomfortably. "But I suppose you're right."

"Tell him we shall probably pay him a visit in Berkeley Square tonight, and to be sure everybody is at home. Oh yes. And the newspapers. There will be reporters here soon, if they're not being held outside already. For the Lord's sake don't say anything yourself. Just say, 'I have no statement to make at the present time,' and refer them to

Sergeant Hamper. He'll tell them what we want given out; he's an old hand. Let's see – I want a newspaper myself, at the moment . . ."

He was already gathering up the objects which had been in Driscoll's pockets. Rampole handed him an old newspaper from the top of a bookcase; he wrapped the crossbow bolt inside it and stowed it away in the breast pocket of his overcoat.

"Right you are. But at least," said the general, "let me give you a stirrup cup before you go." He went to the door and spoke a few words. In a remarkably short time the impassive Parker appeared, bearing a tray with a bottle of whiskey, a syphon, and four glasses.

"Well," he continued, watching the soda foam as Parker mixed the drinks, "this has been an afternoon. If it weren't for poor Bitton and the damnable closeness of this thing, I should even call it entertaining. But I'm bound to say I can't make head or tail of it."

"You wouldn't call it entertaining," Hadley asserted, moodily, "if you had my job. And yet – I don't know." There was a wry smile under his clipped moustache. He accepted a glass and stared into it. "I've been thirty years in this game, General. And yet I can't help getting something like a quickened pulse when I see 'Scotland Yard has been called in on the case.' What's the magic in the damned name? I don't know. I'm a part of it. Sometimes I *am* it. But I'm still as intrigued as a naïve old dodderer like Dr. Fell."

"But I always thought you were dead against amateurs," said the general. ("Thanks Parker.") "Of course you can hardly call the doctor an amateur, but . . ."

Hadley shook his head. "I said once before today that I wasn't such a fool. Sir Basil Thomson, one of the greatest men the Yard ever had, used to say that a detective had to be a jack of all trades and a master of none. The only thing I regret about the doctor here is the deliberate way he patterns himself after the detectives in sensational fiction; of which, by the way, he's an omnivorous reader. His silences. His mysterious 'Aha's!' His . . ."

"Thank you," grumbled Dr. Fell, satirically. He had put on his cloak and his long shovel-hat; he stood, a gigantic and bulky figure, leaning on two canes; and now his face was fiery with controversy. Stumping round near the door he accepted a glass from Parker. "Hadley," he continued, "that's an old charge. An old charge, an outworn maxim, and a baseless slur on a noble branch of literature. Somebody ought to refute it. You say that the detective in fiction is mysterious and slyly secret. All right; but he only reflects real life. What about the genuine detective? He is the one who looks mysterious, says 'Aha!' and assures everybody that there will be an arrest within twenty-four hours. But, despite this pose, he doesn't go so far as the detective in fiction. He doesn't fix the taxpayer with a sombre eye and say, 'The solution of this murder, sir, depends on a mandolin, a perambulator, and a pair of bed-socks,' and send the taxpayer away feeling he's really had the police in after all. He doesn't, because he can't. But he would like to be a master mind and say that, if he could. Who wouldn't? Wouldn't *you*? In other words, he has all the pose, whether he has the knowledge or not. But, like the fictional detective, very sensibly he doesn't tell what he thinks, for the excellent and commonplace reason that he may be wrong."

"All right," said Hadley, resignedly. "If you like. Well, good health, gentlemen . . . !" He drained his glass and put it down. "I suppose, Doctor, this is a preamble to some mysterious predictions of yours?"

Dr. Fell was lifting his glass; but he paused and scowled heavily.

"I hadn't thought of doing so," he replied. "But as a matter of fact, I *will* give you three hints about what I think. I won't elaborate them" – his scowl became ferocious as he saw Hadley's grin – "because I may be wrong. Ha!"

"I thought so. Well, number one?"

"Number one is this. There was some dispute about the time Driscoll died. The only period in which we seem absolutely to be able to fix it lies between one-thirty when he was seen by Parker lighting a cigarette at the rail in front of Traitors' Gate, and ten minutes to two, which is the time Doctor Watson said he died. Mr. Arbor, coming into Water Lane at twenty-five minutes to two, was positive there was nobody near that rail."

"I don't see any implication there," General Mason said, after a pause; "unless it's the implication that Arbor was lying. What's your second hint?"

Dr. Fell was becoming more amiable. He juggled his glass.

"The second hint," he answered, "concerns that crossbow bolt. It was, as you saw, filed sharp into a deadly weapon. Now you are assuming, quite naturally, that this filing was done by the murderer. We have also noticed that the same hand had started to file off those words *Souvenir de Carcassonne,* but had stopped with three letters neatly effaced, and gone no farther . . . *Why weren't those other letters effaced?* When we found the body, we were of course bound to learn of the bolt Mrs. Bitton purchased at Carcassonne, and, since the victim was Driscoll, it would be too monstrous to assume a mere coincidence. I repeat: why weren't those other letters effaced?"

"Yes," said Hadley. "I'd thought of that point, too. I hope you're sure of the answer. I'm not. And the third hint?"

By this time Dr. Fell, and the black ribbon of his eyeglasses, quivered to his chuckle.

"And the third hint," he said, "is very short. It is a simple query. *Why did Sir William's hat fit him?*"

With a capacious tilt of his head he swallowed off his drink, glanced blandly about the group, pushed open the door, and shouldered out into the mist.

10
EYES IN A MIRROR

The great clock in Westminster tower struck eight-thirty.

Dorothy had not been at the hotel when Rampole and the doctor arrived there on their return from the Tower. A note left for Rampole at the desk informed him that Sylvia Somebody, who had been at school with her, was taking her home for a gathering of some of the other old girls. Owing, she said, to previous knowledge of her husband's passionate aversion to jolly little evenings of this kind, she had informed them that he was in the hospital with a violent attack of delirium tremens. ("They'll condole with me so," she explained. "D'you mind if I tell them how you throw plates at the cat and come home every night by way of the coal-chute?") She said he was to give her love to Dr. Fell; and not to forget to pin the name of his hotel to his coat lapel so that the cabman would know where to put him at the end of the evening. Even after more than six months of matrimony, too, she concluded with certain declarations which made Rampole throw out his chest. There, he reflected, was a *wife.*

He and the doctor dined at a little French restaurant in Wardour Street. Hadley, who had gone to Scotland Yard immediately after leaving the Tower, had promised to meet them there for a visit to the Bitton home that night. Dr. Fell was fond of dining in French restaurants; or, in fact, anywhere else. He dug himself in behind a steaming parapet of dishes and a formidable array of winebottles; but throughout the meal he steadily refused to discuss crime.

Those various adventures he had mentioned that afternoon were a surprise even to the young man who knew him so well. He remembered the cottage in the drowsy Lincolnshire countryside. He remembered Dr. Fell smoking his pipe in a little study where three walls were built of books, or pottering about his garden in a broad-brimmed white hat. The sun-dial, the bird-houses the lawns starred with white flowers and asleep in afternoon sunlight: this had seemed to be Dr. Fell's domain. It was incongruous that those words he had used so casually that afternoon, "Cripps, the Notting Hill poisoner," or "that chap with the mirror in his watch," or the tales from the far-off days of the heavy guns. But, none the less, Rampole remembered how once a telegram of five words had brought several quiet armed men from Scotland Yard to do his bidding.

And this evening the doctor would not speak of crime. On any other subject, however, it was practically impossible to stop him. He discussed in turn the third Crusade, the origin of the Christmas cracker, Sir Richard Steele, merry-go-rounds – on which he particularly enjoyed riding – Beowulf, Buddhism, Thomas Henry Huxley, and Miss Greta Garbo. It was eight-thirty before they finished dinner. Rampole, comfortably lazy and warmed with wine, had just sat back for the lighting of the cigars when Hadley arrived.

The chief inspector was restless, and he seemed worried. He put his brief-case down on the table and drew up a chair without removing his overcoat.

"I'll have a sandwich and a whiskey with you," he said, in reply to Dr. Fell's invitation. "Come to think of it, I forgot to get any dinner. But we mustn't waste time."

The doctor peered at him over the flame of the match for his cigar.

"Developments?"

"Serious ones, I'm afraid. At least two unforeseen things have occurred. One of them I can't make head or tail of."

He began to rummage in his brief-case and draw out papers. "To begin with, somebody broke into Driscoll's flat about a quarter to five o'clock this afternoon."

"Broke into . . ."

"Yes. Here are the facts, briefly. You remember, when we questioned that Larkin woman I left orders to have her shadowed. Fortunately, Hamper had an excellent man there; a plain-clothes constable, new man, whose only talent seems to be along that line. He took up Larkin's trail as soon as she left the gates. She walked straight up Tower Hill, without hesitating or looking back. Probably she knew she would be followed; anyhow, she made no attempt to give this man – what's his name – Somers, yes – to give him the slip.

"At the top of Tower Hill she cut across and went into the Mark Lane Underground Station. There was a queue in front of the booking-office, and Somers couldn't get close enough to hear the station to which she booked. But Somers had a hunch. He took a ticket to Russell Square, which is the tube station nearest to where she lives. She changed at King's Cross, and then he knew he was right. He got out after her at the Russell Square station in Bernard Street, and followed her down Woburn Place to Tavistock Square.

"She went into the third entry of Tavistock Chambers, still without looking round. Somers walked straight in after her, like a fool. But it's fortunate he did.

"He describes it as a rather narrow entry, badly lighted by a door with a glass panel at the rear, and with an automatic lift in the centre. The doors to the two flats on that floor are on either side He had seen her closing the door of No. 1 after her. And, at the same time she was going in, a woman slid out of the door of No. 2, darted past the lift, down a couple of steps, and out of the glass door at the back."

"The woman again, eh?" said Dr. Fell, blowing out smoke placidly. "Did he catch a glimpse of her?"

"Wait. Nothing at all definite, you see. There were no lights on, and what with the mist, the darkness of the hall, and the sudden run she made, he could just be sure it was a woman. Of course, he wasn't sure that anything was wrong. But as a matter of caution he went close and looked at the door and then he was sure.

"The lock of the door had been splintered out from the jamb with some sharp instrument like a chisel or a heavy screwdriver. Somers ran down the way she had gone. The glass door opened on a large paved court, with a drive-way going out to the street. Of course, the woman was gone. And Somers came back.

"Now, at the time he didn't know Driscoll lived there; he only knew the Larkin woman did, from what instructions he'd been given. But he struck a match and saw the card on the door, and then he was inside in a hurry.

"The place was in a wild state of disorder; somebody had been searching for something. But I'll come to that in a moment. Somers went out after the porter, and had the devil's own time finding him. The porter is an old man, rather deaf, and he was in a bad state when Somers made him understand what had happened. He said he had been in his room for several hours, and had heard nothing. The only person he had seen there that afternoon was a young man who had been there many times before, and had a key. He knew *he* hadn't burgled the place, because he had met the young man coming out of the door of the flat, and walked out to his car with him, and he knew everything had been in order then. Somers explained he meant a woman, who had been there just a moment ago; and the porter refused to believe him."

Dr. Fell was drawing designs on the tablecloth with a fork.

"Had anything been stolen from the flat?" he inquired.

"We can't tell yet. I haven't seen the place, but one of my best men is up there now. According to Somers's report, the desk had been broken open, every drawer in the flat ransacked, and most of Driscoll's papers were scattered over the floor."

"In search for some sort of letter or document?"

"Apparently. And I think we have an explanation of 'Mary.'"

"I rather thought we should," said the doctor. "Well?"

"One thing in the study struck Somers's eye because it seemed so out of place. It was your typical bachelor digs: hunting-prints, leather chairs, a silver cup or two, sport groups, things like that. But on the mantelpiece were two plaster figures on bases, painted in bright colours – a man and a woman. They wore what Somers called 'old-time clothes, like the ones in Madame Tussaud's,' and they were labelled . . ."

Dr. Fell raised his eyebrows and grunted. "I see. Philip II and Mary Tudor. Rather an unfortunate instance of a romance, though. H'm. They probably got them at some outing together, and kept them for the sentimental remembrance. Well – who was the woman?"

The waiter brought Hadley a ham sandwich and a stiff whiskey and soda. He took a pull at the latter before he answered.

"It looks fairly clear, doesn't it, after what we decided this afternoon?" he demanded. "It had to be somebody who already knew about the murder. She would realize that, with Driscoll dead, his papers would be examined immediately. And if there were any letters that incriminate *her* . . . ?"

"In short, Mrs. Bitton," said Dr. Fell. "No, I don't have any doubt you're right. Let's see. We questioned her before we questioned Larkin, didn't we? And then let her go."

"Yes. And think back, now! Do you remember just before she was about to leave . . . ? Ah, Rampole, *you* remember it, I can see. You noticed?"

The American nodded. "Just for a moment; an expression of real and close terror. She seemed to remember something."

"And do you recall what General Mason had just said? I saw that expression on her face, and I tried to account for it; but I understand now. General Mason had been urging Sir William to go up to his rooms and rest, and he said, 'The Devereux record is in the portfolio on my desk.' And that instantly suggested to her the damning evidence that might be lying in Driscoll's desk for the police to discover. Evidently she has called herself 'Mary' only since he had reason to believe she was being watched."

"But would she have had time to get up to Driscoll's flat and do all this?" Rampole asked. "We didn't talk very long with Mrs. Larkin. And Sir William went out to put Mrs. Bitton into a cab . . ."

"Which she dismissed at the top of Tower Hill for the underground. She could have gone from Mark Lane to King's Cross in less than fifteen minutes; she could have even saved the risk of time lost in changing trains by getting out at King's Cross and walking to Tavistock Square. Oh yes. The taxi would have been much too slow . . . And as for getting into the flat, you've only got to take one look at her to realize that she could have broken open a much less flimsy door with no particular trouble. The deaf porter wouldn't be apt to hear any noise, and the only other person who could have discovered her was Mrs. Larkin – whom she knew to be detained at the Tower."

"That tears it," said Dr, Fell "That undoubtedly tears it. *Hah*!" He put his big head in his hands "This is bad, Hadley. And what I don't like is the symbolism."

"Symbolism?"

"I mean those two plaster figures you've described. God knows, they may have won them throwing balls at bottles at a country fair. But it's a curious and disturbing fact that the woman signed at least one of her letters 'Mary.' Suppose you and your lady-love have two china dolls in which you like to fancy an analogy to yourselves. One of them is labelled 'Abélard' and the other 'Héloïse.' You're very apt to look up Héloïse and Abélard, aren't you, and see who they were? – if you don't already know. And I tell you, Hadley, I didn't like that Bitton woman's much too palpably idiotic prattle about Queen Elizabeth being executed. It wasn't like her."

"What are you driving at?"

"If there *is* a symbolism about those two figures," said the doctor, "we have got to remember two things about Queen Mary Tudor of England and her husband, King Philip II of Spain. One is that all her life Mary was violently in love with Philip, a passion almost as strong as her religious faith; while Philip was never in the least interested in her. And the second thing we must remember . . ."

"Well?"

". . . that they called her 'Bloody Mary,'" said Dr. Fell. There was a long silence. The little restaurant, almost empty of diners, whispered to that suggestion as with the ticking of a clock. There was a little *fine* left at the bottom of Rampole's liqueur-glass, and he drained it hastily.

"Whatever *that* amounts to," Hadley said, at length, with grim doggedness, "I'll go on to the second thing that's happened since I've seen you. And it's the really disturbing one. It's about Julius Arbor."

Dr. Fell struck the table. "Go on!" he said. "Good God! I might have known . . . that chases the cobwebs. Go on, Hadley."

"He's at Golder's Green. Listen:

"They didn't tell us this when we left the Tower, but Sergeant Hamper found it out and phoned to me, and I've just finished tracing down the rest. When Arbor left us, it couldn't have been much more than twenty past six o'clock. You remember, we all looked at our watches to be sure Arbor was right about the time? It was six-fifteen then, and he left shortly afterwards.

"Well, the word had already been carried up to the first tower you enter as you go in – it always confuses me, because it's called the Middle Tower – word had been carried up to let him go through. He told us, you remember, that he'd brought a taxi down there; told the driver to wait, and then couldn't reappear. After some length of time, the driver wondered what was wrong and came down to the Middle Tower to investigate. The Spur Guard barred his way, and the warder on duty said something about an accident. Apparently the driver had happy visions of his meter clicking into pounds; he planted himself there and waited. He waited, mind you, for over three hours. Such is the London cabby."

Hadley finished his sandwich, called for another whiskey, and lit a cigarette.

"Then Arbor came out from the Byward Tower where we were, and started to walk along the causeway between there and the Middle Tower. It was dark then, and still rather misty. But there's a gas-lamp on the parapet of the bridge. The taxi-driver and the warder on duty at the Middle Tower happened to glance along the causeway, and they saw Arbor leaning against the lamp-standard as though he were about to collapse. Then he straightened up and stumbled ahead.

"They thought he was drunk. But when he reached them his face was white and sweaty, and he could hardly talk. Another of those attacks we witnessed, undoubtedly, but a worse attack because, somehow, he'd got a worse fright. The taxi-driver took him over to the refreshment-room, and he drank about half a tumbler of brandy neat. He seemed a bit better, and ordered the driver to take him to Sir William's house in Berkeley Square.

"When he arrived there he again told the driver to wait. He said he wanted to pack a bag and then to go to an address at Golder's Green. At this the driver protested volubly. He'd been waiting over three hours, there was a big bill on the meter, and he hadn't seen the colour of his fare's money: besides, Golder's Green was a long distance out. Then Arbor shoved a five-pound note into his hand, and said he could have another if he would do as he was told.

"Naturally, the taxi-driver began to suspect something fishy. During all the time he spent hanging about the Middle Tower, the warder had let slip a few hints about the real state of affairs. Arbor wasn't in the house long before he came out carrying a valise and a couple of coats over his arm. On the drive to Golder's Green the driver grew decidedly uneasy."

Hadley paused, and turned over a sheet of paper from his brief-case as though to refresh his memory. He spoke while his eye was still running down the typewritten lines.

"Did you ever notice how even the most reticent people will speak freely to taxi-drivers? They'll not only speak, but they'll be quite garrulous. I don't know why it is, unless it's because a taxi-driver is never surprised at anything. If I were going to establish a system of police spies in England, I shouldn't make them *concierges,* as they do in France; I'd make them taxi-drivers . . . Never mind that. Here we are."

He frowned, and then tapped the sheets on his palm.

"Now, but for what this driver knew of the murder, and Arbor's rather remarkable mumblings in the cab, I shouldn't have heard this at all. But the taxi-driver was afraid he'd be mixed up in a murder. So after he drove Arbor to Golder's Green, he came straight back and went to Scotland Yard. Fortunately, he fell into the proper hands, and they sent him to me. He was one of the famous type – stout, patient, rather morose, with a red face and a large greyish moustache and a gruff voice. But, like most Cockneys, he had a flair for description and vivid pantomime. He perched on the edge of a chair in my office, turning his cap round in his hands and imitating Arbor to the life. You could see Arbor, nervous and ultra-dignified, holding to his glasses as the cab bumped, and every two minutes leaning up to ask a question.

"First Arbor asked him whether he carried a revolver. The taxi-driver said 'Ho!' and laughed. Then Arbor suggested he must be a pretty ugly customer in a row. The driver said he could hold his own. Next Arbor wondered whether they were being followed; he began talking about how he wasn't in the directory at all, and he had a cottage at Golder's Green which nobody knew about except some friends near by. He kept hinting that London wasn't as full of criminals as New York; was it? But what the driver especially remembered was his constant reference to 'a voice.'"

"A voice?" Doctor Fell repeated. "Whose voice?"

"Arbor didn't say. But he asked whether telephone calls could be traced; that was the only point he definitely mentioned in connection with it. Well, they reached the cottage, in an outlying district. But Arbor said he wouldn't go in just at the moment – the place hadn't been opened for months. He had the driver drop him at a villa not far away, which was well lighted, The driver noted the name. It was called 'Briarbrae.'"

"The friends of his, I suppose. H'm."

"Yes. We looked it up later. It belongs to a Mr. Daniel Spengler. Now, that's about all. What do you make of it?"

"It looks bad, Hadley. This man may be in very grave danger. I don't think he is, personally, but there's just a chance . . ."

"I don't need you to tell me *that*," the chief inspector said irritably. "If the damned fools would only come to *us* when they get into trouble! That's what we're for. But they won't. And if he is in any danger, he took the worst possible course. Instead of going to a hotel, as he said he intended, he thought he was choosing a spot where nobody could find him. And instead he picked a place ideally suited for – well, murder."

"What have you done?"

"I sent a good man immediately to watch the house, and to phone the Yard every half-hour. But what danger is he in? Do you think he knows something about the murder, and the murderer knows he knows?"

For a moment Dr. Fell puffed furiously at his cigar. Then he said:

"This is getting much too serious, Hadley. Much. You see, I've been basing everything on a belief that I knew how all this came about. I told you this afternoon that everybody liked playing the master-mind. And I could afford to chuckle, because so much of it is really funny . . ."

"*Funny*!"

"Yes. Ironically, impossibly funny. It's like a farce comedy suddenly gone mad. It's as though they introduced a throat-cutting into the second act of 'Charley's Aunt.' . . . Do you remember Mark Twain's description of his experiences in learning to ride a bicycle?"

"I'll be damned," said Hadley, stuffing papers back into his brief-case, "if I listen to any lecture when . . ."

"This isn't a lecture. Listen," urged Dr. Fell, with unwonted seriousness. "He said he was always doing exactly what he didn't want to do. He tried to keep from running over rocks and being thrown. But if he rode down a street two hundred yards wide, and there happened to be one small piece of brick lying anywhere in the road, inevitably he would run over it. Well, that has a very deadly application to this case.

"And I can't keep my pose any longer," the doctor said, with sudden energy. "I've got to separate the nonsense and the happenings of pure chance from the really ugly angle of the business. Chance started it, and murder only finished it; that's what *I* think. I must show you the absurd part of it, and then you can judge whether I'm right. But first there are two things to be done."

"What?"

"Can you communicate with that man you have on guard at Arbor's cottage?" the doctor asked, abruptly.

"Yes. Through the local police station."

"All right. Get in touch with him. Tell him, far from keeping in the background, to make himself as conspicuous as possible. Let him walk about the lawn, if he likes. But under no circumstances – even if he is hailed – to go near Arbor or make himself known to Arbor."

"What's the purpose of that?" the chief inspector demanded.

"I don't believe Arbor's in any danger. But obviously he thinks he is. He also thinks the police haven't any idea where he is. You see, there's something that man knows, which for one reason or another he wouldn't tell us. If he notices your man lurking about his cottage, he'll jump to the conclusion that it's his enemy. If he tries calling the local police, they will find nobody – naturally. It's rather rough on him, but we've got to terrify him into telling what he knows. As you said, the man has no courage at all. Sooner or later he'll seek *your* protection, and by that time we shall be able to get the truth."

"That," said the chief inspector, grimly, "is the only good suggestion you've made so far. I'm glad to see you're waking up. I'll do it."

"It can't do any harm. If he *is* in danger, the obvious presence of a guard will have a salutary effect on the enemy. If he does call the local police and there's a real enemy about, the police can have a look for the real enemy while they pass up your own man . . . The next thing, we've got to pay a very brief visit to Driscoll's flat."

"If you're thinking something is hidden there I can tell you that my men will find it more easily than we can ever . . ."

"No. Your men will attach no importance to what I want to find. I don't suppose they bothered to look at his typewriter, did they?"

"His *what*?"

"Typewriter. You know what a typewriter is," said the doctor, testily. "And also, I want a brief look about the kitchen. If he has one, as I'm sure he has, we shall probably find it stowed away in the kitchen . . . Where's that waiter? I want the bill."

The mist was clearing as they emerged from the restaurant. Narrow Wardour Street was crowded; restaurant signs glowed with dull lights, a barrel-organ tinkled at the corner among a group of small boys, and there was a sound of jollification from several pubs. The theatre traffic had just begun to thin in the glare of Shaftesbury Avenue, and Hadley had some difficulty in manoeuvring his car. But, once out of the centre of Town and across Oxford Street he accelerated the big Daimler to a fast pace. Bloomsbury lay deserted under high and mournful gas-lamps; silent, with the muffled rumble of traffic beyond. They cut across into Great Russell Street, and turned left past the long and prison-like shadows of the British Museum.

"Get that report out of my brief-case, will you?" Hadley requested. "I think Somers said it was on the west side of the square . . ."

Rampole, craning his neck out of the tonneau, watched the street signs. Montague Street; the bare trees and sedate house-fronts of Russell Square; Upper Bedford Place, where Hadley slowed down.

Tavistock Square was large and oblong in shape, not too well supplied with street lights. Along the west side the buildings were higher than on the others, and rather more imposing in a heavy Georgian style. Tavistock Chambers proved to be a red-brick block of flats with four entry halls, two on either side of an arch beneath which a driveway led into the court. Into this court Hadley drove the car.

"So this," he said, "is the way the woman escaped. I don't wonder she wasn't noticed."

He slid from under the wheel and peered about. There was only one lamp in the court, but the mist was rapidly lifting into a clear, cold night. A few windows were alight in the plaster-faced walls which hedged in the court.

"Lower parts of the windows frosted glass," the chief inspector grunted. "I left instructions to question the tenants about her, but it's useless. A red Indian in his war bonnet could have walked out of here without being seen, even on a clear day. Let's see . . . Those are the glass doors giving on the rear of the entry halls. We want the third entry. There it is. That'll be Driscoll's flat, with the light in the rear window. Hum! Evidently my man hasn't left the place yet; I should have thought he'd be finished by this time."

He crossed to the glass door, stumbled over a rubbish-can, and disturbed a hysterical cat. The others followed him up some steps into a red-tiled hall with brown distempered walls. Its only illumination was a sickly electric bulb in the cage of the automatic lift. But a thin line of light slanted out from the door on their left, which was not quite closed, and they saw the splintered wood about the lock.

Flat 2. Rampole's eyes moved to the door facing it across the hall, where the watchful and whaleboned Mrs. Larkin might be peering out from the flap of the letter-slot. It was damp and cold in the hallway, and still except for somebody's radio talking hoarsely on an upper floor.

There was a crash, sudden and violent. The line of light in the doorway of Flat 2 seemed to shake, and the noise echoed hollowly up the lift-well. It had come from that door . . .

While the echoes were still trembling, Hadley moved swiftly across to the door and pushed it open. Rampole, peering over his shoulder, saw the disorder of Philip Driscoll's sitting-room as it had been described a short time ago. But there was another piece of disorder now.

In the wall directly opposite was a mantelpiece with an ornate mirror behind the shelf. And in front of this mantelpiece, his back to the newcomers, a tall and heavy man stood with his head bowed. They saw past his shoulder a foolish plaster figurine standing on the mantelshelf: a woman painted in bright colours, with a tight-waisted dress and a silver hair-net. But there was no companion figure beside it. The hearthstone was littered with a thousand white fragments to show where the other figure had been flung down a moment before.

Just for a moment the tableau held – weird and somehow terrible in its power. The echo of that crash seemed to linger; its passion still quivered in the bent back of the man standing there. He had not heard the newcomers. He seemed weighed down, and lonely, and damned.

Then his hand moved out slowly and seized the other figure. And as he raised it his head lifted and they saw his face in the mirror.

"Good evening," said Dr. Fell. "You're Mr. Lester Bitton, aren't you?"

11
THE LITTLE PLASTER DOLLS

Never before that time, Rampole afterwards thought, had he ever seen a man's naked face. Never had he seen it as for a brief instant he saw Lester Bitton's face in the mirror. At all times in life there are masks and guards, and in the brain a tiny bell gives warning. But here was a man caught blind in his anguish, as nerveless as the hand which held poised that little painted figurine.

And, oddly enough, Rampole's first thought was how he might have looked at this man had he seen him in his everyday existence: going in a bus to the City, say, or reading his newspaper at a club. Where you saw your staunch and practical British business man, you saw Lester Bitton. Well tailored, inclined to corpulence. Clean-shaven face, beginning to draw and go dry at the eyes and mouth, hard but pleasant; thick black hair frizzed with grey, and fresh from the clean hair-tonicy smell of the barber's.

He looked a little like his brother, though his face was inclined to be reddish and have heavy folds. But you could not tell now . . .

The lost, damned eyes stared back at them from the mirror. His wrist wobbled, and the figure almost slid through his fingers. He took it with his other hand and put it back up on the mantelpiece. They could hear him breathing as he turned about. Instinctively his hand went to his tie, to straighten it; instinctively he felt down the sides of his dark overcoat.

"Who the hell" said Lester Bitton, "are *you*?"

His deep voice was hoarse, and it cracked. That almost finished him, but he fought his nerves. "What God damned right have you got to walk in . . ."

Rampole couldn't stand this. It wasn't right to look at him, in the way that man felt; it wasn't decent. The American felt mean and petty. He moved his eyes away, and wished he hadn't come inside the door.

"Steady," said Hadley, quietly. "I'm afraid it's you who have to make an explanation. This flat has been taken over by the police, you know. And I'm afraid we can't respect private feelings in a murder case. You *are* Lester Bitton, aren't you?"

The man's heavy breathing quieted somewhat, and the wrath died out of his eyes. But he looked heavy and hollow, and unutterably tired.

"I am," he said in a lower voice. "Who are you?"

"My name is Hadley . . ."

"Ah," said the other, "I see." He was groping backwards, and he found the edge of a heavy leather chair. Slowly he lowered himself until he was sitting on the arm. Then he made a gesture. "Well, here I am," he added, as though that explained everything.

"What are you doing here, Mr. Bitton?"

"I suppose you don't *know*?" Bitton asked, bitterly. He glanced back over his shoulder, at the smashed figure on the hearthstone, and looked up again at Hadley.

The chief inspector played his advantage. He studied Bitton without threat and almost without interest. Slowly he opened his brief-case, drew out a typewritten sheet – which was only Constable Somers's report, as Rampole saw – and glanced at it.

"We know of course, that you have employed a firm of private detectives to watch your wife. And" – he glanced at the sheet again – "that one of their operatives, a Mrs. Larkin, lives directly across the hall from here."

"Rather smart, you Scotland Yard men," the other observed in an impersonal voice. "Well, that's right. Nothing illegal in that, I suppose. You also know, then, that I don't need to waste my money any longer."

"We know that Mr. Driscoll is dead."

Bitton nodded. His heavy, reddish, rather thickly-lined face was assuming normal appearance; the eyes had ceased to have that dull and terrible glitter; but a nerve seemed to jump in his arm.

"Yes," he said, reflectively. His eyes wandered about the room without curiosity. "The swine's dead. I heard it when I went home to dinner. But I'm afraid it hasn't cut my detective agency off from much money. I was intending to pay them off and get rid of them tomorrow. Business conditions being what they are, I couldn't afford an unnecessary expense."

"That, Mr. Bitton, is open to two meanings. Which of them do you imply?"

Lester Bitton was himself again – hard, shrewd, very clear-eyed; a fleshy and utterly stolid version of his brother. He spread out his hands.

"Let's be frank, Mr . . . er . . . Hadley. I have played the fool. You know I was having my wife followed. I owe her a profound apology. What I have discovered only does credit to her name."

Hadley's face wore a faint smile, as one who says, "Well done!"

"Mr. Bitton," he said, "I had intended having a conversation with you tonight, and this is as good a place as any. I shall have to ask you a number of questions . . ."

"As you wish."

Hadley looked round at his companions. Dr. Fell was paying not the slightest attention to the questioning. He was running his eyes over the small, pleasant room, with its dull, brown-papered walls, sporting prints, and leather chairs. One of the chairs had been knocked over. The drawer of a side-table had been thrown upside down on the floor, its contents scattered. Dr. Fell stumped across and peered down.

"Theatre programs," he said "magazines, old invitations, bills . . . H'm. Nothing I want here. The desk and the type-writer will be in the other rooms somewhere. Excuse me. Carry on with the questioning, Hadley. Don't mind me."

He disappeared through a door at the rear.

Hadley removed his bowler, gestured Rampole to a chair and sat down himself.

"Mr. Bitton," he said, harshly, "I suggest that you be frank. I am not concerned with your wife's morals, or with yours, except in so far as they concern a particularly brutal murder. You have admitted you had her followed. Why do you trouble to deny that there was an affair between your wife and Philip Driscoll?"

"That's a damned lie. If you insinuate . . ."

"I don't insinuate. I tell you. You can hardly be very excited by an insinuation which you made yourself when you put a private detective on her movements – can you? Let's not waste time. We have the 'Mary' notes, Mr. Bitton."

"Mary? Who the devil is Mary?"

"You should know, Mr. Bitton. You were about to smash her on the hearth when we walked into this room."

Hadley bent forward; he spoke sharply and coldly:

"I warn you again, I can't afford to waste time. You are not in the habit of walking into people's houses and smashing ornaments off their mantelshelves because you don't approve of the decoration. If you have any idea that we don't know the meaning of those two figures, get rid of it. We do. You had broken the man and you were about to break the woman. No sane person who saw your face at that moment could have any doubt of your state of mind. Do I make myself clear?"

Bitton shaded his eyes with a big hand, but a crooked vein stood out at his temple. "Is it any of your business," he said at length, in a repressed voice, "whether . . ."

"How much do you know about Driscoll's murder?"

"Eh?"

"Have you heard the facts of Driscoll's murder?"

"A few. I – well, I spoke to my brother when he returned from the Tower. Laura – Laura had come home and locked herself in her room. When I – when I came back from the City, I knocked at her door and she wouldn't let me in. I thought everybody had gone mad. Especially as I knew nothing of this – this murder. And Sheila said that Laura had run into the house as white as death and rushed upstairs without a word." The hand before his eyes clenched spasmodically. "Then Will came in about seven-thirty and told me a little . . ."

"Are you aware, then, that an excellent case could be made out against your wife for the murder of Philip Driscoll?"

Hadley was in action now. Rampole stared at him; a placid merchant ship suddenly running out the masked batteries. Hitherto, the American knew, he had lacked proof of his most vital point, and Bitton had supplied it. There was about him now nothing of the urbanity with which he had treated witnesses that afternoon. He sat grey and inexorable, his fingers interlocked, his eyes burning with a glow behind the eyeballs, and heavy lines tightening round his mouth.

"Just a moment, Mr. Bitton. Don't say anything. I'll give you no theories. I simply intend to tell you facts.

"Your wife was having an affair with Philip Driscoll. She wrote a note telling him to meet her today at one-thirty at the Tower of London. We know that he received this note, because it was found in his pocket. The note informed him that they were being watched. Driscoll, I need not tell you, lived off the bounty of a quick-tempered and far from indulgent uncle. I will not say that if the uncle ever discovered any such scandal he would disinherit his nephew – because even that obvious point is a theory. I will not say that Driscoll saw the vital necessity for breaking off his liaison – because that obvious point is a theory, too.

"But he did telephone Robert Dalrye to get him out of a mess, just after he received that letter. And, later, some one did speak to Dalrye on the telephone, *in a high voice,* and lure him away on a wild-goose chase to this flat. You need not consider the following inferences, because they are theories (1) That Driscoll always ran to Dalrye when he was in trouble, (2) That all Driscoll's family knew this, (3) That Dalrye's level-headedness would have caused the impressionable Driscoll to break off such a dangerous entanglement, (4) That Driscoll was in a mood to break it off, because he had not seen his paramour for several weeks and he was a youth of roving fancy, (5) That his paramour felt convinced she could keep him in line if she saw him once again alone, without the interference of a cool-headed third party, (6) That Driscoll's paramour knew of this morning telephone-call through Sheila Bitton who had also spoken with Dalrye on the phone that morning, (7) That the voice of Driscoll's paramour is, for a woman, fairly deep, and, finally (8) That a voice on the telephone speaking quickly, chaotically, and almost unintelligibly, can pass without detection for the tones of almost anyone the speaker may choose."

Hadley was quite unemotional. He spaced his words as though he were reading a document, and his interlocked fingers seemed to beat time to them. Lester Bitton had taken his hand away from his face, and he was holding the chair-arms.

"I have told you these were inferences. Now for more facts," the chief inspector continued. "The appointment in the note had been for one-thirty. One-thirty is the last time Driscoll was seen alive. He was standing near the Traitors' Gate, and some person approached out of the shadows and touched his arm. At precisely twenty-five minutes to two, a woman answering to the description of your wife was seen hurrying away from the vicinity of the Traitors' Gate. She was hurrying so blindly, in fact, that she bumped squarely into the witness who saw her in a roadway no wider than this room. Finally, when Driscoll's body was found on the steps of the Traitors' Gate, he was discovered to have been stabbed with a weapon which your wife purchased last year in southern France, and which was ready to her hand in her own home."

He paused, looked steadily at Bitton, and added in a low voice:

"Can't you imagine what a clever lawyer could to with all those points, Mr. Bitton? And I am only a policeman."

Bitton hoisted up his big body. His hands were shaking and the rims of his eyes were red.

"Damn you," he said, "that's what you think, is it? Well, I'm glad you saw me so soon. I'm glad you didn't make an unutterable ass of yourself before you told me how good your case was and arrested her. I'll tell you what I'm going to do, I'm going to blow your whole case higher than hell without stepping any further than that flat across the hall. Because *I* have a witness who saw her the whole time she was at the Tower of London, and can swear Driscoll was alive after she left him."

Hadley was on his feet in an instant. It was like the lunge of a swordsman.

"Yes," he said, in a louder voice, "I rather thought you had. I rather thought that was why you came to Tavistock Chambers tonight. When you heard about the murder, you couldn't wait for the usual report of your private detective over there. You had to go to *her* . . . If she knows anything, bring her over here and let her swear to it. Otherwise, so help me God! I'll swear out a warrant for Mrs. Bitton's arrest inside an hour."

Bitton shouldered out of the chair. He was fighting mad, and his usual good sense had deserted him. He flung open the door with the broken lock, and closed it with a slam. They could hear his footsteps ring grittily on the tiles of the hall; a pause, and the insistent clamour of a door-buzzer.

Rampole drew a hand across his forehead. His throat was dry and his heart hammering.

"I didn't know," he said – "I didn't know you were so certain Mrs. Bitton had . . ."

There was a placid smile under Hadley's clipped moustache. He sat down again and folded his hands.

"Sh-h!" he warned. "Not so loud, please; he'll hear you. How did I do it? I'm not much of an actor, but I'm used to little demonstrations like that. Did I do it well?"

He caught the expression on the American's face. "Go ahead, my boy. Swear. I don't mind. It's a tribute to my performance."

"Then you don't believe –"

"I never believed it for an instant," the chief inspector admitted, cheerfully. "There were too many holes in it. If Mrs. Bitton killed Driscoll, what about the hat on Driscoll's head? That becomes nonsense. If she killed him by Traitors' Gate with a blow straight through the heart at one-thirty, how did he contrive to keep alive until ten minutes to two? Why didn't she leave the Tower after she had killed him, instead of hanging about unnecessarily for nearly an hour and getting herself drawn into the mess without reason? . . . Besides, my explanation of the faked telephone-call to Dalrye was very thin. If Bitton hadn't been so upset he would have seen it. Dalrye, of course, never talked to Sheila Bitton this morning and told her Driscoll had made an appointment. But I had to hit Bitton hard and frequently while his guard was down. A little drama also did no harm; it never does."

"But, by God!" said Rampole, "I don't mind telling you it was good." He stared across at the smashed plaster on the hearthstone. "You had to do that. Otherwise you'd never have got Mrs. Larkin's testimony. If she followed Mrs. Bitton, she knows all Mrs. Bitton's movements, but . . ."

Hadley glanced over his shoulder to make sure the door was closed.

"Exactly. But she would never tell them to the police. This afternoon she swore to us she had seen nothing. That was a part of her job; she took the risk. She couldn't tell us she was following Mrs. Bitton without exposing the whole thing and losing her position. More than that – and a much sounder reason – I think she has tidy blackmail schemes in her mind. Now we've knocked *that* on the head . . . She's already told Bitton, of course. So if she won't tell, he will – to clear his wife. But I'll promise to forget what she said this afternoon if she gives us a signed statement. Bitton does all the work of persuading her to talk. Let him apply the third degree; *we* couldn't."

Rampole pushed back his hat.

"Neat!" he said. "Very neat, sir. Now, if your plan to persuade Arbor to talk works as well . . ."

"Arbor . . ." The chief inspector sprang up. "I'd forgotten it. I've been sitting here explaining my own cleverness, and I clean forgot that. I've got to telephone Golder's Green, and do it quickly. Where the devil is the phone? And, incidentally, where's the man who was supposed to be guarding this flat; how did Bitton get in here, anyhow? And where by the way is Fell?"

He was answered without delay. From beyond the closed door, somewhere in the interior of the flat, there was a scrape, a thud, and a terrific metallic crash.

"It's all right!" a muffled voice boomed out to them from some distance away. "No more plaster figures broken. I've just dropped a basket of tools off the shelf in the kitchen."

Hadley and Rampole hurried in the direction of the voice. Beyond the door through which the doctor had gone, a narrow passage ran straight back. There were two doors in either wall; those on the left leading to a study and a bedroom, and those on the right a bath – and a dining-room. The kitchen was at the extreme rear of the passage.

To add to the confusion of the room, Driscoll had never been especially neat in his habits. The study had been cluttered up long before the woman's frantic search that afternoon. The floor was a drift of papers; rows of shelves gaped where whole sections of books had been tossed out; and the drawers of the desk hung out empty and drunken. A portable typewriter, its cover off, had become entangled with the telephone, and the contents of several brass ashtrays were sprayed across carbon paper, pencils, and an overturned bottle of ink. Even the green shade of the hanging lamp, which burned dully above the typewriter, had been knocked awry, and the iron fender pulled away from the fireplace. Apparently the intruder had concentrated her attention on the study.

Hadley glanced quickly into the other rooms as Dr. Fell opened the door of the kitchen. The bed was still unmade in the bedroom. The disarranged bureau was a gallery of large cabinet photographs of women, most of them with rather lurid inscriptions. This Driscoll, Rampole considered, had been a young man to be envied, even though his conquests seemed mostly of the housemaid type. The search here had been more perfunctory, confined to the bureau. And the dining-room had not been touched at all. it had seldom or never been used for eating purposes, but there had palpably been a use for it. Two gigantic rows of empty soda-syphons had been lined up on the sideboard. Under a mosaic dome of lights over the table there mingled in confusion empty bottles, unwashed glasses, a cocktail-shaker, ash-trays, and several sportive pieces of orange-peel. The whole had a dry, sticky appearance. Hadley grunted and switched off the light.

"The kitchen also," Dr. Fell observed at his elbow, "seems to have been used chiefly for mixing drinks. My estimation of the late Mr. Driscoll would have been considerably improved if I had not spotted a tin of that unmentionable substance known as cocoa." He swept his arm about. "You see? That sitting-room he kept tidy for casual visitors like his uncle. This is where he really lived. H'mf."

He was wheezing in the kitchen doorway. Over his arm he carried a large market-basket which jingled with iron.

"You said tools?" inquired Hadley, sharply. "Was that what you were looking for? You mean a chisel or a screwdriver used to force open the outer door of this flat?"

"Good Lord, no!" snorted the doctor, with a grunt that rattled the basket. "My dear Hadley, you don't seriously suppose the woman got into the flat, came back here, found a chisel, and went out again so that she could break open the door for sheer amusement, do you?"

"She might have done just that," said the chief inspector, quietly, "to give the impression it was some outsider who had burgled the flat."

"It's entirely possible, I grant you. But, as a matter of fact, I wasn't interested in the breaking or entering. It was an entirely different sort of tool I was looking for."

"It may further interest you to know," the chief inspector pursued, rather irritably, "that while you have been poking about in the kitchen we've learned a great deal from Bitton . . ."

The doctor nodded several times, and the black ribbon on his glasses swung jumpily. His shovel-hat shaded the top of his face, so that he looked more and more like a fat bandit.

"Yes," he agreed, "I thought you would. He was here to get information from his private detective and you've scared him into forcing her to tell what she knows by making out a thundering case against his wife. I imagined I could safely leave that to you. I wasn't needed. H'mf." He blinked curiously round the passage. "I know you have to get it down for the records, and keep everything in order. But from my point of view it wasn't necessary. I'm rather sure I can tell you what the Larkin woman knows . . . Come over here to the study for a moment, and have a look at Driscoll's character."

"You infernal old stuffed-shirt bluffer . . . !" said Hadley, like one who commences an oration. "You . . ."

"Oh, come," protested the doctor, with a mildly injured air. Tut, tut! No. I may be a childish old fool. I admit that. But I'm not a bluffer, old man. Really, I'm not. Let's see, what was I talking about? Oh yes; Driscoll's character. There are some rather interesting photographs of him in the study. In one of them he . . ."

Sharply and stridently through the silent passage the telephone in the study rang.

12
CONCERNING X-19

"That," said Hadley, whirling about, "may be a lead. Wait a moment. I'll answer it."

They followed him into the study. Dr. Fell seemed about to launch some sort of protest, whose nature Rampole could not imagine but the chief inspector picked up the telephone.

He said: "Hello! . . . Yes, this is . . . Chief Inspector Hadley speaking . . . *Who*? . . . Oh yes . . . It's Sheila Bitton," he said to the others over his shoulder, and there was a tinge of disappointment in his voice. "Yes . . . Yes, certainly, Miss Bitton." A long pause. "Why, I suppose you may, but I shall have to have a look at everything first, you know . . . No trouble at all! When will you come over?"

"Wait!" said Dr. Fell, eagerly. He stumped across. "Tell her to hold on a second."

"What is it?" the chief inspector asked in some irritation, with his hand over the mouthpiece.

"She's coming over here tonight?"

"Yes. She says there are some belongings of Philip's that her uncle wants her to bring to the house."

"H'm. Ask her if she's got anybody to bring her over here."

"What the devil . . . ! Oh, all right," Hadley agreed, wearily, as he saw on the doctor's face that almost fiendish expression which people wear when they want a message transmitted by phone and have to keep silent themselves. Hadley spoke again. "She says she's got Dalrye," he transmitted after a moment.

"That won't do. There's somebody in that house I've got to talk to, and I've got to talk to him *out* of the house or it may be no good. And this," grunted the doctor, excitedly, "is the chance of a lifetime to do it. Let me talk to her, will you?"

Hadley shrugged and got up from the desk.

"Hello!" said the doctor, in what he evidently meant for a gentle tone suitable to women. It actually sounded as though he were gulping. "Miss Bitton? This is Dr. Fell, Mr. Hadley's – um – colleague . . . You do? Oh yes; from your *fiancé*, of course . . . *HEY*?"

"You needn't blow the mouthpiece out," Hadley observed, sourly. "What tact! What tact! Ha!"

"Excuse me, Miss Bitton. Excuse me. I may be, of course, the fattest walrus Mr. Dalrye has ever seen, but . . . No, no, my dear; of course I don't mind . . ."

They could hear the phone tinkling in an animated fashion; Rampole remembered Mrs. Larkin's description of Sheila Bitton as a "little blonde," and grinned to himself. Dr. Fell contemplated the phone with an expression of one trying to smile in order to have his picture taken; presently he broke in.

"What I was trying to say, Miss Bitton, was this. You'll undoubtedly have a number of things to take away, and they'll be quite bulky . . . Oh! Mr. Dalrye has to be back at the Tower by ten o'clock? . . . Then you will certainly want somebody to handle them. Haven't you somebody there who could? . . . The chauffeur's not there? Well, what about your father's valet? What's his name? – Marks. He spoke highly of Marks, and . . . But please don't bring your father, Miss Bitton; it would only make him feel worse. (She's weeping now!" the doctor added, desperately over his shoulder.) . . . "Oh, he's lying down? Very well, Miss Bitton. We shall expect you. Good-bye."

He turned about, glowering, and shook the tool-basket until it jangled. "She burbles. She prattles. And she called me a walrus. A most naïve young lady. And if any humorist on these premises makes the obvious remark about the Walrus and the Carpenter . . ."

He set down the tool-basket with a clank.

"Dr. Watson . . ." Hadley muttered. "Thanks for reminding me. I've got to put a call through to the police station at Golder's Green. Get up from there."

He began a series of relay-calls through Scotland Yard, and finally left his orders. He had just finished informing some mystified desk sergeant on the other wire to phone him here after he had made sure the message was delivered to the guard at Arbor's cottage, when they heard footsteps in the sitting-room.

Evidently it had taken some time for Lester Bitton to persuade Mrs. Larkin that it would be advisable to talk. Bitton was pacing the front room, looking flushed and dangerous. Mrs. Larkin a straight figure with a face more square than ever, was holding back the curtain of the front window and peering out with extreme nonchalance. When she saw Hadley she examined him coldly.

"You tecs," she said, her upper lip wrinkling; "pretty damn smart, ain't you? I told his nibs here you'd got nothing on his wife. He should have sat tight and let you go ahead, and then we could both have got a sweet piece of change out of you for false arrest. But no. He had to get scared and spill the beans. But I've been promised *my* pay for speaking out loud in meeting. So," concluded Mrs. Larkin, lifting her shoulders, "what the hell?"

Hadley opened his brief-case again. This time he was not bluffing; the printed form he opened carried two decidedly un-flattering snapshots, one of which was a side view.

"'Amanda Georgette Larkin,'" he read. "'Alias Amanda Leeds, Alias Georgie Simpson. Known as "Emmy." Shoplifting. Specialty, jewellery, large department stores. Last heard of in New York . . .'"

"You needn't go through all that," interrupted Emmy. "There's nothing on me now. I told you that this afternoon. But go on and get his nibs to tell you what agency I work for. Then you'll tell them, and, *bingo*! I'm through."

Hadley folded up the paper and replaced it. "You may be trying to make an honest living," he said, "if I can be so polite about your profession. We'll certainly keep an eye on you, Mrs. Larkin. But if you give us a clear statement, I don't think I need warn your employers about Georgie Simpson."

She put her hands on her hips and studied him.

"That's fair enough. Not that I've got a lot of choice in the matter. All right. Here she goes."

Mrs. Larkin's manner underwent a subtle change. That afternoon she had seemed all tight corsets and severe tailoring, like an especially forbidding schoolmistress. Now the stiffness disappeared into an easier slouch. She dropped into a chair, saw some cigarettes in a box on the tabouret beside her, selected one, and struck the match by whisking it across the sole of her shoe.

"Those two," she said, with a spurt of something like admiration, "were havin' one hell of a time! They . . ."

"That's enough of that!" Lester Bitton cut in, in a heavy voice. "These – these men aren't interested . . ."

"I bet they're not," said Mrs. Larkin, with cool scepticism. "How about it, Hadley?"

"What we want to know is everything you did today, Mrs. Larkin."

"Right. Well, in my profession a man we always look out for is the postman. I was up bright and early, ready for him. He always puts the letters in the box of Number 1, my place, first, and then goes across the way. I can time it so that I'm picking up the milk-bottle outside my door when he gets out the mail for Number 2. And *that* was easy. Because X19 – that's the way we have to describe people in the confidential reports – X19 always wrote her letters on a sort of pink-purplish kind of paper you could see a mile off . . ."

"How did you know," inquired Hadley, "that the letters were from X19?"

She looked at him. "Don't be funny," said Mrs. Larkin, coldly. "It's not healthy for a respectable widow to get into people's flats with a duplicate key. And it's a damn sight less healthy to be found steaming open people's letters. Let's say I overheard them talking about the first letter she wrote him.

"All right. I'd been warned X19 was coming back to London Sunday night and so I had my eyes open this morning. Well, I admit that I was kind of surprised when I went out to pick up my milk-bottle and found Driscoll picking up *his* milk-bottle just over the way. He never gets up before noon. But there he was, all dressed, and lookin' as though he'd had a bad night. He had his door open, and I could see the inside of the letter-box."

She twisted round, and pointed with her cigarette at the wire cage just below the slot in the door.

"He didn't pay any attention to *me*. Then, while he had the milk-bottle under one arm, and still holding the door open with his foot, he stuck his hand in the letter-box. He pulled out the pink letter and sort of grunted, and put it in his pocket without opening it. Then he saw me, and let the door slam.

"So I thought, 'What ho!' And I knew there was going to be a meeting somewhere. But I wasn't to watch *him*. I'd only been planted opposite so I could catch X19 with the goods."

"You seem to have been a long time in doing it," said Hadley.

She made a comfortable gesture. "Well, we detectives have to take our time, don't we, and be pretty sure before we act? No use finishin' off a good assignment too quick . . . But all the times she's been there I never *saw* anything. The best chance I had was the night before she went away, about two weeks ago. They come in from the theatre or some place, and they was both pretty tight. I watched the door, and everything was all quiet for about two hours, so I knew what was up. Then the door opened, and they both come out again for him to take her home. I couldn't see anything; it was black as pitch out in the hall, but I could hear. By this time she was tighter yet, but he was as drunk as a hoot-owl. And they stood there swearing eternal love to each other; and he was saying how he was going to do a piece of work that would get him a good newspaper job, and then they could get married . . . and oh they had a hell of a time . . .

"But I wasn't certain," explained the practical Mrs. Larkin, "because that's what they all say when they're drunk. And besides, I heard him telling the same thing to a little red-head he had here while X19 was away, so I didn't believe he was as gone on X19 as she was on him. But that night, of course, I wasn't on duty. I was just getting home myself, and he came staggering down the steps with his arm around the red-head, and she was trying to hold him up, and he slipped and fell and said 'Jesus Christ.' . . ."

"*Stop It!*" Lester Bitton suddenly shouted. The cry was wrung from him. He had been standing at the window, staring out, with the window curtain over his shoulder and hiding him. Now he whipped round, started to speak, and sagged. "You didn't," he said heavily – "you didn't put into your report – you didn't say this . . ."

"Time enough. But I am off the subject, ain't I?" said Mrs. Larkin. She studied him. Her hard, square face, which was neither young nor middle-aged, relaxed a trifle. She straightened the puffs of hair over her ears. "Don't take it so hard, mister. They're all like that, mostly. I didn't mean to give you the works. You seem like a pretty decent guy, if you'd come off your dignity and be human.

"I'll go on about today. Oh yes; I know where I was. I've *got* to tell the slops, ain't I?" she said, petulantly, as he turned away again. "Well, I got dressed and went up to Berkeley Square. It's a good thing I did, because she come out of the house fairly early. And believe it or not," said Mrs. Larkin in an awed voice, crushing out her cigarette, "that woman walked all the way from her place to the Tower of London! I damn near died. But I didn't dare take a cab, for fear I'd get too close and she'd see me or I'd lose her in the fog.

"I knew the Tower. My old man took me there once. He said it would be educational. Well, I seen her buying tickets for all them towers, and I had to buy 'em all, too, because I didn't know where she'd go. But I thought, This is a hell of a place to pick for rendyvoo, and then I tumbled to it. She was wise to being watched. I thought probably that trip to the country tipped her off, and her husband had maybe said something to let her guess . . ."

"They had never gone there together before?" interrupted Hadley.

"Not while *I* was watching them. But wait! You'll understand that in a minute."

She was more subdued now when she spoke, and she told her story without comment. It was ten minutes past one when Laura Bitton arrived. After buying her tickets and a little guide, she had gone into the refreshment-room and ordered a sandwich and a glass of milk. All the time she ate she watched the clock with every sign of nervousness and impatience. "And what's more," Mrs. Larkin explained, "she wasn't carrying that arrowthing you had on your desk this afternoon. The only place she could have had it was inside her coat, and when she got through eating she opened her coat and shook it to get rid of the crumbs. I'll take my oath there wasn't nothing there."

At twenty minutes past one Laura Bitton left the refresh-ment-room and hurried away. At the Middle Tower she hesitated, looked about, and presently moved along the causeway, and hesitated again at the Byward Tower. There she consulted the map in her guide-book and looked carefully about her.

"I could see what was in her mind," Mrs. Larkin told them. "She didn't want to hang around the door, like a tart or something; but she wanted to be sure she saw him when he got there. But it was dead easy. Anybody who came in would've had to walk straight along that road – up towards the Traitors' Gate place and the Bloody Tower. So she walked along the road, slow, looking all around. She'd been walking in the centre of the road, and I was just far behind enough to keep her in sight in that fog. Then when she got near the Traitors' Gate place she turned to the right and stopped again . . ."

So that, Rampole reflected, was what Philip Driscoll saw when he "kept looking out of the window" in the general's quarters, as Parker had described. He saw the woman waiting for him down in Water Lane. And soon afterwards he said he would take a stroll in the grounds, and hurried out. In the American's brain the weird and misty scene was taking form. Laura Bitton with her free stride and healthy face; the brown eyes tortured; tapping the pamphlet guide against her hand and hesitating at the rail as she waited for the man who was already there. Driscoll hurrying downstairs, brushing past Arbor outside the King's House . . .

"She'd moved back," Mrs. Larkin went on, "in a doorway on the right-hand side of the Traitors' Gate. I'd flattened myself against the same wail a little distance back. Then I saw a little guy in plus-fours come out from under the arch of the Bloody Tower. He looked up and down, quick; and he didn't see – er – X19 because she was back in that door. I thought it was Driscoll, but I wasn't sure. Neither was she, I guess, for a minute, because she'd expected him to come the other way. Then he starts to walk back and forth, and next he goes over to the rail. I heard him use a cuss-word, and there was a sound like a match striking.

"Now, here's the joker in the deck. I don't know whether you noticed. But that archway thing, where all them spikes in the gate are, sticks out about seven or eight feet on either side of the rail. If you're in that roadway, and looking down it in a straight line, you can't see the rail in front of the steps at all. For the time being it was fine for me, because I could get within a couple of feet of them without being seen.

"So X19 knew it was Driscoll all right. She slipped out of the door and turned the corner towards the rail. I couldn't see her and she couldn't see me, so I came up close. The fog was pretty thick, anyway."

Mrs. Larkin took another cigarette from the box. She bent forward.

"Now, I'm not making anything up. I can tell you every word they said, because there wasn't much of it, and it's my business to remember. The first thing he said was, 'Laura, for God's sake what did you want to bring me down here for? I've got friends here. Is it true that he's found out?' What she said at first I couldn't hear, because it was so low. It was something about that was the reason why she had said to come here, because if either of 'em was seen they could be calling on people they knew. Then he said that was a crazy idea, and was it true that *he'd* found out; he asked that again. She said yes. And she said, 'Do you love me?' And he said, 'Yes, yes, but I'm in a frightful mess.' They was both pretty upset and got to talking louder. He said something about his uncle, and all of a sudden he stopped and said, 'O, my God!' It was frightful to hear him say it like that, I'm telling you, as though he'd just thought of something . . .

"She asked him what was the matter. Here's what he said. 'Laura, there's something I've got to do here and I forgot all about it. It won't take two seconds, but I've got to do it or I'm ruined.' His voice was shaking. It sounded bad. He said, 'Don't stay with me. We might be seen. Go in and look at the Crown Jewels, and then walk up to the parade-ground. I'll join you there inside five minutes. Don't ask me any questions, but please go.'

"There was a kind of shuffling, and I was afraid of being seen, so I backed away. Then I heard him walking and he called out, 'It'll be all right; don't worry.' I heard her walk up and down for a second or two. Then she walked out in the roadway, and I thought for a minute she'd seen me. But she whirled around and started toward the Bloody Tower, and I followed. I didn't see *him*; I suppose he'd gone on ahead. That was about twenty-five minutes to two."

Hadley leaned forward. "You say you followed?" he demanded. "Did you see her bump into anybody?"

"Bump into anybody?" she repeated, blinking. "No. But then I mightn't have. I slipped inside that big arch of the Bloody Tower and up against the wall, in case she turned back. I have a kind of idea that some man passed me; but it was foggy, and under that arch darker than hell . . . I waited a second and followed again.

"I heard her speak to one of them birds in the funny hats and say, 'Which way to the Crown Jewels?' and he directed her to a door not very far on the other side of the arch, and I was still there."

Mrs. Larkin paused to light the cigarette she had been holding for some time.

"That's all," she said in a matter-of-fact voice. "He didn't come near her, because somebody killed him just after he'd left her. But I know *she* didn't, because I took a look in that place where the steps go down – I looked there, mind you, before I followed her up in the Bloody Tower. I was sort of craning my neck around to see up under the arch to the Bloody Tower, and I put out my hand to touch the rail so's

I wouldn't fall over backwards, and naturally I looked over my shoulder. He wasn't there then. And I had her in sight the rest of the time . . . As I said, she went to see the Crown Jewels. So did I. But she didn't look at 'em much. She was kind of white and restless, and she kept looking out the windows. I left before she did. I didn't want to attract notice. And I'd seen that if you went *in* the Bloody Tower and up to a kind of little balcony . . ."

"Raleigh's Walk," the chief inspector said, glancing at Dr. Fell.

". . . Then you could see anybody who came back from looking at them jewels. Unless you went back the way you come there was no other way out. So I waited. And before long she come back, and stood there a while in the road that goes up the hill from the Bloody Tower to that big open space . . ."

"Tower Green."

"Yeah. Well, she started to walk up, kind of listless, and I walked up afterwards. But she didn't do anything. I could see her, because it was high ground and the fog was thin. She sat on a bench, and talked to one of them guards, and kept looking at her watch. But she was patient, all right. *I* wouldn't have waited that long for any man in God's world. She waited over half an hour just sitting on one of them benches in the wet, without moving, and finally she started to leave. You know the rest."

Mrs. Larkin's hard little eyes moved about the group and she drew in a gust of cigarette smoke. "Well. Feenee. There's the words and music. I promised to say 'em, and I did. I don't know who killed Driscoll, but I'm damn sure *she* didn't."

13
WHEREIN MISS BITTON BURBLES

When she had ceased speaking, nobody cared to break the silence. It was so quiet in the little sitting-room that the hoarse mumble of the radio could be heard again from some flat upstairs. They heard footsteps on the tiles of the hall, the clang of an iron gate, and then the long, humming whir of the automatic lift. Distantly, motor horns honked and hooted from the other side of the Square . . .

For the first time Rampole felt how chill it was here, and drew his coat about him. A deeper stamp of death had come on the room, as of fingers slowly pressed into sand. Philip Driscoll was no more than the white fragments of the plaster image scattered on the hearth.

The dancing tinkle of a barrel-organ began to make itself heard in Tavistock Square. Faintly, from upstairs, a creak and another clang; and the hum of the descending lift . . .

Lester Bitton moved the dusty window curtain off his shoulder, and turned about. There was about him now a curious, quiet dignity.

"Gentlemen," he said, "I have done what had to be done. Is there anything more?"

They knew what it had cost him to listen to that recital in the presence of strangers, or alone. He stood quiet, conventional, almost polite, with the pouches showing under his eyes and his bowler hat in his hand. And nobody knew what to say.

At length it was Dr. Fell who spoke. He was sitting spread out in a leather chair, the tool-basket in his lap like a dog, and his eyes old and tired.

"Man," he said sombrely, "go home. You've done some sneaking things in your time, like all the rest of us. But you smashed only one figure when you might have smashed two. You spoke up like a man when you might have denounced her. Go home. We can't keep your name out of this altogether, but we'll save you all the publicity we can."

The doctor's dull eyes moved over to Hadley. Hadley nodded.

Lester Bitton stood for a time motionless. He seemed weary and a trifle puzzled. Then his big hands moved up, adjusted his scarf and buttoned up his coat. He walked rather blindly when he went to the door, but until he reached it he did not put on his hat.

"I – I thank you, gentlemen," he said in a low voice. He made a little bow. "I – I am very fond of her, you see. Good night."

The door with the broken lock closed behind him. They heard the vestibule of the outer hall open and shut wheezily. The tinkle of the barrel-organ grew louder and died.

"That's the Maine Stein Song," observed the doctor, who had been cocking an ear to the music. "Why do people say they don't like street organs? I'm very fond of street organs myself. I always feel like a Grenadier Guard, and throw out my chest, when I pass one. It's like going on errands to band music, as though there were some triumphal *fête* about buying two lamb chops and a bottle of beer. By the way, Mrs. Larkin . . ."

The woman had risen. She turned sharply.

". . . it's not going to be brought out at the inquest, you know, that there was really anything serious between Mrs. Bitton and Driscoll. I imagine you've already been paid to keep quiet." Dr. Fell raised his stick sleepily. "It's money well earned. But don't try to earn any more. That's blackmail, you know. They put you in gaol for it. Good night."

"Oh that's all right," Mrs. Larkin agreed, patting the puffs of hair over her ears. "If you birds are on the level with me, I'm on the level with you . . . y'know what I mean? Men are crazy, anyway," she added, reflectively. The harsh, young-old face was cut into whimsical lines. "If I'd been that dame's old man, I'd have gone home and blacked both 'er eyes. But men are crazy. My Cuthbert was. Still, I loved that old buzzard till he got knocked off in a gun-fight under the Third Avenue L in New York. Every so often he would walk out with some other skirt; and that kept me so upset I never thought of walking out on *him*. That's the way to treat skirts. Keeps 'em in line. Well, I'm off to the pub. G'night. See you at the inquest."

When she had gone the rest of them sat silent. Dr. Fell was wheezing sleepily. And again Hadley began to pace about the room.

"So that's settled," he said. "I think we can take Mrs. Bitton off the list of suspects. I doubt if Larkin's lying. Her information is too exactly in line with all the other facts she couldn't possibly have known. Now what?"

"What do *you* suggest?"

"Not much, for the moment. It all rests on what it was Driscoll remembered he'd forgotten to do when he spoke to Mrs. Bitton in front of the Traitors' Gate. He started for somewhere, but he didn't get very far away, and then he ran into somebody . . . the murderer."

"Fair enough," grunted the doctor.

"Now, first, there's the *direction* he might have gone. Larkin didn't see him go. But we know he didn't go along Water Lane towards the Byward or Middle Tower; towards the gate, in other words. Because Larkin was standing there, and she would have seen him pass.

"There are only two other directions he could have gone." From his invaluable brief-case Hadley took a small map of the Tower, which he had evidently been studying ever since his visit. "He could have gone straight along Water Lane in the other direction. The only place he could have gone in that direction is towards another arch similar to the Bloody Tower and a hundred feet or so away in the same wall . . . the inner ballium wall. From that arch a path leads up to the White Tower, which is almost in the centre of the whole enclosure. Now, unless *all* our calculations are wrong, and there's some piece of evidence we haven't heard, why on earth should he be going to the White Tower? Or for that matter, to the main guard, the store, the hospital, the officers' quarters, the barracks or any place he could have reached by going through that arch?

"Besides, he hadn't got very far away from the Traitors' Gate before he met the murderer. Traitors' Gate is an ideal place for murder on a foggy day. It would have occurred to anybody. But if Driscoll had been starting for the White Tower and met the murderer quite some distance from Traitors' Gate, it wouldn't have been very practical for the murderer to drive that steel bolt through him, pick him up, carry him back, and pitch him over the rail. Physically, it could have been easy; Driscoll's a featherweight. But the risk of being seen carrying that burden any distance, even in the fog, would have been too great."

Hadley paused in his pacing before the mantelpiece. He stared a moment at the idiotic painted face of the doll; and some idea seemed to pinch down the wrinkles round his mouth. But he dismissed it and went on:

"On the other hand, the murderer couldn't say, 'Look here, old man, let's stroll back to the Traitors' Gate; I want to talk to you.' And naturally Driscoll would have said: 'Why? What's the matter with telling me here?' Also he was in a fearful bother and stew to get somewhere and do something. He would more likely have said, 'Sorry. I can't talk to you at all,' and gone on . . . No, it won't do. Driscoll had no business in that direction anyway. So there's only one alternative."

Dr. Fell took out a cigar.

"Namely," he inquired, "that Driscoll went the same direction as Mrs. Bitton did – through the arch of the Bloody Tower?"

"Yes. All indications show that."

"For instance?"

"For instance," Hadley answered, slowly, "what Larkin said. She heard Driscoll walk away, and then Mrs. Bitton walked up and down in front of the rail a minute or so . . . *to give Driscoll time to go on up there ahead of her.* Driscoll said they mustn't be seen together. And once you get inside the inner ballium wall, as Larkin said, you're in view of pretty well everybody; especially as it's high ground, and the fog is thin. Larkin had a positive impression that he'd gone on ahead of Mrs. Bitton. And, above all, that's the reasonable direction for him to have gone, because . . ."

"Because it's the way to the King's House," supplied Dr. Fell.

Hadley nodded. "Whatever he had forgotten, and went to do, was in the general's quarters at the King's House. That's the only part of the Tower he ever had any business in . . . He was going back. There was somebody he had to speak with on the phone, or some message he had to give Parker. *But he never got there.*"

"Good work," said the doctor, approvingly. "I seem to act as a stimulant. Gradually that subconscious imagination of yours, Hadley, is working to the surface. And by degrees everything seems to centre round the arch under the Bloody Tower . . . Hence we perceive the following points: The arch under this tower is a broad tunnel about twenty feet long, and the road runs on a steep uphill slant.

At the best of times it is rather dark, but on a foggy day it is what Mrs. Larkin, who has evidently read Dante, describes as black as hell."

Hadley broke off his fierce musing. He said, petulantly:

"Look here. It seems to me that *I* do all the reconstructing. And when I find the right answer, you wave your hand calmly and say you knew it all the time. Now either you do or you don't, but if you *don't* . . ."

"I am pursuing," Dr. Fell said, with dignity, "the Socratic method. Don't say, 'Bah,' as I perceive you are about to do. I want to lead you along and see where this hypothesis gets us. Hence . . ."

"H'm," the chief inspector observed, struck with an idea. "Now that I come to think of it, by George! I know where all this fictional-detective stuff started in the first place. With that Greek philosopher chap in *Plato's Dialogues.* He always annoyed me. A couple of Greeks would be walking along, not bothering anybody, and up would come this damned philosopher and say, '*Bon jour*' . . . or whatever they said in Athens . . . '*Bon jour*, gents; have you got anything on hand this afternoon?' Of course the other chaps didn't. They never had. There never seemed to be any business to attend to in Greece. All they did was walk about hunting for philosophers. Then Socrates would say, 'Right you are. Now let's sit down here and talk.' Whereupon he would propound some question for them to solve . . . he knew the answer, of course. It was never anything sensible, like 'What do you think of the Irish question?' or 'Who will win the Test Match this year, Athens or Sparta?' It was always some God-awful question about the soul. Socrates asked the question. Then one of the other chaps spoke up, and talked for about nine pages; and Socrates shook his head sadly and said, 'No.' Then another chap took a shot at it, and talked for sixteen pages. And Socrates said, 'Ah!' The next victim must have talked till it got dark, and Socrates said, 'Possibly.' They never up and hit him over the head with an obelisk, either. That's what *I* wanted to do just from reading the thing, because he never would come out and say what he meant . . . That's the origin of your detectives in fiction, Fell. And I wish you'd stop it."

Dr. Fell, who had got his cigar lighted, looked reproving.

"I perceive in you, Hadley," he remarked, "a certain vein of unexpected satire. As well as the germ of an idea most bibliophiles seem to have overlooked. H'mf. I never had much patience with those fellows myself . . . However, stick to your subject. Continue with the murder."

"Er . . . where was I?" demanded Hadley. "This confounded case is beginning to . . ."

"You'd got Driscoll into the tunnel, where he is murdered. So. Now, it was dark in there. Why didn't the murderer dump him against the wall and leave him there?"

"Because the body would be discovered too soon. There's too much traffic in that place. Somebody might stumble over the body before the murderer could make a getaway . . . So he picked Driscoll up like a ventriloquist's dummy, took a quick look to each side in Water Lane, walked across, and chucked him over the rail on the steps."

The doctor nodded. He held up one hand and indicated points on his fingers.

"Driscoll walks into the tunnel, then, and meets the murderer. Mrs. Bitton waits a short time, and follows, because she doesn't know Driscoll is still *in* the tunnel. Now do you see what we've got, Hadley? We've got Mrs. Bitton at one end of the tunnel, Driscoll and the murderer in the middle . . . and our good friend Mr. Arbor at the other end. Haven't we?"

"Every time *you* begin to elucidate," said the chief inspector, "the thing gets more tangled up. But that seems clear. Larkin said Mrs. Bitton went into the arch twenty-five minutes to two. Arbor bumped into her on the other side of it at a coinciding time. Where's the catch?"

"I didn't say there was a catch. Now, following Mrs. Bitton at a little distance is the eagle-eyed Larkin, who enters the tunnel next. All this time you must assume the murderer was still in the tunnel with his victim; otherwise she would have seen him carry the body out. In the tunnel it's very dark and foggy. Mrs. Larkin *hears* somebody moving. That is probably Arbor on his way out from the other side. Thus the tunnel is cleared of traffic. The murderer who has been crouching there with his victim in a deadly sweat of fear he'll be discovered carries out the body, throws it over the rail, and escapes . . . That, I take it, is the summary of events?"

"Yes. That's about it."

Dr. Fell squinted down his cigar "Then," he said, "where does the enigmatic Mr. Arbor fit in? What terrified him? . . . He's out at his cottage now, in a complete funk. Why?"

Hadley slapped the arm of a chair with his brief-case. "He was passing through that dark tunnel, Fell . . . and when he was in such a bad state after he left us, the taxi-driver said he kept repeating over and over something about a '*voice*' . . ."

"Tut, tut," said the doctor. "Do you think the murderer leaned out and said 'Boo!' to him as he passed?"

"I don't expect much from you. But," the chief inspector said, bitterly, "a trifle less heavy humour . . . What are you trying to prove?"

But he was not paying a great deal of attention to what Dr. Fell said, Rampole noticed. His eye kept straying to the mantelpiece, to the smashed figure on the hearthstone, and up again to the other image on the shelf. There was a wrinkle between his brows. The doctor followed his glance.

"Let me tell you what you're thinking, Hadley," he observed. "You're thinking: Murderer. Big man; strength. Powerful motive. Man capable of murder from the emotional depths we saw ourselves. Man with access to crossbow bolt. Man who certainly knew about crossbow bolt. Man so far not even questioned about whereabouts at time of murder . . . Lester Bitton."

"Yes," said Hadley, without turning. "I was thinking just that."

At the door of the flat the bell-buzzer rang. Somebody kept poking it in short bursts. But before Rampole had time to reach the door, it was pushed open . . .

"I'm *so* sorry we're fearfully late!" a girl's voice said, promptly, before the owner saw anybody. "But it was the chauffeur's night off and we didn't want to take the big car, and we tried to use the other car, and it got halfway out into the street and stopped. Fancy. And then a crowd gathered, and Bob lifted the bonnet and started muttering to himself and pulling wires and things, and all of a sudden something exploded, and Bob used the most horrible language, and the crowd cheered. Fancy. And so we had to use the big car, after all."

Rampole found himself looking down at a small face which was poked round the edge of the door. Then by degrees the newcomer got into the room. She was a plump, very pretty little blonde, with two of the most beaming and expressive blue eyes the American had ever seen; she looked like a breathless doll. No shadow of any tragedy, you felt, could ever settle on her. When somebody reminded her of it, she would weep; in the meantime, she would forget all about it.

"Er . . . Miss Bitton?" inquired Rampole.

"*I'm* Miss Bitton," she explained, as though she were singling herself out of a group. "But my Bob is *never* any good at things like that, you see. Because Daddy bought me a cottage at the beach two years ago where all of us could go down, with Laura chaperoning, and I wanted the walls papered, and I had the paper, and Bob and his cousin George said, Ha! They would paper it themselves, and mix the paste, too. But after they spilled paste all over the floor getting it on the paper, then they got all tangled up in the paper with the paste on it. And then they were having the most terrible argument, and swearing and making so much noise the house shook, and a policeman looked in, and they got paper on him, too; and then George got so furious he walked straight out of the house all pasted up in a whole roll of my best paper with blue forget-me-nots on it. Fancy. What the neighbours thought, I mean. But the worst of it was when Bob got the paper on . . . only it *was* a wee bit crooked, and all sort of run together, and not very clean, you know. Because we lighted a fire, and it got warm, and all sorts of ghastly things began happening to the paper, and then they discovered that when they mixed the paste they'd used self-raising flour. Fancy. And that's why I've always said that . . ."

"My dear, please!" protested a mild and harassed voice behind her. Dalrye, thin and blinking, towered over her in the doorway. His sandy hair was disarranged under a hat stuck on the side of his head, and there was a smear of grease under one eye. As he put out his neck to peer into the room, he reminded Rampole irresistibly of one of those reconstructions of prehistoric dinosaurs he saw once in a motion picture. "Er . . ." he added, apologetically, "excuse my hurdy-gurdy, won't you? My dear, after all, you know why we did come here . . ."

Sheila Bitton stopped in mid-flight. Her large eyes grew troubled; and then they wandered about the room. A shocked look came into them when she saw the broken plaster image; of all things, Rampole knew, these figures would appeal to her irresistibly.

She said: "I'm sorry. I . . . I didn't think, of course, and then all that horrible crowd offering suggestions . . ." She looked at Rampole. "You're not . . . oooh no! I know you. You're the one who looks like a football-player. Bob described all of you to me. And you're much better-looking than I thought you'd be from what he said," she decided, subjecting him to a peculiarly open and embarrassing scrutiny.

"And I, ma'am," said Dr. Fell, "am the walrus, you see. Mr. Dalrye seems to have a flair for vivid description. In what delicate terms, may I ask, did he paint a word-picture of my friend Hadley, here?"

"H'm?" inquired Miss Bitton, arching her brows. She glanced at the doctor, and an expression of delight again animated her sparkling eyes. "Oh, I say! You *are* a dear!" she cried.

Dr. Fell jumped violently. There were no inhibitions whatever about Sheila Bitton. After one question to her, a psychoanalyst would have pulled out a handful of his whiskers and slunk back to Vienna in baffled humiliation. It would have embittered his life.

"About Mr. Hadley?" she inquired, candidly. "Oh Bob said he didn't look like anything in particular, you know."

"Gurk!" said Dalrye. He spread out his hands behind her back in helpless pantomime to the others.

". . . and I've always wanted to meet the police, but the only kind I ever meet are the kind who ask me why I am driving down streets where the arrows point the other way; and why *not*? because there's no traffic coming and I can go ever so much faster. And, No, miss, you can*not* park your car in front of the entrance to the fire station. Nasty people. Fancy. But I mean the real kind of police, who find bodies cut up and put in trunks, you know. And . . ." Then she remembered again why she was here, and stopped with a jerk; the rest of them were afraid there would be sudden tears . . .

"Of course, Miss Bitton," the chief inspector said, hastily. "Now if you'll just sit down a moment and . . . er . . . get your breath, you know, then I'm sure . . ."

"Excuse me," said Dalrye. "I'm going to wash my hands." He shivered a little as he glanced round the room, and almost seemed to change his decision. But he shut his jaws hard and left the room. Miss Bitton said, "Poor Phil . . ." suddenly, and sat down.

There was a silence.

"You . . . somebody," she remarked in a small voice, "somebody's tipped over that pretty little figure on the mantel. I'm sorry. It was one of the things I wanted to take back with me."

"Had you seen it before, Miss Bitton?" asked Hadley. His discomfort had disappeared as he saw a possible lead.

"Why, of course I had! I was there when they got them."

"When who got them?"

"At the fair. Phil and Laura and Uncle Lester and I all went to it. Uncle Lester said it was all silly, and didn't want to go, but Laura used that sort of pitying way she has and he said, All right, he'd go. He wouldn't ride on any of the swings or giddy-go-rounds or things, though, and then . . . But you don't want to hear that, do you? I know Bob says I talk too much, and now with poor Phil dead . . ."

"Please go on, Miss Bitton; I should like to hear it."

"You would? Truly? Oooh! Well, then . . . 'M. Oh yes. Phil started ragging Uncle Lester, and it was mean of him because Uncle Lester can't help being old, can he? And Uncle Lester got sort of red in the face, but he didn't say anything and then we got to a shooting-gallery where they have the rifles and things, and Uncle Lester spoke up sort of sharp, but not very loud, and said this was a man's game and not for children, and did Phil want to try? And Phil did, but he wasn't very good. And then Uncle Lester just picked up a pistol instead of a rifle and shot off a whole row of pipes clear across the gallery so fast you couldn't count them; and then he put down the pistol and walked away without saying anything. So Phil didn't like that . . . I could see he didn't. And every booth we passed he began challenging Uncle Lester to all kinds of games, and Laura joined in, too. I tried some of them, but after we came to the booth where you throw wooden balls and try to knock over stuffed cats, they wouldn't let me do it any more; because the first ball I threw I hit the electric-light in the roof, and the second one I threw hit the man who ran the booth behind the ear; and Uncle Lester had to pay for it . . ."

"But about the dolls, Miss Bitton?" Hadley asked, patiently.

"Oh yes. It was Laura who won them; they're a pair. It was at throwing darts, and she was ever so good . . . much better than the men. And you got prizes for it, and Laura got the highest prize for her score, and she said, 'Look, Philip and Mary,' and laughed. Because that's what the dolls have written on them, and, you see, Laura's middle name is Mary. Then Uncle Lester said he wouldn't have her keeping that trash; it was disgraceful-looking, and of course *I* wanted them ever so badly. But Laura said no, she'd give them to Philip if Mary couldn't have them. And Phil did the meanest thing I ever knew, because he made the absurdest bow and said he *would* keep them . . . and, *oh,* I was furious! because I thought he'd surely give them to *me,* you see. And what did *he* want with them, anyway? And Uncle Lester didn't say anything, but he said all at once we ought to go home; and all the way back I kept teasing Phil to give them to me; and he made all sorts of ridiculous speeches that didn't mean anything and looked at Laura, but he wouldn't give them to me. And that's how I remember them, because they remind me of Phil . . . You see, I even asked Bob to see if he could get Phil to give them to me; I asked him the next day . . . that was ages ago . . . when I called Bob on the telephone, because I always make him ring me up every day, or else I ring *him* up, and General Mason doesn't like that . . ."

She paused, her thin eyebrows raised again as she saw Hadley's face.

"You say," the chief inspector observed, in a voice he tried to make casual, "that you talk every day to Mr. Dalrye on the telephone?"

Rampole started. He remembered now. Earlier in the evening Hadley had made a wild shot when he was building up a fake case against Laura Bitton in front of her husband. He had said that Dalrye had informed Sheila of Driscoll's proposed visit to the Tower at one o'clock, because Dalrye talked to her on the telephone that morning; and that, therefore, anybody in the Bitton house could have known of the one-o'clock engagement. Hadley thought it was a wild shot, and nothing more. But, Rampole remembered, *Lester Bitton had shown no disposition to doubt it.* Which was, to say the least, suggestive.

Sheila Bitton's blue eyes were fixed on Hadley.

"Oh, please!" she said, "don't *you* preach! You sound like Daddy. He tells me what a fool I am, calling up every day, and I don't think he likes Bob, anyway, because Bob hasn't any money and likes poker, and Daddy says gambling's absurd, and I know he's looking for an excuse to break off our engagement and keep us from getting married, and . . ."

"My dear Miss Bitton," Hadley interposed, with a sort of desperate joviality, "I certainly am not preaching. I think it's a splendid idea. Splendid, ha! Ha, ha! But I only wanted to ask you . . ."

"You're a dear! You're a dear!" cooed Miss Bitton, as though she were saying, "You're another." "And they rag me so about it, and even Phil used to phone me and pretend he was Bob and ask me to go to the police station because Bob had been arrested for flirting with women in Hyde Park, and was in gaol, and would I bail him out, and . . ."

"Ha, ha," said Hadley again. "Ha, ha, ha . . . I mean, er, how . . . er . . . bad. Shocking. Preposterous. Ha, ha. But what I wanted to ask you, did you speak to Mr. Dalrye today?"

"In gaol," the girl said, darkly, brooding. "My Bob. Fancy. Yes, I did talk to him today."

"When, Miss Bitton? In the morning?"

"Yes. That's when I usually call, you know, or make him call me; because then General Mason isn't there. Nasty old thing with whiskers. He doesn't like it. And I always know when it's Parker who answers the phone, because, before you can say anything, he says, 'General Mason's orderly on the wire!' sort of big and sharp. But when I don't hear it I naturally think it's Bob, and I'm so *jolly* glad to talk to him I say, '*Darling, diddums*!' . . . you know how you'd say that, Mr. Hadley . . . and once I did that, and there was a sound sort of like frying eggs, and then a nasty voice said, 'Madam, this is the Tower of London not a nursery. To whom did you wish to speak?' Fancy. And it was General Mason. And I've always been scared of him, ever since I was a child, and I couldn't think of anything to say, and I sort of wept and said, 'This is your deserted wife,' and rang off while he was still saying things. But after that he made Bob call me up from a public box, and . . ."

"Ho, ho!" chortled Hadley, with ghastly mirth. "Ho, ho! No sentiment to him, is there? No romance, poor fellow . . . But, Miss Bitton, when you spoke to Mr. Dalrye this morning did he tell you that Philip Driscoll . . . your cousin, you know . . . was coming to see him at the Tower?"

She remembered the shadow again, and her eyes clouded.

"Yes," she said, after a pause. "I know, because Bob wanted to know what sort of mess Phil had got into now, and did *I* know anything about it? He told me not to say anything about it to the others . . ."

"And you didn't?"

"Why, of course not!" she cried. "I sort of hinted, that's all, at the breakfast table. Because we didn't have breakfast till ten o'clock that morning, we were so upset the night before. I asked them at the table if they knew why Phil was going to the Tower of London at one o'clock, and they didn't know, and of course I obeyed Bob and didn't say anything more . . ."

"I fancy that should be sufficient," said Hadley. "Was any comment made?"

"Comment?" the girl repeated, doubtfully. "N-no; they just talked a bit, and joked."

"Who was at the table?"

"Just Daddy, and Uncle Lester and that horrible man who's been stopping with us; the one who rushed out this afternoon without saying a word to anybody, and scared me, and nobody knows where he is or why he went; and everything is so upset, anyway . . ."

"Was Mrs. Bitton at the table?"

"Laura? Oh! Oh no. She didn't come down. She wasn't feeling well, and, anyway, I don't blame her, because she and Uncle Lester must have been up all last night, talking; I heard them, and . . ."

"But surely, Miss Bitton *something* must have been said at the breakfast table?"

"No, Mr. Hadley. Truly. Of course I don't like being at the table when just Daddy and that horrible Mr. Arbor are there because mostly I can't understand what they're talking about, books and things like that, and jokes I don't think funny. Or else the talk gets horrid, like the night when Phil told Uncle Lester he wanted to die in a top-hat. But there wasn't anything important that I heard. Of course, Uncle Lester did say he was going to see Phil today . . . But there wasn't anything important. Really."

14
"TO DIE IN A TOP-HAT . . ."

Hadley made a convulsive movement in his seat. Then he got out a handkerchief and mopped his forehead.

"Ha, ha," he said, automatically. He seemed to be getting quite used to it by this time; but the laugh sounded a trifle hollow. "Ha, ha, ha. You never hear anything important, Miss Bitton. It's most unfortunate. Now, Miss Bitton, please try to grasp the fact that some of the meaningless, unimportant conversations you overheard may be of the utmost importance . . . Miss Bitton, just how much do you know about your cousin's death?"

"Nothing much, Mr. Hadley," she said, fretfully. "They won't *tell* me. I couldn't get a word out of Laura or Daddy, and Bob just said there was a sort of accident and he was killed by this man who steals all the hats; but that's the only . . ."

She broke off short, rather guiltily, as Dalrye came back into the room again. He looked more presentable now.

"Sheila," he said, "whatever the things you want happen to be, you'd better go and pick 'em out. That place gives me the horrors. Everywhere I look Phil seems to be sitting there. The place is full of him. I wish I hadn't got any imagination . . ."

He shivered. Automatically he reached for a cigarette in the box on the tabouret, then he seemed to remember, and closed the box without touching one. Rampole extended his case, and Dalrye nodded thanks.

"*I'm* not afraid," the girl announced, sticking out her underlip. "*I* don't believe in ghosts. You've been so long in that musty old Tower of London that you . . ."

"Tower!" Dalrye exclaimed, suddenly rumpling his sandy hair. "Lord! I forgot." He dragged out his watch. "Whoof! A quarter to eleven. I've been locked out three-quarters of an hour. My dear, your father will have to put up with me in the house for tonight. I'm dashed if I stay *here*."

His eye wandered over to a leather couch against one wall, and he shuddered again. Hadley said:

"Now, if you please, Miss Bitton, let's go on. First tell us about this extraordinary business of your cousin wanting to die in a top-hat?"

"Eh?" said Dalrye. "Good God! what's *this*?"

"Why, Robert Dalrye," Sheila Bitton said, warmly, "you know perfectly well . . . Oh no, you don't. I remember now, when you spoke about getting back to that hateful Tower. You had to leave the table early to get there. It was the first night that Mr. Arbor . . . no, it wasn't, because Uncle Lester wasn't there then. Anyway, it was *some* night."

"Undoubtedly, Miss Bitton," agreed the chief inspector. "Never mind the precise date. How did it happen?"

"Yes, I remember now. Just Daddy and Uncle Lester and Laura and I were at the table; and Philip, of course. It was a sort of spooky night, if you know what I mean; and I know just when it was, too, now, because it wasn't a Sunday night at all, and Philip was there. That's how I remember. It was the night before Laura and Uncle Lester went to Cornwall. And Philip was taking Laura to the theatre, because at the last minute Uncle Lester had business and couldn't go, you see; but they were taking the trip to Cornwall because Uncle Lester had lost a lot of money or something, and he was all run down and had things under his eyes, and the doctor advised it . . .

"Oh yes. I couldn't think for a minute. It was a sort of spooky night, you see, with rain and hail coming down, and Daddy never likes any lights in the dining-room but candles, because he says that's like Old England, and a big fire too, and the house is old and it creaks and maybe that's why we all felt the way we did. But, anyway, we started talking about death. And Uncle Lester talked about death, which was funny of him, and he'd got his white tie crooked and I wanted to straighten it, but he wouldn't let me, and he looked as though he hadn't been sleeping much, what with losing all that money. And he asked Daddy how he'd choose to die if he had to die. Daddy was in a good humour that night, which he isn't usually, and first he laughed and said he supposed he'd choose to die like some duke or other who said he wanted to be drowned in a barrel of wine . . . fancy! But then they got serious about it, the way people do, and I was getting scared because they didn't talk very loud, and it was storming outside.

"And finally Daddy said he thought he'd choose some kind of poison he talked about that kills you in one whiff when you breathe it, and Uncle Lester said *he* thought a bullet through the head would be best, and Laura kept saying, 'What rot, what rot,' and 'Come on, Phil, or we'll be late for the first-act curtain.' And when Phil got up from the table Uncle Lester asked him how *he'd* like to die. And Phil just laughed, and, I say, he *was* jolly good-looking with the candles and his white shirt and the way he had his hair combed and everything! . . . And he said something in French and Daddy told me afterwards it meant, 'Always the gentleman,' and he said a lot of absurd things and said . . . Well, anyway, he didn't care so much *how* he died, if he could die with a top-hat on and at least one woman to weep at his grave. Fancy! How absurd of anybody to get that idea, I mean. And then he took Laura to the theatre."

Out in the square, the tireless barrel-organ was still tinkling out the Maine Stein Song. Four pairs of eyes fixed upon her had roused even Sheila Bitton to something like nervousness. As she came towards the end of her recital she was fidgeting and talking faster and faster. Now she cried:

"Please I *won't* . . . I won't have you looking at me like that! And I won't be put upon, and nobody ever tells me anything, and I know I've said something I shouldn't. What *is* the matter?"

She sprang up. Dalrye put a clumsy hand on her shoulder.

He said: "My dear! . . . er . . ." and stopped, because he had nothing to say. He was looking pale. His voice had a sort of rasp and whir like a gramophone running down.

A long silence . . .

"My dear Miss Bitton," the chief inspector said, briskly, "you've said nothing wrong at all. Mr. Dalrye will explain presently. But now about this morning, at the breakfast table. What was it your uncle said about seeing Philip today?"

"I say, Mr. Hadley," Dalrye struck in, clearing his throat. "After all, I mean to say, they treat her like a kid; and when the news came Sir William ordered her to go up to her room and stay there. He made me tell her it was a sort of accident. Do you think it's quite fair . . . ?"

"Yes," Hadley returned, sharply. "Yes, I do. Now, Miss Bitton?"

She hesitated, looked at Dalrye, and wet her lips.

"Why, there wasn't anything, much. Only Uncle Lester said he was going to have a talk with Phil today. And when I said that, about Phil meaning to go to the Tower at one o'clock, he said he thought he'd better run over to Phil's flat in the morning, then, before he got out."

"And did he?"

"Uncle Lester? Yes, he did. I saw him when he came back about noon . . . And I remember, Uncle Lester said to Daddy, 'Oh, I say, you'd better let me have your key, in case he isn't in this morning; I'll sit down and wait for him.'"

Hadley stared. "Your father," he asked, "has a key to this flat?"

"I told you," Sheila answered with some bitterness, "he treats us all like kids. That was one of the things that used to make Phil furious with him. He said he wouldn't pay for Phil's flat unless he could have a key, so that he could see what was going on whenever he wanted to . . . Fancy! As though Phil were a kid. You don't know Daddy. But it was just . . . well, I mean, he didn't really *mean* it, because he never visited Phil except once a month. So Daddy gave Uncle Lester the key."

Hadley bent forward. "Did he see Phil this morning?"

"No, he didn't, truly. Because, as I say, I saw him when he came back. And Phil was out, and Uncle Lester waited half an hour and left. He seemed to be . . ."

"Angry?" prompted Hadley, as she hesitated.

"N-o. Sort of tired and shaky. I know he'd overexerted himself. And . . . funny. He seemed queer, too, and excited; and he laughed."

"*Laughed*?"

"Hold on!" Dr. Fell suddenly boomed. He was having trouble keeping his glasses on his nose, and he held them to look at the girl. "Tell me, my dear . . . Was he carrying anything when he came back?"

"This," she cried again – "this is something horrible to do with Uncle Lester, and I won't *have* it! He's the only one who's really frightfully nice to me, and he *is*, and I won't have it. Even when I was a little girl, he was always the one who brought me bunny-rabbits, and chocolates, and dolls; Daddy said they were absurd. And . . ."

She was stamping on the floor, bewildered, turning suddenly to Dalrye . . .

"I'll be damned," the other flared, "if she answers you another question. Listen, Sheila. Go into the other rooms and see if there's anything you want to take along . . ."

Hadley was about to interpose when Dr. Fell silenced him with a fierce gesture. Then the doctor spoke amiably:

"It's quite all right, my dear. I hadn't meant to upset you, and it wasn't important, anyway. Do as Mr. Dalrye suggests, please . . . But there *is* one thing . . . No, no," as she was about to speak, "no more questions about what you're thinking. You know, I asked you on the telephone whether you would bring somebody along to help you with your things? And I suggested your father's valet . . . ?"

"Marks?" she exclaimed, puzzled. "Why, yes. I forgot. He's out in the car . . ."

"Thank you, my dear. There isn't anything else."

"You go in there and look about, Sheila," Dalrye suggested. "I'll join you in a moment. I should like to talk to these gentlemen . . ."

He waited until the door had closed. Then he turned slowly. There was dull colour under his cheek-bones; he was still visibly shaken, and his mouth worked.

"Listen," he said. His voice was thick. He cleared it with an effort. "I understand all your implications, of course. And you know how much I thought of Phil. But so far as Mr. Bitton's concerned . . . Mr. Lester Bitton . . . Major Bitton . . . I feel the way she does. And I'll tell you you're a lot of damned fools. I know him pretty well. Sheila didn't tell you he was the one who stood up for our marriage when the old man was against it. But *I'll* tell you.

"He's not likeable on the surface, as General Mason is. I know the general dislikes him, because the general's the old roaring, damn-your-eyes type of army man. Bitton's cold and efficient when you just look at him. He's not clever, or a good talker. But he's . . . you're . . . a . . . lot . . . of . . . fools," Dalrye said, suddenly miserable. He struck the back of a chair.

Hadley drummed his fingers on his brief-case.

"Tell us the truth, Mr. Dalrye," he said, after a time. "We've pretty well found out that there was an affair between Mrs. Bitton and Driscoll . . . Well, *I'll* be frank: we know it for a positive fact. Did *you* know about it?"

"I give you my word," said Dalrye, simply, "I didn't. Believe me or not. I only got wind of it . . . well, afterwards." He looked from face to face, and they all knew he was telling the truth. "Phil wouldn't have been such a fool as to tell me. I'd have covered him, I suppose because . . . oh, well, you can see. But I'd have stopped it, somehow."

"And do you suppose Sir William knew of it?"

"O Lord, no! He's the last person who would. He's too tied up with his books and his lectures about how the government is running on senile decay . . . But, for God's sake, find out who killed Phil, and what all this nonsense is about, before we all go mad. Find out!"

"We are going to begin," Dr. Fell said, quietly, "in precisely two minutes."

There was a silence as sudden as the stroke of a gong. "I mean," rumbled the doctor, lifting himself in his chair and raising one cane, "we are going to dispose of the nonsense, and then see our way straight to the sense . . . Mr. Dalrye, will you step outside and ask that valet chap, Marks, to step in here?"

Dalrye hesitated, running a hand through his hair; but at the doctor's imperious gesture he hurried out.

"Now!" urged Dr. Fell, hammering his stick on the floor. "Set that table over in front of me. That's it, my boy; hurry!" He struggled up as Rampole lifted the heavy table and set it down with a thump before him. "Now, Hadley, give me your brief-case . . ."

"Here!" protested the chief inspector; "stop scattering those papers all over the table! What the hell are you doing?"

Rampole stared in astonishment as the doctor waddled over and picked up a bridge-lamp with a powerful electric bulb. Reeling out its cord from the baseboard, he set the lamp at some short distance from the table. Then he rolled a low chair under it, and switched on the light. Rampole found the chief inspector's black notebook thrust into his hands

"That, my boy, is for you," said the doctor. "Sit down here beside me on my left. Have you a pencil? . . . Good! When I give you the word, you are to pretend to be making shorthand notes. Scrawl down anything you like, but keep your pencil working fast. Understand?"

Hadley made motions like one who sees a priceless vase tottering on the edge of a shelf. "*Don't*! . . . Look here, those are all my notes; and if you muck them up! . . . You fat lunatic, what is all this . . ."

"Don't argue," said the doctor, testily. "Have you got a revolver and a pair of handcuffs on you, by any chance?"

Hadley looked at him. He said:

"You're mad. Fell, you're stark, staring mad! They only carry those things in the stories and on the films. I haven't had a revolver or a pair of handcuffs in my hands for ten yea . . ."

"Then I have," the doctor said, composedly. "I knew you'd forget them." With the air of a conjuror he produced from his hip pockets both the articles he had mentioned and held them up, beaming. He pointed the revolver at Rampole and added, "Bing!"

"Look out!" shouted the chief inspector, seizing at his arm. "You blithering idiot be careful with that thing!"

"You needn't worry. Word of honour, you needn't. It's a dummy pistol; even a Scotland Yard man couldn't hurt himself with it. It's just painted tin, you see? The handcuffs are dummies, too, but they both look realistic. I got them at one of those curio-shop places in Glasshouse Street, where you buy all the trick things. Here are some more of them; I couldn't resist buying several. There's a mouse that runs across the table on some sort of roller when you press him down" – he was fumbling in his pockets – "but we don't need 'em now. Ah here was what I wanted."

With manifest pride on his large red face he produced an enormous and impressive-looking gold badge, which he hung on his lapel conspicuously.

"To the man we're going to question," he observed, "we have got to look like a *real* crowd of detectives. That we do not look like the same to the chief of the C.I.D. is of no consequence. But we have got to look the part for Mr. Marks's benefit, or we shall get nothing out of him . . . Now, draw up closely to this table, and look as solemn as possible . . . We have it all arranged now; the light in his face as he sits in that chair I've pushed out; the handcuffs will lie before me, and you, Hadley, will be suggestively fingering the revolver. My young friend here will take down his testimony . . . Turn out those centre lights, will you?" he added to Rampole. "Just the brilliant spotlight on his face, and ourselves in shadow. I think I shall keep on my hat. We now look sufficiently like the classic group, I think, to have our pictures taken . . . Ha!" added the doctor, very pleased. "I feel in my element now. Real detectives don't do this, but I wish to heaven they did."

Rampole inspected them as he went to turn out the centre lights. There *was* a slight suggestion of people having their pictures taken at one of those beach-resort places where you put your head over the top of a cardboard airship and look foolish. Dr. Fell was sitting back sternly, and Hadley looked with a weird expression at the tin revolver hanging by the trigger-guard from one finger. Then there were footfalls in the vestibule. Dr. Fell said, "Hist!" and Rampole hastily extinguished the centre lights.

Dalrye saw the tableau a moment later, and jumped violently.

"Bring in the accused!" Dr. Fell intoned, with a voice strongly suggestive of Hamlet's father's Ghost.

"Bring in *who*?" said Dalrye.

"Bring in Marks," said the Ghost, "and lock the door."

"You can't do it," said Dalrye, after a moment's inspection. "The lock's broken."

"Well, shoot him in," the Ghost suggested, in a more matter-of-fact tone, slightly bordering on irritation, "and stand against it then."

"Right-ho," said Dalrye. He was not sure what was going on, but he caught the cue, and frowned sternly as he ushered in Marks.

The man who appeared was mild, and correct, and very nervous. Not a wrinkle in his neat clothes was out of place, and there was no guile in him. He had a long, lean head, with thin black hair parted sharply in the middle and brushed behind each large ear. His features were blunt and still more nervous. He advanced with a slight stoop, holding a good but obviously not new bowler hat against his breast.

At the sight of the tableau he froze. Nobody spoke.

"You – you wished to speak to me, sir?" he said, in a curious voice, with a slight jump at the end of it.

"Sit down," said Dr. Fell.

Another silence, while Marks's eyes took in the properties. He lowered himself gingerly into the chair and blinked at the bright light in his face.

"Sergeant Rampole," said the doctor, with a massive gesture, "take down this man's testimony . . . Your name?"

"Theophilus Marks, sir."

Rampole made two crosses and a squiggle.

"Occupation?"

"I am employed by Sir William Bitton, of Berkeley Square, sir. I – I hope, sir," said Marks, swallowing, "that this is not in connection with that dreadful business, sir, of Mr. Philip . . ."

"Do I take that down, too?" inquired Rampole.

"Certainly," said the doctor. Obediently, Rampole made a furious row of loops, and ended with a severe flourish. Dr. Fell had for the moment forgotten the voice of Hamlet's father's Ghost. He resumed it with a jerk that made Hadley jump.

"Your last position?"

"For fifteen years, sir, I had the honour to serve Lord Sandival," Marks said, eagerly, "and I'm sure, sir . . ."

"*Aha*!" rumbled the doctor, closing one eye. He looked rather as the Ghost would have looked had he caught Hamlet playing pinochle when he should have been attending to business. "Why did you leave your last place? Sacked?"

"No, sir! It was the death of His Lordship, sir."

"H'm. Murdered, I suppose?" inquired the Ghost.

"Good Heavens, no, sir!"

Marks was visibly wilting. The Ghost became practical. "Now, look here, Marks, I don't mind telling you you're in a very bad corner . . . You've got a good position, haven't you?"

"Yes, sir. And I'm sure Sir William will give me the highest . . ."

"He won't, Marks, if he knows what *we* know. Would you like to lose your position, and go to gaol besides? Think of it, Marks!" rumbled Dr. Fell, picking up the handcuffs.

Marks moved backwards, his forehead damp. He tried to keep the light out of his eyes with a nervous hand.

"Marks," said the Ghost, "give me your hat!"

"My *what*, sir?"

"Your hat. The one you've got there. Quickly!"

As the valet held out his bowler, they could see under the light the large gold letters BITTON on the inside of the white lining in the crown. "Aha!" said the Ghost. "Pinching

Sir William's hats, eh? That'll be another five years. Write it down, Sergeant Rampole."

"No, sir!" Marks cried, through a gulp. "I swear it, sir. I can prove it, Sir William *gave* me that hat. I wear the same size as he does. And he gave me that because he bought two new hats only recently, and if you'll only let me prove it, sir . . . !"

"I'll give you your chance," said the Ghost, ominously. He thrust his hand across the table. It held something round and flat and black; there was a click, and it leaped full-grown into an opera-hat. "Put this hat on, Marks!"

By this time Rampole was so bewildered that he almost expected to see Dr. Fell take from the hat several yards of coloured ribbon and a brace of rabbits. Marks stared.

"*This* is Sir William's hat!" shouted the Ghost. "Put it on. If it fits you, I'll believe what you say."

Without further ado he began to stab with the hat in the direction of Marks's forehead. The valet was compelled to put it on. It was too large; not so large as it had been on the body of Driscoll, but still too large.

"So-ho!" rumbled the Ghost, standing up behind the table. Absently he had been fumbling in his pockets; the Ghost was excited, and making gestures with anything he could lay hold of. Dr. Fell lifted his hand and shook it in the air. "Confess, Marks!" he thundered. "Miserable wretch, your guilt has found you out!"

He crashed his hand down on the table. To Marks's stupefaction, and Dr. Fell's own irritation at the anti-climax, a large rubber mouse with white whiskers popped out of his hand and ambled slowly across the table towards Hadley. Dr. Fell snatched it up hastily and put it into his pocket.

"Hem!" observed the Ghost. Then he paused and added something which really brought Hadley out of his chair.

"Marks," said Dr. Fell, "*you stole Sir William's manuscript*."

For a moment it looked as though the other were going to faint.

"I – I didn't! I swear I didn't! But I didn't know, and I was afraid to tell when he explained it to me . . . !"

"I'll tell you what you did, Marks," said Dr. Fell, forgetting all about the Ghost and threatening in a natural voice. "Sir William gave me all the facts. You're a good valet, Marks, but you're one of the stupidest creatures in God's world. Sir William bought two new hats on Saturday. One of the opera-hats he tried on at the shop was too large for him. But a mistake was made, and they sent the large one to him along with the Homburg, which was of the right size. Ha? You saw it. You would immediately. You wear the same size. But Sir William was going out to the theatre that night. You know what sort of temper he has. If he found a hat that slid down over his forehead, he'd make it hot for the first person he could lay hands on . . .

"Naturally you wanted his hat to be the right size, didn't you, Marks? Otherwise your soul would have been shocked. But there wasn't time to get another hat; it was Saturday evening. So you did the natural thing. You used the same quick makeshift people have been using since hats were invented. You neatly stuffed the band on the inside with paper, the first harmless-looking paper you could find . . ."

Hadley flung the tin revolver on the table. "Good God!" he said, "do you seriously mean to tell us that Marks tightened up the fit of that hat with Sir William's manuscript?"

"Sir William," the doctor said, amiably, "gave us two clues himself which were absolutely revealing. Do you remember what he said? He said that the manuscript consisted of thin sheets of paper folded several times *lengthwise*, and rather long. Try folding over any piece of paper that way, and you'll get a long, narrow, compact set, admirably suited for stuffing the lining of a hat . . . And do you remember what he said besides? The manuscript was wrapped in *tissue-paper.* Taken all together, it was the obvious thing for Marks to use. Like the two labourers in the house where Bitton found it, and the owner of the house himself, Marks couldn't see any importance in a piece of tissue-paper lying idly about . . ."

"But Bitton said it was in the drawer."

"I doubt that," said Dr. Fell. "Was it, Marks?"

Marks brushed a handkerchief over his damp forehead. "N-no, sir," he faltered. "It was lying there on the desk. I – *I* didn't think it was important. It was tissue-paper with some crackly stuff inside, the sort of thing they use to pack objects in cardboard boxes. I thought it was something he'd discarded, sir. I swear I did! If it had been correspondence, or *any* other piece of paper, I take my oath I wouldn't have thought of going near it. But . . ."

"And then," said Dr. Fell, rattling the handcuffs, "you learned next day what you'd done. You learned it was worth thousands of pounds. And so you were afraid to tell Sir William what you'd done, because in the meantime the hat had been stolen." He turned to Hadley. "I rather thought this was the case, from Sir William's description of Marks's behaviour when he interviewed him afterwards. Sir William made us an invaluable suggestion, which he thought was satiric. He said, 'Do you think I go about carrying valuable manuscripts in my hat?' And that's precisely what he did."

"And that," Hadley said in a queer voice, "*that* was why Sir William's hat fitted him. It's what you meant by your 'hint.'"

"It's what I meant by telling you we had got to clear away all the nonsense from this case before we could see the truth. That one little accident precipitated a whole series of ghastly events, like the loss of the horseshoe nail. It was the only point I wasn't sure of. I was staking everything on my belief that that's what had happened. Now I know the whole truth . . . But you can see for yourself why I couldn't have Sir William with me when I was questioning Marks."

The valet removed the opera-hat and was holding it like a bomb. His face was dull and helpless.

"All right," he said in a normal, human, almost even tone. "All right, gents. You've got me. That means my job. What are you going to *do* with me? I've got a sister and three cousins I'm supporting; and respectable, too. But it's all up now."

"Eh?" said Dr. Fell. "Oh! . . . No, Marks. You're safe enough. Now you walk out to the car again, and sit there till you're called. You did a stupid thing, but there's no reason why you should lose your place. *I* won't tell Sir William."

The mild little man thrust himself out violently.

"Honest to God?" he demanded. "Do you mean it?"

"I mean it, Marks."

There was a pause. Marks drew himself up and adjusted his impeccable coat. "Very good, sir," he said in a precise tone. "I'm sure I'm very grateful, sir."

"Turn on the centre lights," Dr. Fell suggested to Rampole, "and give Hadley's notebook back before he gets apoplexy." Beaming, the doctor sat down behind the table and produced the rubber mouse. He pushed his shovel-hat to the back of his head, and set the mouse to running in circles over the table. "This almost marred my effect. I say, Hadley, I'm devilish sorry I didn't think to buy a pair of false whiskers."

As the lights went on, Hadley, Rampole, and a very excited Dalrye almost literally seized him.

"Let me get all this straight," the chief inspector said, heavily. "On Saturday night Bitton walked out of his house with that manuscript in his hat. And this Mad Hatter chap stole the hat . . ."

"Ah," said the doctor, sombrely. He stopped the mouse and scowled at it. "And there you have the inception of the crazy comedy, Hadley. There's where *everything* started to go wrong. If there's one thing in the world young Philip Driscoll wouldn't have done, it was offend his uncle. Over and over, with tears in my eyes, I've implored you to believe that the last thing in the world Driscoll wanted to do was even touch Bitton's beloved manuscript. And so what must have been his horror when he discovered he'd done the one thing in the world he didn't want to do . . . !"

During a frozen silence Dr. Fell picked up the mouse, put it down, and glanced thoughtfully at his companions.

"Oh yes," he said. "*Driscoll was the hat-thief, you see.*"

15
THE AFFAIR OF THE RUBBER MOUSE

"Wait a minute!" protested Rampole. "Wait a minute. They're coming over the plate too fast for me. You mean . . ."

"Just what I say," the doctor answered, testily. "If you didn't see that, I'm surprised you didn't. Nobody could have doubted it from the first. I had proof of it here tonight; but I had to come here and get the proof before you would have believed me. Got a cigar, Hadley?"

He sat back comfortably when the cigar was lighted, the large gold badge still stuck on his lapel and the rubber mouse within reach.

"Consider. Here's a crazy young fellow with a sense of humour and lots of intelligence. I think myself that he was a good deal of a sneak and skunk; but we've got to allow him the nerve, the humour, and the intelligence. He wants to make a name for himself as a newspaperman. He can turn out a good, vivid news-story when he has the facts; but he has so little news-sense that one managing editor swears he wouldn't scent a wedding if he walked through an inch of rice in front of a church.

"That's not only understandable, Hadley, but it's a further clue to his character. His long suit was imagination. The very imaginative people never make good straight reporters; they're looking for the picturesque, the bizarre, the ironic incident; and very often they completely neglect to bother about essential facts. Doing the routine work of covering regular news isn't in their line. Driscoll would have made a thundering good columnist, but as a reporter he was a failure. So he resolved to do what many a reporter has done before him: to *create* news, and the sort of news that would appeal to him. If you'll just think back over everything we know of his character, you'll see what he was up to.

"In every one of these important hat-thefts there was a sort of ironic symbolism, as though the stage had been arranged by an actor. Driscoll loved gestures, and he loved symbolism. A policeman's helmet is propped on a lamp-standard outside Scotland Yard; 'Behold the power of the police!' says the Byronic Mr. Driscoll, with the usual cynicism of very young people. A barrister's wig is put on a cab-horse, which was the nearest approach Driscoll could get towards underlining Mr. Bumble's opinion that the law is an ass. And next the hat of a well-known Jewish war profiteer is stolen and placed on one of the lions in Trafalgar Square. Now, Driscoll is really in his most Byronic vein. 'Behold!' he cries – and it's genuinely comical, as I tried to point out to you – 'behold, in these degenerate days, the British lion's crown!'"

Dr. Fell paused to settle more comfortably. Hadley stared at him, and then the chief inspector nodded.

"Now I shouldn't go into this so thoroughly," the doctor went on, "except that it's a clue to the murder, as you'll see. He was preparing for another coup, a real and final coup, which couldn't help making – in his eyes – the whole of England sit up." The doctor wheezed and chuckled. Putting down his cigar, he pawed among the papers he had taken from Hadley's brief-case. "Here's his notebook, with those notes which puzzled you so much. Before I read them to you again, let me remind you that Driscoll himself gave the whole show away. You recall that drunken evening with Mrs. Bitton, which Mrs. Larkin described for us, when Driscoll prophesied what was going to happen a week before it did begin to happen? He mentioned events which were shortly to occur, and which would make his name as a newspaperman. An artist, when comfortably filled with beer, can talk at length about the great picture he intends to paint, without exciting the least surprise. A writer is practically bound to mention the great novel he will one day write. But when a newspaperman casually mentions what corking stories he is going to turn out about the murder which is to take place next week, there is likely to be considerable curiosity about his powers of foresight.

"But let's return to this big stroke Driscoll was planning, after having built up to it by degrees with lesser hats. First, you see, he carefully stole the crossbow bolt out of Bitton's house . . ."

"He did *what*?" shouted the chief inspector. Dalrye sat down suddenly in a chair by the table, and Rampole found another.

"Oh yes; I must tell you about that," Dr. Fell said, frowning as though he were a trifle annoyed with himself. "But I tried to give you a hint, you know, this afternoon. It was Driscoll who stole it. By the way . . ." he rummaged on the floor at the side of his chair, and brought up the tool-basket. After fumbling inside it, he produced what he wanted . . . "by the way, here's the file he used to sharpen it. It's rather an old file, so you can see the oblique lines in the dirt-coating where he sawed at the barbs of the head. And here are the straighter marks to show where he had started effacing the *Souvenir de Carcassonne,* before somebody stole the bolt from him to use for another purpose . . ."

Hadley took the file and turned it over. "Then . . ." he said.

"I asked you, you know, why that engraving hadn't been entirely obliterated, provided the person who had sharpened the bolt was really the murderer. Let's suppose it *had* been the murderer. He started in to do it, so why in the name of madness didn't he go on? It was obvious that he didn't want the bolt traced, as it would have been and as it was. But he stopped after a neat, thorough job on just three letters. It was only when I realized what was up – an explanation provided by those abstruse notes in Driscoll's notebook – that I realized it wasn't the murderer's doing at all. It was Driscoll's. He hadn't finished his job of effacing when along came the murderer: who didn't care where the bolt came from, or whose it was. But actually this bolt was planned as a part of Driscoll's most daring venture."

"But, good God! *what* venture?" demanded Hadley. "There's no way to associate it with the hats."

"Oh yes, there is," said Dr. Fell.

After he had puffed thoughtfully for a moment he went on: "Hadley, who is the man, above all you can think of, who ranks in the popular eye as England's leading jingo? Who is the man who still makes speeches in private life, as he used to do in public life, about the might of the sword, the longbow, the crossbow, and the stout hearts of old? Who is always agitating for bigger armaments? Who is for ever attacking the Prime Minister as a dangerous pacifist? Who, at any rate, is inevitably the person *Driscoll* would think of in that rôle?"

"You mean – Sir William Bitton . . ."

"I mean just that," nodded the doctor. A grin creased up his chins. "And that insane nephew of his had conceived a design which satisfied all the demands of his sensation-loving soul . . . He was going to steal Sir William Bitton's hat and nail it with a crossbow bolt to the door of Number 10, Downing Street."

Hadley was more than shocked. He was genuinely outraged. For a moment he could only splutter; and Dr. Fell contemplated him with amiable mockery.

"Tut, tut!" said the doctor. "I warned you, Hadley, when the general and I were outlining fantastic schoolboy pranks and you were not amused. I was sure you would never see the back of the design unless you could put yourself into the place of the schoolboy. You've got too much common sense . . . But, you see, Driscoll hadn't. You don't appreciate dummy pistols and rubber mice. That's your trouble. But I do appreciate them, and I can become even as Driscoll.

"Look here." He opened Driscoll's notebook. "See how he's musing about this scheme. He hasn't quite worked it out yet. All he has is the idea of fastening Sir William's hat with this warlike instrument in some public place. So he writes, inquiringly: '*Best place? Tower*?' But, of course, that won't do; it's much too easy, and a crossbow bolt in the Tower would be as conspicuous as a small bit of coal at Newcastle. However, he's got to have his properties first, and he writes, '*Track down hat*,' which is obvious. Then he thinks about Trafalgar Square again, as he inevitably must. But that won't do, because he certainly can't drive his bolt into the stone of the Nelson monument. So he writes, '*Unfortunate Trafalgar, can't transfix*!' But it wasn't so unfortunate, for his burst of inspiration comes – and you note the exclamation points to denote it. He's got it now. He notes down Number 10, home of the Prime Minister. The next words you can easily see. Is the door made of wood? If it's steel-bound, or something of the sort, the scheme won't work; he doesn't know. He must find out. Is there a hedge, or anything that will screen him from observation while he does it? Are there guards about, as there are likely to be? He doesn't know this, either. It's a long chance, and a risky one; but he's jubilant about the possibility, and he means to find out."

Dr, Fell put down the notebook.

"Thus," he said, "I outline to you what I, like Driscoll, intend to call symbolically the Affair of the Rubber Mouse. Let's see what came of it. You *do* see, don't you, Hadley?"

Again the chief inspector was pacing the room. He made a noise almost like a groan.

"I suppose I do," he snapped. "He waited for Sir William's car in Berkeley Street; let's see, that was Saturday night?"

"Saturday night," affirmed the doctor. "He was still youthful and hopeful and all the rest of it. He was up in the clouds – just before the tumble came. And, incidentally, here's another ingenious feature of the scheme. In most cases there wasn't an enormous amount of risk. He stole the hats of the dignified people who wouldn't make a row about it. They certainly wouldn't report the theft to the police, to begin with. And if he were in a tight spot, it's unlikely the victim would give serious chase. That's the cunning feature. A man like Sir William would run halfway across London in pursuit of a man who'd picked his pocket of half a crown. It would be outraged justice. But he wouldn't run a step, for fear of looking a fool, after a man who stole a two-guinea hat . . . Well, reconstruct, Hadley."

"H'm. He waited for Sir William's car in Berkeley Street. Any sort of telephone call to the house, which he could properly have made in his own character, would have got him the information he wanted . . . where Bitton was that night, and the rest of it. And let's see. Bitton said I think, that the chauffeur slowed down to let a blind man with some pencils get across the street . . ."

"Any sort of vender," agreed the doctor, "would have crossed the street for a shilling. And Driscoll got the hat. He bargained on it that Bitton wouldn't give chase. He was right. Still, everything was fine and fair, until . . ."

He peered up inquiringly at Hadley.

"Until Sunday night," Hadley said, slowly. "Then everything came down on him at once when he called at the house."

"We're on debatable ground now. But it's not a question of great importance. H'mf. It's unlikely he discovered until Sunday night that he'd unwittingly pinched the manuscript," said Dr. Fell. "Why should he? You don't pay much attention to paper inside a hat-band.

"But here's the point. On Sunday evening they told him about the theft of the manuscript. Whether he suspected something then I don't know. Undoubtedly he knew all about the manuscript, from Bitton's hints beforehand. But the other affair crashed down on him. Laura Bitton and her husband were back; Laura must have conveyed some hint of the state of affairs; there was a whispered row; Driscoll went wildly out of the house before Laura could make an appointment with him. Otherwise she would have made her appointment then, and not bothered to write. But Driscoll gave her no chance; that was like him."

"Up again, down again," muttered Hadley. "He was afraid of the scandal that might come up; of being cut off by his uncle . . ."

Dr. Fell nodded sombrely.

"And a million other fancies that would come into a head like his. Mr. Dalrye said this flat was full of his presence," the doctor said suddenly, in a louder voice. "What must he have been like when he came home here and discovered, with one of the sickest feelings of horror he ever had, that he'd unintentionally stolen his uncle's most cherished possession? Good God! what would he *think*? In his muddled state he couldn't think at all. What would you think yourself if a ten-thousand-pound manuscript had been stolen, and turned up as stuffing for a hat-band? His difficulties were all childish and all horrible. How could he explain it? Here was his uncle raving, and here *he* was with the manuscript – how had it got into the hat to begin with? Not by any stretch of madness could he have imagined his uncle deliberately putting that fragile thing into a hat of his own accord, and wearing it about the streets. And, worst of all, Driscoll wasn't supposed to know about the manuscript in the first place!

"Imagine that wild, red-headed kid running about here like a bat trying to get out! A moment before, he'd been the reckless adventurer; swaggering, exhilarated – as immortal as a shilling-shocker hero. Women loved him, and he could imagine that men feared him. Now he was threatened with a hellish scandal, with the price of swaggering, and worst of all with his ugly-tempered uncle. I wonder how many drinks he had?"

"If he had been sensible," the chief inspector growled, striking the table, "he'd have gone to his uncle, and . . ."

"Would he?" Dr. Fell frowned. "I wonder if even a sensible person would have done that: at least, with Sir William Bitton. What could Driscoll say? 'Oh, I say, uncle, I'm sorry. Here's your Poe manuscript. I pinched it by mistake at the same time I pinched your hat.' Can you imagine the result? Driscoll wasn't supposed to know about the manuscript; nobody was. Bitton imagined he was being very sly and clever, when he was advertising its presence all the time. To begin with, he wouldn't have believed Driscoll. What would *you* think of somebody who walked in and said, 'By the way, Hadley, you know that thousand-pound bank-note you've been hiding away from everybody in your drawer upstairs? Well, when I was stealing your umbrella last night, I accidentally discovered the bank-note hanging by a string from the handle of the umbrella. Odd, what?' No, my boy. You'd scarcely have been in a receptive mood. And if, to cap the business, your brother later came in and observed, 'Yes, Hadley, and the curious thing is that I discovered in that chap's flat not only your umbrella and your thousand-pound note, but also my wife.' I venture to suggest, old man, that you would have thought your friend's conduct at least a trifle eccentric."

Dr. Fell snorted.

"Perhaps that's what the sensible man would have done. But Driscoll wasn't sensible. Call him anything else you like, but not a clear-thinker. He was wild. *We* can sit here and say how humorous it was, and that he was a half-baked youth who imagined the world tumbling down on him. But he couldn't."

Dr. Fell bent forward and prodded the rubber mouse with his forefinger. It ran round in a circle on the table and bounced off.

"For Lord's sake," cried the exasperated chief inspector, "let that mouse alone and get on with – it! So he wrestled with this thing all night, and in the morning he telephoned Mr. Dalrye here and determined to tell him everything?"

"Exactly."

Dalrye, who had been sitting quietly all through this, turned a puzzled face; he looked like a dishevelled Puritan elder.

"Yes, but there's another thing," he observed. "I say, Doctor, why didn't he come to me straightaway? He phoned in the morning, you know. If he were as upset as all that, he would have come down to the Tower immediately, wouldn't he?"

"No," said the doctor. "And I shall now expound to you, children, why. It is the point which confirmed my suspicions of the whole affair. I mean the second attack on Sir William Bitton."

"Good Lord, yes . . . !" Hadley stopped his pacing and wheeled suddenly. "If Driscoll did all this, why did he steal a *second* hat from Bitton? That wasn't precisely the way to get him out of the scrape, was it?"

"No. But it was a piece of remarkably quick thinking in an emergency, for which we shall have to give him credit."

"Maybe it was," the chief inspector admitted, gloomily. "But it would seem to me somewhat to complicate matters. He'd have another explanation to add to his uncle when he'd finished the ones you were outlining a minute ago. 'Sorry to trouble you again, sir. But I've not only pinched your hat, your manuscript, and your brother's wife, but your first hat wasn't satisfactory, so I just popped round and took another.'"

"Be quiet, will you? Be quiet, and let me talk. Ha. Harrumph. Well. He was going to get Mr. Dalrye's help, but, before he did, he intended to make one last effort to help himself. You see, I rather wondered why he had definitely made the appointment at the Tower for one o'clock, as Mr. Dalrye says, when he could easily have gone down there in the morning. And, having made the appointment, he didn't appear until nearly twenty minutes past one! What held him up? If anything, you would have expected him to be ahead of time . . . What he was going to do was make an attempt to return the manuscript, unknown to his uncle.

"That was rather more difficult an undertaking than it sounds. He knew positively, from what he had heard at the house, that his uncle didn't connect the theft of the manuscript with the theft of the hat. Sir William thought the manuscript was stolen by itself. Suppose, then, Driscoll simply put it into an envelope and sent it back to his uncle by post? . . . Too dangerous! Driscoll knew Arbor was in the house. He had heard Arbor's broad talk at the dinner table. He knew that his uncle was bound to suspect Arbor. But he knew his uncle would never believe Arbor had first stolen the manuscript, and then posted it back again. And if Arbor were eliminated . . . you see?"

Hadley rubbed his chin.

"Yes. If Arbor were eliminated, the only person who could have stolen it was a member of his own household."

"Then what follows? Sir William would know it hadn't been one of the servants; he ridiculed that idea when he talked to *us*. There would remain Lester Bitton, Laura Bitton, Sheila, and Driscoll. Lester and Laura Bitton were definitely several hundred miles away when it was stolen. Only four people could have known about that manuscript, and two of them were in Cornwall! Of the other two, Sheila could hardly have been regarded as the culprit. Inevitably Driscoll must come to be suspected, and be thought to have sent it back in a fit of conscience – which would be precisely like Driscoll, anyway. Rest assured Driscoll knew all this, and he knew that his uncle would suspect it if he posted back that manuscript. But what was he to do? For the same reasons, he couldn't slip into the house and drop the manuscript somewhere so that it would be found. Sir William knew damned well it *hadn't* been mislaid; he'd been over that house with a vacuum cleaner; he knew it wasn't there. The same drawbacks would apply to its being suspiciously 'found' as to its being suspiciously returned in the mail."

"I'm hanged if I can see what he could do," the chief inspector confessed. "Unless he simply sat tight and let his uncle suspect Arbor. That would be the logical thing. But a nervous type like Driscoll would always have the horrible fear that his uncle *might,* somehow, find out. What he'd want most to do would be get the thing out of his hands – quickly. Out of sight, out of mind sort of business."

"Precisely! And that," said Dr. Fell, rapping his stick on the floor, "is where, for a second, he completely lost his head. He wanted to get it out of his hands. It was almost literally burning his fingers. You see what he did? He couldn't make up his mind. He went out, on that misty day, and paced the streets. And with every step he was gravitating towards his uncle's house, with possibilities multiplying and whirling and hammering in his brain, until he lost his head altogether.

"Hadley, do you remember what time Sir William arrived this afternoon at the bar where he met us? It was close on two o'clock. And when he described the theft of his second hat to us, he said, 'It happened an hour and a half ago, and I'm still boiling.' It happened, then, roughly, at about twenty minutes to one. Sir William was ready to make his monthly round of calls, as he told us; and, as he also told us, they rarely varied. It was the afternoon for his monthly call on Driscoll, by the way. I believe he pointed that out . . . His car was standing in the mist at the kerb. His chauffeur had gone down to buy cigarettes, and Sir William had not yet stepped out of the house. And Driscoll was there at the corner, watching it."

"I'm beginning to remember a lot of things Bitton said," the chief inspector answered, grimly. "He told us he saw somebody with his arm through the window of the car fumbling with the side pocket. You mean – Driscoll couldn't stand it any longer; and he wanted to shove the manuscript into the pocket of the car, anywhere out of sight?"

"I do. And he was prevented by Sir William's instant arrival on the scene. Sir William thought he was a sneak-thief. He didn't mind chasing sneak-thieves. He yelled, 'Hi!' and charged – and Driscoll (probably instinctively) did the only piece of quick thinking I've known him do yet. He snatched Sir William's hat and darted away in the mist."

"You mean . . ."

"Instinctive experience, my boy. Because he knew the old man wouldn't chase him. He knew Bitton would simply stand on the pavement and swear."

"Good," said Hadley, in a low voice, after a pause. "Damned good. But you're forgetting one thing. He may really have *put* that manuscript into the pocket of the car, and it may still be there."

Dr. Fell blinked sadly at the mouse he had resurrected from the floor.

"Sorry. I'm afraid you're about eleven hours too late. You see, even in the rush of going to the Tower in Bitton's car, I didn't neglect to examine the pockets this afternoon. It wasn't there. Driscoll never put it in; he left in too much of a hurry."

There was a very faint smile on Hadley's face. Again, Rampole felt, all through this conversation he had been holding himself back; he had been asking Dr. Fell the right questions, and quietly sorting out the pieces of the puzzle he wanted.

"Now, then, let me reassemble my facts," he suggested. "You say Driscoll went out comparatively early this morning, and never came back?"

"Yes."

"He took the manuscript. But the stolen top-hat was here?"

"Probably."

"Also . . . the crossbow bolt was here? The bolt he was filing; likely in a conspicuous place?"

"Yes."

"Then," said Hadley, with sudden grimness, "our case is complete. Lester Bitton came over here to see Driscoll this morning, when Driscoll was out. He let himself in with a key he borrowed from his brother, and returned to his home at noon, where Miss Bitton saw him come in . . . what did she say? . . . 'shaken' and 'laughing.'

"Anybody could have taken that crossbow bolt from the Bitton house. But only Lester Bitton could have stolen it from this flat. Anybody might have stolen Sir William's top-hat. But only Lester Bitton could have taken that top-hat from this flat to put on the head of the man he stabbed at the Tower of London, so that he could give Driscoll the fulfilment of his wish. And Driscoll did die in a top-hat, with at least one woman to weep at his grave."

Dr. Fell let his glasses fall on their black ribbon, and massaged his eyes fiercely. "Yes," he said from between his hands, in a muffled voice, "I'd thought of that, too. I'm afraid it rather sews him up. That's why I asked Miss Bitton whether he was carrying anything when he returned."

They had not realized, in the slow passing of hours, how imperceptibly the night noises of London had faded. Even the muted roar, always in the background, had died until their voices sounded unnaturally loud. They had not been aware of the creaking of boards, or how sharply rose the singing of tires when a late car hummed in the square. But even through a closed door they could hear the telephone bell.

Sheila Bitton's voice could be heard, too, when she answered it. And in a moment she thrust a rather grimy face round the door. She had been crying at one time, too, when she went over the contents of those rooms.

"It's for you, Mr. Hadley," she said. "Something about a Mr. Arbor? Is that *our* Mr. Arbor? You'd better come to the phone, please."

Hadley almost broke into a run.

16
WHAT WAS LEFT IN THE FIREPLACE

Sheila Bitton jumped in astonishment when she saw the expressions on the faces of those who crowded past her. Her own expression indicated that it was undignified. She had discarded hat and coat, to show fluffy yellow hair tousled about her head, and a dark frock with the sleeves now rolled up about the wrists. There was a streak of dirt across her nose where she had jammed her elbow across her eyes; and Rampole had an image of her picking up Driscoll's possessions . . . taking one, discarding one . . . reminded by another of some association, and suddenly sitting down with the tears in her eyes . . .

He reflected that he would never understand the mental processes of women in the presence of death. They were cool and unruffled. And then they became hysterical. Each in its own turn, and intermingling.

Hadley was at the telephone, and Dr. Fell bent over him in the little study. On the doctor's face was an expression Rampole had never seen before: he could not decide whether it was nervousness, or fear, or hope. But Dr. Fell was certainly nervous. Rampole never forgot the weird picture they presented in that time . . . Hadley listening intently to a buzz where words were almost distinguishable in the silent room; his elbow on the table, his back to the door, the dust which Sheila had disturbed settling now round the green-shaded lamp. Dr. Fell bent forward against the line of the bookshelves; the black ribbon on his glasses dangling, his shovel-hat on the back of his head, pinching at his moustache with a hand which still held the small rubber mouse.

Silence, except for the faint, rapid voice in the telephone. A board creaked. Sheila Bitton started to speak, but was hushed by Dalrye. Hadley spoke only once or twice, in monosyllables. Then, without hanging up the receiver, he turned.

"Well?" demanded Dr. Fell.

"It worked. Arbor left his friends, the Spenglers, early in the evening, and Spengler walked with him to his cottage. Our plain-clothes man was watching from the garden; he'd got his instructions already, and he seems to have played up to them . . . Hold on a bit, Carroll," he added into the telephone, and squared himself in the chair. "First Arbor went through the cottage, switching on all the lights, but he immediately closed the shutters after he'd done it. There are diamond-shaped holes in the bottoms of the shutters, though, and the constable worked close enough so that he could look in through the holes in the windows on the ground floor.

"Arbor and his friend were in one of the front rooms, where the covers hadn't been taken off the furniture. They were sitting in front of the fire, playing chess, with a bottle of whiskey between them, and Arbor looked nervous. This, I judge, was about two hours ago. Then the constable got busy. He walked up and down loudly on the gravel, and then dodged round the side of the house. In a moment Arbor's friend, Spengler, opened the shutters and looked out; then he closed them again. That sort of game went on for some time. They phoned for a policeman and the policeman flashed his bull's-eye all round the garden, but of course he didn't find our man. When it had all quieted down again, and our man was back at the window, he decided to rush matters. The whiskey was about half gone and somebody had knocked the chessboard over. Arbor seemed to be trying to persuade Spengler of something, and Spengler wouldn't listen. Then our man went back and rattled the knob of the scullery door.

The next minute he was around the side of the concrete garage, and it's a good thing he was. Somebody opened the scullery door and stuck out a revolver and began firing shots blindly all over the garden. That brought down all the policemen within half a mile; there was a devil of a row and Spengler had to show his pistol permit. When the row quieted down Arbor was all in. He insisted on going to the station with them and getting in touch with me. And he insists on speaking to me personally."

Dr. Fell did not look as pleased as circumstances seemed to warrant.

"What are you going to do?"

Hadley glanced at his watch and scowled. "It's almost ten minutes past twelve . . . H'm. But I'm afraid to put it off until morning. He'll get a return of cheerfulness with daylight, and he may decide not to talk. We've got to catch him while he's in a funk. But I don't want him at Scotland Yard . . . people of his type are very, very reticent when you come the high official over them . . . and I'm hanged if I'm going out to Golder's Green myself . . ."

"Why not bring him here?"

"I don't suppose there would be any objection . . . ?" Hadley looked at Sheila Bitton. "That's best. Dalrye can take Miss Bitton home. Yes, that's it. I'll have him brought in in a police car, so he'll know he's safe. This is as good a base of operations as any."

"Wouldn't he talk over the telephone?" the doctor demanded.

"No. For some reason, the man seems to have developed an unholy horror of telephones . . . Well." Hadley gave brief instructions to the other end of the wire, and hung up. "Fell, what do you think he knows?"

"I'm afraid to tell you what I think. I'm literally afraid. Remember, I asked you the same question when we decided Driscoll was stabbed in the tunnel of the Bloody Tower, with

Mrs. Bitton at one end and Arbor at the other . . ." He had been mumbling, and now he stopped short altogether as he remembered Sheila's presence. The girl was behind Dalrye in the passage, and apparently had not caught words which might have caused unnecessary questions. The doctor peered towards the passage, and chewed the end of his moustache. "Never mind. We shall know soon enough."

Hadley was examining the study. Sheila Bitton had added to its disorder, a thing which nobody would have believed possible a while ago. In the centre of the floor she had been piling all sorts of mementoes: a couple of silver cups, framed photographs of sport groups, a cricket bat, a runner's jersey, a china mug inscribed "Birthday, from Sheila," a stamp-album, a broken fishing-rod, and two warped tennis rackets. In this bleak room now, Rampole thought, memories were gathering and strengthening. It came to him horribly, with a new force: *This man is dead.*

"I wish you men would get *out*!" the girl's voice complained, fretfully. She pushed her way past Dalrye with doll-like aggressiveness, and stood contemplating them. "Everything is in such a *mess*! Phil would never keep tidy. And I'm sure I don't know what to do with his clothes; such a lot of them, all scattered about, and there's one brand-new nice grey hat I know belongs to Daddy, because it's got that gold lettering he uses on the inside, and how it came to be here I can't think."

"Eh?" demanded Hadley, roused out of his musing. His eyes narrowed and he looked at the doctor. "Do you think he came back here after he'd . . . I mean, just before he went to the Tower?"

"I'm fairly certain he did," Dr. Fell answered. "After he'd done what you're thinking about, he still had over twenty minutes to get to the Tower in time for his appointment, you remember. But he was twenty minutes late for it . . . It's all right, Miss Bitton. Just put the hat aside with the other things."

"Anyhow, I hope you'll get out," she said, practically. "Bob, you might call Marks and have him take an armload of those things out to the car. I'm filthy, absolutely filthy. And he's got oil spilled all over the desk where the typewriter is, and a piece of sharp stone I almost cut my finger on . . ."

Hadley turned round slowly to inspect the desk. Rampole had an image of Driscoll sitting under the green-shaded lamp in this cluttered room, patiently sharpening the crossbow bolt which was to be driven into his own heart . . .

"Whetstone," murmured the chief inspector. "And the typewriter . . . By the way, Doctor, you found the tool you wanted, right enough; but I remember you said you were looking for something in his typewriter. What was it?"

Dr. Fell juggled his mouse. "I was looking for the beginning of a certain news-story which gave an account of something before it occured; I mean that little business at No. 10. I wasn't sure he'd started it, but I thought I'd better have a look in case you didn't believe me. It wasn't in his typewriter, but it was on the desk; I have it in my pocket. If he intended to scoop Fleet Street, you see, he wanted time to prepare a corking-good story before the other reporters even heard of it. But there was such a litter of manuscript I almost overlooked it. He's been doing a bit of dabbling with fiction, too, I see. I was about to call your attention to his character in that respect when we went out to interview Mrs. Larkin. The stories have lurid titles, and they seem all of the adventure-mystery school. *The Curse of the Doornaways*, things like that: feudal mansions with galleries and ghosts, and all that sort of thing. I fancy Driscoll always wanted a feudal mansion, and regretted that Sir William's title went no farther back than Sir William."

Sheila Bitton stamped her foot. "Oh, good *gracious*, will you get *out*? I think it's mean of you, when poor Phil's dead, to sit here in his room like this, just talking. And if you want any of that writing, or all those papers, or anything, you'd better tell me, because I'm just going to put it all in a suit-box and take it home for Daddy; he'll want to keep it. Besides, some of it's burnt in the fireplace and you can't have it, and I looked in there because it was written in longhand and it might be a letter . . ." She paused and flushed suddenly: "Anyway, it was just an old story, and all burned, and . . ."

"*O my God*!" said Dr. Fell.

His great bulk lunged across the room to the toy fireplace with its bright-red bricks round the grate. He added, "Get your flashlight, Hadley," and bent to his knees, pushing away the iron fender. There was a startled expression on the chief inspector's own face as he yanked out his flashlight . . .

The fireplace was full of charred and feathered paper. As the bright beam played inside, they saw that the edging of some of the paper not wholly burned was of a dull mauve colour, blackened by smoke.

"The 'Mary' letters," Hadley said, as Dr. Fell tried lightly to lift the mass. "All that's left of them."

Dr. Fell grunted wheezily. "Yes. And here underneath them . . ."

He tried to draw it out gently, but it was only a delicate black shell, and it crumbled to ash. All that remained were a few smoke-fouled inches at the top. It had been a very thin sheaf of damp-stained sheets, folded three times lengthwise, and now open. Holding it gently in his open palms, Dr. Fell put it close to Hadley's light. There had been a title, but the smoke had yellowed and obliterated it; likewise it had obliterated all the letters in the corner except an ornate "E." But, in brown and curly script, they could faintly see a number of lines which the fire had not destroyed:

"Of the singular gifts of my friend the Chevalier C. Auguste Dupin, I may one day speak. Upon my lips he has placed a seal of silence which, for fear of displeasing the eccentricities of his somewhat *outré* humour, I dare not at present violate. I can, therefore, only record that it was after dark one gusty evening in the year 18– that a knock sounded at the door of my chambers in a dim, decaying pile of buildings of the Faubourg St. Germain, and . . ."

They all read it slowly. Dr. Fell did not move; it was as though he were kneeling and offering this piece of blackened paper to a god in the fire.

"There it is," the doctor growled in a low voice, after a pause. "All of him, in the start of one paragraph. The finger on the lip. The suavity, the hint of deadly secrets. The night, the night wind, the distant city, the date mysteriously left blank, the old and crumbling house in a remote quarter . . . H'm. Gentlemen, you are looking at all that is left of the first detective story ever written by Edgar Allan Poe."

Rampole's brain was full of weird pictures . . . a dark man with luminous, brooding eyes, thin shoulders in a military carriage, a weak chin, and an untidy moustache. He saw the candlelight, the mean room, the shabby tall hat hung behind the door, the pitifully thin rows of books. Never in his life would that dark man have anything but dreams, to exchange at last for the cold coin of an imortal name.

Hadley arose and switched off his light. "Well," he said, gloomily, "there goes ten thousand pounds. It's a good job Arbor doesn't have to pay the rest of his agreement to that fellow in Philadelphia."

"I hate having to tell this to Sir William," muttered Dalrye. "Good God! he'll be a maniac. It's a pity Phil couldn't at least have kept the thing . . ."

"*No*!" said Dr. Fell, violently. "You don't see the point. You don't grasp it at all, and I'm ashamed of you . . . What happened?"

"He burnt it, that's all," Hadley returned. "He was so terrified at nearly being caught when he tried to return it, that he came home and chucked it in the fire."

Dr. Fell pushed himself to his feet with the aid of one cane. He was fiery with earnestness.

"You still don't understand. What happened? Who knocked at the door of this man's house in the Faubourg St.-Germain? What terrible adventure was on the way? That's what you *should* think of, Hadley . . . I say to you, to hell with whether this manuscript is preserved for some smug collector to prattle learnedly about and exhibit to his friends like a new gold tooth. To hell whether it costs ten thousand pounds or a halfpenny. To hell whether it makes fools write more books trying to psychoanalyse a dead man of the nineteenth century according to the standards of the twentieth. To hell with whether it's in manuscript, first edition, vellum and morocco, or sixpenny paper . . . What I'm interested in is what magnificent dream of blood and violence began with that knock at the door."

"All right, then . . . to hell with it," the chief inspector agreed, mildly. "You seem a bit rabid on the subject. *I* don't mind. If you're really so curious, you can ask Bitton about the next instalment. He's read it."

Dr. Fell shook his head. "No," he said. "No, I'm never going to ask. That last line will be a deathless 'to be continued in our next' for me to weave answers about it all the rest of my life."

During this unenlightening discussion Sheila Bitton had gone into the bedroom, and they heard her moving things about with sundry suggestive knockings on the communicating wall.

"Well, let's get out," the chief inspector suggested. "Whatever you want to dream about, that fireplace has at least one thing to tell us. The manuscript was lying *under* those burnt 'Mary' letters. Driscoll burnt the manuscript before he left here on his way to the Tower. Mrs. Bitton broke in at five o'clock, and destroyed the evidence against her."

"That's right, I know," the doctor said, wearily. "But look here. I know it's bad taste, and we shouldn't do it, and all that . . . Still, it's warm work, and I've been several hours without a drink. If we could find one hereabouts . . . ?"

"Sound enough," said the chief inspector. "Then I'll outline my case to you."

He led the way out of the little room and down to the forlorn dining-room, where he snapped on the lights of the mosaic dome over the table. Undoubtedly, Rampole thought, that dome had come with the flat; it was of ornate ugliness, with golds and reds and blues jumbled together; and it threw a harsh, weird light on their faces. Curiously enough, the impalpable presence of the dead man was stronger here than anywhere else. It was growing on Rampole with a ghostly and horrible reality. On the mantelpiece of this dusty dining-room, a marble clock with gilt facings had stopped; stopped many days ago, for the glass face was thick with dust. But it had stopped at a quarter of two. Rampole noted the coincidence with a vivid memory of Driscoll lying white-faced and sightless on the steps of Traitors' Gate. He suddenly felt that he could not drink liquor from this man's flat . . .

You might, any moment, hear Driscoll's step in the passage. It wasn't merely that a man died. It was the abrupt severance, like the fall of an axe, the pitching out into nowhere when the marks of his teeth were still visible in the half-eaten biscuit, and the lights still burning against his return. Rampole stared at the pieces of orange peel on the spotted cloth of the table, and shuddered.

"Sorry," he observed, with a sort of jerk and without conscious volition. "I can't drink his whiskey. It doesn't seem right, somehow."

"Neither can I," said Dalrye, quietly. "I knew him, you see."

He sat down at the table and shaded his eyes with his hand.

Dr. Fell turned from rummaging at the back of the sideboard, where he had found some clean glasses. His small eyes were wrinkled up.

"So you feel it too, do you?" he demanded.

"Feel what?" asked the chief inspector. "Here's a bottle nearly full. Make mine strong, with very little soda . . . Feel what?"

"That's he's here," said Dr. Fell. "Driscoll."

Hadley set down the bottle. "Don't talk rot," he said, irritably. "What are you trying to do – throw a scare into us? You look as though you were beginning to tell a ghost story. Give me the glasses; I'll rinse 'em out in the kitchen."

Balancing himself heavily against the sideboard, the doctor wheezed a moment and ran his eyes slowly about the room.

"Listen, Hadley. I'm not talking about ghost stories. I won't even say premonitions. But I'm talking about a wild surmise I had earlier in the evening, when we were talking to Lester Bitton. There was a tiny germ of reason in it, and it frightened me. Possibly it's strong now because the hour's so late and we're none of us at our brightest . . . By God! I'm going to take this drink, and several others, because I genuinely need 'em. And I should advise the rest of you to do the same."

Rampole felt uneasy. He thought he might look a fool or a coward; the strain of the day had made his thoughts more than a little muddled.

"All right . . ." he said, "all right. Pour a big one." He glanced across at Dalrye, who nodded wearily.

"I think I know what you're talking about, Doctor," Dalrye said, in a low voice. "I know I wasn't here, and I'm not sure, but I still think I know what you mean."

"The person *I'm* interested in talking about," Hadley interposes, "is Lester Bitton, as a matter of fact. You're pretty well aware, aren't you, Fell, that he's the murderer?"

The doctor was setting out glasses. He took the bottle from Hadley, waved away the other's suggestion of washing the glasses, and filled them. He said: "Suppose Bitton has an alibi? You've got almost a case to go to the jury on . . . unless he has an alibi. That's what's worrying me. But it's late, and the old man's wits are none of the best . . . Tell me, Mr. Dalrye, when did you last see Sir William Bitton?"

"Sir . . . ?" Dalrye raised his head and regarded the other with puzzled eyes. "Sir William?" he repeated. "Why, at the house tonight. General Mason suggested that I go back with him when he returned from the Tower of London."

"Did the general tell him about who really owned the manuscript? Arbor, I mean? Or did you know about it?"

"I knew about it. Sir William goes about telling everybody," Dalrye answered, grimly, "that nobody knows of the manuscript, and then proceeds to share his secret with everybody. Did he tell you that *you* were the first to hear of it?"

"Yes."

"He's told both the general and myself the same thing. We heard of it weeks ago. But nobody has ever seen it . . . until tonight. Oh yes, I knew about the blasted thing."

"What did he say when Mason told him it belonged to Arbor?"

"That's the funny part. Nothing much. He just said 'I see,' and got very quiet. It's pretty clear that he suspected as much all along. Then he said . . ."

Dalrye looked towards the door with dull eyes. It had become like a warning, repeated over and over until it grows horrible. The telephone bell was ringing again.

There was nothing in that ring which should have sent a chill through anybody. But Rampole went cold. And in the silence beneath the clamour of that insistent bell Dr. Fell said:

"I shouldn't let Miss Bitton answer that, Hadley."

Hadley was out of the door in a moment into the study, and the door closed behind him.

While nobody moved, the rest of them could hear Sheila moving about in the kitchen down the passage. Hadley did not speak for a long time on the phone. He opened the study door presently . . . they could hear the sharp squeak of its hinge. Then he came with slow steps down the passage, entered, and closed the dining-room door behind him.

"It's all up," he said. "Get your coats on."

"What is it?" the doctor asked, in as low a tone as Hadley.

The chief inspector put a hand over his eyes.

"I know what you mean now. I should have seen what sort of mood he was in when he left us. At least, I should have been warned by what Miss Bitton said . . . That was the way he said he wanted to die."

Dr. Fell brought his hand slowly down on the table. "Is it . . ."

"Yes," Hadley answered, nodding. "That's it. Lester Bitton has shot himself."

17
DEATH AT BITTON HOUSE

During the ride in Hadley's car to Berkeley Square, the only words spoken were brief questions and answers on the little Hadley had been told about the tragedy.

"It happened about ten minutes before they phoned," he explained. "That was the butler talking. The household had been up late, and the butler was still sitting up; he'd been ordered to wait for Sheila Bitton's return. He was in his pantry when he heard the shot, and he ran upstairs. The door of Lester Bitton's room was open; he smelled the smoke. Bitton was lying across the bed in his room, with the gun in his hand."

"What happened then?" Dr. Fell demanded.

"Hobbes . . . that's the butler . . . tried to wake up Sir William. But he'd taken a sleeping-draught and the door of his room was locked; Hobbes couldn't rouse him. Then Hobbes remembered Miss Bitton's talking to us, and where we were, so he phoned on the chance of getting me. He didn't know what else to do."

"What about Mrs. Bitton?"

"I didn't ask."

"H'm," muttered the other. "H'm, yes. I suppose it really was suicide . . ."

Rampole, wedged between them in the front seat, scarcely heard them. Inanely, all he could think of in connection with Lester Bitton was that foolish remark of Sheila's, "He brought me chocolates . . ."

The moist, chill air whipped through the open windscreen; the tires of the car sang, and above the roofs there were stars. It had been very quiet, Hadley's handling of the situation. Sheila Bitton had not been told of her uncle's death. They had left her there, with Dalrye to break the news when they were gone.

"I'd better not take her back to the house," Dalrye had said. "She'd only be in the way and she'd get hysterical . . . he was her favourite. I know a great friend of hers, a girl who lives in Park Lane. I'll drive her over there and get Margaret to put her up for the night. Then I'll join you."

The only thing that had surprised Rampole was the doctor's insistence that Hadley should see Arbor.

"Or, on second thought," the doctor had added, with a curious expression, you'd better let *me* see *him*. He still thinks I'm Chief Inspector Hadley, you know. And if we try to explain matters at this stage, when he's in terror of his life, he may suspect all kinds of a put-up job."

"I don't care *who* sees him, so long as he talks," the chief inspector replied, testily. "You can stay here and wait for him, if you like. But I'd much prefer that you came along with me. We can leave Mr. Rampole to talk to him until we get back . . ."

"I have a better idea. Tell them to bring him to Bitton's."

"To Bitton's? But, good God, man! You don't want . . ."

"I have rather a fancy," said the doctor, "to see how he acts there. The idea has been in my mind for some time. Let poor Marks stay in the flat and direct them over when they get here."

It had been arranged that way. Hadley's Daimler flashed through the quiet streets, and the hands of the illuminated clock on the dashboard pointed to nearly one o'clock when they reached Berkeley Square.

The old houses were heavy and sombre against the stars. A thin piping of night traffic drifted up from Piccadilly, and the footfalls of a late passer-by were uncannily loud. A taxi honked its way out of Charles Street. What faint mist was left from the day seemed to have gathered round the high street-lamps and in the thin branches of the trees. When they went up the shallow steps of the Bitton house, Hadley paused with his hand on the bell.

"I know only two quotations," he said, quietly, "but I'm going to tell you one of them now. Do you know what it is?"

Dr. Fell dropped the ferrule of his cane on the step with a hollow thock which had its echo. He stared out at the glow along the roofs towards the south.

"'It must be confessed,'" he repeated, "'it will be confessed; there is no refuge from confession but suicide, and suicide is confession.'"

Hadley rang the bell.

There was no sign of confusion in the house when the heavy door was opened. All the blinds had been drawn and the curtains closed, but every light was on. It was the absolute hush which was sinister. An old, grave-faced man ushered them into a massive blue entrance hall with a crystal chandelier. He closed the door again and fastened a chain across it.

"Chief Inspector Hadley, sir?" the old man asked. "I am Hobbes, sir; I telephoned you. Shall I take you upstairs?" He hesitated as Hadley nodded. "Under such circumstances, sir, I have always heard that it is customary to summon a doctor. But Mr. Bitton was obviously dead and unless you wish it . . . ?"

"It will not be necessary for the moment. Is Sir William up yet?"

"I have not been able to rouse him, sir."

"Where is Mrs. Bitton?"

"In her room, sir. This way, if you please."

Rampole thought he heard a whispering at the back of the hall, near a staircase going down; but still there was that massive calmness and order. The butler took them up a heavily carpeted stair, with bronze figures in the niches and along a passage at the top. It was stuffy up here, and Rampole could distinctly smell the stale reek of cordite.

A bright light streamed out against the gloom of this upper hall. At the door Hobbes stood aside for them to enter.

Here the odour of burnt powder was stronger, but nothing seemed disturbed. It was a high room, with cornices and another long chandelier, severely furnished against a background of dull brown and yellow-threaded walls. A reading-desk, the shade taken off its bright lamp, stood against the foot of the bed, and the drawer was slightly open. But that was all the disturbance. The electric heater was on in the fireplace.

Lester Bitton lay sideways across the bed; they could see his feet from the door. Closer, they could see that he was fully dressed. The bullet had gone through the right temple and emerged about an inch above the left ear; following Hadley's glance, Rampole could discern the splintered place where it had lodged in the ceiling. The dead man's face was curiously peaceful, and there was very little blood. His outflung right hand, turned under at the wrist held a Webley-Scott service automatic of the standard forty-five calibre army pattern. The only really horrible thing, Rampole thought, was the smell of singed hair.

Hadley did not immediately examine him. He spoke in a low voice to Hobbes.

"I think you told me you were in your pantry and heard the shot. You ran up here immediately, and found him just as he is. Did anybody else hear it?"

"Mrs. Bitton, sir, I believe. She came in a moment later."

"Where is Mrs. Bitton's room?"

Hobbes indicated a door near the fireplace. "A dressing-room, sir, which communicates with her own room."

"What did Mrs. Bitton do?"

The butler was very guarded, at the same time as he conveyed an impression of disinterest. "Nothing, sir. She stood looking at him for a long time, and then suggested that I wake Sir William."

"And then?"

"Then, sir, she returned to her room."

Hadley went over to the writing-table, looked at the chair beside it, and turned. "Mr. Bitton was out this evening. He must have returned here before eleven o'clock. Did you see him?"

"Yes, sir. He returned just before eleven, and went directly to the library. He asked me to bring him a cup of cocoa, and when I brought it he was sitting in front of the library fire. When I passed by the door of the library, about an hour later, I went in and asked him if he wished anything more. He was still sitting in the same chair. When I spoke he said, No, nothing more. Then he rose and walked past me and up the stairs . . ." For the first time Hobbes faltered a trifle; the man's self-control was amazing. "That was the last I saw of him, sir, before . . . before this."

"How long afterwards did you hear the shot?"

"I am not positive, sir. Not more than five minutes I should say, and probably less."

"Did his manner seem strange?"

A slight pause before the answer. "I am afraid so, sir. Mr. Bitton has not been exactly himself for the past month. But there was nothing . . . well, sir, *excited* about him. He seemed unlike himself; that's all."

Hadley glanced down at the floor. The carpet was of so thick and smooth a nap that it was almost possible to trace the path a man had taken, as though by footprints. They were standing near the door, and as Rampole followed the chief inspector's glance he could see with terrible clarity what Lester Bitton must have done. For Lester Bitton was a heavy and gigantic man; his footfalls were there where a lighter person's might not have been visible. First he had gone to the fireplace. Then he had walked to the reading-table facing the fireplace, the open drawer telling where the gun had come from. From there he had gone to the bureau, whose mirror was now tilted so that a tall man could look at himself clearly. The impress of his feet, together, was heavy there; he must have stood for some time. Lastly he had walked straight to the bed, stood with his back to it so that he should fall there, and raised the automatic.

"The gun is his own?" Hadley asked.

"Yes, sir. I have seen it before. He kept it in that table drawer."

Softly Hadley punched his fist into his palm, softly and steadily as he looked about.

"There will be little more, Hobbes. I want you to give me a complete account of everything Mr. Bitton did today, so far as you know."

Hobbes's hands plucked at the sides of his trousers. His old, square, bony face was still impassive.

"Yes, sir. I observed him, sir, because I was a trifle concerned about his welfare. I feared he had been over-working. You see, sir" – his eyes shifted slightly – "I have been with Major Bitton for a long time. He left the house this morning at about half-past ten, sir, and returned at noon. I believe he had been to Mr. Philip's flat."

"Was he carrying anything when he returned?"

"Carrying anything, sir? . . . I believe" – a hesitation – "I believe he had a package of some sort, wrapped in brown paper. He left the house again early in the afternoon. I know that he ate no lunch, sir, because on this Monday of the month luncheon is at noon instead of one o'clock, so that Sir William can go out early; I reminded him of this when he returned, and he said he merely wanted a cup of cocoa sent to his room. He left before the . . . unfortunate occurrence at Sir William's car; the thief, sir."

"He left for the City?"

"N-no sir I believe not. As he was leaving, Sir William, who intended to go to the City himself later offered him a lift in the car. Major Bitton said he did not intend to go to his office. He . . . he mentioned that he was going for a walk."

"What was his manner then: nervous, upset . . . ?"

"Well, sir, say restless; as though he wanted fresh air."

"When did he return?"

"I'm afraid I don't remember, sir. Mrs. Bitton had brought back the horrible news about Mr. Philip, and . . ." Hobbes shook his head. He was biting at his lips now, trying to keep calm; trying to stop his voice from shaking and his eyes from wandering to the bed.

"That's all, thank you. Please wait downstairs. I suggest that you make another effort to wake Sir William before you go."

Hobbes bowed and closed the door behind him as he went out.

"I think," Hadley said, turning to his companions, "you two had better go downstairs also. I've got to make an examination . . . just in case . . . and I warn you it won't be pretty. There's no good you can do. I want you to be there for Arbor when he arrives. I wish to God we hadn't got *him* on our hands. So . . . ?"

Dr. Fell grunted. He went over, bent across the body, and held his eyeglasses on while he had a brief look at it. Then he signalled to Rampole and waddled towards the door without a word.

In silence they descended the stairs. Rampole thought he heard behind them somewhere the click of a closing latch. He thought he saw a figure somewhere in the upper hall; but his thoughts were so warped with stealth and murder, and the ghostliness of this ancient house, that he paid scant attention. Of all the districts in London, he had thought, this Mayfair was the place of echoes and of shadows. He liked walking in a strange city by night; and once, he remembered, he had prowled through Mayfair in grey twilight, with a scent of rain in the air, and he had not believed that anybody really lived there. There were gaps in these little streets; unexpected houses, a sudden curve that showed a chimney stack against the sky, and, in the midst of great shuttered houses, lanes full of lighted shops like a country town. All around was the weird realm where people had lived, once, when Becky Sharp rode in her coach and news of Waterloo was fresh, but did not live now. A plane tree rustled. A delivery boy on a bicycle careened past, whistling. Through an opening off Mount Street you could see the rails of the Park, and a few stolid taxicabs burnt patient lamps in the square. Then, presently, the rain began to fall.

You could imagine red buses plunging down past the grenadier pillars of Regent Street; and Ares aiming an arrow at a wall of electric signs; and the crowds spilling out from every byway into the roulette wheel of Piccadilly Circus. But you could not think of this Mayfair as real. It was something out of Thackeray, which Thackeray had got in turn from Addison and Steele.

Rampole, catching up images like cards drawn from a pack, found himself following Dr. Fell down the lower hallway. The doctor had found the library, apparently by instinct. It was another high room at the rear, done in white. Three walls, even around the window spaces, were built entirely of books; the white-painted lines of the shelves showed up startlingly against the dark old volumes. The fourth wall was cream-panneled, with a white-marble fireplace above which hung a full-length portrait of Sir William Bitton in a massive gilt frame. Flanking the fireplace, two long windows looked out on a garden.

Dr. Fell stood in the middle of the dusky room, peering about curiously. A low fire flickered on the brass and irons; a pink-shaded lamp burned on a table amid the heavy upholstered furniture round the fireplace. Otherwise the library was so dark that they could see stars through the blue windows, and the dead shrubbery of the garden.

"There's only one thing now," the doctor said in a low voice, "that I've got to be profoundly thankful for. Arbor still thinks I'm Hadley. I may be able to keep him away from Hadley altogether."

"Thankful? Why?"

"Look behind you," the other said, nodding.

Rampole switched round. He had not heard Laura Bitton come in over the thick carpet. And for a moment he scarcely recognized her.

She seemed much older and much quieter. Nor was she the vigorous young woman with the firm step and the level brown eyes who had walked so confidently into the Warders' Hall that afternoon. The eyes were a trifle red; the face fixed and dull, so that freckles showed against its muddy pallor.

"I followed you down," she said, evenly. "I heard you in the other room." The voice was queer, as though she could not quite understand yet that her husband was dead. Then she added, abruptly, "You know all about it, don't you?"

"All about what, Mrs. Bitton?"

Her gesture recalled some of the determination, the imperiousness; some of the poise and light cynicism.

"Oh, don't quibble. About Phil and me. I knew you would find out."

Dr. Fell inclined his head. "You should not have broken into his flat this afternoon, Mrs. Bitton. You were seen."

She was not interested. "I suppose so. I had a key, but I broke the lock of the door with a chisel I found there to pretend it was a burglar; but it didn't go down. Never mind.

I just want to tell you one thing . . ." But she could not go on with it. She looked from one to the other of them, and shut her lips.

There was a silence.

"Ma'am," said the doctor, leaning on his cane, "I know what you were going to say. You only realized just then how it would sound if you said it. You were going to say you never loved Driscoll. Ma'am, isn't it rather late for that?"

His rumbling voice was colourless; it did not lift or vary, but he studied her curiously.

"Did you see what he had in his hand?"

"Yes," he replied, as she closed her eyes – "yes ma'am, I did."

"Not the gun! The other hand, I mean. He got it out of the drawer. It was a snapshot of me."

She spoke steadily, the brown eyes level and glazed, the jaw firm. "I looked at it, and went back to my room. I have been sitting at the window in the dark, looking out . . . If you think I'm trying to excuse myself, you're a fool. But since I saw him lying on that bed, I think I've seen a thousand, million, God knows how many images; and they're all his. I've seen all my life with him. I can't cry now. I cried today, about Phil's death, but I can't cry now. I know I loved Lester. It was only because his ideas were so different from mine that I had to hurt him. I'm not the first woman who's made a fool of herself. But I loved Lester. I don't care whether you believe me or not, but I wanted to tell you that. Now I'll go. And maybe I can cry."

She paused in the doorway, a hand unsteadily on her rumpled brown hair.

"There was only one other thing," she said, in a quiet voice: "Did Lester kill Phil?"

For a long space the doctor remained motionless, a big silhouette against the lamp, bulked over his cane. Then he nodded his head.

"Keep *that* thought with you, ma'am," he said.

The door closed behind her.

"You see?" Dr. Fell asked. "Or don't you? There's been enough tragedy in this house. I won't add another. Lester Bitton is dead and the Driscoll case is closed. If Hadley is satisfied, there needn't be any publicity. It can go down as 'unsolved'; and Lester Bitton shot himself over money troubles, real or imaginary. And yet . . ."

He was still standing there brooding, under the vast walls of books, when Hobbes knocked at the door.

"Excuse me, sir," said Hobbes. "I have succeeded in waking Sir William. The key was on the inside of his door; I took the liberty of getting a pair of pliers and turning it from the outside. He is upset, sir, and not very well. He has not been well since Mr. Philip's death. But he will be down presently, sir. And there is something else . . ."

"Eh?"

"Two policemen are at the door, sir. A recent guest of ours" – Hobbes spoke slowly, but with a certain inflection – "is with them. A Mr. Arbor. He says Mr. Hadley told him to come here."

"H'm . . . Got a little confidential work for you, Hobbes. Do you follow me?"

"Well, sir?"

"Put those policemen somewhere out of sight. Tell Mr. Arbor Mr. Hadley is here in the library, and send him back to me. You needn't inform Mr. Hadley yet. Got it?"

"Yes, sir."

There was a brief interval while Dr. Fell stumped back and forth on the padded floor, muttering to himself. He turned sharply as the door opened again, and Hobbes ushered in Julius Arbor.

18
MR. ARBOR HEARS A VOICE

Rampole had withdrawn to the fireside. It was all very neat, the hearth-rug not even disarranged. An upholstered chair had been drawn up close, and on a tabouret beside it stood an empty cup with the brown dregs of cocoa inside. Here Lester Bitton had sat quietly, staring at the fire and drinking his cocoa, before he went upstairs to his room. From that blue china cup the American's eyes moved up to the man who was just entering at the end of the room . . .

Mr. Arbor was now imbued with a certain degree of calmness. But he was not at his ease. His glance had gone to the portrait of Sir William, a white eagle in the dusky room, and his discomfort seemed to grow. He had not let Hobbes take his hat or coat; he was much on his dignity. Two lines were drawn about the mouth in the swarthy face; he kept touching his eyeglasses with a light finger, and smoothing the thin black hair that was brushed straight across his large skull.

"Good evening, Inspector," he said. He shifted his hat to his left hand and extended the other in a fishy gesture. Dr. Fell did not notice this. "Tritely, I suppose I ought to say good morning. I . . . er . . . I confess, Inspector, that your request to come here somewhat startled me. I . . . was about to refuse. You must understand that the unpleasant circumstances . . ."

"Sit down there," interrupted the doctor, leading him to the fire. "You remember my colleague here, don't you?"

"Yes. Er . . . yes, of course. How do you do?" Arbor said, vaguely. He added, "Is Sir William about?"

"No. That's it, sit down."

"I presume he has been informed of my purchase of the manuscript?" inquired Arbor, his nervous eye straying to the portrait.

"He has. But it doesn't matter now, you know. Neither of you will ever have it. It's burnt."

The man's finger darted to his eyeglasses to keep them on. He said: "You mean . . . he . . . somebody . . . that is," Arbor made an uncertain gesture. "How was it destroyed? This is terrible, Inspector! I could take the law to prove . . ."

The doctor drew out his pocket-book. Carefully he took from it the only part of the manuscript which remained, and stood weighing it thoughtfully.

"May I . . . may I see that, Inspector?"

He took the flimsy strip of paper in unsteady hands and held it close under the pink-shaded lamp. For some time he studied it, back and front. Then he looked up. "Undoubtedly . . . ah . . . undoubtedly. Inspector, this is an outrage, you know! *I* own this. *I* . . ."

"Is it worth anything now?"

"Well . . ."

"I see that there's some hope for you, then. Now, I'll tell you how it is, Arbor," said Dr. Fell, in an argumentative voice suggestive of the elder Weller. "If I were in your shoes, I should take that bit of paper, and put it in my pocket, and forget all about it for the present. You're in enough trouble as it is, and you don't want more."

"Trouble?" demanded Arbor, in rather too challenging a voice. The way he held the paper reminded Rampole of a man with stage-fright holding his notes on a lecture platform; calm in every way except that betraying flutter of the paper.

"Do you know," continued the doctor, pleasantly, "that all evening I've been of half a mind to let you cool off in gaol for a day or two? You might be able to prove your innocence, but the newspaper publicity would be sad, my friend. Sad . . . Why did you run away?"

"Run away? My dear man . . . !"

"Don't try to deceive *me*," said the doctor, in a sinister voice. It was a rather less blatant resurrection of Hamlet's father's Ghost. "Scotland Yard sees all. Shall I tell you what you did?"

He then proceeded to give a graphic account of Arbor's behaviour after leaving the Tower. It was accurate enough in its details, but so neatly distorted that it sounded like the flight of a guilty man from the law.

"You said," he concluded, "that you had important information to give me personally. I am willing to listen. But I warn you, man, that your position is very bad. And if you don't tell me the whole truth, or I have any reason to doubt what you say, then . . ."

Arbor leaned back in the chair, breathing noisily. The strain of the day, the late hour, all his experiences since the murder, held him limp and nerveless. He kept adjusting his glasses, staring at Sir William's portrait, until he had recovered himself.

"Ah yes," he murmured. "Yes. I perceive, Inspector, that circumstances have put me in a false light. I will tell you everything. I had intended to do so, but now I see I have no choice . . . You see, I felt that I was in a doubly unfortunate and precarious position. I feared that I might not be threatened only by the police, but by some criminal as well."

He got out his ornate cigarette-case and hurriedly solaced himself with a breath of smoke before he went on.

"I am . . . a man of books, Inspector. My life is leisured; I may say sheltered. I do not mingle with the more . . . ah . . . tempestuous portions of the world. You, who are a man of rough existence, and . . . ah . . . accustomed to hand-to-hand encounters with desperate ruffians, will not understand what I felt when I was faced with a bewildering problem of criminal nature.

"It began with that cursed manuscript. I needn't go into details; I gave you enough of them this afternoon. I came here for the purpose of getting the manuscript from Bitton. Not unnaturally" – a querulous note raised his voice – "I wanted my own property. But I hesitated. Due to the unpredictable eccentricities of Bitton's nature, I was placed in a distressing dilemma . . ."

"I see," said Dr. Fell. "What you mean is that you were afraid of Bitton, and so you had to hire somebody to pinch it for you."

"*No*!" Arbor insisted, gripping the arms of the chair in his earnestness. "That is precisely what I do *not* mean. I feared you would think so, as your colleague indicated this afternoon. And I was careful to point out to all of you there could have been no legal steps taken against me had I done so . . . But, inspector, I did not do it. I will take my oath on it. I confess that the procedure had occurred to me; but I dismissed it. It was absurd and mad, and if I were discovered . . . no! I would hire no burglar." He spread out his hands. "When the manuscript was stolen it was as much of a surprise to me as it was to Bitton. The first I heard of the theft, you see, was when he telephoned to my friends, the Spenglers, on Sunday night to . . . ah . . . to see where I was. But *then* . . ."

He caught Dr. Fell's cold eye, and there was a new vehemence in his tone. They knew he was telling the truth.

"Then, considerably later the same night, I received another phone call at the Spenglers'."

"Ah!" grunted the doctor. "From whom?"

"The person refused to give his name. But I was almost positive I knew whose voice it was. I have rather a good ear, and I was sure I knew it, though I had heard it only once before. I thought it was the voice of young Mr. Driscoll."

Dr. Fell jumped. He glared at Arbor, who returned his gaze with a dogged steadiness. Arbor went on:

"I reviewed everything in my mind, and I was sure. I had met this young man at dinner the week before, when I had made almost reckless remarks and exceedingly broad hints about the Poe manuscript. The only other persons who could have heard them were Miss Bitton and Sir William; they were the only others at the table . . . Hence I was sure when this voice spoke. He asked me whether I was interested in a Poe manuscript belonging to Sir William Bitton, and gave such details of what I remembered having said, that I had no doubt. He asked me what price I should be willing to pay, no questions asked, if the manuscript were handed over to me.

"I am . . . ah . . . accustomed to rapid decisions and prompt action, Inspector. I was sure I was dealing with a member of the family. The voice, it is true, was somewhat gruff; but I had little difficulty, in seeing through the disguise. Dealing with a member of the family was very different from dealing with a hired burglar. In case of trouble, there would be no scandal. In any case, there could be no prosecution against me. This person naturally did not know I was the owner of the manuscript; nobody did. If, therefore, he had any ideas of blackmail in his mind after the theft, I could afford to smile. *He* would be the only one to take the risk.

"I reviewed my position in a moment, Inspector, and I perceived that this was . . . ah . . . the easiest solution of my difficulties. After the manuscript came to my hands, I could always drop a note to Sir William explaining my ownership, and referring him to my solicitors in case he did not believe me and wished to prosecute. I knew he would not do so. Besides, it was . . . ah . . . obvious," said Arbor, hesitantly, "that the amount of the commission . . . ah . . ."

"You could promise him whatever he asked," said the doctor, bluntly. "And when you got the manuscript you could give him fifty pounds and tell him to whistle for the rest because you owned it and *he* was the only thief. And the fifty pounds would be much less than you'd have to pay Bitton."

"Considerably less. You . . . ah . . . state matters very succinctly, Inspector," Arbor nodded. He took a few short puffs at his cigarette. "I agreed to what the unknown person said, and asked him whether he had the manuscript. He replied that he had, and again demanded how much I should pay for it. I mentioned rather a large sum; he hesitated, and I named a sum considerably larger. I had nothing to lose. He agreed, and stated that he would name a rendezvous in the course of the next day. I was to be communicated with through the Spenglers. His stipulation was that I must never inquire into his identity; he said he would find a means of concealing it altogether. Again I smiled."

"Well?" prompted the doctor.

"I . . . er . . . naturally I attempted to trace the call, when he had hung up. It was impossible. In fiction it is . . . ah . . . very simple, I have noticed. But my utmost efforts were unavailing; I was told curtly that it was impossible."

"Go on."

Arbor glanced over his shoulder. The nervousness had come back again; he peered into the shadows of the room, and spilled some ash on himself without noticing it.

"I looked forward to it with . . . ah . . . a light heart. The following day, today, I went about my affairs as usual. I paid a long-delayed visit to the Tower of London; and I proceeded exactly as I have told you. When I was detained on my attempt to leave by the news of a murder, I was not unduly upset. I thought, indeed that it would be fascinating to watch the . . . ah . . . famous Scotland Yard at work, and I assumed that it was some member of the underworld who had been killed; I was, if anything, pleased, and I resolved to be a good witness if the police spoke to me."

Again Arbor adjusted his glasses. "You will own, Inspector that it came as a shock when you began your questioning of me by inquiring about Poe manuscripts. Even so, I flatter myself that I was cool and . . . you will pardon me . . . triumphant over you. I was nervous, yes; I fancied all sorts of possibilities, but I effectively deceived you. It was not until you mentioned the name of the dead man that . . ." He drew out the silk handkerchief and mopped his forehead. "My heart, Inspector; I could not see it would make me betray weakness. The possibilities had suddenly become menacing and horrible. Driscoll, at my order, had promised to deliver me that manuscript; and now he was murdered. I must assume even now that he was killed because of it. It occurred to me that in some heinous fashion *I* might come into the case as accessory of some sort. A *murder* case." He shuddered. "I told you, Inspector, that I am . . . a man of books. This ghastly thing . . . I could not see how it might concern me directly, but there were any number of dangers. And where was the manuscript? You had not found it on Driscoll's body; I knew you had not found it at all. I wanted to forget it. As you saw, I wanted no search for it, above all things, because a search might uncover evidence to lead to *me*."

"So far," said the doctor, "very well. What then?"

Rampole was puzzled. If the doctor had insisted on anything in the case so far, he had insisted Driscoll would never attempt to dispose of the manuscript to Arbor. But here he was nodding ponderously and fixing his sharp little eyes on the collector as though he believed every word. And Rampole, too, was compelled to believe Arbor. There was only the possible explanation that Driscoll, in a moment of panic, had made to Arbor an offer whose dangers he saw in a calmer moment the next day, and decided to drop the whole affair . . .

"Now," said Arbor, clearing his throat – "now, Inspector, I come to the amazing, the incredible part of my whole story. It is only fortunate, with my weak heart, that I am not now a dead man. If you could have imagined . . . !"

"Just after you left us in the Warders' Hall," the doctor interposed, slowly, "you got the fright of your life, and it sent you out to Golder's Green in a blind panic. What was it?"

Arbor replaced his handkerchief inside his coat. He seemed to have come to a jumping-off place in his narrative; he hesitated on the brink of the leap, tapping his glasses and peering over.

"Inspector," he said, "before I tell you what you must regard as completely incredible, let me ask you a question or two. I assure you" – he held up his hand as the doctor shifted – "I am *not* trying to divert you . . . In that room where you were questioning me, who was present?"

Dr. Fell regarded him narrowly. "While we were speaking to you, you mean?"

"Yes!"

"H'm. There was Hadley, my . . . my colleague; and Mr. Rampole here; and General Mason, and Sir Wil– Hold on, no! I'm wrong. Bitton wasn't there. He had gone up to Mason's rooms so that we could question you more fr . . . he had gone up to Mason's rooms. Yes. There were just the four of us."

Arbor stared. "Bitton was at the Tower?"

"Yes, yes. But he wasn't in the room with us. Proceed."

"The next thing," Arbor said, carefully, "is . . . ah, what shall I say? . . . an impression, rather than a question. Speaking with some one on the telephone is, in a certain sense, and aside from the mechanical interventions, somewhat like speaking to a person in the dark. You follow me, Inspector? You hear the voice alone. There is no personality or physical appearance to distract you from your impressions of the voice itself. If you heard a voice on the telephone, without having seen the speaker, and later you meet the speaker in real life, you might not recognize him, because his appearance or his personality might destroy the impressions of the voice. But if you heard him in the dark . . ."

"I think I understand."

"Ah! I was afraid, Inspector, that the subtlety of the point I was endeavouring to make would . . . ah . . . not be fully apprehended by . . . by the police," Arbor said, with evident relief. "I feared ridicule or even suspicion." He swallowed hard. "Very well. You dismissed me after the questioning, you will recall, and I went outside.

"The door of the room in which you had been talking to me was not quite closed. It was very dark and quite misty under the arch of the tower there. I stood outside the door to accustom my eyes to the gloom, and to draw my scarf more tightly about my neck. As it was, I was terrified; I admit it. I could with difficulty make a good exit from the room. There was a warder on duty, but he stood at some distance from me. I could hear you talking in the room I had left; a mumble of voices . . .

Then, Inspector," said Arbor, bending forward with his fist clenched, "I think I received the most horrible shock of my life. In the room I had not noticed it, I suppose, because the influence of personalities had overborne the impressions of my hearing; if I may put it that way. But . . .

"As I stood there in the dark, I heard a voice speak from the room. It sounded little louder than a whisper or a mumble. But I knew that the voice I heard from that room was the same voice which has spoken to me on the telephone the day before, and offered to sell me the Poe manuscript."

19
UNDER THE BLOODY TOWER?

This astounding intelligence did not seem to affect Dr. Fell in the least. He did not move or even blink. His wonderfully sharp dark eyes remained fixed on Arbor; he was still bent slightly forward, balanced on the cane.

"I suppose," he said at length, "the voice really came from that room?"

"Why, yes . . . Yes, I assume so. There was nobody else about who could have spoken, and the words were not addressed to me; they were a part of a conversation, it seemed to me."

"What did the voice say?"

Again Arbor became tense. "Now I know, Inspector, that you won't believe me. But I cannot tell you. I have tried until I am ill, but I cannot remember. You must understand the shock of hearing that voice . . ." He moved his arm, and the fist clenched spasmodically. "To begin with, it was like hearing a dead man's voice. I had been willing to swear that the voice over the telephone belonged to Bitton's nephew. Then Bitton's nephew was dead. And suddenly this hideous whisper . . . Listen, Inspector. I told you that the telephone voice seemed disguised; gruffer, as it were; and I had attributed it to Driscoll. But *this was the telephone voice.* Of that I am absolutely certain now. I don't know what it said. I only know that I put my hand against the wall of the tower and wondered whether I were going mad. I tried to visualize with whom I had spoken in the room and I discovered that I could scarcely remember who had been there. I could not remember who had talked, or who had remained silent; it was impossible to think which one of you had uttered what I heard.

"Try to consider what my position was. Everything had gone upside down. I thought I had spoken to Driscoll; yet here was the voice. I had been speaking in that room to somebody . . . certainly a criminal and in all probability a killer. I had outlined completely my position as owner of the manuscript. And somebody (I had forgotten which one) made it clear that if I had employed a thief to take my own property, he could expect only pay for his thievery and not the immense sum I had mentioned I would pay. I . . . well, to tell you the truth, I was not thinking at all. I was only feeling. I felt certain, without knowing why, that the 'voice' had killed Driscoll. Everything had gone mad, and, to make it worse, if I could believe my ears this 'voice' *was one of the police*.

"Otherwise I should have gone back immediately and confessed the whole business. But I was afraid both of having the police on my side, and of having them against me. I suppose I acted insanely. But I could think of nothing else to do. It was only late this evening, when I was certain I heard somebody trying to get into my cottage, that I determined to end the suspense, one way or the other. That's all, Inspector. I can make nothing of it, and I hope you have better luck."

He sat back, bewildered, dejected, with his handkerchief again at his forehead.

"Still," said Dr. Fell, musingly, "you could not *swear* the voice came from that room?"

"No. But . . ."

"And there is not one word you can definitely remember its having said?"

"I'm afraid not. You don't believe me, I dare say . . ."

Dr. Fell drew back his chins and pushed out his chest in a meditative fashion, as though he were about to begin a lecture.

"Now, I've heard you out, Arbor, and I've got a few words to say. We're all alone here. Nobody has heard your story but Sergeant Rampole and myself. We can forget it; that's our business when no crime has been done; but I shouldn't advise you to repeat it to anybody else. You would be in grave danger of being confined either in gaol or in a lunatic asylum . . . Do you realize what you've said?" he inquired, slowly, lifting his cane to point. "There were four people in that room. You must, therefore, accuse the voice of being either the chief inspector of the C.I.D., one of his highest and most trusted officers, or the deputy governor of the Tower of London. If, you retract *that* statement, and decide that the 'voice' actually was Driscoll, you lay yourself open to grave trouble in connection with a murder case. Your status is that of madman or suspected criminal. Do you want to take your choice?"

"But I'm telling you the truth, I swear before . . . !"

"Man," said Dr. Fell, with a real ring and thunder of earnestness in his voice, "I have no doubt you think you're telling the truth. I have no doubt that in your obsession you might have heard anything. You heard a voice. The question is, what voice, and where did it come from?"

"All right," Arbor said, despondently. "But what am I going to do? I'm in an impossible position whichever way I turn. My God! I wish I'd never heard of Poe or manuscripts or any . . . besides, I'm in potential danger of my life . . . What the devil are you laughing at, Inspector?"

"I was merely smiling," said Dr. Fell, "at your fears for your own skin. If that's all you're worrying about, you can stop. We have the murderer, safely. The 'voice' can't hurt you I guarantee that. And you don't want to be tangled up in this affair any farther, do you?"

"Good God, no! . . . You mean you have caught . . . !"

"Arbor, the murder had no concern with your manuscript. You can forget it. You'll feel like forgetting your fears, too, in the morning. You're a secretive beggar and you can hold your tongue when it's to your own advantage; I strongly advise you to hold your tongue now. The murderer is dead. Any inquest on Driscoll will be a private and perfunctory thing; it'll be kept out of the press because it can't serve any useful purpose. So you needn't worry. Go to a hotel and get some sleep. Forget you ever heard the 'voice' on the telephone or anywhere else; and, if you hold your tongue, I'll promise to hold mine."

"But the man trying to get at me tonight . . . !"

"He was one of my own constables, to scare you into telling what you know. Run along, man! You never were in any danger in the world."

"But . . ."

"Run along, man! Do you want Sir William to walk in here on you and make trouble?"

It was the most effective argument he could have used. Arbor did not even inquire too closely into the identity of the murderer. So long as the murderer had no designs on *him*, his aura conveyed that he was averse to the gruesome details of a vulgar murder. When Dr. Fell and Rampole walked with him to the front door, they found Hadley, who had shortly dismissed the two constables, in the front hall.

"I don't think," the doctor said, "that we need detain Mr. Arbor any longer. I have his story, and I'm sorry to say it doesn't help us. Good night, Mr. Arbor."

"I shall walk," said Arbor with cool dignity, "to a hotel. The walk will do me good. Good night, gentlemen."

He was not long in letting himself out.

"You dismissed him damned quickly," growled the chief inspector but without much interest, "after all the trouble he gave us. But I was afraid it might turn out to be a mare's nest. What did he say?"

Dr. Fell chuckled. "Driscoll phoned him and offered him the manuscript. He thought he might get mixed up as some sort of accessory . . ."

"But, good God! I thought you said . . ."

"Blind panic, my boy. Driscoll would never have done it, you can rest assured. And, as you pointed out, it was in blind panic that he burnt the manuscript . . . Then Arbor had some sort of wild idea that he heard the dead man's voice talking to him. You know, Hadley, if I were you I should never bring that man before a coroner's jury. He'd make us all sound mad . . . But you don't need him, do you?"

"Oh no. He wouldn't have been called unless he turned up some evidence bearing on the murder." The chief inspector rubbed a hand wearily over his eyes. "Voices! Bah! The man's as neurotic as an old woman. I wasted people's time for nothing, and made myself look a fool into the bargain. 'Voices'! And all the time that confounded manuscript's been only a red herring . . . Well, I'm glad he didn't complicate matters by trying to identify the murderer's voice."

"So am I," said Dr. Fell.

Stealthily the night noises of the house creaked against the stillness; a ghostly tingle from the crystal pendants of the chandelier, a footfall somewhere which echoed and passed.

"It's all over, Fell," Hadley remarked, in a tired voice. "All over in a day, thank God. The poor devil took the best way out. A few routine questions to go over, and we close the book. I've had a talk with the wife . . ."

"What do you do with the case, then?"

Hadley frowned. His dull eyes wandered about the hall. "I think," he said, "it will go down officially as 'unsolved.' We'll let it die down, and issue a bulletin to the Press Association to handle it lightly. There's no good in the stink of a public inquest, anyway. Don't you think there's been enough tragedy in this house?"

"You needn't justify yourself, my boy. I think there has . . . by the way, where is Sir William?"

"In his room. Hobbes got his door open and waked him up. Did he tell you?"

"Have you told him about . . . ?"

Hadley took a nervous turn about the hall. "I'm not so young as I used to be," he observed, suddenly. "It's only two o'clock in the morning and I'm dog-tired . . . I've told him a little. But he can't seem to grasp it; the opiate hasn't worn off. He's sitting by a fire in his room, with a dressing-gown over his shoulders, as stupid as an image. All he kept saying was, 'See that my guests have refreshment; see that my guests have refreshment.' I think he had a vague idea he was a feudal lord, or a dream had got mixed into his thoughts. He's seventy years old, Fell. You don't think of his age when you talk to him."

"What are you going to do, then?"

"I've had to send for Dr. Watson, the police surgeon. When he gets here I'll have him fix something to wake the old man up; and then" – Hadley nodded grimly – "we'll share the pleasant duty of telling him everything."

They could hear a night wind muttering in the chimneys. Rampole thought of that portrait, the white eagle face, standing with shoulders back, in the library. And he thought again of a lonely man in a lonely house; the old war-eagle now, huddled in a dressing-gown before a low fire in his room, and counting armies in the blaze. He saw the long sharp nose, the tufted eyebrows, the orator's mouth. *He* belonged to this ancient Mayfair which had never existed since it bloomed with flags for Wellington and nodded its head to the tap of ghostly drums.

Hobbes emerged from the rear of the hallway.

"At Sir William's suggestion, gentlemen," he said "I have prepared some sandwiches and coffee in the library, and there is a decanter of whiskey, if you should care for it . . ."

They moved slowly along the hall, back to the library, where a bright blaze was licking up round the coal in the grate, and a covered tray stood on a side-table.

"Stay with Sir William, Hobbes," Hadley directed. "If he –

wakens, come down after me. Admit the police surgeon when he arrives, and show him upstairs."

They sat down wearily in the firelight.

"I got the final proof," Hadley declared, as the doctor did things with a tantalus, "when I talked to Mrs. Bitton a few minutes ago. She said she'd been down here and spoken to you. She said you were convinced her husband had killed Driscoll . . ."

"Did she? – What did *she* think about it?"

"She wasn't so sure until I told her the full story; that's what took me so long upstairs. I couldn't get much out of her. She seemed almost as drugged as the old man. Her idea was that Bitton was quite capable of it, but that he'd be more likely to walk into Driscoll's rooms and strangle him rather than waylay him in a dark corner with a crossbow bolt. And she couldn't reconcile his putting the hat on Driscoll's head. She was willing to swear he didn't think along those lines; he wasn't an imaginative type . . ." Hadley frowned at the fire, tapping his fingers on the arms of the chair. "It bothers me, Fell. She's quite right about that, unless Bitton had unsuspected depths."

The doctor, who was mixing drinks with his back to Hadley, stopped with his hand on the syphon. There was a pause and then he spoke without turning:

"I thought you were satisfied?"

"I am, I suppose. There's absolutely no other person who can fit the evidence. And what makes it certain . . . Did you know Bitton had a gift for mimicry? I didn't, until she told me."

"Eh?"

"Yes. His one talent, and he never employed it nowadays; he didn't think it was – well, fitting. But Mrs. Bitton said he used to burlesque his brother making a speech, and hit him off to the life. He could easily have put in that fake telephone call."

There was a curious, sardonic expression on the doctor's face as he stood up. His eye wandered to Sir William's picture, and he chuckled.

"Hadley," he said, "that's an omen. It's coincidence carried to the *n*th degree. I couldn't have believed it, and I'm glad we didn't hear it at the beginning of the investigation; it would only have confused us. It's too late now . . ."

"What are you talking about?"

"Let's hear the full outline of what Bitton did, as you read it."

Hadley settled back with a chicken sandwich and a cup of coffee.

"Well it's fairly plain. Bitton had made up his mind to kill Driscoll when he returned from the trip. He was a little mad, anyhow, if his behaviour tells everything; and it explains what happened afterwards.

"I don't think he intended at first to make any secret of it. His plan was simply to go to Driscoll's flat and choke the life out of him; and he made up his mind to do it that morning. He was determined to see Driscoll, you know. He borrowed Sir William's key to be sure he could get into the apartment . . . which isn't the course of a person paying a casual visit.

"He arrived there, and Driscoll was out. So he prowled through the apartment. In all likelihood he was looking for incriminating evidence against his wife and her lover. You remember the oil and the whetstone on Driscoll's desk? The oil was fresh; Driscoll had probably been working on that crossbow bolt, and it was lying there conspicuously. Remember that the bolt had a significance to Bitton; *it was one which he and his wife had bought together* . . ."

Dr. Fell rubbed his forehead. "I hadn't thought of that," he muttered; "the omens are still at work. Carry on, Hadley."

"And he found the top-hat. He must have surmised that Driscoll was the Mad Hatter, but that didn't interest him so much as a recollection of Driscoll's wish to die in a top-hat. You see the psychology, Fell? If he'd merely run across a top-hat of Driscoll's, the suggestion mightn't have been so strong. But a hat belonging to his brother – a perfect piece of stage-setting . . . ?

"Suddenly his plan came to him. There was no reason why he should suffer for killing Driscoll. If he stabbed Driscoll at some place which wouldn't be associated with Lester Bitton, and put the stolen hat on the body, he would have done two things: First, he would have put suspicion on the Mad Hatter as the murderer. But the hat-thief was the man he was going to kill! . . . and consequently, the police could never hang an innocent person for murder. Bitton was a sportsman, and I'll give him credit for thinking of that first. Secondly: he would have fulfilled Driscoll's bombastic wish.

"Further, from his point of view the choice of that bolt as a weapon was an ideal one. It had its significance, to begin with. And, though Driscoll had stolen the bolt secretly from his house, *he didn't know that*. Seeing the bolt on Driscoll's desk, he naturally imagined that Driscoll had got it openly – asked for it – and that anybody in his own house would know it was in Driscoll's possession. Hence suspicion would be turned away from his own house! That was what he imagined. He couldn't have been expected to think that Driscoll had carefully concealed a theft of that trumpery souvenir, when it could have been had for the asking . . . Can you imagine what must have been his horror, then, when he found us suspecting his wife?"

The doctor took a long drink of whiskey.

"You've got a better case than I thought, my boy," he said. "The Gentleman who pulls the cords must have been amused by this one. I am listening."

"So, in his half-crazy brain, he evolves a new plan. He knew Driscoll was going to the Tower at one o'clock, to meet Dalrye, because he had heard it at breakfast. He didn't know his wife was going there, of course. His one idea was to get Driscoll alone. If Driscoll went to the Tower, he would be certain to be with Dalrye; and a murder might be devilish awkward.

"You can see what he did. He took the hat and the bolt home with him, and left the house early; before one o'clock. He phoned Dalrye from a public box, imitated Driscoll's voice, and got Dalrye away. At one o'clock he was at the Tower. But Driscoll didn't appear; Driscoll was twenty minutes late . . ."

Hadley drank a mouthful of scalding coffee and set down the cup. He struck his fist into his palm. "Do you realize, man, that, if we look back over our *times* in this case, Driscoll must have walked into the Tower of London no more than a few minutes, or more likely a few *seconds*, before Laura Bitton did? Driscoll was late; she was early. And as soon as Driscoll got up to General Mason's rooms he looked out of the window and saw Laura Bitton by Traitors' Gate . . . In other words, Lester Bitton, lurking about for a suitable opportunity to kill Driscoll as soon as he could, saw both of them come in. He hadn't bargained on *her*. There was to be a meeting, clearly. For fear of detection, he couldn't strike until it was over.

"He waited. As he had thought, a person of Driscoll's wild and restless nature wouldn't sit cooped up in General Mason's rooms. He would wander about, in any event. And he would certainly come down now, for his rendezvous with Laura . . . Fell, when Driscoll came downstairs and met Laura at the rail, Bitton must have been concealed under the arch of the Bloody Tower, watching them."

The doctor was sitting back, one hand shading his eyes. The fire had grown to a fierce heat now. Rampole was growing drowsy.

"He saw the interview, with what rage we can imagine. It must have grown on him until he was tempted to go out and strike them both down. He heard Laura Bitton say she loved him . . . and then, a thing which must have crazed him by its perverse irony, he saw Driscoll leave her, hurriedly and almost contemptuously, and walk towards him under the arch of the Bloody Tower. Driscoll had done more than loved his wife; he had scorned his wife. And now Driscoll was walking towards him in the dark and fog, and the crossbow bolt was ready in Bitton's hand."

Dr. Fell did not take his hand away from his eyes; he parted two fingers, and the bright eye gleamed suddenly behind his glasses.

"I say, Hadley . . . when you talked to Mrs. Bitton, did she say Driscoll really *did* go under the arch of the Bloody Tower?"

"She didn't notice. She said that she was so upset she didn't watch him. She turned away and walked in the roadway – where, you remember, Mrs. Larkin saw her, walking with her back to the Bloody Tower . . ."

"Ah!"

"She didn't conceal anything," Hadley said, dully. "I thought, when I spoke to her, that I was talking to an automaton – a dead person, or something of the sort . . . Driscoll went under the arch. It was all over in a moment: Bitton's hand over his mouth, a wrench and a blow, and Driscoll died without a sound. And when Mrs. Bitton walked through the arch a few seconds later, her husband was holding against the wall the dead body of her lover. When they had gone, he took off Driscoll's cap, opened the top-hat – it was an opera-hat, you know, and collapsible, so that it was easily concealed under a coat – and put it down over Driscoll's eyes. He went out quickly and flung the body over the rail, where it got that smash on the back of the head. Then he went out one of the side gates, unobserved, threw Driscoll's cap into the river – and, I dare say, went to the lunch-room and refreshed himself with a cup of cocoa after his work."

When Hadley had finished, he did not immediately go on eating his sandwich. He stared at the sandwich queerly, put it down; and they were all very quiet. A fierce blaze was roaring and snapping in the fireplace, but it only intensified the stillness of that drugged hour . . . Over their heads, now, somebody was pacing with slow steps. Back and forth, back and forth . . .

A cold wind seethed in the dead shrubs of the garden beyond the windows. They heard a clock strike a musical note; then, very faintly, voices in the front hall, and the boom of the big door closing.

It echoed hollowly through the house. The steps upstairs hesitated, and then resumed their slow pacing . . .

"That'll be the police surgeon," said Hadley. He rubbed his eyes drowsily and stretched stiff muscles. "A bit more routine work, and I'm going home to bed. It's been years since I've taken hold of a regular investigation of this sort . . . I let the others work . . . I'm tired . . ."

"Excuse me," interrupted a voice at the door. "May I see you a moment?"

The tone was such that Hadley spun round. It began levelly, and then gave a sort of horrible jerk. It was a dead voice. Coming out of the shadows they saw Dalrye. His tie was loosened and there was sweat on his face. His eyes, as he moved them from one to the other of these men, were glazed.

"Don't say anything!" Dr. Fell suddenly boomed. He lurched out of his chair and seized the young man's arm. "For God's sake keep your mouth shut! You'll think better of it – you'll . . ."

Dalrye put out his hand. "It's no good," he said . . .

His eyes fixed on Hadley.

"I wish to give myself up, sir," he said, in a clear voice. "I killed Philip Driscoll."

20
THE MURDERER SPEAKS

In the utter and appalled silence of that library, even the footsteps upstairs seemed to have stopped as though they had heard him. The fire drew clearly and quietly; it drew yellow light on the long, pale, dull face. Dalrye mechanically yanked open his collar. His eyes were on the fire as he went on:

"I didn't mean to kill him, you know. It was an accident. I shouldn't have attempted to conceal it afterwards; that was the mistake. So now I don't suppose you'll believe me. I don't care, much. I shouldn't have told you at all if it hadn't been for your suspecting Major Bitton . . . and then his killing himself, and your being sure he'd done it . . . I couldn't stand that. He was – a real – friend. Phil never thought about anybody but himself. But Major Bitton . . ." He fumbled at his eyes. "I've lost my glasses, and I can't see very well without them. May I sit down, sir? I'm all in."

Nobody moved. He stumbled over to the fire, sat down, and as he spread out his hands before it they saw he was shivering.

"You young fool," Dr. Fell said, slowly. "You've ruined everything. I've been trying to cover you all evening, ever since I saw that girl of yours. And now you've wrecked it. There wasn't any sense in your telling. You've only brought more tragedy on this house."

Hadley straightened himself up, almost as though he were trying to recover from a blow in the face. He remained staring at Dalrye . . .

Then Hadley cleared his throat.

"This isn't real," he said. "It can't be. Are you telling me, as a police officer, without any joking . . ."

"I've been walking the streets for an hour," the young man answered. His shoulders were still quivering with cold. "When I kissed Sheila good night over at her friend's place . . . I knew it was the last time I'd ever see her outside the dock. And so I thought I couldn't tell you. But I realized I couldn't go on this way, either. I'm rotten, but I'm not so very rotten. I tried to look at myself while I was walking. I don't know. It's all mixed up." He put his head in his hands. Then an idea seemed to strike him and he peered round. "I heard somebody say . . . *did* somebody say he knew it already?"

"Yes," snapped Dr. Fell, grimly. "And if you'd had the sense to keep your mouth shut . . ."

Hadley had taken out his notebook. His fingers were shaking and his voice was not clear. "Mr. Dalrye," he said, "it is my duty to warn you that anything you say may be taken down . . ."

"All right," said Dalrye. "I'll talk in a minute. I'm cold; O, my God, but I'm cold! Let me sit here. Is that–?" He peered blindly at the drink Rampole was holding out, and clutched it. "Thanks. Thanks. I can use that . . . I suppose there's no good telling you it was an accident is there? He really killed himself, you know; that is, he jumped at me, and in the fight . . . Christ knows, *I* only – I only tried to steal that damned manuscript . . ."

He breathed noisily for a moment.

"This may be true," the chief inspector said, studying him queerly. "But I hope it's not. I hope you can tell me how you answered the telephone in Driscoll's flat at a quarter to two and killed Driscoll at the Tower of London a few minutes later."

Dr. Fell rapped his stick against the edge of the mantelpiece. "It's out now, Hadley. The damage is done. And I may as well tell you that you've put your finger on the essential point. It's where your whole case went wrong . . . You see, Driscoll was not killed at the Tower of London. He was killed in his own flat."

"He was . . . Great God!" Hadley said, despairingly. "All this is nonsense!"

"No, it isn't" said Dalrye. He took another swallow of the whiskey, and it seemed to warm him. "It's true enough. Why Phil came back to his flat I don't know; I can't imagine. I'd taken good care he should be at the Tower. That was why I faked the telephone call to myself. But I – I only wanted to keep him out of the way so that I could steal the manuscript and – and pretend it was some burglar . . ."

His trembling had almost ceased now; he was only dull and drowsily tired. He spoke in a queer, absent-minded voice, like a sick man.

"I feel better," he said, suddenly. "I feel better, now I've told you. I couldn't have kept it up long. I'm not built that way."

"Suppose we get this thing from the beginning," said the chief inspector. "You say you wanted to steal the Poe manuscript . . ."

"I had to," the other said, as though that explained everything. "I *had* to, you see."

"You had to?"

"Oh!" muttered Dalrye. His hand went to his eyes automatically, and found no glasses. "Oh yes. I didn't tell you. It was all on the spur of the moment. Bing. Like that. I don't think I should ever have thought of stealing it out of the house here. That wouldn't have been . . . oh, I don't know! I can't explain it. But when he telephoned me early Sunday evening at the Tower and told me that when he'd pinched his uncle's hat he'd stolen the manuscript with it . . ."

"You knew Driscoll was the hat-thief?"

"O Lord!" said Dalrye, with a sort of feeble irritation. "Of course I did. Of course he'd come to me. I helped him. He – he always had to have help. And of course, you see, he'd have told me, anyway. Because one of his choicest ideas was to get a Yeoman Warder's cap from the Tower of London . . ."

"By God and Bacchus!" muttered Dr. Fell. "I overlooked that. Yes, certainly. Any respectable hat-thief would have tried to . . ."

"Be quiet, will you?" snapped Hadley. "Listen, Mr. Dalrye. He told you about it . . . ?"

"And that's when I got the idea," Dalrye nodded absently. "I was pretty desperate, you see. They were after me, and it would have come out within a week. So I told Phil over the telephone to hang on to that manuscript; not to stir until I found him a plan; and to go round to the house Sunday night and find out what he could before he acted. And in the meantime . . ." He sat back in his chair. "I knew where Arbor was, over the week-end. I'd been out with Sheila Saturday night, and so of course I knew. I wouldn't have dared phone him if he'd been in this house . . ."

"*You phoned Arbor*?"

"Uh. Didn't he tell you? I was afraid he had recognized the voice, and I was panicky tonight when I heard he was coming in . . ."

Hadley stared sharply at Dr. Fell. "What did Arbor mean, then? I thought you told me he said he was sure it was Driscoll . . . ?"

"He did," said the doctor. "But I'm afraid you didn't pay close enough attention to what Miss Bitton said tonight, Hadley. Don't you remember her telling us about how Driscoll had played jokes on her, by telephoning and telling her he was Dalrye here; and she believed it? You've got a voice very much like Driscoll's haven't you, my boy?"

"If I hadn't had," muttered the other, "I couldn't have put this thing over. I'm no actor, you know. But if he could imitate me, then I could imitate him, and talk to Parker on the telephone to change the appointment and send myself up to his flat . . ."

"Hold on!" snapped Hadley. "This is getting ahead of me. You say that first you phoned Arbor and offered him the manuscript, when you didn't have it yet, and then . . . But *why*? Why did you want to steal it?"

Dalrye drained his glass. "I had to have twelve hundred pounds," he said, evenly.

Leaning back in his chair, he stared at the fire. His eyes were wrinkled up and his heavy breathing slowed down . . .

"Let me tell you a little about it," he went on. "Twelve hundred pounds wouldn't be much to most of the people I know. But to me it might as well have been twelve thousand.

"I don't know whether you know anything about me. My father is a clergyman in the north of England, and I'm the youngest of five sons. I never got much, to speak of. I don't suppose I ever wanted much. I got an education, but I had to work for my scholarships, because I wasn't one of these tremendously bright chaps. If I had anything, it was imagination, and I wanted – someday – and this is funny . . . no, I won't tell you what I wanted. It was something I wanted to write. But imagination doesn't help you in passing examinations, and it wasn't easy going to keep at the top. Still, nothing ever bothered me much. I'd been doing some research work on the Tower of London, and I happened to meet General Mason. He liked me, and I liked him, and he asked me to become his secretary.

"That was how I met the Bittons. It's odd . . . but, you know, I admired Driscoll. He was everything I wasn't. I'm tall, and awkward, and near-sighted, and ugly as a mud fence. I was never good at games, either, and women thought I was – oh, nice and pleasant, and they'd tell me all about how they fell in love with other chaps.

"Driscoll – well, you know him. He had the air. And it was the case of the brilliant meteor and the good old plodding cab-horse who helped him out of difficulties. And I told you I was flattered to have my advice taken. But then I met Sheila . . .

"It's damned funny why she looked at me. Other women never did. I'm telling you everything, so I – I – well, I can't tell you how much I worship her. I mean to say, it sounds ridiculous or something . . ."

He glared round him; but every face was expressionless.

". . . and they thought it was funny, too. I mean Phil's friends. And by funny, I mean comical, this time. One nice young dandy made a remark about 'Old parson-face and the moron daughter of Bitton's.' I didn't mind being called parson-face; they all did it. But the other . . . I couldn't do anything then. I had to find another occasion, so I ran into him one night, and said I didn't like *his* face, and knocked it off. He didn't get out of the house for a week. But then they began laughing again, and said, 'Good old Bob; he's a sly one,' and they said I was after Sheila's money. That was awful. And it was worse when Sheila and I knew we loved each other, and told each other so, and the old man learned about it.

"He took me over for an interview and as much as said the same thing. Then I made an ass of myself. I was sick of the whole performance. I don't remember what I said, but I know I told him he could take his dirty money . . . well, you know. That surprised him. Sheila and I were going to be married, anyhow. Then he thought it over, and thought it over, and Major Bitton intervened. Somehow, I don't think the old man was so upset about what I said as I thought he'd be. He came down to see me, and scratched his chin, and all that, and said, 'Well, let's not have a break-up in the family.' He said Sheila wasn't capable of looking after herself, and that if we'd promise to wait a year, and still felt the same way – there it was. I said that was all right, provided I did all the supporting of the new family without any help."

"I'll skip over the next part. Phil said he could tell me a way to make some easy money, and everything would be fine. And I was pretty desperate; Bitton's 'year' only meant – and we both knew it – that at the end of the time he'd say my prospects were no better, were they? And I couldn't expect Sheila to wait for me when she had so many chances for a good match, could I? That was the point of it.

"I got into a jam with my 'money-making.' Never mind that. It was my own fault. Phil . . ."

Dalrye hesitated. "*That's* neither here nor there. We were both in it, but I was the one who did the . . . Anyhow, if it ever got to the old man's ears, I was through. And I had to raise twelve hundred pounds in a week."

He leaned back in the chair and closed his eyes.

"Queer. I can't think of anything except 'old parson-face.' They even used to laugh to see me make cocktails. But then was when I got this wild idea of stealing the manuscript from Phil and selling it to Arbor. It was insane. So was I. I don't excuse it; I was as childish as Phil, when it came to a real difficulty . . .

"You know the scheme. I'd told him on Sunday night to phone me in the morning. He did – wild-eyed. He was in some fresh difficulty. It was the – the wife matter, you know, but I didn't know it then. I had already impressed it on his mind that he had to *conceal* the manuscript; keep it in his room. Over and over I impressed that on him. It was so that I could get it out of the flat.

"And he did. He tried putting it back in the old man's car – you know about that – before he came to the Tower to see me. But my instructions had so impressed him that, before he came to the Tower, he returned to his flat and hid the manuscript at the back of the grate in his study.

"Arranging the fake telephone call had been easy. The first one was genuine. When the second came through, I was in the record-room; I'd simply rung up Parker and spoken as

Driscoll. I knew he would call me on the speaking-tube. Then I would go to the phone again, say 'Hallo, Phil!' to myself, and answer myself in his voice, and Parker would hang up. I thought everything was arranged . . ."

Dalrye brooded a moment, his head in his hands. The fire crackled. Hadley had not moved . . .

"But I had to work fast. The plan was simple. I was going to leave the general's car at a garage in Holborn, hurry to Driscoll's flat, and pinch the manuscript. Then I was going to open a window, ransack the flat a bit, and steal a few odd things so that it would look like the work of a burglar. I didn't have any hesitation about stealing it. I knew Phil would never be blamed for stealing it from the old man; the old man would never know. The only danger Phil ran was in trying to return it. And, by God! if you think I hesitated to steal from the old man . . . I'd pinch his shirt off his back; that's what I think of *him*. The damned . . . Never mind."

He took the bottle of whiskey from the table and poured out almost half a tumbler. He was growing defiant, with a dull stain of colour in his cheeks, and the edge of the bottle clicked nervously against the glass. Dalrye swallowed most of the drink neat . . .

"It sounded good enough. I didn't think Phil would ever suspect *me*. When I got to the flat and found he wasn't there, I had time enough to search. A phone call came from Parker at the Tower while I was searching. I made a mistake by answering it; but I was rattled. Still – later," he choked a little, "later it gave an alibi. It was just before a quarter to two . . .

"Listen! I'd tumbled the study about some, because at first I didn't think of looking in the grate. But I did look there, and found it. I wasn't hurrying, because I thought Phil was safely at the Tower. I found the manuscript, and examined it carefully, and put it in my pocket. I was just going on to rumple up the room some more . . .

"I turned round; heard a noise or something – I don't know. And there was Phil in the doorway, looking at me. I knew he'd been standing there, and he'd seen every-thing."

The rest of the whiskey was tossed off. Dalrye's fixed, absent look had turned horrible. He put one hand a little way out as though he were groping.

"You never saw Phil in one of his rages, did you? When he had them, he was a crazy man. He was standing there, breathing hard, with his mouth pulled back. I'd seen him that way before. He tried to kill a man once, with a penknife, because the man had made fun of something he was wearing. He would go what they call – berserk and he was as dangerous as hell. It was cold and quiet in the room, and I could hear him breathe, and my watch ticking . . . and . . .

"Well, he started to scream. Literally screamed at me. I don't think I've ever heard anybody curse in my life the way he did then. It was so violent it sounded . . . I don't know how to describe it . . . obscene. He had a brown cap, all pulled over one ear. I always knew when he would jump. We'd had boxing-bouts with soft gloves several times; but I stopped sparring with him because I was a better boxer, and when I got inside his guard too smartly he'd fly off the handle and tell me he wanted to fight with knives. And he was dangerous, a sort of wildcat; he'd just as soon kick you below the belt as anything else. I saw him crouch down. I said, 'Phil, for God's sake don't be a fool – ' and he was looking round for something and he saw it. It was that crossbow bolt, lying on a low bookcase beside the door.

"Then he jumped.

"You couldn't avoid him in that little room. I tried to dodge aside and get him by the collar, the way you might a charging dog; I knew if I could get him in a wrestling grip I could keep him quiet. But he landed full. We whirled around . . . I – I don't exactly know what happened. I heard a chair hit the floor. And the next thing I knew we smashed over together, with me on top of him, and I heard a sort of dull crunch . . . and just after that . . .

"F-funny," Dalrye said wildly. "When I was a kid I had a rubber toy once, a sort of doll-like thing that wheezed and squeaked when you punched it. I thought of that. Because the noise he made was just like that toy, only a hundred times louder and more horrible. Unearthly; can you see. Then there was a kind of hiss and gurgle of the toy getting the air in it again. And he didn't move any more.

"I got up. He'd driven that bolt into himself, or my falling on him had done it, until the point hit the floor. The back of his head had hit the iron fender when we went over. There wasn't much blood, except a little stream not much thicker than a lead-pencil, that came out the side of his mouth . . ."

Dalrye sat back with his hands over his eyes.

21
UNSOLVED

For a moment he could not go on. He reached blindly after the whiskey again. Rampole hesitated; and then helped him pour some more. Hadley had sat down now, and he was staring blankly at the fire . . .

"I don't understand," Dalrye muttered in a dull voice; "I don't know why he came back . . ."

"Perhaps," said Dr. Fell, "I can tell you. Sit quietly for a moment, boy, and rest yourself . . . Hadley, do you see now?"

"You mean . . . ?"

"I mean this. It should be plain to you; you gave me the clue yourself. When Driscoll stood there at the Traitors' Gate, at the Tower of London, talking to Mrs. Bitton at one-thirty, he remembered something. The recollection of it startled him nearly out of his wits. He said he had to go and attend to it. What did he remember?"

"Well?"

"Think back! He was talking to her, and he mentioned something about his uncle. *That* was what made him remember, for his outburst followed it. Think! You've heard it a dozen times today . . ."

Hadley sat up suddenly. "My God! it was the afternoon of his uncle's monthly visit to him!"

"Exactly. Bitton didn't intend making the call, but Driscoll didn't know that. He'd forgotten that visit, Driscoll had, in all the excitement of the last two days. *And Bitton had a key to his flat.* He would walk in there . . . and there, in the flat with no attempt to hide them, were the two hats he had stolen.

That was bad enough. But if Bitton grew suspicious, and searched, and found his manuscript . . . ?"

Hadley nodded. "He had to get back to his flat faster than he ever made it before, to head off Sir William."

"He couldn't explain to Laura Bitton, you see. And, if he could, he couldn't take the time. She would want explanations, or to complicate things; and he *couldn't delay.* So he did what many another man has done with a woman. He shooed her away and said he would join her in five minutes. Of course, without any idea of doing it . . .

"And do you see what he did? Remember your plan of the Tower, Hadley. Remember what General Mason told us. He couldn't walk back along Water Lane towards the main gate. The way led *only* to the way out; he couldn't have pretended an errand, and it would have roused the woman's suspicions. So he went the other way along Water Lane, and out one of the other gates to Thames wharf – unnoticed in the fog. That was at half-past one."

The doctor looked down at Dalrye and shook his head.

"You yourself told me, Hadley, that by underground a person could go to Russell Square in fifteen minutes or even less. And it seemed to me, if Mrs. Bitton could do it at five o'clock, why couldn't Driscoll have done it at one-thirty? He would arrive at the flat, in short, about ten minutes to two or a trifle later . . . the time the police surgeon said he died. But, you see, where all your calculations went wrong was in assuming Driscoll had never left the Tower. The possibility never entered your head. I don't think we should have found a warder who saw him go out, even if we had tried, at that side gate. But the thing simply didn't occur to anybody. If it had, it would have been a much more reasonable solution than his remembering an urgent phone call."

"But he was found on the Traitors' Gate! I . . . Never mind," said Hadley. "Do you feel like going on, Dalrye?"

"So that was it," the other said, dully. "I see. I see now. I only thought he might have suspected me . . .

"Let me tell you what I did. He was dead. I saw that. And for a second I went into a sheer panic. I couldn't think straight; my legs wouldn't move, and I thought I must be going blind.

"I saw that I'd committed a murder. I had already prepared the way for a theft, and I was in deeply enough, but here was a murder. Nobody would believe it had been an accident. And where I made my mistake was this: I thought Driscoll had told them at the Tower he was coming back there! I could only imagine that they knew! And I had already definitely proved that *I* was at the flat, because I'd spoken to Parker on the telephone. I thought Driscoll had just changed his mind, and returned – and there I was with the body, when everybody knew we were both there."

He shuddered.

"Then my common sense came back all in a rush. I was cold and empty inside, but I don't think my brain ever worked so fast. I had only one chance. That was to get his body away from this flat, somehow, and dump it somewhere out in the open. Somewhere, say, on the way to the Tower – so that they would think he'd been caught on the way back.

"And it came to me all in a flash – *the car*. The car was in that garage, not far away. The day was very foggy. I could get the car and drive it into the courtyard with the side-curtains on. Phil's body was as light as a kitten. There were only two flats on the floor; and the windows overlooking the court were blank ones; with the fog to help me, there wasn't great danger of being seen . . .

Dr. Fell looked at Hadley. "Quite right. The chief inspector was positive on that point, too, when he was considering how Mrs. Bitton could have got out of the flat. I think he remarked that a red Indian in a war bonnet could have walked out of that court without being observed. It was suggestive."

"Well . . ." Again Dalrye rubbed his eyes unsteadily. "I hadn't much time. The thing to do was to save time by shooting over to the garage by the underground – I could do it, with luck, in two minutes, where it would have taken me ten to walk – to get the car, and come back for the body.

"I don't know how I did it. I don't know what sort of face I put up in front of those garage people. I told them I was going home, rolled out, and shot back to the flat. If I'd been arrested then . . ." He swallowed hard. "I took up Phil's body and carried it out. That was a ghastly time; carrying that thing. My God! I nearly fell down those little steps, and I nearly ran his head through the glass door. When I'd got him stowed in the back of the car, under a rug, I was so weak I thought I hadn't any arms. But I had to go back to the flat to be sure I hadn't overlooked anything. And when I looked round, I got an idea. That top-hat. If I took that along, and put it on Phil . . . why, you see, they would think the Mad Hatter had killed him! Nobody knew who the hat-thief was. I didn't want to get anybody else in trouble, and that way it was perfectly safe . . .

"The chief inspector," said Dr. Fell, "will have no difficulty in understanding you. You needn't elaborate. He had just finished outlining the same idea himself, as being the murderer's line of thought, before you came in. What about the crossbow bolt?"

"I – I left the bolt . . . you know where. You see I'd never seen the damn thing before. I didn't know it came from Bitton's house. I simply assumed it was one of Phil's possessions and couldn't do anybody harm. I didn't see the *Souvenir de Carcassonne*, because – you know why. It was hidden."

Dalrye's nostrils grew taut. His hands clenched on his knees and his voice went high. "But one thing I remembered before I left that flat. I remembered that manuscript in my pocket. I might have killed Phil. I might have been the lowest swine on earth and I was pretty sure I was. But, by God! I wasn't going to put dirty dollars in my pocket by selling that manuscript to Arbor now. It was in my pocket. But it had blood on it. I think I was thinking more about that than even about Phil. I wasn't going to use *that* if I needed it to save me from being hanged. I remember, I took it out. I was so wild that I was going to tear it up and take a handful of the pieces along to throw in Bitton's face. But if I tore it up here . . . oh, well. They'd find the pieces, and there wasn't any use doing Phil dirt, even if I had killed him. Sounds funny, eh. from a murderer? I can't help that. It's the way I felt. I knew I was wasting time, but I touched a match to it and threw it in the grate . . . I had the top-hat, squashed flat, under my coat, and I thought I'd attended to everything. Funny, too. I kept looking around that study, the way you do when you're leaving a hotel room, and you wonder if you've left your toothbrush on the washstand, or something . . ."

"You should have put back the fender in its place," said Dr. Fell. "Nobody merely searching that flat would or could have shoved a solid iron fender round the way you did when you had your fight with Driscoll. Well?"

"Then," said Dalrye, reaching automatically after the whiskey, "then I had the first of my two really horrible shocks. When I was just getting outside the door of the flat, I ran into the porter . . . If I had met him earlier, when I was carrying out Phil! . . . I don't know what I said. I said, 'Ha, ha,' or something of the sort, and told him what a good fellow he was, and for no reason at all I handed him half a crown. He walked out to the car with me . . ."

"Son," said Dr. Fell, with a sudden grunt, "you told an unnecessary lie today, and that car gave you away. When you were telling your story to us at the Tower this afternoon, you said you had never taken the car to the flat at all. You said when you left the flat you had to go to the garage and get it, and then start home. Still, I suppose you couldn't say anything else. But when Mr. Hadley here explained this evening about your having the car there, as the porter told him . . . No matter. Then?"

"I drove away. I was thinking until I thought my head would burst. But I believed I was safe now. I'd put the top-hat on Phil, and stuffed his cap into my pocket. All I had to do was find a side lane somewhere down near the Tower, and pitch him out in the fog. I didn't bother about fingerprints, for, as God is my judge, I'd never touched that crossbow bolt . . . And then, just as I'd laid my plans, and I was getting away from Bloomsbury, do you know what happened?"

"Yes," said Hadley. "You met General Mason."

"Met him? . . . Met him? Do you think I'd have stopped if I'd *seen* him? The first thing I knew he'd hopped on the running-board, and there he was grinning at me, and saying what a godsend this was, and telling me to get over in the front seat, so that he had room to shove in beside me . . .

"I stopped the car dead. I've read in books about how they feel when they think their hearts have stopped. I didn't think that exactly; I felt as though the whole car started to collapse under me. I couldn't move. I tried to move, and my foot jumped so much on the accelerator that I stalled the car. Then I turned my head away and glared out the side as though I were looking at a tire, and I tried to swear at it, but I couldn't seem to get my tongue up out of my throat.

"Then the car got started somehow. I could hear the general talking, but I don't remember anything he said. He was in a very good humour, I know, and that seemed to make it worse. All I thought of, just as though I saw words written on a board, was, 'Come on, parson-face; steady, parson-face; keep your nerve, parson-face,' and I thought that Phil's friends would stare if they saw old parson-face now. I wanted to yell, and slap him on the back and say, 'Glance under that rug in the rear seat, and see what a surprise old parson-face has for you, General.'

"But I didn't. I covered myself by cursing every car that passed so violently that even the general thought something must be wrong. I was headed for destruction now; I could see that. We should go straight back to the Tower, and no power this side of hell could change it. Straight back . . . Excuse me a second . . . a drink. Funny this stuff doesn't seem to have any effect . . . A few drinks will get me tight, usually.

"I had, during that time, about twenty minutes to think and think hard. I'd thought it must be hours since I'd seen Phil dying dead there. But when I looked at my watch I couldn't understand; it was only eight minutes past two. And all the time my brain was going like a machine-shop I was talking to the general – I don't know what we talked about. It began to dawn on me that I had one chance. And that if I worked that chance I might have a real alibi . . .

"You see? If I could get inside the Tower grounds, and dump the body somewhere without detection, no sane person would ever believe I had ridden from Town beside General Mason with a corpse in the rear of the car. It began to seem as though my worst danger might be my – well, my salvation. They would believe, it suddenly dawned on me, that Driscoll had never left the Tower . . .

"I had to nerve myself for one last effort. And I was thankful I'd put on a bad humour and taken to cursing other cars, because now I told the general about the 'fake' telephone call that had lured me away; and I wondered what it was all about . . .

"Then we were inside the Tower grounds as two-thirty struck. I had calculated it neatly, and I knew the place. If there were nobody else about as we went along Water Lane, I knew what I should do. You were quite right, Doctor, in saying that anybody would think of Traitors' Gate as the place to hide a corpse on a foggy day. And this was the place, because *I could stop there without suspicion*.

"You see?" Dalrye demanded, leaning forward eagerly. "I had to let the general out opposite the gate to the Bloody Tower. I waited until he was well up under the archway on his way to the King's House, and then I acted. I opened the rear door, tossed the body over the rail, and was back in the car in a second, driving on . . .

"But, my God! I cut it fine! The general, on his way up, remembered an errand or something in St. Thomas's Tower, and he discovered the body. That – that's about all sir. There's – there's only one other thing. With this terrible thing over me, I'd forgotten about the money Phil had – the money I owed to . . . Well, I'd forgotten it, anyway. When the general sent me after the doctor, and the rest of it, I had to go up to my room to get something to steady my nerves. The reaction was too much. There was a letter on my table. I don't remember opening it; I don't even know *why* I opened it. I found myself standing with a brandy and soda in my hand, and the letter in front of my face. The letter said," suddenly Dalrye gagged, as though he were swallowing medicine, "the letter said, 'Don't worry any more about it. It's paid. Don't mention this to my brother, and don't be such a quixotic young fool again.' It was signed Lester Bitton."

Dalrye got up out of his chair and faced them. He was flushed and his eyes burned brightly. There was a pause, and he had a curious expression of puzzled uncertainty . . .

"I'm drunk!" he said, wonderingly. "I'm drunk. I hadn't noticed it, not till this minute. Old parson-face is drunk. Never mind . . .

"Lester Bitton got rid of what I owed, and never said a word.

"And when you accused him tonight – and he shot himself – you see why I had to tell you . . ."

He stood straight, a little wrinkle between his brows.

"I told you I was a swine," he went on in an even voice, "but I'm not so bad as that. I know what it means. It means the rope. They won't believe me, of course, after what I did to cover myself; and I can't blame them. They shoot you out of a door, and it's all over in a few seconds . . . Don't mind old parson-face. I can't think how I came to be so drunk. I don't drink much, as a rule . . . What was I saying? Oh yes. If you hadn't blamed it on Major Bitton, if you gave out that you hadn't been able to find out *who* the murderer was, I'd have kept quiet. Why not? I love Sheila. Some day I might have . . . Never mind. I'm not going to let you think I'm pitying myself. It's only that I appreciate people who are kind to me. I never had much kindness. People all thought I was too much of a joke. But, by God! old joke parson-face had the police guessing, didn't he?" Momentarily there was a blaze in his face. "Old – joke – parson – face!" said Robert Dalrye.

. . . The fire was sinking now. Dalrye, his hand clenched, stared across the dusky room. He had spoken for a long time. There was a faint hint of dawn in the windows towards the garden; Mayfair lay quiet and dead.

Hadley rose quietly from his chair.

"Young man," he said, "I have an order for you. Go out into one of the other rooms and sit down. I'll call you back in a moment. I want to speak to my friends. There is one other thing. On no account speak a word to anybody until you are called back. Do you hear?"

"Oh, well," said Dalrye. "Oh, well. Go ahead and phone for your Black Maria, or whatever you use. I'll wait . . . By the way, there was something I didn't tell you. I'm afraid I nearly scared that poor devil Arbor into a fit. I didn't mean to. I was in the Warders' Hall on the other side of the Byward Tower, where the visitors were detained, when he was coming out from your conference. And I was talking to your sergeant, only about ten feet away from Arbor. He hadn't recognized my voice before, but I was afraid he did then. It nearly killed him . . . I say! I feel as though I had no legs. I hope I'm not staggering. That would be a devil of a way to go to gaol. Excuse me . . ."

With his shoulders back, he moved with careful steps towards the door.

"Well?" asked Dr. Fell, when he had gone.

Hadley stood before the dying fire, a stiff military figure against the white-marble mantelpiece and in his hand were the notes he had taken of Dalrye's recital. Hadley hesitated. There were lines drawn slantwise under his eyes; he shut his eyes now.

"I told you," he said, quietly, "I was getting old. I am sworn to uphold the law. But – I don't know. I don't know. The older I get, the more I don't know. Ten years ago I should have said, 'Too bad,' and . . . You know what I'm thinking, Fell. No jury would ever believe that boy's testimony. But I do."

"And without speaking of Lester Bitton," said the doctor, "the case can remain unsolved. Good man, Hadley! You know what I think. If this is a tribunal, will you put it up to a vote?"

"Lord help me," said Hadley, "I will. Well, Fell?" He assumed a stern air, but a curious, wise, ancient smile crept about his mouth. "Dr. Fell, your vote?"

"'Unsolved,'" said the doctor.

"Mr. Rampole?"

"'Unsolved,'" said Rampole, instantly.

The dying firelight lit Hadley's face as he half-turned. He upturned his hand; the white note-sheets fluttered from it and drifted down into the blaze. They caught fire and leaped in a puff. Hadley's hand remained motionless, the ancient, wise smile still on his face.

"'Unsolved,'" he said.

The Eight of Swords

Contents

1
EXTRAORDINARY BEHAVIOUR OF A BISHOP

Chief Inspector Hadley had been almost cheerful when he reached his office that morning. For one thing, the diabolical August heat wave had broken last night. After two weeks of brass skies and streets that shimmered crookedly before the eye, rain had come down in a deluge. He had been in the middle of composing his memoirs, a painful labor, at his home in East Croydon; fuming, and guiltily afraid that some of it must sound like braggadocio. The rain restored him somewhat, and also his sense of values. He could reflect that the new police reform bothered him not at all. In a month he would retire for good. Figuratively, he could take off his collar – only figuratively, for he was not the sort of person who takes off collars; besides, Mrs. Hadley had social ambitions – and in a month more the manuscript should be in the hands of Standish & Burke.

So the rain cooled him, while he noted in his methodical way that it began at eleven o'clock, and went more comfortably to bed. Though the following morning was warm, it was not too warm; and he reached Scotland Yard in at least the open frame of mind of the Briton willing to give things a sporting chance, if they don't make too much of it.

When he saw what was on his desk, he swore in astonishment. Then, after he had got the assistant commissioner on the phone, he was still more heated.

"I know it isn't a job for the Yard, Hadley," said that dignitary. "But I hoped you could suggest something; I don't quite know what to make of it myself. Standish has been appealing to me –"

"But what I want to know, sir," said the chief inspector, "is what is the business, anyway? There are some notes on my desk about a bishop and a 'poltergeist', whatever that is –"

There was a grunt from the other end of the telephone.

"I don't know myself exactly what it's about," admitted the assistant commissioner. "Except that it concerns the Bishop of Mappleham. Quite a big pot, I understand. He's been taking a vacation at Colonel Standish's place in Gloucestershire; overworked himself, they tell me, in a strenuous anti-crime campaign or something of the sort . . ."

"Well, sir?"

"Well, Standish has grave doubts about him. He says he caught the bishop sliding down the banisters."

"Sliding down the banisters?"

There was a faint chuckle. The other said musingly: "I should like to have seen that performance. Standish is firmly convinced he's – um – off his rocker, so to speak. This was only the day after the poltergeist had got busy –"

"Would you mind telling me the facts from the beginning, sir?" suggested Hadley, wiping his forehead and giving the telephone a vindictive glare. "It hardly seems to concern us if a clergyman goes mad and slides down the banisters in Gloucestershire."

"I'll let the bishop speak for himself, later on. He's coming to see you this morning, you know . . . Briefly, what I understand is this. At The Grange – that's Standish's country place – they have a room which is supposed to be haunted off and on by a poltergeist. Poltergeist: German for 'racketting spirit'; I got that out of the encyclopedia. It's the sort of ghost that throws china about, and makes the chairs dance, and whatnot. D'you follow me?"

"O Lord!" said Hadley. "Yes, sir."

"The poltergeist hadn't been active for a number of years. Well, it happened the night before last that the Reverend Primley, the vicar of a parish somewhere nearby, had been dining at The Grange –"

"Another clergyman? Yes, sir. Go on."

"– and he missed the last bus home. It was Standish's chauffeur's night off, so they put up the vicar at The Grange. They'd forgotten all about the poltergeist, and he was accidentally accommodated in the haunted room. Then, about one o'clock in the morning, the ghost got busy. It knocked a couple of pictures off the wall, and made the poker walk about, and I don't know what all. Finally, while the vicar was praying away for dear life, a bottle of ink came sailing off the table and biffed him in the eye.

"At this the vicar set up a howl that alarmed the whole household. Standish came charging in with a gun, and the rest of them after him. It was red ink, so at first they thought murder had been done. Then, at the height of the hullabaloo, they looked out of the window, and there they saw him standing on the flat leads of the roof in his nightshirt –"

"Saw who?"

"The bishop. In his nightshirt," explained the assistant commissioner. "They could see him in the moonlight."

"Yes, sir," said Hadley obediently. "What was he doing there?"

"Why, he said that he had seen a crook in the geranium beds."

Hadley sat back and studied the telephone. The Hon. George Bellchester had never been precisely the person he would have chosen as assistant commissioner of the Metropolitan Police; though an able official, he took his duties with some lightness, and above all he had an exceedingly muddy way of recounting facts. Hadley cleared his throat and waited.

"Are you by any chance pulling my leg, sir?" he inquired.

"Eh? Good God, no! – Listen. I may have mentioned that the Bishop of Mappleham claimed to have made an exhaustive study of crime and criminals, though I can't say I ever encountered him in his investigations. I believe he wrote a book about it. Anyhow he swore he had seen this man walking past the geranium beds. He said the man was heading down the hill in the direction of the Guest House, which is occupied by a studious old coot named Depping . . ."

"What man?"

"This crook. I haven't heard his name mentioned, but the bishop says he is a well-known criminal. He – the bishop – had been awakened by a noise, which was probably the racket in the poltergeist's room, he says. He went to the window, and there was the man on the lawn. He turned his head, and the bishop says he could see him clearly in the moonlight. The bishop climbed out of the window on to the roof –"

"Why?"

"I don't know," said Bellchester, rather testily. "He did it, anyway. The crook ran away. But the bishop is convinced that a dangerous criminal is lurking about The Grange for the purpose of mischief. He seems to be rather a formidable person, Hadley. He insisted on Standish's telephoning me and our doing something about it. Standish, on the other hand, is pretty well convinced that the bishop has gone potty. Especially, you see, when the bishop assaulted one of the housemaids –"

"What?" shouted Hadley.

"Fact. Standish saw it himself, and so did the butler, and Standish's son." Bellchester seemed to be relishing the story. He was one of those people who can talk comfortably and at any length over the telephone, sitting back at his ease. Hadley was not. He liked talking face to face, and protracted phone sessions made him fidget. But the assistant commissioner showed no disposition to let him off. "It happened in this way," he pursued. It seems that this scholarly old fellow Depping – the one who occupies the Guest House – has a daughter or a niece or something, living in France. And Standish has a son. Result: matrimony contemplated. Young Standish had just come back from a flying visit to Paris, whence he and the girl decided to make a match of it. So he was breaking the news to his father in the library, asking blessings and the rest of it. He was painting an eloquent picture of the Bishop of Mappleham uniting them in holy matrimony at the altar, and orange blossoms and so on, when they heard wild screams coming from the hall.

"They rushed out. And there was the Bishop, top-hat and gaiters, holding one of the housemaids across a table –"

Hadley made expostulating noises. He was a good family man, and, besides, he thought somebody might be listening in on the wire.

"Oh, it's not quite so bad as that," Bellchester reassured him. "Though it's puzzling enough. He seemed to have got hold of the girl by the back hair and was trying to pull it out, making most unepiscopal threats. That's all Standish told me; and he was excited, anyhow. I gather the Bishop thought the poor girl was wearing a wig. In any event, he made Standish promises to 'phone me and arrange an interview for him with one of our people."

"He's coming here, sir?"

"Yes. Do me a favor, will you, Hadley, and see him? That will probably pacify His Reverence. I want to oblige Standish, and it never does any harm to keep on the good side of the clergy. By the way, Standish is the silent partner in that publishing firm you're writing your memoirs for; did you know it?"

Hadley tapped the mouthpiece thoughtfully. "Um," he said. "No. No, I didn't know that. Burke is the only one I've met. Well –"

"Good man," said Bellchester approvingly. "You see him, then. Good luck."

He rang off. Hadley folded his hands with a patient and gloomy air. He muttered "Poltergeist!" several times, and indulged in some reflections on the evil days which had befallen the Metropolitan Police when the Chief Inspector of the Criminal Investigation Department was required to listen to the maunderings of every loony bishop who went about sliding down bannisters, attacking housemaids, and firing ink-bottles at vicars.

Presently his sense of humor struggled into being again. A grin appeared under his clipped gray moustache, and he fell to whistling as he sorted out his morning's mail. He also reflected, in as sentimental a fashion as his nature would permit, on his thirty-five years in the Force; on all the villainy and nonsense he had seen in this little bare room, with its brown distempered walls and windows that overlooked the sedate Embankment. Each morning he placidly shaved himself in East Croydon, kissed his wife, cast a troubled eye over the newspaper (which always hinted at sinister things, either from Germany or the climate) as the train bore him to Victoria; and took up afresh his duties in murders or lost dogs. Around him was the ordered hum of this clearing-house for both. Around him –

"Come in," he said, in reply to a knock at the door.

A constable, obviously perturbed, coughed.

"There's a gentleman here, sir," he observed, rather in the manner of one making a deduction. "There's a gentleman here." He laid a card on Hadley's desk.

"Um," said the Chief Inspector, who was reading a report. "What's he want?"

"I think you had better see him, sir."

Hadley glanced at the card, which said:

Dr. Sigismund Von Hornswoggle
Vienna

"I think you'd better see him," the other insisted. "He's making a row, sir, and psychoanalyzing everybody he can lay hold of. Sergeant Betts has hidden himself in the record room, and swears he won't come out until somebody takes the gentleman away."

"Look here," said the exasperated Hadley, and creaked round in his swivel-chain. "Is everybody trying to play a game on me this morning? What the hell do you mean, making a row? Why don't you chuck him out?"

"Well, sir, the fact is," said the other, "that – well, I think we know him. You see . . ."

The constable was not a small man, but he was shoved aside by a much larger one; certainly one of five times his girth. The doorway was filled by an enormously stout figure in a black cape and glistening top hat. But the chief inspector's first impression of him was concerned with whiskers. He wore, almost to his cheekbones, the most luxuriant set of black whiskers Hadley had ever seen. His eyebrows were also of the same variety, and seemed to take up half his forehead. Small eyes twinkled behind eyeglasses on a broad black ribbon. His red face beamed, and he swept off his hat in a great bow.

"Goot morning!" he thundered in a rumbling voice, and beamed again. "Haf I der honor of speaking to das chief inspector, yah? Du bist der Hauptmann, meinherr, nicht wahr? Yah, yah, yah. So."

He came over at his rolling gait and set out a chair with great nicety, propping his cane against its side.

"I vill myself sit down," he announced. "So."

He sat down, beamed, folded his hands, and inquired: "Vot do you dream about?"

Then Hadley got his breath. "Fell –" he said. "Gideon Fell . . . What in the name of God," continued Hadley, slapping the desk at each word, "do you mean by putting on that crazy get-up and coming into my office in it? I thought you were in America. Did anybody see you come in?"

"Eh? My goot friend – !" protested the other in an injured tone, "surely you haf yourself mistaken, yah? I am Herr Doktor Sigismund von Hornswoggle . . ."

"Take if off," said Hadley firmly.

"Oh, well," said the other, dropping his accent in a voice of resignation. "So you penetrated my disguise, did you? The chap in New York told me I was perfect in the art. I had a sovereign bet that I could deceive you. Well, aren't you going to shake hands, Hadley? Here I am back, after three months in America –"

"There's a lavatory at the end of the hall," said the chief inspector inexorably. "Go out and take off those whiskers or I'll have you locked up. What do you want to do: make a guy of me in my last month of office?"

"Oh, well," grunted Dr. Fell.

He reappeared in a few minutes, his old self again, with his double chins, his bandit's moustache, and his great mop of gray-streaked hair. His face had grown even redder with the friction of washing off spirit gum. Chuckling, he propped his hands on his stick and beamed at Hadley over his eyeglasses. His headgear had changed to the usual shovel hat.

"Still," he observed, "I flatter myself that I deceived your subordinates. It takes time, of course, to become perfect. And I have my diploma from the William J. Pinkerton School of Disguise. It's what they call a mail-order course. Heh-heh-heh. You pay five dollars down, and they send you your first lesson; and so on. Heh-heh-heh."

"You're a hopeless old sinner," said Hadley, relenting, "but, all the same, I'm devilish glad to see you back. Did you enjoy yourself in America?"

Dr. Fell sighed with reminiscent pleasure, blinking at a corner of the ceiling. Then he rumbled and hammered the ferrule of his cane on the floor.

"He pasted the old apple!" murmured Dr. Fell ecstatically. "Il a frappé l'oignon! Ha, woof! – kill the umpire! I say, Hadley, how would you construe into Latin the following text: 'He poled the tomato into the left-field bleachers for a circuit clout?' I've been debating it all the way across the ocean. 'Poled' and 'tomato' I can manage, but how Virgil would have said 'left-field bleachers' rather stumps me."

"What's all that?"

"It would appear," said Dr. Fell, "to be the dialect of a province called Brooklyn. My friends from the publishing house took me there, thank God, when we were supposed to be attending literary teas. You can't imagine," said the doctor, with unholy glee, "how many literary teas we contrived to miss, or, better still, how many literary people I avoided meeting. Heh-heh. Let me show you my scrap-book."

From beside his chair he took up a brief-case, and produced a volume of cuttings which he spread out proudly on the chief inspector's desk.

"I may mention, to explain some of these headlines," he pursued, "that I was known to the newspapers as 'Gid' –"

"Gid?" said Hadley, blankly.

"It is short, snappy, and fits into a headline," explained Dr. Fell, with the air of one who quotes. "Look at these examples, now."

He opened the book at random. Hadley's eye was caught by the announcement: "Gid Judges Beauty Contest at Long Beach." The accompanying photograph showed Dr. Fell, with cloak, shovel hat, and a beam like a burnished apple on his face, towering among a group of amorous young ladies in almost non-existent bathing costumes. "Gid Opens New Fire-Station in Bronx; Created Honorary Fire Chief," proclaimed another. This cutting was decorated with two snapshots. One showed Dr. Fell wearing a complicated headgear on which was printed the word Chief, and holding up an axe as though he were going to brain somebody. The other pictured him in the act of sliding down a silver-plated pole from the second floor of the fire station; a very impressive sight. It bore the caption: "Did He Fell Or Was He Pushed?"

Hadley was aghast.

"Do you mean to say you actually did all these things?" he demanded.

"Certainly. I told you I had a good time," the other reminded him complacently. "Here is an account of my speech to the convention of the Loyal and Benevolent Order of Mountain Goats. I seem to have spoken very well, though my recollection is hazy. I was also made an Honorary Something of the Order; but I am not sure what my title is, because it was late in the evening and the President couldn't pronounce it with any degree of certainty. Why? Don't you approve?"

"I wouldn't have done all that," said Hadley fervently, "for" – he searched his mind for a suitable inducement – "for a thousand pounds! Close the book; I don't want to read any more . . . What are your plans now?"

Dr. Fell frowned.

"I don't know. My wife hasn't returned from visiting her in-laws yet; I had a wire when the boat docked this morning. I'm rather at a loose end. Still, I happened to run into an old friend of mine at Southampton – a Colonel Standish. He's a member of Standish & Burke, my publishers; though it's only a financial interest, and Burke handles the business for him. Eh? What did you say?"

"Nothing," answered Hadley. There was a gleam in his eye nevertheless.

A long sniff rumbled in the doctor's nose. "I don't know what's the matter with him, Hadley. It seems he'd come down to the boat to meet the son of a friend of his – a fine young fellow, by the way, and the son of the Bishop of

Mappleham. I got to know him pretty well before they locked him up in the brig –"

"Locked him up in the brig?" said Hadley, sitting back in his chair. "Well, well! What was the trouble? Did he go mad too?"

A reminiscent chuckle ran over the bulges of Dr. Fell's waistcoat. With his cane he poked at the edge of Hadley's desk.

"Tut, tut, Hadley. What do you mean, mad? It was only a matter of a pair of lady's – hum – well, undergarments of some description . . ."

"He assaulted the lady, I suppose?"

"I say, Hadley, I wish you wouldn't interrupt. No; good Lord, no! He pinched 'em out of her cabin. Then he and a few other stout-hearted fellows ran 'em up the mast in place of the house flag. They didn't discover it until next morning when a passing ship wirelessed congratulations to the captain. Then, d'ye see, there was a row. This young fellow is a wonder with his fists, by the way. He laid out the first officer and two stewards before they subdued him, and –"

"That's enough," said the chief inspector. "What were you saying about Standish?"

"Why, he seems to have something on his mind. He invited me down to his place in Gloucester for the week-end, and said he had a story to tell me. But the odd part of it was the way he treated young Donovan – that's the bishop's son. He shook his hand sadly, and looked at him in a sympathetic, pitying manner; and told him not to lose heart . . . Incidentally, they're both downstairs in Standish's car now; waiting for me. Eh? What's the matter with you now?"

Hadley leaned forward.

"Listen!" he said . . .

2
"SHOT THROUGH THE HEAD —"

In the short little thoroughfare called Derby Street, which runs off Whitehall to Scotland Yard, Mr. Hugh Answell Donovan sat in the front seat of the car and surreptitiously swallowed another aspirin. The absence of water made him gag, and taste the full vileness of the pill before he could get it down. He pushed his hat over his eyes, shuddered, and stared gloomily at the wind screen.

His dreary outlook was not merely physical; though that was bad enough. His farewell party in New York had become a long, curving bender which did not cease until they put him in the brig when the Aquatic was two days out of Southampton. He was a little better now. Food did not turn green before his eyes, and his stomach had ceased to come together like a collapsing telescope at the sight of it. His hand had begun to regain its steadiness, nor was his conscience crawling through him with such cold feet as before. But there was a worse thing to destroy the pleasure he would have felt at seeing London after a year's absence.

All he had left, he reflected, was his sense of humor, and he had better use it.

Donovan, an amiable and easy-going young man with a dark face, and one of the neatest middleweight battlers who ever came out of Dublin University, tried to say, "Ha ha" to the dashboard. He only gurgled, for he was thinking of his first meeting with his father.

In some ways, of course, the old man was a stout fellow, even if he did happen to be a bishop. He was old-fashioned, which meant that within reasonable limits he believed in a young man sowing an oat or two by the way. But the old man's hobby had been betrayed, and his son shivered to think of the result.

A year's leave had been granted him on the only condition it would ever have been allowed: to study criminology. At the time he had considered it an inspiration. "Dad," he said, straightforwardly and frankly, "Dad, I want to be a detective." And the formidable old boy had beamed. Moodily his son recalled this now. Several times during his stay in America, he had seen photographs in which he had been struck by the really remarkable resemblance of his father to the late William Jennings Bryan. People who had known both of them personally said that the likeness was even more striking than the photographs indicated. There was the same square massive face and broad mouth; the same heavy brow, the long hair curling down behind; the curved nose, fluffy eyebrows, and sharp dark eyes; the same shoulders and decisive stride. Then there was the voice. That the Bishop of Mappleham had the finest voice in the Church of England was never doubted; it was resonant, Bryanesque, and effective as a pipe organ. Altogether, a commanding figure.

His son swallowed another aspirin, automatically. If the bishop had a weakness, it was his hobby. A great criminologist had been lost to the world when Hugh Donovan, Sr., took up holy orders. His information was enormous; he could recite you the details of every atrocity in the last hundred years; he knew all the latest scientific devices for both the advancement and prevention of crime; he had investigated the police departments of Paris, Berlin, Madrid, Rome, Brussels, Vienna, and Leningrad, driving the officials thereof to the verge of insanity; and, finally, he had lectured all about it in the United States. It was possibly his warm reception in America which had induced him to grant his son permission to study criminology at Columbia University . . .

"Gaa," muttered Hugh Junior, and goggled at the dashboard. He had registered there in a burst of ambition, and bought a variety of indigestible books with German titles. Afterwards he had gone no nearer West 116th Street than the apartment of a little blonde who lived uptown on the Drive.

He was now, he perceived, sunk. The old man would be down on him roaring for all the grisly details, and he didn't know one tobacco ash from another. To cap it all, there were mysterious events on foot already. His father had not been at the pier to meet the Aquatic that morning. Instead there had appeared a certain Colonel Standish, whom he vaguely remembered having met somewhere before . . .

He glanced sideways at the colonel, who was fidgeting in the seat beside him, and wondered what ailed the man. Ordinarily the colonel must have been an easy and amiable sort; fleshy and port-wine-colored, with a puffing manner and clipped hair. But he had been acting very strangely. He shifted about. He rolled round a squinted brown eye, and removed it hastily. He had taken to thumping his fist on the steering-wheel, as though he had some sort of internal agony; and several times he accidentally thumped the button of the horn, which let out a squawk that made Donovan jump.

They had driven up from Southampton with a jovial old codger named Fell; and, like a nightmare, Donovan found himself being driven straight to Scotland Yard. There was dirty work here, somewhere. He had a horrible suspicion that his old man, energetic as always, was going to send him before – some sort of tribunal for an examination. The thing became worse because not a word had been said to him about his father, or what was afoot, or –

"Damme, sir," said Colonel Standish, suddenly and energetically. "Damme, damme, damme, damme!"

"Eh?" said Donovan, "I beg your pardon?"

The colonel cleared his throat. His nostrils were working as though at a sudden resolve.

"Young fella," he said in a gruff voice. "Got to tell you. Only right I should. Eh?"

"Yes, sir?"

"It's about your father. Got to tell you what's in store for you, and warn you."

"Oh, my God," said Donovan inaudibly. He slouched down in his seat.

"Happened this way, you see. Poor fellow'd been overworking, and I asked him down to my place for a rest. We'd a comfortable little party: my son – don't think you've met him – my wife, and daughter; hum. Then there was Burke, my partner, and Morgan, the writer fella, and Depping who lives in the Guest House. His daughter and my son – hurrumph, ne' mind. Listen. It started the very first night. The very first night," said the colonel, lowering his voice, "it started."

"What started?" said Donovan, still fearing the worst.

"We'd Lady Langwych to dinner. You know; dem'd suffragette gel used to break all the windows, eh? She was anxious to meet the bishop and talk social reform with him." The colonel was breathing noisily and tapping Donovan's arm. "We were all standing in the hall, hey, downstairs, and talking to Lady Langwych – she'd just got there. All on our best behavior, hey. I remember my wife said: 'The Bishop of Mappleham will be delighted to see you, Lady Langwych.' Old gel said, 'Heh-heh.' My daughter said, 'Damme, yes indeed, damme. When he knows you're here, Lady Langwych, I'm sure he'll be down in a hurry.' Then, all of a sudden – whr-r-r-ree!" goggled the colonel, sweeping out his arm and making a whistling noise like a six-inch shell, "down he came on the bannisters – whr-rree! – one whole flight of stairs – like a demn'd gaitered avalanche."

Donovan was not sure he had heard right.

"Who did?" he demanded.

"Your father, poor fellow. Like a demn'd gaitered avalanche, 'pon my oath!"

The colonel stared, and then chuckled. "Old gel carried it off, too, by Jove! Got to admire her. Your father landed slap at her feet – bing! Like that. Old gel put up her eyeglass and just said it was dashed kind of him to be so prompt. But then was when I began to grow suspicious."

Peering round him to make sure there was nobody there, the colonel assumed an expostulating tone. "I took him aside, and said, 'Look here, old fellow, demmit, this is Liberty Hall, but after all – demmit!' Eh? Then I asked him tactfully whether he was feeling well, and whether I hadn't better have the doctor in, eh? By Jove, he went off the deep end! Swore it was an accident. Said he'd been leaning over the bannisters to look at somebody without being seen; and lost his balance, and had to hang on to save himself from falling. Well, I said, who was he staring at? And he said it was Hilda, one of the housemaids –"

"Great suffering snakes!" said Donovan, pressing his hands to a head that had begun to ache again. "My old man said –"

"He's seeing crooks all over the place, poor fella," grunted the colonel. "Fact is, he thought Hilda was a woman called Piccadilly Jane, a crook, and had a dark wig on. Then he saw the other crook on the lawn. That was the night somebody up and biffed the vicar in the eye with the inkpot. Poor devil. Shouldn't be at all surprised if he thought the vicar was Jack the Ripper in disguise, demmit."

"This is getting to be a little too much for me," said Donovan, beginning to feel ill. "Look here, sir, do you mean that my governor has gone off his onion? Is that it?"

Standish drew a deep breath.

"Didn't like to say it," he grumbled, "but hanged if I see any other explanation. And what makes it worse is that I'm the chief constable of the county. When I wouldn't listen to him, he made me get him an appointment to see the chaps at Scotland Yard, and – s-hhh-sh!"

He broke off suddenly and stared over his shoulder. Following the direction of his glance, Donovan was startled to see what he had been fearing for a long time: a tall, portly figure marching in from Whitehall, with a grim and preoccupied stride as though it were trying to step on every crack in the pavement. Even the top hat had an Onward-Christian-Soldiers look about it. Now and again, out of the massive lined face, sharp eyes would swing left and right, and the Bishop of Mappleham seemed to be muttering to himself. His son noticed this; and also that the bishop looked paler than usual. Even in his incredulous perplexity, a stab of pity went through Donovan. After all, the old man was a stout fellow. He had been warned against overwork. It might be expected, sooner or later, that if a man of such colossal energy didn't constrain himself he would be in danger of a nervous breakdown.

"You see?" said the colonel, in a hoarse barrack-room whisper. "Talking to himself now. Sawbones told me that was one of the first signs, damme. A pity, ain't it? Off his rocker, poor fella. Humor him; be sure to humor him."

Colonel Standish had been under the impression that he was speaking in a whisper. Actually he had been trumpeting down the street, but the bishop did not seem to hear. He saw his son, and stopped. His heavy face lighted up with one of his famous Bryanesque smiles, which were a part of the man's very genuine charm. But the smile had a note of grimness. He hurried over to shake Donovan's hand.

"My boy!" he said. The magnificent voice, which in his younger days could make people believe anything, flowed into Derby Street in its hypnotic fashion. Even Standish was impressed. "I'm delighted to see you back. I should, of course, have been down to meet the boat, but weighty matters demanded my attention. You are looking well, Hugh; very well."

This startling pronouncement added to Donovan's uneasiness. It showed how preoccupied the old man must be.

"Hullo, Dad," he said, and pulled his hat further down.

"You will be able, with your new training," pursued the bishop impressively, "to assist me on a matter of momentous import, which, due to the failure of others to comprehend my plans," – he looked heavily at the colonel and tightened his broad mouth – "they have not as yet fully appreciated. Good morning, Standish."

"Oh, ah. Er – good morning," said the colonel nervously.

The bishop studied him. There was a curious gleam in his eye.

"Standish, I regret to say it to such an old friend, but you are a fool. Duty compels me to say so. I have blundered. I admit it freely. But . . ." He swept his arm about slowly, and there was a roll and thrill in his voice, "stormy waters could not shake me, nor tempests keep me from my path. The humblest man, when clad in the armor of a righteous cause, is more powerful than all the hosts of error."

His son restrained an impulse to cheer. When the old man got to talking in this fashion, he could stampede an audience of mummies. It was not so much what he said; it was the hypnotism of voice and bearing, orchestrated together, with the mesmeric eye and the latent persuasive kindliness.

"Often said so myself," agreed the colonel. "But look here, old fellow; I mean to say, demmit! – why did you cut along from The Grange last night without telling us where you were going? Almost had a search party out after you. Wife frantic, and all that."

"To prove my case, sir," the bishop said grimly. "And I am

pleased to say that I have proved it; and that I have information to lay before Scotland Yard. I travelled to my home for a brief visit, to consult my files . . ."

He folded his arms.

"Be prepared, Standish. I am going to place a bomb under you."

"Oh, my God!" said the colonel. "Easy, old fellow. Come, now; I mean to say, we were at school together –"

"Kindly stop misunderstanding me," interposed the bishop, whose face had assumed a sinister expression. "You were never a man of outstanding intelligence, but at least you can understand this. If I were to tell you –"

"Excuse me, sir," said a voice. A large policeman was addressing Colonel Standish. Young Donovan, who was in no mood to be accosted by policemen that day, backed away. "Excuse me," repeated the law. "You are Colonel Standish?"

"Um," said the colonel doubtfully. "Um. Yes. What is it?"

"Will you step up to the chief inspector's office, sir? The chief inspector understands you were waiting down here . . ."

"The chief inspector? What does he want?"

"Couldn't say, sir."

The bishop narrowed his eyes. "I venture to predict," he said, "that something has happened. Come along; we'll all go. It's quite all right, constable. I myself have an appointment with Chief Inspector Hadley."

Young Donovan manifested a strong reluctance to go, but he could not stand up under his father's eye. The constable led them down Derby Street, into the courtyard where the dark-blue police cars stand under the arches, and into the echoing brick building which had the general appearance and smell of a schoolhouse.

In Hadley's unpretentious room on the second floor, the morning sunlight was full of dust motes, and a noise of traffic floated up from the Embankment through the open windows. Behind a flat-topped desk, Donovan saw a compact man, quietly dressed, with cool watchful eyes, a clipped moustache, and hair the color of dull steel. His hands were folded placidly, but there was an unpleasant twist to his mouth as he looked at them. The receiver of the telephone had been detached from its hook and stood on the desk at his elbow. In a chair near by, Dr. Fell was scowling and poking at the carpet with his stick.

The bishop cleared his throat.

"Mr. Hadley?" he inquired. "Allow me to introduce myself. I am –"

"Colonel Standish?" said Hadley, looking at that fussed gentleman. "There is a phone message for you. I took down its contents, but perhaps you had better speak to the inspector yourself . . ."

"Eh? Inspector?" demanded the colonel. "What inspector?"

"Your county official, under you. You are acquainted with a Mr. Septimus Depping?"

"Old Depping? Good Lord, yes. What about him? He lives in the Guest House on my property. He –"

"He has been murdered," said Hadley. "They found him shot through the head this morning. Here's the telephone."

3
THE EIGHT OF SWORDS

For a moment the colonel only stared at him. His broad-checked sport suit looked wildly out of place in that dingy office. "Oh, look here – !" he protested. "Depping? Can't be Depping, demmit. Depping wouldn't get murdered. Lay you a fiver he'd never think of getting murdered. I say –"

Hadley pushed out a chair for him. Growling, the other stamped over to it and took up the telephone. He had the air of one who was determined to quash this nonsense at the beginning.

"Hallo, hallo, hallo . . . Eh? Murch? How are you? Oh, but I mean to say, what's all this rot? . . . But how do you know?"

A pause.

"Well, maybe he was cleaning his gun and it went off," Standish cut in with an air of inspiration. "Knew a fella who did that once. Fella in the Fifty-Ninth. Blew his foot off . . .

"No, demmit. I see that. He couldn't've done it if there's no gun . . . Right, right. You take charge, Murch. Be down this afternoon. Always something, dash it! Right, right. 'Bye."

He hung up the receiver and regarded it gloomily. "I say, look here! I forgot to ask him – !"

"I have all the facts," interposed Hadley, "if you will explain them to me. Please sit down. These gentlemen . . . ?"

Introductions were performed. The Bishop of Mapplcham, who had seated himself with solid grimness on the other side of Hadley's desk, regarded Standish almost in satisfaction. He seemed genuinely concerned, but he could not help mentioning it.

"Much," he said, "much as I regret the passing of any human being, I must point out that I gave warning of this. It does not in any sense allay the blame, or mitigate the deep damnation of his taking-off. Yet –"

Standish got out a handkerchief and mopped his forehead. "Dash it," he said querulously, "how was I to know the poor devil would get himself done in? Something's wrong. You don't know the fella. Why, he even had a share in my firm!"

Hadley, Donovan noticed, was looking from one to the other of them with an irritated expression. But he addressed the bishop deferentially.

"I must thank you, my lord," he interposed, "for your prompt action and assistance in this matter. When we have heard the facts of the Depping murder, I should be pleased if you would explain further –"

"But, confound it, he slid down the bannisters!" protested Standish in an injured tone. "Smack down the bannisters, like a demn'd gaitered avalanche, demmit, and landed in front of Lady Langwych!"

The bishop froze. He swelled. He looked at Standish as once he had looked at a minor deacon who slipped on the altar steps with the collection plate and sent a shower of coppers over the occupants of the first three pews.

"Those circumstances, sir," he said coldly, "I have already explained, to the satisfaction of any normal-witted person. In an unlucky moment I overbalanced myself, and in order to avoid the consequences attendant upon a disastrous fall, I was compelled to clutch at the bannister and thus – er – expedite my descent somewhat. That was all."

The colonel resented these slurs on his intelligence. "Well, then, why did you chuck ink-bottles at the vicar?" he demanded heatedly. "By Jove, I may not be a bishop, but, damme, I never biffed a vicar in the eye in my life! If you call that a sign of intelli –"

Bluish tints were appearing round the bishop's nostrils. He sat bolt upright, breathing hard, and looked round the circle. His eye rested on Dr. Fell, who was making curious noises behind the hand he had pressed over his mouth.

"You spoke, sir?" inquired His Lordship.

"No, my lord, I didn't," rumbled Dr. Fell guardedly.

"Whoosh! Whee! Gurrunk! N-noo." He clapped on his hand again; but he was shaking all over, and there was a moisture in his eyes.

"I am glad to hear it, sir. But you thought something, perhaps?"

"Well, then," said the doctor frankly, "why did you chuck ink-bottles at the vicar?"

"Gentlemen!" roared Hadley, hammering on his desk. He controlled himself with an effort, and set all the papers straight before him to regain his equanimity. "Perhaps," he went on, "I had better outline the facts as I heard them from Inspector Murch, and you, colonel, can supply the blanks . . . First, however: What do you know of this Mr. Depping?"

"Very good sort, old Depping is," Standish replied defensively. "Related to some good friends of mine in India. Turned up one day five or six years ago; visited me; heard I'd the Guest House vacant; liked it; rented it, and been there since . . . Stiffish sort of fella. Fastidious, d'ye see? All books and what not; over my head. Even carried a special cook with him – liked the fancy dishes," the colonel chuckled. "But you had to know him, damme!"

"What do you mean by that?"

Standish assumed a confidential air. "Why, like this. Didn't know the fella ever drank much; only liked half a bottle of Burgundy – fastidious – bah. But I dropped in on him one night, unexpectedly. There was the old boy without his pince-nez, sitting in his study with his feet up on the desk, and three-quarters of a bottle of whiskey gone – whistle-drunk. Ha. Queerest thing I ever saw. I said, 'Er, damme.' He said, 'Heh-heh!' Then he started to sing and roar, and . . . Look here," said the colonel uneasily. "I don't want to say anything against him, eh? But I think he was a secret drinker, and went on those sprees about every two months. Why not? Did him good, I say. Made him human. Why, before I was married I did it myself. Hum," Standish coughed. "Hey, what's the harm, if nobody sees you? He was anxious for nobody to see him. Dignity. After I'd barged in on him, he made that valet of his sit in the hall outside his study door, every night, damme! – every night, in case somebody dropped in and he wasn't ready."

Hadley frowned.

"Did it every occur to you, colonel, that he had something on his mind?"

"Eh? Something on his mind? Tosh, tosh! Nonsense. What would he have on his mind? He was a widower – he'd got pots of money –"

"Go on, please. What else did you know about him?"

Standish fidgeted. "Not much. He didn't – mix, d'ye see? Fell in with Burke, my partner, and invested a dashed sight with us. Said he'd always wanted to read for a publisher, and, by Jove, he did! He took all the heavy stuff nobody else would touch. You know – somebody's treatise on something, that took seven years to write, or whatnot; bundle about six inches thick, all interlined so you can't read it, and author sending you letters every other day. Bah."

"Had he any relatives?"

Standish's red face was complacent, and then grew uneasy. "I say, this will knock the stuffing out of . . . H'm, yes. He'd a daughter. Dem'd fine gel. None of your hussies, d'ye see, that knock you off the road in a two-seater, d'ye see?" said the colonel viciously. "Fine gel, even if she does live in France. Used to worry Depping no end, what she might be up to. He'd kept her in a convent, though, till she was of age, so maybe she liked France, but God knows why. Ha. I said, 'Right, right; time she was married.' And the gel and my son –" he brooded. "There's always something, – eh?"

Hadley's eyes moved about the group. They rested on the bishop, who seemed about to speak; so Hadley went on quickly:

"Then you never knew of an enemy he might have had? I mean, somebody not in your circle, whom you had never met?"

"Good Lord, No!"

"I asked that," Hadley went on, "because of the circumstances surrounding his death. According to Inspector Murch, who has the testimony of his valet and cook, this is what happened . . ."

He rustled his papers. "His valet, Raymond Storer, says that he came back to the Guest House about seven o'clock, after having been out to tea –"

"Had it with us," grunted the colonel. "We were all pretty bucked about the news: his daughter and my son, I mean. He'd got a letter from her the day before, and he and I talked it over night before last. So he came up to tea yesterday and told the whole crowd."

"Did he seem in good spirits?"

"Good Lord, yes. Tickled pink."

Hadley's eyes narrowed. "Did anything occur, then, while he was with you that – upset him?"

Standish had taken out a cigar, and he was lighting it when an uneasy thought seemed to strike him. He screwed round his neck and looked somewhat malevolently at the bishop.

"Hey . . . Look here, I've thought of something!" His boiled eye protruded. "He did seem down in the dumps when he left, by Jove. And that was just after you took him aside and spoke to him. Eh?"

The bishop folded his hands over his umbrella. His heavy jaw had a curious expression of seeming to move about with repressed satisfaction.

"Quite so, my friend," he replied. "I shall tell the chief inspector about it when he has finished outlining the facts . . . Pray go on, sir."

"The valet testified," Hadley went on, after a slight pause, "that he seemed disturbed when he arrived back at the Guest House. He ordered his dinner to be sent to him in the study. And he did not, as seems to have been usual, dress for dinner.

"His dinner was taken up to him about half past eight, when he seemed to have been even more restless. He told the valet that he had work to do, and would be at home to nobody that night. Last night, you remember, was the end of the heat wave. The storm broke late in the evening –"

"Damme, and what a storm!" grunted the colonel. "Henry Morgan got caught in it, and had to walk three miles to –"

Hadley's temper was wearing thin. "If you don't mind, colonel," he said, "it will be rather necessary for you to know these things . . . Shortly after the storm broke, it blew down a wire or something of the sort, and all the lights went out. The valet, who was on the ground floor closing all the windows, rummaged about until he found some candles. He was about to go upstairs with them when there was a knock at the outer door.

"The wind blew out his candle when he opened the door, but when he had got it lighted again, he saw that the caller was nobody he had ever seen before . . ."

"You have a description of the man, Mr. Hadley?" the bishop put in crisply.

"Not a very good one. He was medium-sized, youngish,

dark hair and moustache, loud clothes, and spoke with an American accent."

An expression of grim triumph drew the bishop's neck in folds over his collar. He nodded. "Pray go on, Mr. Hadley."

"The valet was about to shut the door, saying that Mr. Depping could see no one, when the man put his foot in the door. He said" – Hadley glanced at his notes – "he said, 'He'll see me. Ask him.' Inspector Murch was not very clear about this. The man seems to have pointed to some sort of speaking tube."

"Right," said the colonel. "You know. You whistle in 'em, demmit. Then you talk. Depping only used two rooms to live in: study and bedroom. He'd got a speaking tube running up to the study. It was beside the outer door."

"Very well . . . The man was insistent, so Storer spoke to Mr. Depping upstairs. Mr. Depping finally said, 'All right; send him up,' though the man would give no name. But Depping told the valet to be close at hand, in case he should be needed. Storer suggested that he had better go and see to fixing the lights, whereupon Depping said not to mind the lights; that he had plenty of candles in the study, and they would suffice.

"However, Storer woke up the cook, a man named Achille Georges, and sent him out in the rain with a flashlight – under great protest – to find out whether or not the wires had come down. Meantime he was going about shutting the upstairs windows, and he heard Depping and his guest talking in the study. He couldn't hear anything that was said, but they seemed on amiable enough terms. Presently the cook returned, swearing no wire was down. They had a look at the fuse box, and discovered that there had only been a short circuit of some sort, and that plugging in new fuses restored the lights . . ."

For the first time Dr. Fell, who had been sitting abstractedly filling a pipe, rolled up his big head and stared at the chief inspector. His eyes had a curiously cross-eyed look. A long sniff rumbled in his nose.

"I say, Hadley," he muttered, "That's very interesting. It's the first interesting detail you've mentioned so far. Go on, go on."

Hadley grunted. He looked speculatively at the doctor, and went on:

"By that time it was nearly midnight, and Storer wanted to get to bed. He knocked on the study door, told Depping the lights were repaired, and asked whether he could retire. Depping said, 'Yes, yes,' rather impatiently. So he turned in. There was still a terrific thunderstorm going on, and it kept him awake . . . On reflection, this morning, he thinks he heard the sound of a shot about a quarter past twelve; he noticed it at the time, but he thought it must be a part of a thunderclap, and didn't investigate. Inspector Murch says the police surgeon reports a quarter past twelve to be about the time of death.

"The next morning, when Storer went downstairs, he saw over the transom that the lights were still burning in the study. He knocked at the door for some time, and got no answer; the door was locked on the inside. So he got a chair, climbed up, and looked through the transom.

"Depping was lying forward across his reading desk, with the back of his head shot open directly against the bald spot. Finally Storer plucked up enough nerve to push the transom back, crawl through, and get into the room. Depping had been dead for many hours, and there was no weapon to be found."

Young Donovan found his morning-after head rapidly disappearing. This cool, unhurried, gruesome recital roused his wits and his imagination. That wild talk of sliding down bannisters now seemed a part of yesterday night's tippling; it was the first time he had caught the scent of a man hunt, and he was beginning to understand its fascination. There was a silence. With a return of uneasiness he found the bishop's complacent paternal eye fixed upon him.

"This, Mr. Hadley," said the bishop, "is most interesting. And instructive." He waved his hand towards his son. "My son, Mr. Hadley, is a student of criminology like myself. Hem. I shall see presently what good his studies have done him." He became businesslike, and considered. "There are several suggestive points, I fancy. For example –"

"But, demmit! –" protested the colonel, mopping his forehead, "I say – !"

"– for example," the bishop continued coldly, "you say the door of the study was locked on the inside. Did the murderer escape through a window?"

"No. Through another door. There is an upstairs balcony running along the side of the house, and a door opens out on it. This door – which Storer says is generally locked – was partly open." Hadley regarded him without sarcasm, and very patiently. "Now, then. If you will explain your own part in the matter . . . ?"

The bishop nodded, and smiled at Standish in a kindly fashion.

"With pleasure. Fortunately, Mr. Hadley, I can tell you the name of the man who called on Mr. Depping last night. As a matter of fact, I can show you a photograph of him."

While the colonel stared, he took from his inside pocket a sheet of glazed paper, carefully annotated in a small hand, and bearing two photographs, which he handed across to Hadley. Now that he was vindicated, the bishop's sense of humor seemed to reassert itself.

"His name is Louis Spinelli. In case the name fails to stir your memory, Mr. Hadley, there are a few notes on him at the bottom of the sheet."

"Spinelli –" repeated Hadley. His eyes narrowed. "Spinelli – got it! Blackmail. That's the chap. One of Mayfree's mob, who tried to get into England last year –"

"The only one," the bishop corrected, "who did get into England. This man, Mr. Hadley, is too intelligent to try to walk into this country in his own name in character. Allow me to explain."

This, young Donovan reflected, as he had always reflected, was weird language to hear from a bishop of the Church of England. And the odd part of it was that the old boy carried it off. He talked in this vein as easily as he would have spoken from a pulpit. His son had never quite got used to it.

"At the Police Museum in Centre Street, which is similar to your Black Museum here, their exhibits are classified to represent various types of crime, Mr. Hadley. The commissioner gave me permission to bring back a great deal of interesting lore. This man Spinelli was originally a blackmailer, a lone hand; singled out for notice because of a curious peculiarity he had, which caught him before long.

"He is a young Italian-American, about thirty years old, of decent parents and excellent education. I am told that his manners are good, and that he could pass almost anywhere but for one incredible weakness. He cannot resist the temptation to wear the loudest and most conspicuous attire procurable, in addition to rings and jewelry of all kinds. Look at what you can see of it in that photograph. When he was about twenty-three, they caught him and sent him to Sing Sing for ten years."

The bishop paused. His heavy-lidded eyes moved round the group.

"He was out of prison in three. Nobody knows exactly how it was contrived. According to what I can gather, he realized it was unsafe to play alone. He joined up with Mayfree, who was all-powerful at the time, and nobody could touch him. Then –"

Dr. Fell snorted.

"Look here," he protested, "by God and Bacchus, I hope this little affair isn't going to turn into a dull and stodgy piece of gang-history. Hurrumph. Ha. If there's anything I dislike, it's to see the classic outline of a murder case involved in any such monotonous red tape. I was just becoming interested in that question of the lights . . ."

The bishop shook his head.

"You needn't be afraid of that, my dear sir. You may take my word for it that Spinelli is back on his old lone-hand blackmail tactics. Mayfree's organization is broken up. Nobody knows why, and I know it puzzled the commissioner. It began to decline in power some time ago. The leaders tried to leave the country: some to Italy, some to England, some to Germany. They were refused entrance. But, in some fashion, Spinelli got in . . ."

"We'll soon see to that," snapped Hadley, and spoke briefly into the telephone. He looked at the bishop, and went on rather curtly: "You must know; sir, that this is pure guesswork on your part. I take it you never saw Spinelli face to face?"

"As it happens," said the bishop calmly, "I saw him face to face twice. Once in the police line-up at Centre Street, where nothing was proved against him; that was how I happened to hear the details of his case. And again last night. He was coming out of a public house not far from The Grange. Before that I had seen him at a distance, and in the moonlight, under – hum – somewhat unusual circumstances, in the park of The Grange." The bishop coughed. "It was his clothes which started my memory working, and I thought his face was familiar. But last night I saw him as close as I see you now."

"By Gad!" said the colonel, staring at him with a new expression now. "So that was why you cut away this morning, hey?"

"I do not believe that my story would have been listened to with great respect by the chief constable," the bishop answered frostily. "There, gentlemen, is one of the things I have discovered. The question is –"

Hadley tapped his knuckles moodily on the desk. He glanced at the telephone, which refused to ring.

"The question is," he said, "that we shall have to look into this very carefully, but I think somebody is under a misapprehension. This business of American gangsters shooting scholarly country gentlemen in the wilds of Gloucestershire . . . Pah. Confound it. All the same –"

"I do not think," the bishop said deliberately, "that Louis Spinelli did shoot him. This is no time for going into my reasons. But I should like to ask; Mr. Hadley, what you intend to do."

Hadley was blunt. "It's all up to Colonel Standish. He's the chief constable of his county. If he wishes to call in the Yard, he can do so. If he wishes to handle it himself, it's all the same to me. What do you say, colonel?"

"Personally," observed the bishop in a reflective voice, "I should be most happy to lend the police any assistance in my humble power in this unfortunate business." He pulled out all the stops in the organ of his voice. The massive face swelled, and there was a hypnotic gleam in his eye.

"Got it!" exclaimed Standish, with an air of inspiration. He was tactless. He went on: "Got it, by Jove! There's our man – Fell. Look here, demmit. You promised to come down to The Grange and spend a few days, didn't you? I say, old man. You wouldn't let a demnition foreigner come and blow the daylight out of a friend of mine, hey? Hey?" he turned to the bishop. "This is Fell, you know. Fella who caught Cripps and Loganray and the fake preacher what's-his-name. Look here, what about it?"

Dr. Fell, who had got his pipe lighted at last, rumbled and scowled and poked at the floor with his stick.

"For a long time," he said querulously, "I have protested against these utterly commonplace cases. There's no picturesque or bizarre feature about this thing at all. Where's your drama? Where's –"

Hadley regarded him with a sort of dry and bitter satisfaction.

"Yes. Yes, I know. You are in your element," he agreed, "with the sort of fantastic lunacy of a case which doesn't come our way once in a dozen years, ordinarily. People shot with a crossbow bolt at the Tower of London, or thrown off the balcony of a haunted prison. All right! But what about the featureless, prosaic case that we get week in and out, and that's the hardest to solve? Try your hand at one of them. I don't think you'll make so much fun of the police after that . . . Excuse me, gentlemen. This is merely a little private matter."

He hesitated, and then growled.

"Unfortunately, I've got to tell you something else. There is one small point Inspector Murch mentioned which isn't exactly commonplace. It may mean nothing at all, or even be a possession of Depping's; but it certainly isn't commonplace."

'There are several points," said Dr. Fell, "which aren't commonplace, if you must drive me into saying it. H'mf. Ha. No. Well?"

Hadley rubbed his chin uneasily "Near Depping's hand," he went on, glancing down his notes, "there was a card . . . Yes, that's what I said: a card. It was about the size and shape of a playing card, according to this, with a design beautifully painted in water colour. The design consisted of eight figures which looked like swords, set in the form of a star, and a symbol like water running through the middle of it. There you are. Now go ahead and construct your romance." He threw the notes down on his desk.

Dr. Fell's hand stopped with the pipe halfway to his mouth. He puffed a long breath, wheezily, through his moustache, and his eyes grew fixed.

"Eight swords –" he said. "Eight swords: two on the water level, three above, and three below . . . Oh, Lord!

Oh, Bacchus! Oh my ancient hat! Look here, Hadley, this won't do."

He continued to stare at the chief inspector.

"Oh, all right," said Hadley irritably. "You're in your element again. A secret society, I imagine? The Black Hand, or something like it? A sign of vengeance? – Bah!"

"No," said the doctor slowly, "nothing of the sort. I wish it were a simple as that. This is as mediaeval, and devilish, and imaginative, as . . . Yes, by all means. I shall certainly go down to Gloucestershire. It must be a strange place. And I shall spare no pains to meet a murderer who knows about the eight of swords."

He got up, flinging his cape over his shoulder like a bandit, and stumped to the window, where he stood for a moment staring down at the traffic on the Embankment; with his white-plumed mane of hair ruffled, and the glasses coming askew on his nose.

4
"LOOK FOR THE BUTTONHOOK"

Hugh Donovan saw The Grange for the first time late that afternoon. He had lunched with the bishop, Dr. Fell, and Colonel Standish at Groom's in Fleet Street while they discussed plans. The bishop was affable. When he learned that the stout man in the cloak and shovel hat, who had blinked on everybody with such good humor in Hadley's office, was the celebrated schoolmaster whose amiable eye had singled out half-a-dozen of the shrewdest murderers ever to appear at Madam Tussaud's, then the bishop unbent. He was disposed to make his conversation that of one criminologist to another. But he seemed shocked at the doctor's lack of knowledge, and even lack of interest, with regard to modern criminals and up-to-date scientific methods.

Fortunately, he did not try to draw his son into the discussion. And the latter realized, with silent profanity, that he had missed the best opportunity ever put before him to save his face. If he had known on the boat who Dr. Fell was, he could have explained his difficulties to the old codger, and the old codger would have helped him. You had only to listen to Dr. Fell's rumblings and chucklings, and his roaring pronouncements on the world in general, to be aware that nothing would have pleased him more than a game of this sort. Even now it was not too late. And besides, Hugh Donovan reflected, there was a consolation. Undoubtedly he would be admitted to the shrine now, under the most excellent of false pretenses, and see the high priests making their magic in a real case. He had always wanted to do so. Hitherto the bishop would have instructed him to go and roll his hoop, or some other undignified pastime, while papa had a shot at it. But now he theoretically knew all about ballistics, microphotography, chemical analysis, toxicology, and other depressing studies with figures in them. From the one or two glances he had taken at his textbooks, he had been mystified and annoyed. It was a fake. Instead of giving you something juicy in the way of hints about catching axe-killers, all they seemed to do was babble on about something being four-point-two and one-half plus x more than eleven nought-nought-point-two over y hieroglyphic. It was worst than chemistry.

Morosely he listened to the bishop expounding theories to Dr. Fell, and sipped Groom's excellent beer. All the alluring-sounding things were fakes, anyway: like chemistry. He remembered as a boy being fascinated by the toy chemical outfits in the shops. When they bought him one for Christmas, he had been delighted first off to see instructions for making gunpowder. That, he thought, was the stuff. Your mixture produced a fine black compound, very sinister-looking and satisfying. But it was a failure. He put a mound of it under his father's favorite easy-chair; attached a paper wick, lighted it, and awaited results. All it did was flare out like a flashlight-powder, and scorch the bishop's ankles, though his leap showed his athletic training of old. However, Hugh had to admit, better results were obtained with his manufacture of chlorine gas. By a liberal use of ingredients, he had contrived to paralyse the old man for fully five minutes. But, all in all, he was disappointed, and it had been the same with criminology. He much preferred detective work as set forth in the novels of his favourite author: that distinguished and popular writer of detective stories, Mr. Henry Morgan.

He frowned. This reminded him. If he remembered correctly, Morgan's novels were published by the firm of Standish & Burke. He must ask the colonel who Morgan was, and what he was like, "The nom de plume Henry Morgan," his blurbs always announced, in tones of hushed reverence, "conceals the identity of a figure internationally known in the world of letters and politics, who has turned his genius and his knowledge of police procedure to the writing of the roman policier." Donovan was impressed. He pictured the original as a satanic individual in evening clothes, with forked whiskers and piercing eyes, who was always frustrating somebody's plot to pinch the plans of the latest electromagnetic gun.

But he did not dare question Standish now, not only because the colonel seemed moody and distraught at the lunch table, but because he did not want to attract his father's attention at all. The Bishop of Mappleham was busy with Dr. Fell.

So they left London in Standish's car early in the afternoon, and the bishop was still explaining how his efforts had been misdirected by unfortunate circumstances. How (he freely admitted) he had been mistaken in thinking that Hilda Doffit, a housemaid, was the notorious and light-fingered Piccadilly Jane; and had been led thereby into several equivocal positions. Then, on the night he genuinely did see Louis Spinelli in the geranium beds, his conduct had been misinterpreted by Colonel Standish, due to somebody's idiotic prank at playing ghost on the Reverend George Primley.

This prank, it must be confessed, roused the interest and approval of Hugh Donovan. He looked forward to meeting the person, whoever it might be, who had taken advantage of a poltergeist's notoriously rowdy habits to throw ink at the vicar. But it seemed evident that Colonel Standish was not yet satisfied, and had his own secret doubts about the bishop's conduct.

They made good time through the countryside, and at four o'clock they had turned off the London road at a village called Bridge Eight. It was a hot, still afternoon. The road wound through dips and hollows, overhung by maple trees; and bees from the hedgerows were always sailing in through the windscreen and driving Standish wild. Towards the west Donovan could see the smoky red roofs of the suburbs round Bristol; but this was rural scenery of the thatched-roof and cowbell variety. Here were rolling meadows, frothing yellow with buttercups, and occupied by cows that looked as stolid as a nudist colony. Here were rocky commons, and unexpected brooks, and dark coppices massed on the hillsides. And, as usual when he ventured into the country, Donovan began to get good resolutions. He breathed deeply. He removed his hat and let the sunlight burn his hair to an uncomfortable state. This was health.

He could look back on New York with a mild pity. What asses people were! To be shut into a hot apartment, with twenty different radio programs roaring in your ear; with every light shaking to the thunder of parties on each floor; with children yelling along Christopher Street, and papers blown in gritty over-hot winds, and the rumble of the Sixth Avenue L rising monotonously over the clatter of traffic. Sad. Very sad. Already he could picture his poor friends staggering in and out of cordial shops; wasting their substance by depositing nickels in the slot machines, pulling the lever; and getting only a row of lemons for their pains. Tonight, round Sheridan Square, one poor friend would be measuring out gin drops, with the fierce concentration of a scientist, into a glass jug containing half-a-gallon of alcohol and half-a-gallon of water. Others would be thirstily waiting to drink it, poor devils. Then they would forget to eat dinner; and make love to somebody else's girl, and get a bust in the eye. Sad.

Whereas he . . . The bishop was saying something about Thomas Aquinas, and his son eyed him benevolently as the car sped on. Whcreas he . . .

There should be no more of that. He would rise with the thrush (at whatever hour that exemplary bird does begin raising hell outside your window). He would go for long walks before breakfast. He would decipher inscriptions on gravestones, and meditate on the fallen tower, like those fellows who write the pleasant essays, and who never have any base impulse to go and get plastered at the nearest pub.

And he would listen to quaint bits of philosophy from rustics – those fellows who always tell the local legends to the writers. "Aye," he could hear an old graybeard saying, "aye, it were twenty year come Michaelmas that poor Sally Fevverley drownded herself in yon creek, and on moonlight nights . . ." Excellent. He could already see himself leaning on his ash stick in the twilight as the story was told, looking with sad eyes at the brook, and musing on the villainy of those who drink alcohol-and-water in cities, and then come out and seduce poor girls all over the countryside, and make them drown themselves in brooks. He had worked himself into a high state of virtue, when he was suddenly roused by a hail from the roadside.

"What ho!" cried a voice. "What ho!"

He roused himself, putting on his hat again to shield his eyes from the sun, as the car slowed down. They had come through a cluster of houses, the largest of which was a white-washed stone pub bearing the sign of the Bull, and turned to the left up a long low hill. Midway up on the right was a little square-towered church, a miniature of great age, with flowers round it and the gravestones built up close to its porch. At the crest of the hill the road ran straight for a quarter of a mile; and, far away to the left, Donovan could see acre upon acre of parkland, enclosed along the road by a low stone wall. In the middle of the park lay a vast, low stone house, with its eastern windows glowing against the gold sky.

But the hail had come from closer at hand. On the opposite side of the road, just past the top of the hill, stood a timbered house of the sort that used to be called black-and-white. Its frontage was enclosed by a box hedge as high as a tall man's head. An iron gate in the hedge bore a name plate in small, severe black letters, HANGOVER HOUSE. Leaning on this gate, and gesturing at them with a pipe, stood the lounging man who had called out.

"What ho!" he repeated. "What ho!"

Donovan noticed that his father closed disapproving jaws, but the colonel uttered a grunt of pleasure or relief and swung the car towards the gate. The amiable figure proved to be a lean young man, not many years older than Donovan himself, with a long face, a square jaw, a humorous eye, and tortoise-shell glasses pulled down on a long nose. He was dressed in a loud blazer; soiled gray trousers, and a khaki shirt open at the neck. With one hand he shook the ashes out of his dead pipe, and the other held a glass containing what looked very much like a cocktail.

The colonel stopped the car. "Don't go on saying, 'What ho,' demmit," he complained. "We can't stay. We're in a hurry. What do you want?"

"Come on in," invited the other hospitably. "Have a cocktail. I know it's early, but have one anyway. Besides, there's news. He turned his head over his shoulder; and called, "Madeleine!"

At the sight of the amber-brown contents of that glass, Donovan's feelings underwent a sudden convulsion. On the lawn beyond the hedge he could see an enormous beach umbrella propped up over a table bearing materials which reminded him forcibly of New York. And, unless his eyes were deceiving him, the sides of that great nickelled cocktail-shaker were pale with moisture. A nostalgia swept over him. He was aware that ice for drinks was an almost unknown commodity in rural England. At the young man's hail, a girl's head appeared round the edge of the umbrella and gave everybody a beaming smile.

Getting up from a deck chair, she hurried to the gate. She was a dark-eyed, bouncing little piece of the sort known as a Japanese brunette; and that she was sturdy and admirably fashioned was rendered obvious by the fact that she wore beach pyjamas and one of those short silk coats with the flowers on them. She hung over the gate, inspected them all pleasantly, raised her eyebrows, and said, "Hullo!" as though she were very pleased with herself for thinking of it.

Colonel Standish coughed when he saw the pyjamas, looked at the bishop, and went on hastily:

"Don't think everybody knows everybody. Hum. This is Dr. Fell – detective fella, you know; heard me speak of him, hey? – come down from Scotland Yard. And Mr. Donovan, the bishop's son . . . I want you to meet," he said, rather proudly, "Henry Morgan, the writin' fella. And Mrs. Morgan."

Donovan stared as the introductions were acknowledged. Not even his formidable father could keep him quiet now.

"Excuse me," he said, "you are Henry Morgan?"

Morgan wryly scratched the tip of his ear. "Um," he said in an embarrassed way. "I was afraid of that. Madeleine wins another bob. You see, the bet is that if you say that to me, I pay her a shilling. If, on the other hand, you look at her and make some remark about 'The Old, Bold Mate of Henry Morgan,' then I win it. However . . ."

"Hoora!" gurgled Madeleine delightedly. "I win. Pay me." She regarded Dr. Fell and said with candor: "I like you." Then she looked at Donovan and added with equal impartiality: "I like you too."

Dr. Fell, who was chuckling in the tonneau, lifted his stick in a salute. "'Thank you, my dear. And I'm naturally pleased to meet you both. You see –"

"Hold on a bit!" Donovan interrupted with pardonable rudeness. "You are the creator of John Zed, diplomatist-detective?"

"Um."

Another question, which could not be kept down despite his father's eye, boiled to the surface. He pointed to the glass in the other's hand and demanded: "Martinis?"

Morgan brightened eagerly.

"And how!" agreed the creator of John Zed, diplomatist-detective. "Have one?"

"Hugh!" interposed the bishop in a voice that could quell the most rebellious chapter, dean and all. "We do not wish to take up your time, Mr. Morgan. Doubtless all of us have more important matters to which we can attend." He paused, and his furry brows drew together. "I hope I shall not be misunderstood, my friend, if I add that in the solemn presence of death your attitude seems to me to be somewhat reprehensibly irreverent. Start the car, Standish."

"Sorry; sir;" said Morgan, looking at him meekly over his spectacles. "I mean to say – sorry. Not for a moment would I in my irreverence stay your headlong rush to get at the corpse. All I wanted to tell you was –"

"Don't you mind him, bishop," said Madeleine warmly. "Don't you mind him. You can slide down our bannisters as much as you like, and nobody shall stop you. There! I'll even get a big cushion for you to land on, though I expect," she added, scrutinizing him with a thoughtful air; "you won't need it much, will you?"

"Angel sweetheart," said Morgan dispassionately, "shut your trap. What I was about to say was –"

Madeleine gurgled. "But he won't, will he?" she protested, swinging on the gate. "And what's more, I wouldn't be mean like you, when you said you'd put the goldfish bowl there instead of a cushion. I mean, that isn't nice, is it?"

"Dawn of my existence," said her husband querulously, "all this is beside the point. Whether nature in her abundance has equipped His Reverence with a lower dorsal frontage sufficiently spacious to withstand the shocks of sliding down bannisters all over England, is not only beside the point, but savors of indelicacy." He looked at Standish, and his face suddenly clouded. He moved the loose spectacles up and down his nose, uneasily. "Look here, sir. We don't – well, the bishop is right. We don't take this very seriously, I admit. If it weren't for what Betty would feel about it, I shouldn't be very much cut up about it. I know; de mortuis, and all that. But after all, sir – old Depping was rather a blister wasn't he?"

Standish punched at the steering-wheel, hesitantly.

"Oh, I say!" he protested.

"Right," said Morgan in a colorless voice. "I know it's none of my business. All I wanted to tell you was that I was to look out for you when you arrived and tell you that Inspector Murch has gone home for something to eat; he said to tell you he would be back directly . . . He allowed me to prowl about the Guest House with him, and we found a couple of things . . ."

"And may I ask, young man," said the bishop, stung, "on what authority you did that?"

"Well, sir, I suppose it was rather like your own. There wasn't much to be seen there. But we did find the gun. I should say a gun, though there isn't much doubt it's the one. The autopsy hasn't been performed, but the doctor said it was a thirty-eight bullet. The gun is a thirty-eight Smith & Wesson revolver . . . You will find it," said Morgan, in the negligent manner which would have been employed by John Zed, diplomatist-detective, "in the right-hand drawer of Depping's desk."

"Eh?" demanded Standish. "In Depping's desk? What the devil is it doing there?"

"It's Depping's gun," said Morgan; "we found it there." He noticed that he had a cocktail in his hand, and drank it off. Then he balanced the glass on the edge of the gate, thrust his hands deep into the pockets of the red-and-white blazer, and tried to assume a mysterious profundity like John Zed's. But it was difficult. For the first time Donovan saw the excitability of his nature. He could imagine him striding up and down the lawn with a cocktail in one hand, shifting his spectacles up and down his nose, and hurling out theories to a beaming wife. He said:

"There's no doubt it was his gun, sir. His name on a little silver plate on the grip. And his firearms license was in the same drawer, and the numbers tallied . . . By the way, two shots had been recently fired."

Dr. Fell bent forward abruptly. He made a queer figure against the hot green landscape, in his black cloak and shovel hat.

"Two shots?" he repeated. "So far as we have heard, there was only one. Where was the other bullet?"

"That's the point, sir. We couldn't discover it. Both Murch and I are willing to swear it isn't lodged in the room anywhere. Next –"

"I am afraid we are wasting a great deal of time," the bishop interposed. "All this information can be obtained officially from Inspector Murch. Shall we proceed, Standish?"

There were times, Donovan thought, when his old man was lacking in ordinary courtesy. Still, these constant references to sliding down bannisters must be wearing on his temper; and Madeleine Morgan seemed to be pondering some new remark about cushions. Dr. Fell rumbled something angrily, glaring at the bishop, but Standish was under the influence of that cold ecclesiastical eye, and obediently pressed his starter.

"Right," said Morgan amiably. "Break away as soon as you can," he suggested to Donovan, "and come down and try one of our Martinis . . ." He leaned over the gate as the car backed round. He looked at the bishop. And then up rose Old John Zed himself, to speak in a tone of thunder across the road. "I don't know what deductions you will make, Your Reverence," said Old John Zed, but I'll give you a tip. Look for the buttonhook."

The car slewed round slightly as it sped on. Standish goggled.

"Eh?" he inquired. "What was that he said, hey? What button-hook? What's a demnition button-hook got to do with it?"

"Nothing whatever," said the bishop. "It is merely some of that insolent young man's nonsense. How sensible people can read such balderdash by a young man who knows nothing of criminology, is more than –"

"Oh, look here!" warmly protested the colonel, whose favorite reading was the saga of John Zed. "Murder on the Woolsack, eleventh printing comprising 79,000 copies. Who Shot the Prime Minister? sixteenth printing comprising – well, I don't remember, but a dem'd lot, demmit. Burke told me. Besides," added Standish, using a clinching argument, "my wife likes him."

Dr. Fell, who had been cocking a thoughtful eye at the house along the left, seemed to repress a chuckle. He cast a surreptitious glance at the bishop, and observed dreamily:

"I say, you are in a most unfortunate position, I fear. The impression seems to be widespread that your conduct is at times, humf, a trifle erratic. Heh. Heh-heh–heh. Sir, I should be careful; very careful. It would be unfortunate, for instance, if other lapses occurred."

"I don't think I understand."

"Well, the colonel and I would be compelled to put you under restraint. It would exclude you from the case. It might get into the newspapers. Listen, Your Grace. . ." Dr. Fell's red face was very bland, and his eyes opened wide.

"Let me warn you to walk very softly. Attend to those who want to speak, and what they say; and brush nothing aside as unimportant. Eh?"

Dr. Fell, it was obvious, had been struck with an idea which he continued to ponder while the car turned through the lodge gates of The Grange. The iron gates were shut, and at the porter's lodge a large policeman was trying to maintain a Jovian unconsciousness of the little group of idlers that had gathered outside. He opened the gates at Standish's hail.

"Tell you what," said Standish, "I'll drive on up to the house and tell 'em to make ready for you and get your luggage out. You fellows go along to the Guest House and look about. Join you shortly. The bishop knows where it is."

The bishop assented with great eagerness. He asked the policeman, sharply, whether anything had been touched, looked round him with satisfaction, and then sniffed the air like a hunter as he strode off across the lawn. The three of them, his son reflected, must have made a queer picture. Up beyond them, at the end of a shallow slope, the gables of the low, severely plain house were silhouetted on the yellow sky. Except for a border of elms on either side of the driveway curving up to it, all the ornamental trees were massed behind The Grange in an estate that must have covered eight thousand acres. The Grange was restored Tudor in design, full of tall windows, bearded in ivy, and built on three sides of a rectangle with the open side towards the road. It had almost the stolid aspect of a public building; and must, Donovan reflected, take an enormous income to keep up. Standish could certainly be no army man retired on half-pay.

The Guest House lay on the southern fringe of the park, in the clearing of a coppice which gave it a deserted, mournful, and rather ominous appearance. It was in a hollow of somewhat marshy ground, with a great ilex tree growing behind it, so that it seemed much smaller than it was. If The Grange itself was of plain design, some domestic architect seemed to have spread himself to make this place an unholy mongrel from all styles of building, and to give it as many geegaws as a super-mighty pipe organ in a super-mighty cinema theatre. It looked as though you could play it. Upon a squat stone house rose scrolls, tablets, stops, and fretwork. Every window – including those of the cellar – was protected by a pot-bellied grille in the French fashion. It was encircled by an upper and lower balcony, with fancy iron railings. Midway along the upper balcony Donovan could see on the west side of the square the door by which the murderer must have escaped. It still stood ajar, and a flight of stairs near it led down to the lower balcony. The very bad taste of the house had a sinister look. Despite the sunlight, it was gloomy in the coppice, and the stickiness of last night's rain had not disappeared.

The bishop was leading them up a brick walk, which divided at the house and encircled it, when he stopped suddenly. At the side of the walk that ran round the west end, they could see the figure of a man kneeling and staring at something on the ground.

The bishop almost said, "Aha!" He strode forward. The kneeling figure raised its head with a jerk.

"But they're my shoes!" it protested. "Look here, confound it. They're my shoes!"

5
SOMEBODY'S FOOTPRINT

"Good afternoon, Morley," said the bishop imperturbably. "Gentlemen, allow me to present Morley Standish, Colonel Standish's son . . . What's this about your shoes?"

Morley Standish got up, brushing the knees of his trousers. He was earnest, stocky, and thirty-five; a younger, somewhat more intelligent-looking edition of his father. You could see how he had been molded by that association. He had a heavy, not-unhandsome face, and one of those moustaches recently associated with serious purpose by Herr Hitler. Though he wore a loose sport coat, it was of sombre color, and a black tie apparently from some vague idea of doing the correct thing by the late father of his fiancée. You could almost take it as a symbol of him: correct, O.T.C., hesitantly religious; yet wanting to unbend, and with a streak of impetuousness allied with humor.

"I seem to have blurted out something," he said, after a pause. Donovan could not tell whether it was anger or humor in his eyes. He looked from one to the other of them. "Ever have that experience? Someone startles you by coming on you unexpectedly, and you crack out with the thing that's in your mind?"

The half-smile faded off his face.

"Murch told me, sir, that you and my father knew all about this business. It's pretty bad. I've wired Betty the news, before she should see it in a paper. And I'll attend to all the arrangements. But Murch said you'd probably call in Scotland Yard, and we mustn't touch the body until then. If these gentlemen" – he looked at Donovan and Dr. Fell – "are from the Yard, I hope they'll make a quick examination and let the under-taker carry on."

The bishop nodded. He dearly thought very highly of the practical Morley Standish. "This," he said, "is Dr. Fell, whom my – hum – my good friend the chief inspector sent down to assist us. Our investigation should make excellent headway with him . . ."

He nodded with some stiffness towards the doctor, who blinked amiably upon Standish. "And this is my son, Hugh, of whom you have heard me speak. You are in charge, doctor. Shall we go into the house? You will find Mr. Standish an admirable person to tell us the facts."

"Quite," said Dr. Fell. He jerked a thumb towards the house. "This valet fellow – is he there now?"

Standish had been looking at him with a correct concealment of surprise which thus made itself evident. He had clearly expected Donovan to be a young police official of some description, and he was jarred a little to see Dr. Fell was the man in charge.

"Yes," he said. "Would you care to go in? The cook, Achille, refused to stay. He says there are ghosts in the house. But Storer will stay as long as he is needed."

"No hurry," said Dr. Fell easily. He indicated the few steps which led up to the side entrance of the veranda. "Sit down, Mr. Standish. Make yourself comfortable. Smoke?"

"Surely," observed the bishop, "if we went inside –"

"Rubbish," said Dr. Fell. He settled matters by lowering himself with some difficult on an ornamental bench opposite. Morley Standish, with an expression of great gravity, sat down on the steps and produced a pipe. For a time Dr. Fell was silent, poking at the brick wall with his stick, and wheezing with the labor of having sat down. Then he said with an off-hand air:

"Who do you think killed Depping, Mr. Standish?"

At this unorthodox beginning the bishop folded his arms and looked resigned. It was curiously as though Dr. Fell were on trial, sitting there big and abstracted, with the birds bickering in the trees behind him. Morley Standish looked at him with slightly closed eyes.

"Why," he said, "I don't suppose there's much doubt of that, is there? The chap who came to visit him – the one with the American accent – ?" He frowned inquiringly.

"Spinelli," put in the bishop complacently.

"For God's sake," said Dr. Fell, turning to glare, "shut up, will you? I happen to be in charge here."

Morley Standish jumped. There was a puzzled and somewhat shocked expression on his face. But he answered bitterly:

"You know his name, do you? Well, that reminds me. Bishop Donovan was right. If we'd had the sense to listen to him when he first told us about the fellow, this mightn't have happened. With all my father's good points –" He hesitated. "Never mind. We could have prevented it."

"I wonder," said Dr. Fell. "What traces of him have you found today? I gather Spinelli hasn't been tracked down?"

"Not so far as I know. But I haven't seen Murch since noon."

"H'mf. Now, Mr. Standish, if Spinelli killed your prospective father-in-law, why do you suppose he did it? What connection was there between a studious, harmless old gentleman like Depping, and an American blackmailer with a police record?"

Standish got his pipe lighted, and twitched the match away before he answered. His heavy face had grown more stolid. "I say, Mr. – what was it – oh – Dr. Fell, why ask me? I don't know any more than – well, my father, say. Why ask me?"

"Did you and Miss Depping ever discuss him, for instance?"

"Ah," said Standish. He looked straight at the doctor. "That's rather a personal question, you know. Still, it's easily answered. Betty – Miss Depping – scarcely knew her father at all. And she doesn't remember her mother. From the age of seven or eight she was in a convent at Trieste. Then she was put in one of those super-strict French boarding schools. When she was eighteen she – well, hang it, she's got spirit, and she couldn't stand it; so she broke out and ran away . . ." First Morley Standish's correct face looked somewhat embarrassed, and then he grinned. "Ran away, by Jove! Damned good, eh?" he demanded, and brushed at his Hitler moustache, and slapped his leg. "Then the old ba – Mr. Depping permitted her to live with a hired companion (one of those courtesy aunts) in Paris. All this time she only saw him at long intervals. But she wrote to him at some address in London. About five years ago, when she was twenty, he suddenly turned up and said he'd retired from business. The funny part of it was that though he was always worrying about her, and what mischief she might be up to, he never asked her to live with him –" In full flight Standish checked himself. "I say, you needn't repeat all this, need you? That is, I know more about it than my father, I admit, but . . ."

"Suggestive," said the bishop, drawing down the corners of his mouth. "Very suggestive, doctor. I recall a similar case at Riga in 1876; another in Constantinople in 1895; and still a third in – hum – in St. Louis in 1909."

"You do get about, don't you?" inquired Dr. Fell admiringly. He studied Morley Standish. "What business was Depping in?"

"Oh, something in the City, I believe."

"Um. It's a curious thing," grunted Dr. Fell, scowling, "that whenever a man wants to give somebody a character of sound and colorless respectability, he says that he's something in the City. Why did Depping have a bad character hereabouts?"

Standish's manner became defensive and uncomfortable in a way that was reminiscent of his father.

"Bad character?" he repeated. "What do you mean?"

There was a pause. Dr. Fell only shook his head deprecatingly and continued to look at Standish in a benevolent fashion. For a still longer time he kept on staring, his massive head on one side.

"Er," said Morley Standish, and cleared his throat, "I mean, what makes you think he did have a bad character?"

He spoke with a certain weak truculence, and the doctor nodded.

"Well, one person, at least, appears to think he is a blister, and even your staunch parent didn't contradict it. Besides, you know, you yourself referred to him as an 'old ba – .' Eh?"

"What I say is this," replied Morley, hurriedly and defensively. "What I say is this. While it would have been more dignified, and all that, all the same you've got to look at it from an impersonal point of view. The only reason why anybody thought it was funny, or else disliked it, was because he liked to pay attention to girls only my sister's age, when he was past sixty years old. Maybe his idea of gallantries was ridiculous, but all the same," argued Morley, "it was because he was so prim and studious and fastidious that you couldn't associate it with him. It seemed a little – well, obscene."

Having delivered himself of these sentiments, as though he had been quoting a lesson, Standish bit hard on the stem of his pipe and regarded Dr. Fell in some defiance.

"Old rip with the ladies, was he?" inquired the doctor genially. "I don't suppose he did any real harm, did he?"

Standish's grim mouth slackened. "Thanks," he said in some relief. "I was afraid you'd take it – well, seriously, you know. Harm? Good Lord, no; but he annoyed a lot of people . . . He especially used to put Hank Morgan's back up. A funny thing, because there are few people more broad-minded than Hank. But I think it was Mr. Depping's pedantic mathematics-master way of talking that really annoyed him. This morning, when we got the news, Hank and Madeleine and my sister Patricia and I were having a game of doubles. The tennis courts aren't very far from here, and the first thing we knew Storer came running up the hill, and clawed at the wire, and babbled something about finding Depping dead in his study. Hank only said, 'No such luck,' and didn't even stop serving."

Dr. Fell was silent for a long time. The sun had drawn lower beyond the coppice, and the ugly deformities of the Guest House glittered in level shafts of light.

"We'll come back to that presently," he said, making a gesture of irritation. "Hum, yes. I think we had better go up and look at the body of this very odd combination . . . But first, what was the remark you made when you arrived: something about 'They're my shoes'? You were examining –" He pointed with his stick to the edge of the brick path near the steps.

All this time, consciously or unconsciously, Morley Standish had been keeping one large foot dangling over a tuft of grass in the clayey soil beside the steps. He moved it now. He got up, large and stocky, and scowled.

"It's a footprint," he said. "I may as well tell you it must have been made with one of my shoes."

The bishop, who throughout the recital had been politely trying to see past that blocking foot, strode forward and bent over it. It was close to the edge of the brick path, its toe pointing towards the steps, as though somebody had strayed slightly off the path with the left foot. The impression was sharp and fairly shallow, with a tuft of grass trampled into it: a large square-toed shoe, having some faint but distinct markings in the heelprint like an eight-sided star. Whitish traces clung inside the print and along its edges.

"You see what happened," Standish explained uneasily. "There was the devil of a rain last night, a footprint would be effaced. But that thing is smack in the shelter of those steps . . . I say, don't look at me. I didn't make it. But look here."

He swivelled round and lowered one foot gently into the lines of the impression.

"I must beg of you, Morley," said the bishop, "not to damage that print. If you will step aside . . . ? I have made quite a study of footprints, gentlemen. Hugh! Come here and let me have your assistance in examining this. We are fortunate. Clay, doctor, is by far the most accurate substance for recording an impression. Sand and snow, contrary to the popular impression, are almost valueless, as Dr. Hans Gross points out. The forward impulse of the foot in sand, for example, will lengthen the print anywhere from half an inch to two inches out of its natural dimension. As to breadth – stand aside, please, Morley," He looked round with a tight smile. "We shall certainly have an interesting exhibit to show Inspector Murch when he returns."

"Oh, Murch found it," said Standish, breaking off his effort to lower his shoe gingerly into the print. "He found it right enough. He and Hank Morgan got some plaster-of-Paris and made a cast of it. I knew they'd found a print, but I didn't even go to look at it until this afternoon."

"Oh, ah," said the bishop. He stopped, and rubbed his mouth. "Indeed! That was more of young Morgan's work, I dare say. Unfortunate. Most unfortunate."

Morley stared.

"You're jolly well right it's unfortunate!" he agreed, his voice booming out with sudden nervousness and annoyance. "Look here. It fits. I'm the only person hereabouts with a shoe as large as that. Not only that, but I can even identify the pair of shoes . . . I'll swear I wasn't mucking about here last night, but you can see for yourself that's a fairly fresh print. I wonder if Murch is thinking – ?"

Dr. Fell's voice struck in so quietly and easily that Standish paused. The doctor had lumbered over to blink at the impression in his vague, nearsighted way.

"How can you identify the shoes?" he inquired.

"By the marks on the heel. It's a pair I chucked away . . . To understand that," explained Standish, pushing back his hat, "you'd have to know my mother. She's one of the best, mother is, but she gets notions. She is afflicted by the power of suggestion. The moment she hears of a new food over the wireless, we get it till we choke. If she hears of a new medicine for any ailment whatever, she becomes convinced that everybody in the house has got the ailment, and doses us all silly. Well," said Morley, with brooding resignation, "not very long ago she read a spirited article in a magazine about, Why submit to the tyranny of the cobbler? It proved what a difference you could make to your household budget if you bought rubber heels at cost and tacked 'em on your own shoes when the old heels wore out. It impressed her so much that she sent to town for great quantities of rubber heels; thousands of rubber heels; God knows how many rubber heels. I never knew there were so many rubber heels in the world. The house was swamped in 'em. They turned up everywhere. You couldn't even open the medicine chest in the bathroom without getting a shower of rubber heels. But worst of it was that you were supposed to nail 'em on yourself – that was a part of the diabolical design, to teach the British household a useful art. The result was –"

"Kindly come to the point, Morley," said the bishop; "I was about to go on explaining –"

"The result was," went on Morley, embarked on a grievance, "that you either soaked the nail clear through the shoe so that you couldn't walk on it, or put it in so loose that the heel would come off just as you started downstairs. I never heard my governor use such language before or since. Finally we rebelled. I told Kennings to take the only pair I'd mutilated and throw it away . . . And that's it," he declared, pointing to the print. "I'd know it anywhere; the heel was too large for the shoe anyhow. All I'm sure of is that somebody is using them. But why?"

The bishop pinched at his lower lip. He said:

"This, doctor, begins to grow serious. It seems to indicate that somebody at The Grange itself is trying to throw suspicion on Morley . . ."

"I wonder," grunted Dr. Fell.

". . . for it is obvious to the most elementary intelligence," the other went on benevolently, "that Morley himself never wore them. Stand over there, Morley, and put your foot down in the clay beside that print. Now walk in it there. You see the difference?"

There was a pause. Morley examined the print he had made.

"What ho," said Morley, and whistled. "I see. You mean the print I make is too deep."

"Exactly. You are very much heavier than the person who stepped there, and your own impression is half an inch deeper. You follow me, doctor?"

Dr. Fell seemed to be paying no attention. He had lumbered away, thoughtfully, his shovel hat pulled down on his forehead; and he turned again to examine the Guest House with a curiously blank, cross-eyed stare. "I'm very much afraid," he said, "that you miss the point of that footprint altogether . . . When did you last see those shoes, Mr. Standish?"

"See – ? Oh, months ago. I gave them to Kennings."

"And what did Kennings, whoever he is, do with them?"

"He's the first footman. He runs mother's junk closet. He . . . I say!" Morley snapped his fingers. "Got it! Ten to one he put 'em in the junk closet. That's mother's idea. It's for the heathen. Whatever there is in the house that we can't possibly want, it's chucked into the junk closet, and once or twice a year mother sorts everything out with the idea of sending it to the heathen. After six months' cool reflection, however, she generally decides she can find a use for most of the things that have been thrown away, so the heathen don't profit much after all."

"And this junk closet is accessible to everybody?"

"Oh, yes. It's a room, really," Morley glanced at the bishop, and one of his eyelids drooped. "It's next door to the room, by the way, where that poltergeist of ours made such a murderous attack on the Vicar of Pucklechurch."

The bishop looked at Dr. Fell, and Dr. Fell looked at the bishop. Hugh Donovan had an uneasy feeling that nonsense was beginning to assume the colors of ugly purpose.

"Let's go inside," said Dr. Fell abruptly, and turned. They went round to the front of the house. The marshy smell had grown strong with the declining sun, and gnats flickered in the shadow of the porch. All the dull-red blinds were drawn on the lower floor. Poking at the bell push with his stick, Dr. Fell glanced along the line of windows.

"There's more in this business," he said, "than shoes or poltergeists, or even murder. The queerest riddle of all is old Depping himself. H'mf. Look at this atrocity!" He rapped the stone wall of the house. "Here's a man noted for his fastidiousness of taste in dress, in letters, and in bearing. He is a gourmet who employs a special cook to prepare him dishes that must be exactly right. And yet he lives in a house like this! He's an austere fellow with the nicest sort of taste in wines, and yet he goes on periodical whooping sprees of secret drinking with a servant posted outside the door so that nobody may disturb him. In addition to this, he interrupts periods of hard study to go slobbering after girls young enough to be his granddaughters. This is bad. There's something mad and unholy about it, and this ascetic old satyr is the worst of all. Archons of Athens! – behold Hadley's idea of a nice, featureless, commonplace case. The eight of swords is only an item . . . Ah!"

The door, whose upper panel was made of red-and-black chequered glass, glowed out eerily as somebody switched on a light inside. It was opened by a thin man with a melancholy nose and an air of having looked on all the follies of earth without any particular surprise.

"Yes, sir?" said the nose; he talked through it.

"We're from the police," said Dr. Fell. "Take us upstairs. – Your name is Storer, isn't it?"

"Yes, sir. You will wish," observed the nose, exactly as though it spoke of a living person, "to see the corpse. Please come this way."

Now that they were approaching it, Hugh Donovan felt a nauseous reluctance to see Depping's body at close range. Nor did he like the hall through which Storer led them. It was without windows, and smelt of furniture polish: a mysterious circumstance, inasmuch as none of the heavy dark furniture ever seemed to have been polished. Two meagre-looking electric bulbs descended on a long chandelier from the high ceiling. On the floor and staircase lay matting which had once been yellow, and there were ghostly black portieres over several doors. A speaking tube projected from the wall beside one of them; Dr. Fell inspected it before he followed the procession upstairs.

The study was the front room on the west side. Storer seemed to resist an inclination to knock before he pushed open the door.

A large room with a high ceiling. In the wall facing the door by which they entered, Donovan could see the door to the balcony: its glass panel chequered, like the lower one, in red-and-black glass. It was flanked by two windows, their black velvet curtains drawn back, with the pot-bellied iron grilles outside. Three more windows were in the right-hand wall at the front, furnished in a similar fashion. And all the windows were open.

The trees round the Guest House were so thick that only a greenish twilight fell into the study, but it was sufficient to show dully the room's chief exhibit.

Hugh Donovan never forgot his first sight of violent death. In the left-hand wall – as he faced the door to the balcony – was a low fireplace of white marble. Three or four feet out from it, the late Dr. Septimus Depping lay forward across a flat-topped desk, with his face turned away from the newcomers and his back to the fireplace. He was leaning out of a low leather easy-chair. His legs were doubled back against it. His right arm hung down limp, shoulder on the edge of the desk, and his left rested out across the blotter. The late Mr. Depping wore an old-fashioned smoking jacket and a high collar; his trousers were evening trousers, and he wore black socks and patent-leather shoes. But, most prominent of all, the watchers could see the back of the head that was turned towards them. The hair was well-brushed, scanty, and grizzled-gray. On the crown there had once been a small bald spot, which was now scorched black where the bullet had been fired close against the head.

It was all quietly horrible, the more so because the birds were piping outside, and an indifferent robin was regarding something else from the top of the balcony railing beyond one window.

Hugh Donovan tried to look at something else also. He noticed that even his formidable father was much more human, and not quite so ghoulishly eager as before. Hugh tried to shake up his wits as he would have shaken up a medicine, sharply for sooner or later he would be required to express an opinion. But in the terrible grimness of that picture he did not understand how anybody could be cool and scientific. He peered round the study. The walls were lined with books, even between the window spaces, in neat sectional cases. Everything was scrupulously neat. On a side-table, with a straight chair drawn up before it, was a dinner tray covered by a white cloth; a silver bowl of roses, still unwithered, stood beyond it.

Donovan's eyes moved back, only skirting the desk. A leather chair had been drawn up facing the desk, as though X had been sitting there for a chat. There was a standing ashtray, without ashes or stubs, beside it. A metal filing cabinet stood against the desk; a small table bearing a covered typewriter; and another standing ashtray. Over the desk hung a single powerful electric bulb in a plain shade, which, with the exception of a bridge lamp in one corner, appeared to be the only means of illumination. On the large clean desk blotter was a wire basket containing several bundles of manuscript to which were clipped blue type-written sheets; a tray of pens and colored pencils, an inkpot, a box of clips holding down several sheets of stamps, and a large silver-mounted photograph of a girl. Finally, almost in a line with the chairs of Depping and X, there stood on the edge of the table a holder containing a half-burned candle.

Yes . . . when the lights went out. Hugh saw another candle on the edge of the mantelpiece. On one side of this mantelpiece was a curtained door, and on the other a side-board wedged cater-cornered in the angle of two walls of books. But his eyes always kept coming back to the bullet hole in the dead man's head; to the quiet orderliness of the murder, and to the glimmer of a painted card he could see just under the fingers of the dead man's left hand.

The first to move was Dr. Fell. He lumbered through the

door, his stick bumping heavily on the carpet against stillness. Wheezing, he bent to peer at the body, and the black ribbon on his glasses brushed the candlestick. Then, still bent forward, he looked slowly round the room. Something seemed to bother him. He went to the windows, looked at the floor under them, and felt the curtains of each one. He was bothered still more.

"Why," he said, suddenly, "why are all the windows open?"

6
THE WRONG VISITOR

Storer, who had been waiting patiently with his nose inclined, frowned at this beginning. He said:

"I beg your pardon, sir?"

"Were these windows open when you found the body this morning?"

"Yes, sir," replied Storer, after inspecting each one. The doctor removed his shovel hat; and, on the sudden realization, everybody else did the same; though the doctor's action had been prompted less out of veneration for the dead than to mop his moist forehead with a gaudy bandana. And, as though that action had broken a sort of spell, everybody moved into the room.

"H'm, yes. The floor over here is half an inch deep in water, and all the curtains are soaked . . . About this storm last night: What time did it commence?"

"About eleven o'clock, sir."

Dr. Fell seemed to be talking to himself. "Then why didn't Depping close his windows? Why leave all five of them open, with a thunderstorm blowing in? It's wrong; it's illogical; it's . . . What were you saying?"

Storer's eyes had grown sharp with a memory; his cheeks puffed slightly, and for a moment he looked less disillusioned.

"Go on, man," said Dr. Fell testily. "The storm begins at eleven. Depping is alone then. His visitor arrives shortly afterwards – the visitor goes upstairs, and is entertained – and all this time the storm is coming full blast through five open windows. That's wrong somewhere . . . what were you thinking of?"

"Something Achille said, sir." The valet looked at Depping, and seemed puzzled. "I forgot it, and so did Achille, when the other police officer was speaking to us. That's Achille Georges – the cook, you know . . ."

"Well?"

Storer stood on his dignity, and would not be hurried. "After the storm had begun, and that American went upstairs to see Mr. Depping, you see, sir. I sent Achille out to see what had gone wrong with the electric wires. They put the lights out, you see –"

"We know all that."

"Yes, sir. While Achille was out in the rain, he saw Mr. Depping and the American up here going about and raising all the windows. He said they seemed to be waving the curtains too."

Dr. Fell blinked at him. "Raising all the windows? Waving the curtains? – Didn't that seem at least a trifle odd?"

Again the valet contemplated the follies of the world and was not surprised. "Mr. Depping, sir," he answered stolidly, "was a man of moods."

The doctor said, "Bah!" And the bishop of Mappleham, who had recovered himself by this time, moved into first place with stately serenity.

"We can go into all that presently," he suggested. "Ah, might I inquire – Inspector Murch went over this room, I presume, for fingerprints? We shall not be disturbing anything if we investigate?"

"No, sir. There were no fingerprints," said Storer in a rather approving manner. He regarded the body as though he appreciated a workmanlike job, and then stared out of the windows.

"First," observed the bishop, "a look round . . ." He approached the desk, his son following, moved round it, and inspected the dead man's face. Death had been instantaneous. There was even a rather complacent expression on Depping's face, which was smirking out towards the windows with its cheek against the blotter. It was a long, dry, nondescript countenance, which might have borne any expression in life. The eyes were half open, the forehead bony, the mouth furrowed; and a rimless pince-nez still clung to his high-bridged nose.

From under his fingers the bishop drew the card. It was of white glazed cardboard, neatly cut out from a sheet such as you buy at any stationer's. Eight tiny broadswords drawn in India ink, their hilts painted black and their blades gray with watercolor, were arranged in a sort of asterisk along a blue painted line which was evidently meant to represent water. "If," said the bishop, as though offhand to his son, "Dr. Fell really has some notion as to what this means . . ."

Dr. Fell did not reply. He was lifting the white cloth over the dishes on the side table. After fingering the card impatiently, the bishop circled the desk, peering, and opened the right-hand drawer. From it he took out a thirty-eight calibre Smith & Wesson revolver with an ivory handle. He sniffed at the barrel, and then broke it open as though he had been handling firearms all his life. Then he replaced it, and closed the drawer with a bang. He seemed more at a loss than Hugh had ever seen him.

"Two shots," he said, "and no other bullet found here . . ."

"No, sir," said the valet complacently. "The police officer and Mr. Morgan allowed me to stay here while they made their examination, sir. They even conceived an idea that it might have gone out one of the windows, and they sighted lines from all parts of the room to see if they could find its direction. But Mr. Morgan, sir – Mr. Morgan pointed out it would be most unusual if a bullet went out there without touching any of the bars. They are not more than half an inch apart, any of them. He said it would be freakish, sir," amplified Storer, testing the word with a little tilt of his nose, and finding it good; "freakish. If you'll excuse me."

"A very clever young man," said the other coldly. "But what we want are facts. Let us proceed to the facts." He stood heavy and sharp-jawed against his light, flapping his hands behind him, and his hypnotic eye fixed the valet. "How long have you been with Mr. Depping?"

"Five years, sir. Ever since he came to live here."

"How did he come to employ you?"

"Through a London agency, sir. This is not," replied Storer with a touch of austerity, "my part of the country."

"Do you know anything of his past life – before he employed you?"

"No, sir. I assured the police officer of that this morning."

He went over his story in a patient fashion. Mr. Depping had been a man of moods; touchy, irritated by trifles, apt to go into a rage with the cook if his meals were not shaded exactly to his fastidious palate, fond of quoting Brillat-Savarin. Very learned, no doubt, but not a gentleman. Storer appeared to base his sad deductions to this effect on the statements that (a) Mr. Depping tended to call the servants by their first names when he was drunk, and to mention his business affairs, (b) he used American expressions, and (c) he was freely and often – said Storer – vulgarly generous with his money. At one time (while devoted to his whiskey drinking) he had said that the only reason why he employed Storer was because the valet looked so bloody respectable: and the only reason why he employed Achille Georges was because the world considered a taste for fine foods and wines to be the mark of a cultured man.

"That's what he said, sir," affirmed Storer; with an expression which on any less dismal face would have been sly. His nose sang on: "'The world is so full of fools, Charley,' – which is not my name, sir – 'the world is so full of fools,' he said to me, 'that anybody who can get emotional over an omelette, or tell you the vintage of a wine, is considered a very superior sort of person.' Then he would glare over those half-glasses of his, and grip the whiskey bottle as though he meant to throw it."

The valet's eyes wheeled round his narrow nose as though he appreciated this too. "But I must say, sir, in all justice, that he said he would have kept Achille anyway, because of the soups he could make. They were good soups," agreed Storer, judicially. "Mr. Depping was very fond –"

"My good man," interposed the bishop testily, "I am not at all concerned with his tastes in food –"

"I am," said Dr. Fell suddenly. He had wheeled round as the valet's narrative went on. "Was he fond of crawfish soup, by any chance?"

"He was, sir," replied Storer imperturbably. "It was his favorite. Achille had been preparing it frequently of late."

Dr. Fell removed the cloth again from the dinner dishes of last night, and nodded towards them. "Then it's damned funny," he said. "Here's crawfish soup, nearly untasted. On the other hand, he seems to have been especially rough on a kind of pineapple salad. He's eaten most of his dinner except the soup . . . Never mind. Carry on."

The bishop of Mappleham, who had paid no attention to this, fixed on an idea which had been growing in his son's mind for some time.

"One thing is evident," he declared. "Every bit of evidence we have heard points towards it. I do not wish to defame the memory of the dead, but this man Depping was not what he seemed. His past life – his unaccountable past life – his actions, and contradictions, are all those of a man who is playing a part . . ."

"Yes," said Dr. Fell, with a sort of obstinacy; "that's too evident to mention. But who's been eating his dinner?"

"Confound his dinner!" roared the bishop, letting off steam for the first time. "You know it, Storer. I believe you know it too, Morley . . ."

He swung round to young Standish, who had remained near the door with his hands jammed into his pockets. Morley lifted his eyes. Morley said equably:

"Sorry, sir. I don't know anything of the kind."

"It does not surprise me," pursued His Reverence, "that Depping should have been consorting with criminals. In all likelihood he has been a criminal himself in the past, and he has been living here to assume a guise of respectability. He knew Louis Spinelli. Louis Spinelli tracked him down for the purpose of blackmailing him . . . Depping's business! What was his business? Does anybody know anything about it?"

"Excuse me, sir," observed the valet. "He had – he informed me – a large financial interest in the publishing firm of Standish & Burke. But, as I told the police officer this morning, he was trying to get rid of that interest. You see, he told me all about it when he was – indisposed the last time."

"I meant his business previous to five years ago. He never mentioned that to you, I dare say? . . . I thought not."

His Reverence was regaining his self-confidence. He moved one hand up and down the lapel of his ponderous black coat. "Now, let us reconstruct what happened last night, if we can. Shortly after the storm began, around eleven o'clock, this stranger – I mean the American, whose name we know to be Spinelli – rang the doorbell and asked to see Mr. Depping. That is correct, Storer? Thank you . . . Now, as a matter of form I must ask you to identify him. I have two photographs here" – he produced them from his inside pocket and handed them to the valet. "That is the man who called on Mr. Depping, is it not?"

Storer looked at the snapshots with care. He handed them back.

“No, sir,” he said apologetically.

With a feeling that somebody had gone mad, Hugh Donovan peered into the man’s face. There was a silence, during which they could hear Dr. Fell unconcernedly poking with his stick in the fireplace behind the dead man’s chair. Behind this chair Dr. Fell rose to the surface like a red-faced walrus, wrinkled his moustache with a beaming air, and sank down again. The bishop only stared, blankly.

“But this . . .” he said, and swallowed hard. He assumed a persuasive air. “Come, come, now! This is absurd. Utterly absurd, you know. This must be the man. Come look again.”

“No, sir, it isn’t the same man,” Storer answered with an air of regret. “I only had a brief look at him, I know, and the candle didn’t give a great deal of light. Perhaps, sir, I might not even be able to identify him positively if I saw him again . . . But – excuse me – this is not the same man. The whole face is different, except for the moustache. This man’s face is very broad and low, and has heavy eyebrows. It doesn’t look anything like the man I saw. And, besides, the man I saw had projecting ears, noticeably projecting, sir.”

The bishop looked at Dr. Fell. The doctor was stirring a mass of heavy black ash in the fireplace, and one eye caught the ecclesiastical appeal.

“Yes,” he said, “yes, I was afraid of that.”

Somebody brushed past Donovan. Morley Standish had come up to the desk.

“This man’s lying,” he said heavily. “He’s either lying, or else he’s working with Spinelli. It must have been Spinelli. The bishop is right. There’s nobody else –”

“Tut, tut,” said Dr. Fell, rather irritably. “Calm yourselves a moment, while I ask just one question, and then I may be able to tell you something. I say, Storer, it’s rather an important question, so try not to make any mistake.”

He indicated the door to the balcony. "It's about that door. Was it usually locked or unlocked?"

"The door . . . why, always locked, sir. Invariably. It was never used."

Dr. Fell nodded. "And the lock," he said musingly, "isn't a spring-lock. It's the old-fashioned kind, d'ye see. Where's the key for it?"

The other reflected for some time. "I believe, sir, that it's hanging up on a hook in the pantry, along with some other keys for rooms that aren't used."

"Cut along then, and see if you can find it. I'll give you odds it isn't there, but have a look anyway."

He watched owlishly until the valet had left the room.

"Let's pass over for the moment," he went on, "the identity of the man who came to see Depping last night. Let's only assume that somebody came here for the purpose of killing Depping, not blackmailing him, and go on from there. Come here a moment, will you?"

They followed him uncertainly as he went over to the bridge lamp near the front windows.

"The electric fittings in this place," he continued, "are of a rather old-fashioned variety. You see that socket along the baseboard of the wall? This plug," – he picked up a length of wire from the lamp – "this plug, which is loose now, is screwed into that socket. In the modern ones the plug has only two prongs, which fit into the socket, and the live part isn't exposed for somebody to touch accidentally and get the devil of a shock. But the live part is exposed there; you see?"

"Certainly," said the bishop. "What about it?"

"Well, I've found the buttonhook."

"What?"

Dr. Fell raised his hand for silence as Storer hurried back into the room. "The key isn't there, sir," he reported.

"H'mf, yes. Now, then, just let me get one or two points corroborated, and then you may go. Last night the storm began just before eleven o'clock. You didn't speak to Mr. Depping then, or he to you. You went downstairs to shut the windows, and you were down there when the lights went out. You rummaged after candles down here, which took – how long, should you think?"

"Well, sir, say five minutes."

"Good. Then you started upstairs, and were going up to see whether your employer needed any candles when the knock came at the door, and you saw the mysterious man with the American accent. He wouldn't give any name, but pointed to the speaking tube and said to ask Mr. Depping whether he couldn't go upstairs. Which you did, and the visitor went up. Is all that correct, as we heard it?" "Yes, sir."

"That's all. And be sure you go downstairs now, please," Pushing out his cloak, Dr. Fell lowered himself into an easy-chair near the lamp. He regarded his audience with an argumentative stare, and said: "I wanted to be sure of that, gentlemen. It struck me, when I heard it this morning, that the story had a distinctly fishy sound. Look here. Put yourselves in Depping's place for a moment.

"You're sitting here in this room one evening, reading or whatnot, and all of a sudden – without the slightest warning – every light in the house goes out. What would you do?"

"Do?" repeated the bishop. He frowned. "Why, I suppose I should go out and find out why –"

"Precisely!" rumbled Dr. Fell, and struck his stick against the floor. "It's the normal, inevitable thing. You'd be furious; people always are when that sort of thing happens. You'd go out and bawl over the bannisters as to what the thus-and-so was going on in that place. Depping, a man who was annoyed more than anything by trifles, assuredly would. But that's the point. He didn't. He didn't even call downstairs to inquire what was wrong.

"To the contrary, he evinced a singular lack of interest in those lights. He was willing to entertain a man – who wouldn't give his name – with only a candle or two for illumination. He even, you recall, instructed Storer not to bother about seeing that they were repaired. Now, that isn't reasonable. And, actually, what was wrong? Something had blown out the fuses. I thought it might be interesting to inquire into causes. Here is the cause."

From the floor beside the chair Dr. Fell took up a long steel buttonhook, now corroded and blackened.

He turned it over in his palm, musingly.

"You see that live socket? Eh? Well, this buttonhook was deliberately thrust into it, in order to short-circuit the lights. You have only to look at the buttonhook to see that. I found it lying near the open socket. In other words, the lights were put out from this room . . . What do you make of it?"

7
"WHO'S BEEN SITTING IN MY *CHAIR?"*

The bishop was a gentleman and a sportsman. He rumpled at the bird's nest of hair curling back over his big head, and then he smiled. "My dear doctor," he said, "it begins to be borne in on me that I should have done better to remain silent. Pray go on."

"Tut!" grunted Dr. Fell amiably. "Let's pursue this line of reconstruction a little further. Il saute aux yeux la question: Why under sanity should Depping want to put out his own lights? The obvious answer is that he wanted to entertain a visitor who must not be recognized by his servants.

"From this we proceed to inference that (1) Storer did know the person who was to call on him, but (2) he was in such fashion disguised that Storer would not know him if he were seen only by the very uncertain light of a candle. Hence the short-circuiting of the lights. This is decidedly supported by the conduct of the visitor. Mind, he is never supposed to have been inside the house before, and is a complete stranger. Yet he points to the speaking tube on the wall and tells Storer to speak to his employer. That isn't the ordinary behavior of a caller who wants an interview with the master of a house; far from it."

The bishop nodded. "Unquestionably," he agreed. "There can be no doubt of it. That is the explanation."

Dr. Fell scowled. His eyes wandered drowsily about the room, and then a capacious chuckle ran down the ridges of his waistcoat.

"No, it isn't," he said.

"I beg your pardon?"

"It isn't. I didn't say it was the explanation; I only said those were inferences to be drawn from the hypothesis that Depping put out his own lights. And I wish it were as simple as that. But let's proceed for a moment on that assumption, and see what we find.

"H'm. Harrumph. There is a very, very grave objection to this theory. If Depping wished to entertain a secret visitor, why did he indulge in all that elaborate and dangerous mummery? Why go to all the trouble of putting a loud check suit and a false moustache on his visitor, dousing the lights, and mysteriously bringing him in at the front door? Why not simply bring him up to the balcony, and through the balcony door unknown to anybody? Why not smuggle him in at the back door? Why not bring him through a window, if necessary? Why not adopt the simplest course of all: send the servants to bed and let him in himself – front door, balcony door, or back door?

"You see, that theory won't work. Nobody but a lunatic would have arranged a meeting like that. There must have been a very good reason why it was done in that way."

He paused for a long time.

"To see whether we can explain it, remember that the balcony door, which is always kept locked, was found open this morning. Not only was this door usually locked, but the key was not in it at all; it hung on a nail in a pantry downstairs. And it is gone now. Who took that key, and who opened the door? The murderer left that way, and it must have been unlocked either by Depping or by the murderer. Keep that fact fixed in your mind while we consider the problem.

"Whoever the visitor was, or why he was admitted under such circumstances of hocus-pocus, look at the facts and see what happened afterwards. Depping and X are closeted together, amiably enough to all purposes, and some very extraordinary things occur. They are seen by the cook putting up all the windows in the midst of a blowing thunderstorm . . . What does that suggest to you?"

The bishop was pacing about at a measured and thoughtful gait.

"I can scarcely imagine," he replied, "that they did so because they wanted to air the room."

"But they did," said Dr. Fell. "That's exactly what they wanted to do. Haven't you looked in the fireplace? Haven't you wondered about a fire in the hottest part of August? Haven't you seen that heavy, clotted mass of ash? Haven't you wondered what must have been burned, so that all the windows had to be raised?"

"You mean –"

"Clothes," said Dr. Fell.

There was an eerie pause. "I mean," the doctor went on, his voice rumbling through the quiet room, "I mean that glaring check suit worn by the visitor. You can still see traces of it in the fireplace. Now, mark you, these two are acting in perfect accord and understanding. The more we examine the problems as it seems to be, the more we must realize that it's mad, and there must be something wrong with the facts as they have been presented to us. Here is Depping admitting a visitor as he does, when he could easily have let him in through the balcony door without fuss. Here are Depping and his visitor sitting down to burn the visitor's clothes: which, I can assure you, is a social pursuit somewhat rare in the British Isles. Finally, we have the visitor not only shooting Depping with Depping's own gun, but (a) taking the gun out of the drawer without any protest, (b) getting behind Depping with it, also without protest, (c) firing two bullets of which one has mysteriously vanished, (d) carefully replacing the gun in the drawer, and (e) leaving this room by means of a balcony door which is always kept locked, and whose key is downstairs in the pantry."

Wheezing, the doctor took out his pipe and tobacco pouch with an air of gentle protest. Morley Standish, who had been staring out of the window, turned suddenly.

"Hold on, sir! I don't follow that. Even if Depping didn't let the man in, he might have got the key out of the pantry and put it in the door so that he could let the visitor out afterwards."

"Quite so," agreed Dr. Fell. "Then why isn't the key there now?"

"Why isn't – ?"

"H'mf, yes. It's not very complicated, is it?" the other asked anxiously. "If you're a murderer leaving a room in comparative haste, throwing the door open and ducking out, does it generally occur to you to pinch the key on your way out? Why should you? If you wanted to lock the door behind you, I could understand the position. Lock the door; chuck away the key. But why, if you intend leaving the door ajar, do you want a dangerous souvenir like that?"

He lit the dregs of his pipe.

"But let's not consider that just yet. Let's tear some more flimsy shreds out of the situation as it seems. If we come back to that problem of the mummery round the entrance of Depping's visitor, I think we shall see it isn't sensible either way. If for some reason the thing were an abstruse piece of deception, with all details arranged between them beforehand, look at the fantastic nature of one of the details! I refer, gentlemen, to Depping's apparent means of putting out the lights. I can think offhand of several easy and perfectly safe means of short-circuiting 'em . . . But what, apparently, does Depping do? He picks up an all-steel button-hook and shoves it into a live socket – !

"There's the buttonhook. Will any of you volunteer to do it now?"

Morley ran a hand through his sleek dark hair.

"Look here!" he protested plaintively, "I mean to say, come to think of it, if you tried that you'd get a shock that would lay you out for fifteen minutes . . ."

"If not considerably worse. Quite so."

Hugh Donovan found his voice for the first time. His father had ceased to be formidable now. He said: "I thought you'd just proved, doctor, that the buttonhook was used. And yet anybody would know better than to do a thing like that."

"Oh, it was used right enough; look at it. But go a step further. Can you think of any means by which it could have been used in perfect safety?"

"I confess I scarcely follow you," replied the bishop. "I cannot conjecture that it was in some fashion propped up so that it would fall into the socket at the required moment . . ."

"No. But what about rubber gloves?" inquired Dr. Fell.

There was a pause.

"H'mf. I'm only theorizing now, of course," the doctor rumbled, "yet, when you ally it with a few other points I shall indicate in a moment, it is an alluring theory. That's the only way the trick could have been worked. Yet again the total adds up to foolishness if we conceive that – as a part of this intricate design – Depping provided himself with a pair of rubber gloves to put out his own lights, when (as I have insisted) other and simpler methods were at hand . . . Nevertheless, there is another connotation of rubber gloves. If a man desires to leave no fingerprints, and yet have a free and delicate use of his hands, rubber gloves are the best sort of protection."

The bishop made a massive gesture. "My dear Dr. Fell," he intoned, almost sepulchrally, "you are getting into the realm of fantastic nonsense. Why should the late Mr. Depping have cared whether or not he left fingerprints in his own study?"

Letting out a gust of smoke, Dr. Fell leaned forward with a sort of fierce intensity and pointed his pipestem. His wheezing breath grew louder. He said:

"Exactly! Why should he? There's another 'why should he' for this incredible collection. Why should he at least not make a pretense of wondering why the lights went out? Why didn't he play his part like an artist, and come out of his room to ask Storer what was wrong? Why didn't he show himself? Why did he help the visitor burn his clothes? – And last of all," said the doctor, lifting his stick and jabbing it towards the dinner tray, "why did he sample everything on that tray except his favorite soup?"

"I say, this bears a curious resemblance to the classic history of the three bears. 'Who's been sitting in my chair? Who's been drinking my porridge? Who –' Gentlemen, I think you are beginning to perceive by this time that the man in this room was not Depping at all."

The bishop muttered something to himself. A sudden dazzling suspicion seemed to make him wheel round and look at the smirking face of the dead man . . .

"Then Depping –" he said. "Where was Depping all this time?"

"Why, I'll tell you," responded the doctor, and made a hideous pantomime face by way of emphasis. "He was decked out in an eye-splitting check suit, bogus jewellery, a wig, a false moustache, and actor's cement behind his ears to make them protrude. He was ringing his own doorbell and paying a call in his own house . . . There it is, you see. In this masquerade the rôles were simply reversed, and that's what I meant by saying we should have to tear apart the facts as they seemed, or we should never understand the truth. It was X, the mysterious stranger, who posed as Depping in this room. And it was Depping – eh?"

"Can you –" said Morley Standish, "can you prove this?"

He was breathing hard, and his heavy dark face, with its absurd-looking moustache, had a sudden look of relief.

"I rather think I can," said Dr. Fell modestly.

"But – ah," observed the bishop, "I – that is, I am bound to remark that this fresh approach would seem to make the matter quite as complicated and incomprehensible as it was before."

"Eh? No. No, I don't agree. Give me this reversal of rôles," urged Dr. Fell, with a persuasive air, "and I'll undertake to simplify it. Heh. Yes."

"I can understand," pursued the other, "how Depping's appearance could have deceived Storer with only one candle burning. The very clothes alone would have had the effect of distracting his eye much as a conjuror does; which is – ah – the first principle of disguise, and, I am told, the only really effective one." It was a struggle for the bishop to include that "I am told"; but he did it. He brooded. "I can even understand the change of voice, allied to the American accent . . . But there is a more difficult imposture to account for. How do you account for the voice of the man in this room, imitating Depping's? Surely Storer would have known it was not the same?"

The doctor chuckled, and spilled ashes down his waistcoat.

"He would," the doctor agreed, "if he had heard it anywhere else but through a speaking tube." He pointed to the wall. "Of all the ghostly and disembodied effects in the way of communication, commend me to the speaking tube. You yourself would sound like a spirit-voice. Have you never used one? It isn't like a telephone, you know. Go downstairs, and let each of us speak to you in turn; and I will defy you to identify your own son.

"And, you see, it was only over the speaking tube that the bogus Depping spoke to Storer. The 'visitor' went upstairs, entered this room, and the door closed. Afterwards, of course, the real Depping spoke, and there was no deception to puzzle our observant valet."

"For the present," said the bishop, "let's accept the hypothesis . . . I must insist that we still have as inexplicable a situation as before. Why should Depping and X have put up this imposture between them?"

"I don't think they did."

The bishop remained calm. He said: "Most extraordinary, doctor. I was under the impression that you said –"

"I do not think they put it up between them, confound it," snorted Dr. Fell. "Remember, if you please, that we have only got a reversal of rôles. It doesn't alter any of the circumstances. If you say there was collusion between those two, you must explain the same riddles as before. The queer behavior of the man in this room isn't greatly altered because his name is X instead of Depping. Why, if X is working with Depping from the beginning of a carefully conceived plan, does he want the rubber gloves? If Depping brought a disguised X through the front door instead of smuggling him up the balcony, why didn't X do the same for a disguised Depping? . . . Be calm, my dear sir; I know you yourself pointed out those difficulties. So let's begin with the dinner. Depping didn't eat it, but X did. Whispering to the inner ear, echoing through the halls of consciousness," said Dr. Fell with relish, "comes the sinister question: Why didn't Depping eat his dinner?"

"Maybe he wasn't hungry," said Morley Standish, after considering the problem.

"Brilliant," said Dr. Fell testily. "The helpfulness of my colleagues is inspiring. Surely, gentlemen, your innate shrewdness, your native cunning, can provide a better answer than that – ? It must have occurred to you that he didn't eat his dinner because he wasn't here, and X did eat it because he was here. The dinner was brought up at half-past eight. Depping was here then, restless and nervous, I think the report was. And he must have left the house shortly after that, in his fancy disguise. He must, therefore, have gone out the balcony door. Eh?"

"Quite," said the bishop. "And – that provides us, it is obvious, with an important piece of evidence. He had the key to the balcony door."

"Good. We progress. So what follows?"

"I do not agree with your statement that no plot was arranged beforehand between Depping and X," said the bishop. He was stalking about now, in a fervor of enlightenment. "Everything points to that. While Depping was away –"

"For nearly an hour and a half –"

"– for nearly an hour and a half, then, X was in this room. Doctor, every detail fits into place. Depping, in disguise, left here for a nefarious purpose, an illegal purpose . . ."

Dr. Fell stroked his moustache. "It is considered so. Yes. He took his gun along, you see . . . Are you beginning to have a nebulous idea as to what happened to the missing bullet?"

"Oh, my God!" said Morley Standish suddenly.

"Ghosts of the past will now gather round," continued Dr. Fell, "to gibber that crusty old Depping was a very, very dangerous man on whom to try any games. I expect his use of American words, when drunk, came naturally to him . . . It occurs to me that poor old Louis Spinelli will never try any blackmailing tricks again. If he isn't as dead as Garibaldi at this moment, I am very much mistaken."

They all looked at the dead smirk on Depping's face; at the neatness of his clothes, the orderly books, and the silver bowl of roses on the dinner table.

"My friend," declared the bishop, as though he were beginning a speech, "on the admirable completeness with which you have conjured a case out of evidence which does not exist and facts which have not been demonstrated, I must offer my sincerest congratulations . . . Hem. On the other hand, you must be aware that everything you have said indicates a plot between Depping and X. Depping was going out to commit a murder. It is simplicity itself. He left a colleague here to prove him an alibi."

Dr. Fell ruffled the hair at his temples. For a long time he blinked across the room. A new, disturbing idea seemed to strike him.

"You know . . ." he said. "By the Lord, I believe it would be better, if for the present, we agreed on that. I don't believe it is precisely true; and yet my own idea – which is not so very different from yours in essentials – is open to such an overpowering objection that . . . Yes, let's assume what you say. Let's say Depping left somebody here, to growl something through the door in case he should be approached –"

"And this person," interposed the bishop grimly, "came here determined to kill Depping just as Depping meant to kill Spinelli."

"Yes. Now we are on safe ground. Gentlemen, no more beautiful opportunity for murder ever presented itself with a proof of innocence attached. Look at it! If Depping thought he was safe to kill Spinelli, then X must have roared with mirth to see how safely he could kill Depping . . .

"Don't you see," he demanded, pounding his fist on his knee, "how it would work out? It explains our problem as to why Depping walked through the door in disguise. In the original plan, Depping had never intended to do that. To do that, after he had killed Spinelli, would have been idiotic and dangerous. His alibi was planted in his study. He should have returned there as he left – by the balcony door, unseen, to shed his disguise. A suspicious man in loud clothes, with a mysterious manner and an American accent, who deliberately walked in his front door . . . why, it would have started every tongue in the countryside wagging. If Spinelli were discovered dead – another suspicious American – then inquiries would lead straight to Depping to ask what he knew about it. They might not prove him guilty of murder, but your respectable, studious country gentleman would be in for an uncomfortable lot of explaining."

Morley Standish cleared his throat. "Then, hang it, why did he?" he asked.

"That's the infernal beauty of X's scheme . . . Depping came in the front door because he couldn't get in any other way. Do you see it? X caught him in the neatest kind of trap. Depping had gone out the balcony door, leaving the key in it; instructing X to lock it behind him, and admit him when he returned . . . Remember, that's your theory; I told you that in many features mine is different . . . but, anyway, Depping returns just as the thunderstorm breaks, and he can't get in "

"Because X won't let him in," said the bishop.

"Well, it can scarcely have been so crude as that. That's where your hypothesis wobbles a bit; to keep Depping unsuspicious, X would have had to spin some yarn about losing the key. It would sound improbable. I think I have a better explanation, but it works out on the same principle . . . And there you are. There's the door locked, and bars on every window. There's Depping fairly caught out in a heavy storm, in a disguise he can't possibly explain!

"The stiff and scholarly Mr. Depping known hereabouts," he went on musingly, "wearing a music-hall suit . . . Where can he go? How can he dispose of that garb? Picture yourself, Bishop Donovan, caught in an English village at night and in a storm, dressed up as Charles Chaplin just after having committed a murder . . . Depping was fairly in the soup. He'd got to get into his house unsuspected, and all the windows were barred. And he had to get in quickly; every minute his accomplice remained there increased the danger of detection both for himself and his accomplice. He could even talk to his accomplice, through the bars of the balcony window, but he couldn't get in.

"And here's X with a suggestion – you know what it was. Lights short-circuited, American visitor enters, identities are restored. It was a dangerous risk, but the lesser of two bad positions for Depping. For X it was the boon of an American visitor who would be supposed to have shot Depping when, later on, Depping was found murdered. And it very nearly succeeded."

The bishop went over the desk, and for a time he looked down at the dead man with an expression in which were mingled compassion and disgust.

"'The Lord gave – '" he said, and stopped. When he turned again, there was a quizzical expression in his eyes.

"You are a persuasive speaker, doctor," he said. "An unusually persuasive speaker. All this has been explained so coherently that I have been forgetting the basis on which all the assumptions rest: that is, the death of Spinelli. I have read of brilliant pieces of deduction to unravel crimes. But I must compliment you on your brilliance in unravelling a murder we don't know has been committed."

Dr. Fell was not abashed. "Oh, I'm a bit of a charlatan," he acknowledged affably. "Still, I'll wager you two junior mathematics masters against a curate that it took place as I've indicated. That door over there leads to Depping's bedroom. If you care to make a search, you'll probably find evidence to support me. Personally, I'm lazy . . ."

"Look here," said Morley Standish. "There's something you've got to promise. You say old Depping was a crook in the past, and probably worse; that's what you believe, anyhow . . ."

His big stride brought him to the side of Dr. Fell's chair; and his face was painfully earnest; he had the uncertain look of a man who feels that showing an emotion would be an incorrect thing, but is determined to force it over by lowering his voice and speaking very fast.

"Well, I'll tell you the truth. I'm not surprised. I've been thinking – things, myself. You'll say that's disloyal –"

"Tut," grunted Dr. Fell. "Why?"

"– but there it is. Now do you realize what a mess we'll all be in when this gets out? Scandal, publicity, slime . . . My God, don't you see it? They may even try to stop my marriage; they will try, if I know my mother. They won't succeed, but that's not the point. Why does everybody have to be subjected to this? Why . . ." His puzzled expression as he glanced at each of them, puzzled and baffled and rather desperate, seemed to demand the reason for the injustice of having criminals in the world just when he was on the point of matrimony. "What good purpose will it serve to drag all this out? Can you tell me that?"

"I take it, my boy," said the bishop, "that you do not care whether your fiancée's father had been a criminal? Or a murderer?"

Two muscles worked up the sides of Morley's jaws. His eyes were puzzled.

"I don't care," he said simply, "if the old swine committed every murder in Chicago . . . But why does it have to be made public?"

"But you want the truth to come out, don't you?"

"Yes, I suppose I do," admitted Morley, rubbing his forehead. "That's the rules. Got to play fair. But why can't they just catch him and hang him quietly, without anybody knowing . . . ? I'm talking rot, of course, but if I could make you understand what I mean . . . why do the damned newspapers have a right to splash out all the scandal they like just because a man's been murdered? Why can't you administer justice in private, the same as you make a law or perform an operation?"

"That, Mr. Standish," Dr. Fell said, "is a problem for discussion over half-a-dozen bottles of beer. But for the moment I don't think you need worry about scandal. I was coming to that: I mean our plan of campaign . . . Do you see what we've got to do?"

"No," said Morley hopelessly. "I wish I could."

"It's an ugly thing to face, then, but here it is. The murderer of Depping – X – the decidedly brainy person who worked out this design – is here. He's no fanciful gangster. He's a member of the community in an English village, and probably not a mile away from us now. That's why I've gone through this laborious explanation: so that we could center our activities. As it stands now –"

He leaned forward, and beat his finger slowly into his palm.

"– as it stands now, he thinks he is safe. He thinks we have laid the murder on Louis Spinelli. That's where we have the advantage, and the only way we shall be able to trap him unawares. Therefore, for the time being, we shall keep silent about everything we know, including our suspicions as to Depping's past. I shall have to report it all to Hadley, and the past can be investigated from London. But our information we will keep to ourselves.

"Besides, gentlemen, we have several valuable clues. The murderer made one or two mistakes, which I needn't outline at the moment, but his greatest mistake was leaving the eight of swords. It supplies a direction in which to look for the motive."

"Are you at last prepared, then," said the bishop, "to tell us what this eight of swords means?"

"Oh, yes. I don't know whether you've noticed on Depping's shelves a number of works dealing with –"

From outside the house there rose a murmur a voices and a trampling of feet. Morley and the bishop, who were near the windows, glanced out.

“Here comes a whole procession,” said the former. “My father, and Inspector Murch, and my sister; and Dr. Fordyce, and two constables. I –”

Apparently the colonel could not restrain himself. Through the quiet of the coppice, eager and jubilant, his hoarse voice came floating from below.

“I say! Come down here! It’s all up, you know; all up!”

The bishop tried to peer out through the rounded bars. He hesitated, and then called: “Kindly refrain from yowling like that, Standish. What’s all up?”

“Why, we’ve got him, you know. Murch has got him. Make him talk now.” “Got who?”

“Why, Louis Spinelli, demmit! He’s down in the village, and Murch has got him under technical arrest.”

“Whoosh!” said Hugh Donovan, and turned to stare at Dr. Fell.

8
AT THE CHEQUERS INN

At this point, the chronicler of Dr. Fell's adventures should, strictly speaking, apologize for introducing that luscious little ginch, Patricia Standish. "Ginch," Hugh Donovan has frequently assured the chronicler, is the word that best describes her; a mysterious term whose definition will presently be made clear. It is pronounced to rhyme with "cinch," for more reasons than one.

This apology should come from the fact that on one point all the leading authorities are agreed: to introduce a heroine (whether or not the tale be fact) is bad. Very bad. As Henry Morgan says, you know what I mean: the gray-eyed, fearless Grace Darling with the cool philosophy, who likes to poke her nose into trouble and use a gun as well as the detective, and who requires the whole book to make up her mind whether she is more than casually interested in the hero.

But in extenuation it must be urged, first, that this is a true story, and second – by the splendid grace of God – Patricia Standish had none of the traits just mentioned. She was not cool-headed or strong-minded. She could no more have accompanied the detectives with a gun than she could have brought down the villain with a flying tackle. Quite to the contrary, she was content to leave that sort of thing to the proper people; to beam up at you as though she were saying, "What a man!" – and you threw out your chest, and felt about nine feet tall, and said, "Ha, ha." Nor, in her case, were there all those persistent attempts to freeze or embarrass the hero until the very last. She tumbled into Hugh Donovan's arms from the start, and stayed there, and a very good thing too.

Some magnificent premonition of this stirred in his mind the moment he saw her. She was walking up the brick path, against the dark trees that were now glowing fiery with sunset, and she was in the midst of a small procession. Patricia Standish had her arm through that of the ruddy-faced colonel, who was expounding something to a large man in uniform. Behind them walked two constables and a melancholy medical man who seemed to be thinking glumly about a lost tea.

Against this background she stood out vividly. She was a blonde, but not a fluffy blonde or a statuesque blonde. And she was dexterously made, as though nature had added just that extra touch and fillip to the curves in the right places, for a frock to adhere to. Her air was at once hesitant and vigorous; and her skin seemed to glow with that brownish flesh tint which is so rarely to be seen in real flesh. Dark hazel eyes contemplated you with that interested, rapt, "What-a-man!" look already referred to; her high eyebrows gave her a perpetual air of pleased surprise; and she had a pink, rather broad mouth which always seemed to have just finished smiling.

Thus Hugh Donovan saw her coming hesitantly up the path, in a white tennis frock without sleeves, against the dark fire-edged trees. Along with the bishop, Morley, and Dr. Fell, he had come downstairs to the porch of the Guest House. And there she was, arching her neck to look rather fearfully at the balcony door, while the colonel spoke to Inspector Murch. Then she looked towards the porch, and at Donovan.

His immediate sensation was that of one who goes up a staircase in the dark, and puts his foot down on a nonexistent top step – you know. And this was followed by a sort of stupendous emotional clang: as though he had put a rifle to his shoulder, fired, and hit the loudest bell in the shooting-gallery first shot. Clang – like that, and hot and cold all at once, and a number of other mixed metaphors.

He knew, right then and there.

Furthermore, he knew that she knew also. You can feel that kind of thing emanating from ginches, in waves or vibrations or something, and the person who says you can't is a goof who does not deserve to have the vibrations launched in his direction. Hugh Donovan knew she knew, also, by the way their eyes did not meet. They took a sort of quick flash and slid away from each other. He and Patricia Standish made an elaborate pretense that they were not aware of each other's presence; that they would scarcely be aware of each other's presence after they had been properly introduced; and these are excellent signs indeed. Patricia was contemplating a stone peacock on the roof of the Guest House, her head high and her manner casual.

All these emotional fireworks were not obvious to Colonel Standish. The colonel made noises of satisfaction, and pushed forward Inspector Murch. Inspector Murch was large, and had an aggressive moustache; his method of standing at attention made him look as though he were tilted slightly backwards, and in danger of toppling over if you gave him a shove. His expression of conscientiousness remained fixed; but he seemed pleased with himself.

"Tell 'em, Murch," said the colonel. "Speak out, now. Oh, yes; that's Dr. Fell, and the Bishop of Mappleham, and Mr. Donovan . . . Inspector Murch, and this is Doctor Fordyce – goin' to take the bullet out now. Oh, yes, h'rrm – I forgot. And my daughter Patricia. Tell 'em, Murch."

Patricia gave a small inclination of her head. The inspector was more conscientious than ever; he fingered his sandy moustache, cleared his throat, and fixed a pale blue satisfied eye on Dr. Fell. He spoke confidentially, in a throaty voice.

"I would like to call this an honor, sir. And I would explain why I was unable to do me duty in being here to welcome you." He took a notebook. "After making investigations here, I took the liberty of going home for me tea. This was not a dereliction of duty, look; I took with me a selection from Mr. Depping's correspondence – letters, sir," he translated, tapping the notebook, "which were revealin'. Meanwhile, I had been making inquiries about the man who visited Mr. Depping last night.

"The landlord of the 'Bull' told me that a man answering to the description had been seen frequently in these parts for more than a week. He was often at the 'Bull', and asking questions about everybody at The Grange; and news do get about, sir," observed Inspector Murch, shaking his head. "But this man had not been there last night.

"'Owever; while I was drinking me tea, I received a call on the telephone from Detective Sergeant Ravens, at Hanham, saying he thought the man I wanted was stopping at the Chequers Inn – which I must explain is down Hanham way, by the river, about four miles from here . . ."

"Interesting," put in the bishop, looking sideways at Dr. Fell. "The man is not dead, then?"

"Dead?" said Murch, blankly. "Dead? Gaawdblessmes'ul, no! Why should he be dead?"

"I was only endeavoring to ascertain the facts," said the other, with a negligent gesture and another satisfied look at Dr. Fell. "Go on, Inspector."

Dr. Fell was not at all disconcerted.

"It would seem that for the moment I am in disgrace," he wheezed affably. "H'mf. No matter. Sexton Blake will yet be triumphant. I don't think it matters in the least – did you go over to see him, Inspector?"

"Yes, sir. First I telephoned to The Grange, to ascertain whether Colonel Standish had returned. He had not. I then borrowed a car and drove to the Chequers Inn. At this time I did not know his name was Spinelli, or 'oo the chap was at all.

"He was known at the Chequers as Mr. Travers, and he'd not made any attempt to bolt. I found him sitting out on the porch, drinking his half-pint, as cool as you please. A very well-spoken person, sir; like a gentleman. In process of law," intoned Inspector Murch, "I cautioned him, informing him he was not under oath, but 'ad better answer such questions as I put in process of law. He made a certain statement, not under oath, which he initialled."

Clearing his throat, Murch opened his notebook.

"'My name is Stuart Travers. I am a theatrical impreesorrio, retired. I lived at the Deword, Broadway and Eighty-Sixth Street, New York City. I am travelling in England for pleasure. I do not know Mr. Depping. Yes, I know what happened last night; everybody here knows all about it. Yes, I know I am under suspicion. I was not near the Guest House at any time last night. If the man who called there was seen, they will tell you it was not me. I have nothing to be afraid of. I went to my room last night at half-past nine, and did not leave it until this morning. That is all I have to say until I have consulted my lawyer.'"

During the reading, Inspector Murch had been leaning farther and farther backwards. Now he looked up with a heavy and crafty smile.

"I had not any warrant," he pursued, "and could not hold the accused until properly identified. I asked him to accompany me 'ere to be identified, and he would not, sir, he said, until he had telephoned to London and talked to his lawyer. Very cool. Afterwards, the accused said he would come gladly, and meantime he would stop in charge of Sergeant Ravens. So he won't run away, sir, look – but, in secret, I obtained pieces of evidence which is most significant."

"Dashed good work, that," said Colonel Standish approvingly. "Hear that? Listen again. Hang him without a doubt. Eh, Murch?"

"Thank you, sir. We can hope so," replied Murch, with heavy modesty. "Well, sir, to go on. Mr. Travers was not in his room last night at the time indicated as per statement. It is true he be and went there at half-past nine. But he left it, because he was seen at close on ten o'clock, climbing back into the window of 'is room – which is on the ground floor. Funny thing; he was sopping wet, though the rain hadn't started, as wet as though he'd been and fallen in the river . . ."

"In the river," interrupted Dr. Fell, musingly. "Not bad, not bad. How do you explain that?"

"Well, sir, I don't. But that's not the important thing, you see. Mrs. Kenviss, the landlord's wife at the Chequers, saw him doing it when she was coming back from taking the cloths off all the little tables in a sort of restaurant arbor they have outside. She wondered what was up, and watched . . . In less than five minutes, out this Mr. Travers climbed again, with 'is clothes changed, and hurried off somewhere. That's the important thing. A good walker could easy cover four miles between the Chequers and this house here in less than an hour. He'd have reached here by eleven o'clock . . ."

"So he would," agreed Dr. Fell. "In time for a blackmailer to have seen a great deal."

The inspector frowned. "Seen, sir?" he repeated, with a sort of hoarse jocosity. "'M! 'Tisn't what he'd've seen, not much. That's the time he walked straight in that door there, after the lights went out, and upstairs – as we know. And shot poor Mr. Depping. He didn't get back to the Chequers until half-past one. Mrs. Kenviss," the inspector said virtuously, "said it was her bounden duty to sit up, and watch that window, and see what was what. Blessmes'l, she and

Mr. Kenviss do get a scare when they learn this morning what's happened! And they didn't dare speak to Mr. Travers; so she hurries out after Sergeant Ravens, and that's how I know. But," announced Murch, tapping his notebook with heavy emphasis, "we don't give our knowledge away, Ravens and me. To Mr. Travers, I mean. I thought I'd best nip back here straightaway, get that Storer chap, take him and identify Mr. Travers, and we've got him."

He closed his notebook. "My superior officer; the chief constable," he continued, with an air of putting on the final touch, "has made the information against him as being one Louis Spinelli, and that completes it. I have now my warrants for arrest and search."

"Got him, eh?" inquired the colonel, glancing from one to the other of the figures on the porch. "Got him drunk on parade – dead to rights, damme! Sorry to have pulled you down here for nothing, Fell. Still . . . Hallo, I'm sorry; I forgot! . . . Let me introduce, Dr. Fordyce, my daughter Patricia . . ." He whirled round with an air of inspiration.

"How do you do?" said Hugh Donovan instantly.

"You've already introduced everybody," said the sad-faced medical man with some asperity. "And since the police seem to have finished, I'll be thankful to get on with my postmortem and be off."

"Oh, yes. Carry on, then," said Dr. Fell, with an absent-minded air. He waited until the doctor and the two constables had tramped past him into the house. Then he looked round the little group, and fixed Murch with a sombre eye. "So you came back here for an identification of Spinelli from the valet, Inspector?"

"Yes, sir." Murch wheezed out a breath of relief. "And, by George, sir! I'm free to confess how glad I am it was this man Travers, or Spinelli; one of those there gunman chaps, that'd as soon shoot as look at you, like you see in the films; and not one of our own folk. Ah, ah, he'll soon learn you can't do that business over here, by Gearge!" Another breath of relief, which agitated the ends of his sandy moustache. "Ah, ay, a good thing. I'm bound to admit I was having ideas, sir."

"Ideas?"

"Ah," agreed the inspector. "'Tis nonsense, sir, but there it is." A broader strain had crept into the good inspector's speech now that the burden of an official report had been removed. "Ah, but when an idea cooms to you, blest if you can drive 'ee oot. There he is, and there he stays. Eh zed to meself, Eh zed, by Gearge!" proclaimed Murch, illustrating what he said to himself by sweeping a big arm through the air and snapping his fingers as though he had just thrown a pair of dice, "is that true? Eh zed. 'Tis queer, when I heard some of the things that are being said hereabouts – hints, like – and had a look at his letters, then I had ideas. Both Mr. Morgan and I had ideas; yon's a clever lad, Mr. Morgan; he helped me this morning. Aa-hh-ha, yes. But Eh zed to meself. Eh, zed, 'Luther Murch, you'm dimp!' And a small matter now too, with us having the murderer."

He threw out his big hands, dismissing it, but not without a frown. Dr. Fell regarded him steadily.

"I shall want to hear those ideas, Inspector. H'm, yes. Together with all the evidence you have collected today; we haven't done much but talk. Please come upstairs. I'm afraid I've bad news for you."

The colonel interposed. He said:

"Well, well, what are we waiting for; demmit?" in a querulous tone. "Time we were busy. I've got to drive six miles to a telegraph office, confounded nuisance, just to tell Hadley we've caught our man . . . Morley! What the devil are you doing here, eh? Come along with me; I can't write telegrams; never could . . . You, Patricia! Dash it, this is no place for you, you know!" he protested, rather defensively.

She spoke for the first time. It was one of those warm,

soft, ginch-like voices also. She looked down from her contemplation of the stone peacock.

"Of course not, Dad," she agreed, with such readiness that the colonel stared at her.

"Eh?" he said.

"Of course not." The hazel eyes grew sombre. They flickered past Hugh, and then looked squarely at him for the first time. They had such an overpowering effect that the shooting-gallery bell clanged six times in rapid succession, and with unnerving noise. Patricia went on in bright helpfulness:

"Shall I take Mr. Donovan up to The Grange and introduce him to Mother? And I'm sure he must be dying for a dr – for something to eat."

She smiled. The colonel caught up with the suggestion with his usual air of inspiration.

"That's it, by Jove!" he assented warmly. "Take him along. Introduce him. Oh, yes; and that reminds me . . . Patricia, this is Joe Donovan's son. Hugh, my boy, let me present my daughter Patricia. Patricia, this is Hugh Donovan."

"How do you do?" said Donovan obediently.

"Are you sure you've got it clear now?" she inquired. "Right-ho, then! Come along with me; do."

9
THE DEDUCTIONS OF OLD JOHN ZED

That was how, in a few short moments, he found himself walking away beside this lithe, bright-eyed, altogether luscious ginch in the tennis frock – walking rather hurriedly, because he was afraid he would hear his father's stern hail from the porch, bidding him back to duty and the lighthouse. If possible, that last remark of hers drew her closer to him than ever, a powerful, unspoken, dazzling sympathy. "He must be dying for a dri –" She knew. This must be the sort of thing Elizabeth Barrett Browning wrote about in the sonnets. It was not only sympathetic feminine intuition on her part, but he realized that the very sight of this girl had made him want to reach for a cocktail; some women have that effect. Such a glamour must have attended all the great sirens of the ages. In its absence there are unfulfilled romances. If, when Dante met Beatrice that famous time on the what's-its-name bridge, Beatrice had smiled at him and whispered, "Look here, I could do with a slug of Chianti," then the poor sap would have tried to find out her address and telephone number; instead of merely going home and grousing about it in an epic.

Here in the twilight coppice the strength and reasonableness of this theory grew on him; and, as he looked down at the hazel eyes which were regarding him inquiringly over her shoulder, he was struck with inspiration.

He burst out suddenly:

"There once was a poet named Dante,
Who was fond of imbibing Chianti –
He wrote about hell
And a Florentine gel,
Which distressed his Victorian auntie."

Then he said, "Hah!" in a pleased, surprised tone, and rubbed his hands together as though he were waiting for the gods to throw him another.

"Hullo!" observed Patricia, opening her eyes wide. "I say, that's a nice opening speech from a bishop's son! Your father told me a lot about you. He said you were a good young man."

"It's a contemptible lie!" he said, stung to the depths. "Look here! I don't want you to go believing any such –"

"Oh, I don't believe it," she said composedly. "H'm. What made you think of it? That limerick, I mean?"

"Well, to tell you the truth, I think it was you. That is, it was a sort of inspiration – the kind that's supposed to soak you on your first sight of Tintern Abbey, or something of the sort. Then you rush home, and wake up your wife, and write it down."

She stared. "Ooh, you villain! You mean to tell me that looking at me makes you think of a limerick? I don't think that's nice."

"Eh? Why?"

"H'm. Well," she admitted, lifting an eyebrow meditatively, "maybe we weren't thinking of the same limerick . . . Why do you wake up your wife?"

"What wife?" said Hugh, who had lost the thread of the discourse.

She brooded, her full pink lips pressed together. Again she looked at him over her shoulder, with an air of a suspicion confirmed.

"So you've got a wife, have you?" she said bitterly. "I jolly well might have known it. Secret marriages are all the fashion. I bet you didn't tell your father, did you? One of those forward American hussies, I suppose, who – who let men – h'm."

From experience on both sides of the Atlantic, Donovan was aware that one of the most stimulating qualities of the English girl is her bewildering use of non-sequitur. He wanted wildly to disclaim any foreign entanglement. Yet the statement roused his stern masculine pride.

"I am not married," he replied with dignity. "On the other hand, I have known any number of very pleasant ginches on the other side, who were certainly fond of h'm."

"You needn't bother," she said warmly, "to regale me with any account of your disgusting love-affairs. I'm sure I'm not interested! I suppose you're one of those nasty people who think women are toys, and oughtn't to have careers and do some good in the world –"

"Right you are."

"Bah!" she said, and gave a vigorous toss of her head. "That's just it. I never thought anybody could be so stupid and old-fashioned in this day and age . . . What are you thinking of?" she asked in some suspicion.

"H'm," said Donovan enigmatically. "You are a little liar. And you keep straying away from the subject. What I originally said was that merely seeing you inspired me to burst into limericks, like Keats or somebody. The idea of you having a career is unthinkable. Preposterous. If you became a doctor, your patients would wake up out of the strongest anaesthetic the moment you felt their pulses. If you became a barrister, you would probably throw the inkstand at the judge when he ruled against you, and . . . What ho! That reminds me . . ."

Patricia, who was beaming, followed his expression. "Go on," she prompted, rather crossly. They had come out of the gloom in the coppice to the warm slope of parkland, drowsy and almost uncannily still as the evening drew in. After the clanging of cities, this hush made him uncomfortable. He looked up at The Grange, with the poplars silhouetted behind it, and he remembered what Dr. Fell had said about a killer. He remembered that, after all, they were still as far away as ever from knowing the murderer's name. Old Depping made a pitiable ghost. These people went on their easy ways, interested in the gossip, but certainly not mourning him. And something that had persisted in Hugh's mind wormed to the surface again.

"Throw the inkstand . . ." he repeated. "Why, I was only thinking of your poltergeist, and what it did to the vicar . . ."

"Oh, that?" She raised her eyebrows quizzically, and grinned. "I say, we did have a row! You should have been here. Of course none of us believed your father was mad, really – except maybe my father – but we didn't believe him when he told us about that American what's-his-name –"

"Spinelli?"

"'M. But that's what made it worse when we heard this morning . . ." She dug the toe of her shoe round in the grass, uneasily. "And that reminds me," she went on, as though she would dismiss the subject. "We don't really want to go up to the house now, do we? If we went along to Henry Morgan's, and maybe had a cocktail . . . ?"

The power of sympathy showed the answer in both their faces. They were beginning to turn round and head the other way almost as soon as she had uttered the words, and Patricia gave a conspirator's gurgle of enjoyment. She knew, she said, a short-cut; a side gate in the boundary wall, not far from the coppice where the Guest House stood, which would lead them out to Hangover House.

"I don't know why," she continued, as though she hated thinking about the matter, but was determined to flounder through it; "I don't know why," she went on suddenly, "that

Spinelli man should want to kill Mr. Depping. But he did do it; and Spinelli's an Italian, and probably a member of the Black Hand, and they do all sorts of queer things – don't they? You know. You know all about criminals, don't you?"

"Um," said Hugh judicially. He was beginning to feel remorseful. He wanted to explain everything to this little ginch, but for some reason he found he couldn't.

"All sorts of queer things," she repeated, evidently satisfied by this logic. "Anyway, I'd be a hypocrite – and so would most of us – if we pretended we'd miss Mr. Depping. I mean, I'm jolly sorry he's dead, and it's too bad, and I'm glad they've caught the man who killed him . . . but there were times when I wished he'd move away, and – and never come back." She hesitated. "If it hadn't been for Betty, the few times we've seen her, I think we'd all have flown against Dad and Mr. Burke and said, 'Look here, throw that blighter out.'"

They were skirting the boundary wall, and she slapped at it with sudden vehemence. It was beginning to puzzle Hugh all the more.

"Yes," he said. "That's the queerest part of it, from what I've seen . . ."

"What is?"

"Well, Depping's status. There doesn't seem to be anybody who more than half defends him. He came here as a stranger; and you took him up and made him one of you. It sounds unusual, if he was so unpopular as he seems to be."

"Oh, I know! I've had it dinned into me a dozen times. Mr. Burke is behind it. He puts Dad up to speaking to us about it. Dad sidles up with a red face and a guilty look, and says, 'Burpf, burpf, eh, what?' And you say, 'What?' Then he splutters some more, and finally says, 'Old Depping – very decent sort, eh?' And you say, 'No.' Then he says, 'Well, damme, he is!' and bolts out the most convenient door as though he'd done his duty. It's Mr. Burke's idea, but he never says anything at all."

"Burke? That's –"

"'M. Yes. Wait till you meet him. Little, broad-set man with a shiny bald head and a gruff voice. He always looks sour, and then chuckles; or else he looks just sleepy. Always wears a brown suit – never saw him in anything else – and has a pipe in his mouth. And," said Patricia, embarked on a sort of grievance, "he has a way of suddenly closing one eye and sighting at you down the pipe as though he were looking along a gun. It takes some time to get used to him." Again she gave the little gurgle of pleasure. "All I'm sure of about J. R. Burke is that he hates talking books, and he can drink more whiskey with absolutely no change of expression than any man I ever saw."

Hugh was impressed. "That," he declared, "is a new one." He pondered. "I always had a sort of idea that everyone connected with a publishing house had long white whiskers and double-lensed spectacles, and sat around in darkish rooms looking for masterpieces. But then I also thought Henry Morgan – I've met him, by the way – that is, the blurbs on the jackets of his books said . . ."

She gurgled. "Yes, they're rather good, aren't they?" she inquired complacently. "He writes them himself. Oh, you're quite wrong, you know. But I was telling you about Mr. Depping. I don't think it was so much the money he'd invested, though I gather that was quite a lot. It was a sort of uncanny ability he had to tell what books would sell and what books wouldn't. There are only about half-a-dozen people like that in the world; I don't know where he got it. But he always knew. He was invaluable. The only thing I ever heard Mr. Burke say about him was once when Madeleine and I were giving him what-for; and J. R. was trying to sleep in a chair with the Times over his face. He took the paper away and said, 'Shut up'; and then he said, 'The man's a genius,' and went back to sleep again . . ."

They had come out into the main road now, cool and shadowy under the trees that lined it, and the high hedges of hawthorn. Almost opposite were the gables of Hangover House. As they approached the gate there became audible an energetic and muffled rattling, which appeared to proceed from a cocktail shaker.

"Light of my life," said an argumentative voice, between rattles, "I will now proceed to expound to you the solution of this mystery as it would be explained by John Zed. To begin with –"

"Hullo, Hank," said Patricia, "may we come in?"

A very pleasant little domestic scene was in progress on the lawn before the house, screened by the high hedge. Madeleine Morgan was curled up in a deck chair under the beach umbrella, an expression of bright anticipation on her face. Alternately she raised to her lips a cocktail glass and a cigarette, and she was making noises of admiration between. In the faint light of the afterglow, the newcomers could see her husband pacing up and down before the table; stopping to administer a vigorous rattle to the shaker, wheeling round, slapping the back of his head, and stalking on again. He turned round at Patricia's greeting, to peer over his spectacles.

"Ha!" he said approvingly. "Come in, come in! Madeleine, more glasses. I think we can find you a couple of chairs. What's up – anything?"

"Didn't I hear you say," remarked Patricia, "that you were going to explain the murder? Well, you needn't. They've found that American, and everything seems to be finished."

"No, it isn't," piped Madeleine, with a pleased look at her husband. "Hank says it isn't."

Chairs were set out, and Morgan filled all the glasses. "I know they've found the American. I saw Murch on his way back from Hanham. But he isn't guilty. Stands to reason. (Here's loud cheers – down she goes! –)"

A general murmur, like the church's mumbled responses when the minister reads the catechism, answered the toast. The Martini's healing chill soothed Hugh Donovan almost at once. He relaxed slowly.

Morgan went on with some warmth:

"Stands to reason, I tell you! Of course, I'm interested in truth only as a secondary consideration. Chiefly I'm interested in how this murder ought to work out according to story standards, and whether a plot can be worked up around it. You see –"

"I say, why don't you?" interrupted Patricia, inspired. She took the glass away from her lips and frowned. "That's a jolly good idea! It would be a change. To date," she said dreamily, "you have poisoned one Home Secretary, killed the Lord Chancellor with an axe, shot two Prime Ministers, strangled the First Sea Lord, and blown up the Chief Justice. Why don't you stop picking on the poor Government for a while and kill a publisher like Depping?"

"The Lord Chancellor, my dear girl," said Morgan with a touch of austerity, "was not killed with an axe. I wish you would get these things right. On the contrary, he was beaned with the Great Seal and found dead on the Woolsack . . . You are probably thinking of the Chancellor of the Exchequer; in The Inland Revenue Murders. I was only letting off a little steam in that one."

"I remember that one!" said Hugh, with enthusiasm. "It was damned good." Morgan beamed, and refilled his glass. "I like those stories," Hugh pursued, "a lot better than the ones that are so popular by that other fellow – what's his name? – William Block Tournedos. I mean the ones that are supposed to be very probable and real, where all they do is run around showing photographs to people."

Morgan looked embarrassed.

"Well," he said, "you see, to tell you the truth, I'm William Block Tournedos too. And I thoroughly agree with you. That's my graft."

"Graft?"

"Yes. They're written for the critics' benefit. You see, the critics, as differentiated from the reading public, are required to like any story that is probable. I discovered a long time ago the way to write a probable and real story. You must have (1) no action, (2) no atmosphere whatever – that's very important – (3) as few interesting characters as possible, (4) absolutely no digressions, and (5) above all things, no deduction. Digressions are the curse of probability . . . which is a funny way of looking at life in general; and the detective may uncover all he can, so long as he never deduces anything. Observe those rules, my children; then you may outrage real probability as much as you like, and the critics will call it ingenious."

"Hooray!" said Madeleine, and took another drink.

Patricia said: "You've whipped your hobbyhorse to death, Hank. Go back to the problem . . . Why couldn't this be a story; I mean, from your own preferences in stories?"

Morgan grinned, getting his breath. "It could," he admitted, "up to and including the time of the murder. After that . . ." He scowled.

A sharp premonition made Hugh look up. He remembered that this was the person who had told them to look for the buttonhook.

"What do you mean, after that?"

"I don't think the American is guilty. And," said Morgan, "of all the motiveless and unenterprising sluggards to gather up as suspects, the rest of us are the worst! At least, in a crime story, you get a lot of motives and plenty of suspicious behavior. You have a quarrel overheard by the butler, and somebody threatening to kill somebody, and somebody else sneaking out to bury a blood-stained handkerchief in the flower bed . . . But here we've nothing of the kind.

"Depping, for instance. I don't mean he had no enemies. When you hear of a man who is said to have no enemies, you can practically sit back and wait for somebody to murder him. Depping was a harder sort of problem. Nobody liked him, but, God knows, nobody hereabouts would have gone to the point of doing him in. – And in your wildest imagination, now, can you picture anybody as the murderer? The bishop? Colonel Standish? J. R. Burke? Maw? Let me fill up your glass again."

"Thanks," said Hugh. "Who's Maw?"

Patricia wriggled delightedly in the deck chair. The windows of the house behind her were still glowing, though the lawn was in shadow; there was a light on her blonde hair, and even that vibrant brownish-gold skin seemed to reflect it. She lounged back in the chair, her eyes bright and her lips moist, ticking the glass against her teeth. One bare leg in a tennis shoe swung over the side. Patricia said:

"Oh, yes. I'd better explain that before you meet her, so that you'll know how to handle her . . . It's my mother. You'll like her. Nowadays she's a sort of tyrant who can't tyrannize, and it makes her furious. Coo! We all used to be afraid of her, until an American friend of Hank's found the solution . . ."

"Um," said Donovan. He resisted a powerful impulse to go over and sit down beside her on the foot-rest part of the deck chair. "Yes, I remember your brother said something about that."

"Poor Morley is still shocked. But it's the only way to deal with her, really. Otherwise you'd always be eating turnips, or doing exercises in front of an open window, or something. It only began by everybody calling her Maw . . . So remember. When she comes sailing up to you and orders you to do something, or tries to dragoon you into it, you look her straight in the eye and say, firmly, 'Nuts, Maw.' Just like that. And then even more firmly, 'Nuts.' That closes the subject."

"'Nuts,'" repeated Donovan, with the air of one uttering a talisman. "'Nuts, Maw.'" He drew reflectively on his cigarette. "But are you sure it works? I'd like to try something like that on my old man, if I could muster up the nerve . . ."

"It takes a bit of doing," Morgan admitted, rubbing his jaw. "Colonel Standish can't manage it even yet. Of course, he got off on the wrong foot. The first time he tried it he only rushed up to her and said, 'Almonds, damme, almonds'; and waited for something to happen. And it didn't. So now –"

"I don't believe that story," said Patricia defensively. "He tells that to everybody," she appealed to Hugh, "and it never happened at all. It –"

"On my sacred word of honor," said Morgan, raising his hand with fervor, "it did. I was outside the door, and heard it. He came out afterwards and said he must have forgot the demnition countersign, and now he'd have to take cod-liver oil after all. But there you are; there's a good example . . . Try to find a murderer among people like that! We know these people. I can't seem to find one who would fit into the part; not one of the whole crowd we could hang for murder – !"

"Certainly you can, dear!" his wife maintained stoutly. Her flushed face looked round at the others in some defiance. She swallowed a sip of her cocktail, said, "Urk!" and then beamed on them. "You just keep on trying, and you'll find somebody. I know you will."

"But you don't need to find anybody, old boy," said Patricia. "This is real life, you see; that's the difference. This American Spinelli shot him, and there's no detective story plot about it."

Morgan was stalking up and down, gesturing with his dead pipe. Even his striped blazer was growing indistinct in the dusk. He wheeled round.

"I am prepared to outline you a theory," he declared, "and to prove to you that what's-his-name didn't. I don't know whether I'm right. I'm only looking at it from poor old John Zed's viewpoint. But I shouldn't be surprised if it were true. Anyway, it's what I meant by saying the first part of it would make a good story . . ."

None of them had heard stolid footsteps coming along the road. But now an indistinct figure leaned over the gate, and seemed to be looking from one to the other of them. They could see the bowl of a pipe glowing.

"You still talking, eh?" growled a gruff voice, with a faint chuckle under it. "May I come in?"

"What ho," said Morgan. "Come in, J. R. Come in." He was apologetic but determined. "I'd like to have you hear this, if you think I generally talk nonsense. Mr. Burke, this is the Bishop of Mappleham's son . . ."

10
A QUESTION OF KEYS

The great J. R. Burke came in with his short solid steps, head slightly down. Hugh could see him better when he moved out of the darkness near the gate, and into the faint glow that lingered over against the house. Patricia had correctly described him, except that now his large bald head was hidden under a sort of piratical hat with its brim turned up in front. A short, stocky man in a brown suit, who always seemed to be looking up at you in that squinting, sighting fashion over half-glasses. First he would preserve a Chinese-image expression, with the corners of his mouth drawn down. Then, as he seemed to see nothing dangerous on the horizon, he would grunt, assume a quizzical expression, and attain a faint twinkle of the eye.

This, as indicated, was the great J. R. Burke, potent discoverer of authors, manager of finances, and hater of books; urbane, genial, cynical, immensely well-read, frequently drunk, and always at ease. He stumped across now, sighting at everybody.

"I've been sittin' on a log," he grunted, with a sniff which seemed to indicate what he thought of nature in general. "I hate sittin' on logs. If I sit on a log for two minutes, all the rest of the day I think things are crawling all over me . . . Hum. Let us have a little causerie."

Morgan brought out another chair, and he established himself. "Go on talking," he said to Morgan. "You will anyhow. Humph. Eh? Yes, whiskey, please. Ah! – that's enough. Stop a minute. They tell me Scotland Yard's sent Gideon Fell down to look into this business. Is that true?"

"It is. Do you mean to say you haven't been about all afternoon?"

"Good man, Fell," said J R. gruffly.

He spread himself out, squaring his arms; tasted his whiskey, and then looked quizzically at everybody, blinking over the half-glasses. The pipe went back into his mouth.

"Humph," he added. "I've been taking a walk in quiet country lanes. I won't do it again. Every time I try to walk in quiet country lanes, they are suddenly as full of automobiles as Regent Street at five o'clock in the afternoon. Twenty times I was nearly run over by bicycles coming up behind. I hate being run down by bicycles; there is something insulting about being run down by bicycles, damn it. They sneak up on you. When you do see them, neither you nor the cyclist can decide which way to go; so you both stagger all over the road, and finally he sideswipes you with the handlebar. Humph."

"Poor Mr. Burke!" said Madeleine, keeping her face straight with an expression of concern. "Diddums get hit by a mean old bicycle?"

"Yes, my dear," said J. R., and squinted sideways with his rifle-barrel glare, "yes, I did. And on the main road. I was deliberately assaulted by a bicycle on the main road – after having successfully dodged twenty-four of them in all the back lanes of Gloucestershire. Fellow coming down this hill at a speed that ought to be prohibited. It's a blind corner. I didn't see him. Bang."

"Never mind, sir," said Morgan consolingly. "You were just off your game, that's all. You'll fool him next time."

J. R. looked at him.

"Fellow got up off the road dizzy, and helped me get up. Then he said, 'Are you Mr. J. R. Burke?' I said yes. He said, 'I've got a telegram for you.' I said, 'Well, this is the hell of a way to deliver it, isn't it?' Imagine his confounded nerve. 'What is your procedure.' I said, 'when unusual circumstances compel you to deliver a telegram at somebody's house? Is it necessary to use a tank, or do you only wrap the telegram round a hand grenade and chuck it through the window?'" Evidently satisfied by this retort, J. R. recovered some of his good humor. He growled something into his glass, and glanced sardonically at Morgan. "By the way, it was from Langdon, Depping's solicitor in London. You people at The Grange – I don't suppose anybody thought to do that, eh? Fine practical minds. Suppose you thought his affairs would take care of themselves."

"Any ideas," said Morgan, "about the murder?"

J. R. looked at him sharply. "No. It's a bad business, that's all I know. Going to hurt us – plenty. Why theorize? They've caught the murderer . . ."

"Have they?"

"If you're trying to apply theories . . . " The corners of the other's mouth turned down, and he surveyed his glass; looked around it, and over it, and under it. "I'll give you advice. Stick to John Zed, and let real life alone. Don't touch this business, anyway. It's mucky."

"Well, that's what I was wondering. The police are likely to be asking you what you know about Depping; his past, and the rest of it –"

"You mean Gideon Fell will. Humph . . . What of it? I can't tell him any more than I can tell anybody else. Depping's credit's perfectly sound and Bank-of-England. Otherwise he had – useful qualities. Standish vouched for him. If Fell wants any further information, he'll have to ask the solicitor. Langdon will be here tonight or tomorrow morning."

Morgan evidently saw that J. R. (if he knew anything) had no disposition to talk. But Morgan talked. He stood in the middle of the darkened lawn and proceeded with a recital which raised Donovan's hair – for, in essentials, it was inference for inference almost exactly the same explanation as Dr. Fell's.

Less closely reasoned, more discursive, and with a few points missing, he had nevertheless contrived to evolve the whole scene with the imaginative vividness of a story-teller. He started with the buttonhook, and went on with a multitude of details – after the fashion of the novelist – which were new to Donovan. When he announced his first surprise, Depping's disguise and imposture, Patricia gave a hoot of derision, and J. R. peered over his glasses in tolerant mockery. But presently he began pounding in his details, and the others were silent.

"And I can prove my assumptions," he went on, striding back and forth among them, and addressing himself to Burke, "on points I noticed when Murch and I examined the room this morning. I decided that there had been an imposture, and I examined the body first of all . . ." He turned to Donovan. "You were with Dr. Fell when he went to the Guest House. Did he examine the body carefully?"

Donovan was cautious. "Well, no. That is –"

"On the upper lip," Morgan proceeded, "there were traces of spirit-gum for the moustache; you can't take it off with water. Traces of the actor's cement were behind his ears. In the fireplace were not only remnants of burned clothing, but a scorched tuft of black hair from the wig . . . Then I went into his bedroom and bathroom, which adjoined the study. If there had been any further need for confirmation, it was there. On either side of the mirror over the washbowl in the bathroom, two candles had been propped up – to give Depping light in taking off his make-up, immediately after his return. Stuck in the drain was one of those strips of transparent fishskin that are used for drawing in sagging flesh round the cheeks and eyes, to present an appearance of youth. There were wet socks and a suit of wet underclothing across a chair; the rest had been burned. I didn't find any box of cosmetics, but Murch was watching and I couldn't make a thorough search. All this puzzled Murch considerably." Again he peered at Hugh in the gloom. "What did Dr. Fell make of it?"

This time Hugh was caught off guard. "We didn't go in there," he replied. "When he deduced all you've said, it was only from the facts we'd heard –"

There was a silence. He heard his own words as though they had come back to him in an echo. Suddenly he tried to stumble into another explanation, but he could think of nothing. In the hush Morgan walked across, his head bent forward.

"Good God," he said, "do you mean to tell me that I'm right?"

There was a sort of staggered incredulity in his tone which puzzled Hugh still more.

"Right?" he repeated. "Well, if you've been saying all this –"

"I know," said Morgan, and passed a hand over his eyes. Then he started to laugh. "I'd convinced myself of it, but . . . well, it seemed too good to be true. It was so exactly the way it should have happened according to romance that I didn't really believe it myself. That was why I was testing it out on all of you. Betrayed, by the Lord! Mastermind betrayed into telling the true facts too soon." He picked up the cocktail shaker, found it was empty, and set it down irritably. "Why the devil couldn't I have waited and hit the bishop in the eye with it? I'll never forgive myself for this."

He sat down. J. R. was making protesting noises. "Look here," he said, "do you mean to tell me Gideon Fell believes all this tommyrot?"

"I'd be willing to bet," said Morgan thoughtfully, "that you believe it yourself."

"Tommyrot!" snapped J. R. "You're making Depping out as an ex-criminal, who wanted to kill Spinelli –"

"I only said there was something highly unsavory in his past."

"Humph." After a time of lowering his head and grunting, the other's tone changed again to tolerant sarcasm. "It would look well enough for a book, my lad, but it won't do. There's one great big thundering hole in it. Know what it is? Shut up. Let me talk. I'll see to what lengths of nonsense you're willing to go before I explode the thing . . . Suppose it's true. Which I don't admit, mind. What then?"

"Why, we come back to the fact that the murderer is somebody in our midst." Morgan got up again, stared at the darkening sky, and began to move about rather uneasily. He had the air of one who has started up more than was his intention. "That is . . . Look here, is this what Dr. Fell thinks? For God's sake, man, tell me the truth!"

Donovan, who had been cursing himself, made an attempt at mysteriousness that was not very successful. He shrugged his shoulders. Patricia was brooding with her chin in her fists. Morgan went on:

"This was Depping's world. If he wanted a confederate to keep guard in his room while he went out after Spinelli . . ."

"Rubbish," said J. R. "And I'll tell you why . . . Assume what you say is true. His having a confederate for this business is fantastic. Worse than the idea he was a criminal in the past. Much. Pah! Listen to me." The red bowl of his pipe stabbed out in the gloom. "What did Depping most want to do?"

"About what? I don't follow you."

Patricia passed a hand over her hair and then gestured like one who wants silence in which to think. "I say, wait a bit. I think I follow." She turned accusingly to J. R. "At least you'll admit this. You've always thought he was playing some sort of part – now, haven't you?"

"Got nothing to do with it. Don't ask me questions," growled the other. "Go on."

"He wanted to be thought a scholarly and well-bred country gentleman; that's what he wanted," said Patricia with emphasis.

"Humph. Which he may have been, mind . . . Anyhow, that's what I meant. He wanted to establish his position for that; he'd been working towards it for five years. Humph." J. R. gathered his shoulders together. His face was barely visible in the gloom; but they could feel the Chinese-image expression hardening and staring out as though to convince them by weight of personality, like the bishop. "Then is what you say very likely? – Would he go up to one of the people hereabouts and say, 'Look here. Sorry to deceive you all this time, but the fact is I'm really an ex-criminal and baby-killer. There's a fellow I used to know, who's been trying to blackmail me, and I've got to bump him off. Give me a hand, will you? Take my place in the study while I go out and attend to him; there's a good fellow. I'll do the same for you sometime.'" He snorted. "Nonsense!"

Morgan had been lighting his pipe. The match abruptly stopped just above the bowl; it showed his face gone tense, and rather strained, and he was staring at the beach umbrella. Then the match went out.

He said slowly: "No. Depping needn't have said that at all."

"More theories – ?"

"The only theory," Morgan answered in a queer voice, "that will account for all the facts. A theory that turns half-a-dozen of the most harmless people in England, including myself, into a group of potential murderers."

Another pause. Hugh stared at the sky, turning to colors of pale white and purple after sunset, and he was conscious of a chill that had taken hold of everybody. Madeleine said,

"Don't talk like that –" all of a sudden, and struck the side of the deck chair.

"Let's hear it," said J. R. sharply.

"I'm rather muddled myself," Morgan admitted, with his hand over his eyes; "and there have been so many cross-deductions that we're apt to tangle up what we know with what we only suspect. But here it is . . .

"The last part of the hypothesis I told you – that is, the murder of Depping by his confederate – was based on the assumption that the confederate was a willing accomplice, who knew what Depping meant to do; and, second, that this accomplice had meantime devised his own plan for killing Depping. That he went to the Guest House prepared with rubber gloves. That he left Depping locked out on the balcony, pretending that the key was lost; that he made Depping come up through the front door to provide an alibi . . . Is that correct?"

"Fair enough," said Hugh. "What then?"

Morgan replied quietly: "Only that the accomplice was nothing of the kind, and had at first not the slightest intention of killing Depping."

"But, look here –"

"J. R's objection is perfectly sound. It's convincing, and it's true. Depping would never have suggested to anybody hereabouts that they assist him in a murder; or even have hinted at an unsavory past, until . . . Wait a bit. But there would have been any number of harmless people in this vicinity quite willing to assist Depping in what they thought was a lark."

Burke snorted. "A lark! You've an odd notion of the people in your circle, my boy, if you think they're addicted –"

"Have you forgotten the poltergeist?" said Morgan.

After a silence he went on steadily:

"Somebody was willing to cut up that row with the vicar, and probably enjoyed it. I should have enjoyed it, personally . . . I still insist that several people could have been drawn in to assist Depping, unwittingly, if they had been persuaded it was a show of that sort. It wouldn't be hard to spin up a tale that would plant an unconscious confederate in that study. Depping meant to go out and kill Spinelli. But the accomplice didn't know that."

"In that case," said Donovan, who was trying to hold hard to reason, "what becomes of the plot to kill Depping? What about the rubber gloves – and the key that accomplice pretended to have lost – and – ?"

"They are all suppositions," said Morgan coolly.

Hugh peered at him. "Good God, man, I know they are! They're your suppositions. What happens to them now?"

"Put it this way. Depping, in disguise, was locked out. He was locked out for an obvious reason which doesn't seem to have occurred to anybody: that the accomplice really couldn't find the key. Depping had sneaked out the front door of the house intending to return by the balcony. But he had forgotten the key – left it behind in his other clothes, and it couldn't be found. Meantime, Depping can't wait in the rain. He conceives the idea that he can get in through the front door, if the other person will blow out the fuses . . ."

"How?" demanded Hugh. "I thought we'd agreed about the buttonhook. Nobody with bare hands would have tried blowing the fuses like that."

"Certainly not. But it could have propped against that low socket, and pushed in to make a contact . . ."

"With what?"

"With the sole of a tennis shoe," said Morgan, and struck another match. "We mustn't be too sure of those rubber gloves, you know. And thus we destroy the only basis for believing that the accomplice intended to kill Depping . . . with the sole of any ordinary tennis shoe."

Donovan searched his mind for a suitable observation, and eyed his host with malevolence. "Nuts!" he said violently, after some consideration. "Nuts."

Patricia let out a protesting gurgle.

"I say, Hank, it won't do!" she insisted. "I thought you said that, after Mr. Depping was shot, the murderer got out the balcony door, and the door was left open . . . If that's so, and the murderer really couldn't find the key, how did he get out that way?"

Morgan was afire with his new idea. He went stalking up and down, banging into the table in the gloom, and bumping against chairs indiscriminately.

"As simple as that!" he almost shouted. "Ha. Ha. Of course. When his accomplice can't find the key, Depping is hopping mad. Depping is hop . . . 'm. Let the euphony pass. He comes upstairs in his disguise. He does exactly what you yourself would have done under the circumstances. 'Are you blind?' he says. 'Look here, you fathead!' – or words to that effect, however Depping would have phrased it. He goes in and finds the key himself and produces it before the other person's eyes. In moments of great emotional stress, that's precisely the sort of silly thing a person would do. Can't you see Depping, wet to the skin, nervous, vicious; with his loud clothes and his wig coming askew; standing there shaking the key before the other person? Even with the murder of Spinelli on his mind . . ."

"I don't know whether you are aware of it," said Hugh with great politeness, "but Spinelli happens to be alive."

"Which," said Morgan, "Depping didn't know. He thought Spinelli's body was safe in the river . . . Murch told me what happened at the Chequers last night. Depping didn't know his attempt was a failure. And what then?"

Morgan's voice sank. "Now he has the accomplice utterly at his mercy. I can see Depping with that little smirk he used to have – remember it? – on his face, and the stoop of his shoulders, and his hands rubbing together. He goes into the bathroom and painstakingly removes his disguise. He brushes his hair and puts on other clothes. His accomplice is still mystified; but he has been promised an explanation, after the clothes and evidences have been destroyed. Presently Depping sits down, facing the other person, and smiles again.

"'I have killed a man,' he says in that dry voice of his. 'You will never dare betray me, because I have made you accessory before and after the fact.'"

Morgan's voice had unconsciously fallen into an imitation. Hugh had never heard Depping's voice; but it was just such a one as he would have believed Depping to have possessed – level, thin, harsh, and edged with malice. The man had suddenly become alive here in the dusk: a puzzle and a monstrosity, rubbing his hands together. Donovan could see him sitting up stiff in his leather chair, with a candle burning on the desk before him, and the storm roaring outside. He could see the long furrowed face, the grizzled hair, the dry leer out of the eyes.

Across from him sat X.

"You know how he repressed himself when he was with us," Morgan went on abruptly. "You could feel it. You knew he hated us, that he was thinking differently, and his mind was boiling the whole time. He'd got his new life; but he could never get used to it. That was why he went on those drinking sprees.

"I don't know what there had been in his past life. But I think that murder had probably been one of the least of his offenses. I think he sat there and carefully explained to his accomplice what he had been, and what he was; that all his spite came out; and that he pointed out carefully how the accomplice was caught. He couldn't be betrayed, or Depping would swear both of them were concerned in the murder. What the confederate had thought a lark was really a crime that put him at Depping's mercy. Depping displayed the pistol, laid it on the table. And I think something was said – I don't know what; this is only a guess – that made one of our nice, harmless, inoffensive community go slightly insane. Maybe it was the way Depping smirked and moved his head. I don't know, but I could have killed him, myself, more than once. I think one of our harmless community found an excuse to get behind Depping – snatched up the gun from the table, and –"

"Don't!" cried Patricia out of the dark. "Don't say that! You almost sound as though you'd been there! . . ."

Morgan lowered his head. He seemed to catch sight of his wife, who was huddled back silently into the deck chair. Moving across, he sat down beside her and said in a matter-of-fact voice:

"What price horrors? Actually, what we all want is another cocktail. Wait till I get the lights on, and another bowl of ice, and I'll mix a new shaker . . ."

"You don't get out of it," said Hugh grimly, "so easily as that."

"No. No," the other replied in a reflective voice, "I didn't suppose I should. Well, the only question is: Which one of us would old Depping select for his lark?"

The implication of his remark was setting slowly into all their minds when, with only a preliminary grunt, J. R. Burke spoke out. He said in a meditative voice:

"I dare say I'm obstructing justice."

"Obstructing – ?"

"Don't mind obstructing justice, I don't," growled J. R. "Officious, that's what the police are. Ought to be a law against it. Still – if Gideon Fell thinks all this, got to tell it. Young fella, you think there was an accomplice, do you? What time do you think this accomplice came to see Depping at the Guest House?"

Morgan peered at him oddly. "I don't know. Any time

after Depping's dinner tray was taken up; half-past eight to nine o'clock, maybe."

"Humph. Well, you're wrong."

"How do you know?"

"Because," said J. R. equably, "I was talking to Depping at that time . . . Don't gape at me, confound it!" He unscrewed his pipe and blew down the stem. "Now you'll call it suspicious behavior; won't you? Bah. Man pays a perfectly ordinary visit, and there you are."

Morgan got up. He said: "Holy Saint Patrick! And the suspicious behavior had to come from you . . . Did you tell this to Murch?"

"No. Why should I? But now they've brought on all this funny business . . ."

"Excuse me, sir," said Hugh, "but did you make any foot-prints?"

J. R. used some bad language. He said it was a matter of indifference to him whether he had made any footprints, and also that he didn't know, and what was this all about anyway?

"I mean," Hugh persisted, "did you go to see him in Morley Standish's shoes?"

J. R. dwelt fancifully on this theme. He pointed out the infrequency of his necessity for borrowing a pair of shoes in order to pay business calls on his associates. Then Morgan remembered the footprint of which he and Murch had taken a plaster cast; and Hugh explained its origin.

"But the valet," he went on, "didn't mention any other visit last night, and I only wondered whether you might have gone up by the balcony door . . ."

"I did go up by the balcony door," returned Burke. "Ah, I see, I see. You're itching to turn inquisitor on me; I can smell it in the air. There's no good damned reason why I should tell it, but I will." He craned his neck aggressively. "I went up because I saw his light, and that's the only room he ever uses. Why shouldn't I go up by the balcony door? Much easier."

There was a strained and polite silence. Morgan coughed. No better spur could have been applied.

"I'd just as soon break down your theories by telling you. Humph. All this business about keys – ! Listen. I went to see Depping last night just after dinner; it was about a quarter to nine, and just getting dark. And I'll give Gideon Fell another tip, for what it's worth. Depping was leaving England.

"Don't ask me where or why. What I saw him about was business, and that doesn't concern you. But I'd be willing to swear he wasn't expecting anybody at all that night . . . I went up on the balcony and looked through the glass in the upper part of the door; you can see through the white squares in the chequering. He was standing by the desk with his coat, shirt, and collar off, and rummaging in the desk drawer. I couldn't see what he had in his hand. Still, I'll admit it may have been a wig."

Morgan whistled.

"Pleases you, don't it," said the other, "when somebody really gets into a situation like that? Tell you frankly, it didn't please me when I heard about the murder this morning . . . Humph. I was telling you. When I tapped on the door, Depping almost jumped out of his shoes. He'd got a wild-eyed look about him. Wondered if he'd been drinkin' again. He said, 'Who's there?' Would he have looked like that if he'd been expecting somebody eh?"

"Well . . ."

"Well, nothing. He took a key out of his pocket – yes, out of his pocket – and came over and unlocked the door. He smelled of whiskey. He said, 'I can't see you tonight.' I said, 'This is important, and I don't want you going off drinking again.' We talked for a while, but every minute or so he'd look at his watch; and he didn't ask me to sit down. Finally I said, 'All right, go to the devil; and walked out . . . He locked the door after me, and put the key in his pocket. That's all I know. It may be still there."

"It wasn't there," said Morgan, "when Murch searched his clothes. And it wasn't in any of the suits in his wardrobe. I wonder . . ."

They sat quiet for many minutes. It was Patricia who finally suggested that they ought to be returning to The Grange for dinner; and, when she put her hand on Hugh's arm as she rose, he thought that it trembled.

11
THE POLTERGEIST AND THE RED NOTEBOOK

There was no regular dinner that night at The Grange. When they hurried up to the house, well after seven o'clock, they received the news that Mr. Theseus Langdon, the dead man's solicitor, had arrived shortly before, accompanied by Miss Elizabeth Depping, who had taken the afternoon plane from Paris. The former was closeted in the library with Dr. Fell and Inspector Murch; the latter was indisposed, and kept to her room – probably, Patricia said with candor, less from her father's death than from her usual airsickness. But this indisposition was highly romanticized by Colonel Standish's good lady, who sailed about in a tempest of activity and set the house into an uproar. She presided at Betty Depping's bedside much as she might have presided at a ladies' club meeting; Patricia joined her, and there would seem to have been a row of some sort. Anyhow, only cold refreshments were set out on a sideboard in the dining-room, and disconsolate guests wandered about eating surreptitious sandwiches.

Of the celebrated Maw Standish, Hugh caught only a brief glimpse. She stalked downstairs to bid him welcome – a handsome woman, five-feet-ten in her lowest-heeled shoes, with a mass of ash-blonde hair carried like a war banner, and a rather hard but determinedly pleasant face. She told him firmly that he would like The Grange. She stabbed a finger at several of the portraits in the main hall, and reeled off the names of their artists. She tapped the elaborately carved frame of a mirror in the great alcove where the staircase stood, and impressively said, "Grinling Gibbons!" Donovan said, "Ah!" Next she enumerated the distinguished people who had visited the house, including Cromwell, Judge Jeffreys, and Queen Anne. Cromwell, it seemed, had left behind a pair of boots, and Jeffreys had smashed a piece out of the panelling; but Queen Anne seemed to have retired in good order. She fixed him with a stern, faintly smiling look, as though she wondered if he were worthy of this heritage; then she said that the patient required her attention, and marched up the staircase.

The Grange, he discovered, was a pleasant house: cool and sleepy, with its big rooms built on three sides of a rectangle. It had been modernized. The electric lights, set in wall brackets or depending from very high ceilings, had a rather naked look; but the only touch of antiquity – and a spurious one at that – was in the stone-flagged floor of the main hall, its great fireplace of white sandstone, and red-painted walls full of non-family portraits in gilt frames. Behind the main hall was a funereal dining-room, outside whose bay windows grew the largest ilex tree he had ever seen; and here J. R. Burke sat drinking beer in stolid thoughtfulness.

Wandering off into the west wing, Hugh found a drawing-room which some ancestor had decorated in opulent and almost pleasant bad taste. The walls were a panorama of Venetian scenes, with everybody leaning out of gondolas at perilous angles; gold-leaf mirrors; cabinets overlaid in china ornaments; and a chandelier like a glass castle. From across a hallway he could hear a mutter of voices behind the door to the library. A tribunal seemed to be going on there. As he watched, the door opened, and a butler came out; he could see momentarily a long room full of cigar smoke, and Dr. Fell making notes at a table.

The drawing-room windows were open on a stone-flagged terrace, where a cigarette was winking in the gloom. Hugh went outside. The terrace looked down over shelving gardens towards the rear, colorless under the white-and-purple dusk; and a few mullioned windows were alight in the pile of the west wing. Against the stone balustrade Morley Standish leaned and stared at the windows. He peered round as he heard a footstep.

"Who – ? Oh, hullo," he said, and resumed his scrutiny.

Hugh lit a cigarette and said: "What's been going on? Your sister and I were down at Morgan's. Have they found – ?"

"That's what I'd like to know," said Morley. "Seems to me they're devilish secretive. I don't seem to count for anything. Mother says I oughtn't to see Betty. . . Miss Depping, you know, she's here. I don't know what they're doing. They've had every servant on the carpet over there in the library. God knows what's going on."

He flung away his cigarette, hunched himself up, and brooded over the balustrade. "Beautiful night, too," he added irrelevantly. "'Where were you on the night of the murder?'"

"I?"

"They've been asking us all that – just as a matter of form. Beginning with the servants to make it look better. Where would we be? Where is there to go after dark? We were all tucked up in our beds. I wish I could explain those confounded shoes."

"Did you ask about them?"

"I asked Kennings: that footman I was telling you about. He doesn't know. He remembers putting the shoes in the junk closet right enough, some time ago. Anybody could have taken 'em out. There's no mistake. They're not there now . . . Hullo!"

Hugh followed the direction of his glance. Another light had appeared in the west wing. "Now I wonder," said

Morley, rubbing his forehead with a heavy hand, "who's in the oak room at this time?"

"The oak room?"

"Where our poltergeist hangs out," Morley told him grimly. After a pause, during which he stared at the light, he said: "Am I getting idiotic notions? Or do you think we ought to go up and see?"

They looked at each other. Hugh was conscious of a tensity in the other's bearing; almost an explosiveness which the stolid Morley had been concealing. Hugh nodded. Almost in a rush they left the terrace. They were climbing the main staircase before Morley spoke again.

"See that fellow?" he asked, pointing to a bad portrait on the landing. It was that of a fleshy-faced man in a laced coat and full-bottomed periwig, with plump hands which seemed to be making an uncertain gesture, and an evasive eye. "He was one of the Aldermen of Bristol, supposed to have been concerned in the Western Rebellion of 1685. He didn't actually do anything – didn't have the nerve, I suppose – but he was rumored to have favored Monmouth. When Chief Justice Jeffreys came down for the assize to punish the rebels, he had all his goods forfeited. Jeffreys was staying here, with a Squire Redlands who owned The Grange then. That man, Alderman Wyde, came here to plead with Jeffreys against the sentence. Jeffreys foamed, and preached him a long sermon. So Wyde cut his throat in the oak room. Hence . . ."

They were moving along a passage that led off the main hall upstairs: a narrow passage, badly lighted, and Morley was peering about him as though he expected to find somebody following. The whole house might have been deserted. Morley stopped before a door at the end. He waited a moment, straightened his shoulders, and knocked.

There was no answer. An eerie feeling crawled through Donovan, because they could see the light shining out under the door. Morley knocked again. "All right!" he said, and pushed the door open.

It was a spacious room, but gloomy, because it was panelled to the ceiling. The only illumination was a lamp with a frosted-glass shade, which stood on a table by the bed: a canopied bed, unmade and uncurtained. In the wall facing them was a wooden mantelpiece, with leaded windows in embrasures on either side. There was another door in the right-hand wall. And the room was empty.

Morley's footsteps rattled on the boarded floor. He called, "Hallo!" and moved across to the other door; which was shut but unlocked. He pulled it open and glanced into the darkness beyond.

"That," he said, "is the junk closet. It –"

He whirled round. Hugh also had backed away. There had been a sharp creak near the fireplace, and a flicker of light. A section of the panelling between the fireplace and the window embrasure was being pushed open: a hinged section, nearly as high as a door. The Bishop of Mappleham, with a candle in his hand, appeared in the aperture.

Hugh had the presence of mind not to laugh.

"Look here, sir," he protested, "I wish you wouldn't do that. Mysterious villains have a monopoly on entrances like that. When you appear –"

His father's face looked tired and heavy over the candle flame. He turned to Morley.

"Why," he said, "was I not told of this – this passage?"

Morley only returned his gaze blankly for a moment. "That? I thought you knew about it, sir. It isn't a secret passage, you know. If you look closely, you can see the hinges. And the hole where you put your finger to open it. It leads –"

"I know where it leads," said the bishop. "Downstairs, to a concealed door opening on the gardens. I have explored it. Neither end is latched. Do you realize that any outsider could enter this house unseen at any time he chose?"

Morley's dark, almost expressionless eyes seemed to recognize what the other was thinking. He nodded, slightly. But he said:

"For that matter; an outsider could walk in the front entrance if he chose. We never lock doors."

The bishop set down his candle on the mantelshelf, and fell to brushing dust from his coat. Again his face was heavy and clouded, as though from anger or loss of sleep. "However," he said, "it has been recently used. The dust is disturbed. And over there is the closet from which your shoes were taken . . ."

Heavily, with a forward stoop of his shoulders, he moved over towards the bed. Hugh saw that he was looking at a splattered red stain on the wall and on the floor. For a moment a vision of throat-cuttings, and periwigged gentlemen out of the seventeenth century, invaded the shrivelled old room; then, with a drop of anticlimax, Hugh remembered about the ink. This was where the poltergeist had been active. The whole thing was at once baffling, ludicrous, and terrible.

"Since our authorities," he went on with bitter heaviness, "Dr. Fell with his great knowledge of criminals, and that brilliant detective Inspector Murch, have not seen fit to take me into their confidence this afternoon – well, I have conducted my investigation along my own lines . . . Tell me: This room is not generally used, is it?"

"Never," said Morley. "It's damp, and there's no steam heat. Er – why do you ask, sir?"

"Then how did Mr. Primley happen to occupy it on the night of – on the night someone was assumed to be exercising a primitive sense of humor?"

Morley stared at him. "Well, you ought to know, sir! You

were with us when it was arranged. It was because he asked . . ."

The bishop made an irritated gesture. "I am putting these questions to you," he said, "for my son's benefit. I wish him to understand exactly how the proper sort of examination is conducted."

"Oh!" said Morley. A slightly humorous look appeared in his eyes. "I see. Well, you and my father and Mr. Primley and I began talking about the story of the man who'd killed himself here, and 'the influence' or whatever you call it. So when Mr. Primley had to spend the night here, he asked to be put in this room . . ."

"Ah. Yes. Yes, quite so. That," nodded the bishop, drawing back his chin, "is what I want to establish. Listen, Hugh. But Mr. Primley had not originally intended to spend the night, had he?"

"No, sir. He missed the last bus back home, and he –"

"Consequently, I must point out to you, Hugh: consequently, no outsider could even have known of the vicar's intention to stay the night, even in the doubtful event an outsider knew he was here. It was a sudden decision, made late in the evening. Much less could any outsider have known Mr. Primley intended to occupy this room . . . Therefore this affair could not conceivably have been a joke put up on Mr. Primley by an outsider."

"What ho!" said Hugh, after a pause. "You mean somebody sneaked up that passage to get into the junk closet and steal those shoes; but he didn't expect to find this room occupied . . ."

"Precisely. I am afraid you run ahead of my logic," the bishop rebuked him in a somewhat annoyed voice: "a practice against which I must caution you. But that is what I do mean. He did not expect to find the room occupied; and, either coming in or going out – probably the latter – he woke Mr. Primley. He raised a very brief ghost scare to cover himself." The bishop's furry brows drew together, and he put his hand into his pocket. "What is more, I can tell you exactly the person who would be apt to do that, and I can prove that he was here."

From his pocket he drew a small notebook of red leather; smudged over with dirt. There were gilt initials stamped upon it.

"This interesting little clue was dropped in an angle of the stairs that go down inside that passage. Do me the favor of looking at it. It is unfortunate that it was lost; it bears the initials H.M. Do I need to expatiate at length on the traits of character belonging to young Mr. Henry Morgan, or to point out his suspicious eagerness to lead Inspector Murch by the nose in this case? It was he, I believe, who called Murch's attention to that footprint by the Guest House, and kindly offered to take a plaster impression of the evidence."

"ROT!" said Hugh violently. He swallowed hard. "I mean – excuse me, sir, but that's fantastic. It won't work. It's –"

Morley cleared his throat.

"You'll have to admit, sir," he urged persuasively, "that it takes some believing. I don't mean the evidence! – but about Hank. He would be quite capable of playing a joke of that sort on Mr. Primley or anybody else who slept here, but the rest of it can't be right."

The bishop spread out his hands. "Young man," he said; "I urge nothing upon you. I simply inform you. Did Henry Morgan know Mr. Primley was here at all that night?"

"N-no. But he could have seen him come in, possibly."

"Yet he could not under any circumstances have known Mr. Primley was staying the night?"

"I suppose not."

"Or, above all, the room he would occupy? Ah. Thank you." He placed the notebook carefully back in his pocket, patted his waistcoat, and assumed a benign air. "I think that I shall presently wait upon our good authorities in the library. Shall we go downstairs now? Morley, if you will blow out that candle . . . ? No, leave it there. We shall probably need it presently."

They were walking along the hall again before Morley spoke.

"I tell you, sir," he said, "your assumption is – well, ridiculous; not to put too fine a point on it. I told you Hank didn't like the old boy; all right; everybody will admit that, including Hank himself. But that's no reason for . . ." He hesitated, as though he could not use the word, and went on stubbornly: "And as for sneaking upstairs to get my shoes – ! No, no. That won't work. That's pure theory."

"My boy, be careful. I wish it distinctly understood that I accuse nobody. I have not yet, even in my own thoughts, gone so far as any accusation or implication of – ah – homicide. But if this estimable gentleman, Fell, chooses to exert the letter of his authority in excluding me from his puerile councils, then he cannot be chagrined if I take steps to circumvent him."

Hugh had never before seen his father's hobby take such a violent and spiteful hold. More than this, he suddenly became aware that the bishop was growing old, and unsteady. Nobody in the past, whatever the satirical remarks about him, had ever doubted his fairness or his intelligence. Now Hugh seemed to see only a large grizzle-headed shell, with flabby jowls, and a bitter mouth. He had lived too long, too aggressively, and now there was a faint childishness creeping into him. In only a year . . . Hugh realized, only then, what must have been the effect on him of being betrayed – as though the very Providence he extolled were conspiring to make a fool of him – into the ludicrous antics over which everybody had got so much amusement. It wasn't humorous. The maddest joke of all was just that; he took it seriously. There must be a moral somewhere . . .

Nor did Hugh believe that Morgan was guilty, if only because he felt vaguely that people like Morgan do not commit murders; especially as they are always writing about them in books, and treat murderers as fascinating monstrosities apart from human life, like unicorns or griffins. He doubted whether his father believed it. But he had an alarming idea that the bishop was willing to accuse anybody, regardless of belief, if he could find any sort of case.

Meanwhile, his thoughts were complicated by the mess of the whole affair, and how soon he could see Patricia, and why the mess had to occur at just this time anyway. As he followed his father through the drawing-room, a door slammed violently. It was the library door. Stumping through the drawing-room came J. R. Burke, a sardonic expression on his face, and a reminiscent gleam of battle over his half-glasses. He peered at the newcomers, and grinned. Then he took the pipe out of his mouth to point over his shoulder.

"Evenin'," he said to the bishop. "They told me to fetch you. And also you, young fella. I've given my evidence, and they can put it in their pipes and smoke it. Hum, hum." He cocked his head on one side in pleased reflection. "Go on in. The more the merrier. There's hell poppin' in there."

The bishop drew himself up. "I fancied," he replied, "that sooner or later my presence might be requested. I also fancy I shall somewhat astonish them – What is going on in there, Mr. Burke?"

"It's about Depping's lawyer," explained J. R., chuckling. "It turns out that, in addition to being Depping's lawyer, he's also Spinelli's. And trimming both sides as neat as you please . . . Join up. You and your son are both wanted."

12
SPINELLI READS THE TAROC

The library was a long, narrow room, on one side of which were windows opening on the terrace, and on the other built-in bookshelves and a built-in fireplace. Its color scheme was both dark and florid; there were heavy brown drapes at the windows, and across double doors at the far narrow end of the room. All the wall lamps were burning behind yellowish shades; and the glass chandelier was also in full blaze. Blue sheets of smoke hung under it. At a cluttered table beneath the smoke, Dr. Fell sat spread out with his chins in his collar, absently drawing pictures on a pad. Inspector Murch, a whole brief-case-full of papers spread out before him, was teetering backwards and bristling over his sandy moustache. His pale blue eye looked angry and baffled. Evidently he had just finished some remarks to the smiling gentlemen who sat on the divan beside the table.

"– and you will appreciate, I am sure," the latter was saying smoothly, "the difficulties, both ethical and legal, in which I find myself. You are a reasonable man, Mr. Murch. We are all (I hope) reasonable men. Ahem." He turned his head as the Donovans, père et fils, entered.

Dr. Fell blinked up from his drawing, and waved a hand. "Come in," he invited. "This is Mr. Langdon. Sit down. We're very much in need of help."

Mr. Theseus Langdon was one of those smiling and expansive gentlemen, smooth of gesture and rather too practised of poise, who are all of an engaging frankness. They seem always to impart confidences, with low-voiced diplomacy and a deprecating smile. They can speak of the weather as though they were telling international secrets. In person Mr. Langdon was inclined to portliness. He had a pink scrubbed face, thin brown hair brushed back from a low forehead, eyes like those of an alert dog, and a broad mouth. He sat back on the divan with both ease and dignity, his well-manicured hands in his lap. His cutaway and striped trousers were unwrinkled, and his wing collar looked cool despite the heat. He rose, bowing to the newcomers.

"Thirty-seven, Gray's Inn Square," said Mr. Langdon, as though he were making an epigram. "Gentlemen! At your service!" Then he sat down again and resumed in his easy voice: "As I was saying concerning this dreadful affair, Inspector, you will appreciate my difficulties. Whatever information I possess is at your disposal, I need not tell you. But, as Mr. Burke so admirably put it a moment ago, Mr. Depping was an oyster. Precisely so. A veritable oyster, I assure you."

Murch glowered at him. But his dogged, gruff voice persisted. "'Tes this, then. Which you won't deny. You'm the solicitor both for Mr. Depping that was, and for Louis Spinelli –"

"Excuse me, please. For Mr. Stuart Travers."

"Eh, eh! I be and told you his name is Spinelli –"

"So far as I have any knowledge, Mr. Murch," said Langdon, smiling composedly, "my client's name is Mr. Stuart Travers. You see?"

"But Spinelli has told us –"

At this point Dr. Fell rumbled warningly. Inspector Murch nodded, and fell back. For a time the doctor sat tapping his pencil against the writing pad, and blinking at it. Then he raised his eyes.

"Let's get this straight from the beginning, Mr. Langdon. We happen to know that Spinelli, or Travers, put in a trunk call to you this afternoon. What you advised him is neither here nor there, at the moment. Let's concern ourselves with

Depping. You have told us" – he held out his pudgy fingers and checked off the points – "that you have been his legal adviser for five years. That you know nothing about him, except that he was a British subject who had spent some years in America. That he made no will, and leaves an estate which you estimate at about fifty thousand pounds –"

"Sadly depreciated, I fear," interposed Langdon, shaking his head with a sorrowful smile. "Sadly."

"Eh. Very well then. How did Depping come to you in the first place?"

"I believe I was recommended to him."

"Um," said Dr. Fell, pinching at his moustache. "By the same person who recommended you to Spinelli?"

"I really can't say."

"Now, it's a very curious thing, Mr. Langdon," rumbled Dr. Fell, after a time of tapping the pencil on the pad, "about this information you volunteer. After telling you nothing of himself for five years, according to what you say, Depping walked into your office about two weeks ago and told you several things of a highly private nature. – Is that what you told Inspector Murch?"

Langdon had been sitting back, all polite attention, smiling mechanically; but his alert eyes had been disinterested. They strayed. He touched the sharp crease in his trousers, and seemed pleased. But now the eyes came round sharply to Dr. Fell. His faint eyebrows rose. It was as though the satisfaction of some exceedingly shrewd piece of business gleamed out.

"Quite true," he said. "Shall I – would you like me to repeat my statement, for the benefit of these gentlemen?"

"Langdon," the doctor said suddenly, "why are you so damned anxious for everybody to hear it?"

He had raised his voice only slightly, but it seemed to boom and echo in the room. This somnolent fat man took on an expression which caused Langdon's own expression to veil immediately. But the doctor only said, between wheezes:

"Never mind. I'll repeat it. Depping said, in effect, 'I'm sick of this sort of life, and I'm going away; probably for a trip around the world. What's more, I'm taking somebody with me – a woman.'"

"Quite so," affirmed Langdon pleasantly. He glanced at the newcomers. "Say, however, a lady. A lady of your own charming community here, he told me."

Hugh looked at Inspector Murch, and then at his father. The inspector was muttering with suppressed anger, his eyes half-shut and his moustache bristling. The bishop sat upright, and all the muscles of his face seemed to stiffen with some thought that had come to him. His hand moved slowly towards his pocket . . . For possibly a full minute each of that group was locked up with his own buzzing thoughts. Then Inspector Murch's voice fell heavily into the silence.

He said to Dr. Fell: "I don't believe it. S'help me, sir, I don't believe it."

Langdon turned on him. "Come, come, my friend! This won't do, you know – really it won't. I should have thought that the word of an honorable man would be sufficient. Have you any reason for doubting it? No? I thank you." He went on smiling.

"And he told you all this – ?" Dr. Fell prompted.

"À propos the matter which Inspector Murch was mentioning a while ago. Those rather spirited letters between Mr. Depping and Mr. J. R. Burke," he nodded at the papers on the table, "which the inspector found in Mr. Depping's files. Mr. Depping had invested quite a large sum in Mr. Burke's firm. When he decided to leave England, he wished to withdraw it: a sudden and highly irregular proceeding; but then Mr. Depping was never a business man. You heard what Mr. Burke said a moment ago – it would have been highly inconvenient, not to say impossible, to allow this at the present time; especially on such short notice. Besides, as I pointed out, it was an excellent investment."

"What did he decide?"

"Oh, it was settled most amicably. Mr. Depping was content to let it stand. He was – may I say so – a strange combination of wisdom and irresponsibility."

Dr. Fell leaned back in his chair and asked offhandedly:

"Got any explanation of his death, Mr. Langdon?"

"Ah. Unfortunately, no. I can only say that it is a dreadful business, and shocks me beyond words. Besides" – again the solicitor's eyes narrowed, and his voice grew soft with suggestion – "you can hardly expect me to express an opinion, either private or professional, until I have had the opportunity of conferring with my other client, Mr. Travers."

"All right," said Dr. Fell. He hoisted himself to his feet, wheezing. "All right. That's fair enough . . . Inspector, bring in Louis Spinelli."

There was a silence. Clearly Langdon had not expected this. One of his well-manicured hands moved to his upper lip and caressed it; he sat stiffly, but his eyes followed Murch as the inspector went to the windows. Murch put his head through the curtains and spoke some words outside.

"'Mf. By the way," the doctor remarked, "you'll be interested to know that Spinelli is willing to talk. I don't think he's satisfied with your legal counsel, Mr. Langdon. In return for certain favors –"

Murch stood aside. Followed by a constable, Spinelli moved into the room and looked round him coolly. He was a thin and wiry man, but with a broad, low face. His chin was weak, and his eyes had a look of assumed easiness. Hugh Donovan could understand at once why the rather vague descriptions of him always insisted on "loud clothes," though, strictly speaking, it was erroneous. In no particular was he noticeably loud, yet the effect of the whole – a trick of gesture, a ring on the wrong finger, a necktie adjusted too studiedly at one side – was blatant. His fawn-colored hat was a little too narrow in the brim, and too rakish; his sideburns were exaggerated, and his moustache shaved to a hairline. Now he looked coolly round the library, as though he were appraising it. But he was nervous. Most unpleasant of all, Hugh was conscious of a faint medicinal smell which clung to him.

"How are you?" he said to the company in general, nodding. He removed his hat, smoothed back his sharply parted hair, and looked straight at Langdon. "Fowler told me you were a crook, Langdon. But of all the crude work I've ever had pulled on me, your advising me to hand over my passport to 'em was the worst."

Spinelli's air was compounded of vindictiveness and a nervous desire to please. His voice had a rasping softness. He turned to Dr. Fell. "That fellow – my counsel; my counsel, mind you! – didn't waste any time. I knew I was in a spot. And then I knew he was out to sell me. 'Certainly, let them see your passport.' So they'd cable to Washington, and then where am I?"

"In Dartmoor," replied Dr. Fell blandly. He seemed to be enjoying this. His sleepy eye wandered towards Langdon. "Why should he be trying to sell you, do you think?"

"Cut it," said Spinelli, with a curt gesture. "That's your business to find out. All I want is to understand your proposition – the proposition this fellow," he nodded at Inspector Murch, "put up to me. I'm not running foul of any English dicks if I can help it, and that's flat."

Langdon had risen, and was smiling paternally. He began:

"Tut, tut! Come, you mustn't misunderstand me, Mr. Travers! Be reasonable. I advised you for your own good . . ."

"As for you –" said Spinelli. "You're thinking, 'How much does he know?' You'll find out . . . So this is the proposition. I'm to tell you everything I know. In return for that, you promise not to prosecute for using a faked passport, and allow me one week to get out of the country. Is that it?"

Langdon moved forward. His voice went up shrilly. he said:

"Don't be a fool – !"

"Knocks the wind out of you, does it?" asked Spinelli. "I thought it would. Keep on thinking, 'How much does he know?'"

The American sat down opposite Langdon. With the lights just above his head, his face was hollowed out in shadows; under the eyes and cheekbones, and in sharp lines down his jaws; but his hair had a high gloss like his small defiant eyes. Then he seemed to remember that he had not been acting exactly in the character of a cultured and cosmopolitan traveller. His manner changed, with a jerk. Even his voice seemed to change.

"May I smoke?" he inquired.

This attempt at suavity, considering the haze of smoke round him, was not a success. He seemed to know it, and it angered him. He lit a cigarette, twitching out the match with a snap of his wrist. His next remark was obviously more sincere; as his eyes were roving round the room, he appeared surprised and rather puzzled. "So this," he said abruptly, "is an English country house. It's disappointing, I don't mind telling you. That thing" – his cigarette stabbed at another of the bad Venetian scenes – "is an eyesore. So is that. Your imitation Fragonard over the fireplace would disgrace Pine Falls, Arkansas. Gentlemen, I hope I'm in the right place?"

Inspector Murch was insistent. "Never mind that. You see you do stick to the subject; look." He scowled. "I don't mind saying, myself, that I do favor no bargains with you. 'Tes Dr. Fell who's done it, and it's done, and he's responsible to Scotland Yard; now we'm here to get the benefit from it . . . if you do satisfy us that you'm not the one who shot Mr. Depping. First, we want to know –"

"Nonsense, inspector!" said Dr. Fell affably. His wheezy gesture bade Spinelli continue on whatever line he liked; he folded his hands over the ridges of his stomach and assumed an almost paternal air. "You're quite right, Mr. Spinelli, about the pictures. But there's a more interesting one, in watercolor, on the table beside you – that card. Look at it. What do you make of it?"

Spinelli glanced down; he saw the card with the eight swords painted on it, and forgot his lethargy.

"Hell's bells! The taroc, eh? Where did you get this?"

"You recognize it? . . . Good! That was better than I had hoped for. I was going to ask you whether Depping, when you knew him, ever dabbled in pseudo-occultism of this kind. I presumed he did; he had several shelves of books dealing with the more rarified forms – people like Wirth, and Ely Star, and Barlet, and Papus. But nobody seemed to know anything about his interest in such matters, if – h'mf – if he had any."

"He was a sucker for it," Spinelli answered simply. "Or for anything in the line of glorified fortune-telling. He didn't like to admit it, that's all. Actually, he was as superstitious as they make 'em. And the taroc was his favorite."

Inspector Murch lumbered over and seized his notebook.

"Taroc?" he repeated. "What's this taroc?"

"To answer that question, my friend, fully and thoroughly," said Dr. Fell, squinting at the card, "you would need to be initiated into the mysteries of theosophy; and even then the explanation would baffle any ordinary brain, including my own. You'll get some idea of the modest functions it is supposed to have if I tell you some of the claims they make for it. The taroc reveals the world of ideas and principles, and enables us to grasp the laws of the evolution of phenomena; it is a mirror of the universe, wherein we find symbolically the threefold theogonic, androgonic, and cosmogonic theory of the ancient magi; a double current of the progressive materialization or involution of the God-mind, and the progressive redivinisation of matter which is the basis of theosophy. It is also –"

"Excuse me, sir," said Inspector March, breathing hard,

"but I can't write all that down, you know. If you'd make yourself a bit clearer . . ."

"Unfortunately," said the doctor; "I can't. Damned if I know what it means myself. I only inflicted that explanation, as I have read it, because I am fascinated by the roll and stateliness of the words. H'm. Say that according to some people the taroc is, in summo gradu, a key to the universal mechanism . . . In substance it is a pack of seventy-eight cards, with weird and rather ghastly markings. They use it like a pack of ordinary playing cards, for what Mr. Spinelli has called glorified fortune-telling."

Murch looked relieved and interested. "Oh, ah. Like reading the cards? Ah, ay; done it meself. Me sister's cousin often reads the cards for us. And tea leaves as well. And, lu' me, sir," he said in a low earnest voice, "if she don't 'ave it right, every time . . . !" He caught himself up, guiltily.

"Don't apologize," said Dr. Fell, with a similarly guilty expression. "I myself am what Mr. Spinelli would describe as a sucker for such things. I am never able to pass a palmist's without going in to get my hand read, or my future revealed in a crystal. Hurrumph. I can't help it," he declared, rather querulously. "The less I believe in it, I'm still the first to howl for my fortune to be told. That's how I happen to know about the taroc."

Spinelli's lip lifted in a sardonic quirk. He sniggered. "Say, are you a dick?" he asked. "You're a funny one. Well, we live and learn. Fortune-telling –" He sniggered again.

"The taroc pack, inspector," Dr. Fell continued equably, "is supposed to be of Egyptian invention. But this card has the design of the French taroc, which dates back to Charles VI and the origin of the playing card. Out of the seventy-eight cards, twenty-two are called major arcana and fifty-six minor arcana. I needn't tell you such, a pack, or even the knowledge of it, is very rare. The minor arcana are divided into four series, like the clubs, diamonds, hearts, and spades; but in this case called . . . ?"

"Rods, cups, pence, and swords," said Spinelli, examining his finger nails. "But what I want to know is this: Where did you get that card? Was it Depping's?"

Dr. Fell picked it up. He went on: "Each card having a definite meaning. I needn't go into the method of fortune-telling, but you'll be interested in the significance . . . Question for question, Mr. Spinelli. Did Depping ever possess a taroc pack?"

"He did. Designed it himself from somebody's manual. And paid about a grand to have it turned out by a playing-card company. But that card didn't come from it . . . unless he made a deck for himself. I'm asking you, where did you get it?"

"We have reason to believe that the murderer left it behind, as a sort of symbol. Who knows about high magic in the wilds of Gloucestershire?" mused Dr. Fell.

Spinelli looked straight in front of him. For an instant Hugh Donovan could have sworn the man saw something. But he only sniggered again.

"And that card means something?" Murch demanded.

"You tell him," Dr. Fell said, and held it up.

The American relished his position. He assumed a theatrical air; glanced first to one side and then the other. "Sure I can tell you, gentlemen. It means he got what was coming to him. The eight of swords – Condemning justice. It put the finger on old Nick Depping, and God knows he deserved it."

13
BULLET-PROOF

Again they were all locked up with their own thoughts, because each new development seemed to lead the case in a different direction; and each box opened up like a magician's casket, to show only another box inside the last. It was growing hot and stuffy in the library. Somewhere in the house a clock began to strike. It had finished banging out the hour of nine before Dr. Fell spoke again.

"So that's established. Very well. Now tell us what you know about Depping himself, and what happened last night."

"As your legal adviser, Mr. Travers –" began Langdon, suddenly thrusting himself into the conversation as he might have made up his mind to jump out of bed on a cold day; a more incongruous fancy because the man was sweating – "as your legal adviser, I must insist that you confer in private with me before taking any unwise steps . . ."

Spinelli looked at him. "Burn, damn you," he said cryptically, leaning forward in fierce vindictiveness. "Burn. Sweat. Go on; I like it . . ."

"I can give the whole thing to you," he went on, relaxing again, "in a couple of words. Nick Depping – he didn't call himself Septimus then – was the slickest article that ever came out of England. By God, he had brains! I'll give him that. He came over to the States about eight or nine years ago with the idea of making his fortune, like a lot of Britishers; only he'd thought it all over, and he'd decided that the best way was to teach them new rackets in the home of rackets. I don't know how he got hold of Jet Mayfree. Mayfree didn't amount to a row of beans then; he was one of those two-for-a-nickel ward heelers that hang around speakeasies and maybe can get a few muscle-men to do somebody else's dirty work – but that's all. Well, I'm telling you, Depping made Mayfree a big shot as sure as God made little apples. Depping blew into New York and lived in speaks until he found the man he wanted for his front, and in a year . . ." Spinelli gestured.

"I don't mean booze, you understand. That's small change. I mean protection, politics, swindles, blackmail – holy Jesus, he could put a new angle on each one of 'em that nobody else would have thought of in a million years! And he wasn't crude: no guns, unless it couldn't be helped, and even then no stuff that looked like a gang killing. 'Why advertise?' he said. 'Let somebody else take the rap.' At one time he was running a real badger-game syndicate: twenty-two women working the hotels for him. An assistant district attorney got nosey. Nick Depping worked it out, planted evidence, and had the man poisoned so that there was clear proof his wife had done it; and the d.a.'s wife went to the chair for it."

Spinelli leaned back and smoked with a sort of malignant admiration.

"Do you get it? He organized all the little rackets, that the big shots had never bothered with. He never tried to muscle in on them, and they let him alone. Extortion, for one thing. That was how he ran into me. I wouldn't join his union. And what happened? Why, he got me sent up the river for five years."

The man coughed on some smoke. He brushed a hand over his eyes, which had become watery. Side-burns, hair-line moustache, broad face with nostrils working, all the offensiveness of the man seemed to gather into one lump; to grow poisonous, and writhe on the brown sofa.

"All right!" he said hoarsely, and then controlled himself. He remembered his suavity. "I've forgotten that, now. All I was thinking – it was queer to see that dry old bird . . . He looked and talked like a college professor, except when he was drunk. I had one interview with him, the first time I ever saw him; and I was curious. He had an apartment in the East Sixties, lined up with books, and when I saw him he was sitting at a table with a bottle of rye and a pack of taroc cards . . ." Spinelli coughed.

"Steady on," said Dr. Fell quietly. His dull eyes opened wide for a moment. "There's a lavatory just off here. Would you care to, humph, retire for a minute or two. Eh?"

The other rose. At Dr. Fell's gesture, a mystified Inspector Murch followed to stand at the door. During the heavy silence of the room, when he had gone, Dr. Fell glanced round the group. He picked up a pencil, placed it against his arm, and made a motion of one pressing a plunger.

"Let him alone," he said gruffly. "He'll be with us shortly."

All during this recital, the bishop had been sitting with his head in his hands. He straightened up, and said, "This is sickening. I – I never realized . . ."

"No," said Dr. Fell. "It isn't pleasant when you really see it at close range, is it? Far different from looking at criminals all preserved and ticketed behind glass cases; and reading the Latin titles on the reptile exhibits with your handkerchief to your nose? I've found that out. I found it out long ago, for my sins. But I ought to have warned you that you will never see clearly to the heart of any crime until you can honestly repeat, 'There but for the grace of God –'"

Mr. Theseus Langdon again took his jump, but this time with more ease.

"Come!" he said persuasively. "I am afraid I must insist, in justice to my client, that we must not place too much credence in what he says at this time. If you will allow me to join him and speak to him in private, as my prerogative is . . . ?"

"Sit still," rumbled Dr. Fell. He made only a slight gesture with his pencil, but Langdon subsided.

Spinelli was soothed and urbane when he returned, though a muscle seemed to jump in his shoulder. He stared round with a toothy smile; apologized, and lowered himself with a sort of stage grace into another chair. After a time he went on:

"I was – ha, ha – speaking of poor Nick Depping the first time I saw him. He said, 'They tell me you're a man of some education. You don't look it. But sit down.' That was how I came to know him, and, take my word for it, I knew him pretty well. So I entered his organization . . ."

"Stop a bit!" said Dr. Fell. "I thought you told us a while ago that you refused – ?"

The other smirked. "Oh, I had outside interests. Listen! I still think I'm as smart as he was; yes, and as well-educated too, by God, though you mugs wouldn't believe it . . ." His wrist jerked viciously as he lit another cigarette. "Never mind. He found it out, and I went to the Big House. But in the meantime I was his sparring partner for what he thought of books, and I read his fortune in that taroc pack until I knew it better than he did. Mind, I expected him to go far. He used to call me the court astrologer, and once he nearly shot me when he was drunk. If it hadn't been for the drinking, and for one outstanding weakness –"

"What was that?"

"Women. He blew in plenty of money on them. If it hadn't been for that . . . yet," said Spinelli, who seemed to be jabbed by an ugly memory, "he honest-to-God had a real fascination for them. They fell for him. I told him once, when I'd had a few drinks myself, 'I'm a better man than you, Nick; by God, I am. But they don't seem to fall for me. It's your money.' But, somehow . . ." Spinelli fingered his sideburns. "I used to hate that conceited old rat because the women did go after him, and they wouldn't admit it. They'd pretend to laugh at him in public. But he – he hypnotized them, or something. Why can't I have his luck?" he demanded, almost at a whine. "Why won't they go for me? He even had one high-class dame with a Park Avenue manner, even if she did come from Ninth Avenue – and stuck to her – and she stuck to him; until he threw her over . . ."

Spinelli checked himself, as though he had just remembered something. He glanced at Langdon.

"You were saying – ?" prompted Dr. Fell.

"I was telling you." He drew a deep breath. "I got sent to the Big House. But he was blowing in his money. And if he'd kept his head, and not thrown it around everywhere, he'd have been worth about six million, instead of only fifty thousand pounds in your money."

Dr. Fell opened one eye. He wheezed thoughtfully, and then said in a gentle voice:

"That's very interesting, my friend. How do you happen to know he left an estate of fifty thousand pounds?"

Nobody moved. Spinelli's eyes remained fixed and glazed. At length he said:

"Trying to trip me up, are you? Suppose I won't answer?"

They could hear his harsh breathing. Dr. Fell lifted his cane and pointed with it across the table.

"I wish you would endeavor to get it through your head, my friend, that there is at present quite enough evidence to hang you for the murder of Depping . . . Didn't I mention that?"

"No, by God, you didn't! You said –"

"That I wouldn't press the passport charge; that's all."

"You can't bluff me. This dick," he nodded at Murch, "told me this morning I was supposed to have visited Nick

Depping last night. Well, I didn't. Show me that servant who says I came to visit him, and I'll prove he's a liar. You can't bluff me. And, if you try, I'll be damned if I tell you what did happen."

Dr. Fell sighed. "You'll try to avoid telling it anyway, I'm afraid. So I shall have to tell you, and I am afraid you'll hang anyway. You see, there are points of evidence against you which Inspector Murch neglected to mention. We don't think you were the man who rang Depping's doorbell and went upstairs at all. The evidence against you concerns that visit you paid to his house late on the same night – during the rainstorm – when you followed him back after he'd tried to kill you."

Spinelli jumped to his feet. He said shrilly: "By Christ, if any squealer –"

"You'd better listen to me, I think. Personally, I don't care a tuppenny farthing what happens to you. But if you value your own neck . . . Ah, that's better."

There was something rather terrifying in the wide-open stare of the doctor's eyes. He got his breath again, and went on:

"While you were in prison at Sing Sing, Depping left the States. He was tired of his new toy called racketeering, tired of making his fortune – just as later he tired of the publishing business. He cut loose from Mayfree and returned to England." Dr. Fell glanced at the bishop. "You remember remarking this morning, Bishop Donovan, how Mayfree suddenly lost all his power and influence about five years ago? Umph, yes. I think Spinelli has provided us with a reason. You, Spinelli . . . After you got out of prison, you went in with Mayfree; you discovered his influence was gone; and you very prudently deserted also. Then you came to England . . ."

"Listen, you," said Spinelli, jabbing his forefinger into his palm. "If you think I came over here to find Depping – if anybody thinks that – it's a lie. I swear it's a lie. I was only – on a vacation. Why shouldn't I? It was an accident. I –"

"That's the odd part of it," Dr. Fell observed reflectively; "I think it was. I think it was completely by accident that you ran across your old friend Depping, while you were looking for fresh fields in England. Although, of course, you had prudently provided yourself with a solicitor in case of trouble. Somebody recommended you the same solicitor who had been recommended to Depping; rather a natural thing in the fraternity . . . Of course, Mr. Langdon may have told you about Depping . . ."

Spinelli's lip twisted. "No fear. Say, no fear of him telling about a good thing! I didn't know he had anything to do with Depping, until –" He checked himself. A sharp glance passed between him and Dr. Fell; it was as though they read each other's thoughts. But the doctor did not press the obvious lead. Besides, Langdon was sputtering.

"This," he said, with a sort of gulp, "all this is outrageous? Insufferable. Dr. Fell, I must ask to be excused from this conference. I cannot any longer sit and listen to insults which –"

"Park yourself," said Spinelli coolly, as the other got up, "or you'll wish you had . . . Got any other remarks, Dr. What's your name?"

"H'mf, yes. You found Depping posing as a respectable country gentleman. It struck you as a heaven-sent opportunity to exercise those peculiar talents of yours – eh?"

"I deny that."

"You would, naturally. Let us say that you wanted to present your compliments to Depping and arrange a meeting to chat about old times. But the terms of the meeting, as suggested by Depping, roused suspicions in your none-too-trusting nature. He didn't ask you to his house, for this chat. A meeting in a lonely neighborhood, beside the river half-a-mile from the inn where you were stopping; and so far away from where Depping lived that, if your body were found floating in the river some miles still further down, he would scarcely be connected –"

Dr. Fell paused. He flipped up his hand as though he were tossing something away.

"You know a hell of a lot, don't you?" the other asked quietly. "Suppose I admitted it? You couldn't prove any blackmail charge. We arranged a friendly little conversation; that was all."

"Agreed . . . Well, how did you manage it?"

The other seemed to come to a decision. He shrugged his thin shoulders. "O.K. I'll risk it. – Bullet-proof vest. I trusted old Nick Depping about as far as I can throw that desk. Even so, he nearly got me. I was standing on the river bank – that little creek they call a river – at the foot of a meadow where there's a dump of trees. We'd arranged to meet there. It was moonlight, but clouding up already. I didn't know he was going to start anything. I thought maybe he'd come to terms, like any sensible man who was caught with the goods . . ." He thrust out his neck and wriggled his head from side to side; his collar seemed to be too tight. They could see his teeth now.

"And then I heard a noise behind a tree. I whirled around, and there was somebody steadying a rod against the side of a tree, and taking a flat bead on me so close he couldn't miss. It didn't look like Nick – this guy with the rod, I mean. He looked young, and had a moustache, from what I could see in the moonlight. But I heard Nick's voice, all right. He said, 'You'll never do it again.' And then he let me have it, and I saw one of Nick's gold teeth.

"I didn't think of falling in the river. The slug knocked me in; square in the chest – through the heart if I hadn't been wearing that vest. But once I was in the water I got my senses back. It's deep, and there's hell's own current. I went downstream underwater as far as I could, and came up round a bend. He thought he'd got me."

"What then?"

"I went back to that little hotel where I'm staying. I changed my clothes, and I went to bed. Now get this! – get it straight. You're not going to pin any rap on me. This talk about my following Nick Depping home is bluff, and you know it." He was fiercely trying to hold Dr. Fell's eyes, as though to drive belief in like a nail. "Bluff. Every word of it. I didn't stir out of that room. You think I wanted more heat? I wasn't going to face Nick Depping. I never handled a rod in my life, and I never will. Why should I?"

His voice was cracking with intensity. "Look up my record and see if I ever handled a rod. I'm as good a man as Nick Depping ever was, but I wasn't going back there; I wasn't mad at him for trying to iron me. Fortunes of war, see? Kill him? Not me. And if I did want him to – ah, advance me a little loan, do you think I'd be crazy enough to try anything like that?" He hammered the arm of his chair "Do you?"

Throughout all this, Inspector Murch had been trying to take rapid notes; he seemed to be struggling with the idiom, and several times on the point of protest. But now there was a tight smile on his sandy moustache. Hugh Donovan could see what was going on in his mind; he had still against Spinelli that evidence of his having changed clothes and crawled out the window of the Chequers Inn a second time . . . Then Hugh saw that Dr. Fell was also looking at the inspector. Murch, who had just opened his mouth to speak, stopped. His boiled eye was puzzled.

And Dr. Fell chuckled.

"Bluff?" he said musingly. "I know it."

"You – you know . . . ?"

"H'm, yes. But I had to persuade you to talk, you see." the doctor said. "As a matter of fact, we are fairly well satisfied that you had nothing to do with the murder. I neglected to tell you," he beamed, "that you were seen by the landlord's wife at the Chequers, climbing back into the window of your room, soaking wet, at about ten o'clock."

"And not leave it again – ?" Spinelli asked the question after a very brief pause; he seemed almost to have stopped breathing.

"And not leave it again. There, my friend, is your corroboration."

After this thundering lie, Dr. Fell looked as benevolent as Old King Cole. Spinelli's shoulders jerked.

"You mean – I can go? You're not going to hold me? Even as a material witness?"

"You may go. Get out of the country in forty-eight hours, and you shall not be held."

A sort of wild, malignant hope was in Spinelli's face.

He had drawn himself back, with one hand against his chest. You could see that he was thinking fast, sifting chances, wondering, feeling for a trap; but he could not help saying: "Say; you told me a week! A week to leave the country, that's what you said. A week –"

"Man," interposed Dr. Fell softly, "will you never let well-enough alone? There are a number of dangerous questions I could have insisted on your answering; and you evaded them. Very well. Since I don't believe you shot Depping, I am willing to let that pass. But, by God, my friend! – if you question me, or argue with me, or try to quibble about time limits, you will get no mercy at all." He struck the handle of his stick on the table. "Speak up! What's it to be? Freedom, or gaol?"

"Oh, I'll go! Listen, governor, please! I didn't mean anything. I wasn't trying to give you any back-talk . . ."

The man spoke with a sort of eager and slobbering whine. "All I meant was – well, it's sudden. And I'd like," here he spoke slowly, as though he were watching the doctor with furtive care to see the effect of his words, "I'd naturally like to speak with my mouth-piece – my lawyer – and sort of – arrange things, you know; but he's tied up here, and I thought maybe I might have more time. That's all I meant."

For an instant, as the doctor bent over to pick up a matchbox he had knocked on the floor, Hugh saw the faintest twitch of a smile under his moustache. With a grunt Dr. Fell hoisted himself again.

"Humph. Well, I see no objection to that. Unless, of course, it comes from Mr. Langdon? I think he said a while ago that your conduct was insufferable, and that he was inclined to wash his hands of –"

Langdon was instantly all smiles and deprecation.

For some reason he seemed as relieved as Spinelli at the turn matters had taken. He almost clucked. Rolling his dog's eyes about, talking with a glutinous ease, he assured them that his first duty (after all) was to his client; that he had spoken with unintentional warmth, and under pardonable stress; finally, that he would be most happy to assist his client with any advice in his power.

"I mean," insisted Spinelli, still watching Dr. Fell, "could you let us talk now – in private? Listen, if I've got to get out of England in a hurry, then I won't have time to see him . . . !"

The doctor seemed reluctant, but allowed himself to be persuaded. Murch, who was plainly mystified, agreed. The drawing-room was put at the disposal of Spinelli and Langdon, and they were ushered out by the constable. Langdon stood in the doorway to deliver a little speech, flashing his smile and assuring them that he would be only a few minutes; then he faded out after Spinelli with a rather ghostly effect of disappearance. The door closed.

Inspector Murch watched it close. He swung round on Dr. Fell.

"Well, sir! You'm got some idea in this! What is it? Ah, but now yon pair do have a chance to put their heads together!"

"Yes," agreed the doctor. "Never have I accomplished a design with less trouble. They clamored for it. Gentlemen, the game is getting rapid now, and somebody is going to lose a number of tricks in a very short time. I wonder –"

"Eh, sir?"

"I wonder," said the doctor musingly, and poked at the table with his cane, "whether Spinelli is still wearing his bullet-proof vest? I rather suspect he will find it valuable before long. Steady, now! In the meantime, I want to talk about ladies."

14
THE DEVIL AND MAW STANDISH

Uneasily Murch rubbed a hand across his sandy cropped hair. He glanced at the bishop, as though he wondered whether such matters should be discussed in the episcopal presence.

"About ladies, sir? You mean – what Mr. Langdon said about a lady from hereabouts? Ah, ah! S'help me, I hate to say it – !"

The bishop, who all this time had been staring at the windows, turned heavily. His face looked dull and uncertain.

"Is all this necessary?" he asked. "I confess, doctor, that I am – much troubled. And confused. Villainy – ah – in general I have always regarded as an abstract thing, like a chemical reaction. Seeing it here . . ."

"Nevertheless, we have got to talk about it. Those remarks between Spinelli and Langdon, especially the things they didn't say, were the most revealing clues we have had up to this time. I am interested now not so much in what things were said, as why they were said. H'm." A thoughtful sniff rumbled in the doctor's nose. "For instance, Langdon's insistent statement that a lady from what he calls 'your charming community' was prepared to run away with Depping. True or untrue – why did he say it? Definitely he had some purpose, in desiring that everybody should know he knew it. I don't think we can doubt that Langdon knew a great deal more about Depping than he was willing to tell us. But he chose that little item to parade before us."

"To throw suspicion on a woman, one would think," suggested the bishop. "To let us know he knew more about the murder than he was willing to tell."

"And yet I doubt it. Surely it leads in another direction as well . . . It's an unpleasant business, but I think we shall have to listen to a little gossip and opinion. Humph, brr-r; yes. Preferably strong-minded gossip and opinion. Inspector, will you step outside and tell the butler to ask Mrs. Standish to step downstairs? We haven't yet heard her views. And I lack something. I know who the murderer is, but –"

The bishop lifted his head. "You know, doctor?"

"I'm afraid I do. I knew it this afternoon. You see," Dr. Fell's hands slid out and played with the silver inkstand, "you see, the murderer made one terrific slip, which has not received the proper attention . . . Never mind. We can discuss that later. Stop a bit, Inspector! Before you go, in case Spinelli and Langdon should get through their conversation prematurely, you must have your instructions."

"Yes, sir?" said Murch gruffly.

"When Spinelli comes back to this room, you will be informed that neither you nor your constable will be needed further tonight. Both of you will leave here, ostentatiously . . ."

"Ah! And follow Spinelli?"

"Tut, tut. Nothing of the kind. Those uniforms of yours would be spotted half a mile, especially if Spinelli has reason to believe he is under surveillance. The constable will go home. You, after pretending to do so, will take a long way round and go to the Guest House. This is merely a guess of mine, but we shall have to play a long chance."

Murch stroked his moustache. "But there's nobody at the Guest House, sir! You be and sent the man Storer away to the 'Bull' –"

"Exactly. You won't go inside, but keep in concealment close to the house, and watch what may happen. Meanwhile . . ."

He turned to Hugh Donovan, and smiled quizzically. "You look like a stout young fellow who could take care of himself if it came to trouble. So I'll tell you why I wanted you here to listen to what we've heard tonight. You've – hum – studied academic criminology, they tell me." He coughed meaningly, and as Hugh met the glance over the doctor's spectacles he knew that this fat bandit knew his own particular guilty secret.

"Would you like to try a little practical work?"

"Would I!" said Hugh fervently.

"Think you could follow Spinelli wherever he went, and keep out of sight?"

"Absolutely."

"I don't like to do this, but you're the only person here who might conceivably do it. And before you agree, I want to impress on you exactly what you're doing." Dr. Fell looked sharply at him, at the bishop, and at the scowling Inspector Murch. "If I'm right, you see, that man Spinelli is going to walk straight into a death- trap."

He waited to let that statement sink in, and for his listeners to use their imaginations on it. The bright, hot library had become full of suggestion.

"In other words, my boy, this placid little rustic corner – where nobody has any motive – contains a killer who would just as soon put a bullet into you as into Spinelli. A killer possibly without deep intelligence, but a quick thinker with an incredible amount of nerve. I can't say for certain whether Spinelli will try the same tactics as he tried with Depping, but I believe he will. And if he attempts it at all, it will have to be immediately, because I've forced his hand; he has got to leave England, and he must act at once . . . Do you understand?"

"Enough to try it, doctor."

"Very well." He turned and nodded towards the closed portieres over the doorway at the far end of the library. "I don't want Spinelli to see you when he comes back. Go into the billiard-room there, and keep watch behind those curtains. We'll maneuver him out the same way he came in: through the windows to the terrace. The terrace runs all the way round this side of the house, including the billiard-room, and there's a door opening on it from there. When you see Spinelli leave, slip out the door from the billiard-room to the terrace, and follow. Whatever you do, for God's sake don't lose him. That's all. Very well, Inspector; go and see if you can find Mrs. Standish."

Hugh was already feeling the excitement of the thing, as though it had been a game. He had a wholesome love of play-acting, and he could not even yet bring himself to believe that following people was anything else. If he had not seen that dead man . . . but the image flashed across his mind as he put his hand on the portieres at the end of the room. It was effective.

There was a bright moon that night. Its light fell into the dark billiard-room through a row of diamond-paned windows high up on the wall to the right, and there were other windows at the far end. In the right-hand wall there was also a glass-panelled door standing open on the terrace. Like the library, this room was high and narrow. He could dimly see the billiard table in the middle, and the marking-board and racks of cues against the wall.

It was cool here, after the stuffy air of the other room. The portieres had a sound-deadening effect; he could hear his father's voice only faintly as the bishop expounded something to Dr. Fell. Parting the curtains about half an inch, he groped into the shadows after a chair. Cool here, and a faint breeze. The glass door moved slightly; a swish of trees went murmuring round the house; and the thin line of light from between the portieres trembled across the billiard table. This, it occurred to him, would be an excellent house in which to play any sort of game that entailed wandering about in the dark; say that noble pastime called sardines. Which suggestion turned his thoughts inevitably to Patricia Standish and the pleasures of darkness. But he had to attend to business. Discovering a chair, he had just drawn it up to the opening between the curtains when a new voice rose, commanding and majestic, from the library.

"I do not ask to know what this means," it proclaimed; "but I demand to know what it means. Certain remarks and hints have been made to me, which, in justice to the memory of dear, dear Septimus – to say nothing of poor; poor Betty – I will have explained. Furthermore . . ."

Hugh peered through the opening. Standing before Dr. Fell was the handsome and aggressive figure of Maw Standish. Her chin was up, her ash-blonde head and square face determined; she was a Matterhorn in white lace, staring down over the icy slopes of herself. She stood with her arm round the shoulders of a pretty little brown-haired girl who, Maw's gesture indicated, was Betty Depping. Betty Depping looked tired, and nervous, and, most of all, embarrassed. Instinctively Hugh liked her. In appearance she would not have qualified for the name of Ginch: despite her neatness, her pale fine face, and dark blue eyes set rather wide apart, she looked sturdy and capable. Her lips were full, but her chin strong. The brown hair was drawn back severely behind her ears, and – had he been closer – Hugh would have expected to find a freckle or two round her nose. As she glanced at Maw Standish, there was in her eyes a sort of weary cynicism. You felt that she would never shed many tears; but that they would be bitter ones.

Her presence complicated matters. Hugh could only see the back of Dr. Fell's head, but he could imagine the doctor rumbling and scowling at bringing in Depping's daughter at this juncture. However, Maw Standish was giving nobody a chance to protest.

". . . furthermore," she continued, shaking Betty by way of emphasis in spite of the girl's efforts to free herself, "I demand to know the reason why this house has been filled with objectionable people. In the drawing-room at this minute – at this very minute," said Maw Standish, as though that made the fact more sinister, "there is a horrible creature with a fawn-colored hat and a red pin stripe in his suit. Why must this house be filled with objectionable people? Think of the dear, dear bishop's feelings. Think of my own feelings. I am sure the dear, dear bishop must be outraged . . ."

The dear, dear bishop made a coughing noise, and backed his chair away.

"Ma'am," said Dr. Fell urbanely, "one of the most unfortunate features of police work is that it brings us into contact with people whom we should otherwise run a mile to avoid. Pray accept my assurance, ma'am, that nobody appreciates this more than I do."

Maw sniffed, and after considering this she looked at him sharply.

"Is it possible, Dr. Fell; can it be possible – and in the presence of the dear, dear bishop at that – that I scent an ulterior meaning in what you say?"

"Ma'am, ma'am," said the doctor; with a touch of reproof. "Heh. Heh-heh-heh. Pray control yourself. I am sure His Reverence must resent your statement that his presence stimulates your olfactory senses. I must ask you to respect his cloth."

Maw stared at him as though she could not believe her ears. She stiffened, turned livid, and emitted a sound like the whistle of a peanut vendor's machine on a cold day.

"Well, of all – !" she gasped, "of all the – of all – Gorooo! Sir, will you trifle with me?"

"Madam!" rumbled Dr. Fell. He chuckled. Hugh could imagine his wide-open eyes as he looked at her. "Reluctantly, I am afraid I must decline. I trust you are familiar with that classic anecdote which concludes, 'Ma'am, I am a married man myself, and I would rather have a glass of beer.' Just so. Nunqum nimis nunquam satis. Speaking of beer –"

Maw was in a dangerous condition. She turned to the bishop, as though to appeal for assistance. That worthy gentleman narrowly missed doing something which would forever have condemned him in the maternal presence; he turned mirth into a cough at just the right time. Then he looked very ecclesiastical.

"Of all," said Maw; breathlessly, "of all the insufferable –"

"Yes. So Mr. Langdon said. Now, I'll tell you what it is, Mrs. Standish," said Dr. Fell sharply. "You are here for the purpose of giving evidence; not orders. You were expressly instructed to come here alone, furthermore. Certain things we have discovered today will not make very pleasant hearing for Miss Depping."

Betty Depping looked up. There had been a sort of weary humor in her eyes; but now she spoke dully, in a pleasant voice which always seemed to ask a question of her future mother-in-law.

"Isn't that," she said, "why I have a right to be here?" Subtly, it brought a new element into the conversation. You could feel in what she was thinking a vitality, an intensity, even a tragedy about which nobody had bothered to think. Maw's attack was broken, but she went on in a lower voice:

"I wish this nonsense dispelled, that is all. If you cannot be sufficiently courteous – ! I refer to hints. From Patricia, and especially (in a mealy-mouthed fashion, which I detest) from Morley. As though to prepare me for something." Maw shut her jaws hard, and looked from Dr. Fell to the bishop. "If I must speak of it, it concerns rumors of poor dear Mr. Depping's past life."

Again Betty Depping looked at her, curiously.

"Could it make any difference?" she asked in a low voice.

For a time Hugh could hear the slow tapping of Dr. Fell's pencil on the table. "My dear," he said suddenly, "since you are here . . . did you ever have any knowledge of your father's past life?"

"N-no. No knowledge. I – suspected something. I don't know what."

"Did you tell this suspicion to anybody?"

"Yes. I told Morley. I thought it was only fair." She hesitated, and a sort of puzzled, protesting fierceness came into her face. "All I wanted to know is, why should it matter? If father had lived – if he were living now – nobody would have known it or asked questions about it. Now that he's dead, if there's anything against him it's bound to come out . . ."

She looked away, at a corner of one window, and added in a very low voice: "I never had a great deal of happiness, you see. I thought that I was going to have it, now. Why should – somebody – have spoiled it?"

Again the night breeze went wandering through the trees round the house, with a rustling of turmoil far away; and you knew that it was agitating the beeches and maples round the Guest House as well. All the time Dr. Fell's pencil was slowly clicking against the desk; tap – tap – tap – as though it were a brain endlessly asking the same question.

"How long have you suspected anything in your father's past, Miss Depping?"

She shook her head. "There never was anything definite. But I think I started to wonder as much as five years ago. You see, he sent for me to join him in London suddenly. I thought he had always been there; I wrote him once a week, in care of Mr. Langdon, and he would reply about once a month, with a London postmark. So I came over from France; naturally I was pleased to get away from school. He told me he was retiring from whatever it was he did in the City, and going into the publishing business with a Mr. Standish and a Mr. Burke.

"Then – we were sitting in the lobby of the hotel one afternoon, and all of a sudden he caught sight of somebody walking towards us, and he was – I don't know – flustered. He said, 'That's Burke; he didn't say he was coming here. Listen: don't be surprised at anything I say to him in the way of business. So far as you know, I've spent a year in India, where – remember this – where my closest friend was a Major Pendleton.' Then he hushed me." She brushed a hand back across her shining brown hair. It was as though she had an insupportable headache, and tried to smile in spite of it. "You . . . well, you wonder about things like that. But I never knew. That's why I say I have a right to know."

Again she hesitated, stared at Dr. Fell, and could not ask the question. It was Maw Standish who fired it out.

"That's precisely it. That's why I demand to know. I still tell you this is impossible! Poor Mr. Depping . . . I have even heard rumors from the servants' hall – from the servants'hall, I assure you. To the outrageous effect – that he was a criminal. A criminal." Maw gulped out the word.

"We had better settle this," declared Dr. Fell, "before we can go on." His voice became gruff. "I am sorry that I must give you the facts brutally, but it will be best this way. The rumor was correct. Depping was not only a criminal; he was a criminal of the meanest and most damnable variety; a racketeer, an extortionist, and a killer. Do not ask for any of the details. They are not pretty."

"Impossi –" said Mrs. Standish, and stopped. She stared at the bishop, who nodded slowly.

"I am sorry, madam," he said.

"God – help – us . . ." She touched her white face, her handsome face where you could see the faint wrinkles now; "This – this alters – this – that is . . ."

Her gaze turned towards Betty Depping, who was looking blankly at Dr. Fell.

"Betty darling!" said Maw, with a brisk abrupt smile. "I see that I should not have brought you down here at all. You were upset enough to begin with. These trying events, these monstrous accusations . . . Child! Do as I tell you. Go upstairs this instant, and lie down. Now, now; I won't hear a word! Lie down like a good child, and tell Patricia to put the ice bag on your head. I will stay here and thrash this matter out. There is a mistake somewhere – surely there is a mistake. You will need all your strength presently. Depend on it, I will do my best for you. Run along, now!"

She disengaged her arm from the other's shoulder. Betty Depping was looking at her steadily. Again Betty was sturdy and capable; with the cool cynical eyes and the strong chin. She smiled.

"Yes, it does alter matters, doesn't it?" she asked softly. "I – I don't think I care to hear anything more."

She inclined her head to the group and walked to the door, but she turned there. She had become tense and fierce, with color in her cheeks: a fighter; and dangerous, and her eyes had a hot blue brilliance. Yet her lips hardly seemed to move.

"The only one who matters in this affair," she said, still in a low voice, "is Morley. Understand that. What he thinks, and what he cares" – her breast rose and fell once, with a sort of shudder – "is what I think and care. Remember that, please."

"Child!" said Maw, lifting her chin.

"Good night," said Betty Depping, and closed the door.

The warmth and strength of her personality was still in

that room. Even the colonel's lady felt it. She tried to adjust herself to the new state of affairs; to stare down Dr. Fell and the bishop; to preserve a high-chinned dignity and yet keep an appropriate aloofness.

"Will you kindly," she said in a tense voice, "stop tapping that pencil on the table? It has been driving me insane . . . Thank you so much. Now that Miss Depping has gone, will you be so good as to substantiate these lurid statements of yours? They can be substantiated, I hope?"

"Unquestionably."

"Dear, dear, dear, dear . . . and – and will there be a scandal?"

"Why should there be a scandal, ma'am?"

"Oh, don't be so dull-witted! This is the most abominable and – and – incredible thing I have ever heard. I can't believe it. Poor, dear Mr. Depping . . . why, the filthy wretch! The –"

Tap-tap-tap-tap, as measured as the ticking of a clock, Dr. Fell's pencil clicked on the table. Hugh Donovan wished he could see his face. The doctor was gathered together into a great mass, his head down.

"Mrs. Standish," he said, "who was the lady whom Depping had persuaded to elope with him?"

15
A MAN WALKS IN THE DARK

The bishop got up abruptly from his chair, went to one window, and pushed it open for more air. Mrs. Standish did not seem to grasp the question. After a sideways glance, she repeated:

"Lady? Elope? – What on earth do you mean? My dear sir, you must be mad!" She edged backwards to a chair, and sat down.

"The ancient and melodious refrain to which," said Dr. Fell musingly, "to which I have got accustomed after all these years. 'Fell, you must be mad.' It is Chief Inspector Hadley's favorite ditty. Well, I don't mind. Believe me, ma'am, the subject is distasteful. I mention it only because I believe it has rather a terrible bearing on the murder."

"I'm sure I don't know what you mean."

"H'm. Perhaps I had better start from the beginning. Do you mind if I smoke?"

She sniffed the air. "It does not seem to have been necessary for you to get permission, doctor. Do not let my presence interfere with you, please . . . What were you saying?"

Dr. Fell sat back with a grunt of satisfaction, and clipped the end of a cigar. "Thank you. Beer and tobacco, ma'am, are the twin warming pans of my declining years. Both have curious histories. To the first I have devoted an entire chapter of my work, The Drinking Customs of England from the Earliest Days. Do you know, for example, the first time that what is humorously called a prohibition law was ever in effect in history? Heh-heh. It affords me amusement to think that our friends the Americans believed they had something new. The first prohibition law was enacted in Egypt by the Pharaoh User. maat.-ra, or Rameses the Great, about the year 4000 B.C. It was an edict designed to prevent his subjects from getting sozzled on a species of barley beer and manufacturing whoopee in the streets of Thebes. Prohibitionists asserted that the next generation would never know the taste of the villainous stuff. Ha, hum, alas. The law failed, and was revoked. Tobacco, now . . ."

He struck a match, argumentatively. "Tobacco, now – h'rrm; puff – puff – aaah! Tobacco, as I was saying, has a history which has been much distorted. Christopher Columbus saw American natives smoking cigars as early as 1492. It is a curious and fantastic picture, almost as though they had been described as wearing top hats and gold watch chains. Jean Nicot . . ."

"Will you get on with what you were saying?" she interrupted, clenching her hands.

"Eh? Oh, if you like . . ." He seemed to reflect. "I am given to understand, Mrs. Standish, that Mr. Depping was much addicted to gallantries."

"'Gallantries' is precisely the word. He was gallant, in an age where men seem to think it most unnecessary."

"I see. And the ladies liked it?"

"Humph. I thought him a very charming man. The old hypocrite."

"Undoubtedly a man of singular gifts. But there was no one to whom he paid particular attention, was there?"

"There was not," she answered decisively. The lines tightened round her handsome mouth. "For instance, he took pleasure in reciting selections from the great poets to my daughter Patricia. I approved the practice. Young people are entirely too prone to neglect matters cultural in this lax generation; dear Canon Dibson said so over the wireless only last week, and I must say that I agree with him . . . But Patricia did not like Mr. Depping, and Madeleine Morgan positively detested him. H'm. H'm." She pondered, one eye narrowing. "Now I wonder . . . it couldn't, of course it couldn't have been dear Lucy Mellsworthy, from Bath. One of my very dearest friends, Dr. Fell, though of course much older. Nevertheless, I have always said there was a little something – something – something suspicious about that whole family, since her cousin Nell ran away with that dreadful man who was owl-catcher for the zoo. Heredity tells; that's what I always say to my husband. Don't you agree?"

"I hardly think we need consider this Miss Mellsworthy –"

"Mrs. Mellsworthy," she corrected stiffly. "Indeed not. Besides, I do not think they were acquainted. All I said was, heredity tells. And I will tell you frankly, doctor: I do not like gossip. This nonsensical rumor of Mr. Depping running away with somebody: I will not stand for it in my house, and I wish you distinctly to understand that. – Where did you hear it?"

Dr. Fell chuckled. "You don't believe it's true, then?"

"I am bound to admit I never saw anything." She shut her lips firmly, peered over her shoulder, and edged forward. "Though, if the man was a criminal, I would not put anything past him. When I think that a son of mine almost married the daughter of a man who might have cut our throats any night, why, why – !" She shuddered. "I needn't tell you that I shall instruct my husband to take immediate steps about that. Such silliness in young people should be shaken out of them, anyhow. Besides . . ."

Trying to make no noise, Hugh slid his chair back. It was here now. Behind Maw Standish the door giving on the passage to the drawing-room had opened. Spinelli, twirling his hat on one finger, a satisfied smirk on his face, preceded Langdon into the room. The solicitor, Hugh noticed, did not look so happy. Spinelli's gaze rested briefly, without recognition, on Mrs. Standish; flickered past, and rested good-humoredly on Dr. Fell.

"Thanks, governor. I'm all set now," he vouchsafed. "So I'll be pushing off. Got a hired car down by the 'Bull'; I'll get back to Hanham, check out, and hop a night train to London. I'll be on a boat tomorrow, if there is one. If not, I'll see if they'll let me into France before I head back to the States. Well . . ."

"Dr. Fell," the colonel's lady said with mounting exasperation, "will you kindly inform me what this objectionable person is doing in my house?"

Spinelli looked over his shoulder. "Kind of feeling your oats, aren't you, mother?" he asked coolly. Then he turned back. "Tiens, qui est la vielle vache? Je crois que son mari a couché sur la pin de sa chemise. Which reminds me, doc. Be a sport and don't try to keep me out of France, will you, eh? I'd like to brush up my French. I noticed you sent that fellow Murch and his harness-bull away; saw 'em go. Thanks. That's a square guy. Well, I'll be seeing you. If you'll show me the front door of this joint –"

"Indeed?" said Maw Standish. "You have great presumptions, I think, my man. Doctor, will you ring for somebody? If we can arrange to show this person out by way of the cellar –"

Spinelli hid his face with his hand, and took it away in a gesture of his wrist. On his face there was plastered such a quirk of impudence that Hugh had a strong inclination to assist his progress with a kick.

"O.K., mother. O.K.! I'll use the window, then. I don't think much of your country houses anyway. Lousy pictures, imitation antiques, Bowery manners –"

"Get out of here," said Dr. Fell, and surged to his feet.

It was the last Hugh saw. He hurried across the billiard-room to the glass door, kept himself in the shadows, and peered along the terrace. Fortunately, he was wearing a dark suit. The luminous dial of his wristwatch showed that it was half past nine. And he was a trifle surprised to find his heart beating heavily.

No wind now, but a cool moist air that smelt of grass and flowers. The moon was still low, but very bright; long shadows were close at hand, lawns dully gleaming, and a haze in the hollows of trees that sloped down towards the east. Half a mile away he could make out the lights of a bus passing along some unidentifiable road. A dog was barking faintly.

Along the terrace a window creaked open, letting out yellow light. Spinelli stepped out, pushing aside curtains, and closed the window behind him. He hesitated, and seemed to be staring up at the moon. Hugh could dimly see his face; he was smiling. The smile died. He looked sharply left and right; saw nothing, and seemed reassured. Leisurely he struck a match and lit a cigarette. Then he descended some shallow steps to the lawn, looked round again, and finally sauntered along below the terrace towards the direction in which Hugh was hiding. As he passed the door to the billiard-room, he was trying to read his watch by the moonlight, and humming, "The Gay Caballero." His footsteps crunched on the gravel path.

Hugh was after him as he turned the corner of the house. Keeping to the grass border against the house, the pursuer was entirely in shadow, and could move soundlessly; though once he nearly tripped over a playful lawn mower. The crunching steps moved ahead, steadily and jauntily. As the driveway curved down through the avenue of elms towards the lodge gate, Hugh had to negotiate a broad patch of moonlight to cross the drive and duck into the shelter of the trees on the right hand side. He jumped the stretch of gravel and dodged behind a laurel bush. What he believed to be the absurdity of this performance began to grow on him. He liked it well enough, this crawling about wet lawns on the knees of your trousers, and peering round bushes as though you were playing I Spy. But you would look damned silly if anybody happened to see you . . .

His blood was heating already. He slid into the shadow of the elm avenue and walked upright in comparative safety, though Spinelli was only twenty yards ahead. Spinelli's feet were making such a rattling noise on the gravel that any minor noises Hugh might make, a breaking twig or a crackly leaf, would go unnoticed. His quarry was muttering to himself; scuffling the gravel, and frequently giving it a kick. Once he cursed to himself, and stopped to assume some sort of defiant attitude, swinging back his cigarette as though he faced an adversary. Then he muttered again as he continued down the drive. At length he said aloud, "Ah, to hell with it!" and fell to whistling, loudly. But often again he would throw out his narrow shoulders for a heroic posture.

Hugh was forced into more sprinting and dodging when they reached the open lodge gates. Without hesitation Spinelli struck off down the hill in the direction of the village. There were no cars or pedestrians; the asphalt road ran bare under the moon and the high hedgerows; and Spinelli, a strutting little figure in an absurd hat, had not once looked around. As they came to Morgan's house, Hugh was in a sweat lest somebody should be hanging over the gate, and hail him as he crouched past in the shadow of the hedge. But he passed it in safety, passed the ghostly church, and came down to the cluster of dull lights that marked the village.

Here there was real danger of being seen, even though there were no street lamps. The only tolerable illumination (all of which came from oil lamps anyway) was in the public house. This building was set back from the road in a muddy yard, smelling of straw and dung: a low, heavy stone structure that had once been whitewashed, with a thatched roof and two wings running out to form a court in front. Its lattices were all open, and shadows passed the smoky oil flames inside.

Hugh slipped off the road about thirty yards away. From the pub issued a noise of jollification; people were stamping time to a piano and an asthmatic accordion, and roaring with applause as somebody sang a comic song. Hugh remembered that it was Saturday night. This was a fool game anyhow, stumbling about in the mud; his nerves crawled for a smoke, and he thought passionately of cool beer. In complete darkness he moved round towards the side of the 'Bull' and bumped into an automobile parked there with its lights out. The pain of the collision brought his wits alive again. Probably Spinelli's car. God knows what the man meant to do; go back to the Guest House, Dr. Fell thought; but it might not be a bad idea to take out the spark plugs, just in case he tried to use it.

Meantime, Spinelli was standing in front of the 'Bull,' his shoulders hunched, smoking reflectively. He seemed to come to a decision. The red end of his cigarette sailed away, and he sauntered up towards the steps that led into the court. Hugh had edged round to the front of the two-seater, lifted the clamps that held down the bonnet, and was raising it softly, to avoid creaks, when he heard footsteps squashing towards him. An unpleasant (and unreasonable) qualm took his stomach as he looked up. Spinelli had altered his direction, and was making straight for the car.

The bonnet seemed to scrape with hideous loudness as he lowered it. He ducked back towards a maple tree and waited, conscious that his heart was beating heavily again. It was impossible that he could have been seen. Then he heard Spinelli fumbling with the car in the dark not a dozen feet away; a door opened, there was a click, and the lights went on, off, and on again, until only the dashboard lamps were glowing. Clear in that little spot of light, Spinelli raised his head to peer about. Hugh could see his face clearly . . .

For the first time that night, dread took hold of him. The man's lower lip was shaking, and there was sweat on his forehead. A bead of it dropped down past his cheek and sideburn as he twisted his head. Spinelli tried to mutter a little laugh, and failed. His hand slid into the side pocket of the front seat; fumbled, and pulled out a belt and shoulder holster that showed the butt of a heavy automatic pistol.

Hugh whispered, almost aloud: "By God, it's not a game . . ." And his heart bumped for fear he had been heard. Crouching down over the dashboard, Spinelli drew out the automatic and examined it. He slid the cartridge clip into his palm, turned it over, replaced it.

Finally, with a timorous finger, he released the safety catch and stuffed the weapon back into its holster. Peering round again, he removed his coat and began to buckle the holster under his left armpit. He was wearing a blue-and-white striped shirt, which clung to him damply. Even at that distance Hugh could hear him breathing.

A dim wind rustled in the trees. From the 'Bull' issued a roar of merriment, and an applauding rattle of glasses on wooden tables. The accordion let out a few preliminary bleats, as though it were clearing its throat, and then began to punch out the accompaniment to somebody's song. The uproar died down; a mincing tenor voice floated out on the silence:

"I'm Burlington Bertie,
I rise at ten-thirty
And saunter about like a toff . . ."

Somebody laughed. The accordion hit each syllable with rising and falling emphasis. A voice called, "Eigh! Two more bitters, eigh." Spinelli, breathing hard, buttoned up his coat again. Whatever sort of rendezvous he would meet, he intended to keep it, then. Wiping off his forehead with a silk handkerchief, he adjusted his hat, switched off the lights of the car, and moved away.

He was going into the 'Bull.' Circling the car after him, Hugh was not certain what to do. There was undoubtedly a back entrance to the place, and, if he had any reason to throw off an even imaginary pursuit, the pursuer might be lost. On the other hand, Hugh did not wish to risk coming face to face with him.

But there seemed to be a large crowd inside, and he wanted a drink. He waited only long enough to complete his original design of removing the spark plugs. Then, as the door closed behind Spinelli, he strolled up the court after him.

16
THE PUZZLE OF THE SHOES

Thus guiltily excusing himself from the fact that, even in the midst of adventure, he could not resist the temptation to stop and have a glass of beer, Hugh walked up the court and through a low door. The place smelt heavily of beer; earth, and old wood; and the walls, he judged, must be four-feet thick. Nobody could tell when or why this house had been built, except that two cloister-like structures along the court, full of disused hay carts and straw, suggested a stable. Inside there was an even larger crowd than he had expected, comfortably tipsy, wandering and bumping in the narrow passages. Through the windows he could see a public-room in each wing, and there was a bar at the rear. Spinelli had turned into the room on the right.

Lowering his head in the passage, Hugh penetrated back to the bar. A couple of oil lamps smoked against perspiring walls. Most of the crowd had gathered in the room across the way, where somebody was strumming the piano, and two loud voices were arguing about a song. The room Hugh entered was low and raftered, with high-tacked settles and long tables; polished brass jugs along the tops of the settles; walls patched up in grimy linoleum of different patterns; a wooden mantel-piece bearing an ancient clock without hands; and, squeezed into one dark corner, a fly-blown picture of Prince Albert in Highland costume. Prince Albert looked disapproving. Just beneath him, two or three grimy sages in cloth caps huddled about a table, flourishing pewter mugs as they argued, their long necks rising and wriggling above brass collar studs. One said: "Don't 'ee be a bloody fool, now!" and turned sulkily and banged his mug down on the table. "Tell 'ee 'tes nowt 'ow the Princess Mary was blowed up, and if the' can't take the ward of a gunner in 'Is Majesty's Sarvice, look, then Gawd bless me, look! I'll –" Bang! went the tankard again, and he glared at his opponent. A stout harassed barmaid hopped past with a tray of glasses; she seemed to be moving her head to avoid the layers of tobacco smoke, and giving an absent-minded smile to everybody. She said, "Tcha, tcha!" to the contestants, who then appealed to the proprietor. This latter was a pacifying dignitary in shirt sleeves, with a wary eye out: he stood behind the bar in a wilderness of beer cases, his arms folded; but he would jerk to life the moment a hand was raised for more beer. He sprang forward as Donovan approached the bar.

Hugh changed his mind, said, "Whiskey and soda," and fixed his eyes on a polished brass plate on a shelf beside him. Despite the smoke and blur, he could see the door to the passage and the other room reflected there. Spinelli was directly in line with it. The other room seemed to be a sort of parlor; and Spinelli slouched in a large tasselled chair, defiantly. Even Hugh could hear the whispers in the noise there – "that gen'lman," "dreffle murder," "Sh-shh!" drowned out by the bang of the piano. Subtly, the news was going all around. Even the three sages finished their beer all together, as at a drill order; and peered round . . .

Squirting soda into his glass and watching the brass plate from the corner of his eye, Hugh turned quickly towards plate and wall. Spinelli had got up. He strode out of the room, into the passage, and through to the bar; he looked angry. People drifted out to follow him, obtrusively interested in their drinks. An insistent voice kept calling, "Sing 'Old John Wesley!'"

Spinelli strode up to the bar.

"Is it possible," he said in a voice of freezing dignity which somehow reminded Hugh of Maw Standish, "is it possible, my man, or isn't it, to get any service in this place?"

A part of the clamor had died down to a buzz; there were many people straining their ears. Spinelli's elaborate unconsciousness of everything, his airs and dignity, made a rather ludicrous spectacle. The proprietor sprang forward.

"I'm sorryzir! I'm sorry! Thought they do be and attended to 'ee, zir! Yeszir?"

"I'll have brandy," said the other; aloofly fingering his tie. "If you have any. Your best. Bring the bottle, and give me a glass of beer with it. Would you like a drink?"

"Ah! Thank 'eezir. Eh don't mind."

If Spinelli got a good view of him, Hugh was thinking . . . He turned still farther away. But the American was not noticing. Pouring out a large dose of brandy, he swallowed it neat and followed it with a draught of beer. Then he poured another. The landlord, with a great carelessness of manner, was opening a bottle of home-brewed.

"Nice weather we'm 'aving, Mr. Travers," he observed critically.

"Uh."

"Ah! Bit waarm, though," the landlord qualified with a judicial air. The bottle cap went Sss-t! and the landlord frowned still more judicially as he poured out his beer. "Still, zir, the' get him much waarmer in the States, I expect?"

"Plenty. Fill up that glass again."

"Ah! Fine country, the States! Did Eh tell 'ee, zir, Eh've a wife's cousin's step-brother that lives in Kansas City? – Ah, ay!" He nodded approvingly. "Lived there farty year' now, 'e 'as. Gearge Loopey 'is name is. Maybe you've 'eard of him, zir; Gearge E. Loopey? 'E do run a big lumber yaard,

I've 'eard. No! Ah, well; 'tes a big place . . . Your good 'ealth, zir!"

Never before had Hugh appreciated so thoroughly the restraint of the English people. Everybody in that house was exploding with curiosity as to what had been happening at The Grange; it must have been the chief topic of conversation all evening; and here was the chief actor – supposed to have been already under arrest – in their midst. Yet conversation, even though strained, went on as usual. Not a glance was obviously turned towards Spinelli. The landlord pattered on.

"The'll be staying with us some time, now, I hope, Mr. Travers?"

"No," said Spinelli. "I'm leaving tonight."

"Ah?"

"Tonight. And damned glad to get away. Listen . . ." He finished his third brandy with a swaggering gesture, and leaned against the bar. Whether it was the brandy, or some deliberate purpose, or merely a love of being in the limelight – for, as he spoke, a rustling quiet settled down, and his voice rang loud against it – Hugh never knew. But Spinelli was aware that he was talking to the house. And three double-brandies, on top of his nervous strain, did things to his tongue. He cleared his throat. His spiteful little eyes rolled round at the assembly with some satisfaction, but he turned back to the landlord.

"Come on, admit it! Don't stand there lapping up that beer and trying to be polite. I know what you're thinking about. The murder. Yeah. And wondering, in your charitable way, why they haven't got me in the can for it right now. Eh?"

The landlord tried to play his part by also seeming unconscious of all the others. He assumed a look of diffidence.

"Well, zir, now that you do mention it – ! Of carse, us've 'eard all about it, and what a 'orrible business he was," he polished the bar vigorously, "and, ah, ah, we do feel sorry for the poor gen'lman . . ."

"Push that bottle over here. Horrible business, nuts! They tried to hook me in on it. And couldn't. Tell that to your friends. Because I didn't happen to have anything to do with it, and I proved it."

The landlord beamed. "Why, Eh'm sure Eh do congratulate you, Mr. Travers! Us thought nothing against 'ee, mind, zir! Only 'twas said 'ereabouts – you know what gossip is! –" he lowered his voice, "only that you'd paid poor Mr. Depping a visit, and a lot of dimp people –"

"You're telling me? Listen." He drained his glass, set it down with a thump, and poked the proprietor in the chest. "I was never inside his house. The man they thought was me was old Nick Depping himself got up into a fancy disguise so nobody would recognize him. Tell that to your friends, and your dumb flatfeet too."

"Zir?"

"It was Depping, I tell you! Trying to tell me I'm a liar?"

The landlord was so obviously puzzled that even Spinelli did not press it. He grew confidential, almost paternal.

"Listen. I'll tell you how it was. Old Nick Depping wanted to get out of his house; see? Never mind why. I'm not telling that. But he wanted to get out of his house; see? All right. He goes up to London and buys a make-up box at a theatrical outfitter's, and he goes to a ready-made clothes store and buys a suit there. All right; you can do all that without anybody being suspicious of you. But Nick was an artist, see? – a real artist; I'll give him credit for that. And, if he left any footprints anywhere, he didn't want the footprints traced to him. He even wanted to have the shoes a different size from his own. All right! But you can't go into a shoe store and ask for a pair of shoes three or four sizes too large. That's nutty; and they're going to remember it in the store, and, if there's any trouble afterwards, maybe the dicks can trace you; see?"

Spinelli leaned across the bar and thrust a flushed countenance within an inch of the landlord's. He went on rather hoarsely:

"So what does Nick do? He goes up to that big place they call The Grange; the one with the lousy furniture in it, and pictures I wouldn't put in my coal cellar. Well, he goes up one afternoon with a satchel that's supposed to have books in it; get me? He goes back to a room where they store a lot of junk, and swipes an old pair of somebody's shoes to wear; and then if he does happen to make any footprints anywhere, why, it's going to be just too bad for the bird who owns the shoes. See? That's what Nick does, and all because he wants to get out of his house and . . ."

Hugh did not hear the last part of the sentence. He was so startled that he almost faced round and spoke to Spinelli. He remained motionless, his empty glass to his lips, staring at a placard behind the bar whereon a high-stepping figure of Johnny Walker grinned back with a rather sardonic leer. Down came one of the props of the case, shattering every hypothesis built on it; a due blown up, shot to pieces; ashes and smoke: viz., the mysterious shoes that belonged to Morley Standish. All sorts of explanations had been, and might be, propounded. The simplest explanation of all – that Depping himself had used them for his masquerade – had been overlooked or at least not mentioned. What became now of his father's fantastic picture of Henry Morgan playing poltergeist in order to steal the shoes?

He risked a short sideways glance at Spinelli. The latter was too preoccupied; too malicious, too full of new alcoholic courage, too greedy of the limelight, even to turn his head or lower his voice. Spinelli laughed. His foot groped vainly for a rail under the bar.

"And that's how it was," he said, tapping the counter; "that he got mistaken for me, see? Because he wanted to get out of his house, and nobody to know it. That's old Nick Depping for you! And when he got back to his house he couldn't get in. Because why? Because he'd lost the key out of his pocket while he was on his little expedition, that's why. Ha. Ha ha ha. Don't tell me. I know."

All this was so much gibberish to the landlord. He stole a look at the brandy-bottle, thoughtfully, and coughed.

"Ah, ay. Well, zir, after all," he suggested in a persuasive manner, "after all, Mr. Depping was a strange sort of gentleman, look. Ah, ay. (Shall Eh sarve the' some Gearges' home-brewed, zir? Mind, he's good!) And if poor Mr. Depping do wish to dress 'imself up 'ow 'e likes, why, we've no right to complain, have us?"

Spinelli whirled. "You don't believe me, eh? Listen. I'm telling you this, I'm telling the world, just what kind of a heel Nick Depping was. I'm going to tell you about him, and I want everybody to know it, by God! Because –"

"Mr. Travers, zir! Ladies present!"

"And, anyway, somebody was smarter than he was. Somebody'd got in there with a duplicate key while he was out, and then pretended they had no key. But that's not what I want to tell the world. What I'm going to tell all you people who thought Nick Depping was a nice, high-hat, Park-Avenue swell; well, I'm going to tell you . . ."

Exactly how far he would have gone Hugh could not guess. He realized that Spinelli's idea was to take the only revenge on Depping now possible. But the proprietor interrupted it. He glanced at his watch, gave a start of realization, and with a voice of surprising power bellowed through the house: "Last or-ders! Last or'rders, ladies and gentlemen, if you please! Ten minutes apast closing! Come, come if you please – !" His voice held that note of extraordinary agony which seems to galvanize publicans like a cramp, and comes as suddenly as a cramp at ten o'clock. In an instant he had become all bustle. He exhorted his listeners, in almost lachrymose entreaty, not to make him lose his license. In the ensuing rush on the bar for final drinks, Hugh was able to crowd himself out into the passage unseen, and wait there to see which direction Spinelli would take.

From the darkness he could see his quarry's face. Indubitably there had been a let-down in the man's elation. There was an oil lamp just over his head; and he looked hunted. The old fears were coming back. This man wanted desperately to cling to lights and company; now they were all fading, and he would have to walk down a dark road to his interview. There could be no doubt that he was meeting the murderer; meeting him tonight, and at the Guest House. Hugh Donovan had at that moment a cold premonition, a conviction so growing and certain that he could have spoken it aloud.

This man is going to his death.

He had, furthermore, an almost maniacal impulse to elbow his way to Spinelli, grab him by the shoulder, and shout, "Look here, you damned fool, don't do it! Stay away from there. Stay away from there, or you'll get what Depping got as sure as he got it." He could have sworn to his conviction. In this babbling crowd, death was as palpable as the tobacco smoke round Spinelli's frightened face.

Spinelli was buying the bottle of brandy, stuffing it hurriedly into the pocket of his coat. And he was buying two packs of cigarettes, which probably meant that there was still some time to pass before his interview. Nobody paid any attention to him; each was elaborately unconscious of his presence. As the first to leave began drifting out the door, he took a sudden resolution and followed them.

Groups were breaking up in the moonlit road before the house. An argument waxed, passed, and faded away under ringing footfalls down the road. Somebody, in an unmusical baritone, was singing, "Me Old Corduroys"; and the countryside was so quiet that the loud voice almost seemed to have an echo from the sky. A woman, giggling-tipsy, went skipping towards the bus-stop on somebody's arm. Already the lights were going out in the house.

Presently it was dark and silent again; an incredible silence, in which Hugh hardly dared to breathe. He was against the side of the tavern, wondering vaguely whether they let loose a dog at night. Somebody raised a window over his head, and afterwards he could even hear a creak as somebody tumbled into bed.

Spinelli was sitting in the front seat of his parked car, no lights on. He had not attempted to start it. He shifted constantly; at intervals he would strike a match for a cigarette, and peer at his watch; and he seemed to be steadily drinking. Afterwards Hugh could never tell how long a time it was, but he had a cramp in every muscle. The moon had begun to decline: a watery moon, with heat clouds banning up around it . . .

There was a faint thunder, as stealthy as somebody's footstep. Hugh could hear cattle stirring in the stable yard. Stiff and half drowsy, he jerked alert as he heard the door of the car opening softly. His quarry slid down, and the bottle bumped against the door. Then he was off up the road; he seemed cold sober.

Until he was out of hearing of the tavern, Spinelli moved with great care, and Hugh had to exercise a greater. But halfway up the hill Spinelli stepped out into the center of the road. At the low stone wall bordering the churchyard he unexpectedly stopped, and leaned on the wall. He giggled to himself. He looked up at the square church tower, where the moon made shadows with the ivy, the queer little porch, and the toppling headstones in the yard. Then he made a magniloquent gesture.

"'Each in his narrow cell forever laid,'" Spinelli said aloud, "'the rude forefathers of the hamlet sleep.' Nuts!"

Something described a circle in the air, and there was a smash of a bottle breaking against stone.

Spinelli moved on.

That defiance, which had genuinely shocked Hugh, seemed to give Spinelli a fresh courage. For the pursuer's part, his impulse was now to overtake Spinelli, tap him on the shoulder, measure him for one on the jaw, and lay him out senseless along the side of the road. A neat, clean proceeding which anybody must approve of, and which would avoid endless trouble; certainly ease the strain of this night. He had no particular fear of the man's gun. He doubted that Spinelli, even in an extremity, would have the nerve to use it. In a rather vague way, as he considered his idea, he puzzled over the intricacies of the man's character as he had seen them revealed that night; Spinelli was a case for either a well-administered beating or a mental specialist, according to your view of the matter. He –

Hugh drew up short. Almost opposite Morgan's dark house, Spinelli had stopped. He moved to the left-hand side of the road, towards the boundary wall of The Grange park, groped, struck a match, and touched the wall. Towards the Guest House, no doubt of it. Hugh was pressing back against the hedge on the opposite side. He crept forward softly . . .

Somebody grasped his arm from behind.

It was the most horrible shock he had ever had. Hugh stiffened, momentarily unable to think; motionless, without turning round. All he could think of was a murderer. He gathered himself to pivot suddenly and hit out. Then a voice spoke close to his ear, in such a whisper that he thought he must have imagined it; it was lower than the rustle in the hedges.

"It's all right," the voice said; "I've been watching. May I come along? You might need help."

The almost inaudible whispering ceased. Turning softly, Hugh saw that his back was directly against the gate in the hedge round Morgan's house. A fugitive spark of moonlight struck Morgan's glasses. He was leaning over the gate, invisible except for that. Hugh bent his shoulders to indicate an assent, and risked a whisper for silence. He wanted company. To his strained nerves he thought the gate creaked perceptibly as Morgan vaulted it, and landed on tennis shoes in the wet grass outside.

No; it was another gate creaking, a little way up the wall. Spinelli had found the entrance to the Guest House in the boundary wall. They could hear his foot scraping in coarse grass; he was striking a match now, and propping the gate open. A good job. With Morgan following, Hugh went down on his hands and knees to dart across the moon-splashed road; he dodged into the shelter of the wall, breathing hard. The touch of rough stone was reassuring. Then they worked their way up and through the gate . . .

A momentary uneasiness gripped him. He could not see or hear Spinelli now. Damp trees overhung the path, and seethed faintly; the clouded moon could not penetrate, and only distorted the darkness. There were queer strands of cobweb floating across the path; they caught in your mouth as you moved. Hugh felt Morgan poke him in the back, and he crept on up in this wild game of hide-and-seek, up an endless path under the trees . . . The end of it came abruptly, at a turn. There was the clearing, with the fantastically ugly house in the middle. Its barred windows were gleaming dully. And they saw Spinelli again.

He had come out into the clearing, slowly, and this time he had the pistol in his hand. He was bracing himself against a sundial, moving the gun about in a slow circle as though he were searching the whole open space. Nothing stirred . . .

Then he moved out of their line of vision, over towards the brick path that lead away in the direction of The Grange. They could hear the low swish-swish of his feet in wet grass; hesitant, exploring.

Silence. Then it was as though the air were full of vibrations; as though they could feel the jerk and gasp he gave. His voice rose, not loudly, but muffled and yet of piercing intensity:

"Come out of there! Come on, step out! No tricks – no tricks, now, by God – yes, I've got you covered – come on –"

The murderer . . . ?

17
NO LONGER BULLET-PROOF

Hugh's uppermost thought was that he had got to see this, even if he blundered and wrecked all the plans. It occurred to him – where was Inspector Murch? Murch was supposed to be here, in hiding. If by any ironical chance Spinelli had stumbled on Murch in mistake for the man he hoped to meet, there was an end to everything.

He swallowed hard; tried to control his inexplicable trembling; and slid forward boldly into the mouth of the clearing. Mud squished under his foot, but he paid no attention to it.

Its scrolls and deformities darkened, but its barred windows gleaming almost hypnotically, the Guest House seemed to be watching too. Hugh had a sharp feeling that this was not fancy at all; that it literally was watching, or that somebody was watching in a dead man's place. The cool air struck his face again. He peered to the right, and drew back.

About thirty feet away, back turned towards him, Spinelli was standing and facing a thick oak tree beside the brick path. His pistol was held close in against his side, to avert its being knocked away.

"Come out," he was muttering, with a rising inflection that sounded like hysteria. "I can see your hand – give you just a second more – don't stand there; I'm not going to hurt you; but you're going to pay me, and keep on paying me, get me?"

Some faint words were whispered, too indistinct to be heard at that distance. Hugh dropped on his hands and knees and wriggled closer. Spinelli was backing away, towards a dappling of moonlight.

"Know you?" said Spinelli. For the first time Hugh saw him sway a little; the man was almost blind drunk, and holding himself together on sheer nervous excitement. He lost all caution, and his voice screeched out aloud. "Know you? What the hell are you trying to do? You try any tricks on me, and see what you get . . ." He gulped; he seemed hardly able to breathe. "I got your gun first last night, or you'd 've got me the way you got Nick . . ."

Closer yet in the long grass . . . Hugh raised his head. He was touching the brick path, but he had had to circle backwards, so that Spinelli was now turned partly sideways to him, and whoever stood behind that oak tree was completely hidden. A dappling of moonlight touched Spinelli's face; he could see the loose mouth, and he even noticed that there was a little colored feather stuck in the man's hatband. Now a voice spoke, very low, from behind the oak. It whispered: "Thank you, my friend. I thought so. But I'm not the person you think I am. Put up your gun, put up your gun – ! Sh-sh!"

Spinelli's hand shook. He lurched a trifle, and tried to rub clear sight into his eyes. Twigs cracked as somebody stepped out.

"You dirty rat –" said Spinelli suddenly. He choked; it was as though he were going to weep as he saw the other person. The word "rat" had an incredulous, shrill, despairing echo. He took a step forward . . .

It was pure chance that Hugh looked round then. He wanted to see whether Morgan was behind him. As he craned his neck round, his eyes fell on the house some distance behind Spinelli, and he stared. Something was different about it. Even his vision seemed blurred with doubt, until he realized that the difference was in the line of shimmering windows. There was a half-blank where one of the windows should have been, growing slowly, because one of the windows – that nearest the front door – was being slowly pushed up.

Spinelli did not see it. But the other man, the man behind the oak tree, let out a sound that resembled a gurgling, "Chua!" followed by a horrible rattling of breath. He jumped forward, seizing Spinelli by the shoulders as though he would hide himself.

From that window there was a tiny yellow spurt, less than a needle flash, but an explosion that shook the moonlight; so shattering in that hush that it was like a blow over the head. Hugh tried to lurch to his feet. He heard Morgan say, "Chri . . ." behind him; but he was conscious only of Spinelli. The man's hat, with its little colored feather, had fallen off. His leg gave; he suddenly began to reel round like one who had been thrown off the end of the line in a game of crack-the-whip; then his other leg buckled; and Hugh saw that the man was being sick at the very moment he pitched forward with a bullet through the brain.

The other man screamed. It blended horribly with a squawking and stirring of birds roused out of the ivy by the crash. His body seemed paralyzed, though with one hand he wildly gestured towards the window as though he would push Death away. He fell on his knees and rolled, kicking; he tried to dive for the underbrush . . .

Crack! There had been another cool pause, as though the person in the window were taking deliberate aim. The man behind the oak was staggering to his feet just as the bullet took him; he flapped against the bole of the tree, screamed again . . .

Crack! The cool, inhuman precision of the sniper in the window was adjusted with hideous nicety; he fired at intervals of just five seconds, drawing his sights to a fraction of an inch . . .

Crack! – Somebody was thrashing through the underbrush, still screaming. Hugh couldn't stand it. He got to his feet just as Morgan seized his ankle and brought him down toppling. Morgan yelled: "Don'tbeabloodyfool; he'llpicku-soffas-we-get-up – ! Ah!"

He grunted as Hugh jerked loose. Nobody would have believed that mere birds could have made such a racket; the clearing was alive with their noise, and they wheeled in clouds on the moonlight. Round the side of the house ran a clumsy figure, making indistinguishable noises. It was a wild-eyed Inspector Murch. He ran up the side steps of the porch, waving a flashlight whose beam darted crazily over the house, and he had something else in the other; and even then he was shouting out some nonsensical words about the name of the Law.

Nobody has a clear recollection of exactly what happened. Morgan gasped something like, "Oh, all right!" and then he and Hugh were running up the lawn, zigzag fashion, towards the house. Murch's light glared momentarily in the sniper's window; and something jerked back like a toad. The sniper fired high, off balance, shattering the glass in his own window. They saw it spurt and glitter out against a white mist of smoke and the pot-bellied bars that guarded the window. Then there were more flashes in the smoke, because Murch forgot police rules, and he was firing in reply. When the three of them came together on the porch, he was dangerously ready to drill anybody he saw; but Morgan cursed him in time, and prevented a shot as the inspector whirled round. The sniper was gone. All Murch did was stand and shake the bars of the window, until somebody said, "Door!" and they all charged for it.

It was unlocked. But even as Murch kicked it open, a faint bang from another door at the rear of the house announced which way the sniper had gone . . .

Five minutes later they were still aimlessly beating the brush, and finding nobody. The only result was that Murch had stumbled on something and broken his flashlight. Not, they silently agreed as they looked at each other, a very dignified spectacle of a man hunt. Even the querulous birds were angrily dozing off again. The sharp mist of smoke had begun to dissolve before a shattered window; a breeze had come back – rather complacently, you felt – to the long grasses; and the clearing was quiet. But, from the porch where they had reassembled, they could see Spinelli's body lying spread-eagled on the brick path near the oak. That was all.

Morgan leaned against the porch. He tried to light a cigarette, shakily.

"Well?" he said.

"'E can't get away, I tell the'!" insisted Inspector Murch, who was nearly unintelligible from wrath and uncertainty. He shook his fist. "We know! He's going to The Grange, every time! We know it – we – aaah!" He panted for a moment. "You two see if the' can do anything for them that was shot, down there. I'll go to the big 'ouse. That's where our man is, and we know it."

"Do you think you hit him?" Hugh asked, as calmly as he could. "When you fired through the window, I mean? If you did –"

"Ah! I was off me head for a moment, d'ye see." Murch looked blankly at the weapon in his hand. "I don't know. 'Twas so sudden; I don't know. Stand guard, now. There's another one that was shot at – where's he? Who was 'e?"

"Damned if I know," said Morgan. He added bitterly: "We're a fine parcel of men of action. This is one to remember for the book. All right, inspector; cut along. We'll look for your missing body. Though, personally, I'd rather take castor oil."

He hunched his shoulders and shivered as he went down the lawn. Hugh could still hear the stupefying crash of the shooting; and the emotional let-down was fully as stupefying. He accepted one of his companion's cigarettes, but his hand was not steady.

"Is this real?" Morgan demanded in an odd voice. "Hell-raising – gunplay – all over in a second; feel like a wet rag . . . No, no. Something's wrong. I don't believe it."

"It's real enough," said Hugh. He forced himself to go close to Spinelli's body. All around there was a smell of sickness and the warm odor of blood. As Morgan struck a match, the glimmer shone on bloodstains in the brush round the oak tree, where the second man had tried to crawl for safety. Hugh added: "I don't suppose there's any doubt . . . ?"

Spinelli lay on his face. Morgan, who was looking white, bent over and held the match near his head. It burned his fingers, and he jumped up again.

"Dead. No doubt. They – they got him through the back of the head, just over the hair line. Euh . . . I imagine," he said blankly, "that's rather like what a battle must be, that business. I can't tell just yet what did happen," He shivered. "I don't mind admitting that if anybody leaned out and said. 'Boo!' to me at this minute, I'd jump out of my skin. But, look here . . . H'm. One thing about it, that little marksman in the window was out to get Spinelli and the other chap; deliberately knock over those two, and nobody else. He didn't take a shot at either one of us, though he must have seen us easily."

"He shot at Murch."

"'M, yes. But a wild shot, over his head, to keep him back. Not the way he picked off Spinelli. Like a sitting bird. Ugh! And the other fellow. Or maybe he lost his nerve. I don't know. God, I don't know anything . . ."

He began to pace back and forth. "Come on. We've got to look for the other man, if it kills us. Who was he? Do you know?"

"I didn't see him either; at least, to recognize him. Here, I've got a cigarette lighter. That will be better than matches. If," said Hugh, feeling a little sick, "we follow that trail of bloodstains . . ."

But neither of them was anxious to start. Morgan made a gesture which said, "Let's finish our cigarettes." He said aloud:

"I was just thinking who it might be." The thought, to Hugh, was as terrifying as anything that had gone before. They would need to penetrate only a little way among the trees, because the sniper had been too deadly a shot for his second victim to have got very far. But his mind was full of formless conjectures that were all horrible. Morgan seemed to meet his thought. He went on swiftly:

"Uh. A dead shot, and cool. My God, what's going on in this nice placid corner of the universe? Who's the maniac can sit at a window and break people's heads like clay pigeons? I told you how impossible it was. And yet it happened. 'Keep your stories probable.' I'd like to know what the hell a probable story is," he said rather wildly, "if this is one . . . Keep on talking; it'll whistle our spirits up. That reminds me, I'm carrying a flask. Like a drink?"

"Would I!" Hugh said fervently.

"Two amateur criminologists," jerked out Morgan, handing over the flask, "afraid of the bogey man. The reason is, you and I are afraid there's somebody we know only too well lying in there with a couple of bullets through him."

Hugh drank whiskey greedily, shuddered at the bite in his throat; but he felt better. "Let's go," he said.

The pocket lighter made a surprisingly broad flame. Holding it low, Hugh stepped across the brick path towards the oak tree. The path here was bordered with foxglove, white and reddish-purple above the fern; but it had been torn and kicked about, and much of the red was blood. It was not difficult to follow the trail. Somebody had ripped himself loose from the thorns of a blackberry bush, and penetrated in where the trees were thickest. It was chill and marshy now, and there were gnats. More blood in a clump of bracken, which bore an impress as though somebody had dragged himself forward on his face, weakening . . .

Something rustled. The flame moved right and left, writhed in a draught, and almost went out. Their feet crackled on dead plants. Branches scratched past Hugh's shoulder; their snap and swish knocked his arm, and he had to spin the wheel of the lighter again.

"I could have sworn," said Morgan. "I heard somebody groan."

Hugh almost stepped on it. It was a highly polished black shoe, scuffing in dead leaves at the bole of a maple tree. As they looked it jerked once, showed part of a striped trouser leg, and became only a shoe again. There were whitish rents in the bark of the tree where the owner of the shoe had scratched it as he fell. He was lying on his side in a dump of foxglove, shot through the neck and shoulder. They heard him die as Hugh's light flickered on him.

Morgan said: "Steady. We can't go back now. Besides –"

Kneeling, Hugh wrenched the portly figure over on its back. Its face was dirty, the mouth and eyes open; and blood had not made it more attractive. There was a long silence as they stared at it.

"Who the devil is that?" Morgan whispered. "I never saw . . ."

"Hold the lighter," said the other; gagging in sudden nausea, "and let's get out of here. I know him. He's a lawyer. His name is Langdon."

18
DR. FELL MEETS THE MURDERER

They got back into the clearing somehow. Even then, Hugh remembered accidentally kicking Spinelli's hat as they crossed the brick path. By common consent they made for the Guest House. It was full of ugly suggestions and memories, but it was better than that area where the sniper had left his messy trophies.

Morgan peered at the house, and stopped. "I know what's wrong," he said. "Funny. It never occurred to me before. Do you know what we've done? The lights, man!" He pointed. "We've chased somebody we couldn't find all over the house and the grounds, and we never once thought to turn on the lights inside . . . Add psychological quirks, if you can add anything. What am I talking about anyway? Anyway, what we need is light . . ."

He ran up on the porch, and groped round inside the open front door. The electric lights of the hall glowed out; gloomy enough, but better than the darkness. They stood in the light as they might have stood before a fire on a cold day.

"All we can do," said Hugh, sitting down on the step, "is to take it easy and wait until Murch gets back with some – some minions," (That, he thought, was an idiotic word to use; like somebody in a bad play. "Minions!" What put that into his head?)

Morgan nodded. He stood bracing himself against the doorway, the collar of his blazer drawn up, and his face turned away.

"Uh. Yes, that's all. Question is, who is this Langdon down there, and why should he get killed?"

"I don't know why he should get killed. As to who he was, you'd have to hear all about what happened tonight. It's a longish story, and I don't feel up to it. Not just yet, anyhow. But –" an idea occurred to him, "but at least there's something about it you ought to know."

Automatically Morgan took out his flask and handed it over.

"Fire away," he said.

"Well, the fact is that my old man – the bishop, you know – got an idea into his head that you were the murderer; or, at least, a pretty suspicious character."

The other did not seem surprised. He let out a long breath, as though facts were being faced at last. "Ah! Enfin. I've been waiting for that. It was sure to occur to somebody, and I'm not surprised it was your father; I could see he had his eye on me. But why?"

"Chiefly it was about that footprint; the one around the side of the house here, made with Morley Standish's shoe. He had a theory that you had gone up to The Grange to steal those shoes; gone in through the secret passage in the oak room to get to the junk closet, without knowing anybody was sleeping there; and, when you find it had an occupant, you played poltergeist to cover your retreat."

Morgan turned, staring.

"Holy – !" he said, and struck the back of his head. "Now there's a suggestion that hadn't occurred to me. About the shoes, I mean. But the rest of it – yes, I was expecting it to happen."

"The idea's all wrong, of course. Spinelli proved that tonight. It was Depping himself who wore the shoes for his masquerade; I heard Spinelli say so. Afterwards he probably hid them somewhere in the house. But my old man worked up rather a plausible theory, proving that you couldn't have known the vicar was in the house, and the rest of it. Doesn't matter now. We know you weren't the poltergeist . . ."

Morgan frowned. "Certainly I was the poltergeist," he said. "That's just it. Do you mean to say you didn't find the clue I deliberately left? That's what I was worried about. I wanted to be true to tradition, and, besides, I was full of cocktails; so I dropped a little red notebook with my initials on it. After all, damn it," he pointed out argumentatively, "the sleuths ought to have something to work on."

"You mean . . ."

"Uh. It gave me some bad moments, when I thought about it afterwards." He kicked moodily at the jamb of the door. "Penalty of childishness. It makes me want to kick myself when I think of – of this. Not so entertaining, is it, when it's real? But I was the poltergeist, all right. And it's perfectly true: I didn't know the vicar was sleeping in that room. I didn't know he was in the house at all."

After a pause, he turned again with a guilty expression.

"As a matter of fact, that demonstration was intended for your old man . . . It was like this. I've got a habit of taking about a six-mile walk every night, late – incidentally, I was caught out in that storm last night, and hadn't any alibi; never mind. Well, I knew the bishop was staying at The Grange; he'd made a point of sitting on me hard and frequently, because of the detective stories. On the poltergeist night I was coming back from my walk, and cutting across the park, when I saw a light go on in the oak room. I thought, 'What ho!' and I put two and two together, because the room isn't usually occupied. And the bishop knew the story of the haunting. But, just to make sure, I sneaked round to the side door of the servants' hall, and collared old Dibbs – that's the butler. I said, 'Where is His Reverence sleeping?' And Dibbs said, 'In the oak room.'"

Wryly Morgan moved his glasses up and down his nose. "Well, what did I naturally think? I didn't know it was poor old Primley. I swore Dibbs to silence with a new, crisp jimmy-o'goblin – and I'll bet he hasn't betrayed me yet. Ha. The more I thought about it, the better I liked the idea. I went home, and had a few drinks with Madeleine, and the idea got better and better. You know the rest."

He came over and sat down on the step.

"And I saw Spinelli that night," he said abruptly. "Going down over the hill to the Guest House here, just as the bishop said. But I couldn't tell the colonel so, could I? And nobody believed the bishop – and this business came on." He stabbed his finger down the lawn.

The moon was low now, a deathly radiance through the trees towards the west. A mist had begun to creep over the lawn, in the hour of suicides, and the black despair of those who lie awake; a cold, luminous mist, that came out to take Spinelli's body. Hugh felt an increasing sense of disquiet. A party from The Grange should have arrived by this time. "It's a wonder," he said, "that the whole county wasn't wakened by that shooting. Why there isn't anybody here – why we've got to sit like a couple of corpse-watchers –"

"Madeleine!" said Morgan, sitting up straight. "My God, she must have heard it as plainly as we did. She'll be picturing me . . ." He jumped up. "Look here, this won't do. Post of duty or no post of duty, I've got to hop back to my place – for a few minutes, anyhow – and tell her I'm alive. I'll be back in five minutes. Is it all right?"

Hugh nodded. But he wished very fervently that half-a-dozen people, talkative people, would come into that clearing with lights and sct about removing the sniper's trophies. As Morgan strode off down the misty lawn, he moved into the exact center of the light that streamed from the open door. What he ought to do was go into the house and switch on every lamp. Besides, it was devilish cold; he could see his breath. But whether it would do any good, even if the whole house blazed like a cinema theatre . . .

Hesitantly he went into the hall. It was even more depressing than it had looked that afternoon: the soiled yellow matting, the black portieres, the black furniture smelling of stale furniture polish, the speaking tube in the wall. He understood a little better now. It was not only empty at this moment, but it had always been empty. Old Depping had never actually lived here. It had only been the place where he hung up one of his masks; an unsatisfied genius, as brilliant as unpleasant, whose fingers had touched everybody in this case, and whose fury was the one thing that made it vivid. You might think to see him coming down those stairs now in his high, prim collar: a sort of grizzle-haired satyr, peering over the bannisters.

Uneasily Hugh wondered whether the body upstairs had been removed. He supposed it had; they were speaking of it this afternoon; but you did not like to think the old man might still be lying with his dead smirk across the desk . . . Automatically Hugh did what he and Murch and Morgan had done when they first entered the house a while ago: he went to the door on the right and glanced through to the room where the sniper had hidden.

There were no electric lights here. Hugh did not try to put on the gas; he kindled his pocket lighter and saw, as before, nothing. A dreary and unfurnished place, which might once have been a drawing-room, smelling of damp wallpaper. But they had kept it clean and dusted. The floor, varnished round the edges and bare-boarded in the middle where a carpet should have been, held no footprints. Nor were there any traces that the sniper had been hit by Murch's fire, though the mantelpiece was gouged with bullets and one of them had smashed the mirror that was a part of it. Only stale cordite fumes, and slivers of broken glass round the window.

His foot creaked on a loose board. In the act of blowing out the lighter, he whirled round. Somebody was moving about in the house.

Impossible to tell the direction of sounds. The noise he heard seemed to have come from upstairs. It would be . . . queer how these inapt words struck him. What he had thought was, it would be embarrassing if old Depping were to walk down the steps now. The bright hallway was full of creakings. Another explanation occurred to him. There was no actual evidence to prove that the murderer had ever left the house at all. They had seen nobody. A slammed door; nothing else. And, if the sniper were still here, there would still be a bullet or two in reserve . . .

"Good morning," said a voice from the back of the hallway. "How do you like your job?"

He recognized the voice, as well as the lumbering step that followed it, in time to be reassured. It was Dr. Fell's voice; but even then there was a difference. It had lost its aggressive rumble. It was heavy, and dull, and full of a bitterness that very few people had ever heard there. Stumping on his cane, catching his breath harshly as though he had been walking hard, Dr. Fell appeared round the corner of the staircase. He was hatless, and had a heavy plaid shawl round his shoulders. His reddish face had lost color; his great white-streaked mop of hair was disarranged. The small eyes, the curved moustache, the mountainous chins, all showed a kind of sardonic weariness.

"I know," he rumbled, and wheezed again. "You want to know what I'm doing here. Well, I'll tell you. Cursing myself."

A pause. His eyes strayed up the dark staircase, and then came back to Donovan.

"Maybe, yes, certainly, if they'd told me about that passage in the oak room . . . Never mind. It was my own fault. I should have investigated for myself. I allowed this to happen!" he snapped, and struck the ferrule of his cane on the matting. "I encouraged it, deliberately encouraged it, so that I could prove my case; but I never meant it to happen. I intended to set the bait, and then head off . . ." His voice grew lower. "This is my last case. I'll never play the omniscient damned fool again."

"Don't you think," said Hugh, "that Spinelli got not very far off what he deserved?"

"I was thinking," said Dr. Fell in a queer voice, "of justice, or what constitutes justice, and other things as open to argument as the number of angels that can dance on the head of a pin. And I couldn't see my way clear as to what to do. This new business" – he pointed toward the door with his cane – "has almost decided it. But I wish it hadn't. I tried to prevent it. Do you know what I've been doing? I've been sitting in a chair in the upstairs hallway at The Grange, after everybody else had gone to bed. I've been sitting there watching the entrance to a passageway giving on a line of bedrooms, where I knew Somebody's bedroom was. I was convinced Somebody would come out of there when the house was asleep, go downstairs, and out for a rendezvous with Spinelli. And if I saw this person, I would know beyond a doubt that I was right. I would intercept this Somebody, and then . . . God knows."

He leaned his great bulk against the newel post of the stairs, blinking over his eyeglasses.

"But in my fine fancy conceit I didn't know about the secret passage in the oak room, that leads outside. Somebody did come out – but not past me. It was very, very easy. Out of one room in a step, into another, down the stairs; and I suspected nothing until I heard the shots down here . . ."

"Well, sir?"

"Somebody's room was empty. Across the corridor, the door of the oak room was partly open. A candle had been indiscreetly left there, lighted, on the edge of the mantel –"

"My father put that candle there," said Hugh, "when he explored –"

"It had been lighted," said Dr. Fell, "against Somebody's return. When I saw the piece of panelling open –"

There was something odd in the doctor's manner; something labored; he went on talking as though he were giving a long explanation for the benefit of some person unseen, and using Hugh only as an audience.

"Why," said the latter, "are you telling me this?"

"Because the murderer did not return," replied Dr. Fell. He had raised his voice, and it echoed in the narrow hall. "Because I stood at the entrance to the secret passage on the outside, and waited there until Murch came up over the hill to tell me the news. The murderer could not get back. The murderer was locked out of that house, with all the downstairs windows locked, and every door bolted; shut out tonight as certainly as Depping was shut out here just twenty-four hours ago."

"Then –"

"The whole house is aroused now. It will only be a matter of minutes before the one room is discovered to be empty. Murch knows it already, and so do – several others. A searching party, with flashlights and lanterns, has begun to comb the grounds. The murderer is either hiding somewhere in the grounds, or" – his voice lifted eerily – "is here."

He took his hand off the newel post and stood upright.

"Shall we go upstairs?" he asked gruffly.

After a pause Hugh said quietly, "Right you are, sir. But I suppose Murch told you the fellow's a dead shot, and he's still armed?"

"Yes. That is why, if Somebody is here, and could hear me, I would say: 'For God's sake don't commit the madness and folly of shooting when you are cornered, or you will certainly hang. There is some excuse for you now, but there will be none if you turn your gun on the police.'"

Dr. Fell was already climbing the stairs. He moved slowly and steadily, his cane rapping sharply on every tread; bump – rap, bump – rap; and a great shadow of him crouched ahead on the wall.

"I do not intend to look for this person," he said over his shoulder. "You and I, my boy, will go to the study and sit down. Now I am going to turn on the lights in the upstairs hall, here."

A silence. Hugh felt his heart rise in his throat as the switch clicked; the bare, desolate hallway was empty. He thought, however, that he heard a board creak and a door close.

Tap-tap, tap-tap . . . Dr. Fell's cane moved along the uncarpeted floor. His boots squeaked loudly.

In desperation Hugh tried to think of something that would help him. The doctor spoke with quiet steadiness. He was trying to draw the murderer out into the light, delicately, with gloved hands, as you might handle a nest of wasps. And the house was listening again. If the murderer were here, he must have heard in desperation each hope of escape taken from under him; and each tap of the cane must have sounded like another nail . . .

Hugh expected a bullet. He did not believe the sniper would submit without a fight. Nevertheless, he played up to the doctor's lead.

"I suppose you can prove your case?" he asked. "Would it be any good for the murderer to deny guilt?"

"None whatever." Dr. Fell leaned inside the study door. He stood there a moment, looking into darkness, silhouetted against the light if there were anybody inside. Then he pressed the electric switch. The study was as neat as it had been that day, and the body of Depping had been removed. The bright hanging lamp over the desk left most of the room in shadow, but they could see that the chairs still stood as before, and the covered dinner tray on its side-table with the bowl of withered roses.

Dr. Fell glanced round. The door to the balcony, with its chequered red-and-white glass panel, was closed.

For a time he stood motionless, as though musing. Then he walked to one window.

"They're here," he said. "Murch and his searching party. You see the flashlights, down there in the trees? Somebody seems to have a very powerful motorcycle lamp. Yes, they've covered that end of the grounds, and the murderer isn't there. They're coming this way . . ."

Hugh could not keep it back. He turned round, his voice was almost a yell: "For God's sake, you've got to tell me! Who is it? Who –"

A beam of white light struck up past the windows. Simultaneously, somebody cried out from below. The number of voices rose to a shouting; feet stamped and rustled in the underbrush, and more beams were directed on the balcony.

Dr. Fell moved over and touched the glass of the door with his stick.

"You'd better come in, you know," he said gently. "It's all up now. They've seen you."

The knob began to turn, and hesitated. There was a clink of glass as the muzzle of a firearm was jabbed towards them against the panel; but Dr. Fell did not move. He remained blinking affably at it, and at the silhouette they could see moving behind the door in the broadening white glare of the flashlights . . .

"I shouldn't try it, if I were you," he advised. "After all, you know, you've got a chance. Ever since the Edith Thompson case it's been tacitly agreed that they will not hang a woman."

The steel muzzle slid down raspingly, as though the hand that held it had gone weak. A sort of shudder went through the person on the other side of the door; the door wavered, and then was knocked open.

She was pale, so pale that even her lips looked blue. Once those wide-set blue eyes had been determined, and not glazed over with despair. The fine face seemed as old as a hag's; the chin wabbled; only the weariness remained.

"All right. You win," said Betty Depping.

The Mauser pistol rolled over a hand weirdly encased in a yellow rubber glove, and fell on the floor. Dr. Fell caught the girl as she slid down in a dead faint.

19
A HIGHLY PROBABLY STORY

The story, it is to be feared, has already been told too many times. It has been featured in the public prints, made the subject for leading articles, controversies in women's magazines, homilies, sermons, and the tearful "humanists" of the family pages. Betty Depping – whose name was not Betty Depping, and was no relation to the man she murdered – told the story herself a week before she poisoned herself at Horfield Gaol in Bristol. And that is why Dr. Fell insists to this day that the case was not one of his successes.

"That was the key fact of the whole business," he will say. "The girl wasn't his daughter. She had been his mistress for two years during the time he lived in America. And this was the explanation I had only begun to guess at the end. From the evidence on hand, it was easy to fix on her as the killer; that was fairly obvious from the beginning. But her motive puzzled me.

"Now we have the answer, which would appear to lie in Depping's character as well as her own. You see, she was the one woman who had ever succeeded in holding Depping's fancy. When he grew tired of making cutthroat money in the States, and decided to chuck it up and create another character for himself in England (I do not, at this juncture, make any comparisons), he took her along with him. She, by the way, was the 'high-class dame with the Park-Avenue manner' of whom Spinelli spoke to us.

"I think we can read between the lines of her confession. She maintains that his original intention was to present her as his wife when he assumed his new character, but that chance prevented it. She says that Depping, in his desire for terrific respectability, overdid it. When he was just completing arrangements to buy a share in the publishing firm, without having said anything of his domestic arrangements, quite by accident J. R. Burke encountered him and the girl unexpectedly in a London hotel. (You may remember that she told us a rather similar story, while pretending she really was his daughter?) Depping, playing his part clumsily, and flustered at being discovered with a young and pretty girl without a wedding ring, imagined that it might hurt his chances for social respectability; and at a somewhat crucial time. So he blurted out that she was his daughter, and was afterwards obliged to stick to his story. Hence, if scandal were to be averted, the girl must live abroad. If she lived in the same house, he might forget himself and become too loverlike where others – such as servants – could observe it. The scandal attendant on a supposed 'father' making love to his daughter would make the other affair seem innocuous by comparison.

"This, as I say, is her version. You may accept it if you like, but I should have thought Depping to have been too careful and far-seeing a plotter to have been forced, by an unexpected encounter; into such an awkward strategem. I think he maneuvered the girl into this position so as to be quit of her – except on such occasions as he could forget his rôle of country gentleman and pay her amorous visits at not-too-frequent intervals. Hence the flat in Paris, the supposed 'lady companion' (who did not exist), and the whole fiction manufactured about her past life. Depping, you see, really believed that he could will himself into his new character. He saw no necessity for putting her out of his life. His arrangement, he thought, was ideal. He had a genuine love of scholarship and his new pursuits; and, if he placed her in this position, no mistress could make awkward demands on his time. He could see her when he wished; at other times, she would be kept a convenient distance away. A good deal of Depping's character is in that proceeding.

"But, as was inevitable, he grew tired of his new life. A good deal, I suspect, because his circle had made it pretty uncomfortable for him. They didn't like him, or 'admit him,' or give him the sense of power to which he had been used. They made it clear that he was being put up with only because of his value to business. Hence his outbursts and his fits of drinking.

"At length he determined to chuck it up and go away; to start a new life among new people. He should keep a certain 'respectability,' and take the girl along either as wife or mistress. And at that juncture, two complications appeared, grew, and wrecked everything. Spinelli appeared, and the girl had fallen in love – genuinely, she declared – with Morley Standish.

"I recommend that you read her confession. It is a curious document: a combination of sincerity, cynicism, school-girl naïvete, matured wisdom, lies, and astonishing flights of cheap rhetoric. Make what you can of it. 'Patsy Mulholland' she signs herself. During all her association with Depping she seems at once to have hated considerably, loved a little, despised a little, and admired a good deal. She had a sort of instinctive gentility and poise; small education, but the wit to conceal that; and a good taste that Depping would never have.

"Inevitably, he had to bring her to England at intervals. At The Grange they liked her, and Morley Standish fell in love with her. She fell in love with him, she says. I remember one passage in her evidence. 'He was comfortable,' she said. 'The sort I wanted. One hates (sic!) one hates existence with a combination ice box and tiger.' When I think of that girl, cool to the last, sitting before the magistrates and talking in this fashion . . .

"Whatever the truth of the matter, it was a dazzling opportunity. She must play it coolly. To Depping she must laugh at his infatuation, and Depping will even assist and encourage it; because, he thinks, it will bring about his revenge on the people who have slighted him.

"Depping, you see, was already perfecting his plans for departure with her, and she was agreeing to them. 'Encourage him!' says Depping. 'Get engaged to him; flaunt it in their faces.' It inspired him with a triumphant delight. Then, when the news of the engagement was published, he himself would announce the real state of affairs, bow ironically, and sail away with the bride. If you can readily conceive any better way to make a laughing stock of people you hate, I should be interested to hear it.

"In fact, it was a bit too perfect. Betty (let's call her that) had no intention of permitting it. The issue was clear-cut. She was going to become Mrs. Morley Standish. The only way she could become Mrs. Morley Standish, and put the past entirely behind her, was to kill Depping.

"It was not merely a case of cold resolve, though that was the beginning of it. The girl seems to have indulged in a sort of self-hypnosis; of convincing herself that she had been bitterly and unfairly treated; of working up the state of her wrongs in her own mind until she genuinely believed in them. In her confession, a hysterical outburst against Depping precedes a statement wherein she prides herself on the workmanlike way she set about to plan his murder.

"For Spinelli had already appeared. And Spinelli was a serious threat to both of them. That Spinelli, when he accidently came across Depping in England, knew Depping's former mistress was still with him in the pose of his daughter, I am inclined to doubt. But Depping decided he must be put out of the way. To begin with, he might spoil Depping's last 'joke' – engaging his supposed daughter to Morley Standish – before Depping was ready to reveal it.

But most of all because he would now be a blackmailing leech on Depping wherever he went, and in whatever character he chose to assume. In brief, he was not so much a menace as a nuisance. And Depping had a curt way of dealing with nuisances.

"Betty Depping encouraged his design while she was formulating one of her own. Spinelli could be a very deadly danger to her. She corresponded with Depping about means for putting Spinelli out of the way: monstrously indiscreet letters. Depping wisely destroyed all she sent him, but a packet of his letters was found in her flat in Paris. One, dated two nights before the murder, informs her that he had procured 'the necessities,' and 'arranged a meeting with S. in a suitably lonely spot for Friday night.'

"The details I dare say she did not know. The interesting thing is that by this time she had worked herself into a bitter, wild, virtuous, crusading rage against Depping, mixed with a certain music-hall theatricality. 'I felt,' she says – and almost seems to mean it – 'that I would be ridding the world of a monster.' Did anybody ever really talk like that? Oh, yes. Talk. But her actions show the intrinsic falsity of the emotion. I don't wish to do the woman an injustice; and I thoroughly agree that the world was well rid of Depping. I am only pointing out that she slightly overdid her emotion when she painted that little card of the eight swords . . ."

This is what Dr. Fell will say before you ask him to explain his means of determining the guilty person.

Hugh Donovan, in the ensuing months, heard the details many times. It has always been a favorite topic of conversation at The Grange, where he has been a frequent visitor, due to asking Patricia Standish to marry him, and being accepted, and also learning firmly to utter a certain vigorous phrase to his prospective mother-in-law. Maw Standish maintains (between listening to the wireless, and assuring the colonel that his mind, for the head of a great publishing house is in a deplorable state and needs improving), Maw maintains she knew of Betty Depping's perfidy all the time; and also that the trip around the world is doing Morley good. These endings are eminently commonplace and probable, you will perceive, and serve fittingly to conclude a probable story.

But, as regards explanations, Hugh remembers best a conversation in J. R. Burke's office, one wet and murky October afternoon in the same year, when several of the characters were sitting round a fire, and Dr. Fell talked.

Dr. Fell was smoking J. R.'s cigars, which were kept rather for effect than for use, and leaning back amicably in a leather chair. Outside the rain was pattering in Paternoster Row, and the dingy tangle of window fronts that straggle under the shadow of Paul's dome. The fire was bright, the cigars good; and J. R., having locked the door of the book-lined room against his secretary, had produced whiskey. Henry Morgan was there, having just brought up to London the completed manuscript of his new book, Aconite in the Admiralty. Hugh was there also, but not the bishop. And Dr. Fell had been talking in the fashion indicated, when J. R. interrupted him.

"Get on to the point," he grunted. "Tell us why you thought the girl was guilty. We don't want these characterizations. Not in a detective story, anyhow. The public will only glance at this chapter, to make sure it hasn't been cheated by having evidence withheld. If you've got any reasons, let's hear 'em. Otherwise –"

"Exactly," agreed Morgan. "After all, this is only a detective story. It only concerns the little emotions that go into the act of murdering somebody."

"Shut up." said J. R. austerely.

Dr. Fell blinked at his cigar. "But that's quite right, nevertheless. It wouldn't be true to life. It wouldn't be true to life, for instance, if a modern novelist devoted to motives for murder the same profound and detailed analysis he devotes to little Bertie's early life among the dandelions, or the sinister Freudian motives behind his desire to kiss the housemaid. Humph. When an inhibition bites a man, it's a fine novel. When a man up and bites an inhibition, it's only a detective story."

"The Russians –" said J. R.

"I knew it," said Dr. Fell querulously. "I was afraid of that. I decline to discuss the Russians. After long and thoughtful reflection, I have come to the conclusion that the only adequate answer to one who begins rhapsodizing about the Russians is a swift uppercut to the jaw. Besides, I find it absolutely impossible to become passionately interested in the agonies and misfortunes of any character whose name ends in 'ski' or 'vitch.' This may be insularity. It may also be a disturbing sense that, from what I read, these people are not human beings at all. Ah, God," said Dr. Fell musingly, "if only somebody would make a bad pun! If only Popoff would say to Whiskervitch, "Who was that lady I seen you with last night?" Try to imagine a conversation, in the after life, between Mark Twain or Anatole France and any of the leading Russians, and you will have some vague glimmering of what I mean."

J. R. snorted. "You don't know what you're talking about. And, besides, get back to the subject. This is the last chapter, and we want to get it over with."

Dr. Fell mused a while.

"The extraordinary feature about the Depping murder," he rumbled, after refreshing himself with whiskey, "is that the thing explained itself if you only bothered to inquire what the facts meant.

"I had a strong inkling of who the murderer was long before I had met her. The first fact that established itself beyond any question was that the murderer was definitely NOT one of the little community at or around The Grange.

And the murderer was not only an outsider, but an outsider who had known Depping in his past (and, at that time) unknown life."

"Why?"

"Let us begin with the attempted murder of Spinelli by Depping, at the point in our previous deductions where we had decided that it was Depping who left the house in disguise and came back to it through the front door. The problem was this: Was Depping working with a confederate whom he had planted in that room as an alibi? Or was he working alone, and X somebody who had come unexpectedly to that room with the intent to kill – only helping him in his deception when X saw the opportunity of an alibi for him (or her)self? In either case, were there any indications as to X's identity?

"Very well. Now, all the weight of evidence lay against Depping's having a confederate. To begin with, why did he NEED a confederate at all? It's a very poor alibi, you know, merely to put somebody in a room; somebody who can't show himself or act for you, or prove you are there. If Depping had genuinely wanted an alibi for his presence in that room, he would have had a confederate do something that could have testified to his presence . . . running the type-writer; for example. Or even moving about or making conspicuous sounds of any sort. But it didn't happen. And what's the good of an alibi that doesn't alibi, but merely puts you into the power of your confederate? Why share a secret that you don't have to share at all?

"Which brings us to the second and most powerful objection. Depping was acting a part before that community. The last thing in the world he would think of doing would be to reveal himself: to tell what he was –"

"Hold on!" interrupted J. R. "I made that objection myself. He couldn't tell anybody what he'd been, or that he intended to go out and murder Spinelli; he didn't know or trust anybody well enough for that. But somebody" – he sighted over his eyeglasses at Morgan – "invented a long yarn about an 'innocent victim,' who had been persuaded by Depping to stay there on the grounds that he was playing a practical joke on somebody, and afterwards the accomplice couldn't reveal the plot without incriminating himself."

Dr. Fell followed the direction of his glance at Morgan, and chuckled.

"Consider it," he said. "Can any of you conceive of a person from whom an excuse of that sort would come with less plausibility than from Depping? Could any of your community, Morgan, imagine Depping in the role of light and graceful practical joker? If he had come to you with a proposition of that sort, would you have believed him or assisted him? . . . I doubt it. But the real objection lies in the eight of swords. If you believe in an innocent confederate, what becomes of that symbol and trade-mark of the murderer? How did it come there? Why did an innocent confederate bring it there to begin with?

"We will consider that card next. For the moment, we establish in theory that Depping had no confederate (a) because he didn't need one, and (b) because he would not have dared to reveal himself: which thesis I can prove in another way. As actual evidence of this, we have your evidence, J. R. . . ."

"Hated to give it," said the other. "Thought it might give you ideas." He snorted.

"When you called on Depping, he was startled to hear a knock even when he couldn't see you. That's not the behavior of a man expecting an accomplice. Furthermore, he first took the key out of his pocket to unlock the door, and later you saw him through the glass putting it back in his pocket when he'd locked the door after you.

"In brief, he was going out alone, and he was going to lock the door and take the key when he went to kill Spinelli."

Dr. Fell tapped his finger on the chair arm.

"In deciding where to look for Depping's murderer – the person who had come into that house unseen, and was waiting for him when he returned – there were several suggestions. One of them is so obvious that its comic."

"Well?"

"The murderer," said Dr. Fell, "ate Depping's dinner." There was a silence. Then the doctor shook his head.

"Reflect, if you please, on the monstrous, the solemn, the glaring give-away of that fact. Look at it from all angles, if you would try to convince me that the murderer was somebody from that community. Study the fantastic picture of Colonel Standish, of Mrs. Standish, of Morley Standish, of Morgan, of yourself . . . of anybody you like to name, going up to kill Depping, finding him not at home, and then whiling away the time by sitting down and eating a hearty meal off the tray of the man you shortly expect to kill! Of, if you prefer, imagine any one of those people paying an ordinary social visit, unexpectedly, and eating the dinner they happen to find conveniently on a tray! It's not only absurd; it's unthinkable.

"That's why I remarked that the case explained itself. There is only one explanation that can account for it. When I was meditating over this astonishing behavior of X, I said, 'Why did he eat Depping's dinner?' Morley Standish triumphantly replied, 'Because he was hungry.' But it didn't seem to occur to anybody that X was hungry because X had come from some distance away, and in a hurry. It did not seem plain that people who eat normal dinners in the neighborhood of The Grange are not apt to behave in this fashion.

"The corollary to this not-very-complicated deduction is that X not only came from some distance away, but was so thoroughly intimate with Depping that he (or she) could sit down and eat a dinner like that without ever thinking twice about it. It's the sort of thing you might do with a close relative, but few other people. You have only to ask yourself, 'How many people were close enough to Depping to fit into this picture?' And on top of that you will inquire about the key. How many people would have a key which fitted Depping's balcony door? Depping locked it when he went out, and X had to get in."

"Yes, but X might have come in the front door –" Morgan was beginning, when he saw the flaw and stopped. "I see. It would be the same whichever door was used. X couldn't ring and be let in by the valet."

"Certainly not for the purpose in mind," said Dr. Fell; "that is, murdering Depping. Now, to the combination of these two things, a person with keys to the house yet living a great distance away, is added another significant circumstance . . . After his attempted murder of Spinelli, Depping returned. It was then he discovered that somewhere on the way he had lost his key to the balcony door. He went up, looked through the window, and saw X in possession. Would he have revealed himself so readily to some member of the neighborhood; gone into conversation; agreed to the scheme for walking in the front door; unless the person inside had been . . . who? And the answer that occurred to me in my innocence was: a daughter; who, being a daughter, he thought would not betray him. The fact that she was his mistress I didn't know, but the rule still works.

"Now we come to that mysterious eight of swords. The curious part there was that not only was there nobody there who knew what it meant, but that nobody had ever heard of Depping's interest in the occult. He never mentioned it, he never played with fortune-telling packs, though his bookshelves were stuffed with works on the subject . . . I filed away the idea, still wondering, when – as soon as

Spinelli appeared on the scene – he recognized it. It was definitely a part of Depping's dark past. The murderer, then, was somebody who had known Depping in America; or, at least, known something of Depping that nobody else did.

"With my growing suspicion of the daughter in my mind, I tried to couple it with this fact. It was corroboration, even though it had never entered my head to suspect the daughter of being anything else than she pretended until Spinelli and Langdon were on the scene.

"I noticed how all references to the daughter were scrupulously kept out of their talk. What Langdon did was to hint at a 'mysterious woman' with whom Depping was going to run away: Why did he do that? Then Spinelli made a slip and revealed that he knew the amount of Depping's estate. Whatever you deduce from this, you will admit that these two – between them – knew something about Depping's past life out of which they both believed they could make capital.

"Spinelli I could understand, because I believed he knew who the killer was. But what could both of them have known, which would be of profit? What had Langdon found out? And the first faint suggestion began to come to me, though I didn't believe it. This daughter, who didn't live with her father, although – vide Morley Standish – he was 'always worrying about her, and what she was doing'; this card of the taroc that Depping only used in America, and whose painting in watercolor suggested a woman; this queer attitude of the lawyer . . .

"For, you see, if Betty Depping were not really his daughter, it would be an excellent thing for Langdon. I mean blackmail. 'Split half the estate with me, or you get none.' And it would fit in exactly . . ."

Dr. Fell waved his hand.

"What happened was simply this. We know it from the girl's confession. She came over from Paris that Friday night with the intention of killing Depping. She didn't know where

Depping would be, except that he would be out on Spinelli's trail, and she wanted him to do that piece of work for them both before she shot him. She was prepared with a pistol – the same one she later used on Spinelli and Langdon.

"She came up on the balcony and let herself in through the door. Depping had already gone. But she saw . . . you understand?"

Morgan nodded, abstractedly. "His disguise preparations, his own clothes left behind, and all the traces of that masquerade."

"Exactly. She knew he was out after Spinelli in disguise. As yet the brilliant idea had not occurred to her. She could not have known Depping had lost his key. But it did occur – she says with some pride – when she heard Depping fumble at the door, and say he was locked out. You know what happened. She short-circuited the lights with her rubber glove, and the comedy was played.

"Meantime, Spinelli had followed Depping back from the river. He saw everything, and heard everything at the window. The woman got Depping back into his ordinary clothes, her stage set; and then she did not have to use her own pistol at all. She picked up Depping's own gun from the desk – not wearing her gloves, of course – sat on the arm of his chair, and shot him. Afterwards she wiped off the gun, blew out the candles, and left . . . to meet Spinelli on the lawn below.

"He was careful. He took away the handbag in which she carried the other pistol; got it out of her grasp first, and removed the bullets, before he talked business. He had her cornered. She couldn't give him all he demanded; she protested that Depping hadn't been as rich as Spinelli thought. But let her get away from the place, she swore, and she would arrange something, and agreed to meet him on that spot the following night to discuss terms.

"Eheu! Naturally she never went back to Paris at all. She caught the last bus to Bristol, where she had a hotel room under another name. She then took a morning train to London; put through a trunk call to Paris, to the maid at her flat (who had been well coached from the beginning) and found that the telegram informing her of her father's death had arrived. So, allowing a reasonable time, she called on Langdon in Gray's Inn Square, and asked him to accompany her down to The Grange . . . But Langdon, you see, knew she was not really Depping's daughter. On the way down, he informed her of it. Depping had been indiscreet, and told him the whole story.

"He wanted half, to which she agreed. Meanwhile, Langdon was wondering how he could connect up this murder with the phone call he had had from Spinelli, saying that he (Spinelli) was on the point of being arrested for murder and asking for advice. Langdon jumped to the conclusion which was true – that Spinelli knew the facts of his own case: viz., that the girl was not Depping's daughter. Langdon hinted as much to her.

"And she invented a brilliant scheme for disposing of them both. She said that Spinelli did know, and was asking for his share of hush money. She told him that she was to meet Spinelli at the Guest House that night: Would he, Langdon, be along, and use moral terrors, or legal terrors, or both, in an attempt to intimidate Spinelli?

"It nearly fell through; because, you see, we confronted Spinelli with Langdon, and they had the opportunity to confer in private. You can understand now Langdon's horror and nervousness when I announced that Spinelli was ready to talk. He thought I meant talk of what he knew about the girl. But the girl's scheme worked because Langdon's suspicions were aroused at Spinelli's talk, and he wondered whether 'Betty Depping' mightn't have deeper reasons for wishing silence all around than that matter of her identity.

"We shall never know what passed between Spinelli and Langdon at their interview. Langdon realized that Spinelli knew something more; but he kept his own counsel, and determined to be present that night – unseen and unheard – at the rendez vous between Spinelli and the girl."

Dr. Fell threw his cigar into the fire. He leaned back and listened to the rain.

"They were both marked," he said. "You know what happened."

"Moral observations," remarked J. R., after a silence, "are now in order. Somebody will have to talk for a page or two on the futility and sadness of it, and how she would have been safe if only she hadn't left one-little-damning clue behind . . ."

"It won't go, I'm afraid," said Dr. Fell. He chuckled. "The one-little-damning clue was a large and many-caloried dinner, steaming before your noses. You might as well say that the Guiness advertisements plastered over the hoardings are a clue to the theory that somebody is trying to sell stout."

J. R. scowled. "All the same," he said, "I'm glad that the only detective plot in which I ever took part was not full of improbabilities and wild situations, like – well, like Morgan's Murder on the Woolsack or Aconite at the Admiralty. There are no fiendish under-clerks shooting poisoned darts through keyholes at the First Sea-Lord, or luxurious secret dens of the Master Criminal at Limehouse. What I mean by probability . . ."

Hugh looked round in some surprise to see that Morgan was gurgling with rage.

"And you think," Morgan inquired, "that this is a probable story?"

"Isn't it?" asked Hugh. "It's exactly like one of those stories by William Block Tournedos. As Mr. Burke says . . ."

Morgan sank back.

"Oh, well!" he said. "Never mind. Let's have a drink."